P9-AQR-909

The Trench

ALSO BY THE AUTHOR

Cities of Salt

THE
TRENCH

VOLUME TWO OF THE *CITIES OF SALT* TRILOGY

Abdelrahman Munif

◆ TRANSLATED FROM THE ARABIC BY PETER THEROUX ◆

Pantheon Books · New York

English translation copyright © 1991 by Cape Cod
Scriveners

All rights reserved under International and Pan-
American Copyright Conventions. Published in the
United States by Pantheon Books, a division of
Random House, Inc., New York, and simultaneously
in Canada by Random House of Canada Limited,
Toronto.

Originally published in Arabic as *al-Ukhdūd* by The
Arab Institute for Research & Publishing, Beirut,
Lebanon, in 1986. All rights reserved.

A portion of this translation was originally published
in *Grand Street* #37, Volume 10, Number 1.

Library of Congress Cataloging-in-Publication Data

Munīf, Abd al-Raḥmān.
[*Ukhdūd*. English]
The trench / by Abdelrahman Munif; translated from
the Arabic by Peter Theroux.
p. cm.
Translation of: *al-Ukhdūd*.
I. Title.
PJ7850.U514U3513   1991 892'.736—dc20 91-52622
ISBN 0-394-57672-1

Book Design by Guenet Abraham

Manufactured in the United States of America
First Edition

The Trench

1

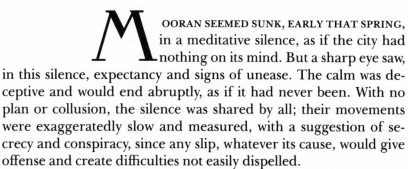

MOORAN SEEMED SUNK, EARLY THAT SPRING, in a meditative silence, as if the city had nothing on its mind. But a sharp eye saw, in this silence, expectancy and signs of unease. The calm was deceptive and would end abruptly, as if it had never been. With no plan or collusion, the silence was shared by all; their movements were exaggeratedly slow and measured, with a suggestion of secrecy and conspiracy, since any slip, whatever its cause, would give offense and create difficulties not easily dispelled.

For the death of Sultan Khureybit, which came as a surprise to so many and seemed to them one of the terrible catastrophes of all time, had actually been foreseen, expected momentarily, in fact, from the day the news of his illness spread. He had gone blind and there were rumors of delirium. Some found his death slow in coming; most were surprised that he had lasted so long. When Dr. Subhi Mahmilji arrived in Mooran, with all the fuss that entailed, and the tense traffic between the Rawdh Palace and the Bakri Pharmacy, some people said that death was imminent, especially after they heard what Hommoud al-Kayed, who worked in the pharmacy, had said. Two of his cousins had just come from al-Rehaiba seeking medicine to save Sheikh Muhaisen's son, "whose belly is so full of worms that they are coming out his ears"; they said he swallowed enough squash seeds to feed a two-year-old horse, but it did no good. Hommoud didn't listen to the two men, but told them casually that "The old man will die tonight—tomorrow at the latest." This seemed confirmed by Dr. Mahmilji's two anxiously watched visits to the pharmacy, accompanied by aides and guards, who demanded that everyone else leave the premises, "so that the *dakhtoor* can think clearly and not make a mistake." As a rule, Sadeq al-Bakri, the owner of the pharmacy, never let anyone even come near his glass cases. He hadn't even let Hommoud enter the little room where prescriptions were mixed until he had worked there for years, and he was satisfied, after watching him like a hawk, that he was trustworthy; but now he instinctively made room for his visitors and gestured for them to crowd behind the glass cases. He had a long meeting with the doctor in the prescriptions room. The longer the doctor stayed, the more fearful and pessimistic Bakri seemed; so much so that he made several small mistakes until at last he dropped a large blue flask, causing himself immense embarrassment and vexation; he broke out in a sweat and apologized profusely. Bakri accompanied Dr. Subhi to the door when he left, and stood there even after the cars of the aides and bodyguards had careened around to the right and disappeared.

Hommoud al-Kayed replaced and rearranged the medicines, trying to analyze what symptoms or maladies they would be used to treat, but he could find no hopeful signs—all they conveyed were the agony of the disease and the dire state of the patient. When his employer began to add up the bill, it was different from any past bill: the word *PALACE* was scrawled across it. The patient could be none other than the Sultan.

"Who is the patient, sir?" whispered Hommoud, leaning close to Sadeq.

Sadeq started at the question, which had interrupted his train of thought. He thrust out his lower lip and spoke without looking at him. "Keep your mind on your work, son, and never mind."

Hommoud had no need to ask. It was not his employer's habit to answer him that way: if he waited patiently for one more minute he would get his answer. Abu Bakri could not keep a secret any more than he could contain a sigh or a yawn in his chest, especially since everyone in the market was gazing expectantly at the pharmacy, closely watching the arrival of Dr. Subhi, Crown Prince Khazael's aides and their bodyguards, and given the fear and concern the visit generated.

"God heal him and give him long life," murmured Abu Bakri sadly.

This answer convinced Hommoud that he had been right. When the two men returned to pick up the medicine, he told them, "You'd better get back to your boy before the worms eat him." He paused and leaned over slightly, so that no one else could hear him. "I don't think the old man has to worry about worms—yet!"

The men looked surprised and turned around. He accompanied them past the door and spoke with pronounced clarity.

"That medicine they took will only give him gas." He gazed at the sky and went on as if talking to himself. "Even if the old man lives through the night, it will be his last. You'll see."

The two men lingered in Mooran. Every passing hour brought more detailed news of the Sultan's worsening health, and there were ever-varying versions of the story as the number of storytellers increased; what the men had been told by Hommoud al-Kayed, for example, meant nothing later.

Many people had sprawled out on the pavement outside the Rawdh Palace to watch everyone leaving and entering, monitoring the slightest and most trivial movements. They debated it all at the top of their voices and kept a watchful eye on the al-Bakri Pharmacy, as new medicines were brought from the stockroom, and Sadeq and Hommoud worked together carefully to clean the room where prescriptions were filled. They took care to move some of the things from this room to a more secure place, out of public view.

These were essential measures, for what Sadeq al-Bakri had anticipated now occurred: Dr. Subhi came back to the pharmacy. He examined the drug specimens very carefully and thumbed through the volume that Sadeq drew from the lower drawer of the desk where he sat when he wanted to rest or meet with doctors.

After the two finished studying the drugs together, the doctor had to mix the needed drug that he could not find. He returned to the pharmacy a third time that night, where with Sadeq, by the light of a flashlight and some matches, he filled a blue flask and took it to the palace. But it was too late.

On the morning of the third day the al-Rawdh Palace issued a bulletin:

" 'In the name of God, the Compassionate and Merciful. O soul now at rest, return to your Lord, pleased and content. Enter the ranks of the faithful in my Paradise.' Thus saith the Lord God."

Sultan Khureybit was dead.

2

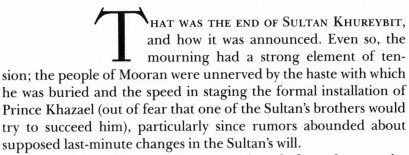

THAT WAS THE END OF SULTAN KHUREYBIT, and how it was announced. Even so, the mourning had a strong element of tension; the people of Mooran were unnerved by the haste with which he was buried and the speed in staging the formal installation of Prince Khazael (out of fear that one of the Sultan's brothers would try to succeed him), particularly since rumors abounded about supposed last-minute changes in the Sultan's will.

Dr. Subhi had visited Mooran many times before, always at the invitation of Prince Khazael, without attracting attention, but now, on this visit, he seemed different—distinguished, even. Every eye followed him; the Sultan's life was in his hands. Even his assistant Muhammad Eid, who had stayed behind in Harran during these events, and barely discussed them with the doctor after his return, was soon broadcasting accounts of the Sultan's last hours: how he'd rallied, thanks to Dr. Subhi's drugs and healing powers; how the doctors who had previously treated him, and their numerous errors, hampered the recovery. Nevertheless, the Sultan expired restfully and painlessly. In his last wakefulness, a full hour before his death, he asked the doctor to read his will, which decreed three times, clearly, that Prince Khazael was to succeed him. As the doctor read the will, those present were overcome with sorrow, and tears streamed down their faces, though they hardly noticed it. The Sultan sealed the will with his signet, and Dr. Subhi witnessed it.

This was Muhammad Eid's story of the Sultan's sickness and death, though he often changed it by adding or subtracting details, so that numerous versions of the Sultan's death and the other events of those hours circulated throughout Harran.

Mooran masked its sorrow and curiosity in silence, but could not rest, not understanding why Dr. Subhi left town after three days. He should have stayed and stood by Prince Khazael; they were old and dear friends. He should have behaved differently from the foreigners and the delegations that came for a day, or part of a day, to extend their condolences, then went home.

When Dr. Subhi left Mooran unexpectedly, some of Prince Khazael's men said, "The man has been blinded by money, and one of these days that money will kill him." It was not known whether they were referring to the money it was assumed he would be paid for treating Sultan Khureybit, or to his haste in returning to Harran to attend to his business there. Zaid al-Heraidi stood beside the doctor's car and had a long conversation with him, but the men could not hear what was being said. When his aides asked him, rather suggestively, about the doctor's departure, he only smiled and shook his head, so no one knew or could even guess.

When the doctor returned in the morning exactly one week later with a large delegation from Harran, he seemed, to everyone who saw him, a totally different man. He was not dressed in the often flashy European clothes he had always worn, which set him apart from all around him, and whose neatness and elegance were his foremost concern. On this visit he was lost, like a puppet, in a set of gaudy Arab robes that he had not yet learned to arrange. He kept tripping over them. The beard he had allowed to grow over the past few days was not as full as the beards of the men around him and made him look as though he had forgotten to shave. In the shadow of the red-and-white-checked headcloth he wore, he looked like a fugitive; his whiskers grew unevenly and looked like irregular smudges.

Something unexpected happened when the doctor arrived at the head of the Harrani delegation. Those who had said that he'd fled to Harran with large sums of money, afraid of losing it or being robbed in Mooran, refused to believe that this stranger, stumbling over his clothes like a boy in his ritual circumcision robes, was in fact the doctor. When Prince Khazael came near him with two Harranis and whispered something in his ear, however, and the doctor nodded vigorously and turned around several times, as if looking for something or someone, and his face showed clearly, the doubters recognized the doctor himself. The doctor stayed in Mooran for several days with no sign of leaving, in his Arab clothes, which gradually grew neater and suited him better, his beard more elegantly trimmed, so that it looked extremely handsome, coal-black against his fair, rosy complexion—with this new development, a great number of people grew depressed, guessing that a new era of bad luck had begun.

Farhan al-Madloul, who poured the emir's coffee, looked around carefully before joining a discussion about Dr. Subhi.

"Be patient, my friends, just be patient. The Rawdh Palace has seen a lot of his kind come and go!" He added nostalgically a moment later, "And we swept away their bones with our own feet!"

The men took this view of the doctor because a number of them remembered Prince Khazael's visit to Mooran: how this "devil" had thoroughly ingratiated himself with the prince not in a matter of days but of hours, as none of them had been able to do in their years of service to the prince. Others recalled the green automobile, intended for the emir of the central province—for it was whispered, after the twenty-three cars had been delivered, that at the last minute the orders were changed and the car given to Dr. Subhi. That was at a time when many people considered themselves far above him and expected to receive cars for themselves. Although Prince Khazael himself no longer remembered this gift, for it was so small compared to the extravagant gifts he had given to the doctor subsequently, that very automobile had sown bitter envy in many hearts, and this envy mounted after the doctor's second visit to Mooran.

Barely a month after Dr. Subhi's arrival, a young man whose precise age no one could guess appeared in Mooran: of medium build, rather short, with a full black mustache in a florid face. This young man was very vain about his mustache; the thumb and forefinger of his right hand were always slightly open, a fixed distance apart, constantly stroking his mustache.

He had arrived unexpectedly in Mooran, and his name was the source of puzzlement and derisive amusement when he presented himself at the Rawdh Palace. The guards called the palace overseers repeatedly, and it was said that even the Sultan was asked about his name. When at last everyone had denied knowing him and why he had come and who might have summoned him, he was referred to the emirate; and from there, after several telephone calls, Muti Shakhashirou was sent to Prince Khazael's palace.

After delays and confusion, the prince was told that the young man had been summoned by Dr. Subhi Mahmilji—to come, in fact, as quickly as possible; and that they were related. The prince seemed pleased and reassured, though the purpose of Muti's errand seemed no more comprehensible than before. The doctor had always said that the prince needed a personal secretary, and that such a secretary could deputize for the prince in countless small matters, but these matters, which seemed so urgent and momentous when the doctor discussed them, saying with a smile that he had the very man made for the job, were not specified. It seemed that there were many diverse, undefined tasks. Now the prince gazed at the young man and spoke so that he would not mislead him about what he was supposed to do.

"Rest now, my boy, and later on you can see our brothers and do what God has given you the strength for."

Muti did not know what precisely these words meant, but the others understood: this foreigner had come to compete with them and create problems. They looked at him apprehensively and even fearfully, each sensing that he was looking at an enemy, or at least a potential enemy, which led them all to watch him carefully and fall silent whenever he came near or asked them a question, on the pretext that "they did not understand what he was saying." But

Muti was not in a hurry, and accepted their silence and secret war without any word of complaint; he even exaggerated his serenity, seeming grateful for every word and glance, even the things that the guards and servants said—shrugging or nudging each other when he stroked his mustache with his thumb and forefinger. He did not notice their laughter or derision, or did not realize that it was directed at him.

So it went for a short time, until Muti Shakhashirou asked for the prince's permission to go on a tour through the various provinces of the Sultanate, to acquaint himself with the nature and climate of each, the better to deal, he said, with journalists and visitors. The prince thought this a very wise and ambitious proposal and immediately gave his consent. Actually, Muti wanted to go to Harran to meet his Uncle Subhi to try to find work with him, or to manage on his own "in this goddamned desert." His ambitions lay far beyond "these deadly evenings where they tell the same story a hundred times, as loudly as possible and with the most idiotic gestures, and get nothing at all done."

Many in the Rawdh Palace recalled the doctor's third visit to Mooran, where he was privileged to be received by the Sultan and dine with him, exchanging stories and gossip. It was on this visit that Muti's position was settled once and for all. Muti was by the doctor's side at all times and seemed, on this visit and subsequently—for a long time afterward—at the pinnacle of bliss and self-confidence. He played his role perfectly, as the Sultan observed, when the conversation turned to Master Muti and the momentous role he would play, and the great services he would render to the Sultanate, and to the Sultan particularly.

3

THE PEOPLE GRADUALLY FORGOT MUTI'S early days in Mooran. Even his family ties to the doctor meant nothing as long as he was off in Harran, but then Mahmilji moved to Mooran and settled there for good, and their fears and reservations stirred again.

Now Muti was a little uneasy with the three guests he had summoned to the Ghadir Palace. He did not know how to begin his speech. He said, to explain his sorrow at the death of the Sultan: "He was a father to us all. He looked after the great and the small. . . ." He paused a moment and added emotionally, "I remember, a week before he died, God's mercy allowed him to hear some of the Koran, and the tears streamed from his eyes, down his cheeks and into his beard, and he couldn't budge to wipe them away!"

He drew a sobbing breath and continued.

"It is a great loss, one that can never be compensated. We can only be patient and wait for the day when we join him in eternal rest!"

The three guests believed and did not believe what they were hearing. They were certain that he was holding back something quite different from what he was now saying, and that what was on his mind was not the death of the Sultan, but they kept silent.

After a long silence heavy laden with remembrance, he went on in an emotional tone.

"Dr. Subhi still wishes to remain in Harran. We all tried to convince him to move, to settle here, but he says, 'I'm used to Harran, I have my friends there. The Shifa Hospital is the only one in Harran—how can I leave the sick? Who will take care of them?'"

He shook his head in profound grief.

"Had it not been for the Sultan's insistence, no other power on earth could have forced him to change his mind!"

This subject struck the three men as strange. They may have heard of Dr. Subhi or seen him, or heard talk about his superhuman efforts to save—or kill—the Sultan, but they did not understand why the private secretary of Sultan Khazael had summoned them to discuss the doctor.

"So if he likes Harran, let him stay in Harran," said Shamran al-Oteibi.

"And what of the views of His Majesty the Sultan?" hissed Muti, shocked and contemptuous.

"There are loads of pharmacies here and doctors too. Harran has no one—let him stay in Harran."

"And what of His Majesty's views of the matter, Abu Nimr?"

"And the people of Harran, aren't they our own, and the Sultan's subjects too?"

"But the Sultan wants him here."

"Then it's in God's hands—the Sultan must have his wish," replied Shamran with subtle contempt.

Again silence fell. Both sides realized that what had been said was only a preface to what was coming, or rather a rehearsal for the true or serious part. Fahaid al-Olayan spoke up to change the subject.

"If it doesn't rain once or twice between now and Ramadan, everyone is either going to leave here or die."

"Trust in God, men," said Abu Nimr very ironically. "Now that His Majesty is here, our troubles are over forever."

"Everything that comes to pass is God's will, my friends," said Muti, who sensed that the discussion was slipping away from him, "and I believe that the days to come will bring much good with them." He waited for no reply or comment, but added in a new tone of voice, "My friends, His Majesty the Sultan has asked me to meet with you, and there is a favor he wishes to ask of you."

They looked at him and they looked at one another, silent and expectant.

"His Majesty wants Dr. Subhi to be near him, and he wants the new hospital to be convenient. The land west of the Ghadir Palace belongs to Sheikh Shamran. We want that land, Abu Nimr, and will pay whatever price you want!"

Muti paused a moment to adjust his sitting posture, turned slightly and resumed.

"We want to build a hospital either on the land between al-Hawooz and the market, or between the wall and Duleyi Alley. It will be the biggest hospital in Mooran, open to all and treating all diseases. So what do you men say?"

The negotiations were brief, full of pressure and inducements, and interrupted at one point by the chief of police, who brought two of Shamran's sons; they were made to understand that the matter at hand left no room for refusal or stubbornness; it was the wish of the Sultan himself. Finally it was agreed that Dr. Subhi would buy the lot west of the Ghadir Palace and the one between al-Hawooz and the market. The price of the lots would be set by a committee of three persons: one would be chosen by Dr. Subhi, the second by the chief of police, and the third by Fahaid al-Olayan for his land. Shamran al-Oteibi remained stubborn, moving one of his friends to join the committee. "Otherwise," he was told, "you'll lose the land and get no price for it, and you, Abu Nimr, will pay the tax and surveying charges from your own pocket."

After the transaction Dr. Subhi was compelled to go back to Harran, "because the government has decided to buy the Shifa Hospital, so I have to visit the patients and check on them and discuss their cases with the doctors and staff replacing me. And I have to say my formal good-byes to the emir, and to all the dear friends I have there."

4

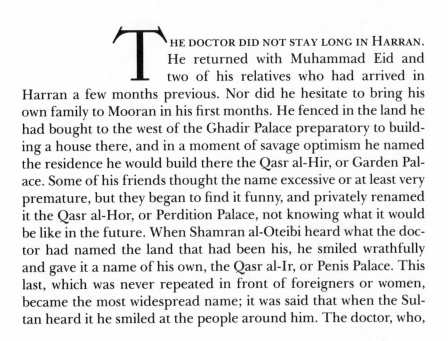

THE DOCTOR DID NOT STAY LONG IN HARRAN. He returned with Muhammad Eid and two of his relatives who had arrived in Harran a few months previous. Nor did he hesitate to bring his own family to Mooran in his first months. He fenced in the land he had bought to the west of the Ghadir Palace preparatory to building a house there, and in a moment of savage optimism he named the residence he would build there the Qasr al-Hir, or Garden Palace. Some of his friends thought the name excessive or at least very premature, but they began to find it funny, and privately renamed it the Qasr al-Hor, or Perdition Palace, not knowing what it would be like in the future. When Shamran al-Oteibi heard what the doctor had named the land that had been his, he smiled wrathfully and gave it a name of his own, the Qasr al-Ir, or Penis Palace. This last, which was never repeated in front of foreigners or women, became the most widespread name; it was said that when the Sultan heard it he smiled at the people around him. The doctor, who, it was said, had no secrets from His Majesty, showed no sign of anger. Muhammad Eid tried to convince him, using twisted and ribald means, not to give the property any name at all, arguing that in Mooran and Harran and most other cities houses were simply not given names. The doctor gnashed his teeth.

"Listen, my boy, and learn something now: the doctor has come to this place to change things: minds, people, and names too! And you'll live to see it!"

Despite this conviction, which colored all the doctor's thinking and gave him his self-confidence and ability to ignore what people said, he trembled a little when he arrived in Mooran to settle there for good: this city, which resembled no other city on earth, sunk in a distant, forgotten desert, with its brackish, bitter water, seemed almost uninhabitable. He grew worried, troubled by insomnia or even illness, just as had happened to him when he'd first moved to Harran. He remembered what he had told Muti more than a year before, when he'd brought him, grumbling and complaining, to Harran, and he laughed when he thought back on his solemn words, as he tried to convince Muhammad Eid to accompany him to Mooran.

"Listen, Muhammad, you're as dear to me as my own son Ghazwan, or even dearer. I've spent more time with you than I have with my own children." He laughed with remembrance and went on. "I know more than you do, Muhammad; as the proverb says, 'Older by a day, wiser by a year.' I want you to be with me in Mooran. I promise you won't regret it!"

The doctor described in great detail what a spacious and elegant city Mooran was and what its people were like. It was nothing like Harran, which had become a refuge for brigands, thieves, smugglers and the idle unemployed. It was unlike Ras Badra or Awali or any other city. The doctor remembered what he'd said at the end of his speech.

"Once you get there and settle down, you won't believe how happy and easy things are. You'll regret every moment you spent in Harran!"

Muhammad Eid did not need all this persuading: he was not as hesitant as the doctor thought. But in order not to seem rash or servile, he asked how many people lived there and what the climate was like. He asked whether the doctor would open a hospital there like the Shifa Hospital, or a bigger one. The doctor gave brief and ambiguous answers; he did not want to bother himself with problems and ideas whose time had not yet come.

He told Muhammad Eid, who was busy packing firearms presented to the doctor by the Emir of Harran: "The only problem, my little Eid, is that we have to get used to the clothes these fools wear!"

Muhammad Eid paused, looked at the doctor, who had already dispensed with most of his old wardrobe, and smiled.

"The truth is, Doctor, no one could tell you weren't one of them!" His smile broadened until he almost laughed out loud. "Until you open your mouth!"

The doctor thought back on this and other things as he paced the balcony: the day he had arrived in Harran, the day he became a man of rank there, and how he had found his feet and "put down roots," as he liked to say. He had helped to build the city, had founded a hospital, and joined the Chamber of Commerce. He recalled the large sum of money he had donated to build the Great Mosque. He was not only a partner in the construction of the huge downtown buildings, but one of the three major shareholders, and he had made decisive changes both in the planning and construction stages.

Not only that, he was one of the most admired men in Harran: people were proud of everything he had done. His ideas and comments were repeated everywhere, and even the jokes he made with the emir and his friends were the stuff of gossip. Of course they got changed, and he was sometimes put out when he heard them repeated in their new, distorted versions, or when people retold them without his flair, but deep down he was pleased. So it had been in Harran: he was respected. He felt his reputation was complete when, after deciding to leave Harran and informing the emir that he was compelled to resettle in Mooran, the emir clutched his forehead and squawked.

"Who can take your place, Abu Ghazwan?"

He explained, keeping his eyes on the floor so as not to embarrass the emir further.

"By God, Abu Ghazwan, Harran is dead when you go away on a

trip—how will it be when you've left for good?" asked the emir in a sincerely pained voice. He paused and added resignedly, "If these are His Majesty's orders, then of course we must obey." He sighed deeply. "Perhaps I'll come along too, Abu Ghazwan!"

Here, in Mooran, it was easy to get rich, it was possible to live, but the people here were something else again. They were like desert animals: scaly, rough and mean, thick-skinned and unknowable. Even their laughter was short and gruff, and when they did speak their minds they spared nothing and no one. They gnawed even at themselves. Why had he come here? To offer them his flesh to eat day and night? To help pass their long, empty nights?

This was how he thought as he reviewed his life, when he felt regretful or nostalgic for the irrecoverable past. He said to himself, with a challenge, *It is men who create places and leave their stamp upon them when their minds and hearts catch fire from a great cause. If they seek only water, shade and the easy life, they die off like insects and leave nothing behind.*

The doctor paced the wide balcony of the house he had rented near the Rawdh Palace and raised his arms level with his shoulders as he breathed; this is what he had been taught as a student, for it was the healthy way, and he had taught his children to do it. He remembered how he had said, smiling, in his loudest voice: "I and Mooran, and the time is now!"

He laughed delightedly at this purest of poetry.

5

OORAN WAS, IN THOSE YEARS FOLLOWING
midcentury, still a desolate and forgotten
settlement: more than a village but not
quite a city, much like the little towns strewn along the trade routes
or in the larger oases. The people there lived humble, even rough
lives. Fathers inherited from their forefathers a simple view of life
and death; and because they did not expect much of life or fear
death during the years they spent on earth, toiling for a crust of
bread, and though the crust was hard or remote most of the time,
they did find ample time to contemplate their surroundings, and
took delight in memorizing poetry, verses from the Koran and old
folktales. On the long summer nights they found their spirits de-
parting beyond life and death and their eyes wandering the heavens to locate the stars and planets or trying to read in the wind the
signs of dust storms, locusts and catastrophes.

Because of Mooran's desolate, isolated location, no one ever went there unless it was his actual destination, so the townspeople knew each other intimately; the complex relations and blood relationships were part of their lives. An outsider had no chance of penetrating the thick shell enclosing these people and their lives; he might succeed only after long years of grueling effort. The people of Mooran had seen any number of foreigners arriving or passing through and had, for the most part, shown no fear or unease, for within the cocoon that protected and warmed, and in light of their own profound interrelations, they knew how to protect themselves, how to react to everything that happened around them. They were confident that foreigners had no patience and knew none of the hidden paths into the depths of the desert or of men; they would not stay long. Those who'd come to settle were soon overcome with unease, and fear slew them with the onslaught of the searing, dust-tormented days, as they realized that their choice was either to die or to leave. Those who had no place else to go and were full of resolve to stay were slowly transformed into a species of people no different from the Mooranis themselves, in their appearance, their mannerisms, their facial features and the will that bred the power to endure. As to those consumed by nostalgia, their tongues stung by the bitter salt of the water here, they felt besieged, as though Death were lurking near and would suddenly assault them. Then, one summer night, they would be gone, with a caravan or camel driver, having told no one, and no one the wiser. With their flight, all news of them was lost and the absence was total. No stranger, having left, ever came back to Mooran.

So Mooran had been for hundreds of years. True, it had grown and expanded in some eras, only to shrink and decline in others, and plagues, famines and mourning had nearly effaced the town, but it always rose again from the sands to live again.

It was an eerie city. The tales children heard from their grandmothers were full of evil genies and demons, of hidden voices and flashes of lightning. The city baffled young and old, who looked all around them, masking their fear and anticipation with silence.

Mooran's rulers feared the city more than they loved it, always expecting the earth to crack open and destroy everything. This fear, which had guided the rulers since Mooran was founded, and for which they could find no conscious reason, filled them with a truth that dominated them always: to live for today, not to wait for tomorrow, for one day tomorrow would not come. This truth slowly and secretly infected Mooran with a state of constant apprehension, a waiting that did not know boredom. The eyes of the people never left the palace of the Sultan, no matter which Sultan it was.

Every city has its own mood and character, and Mooran was at times filled with joys or fears, but with the death of Sultan Khureybit Mooran took on an intensely brooding aspect. Its people were watching and waiting for something, but if asked they would have been unable to say what.

Shamran al-Oteibi heard the news of the Sultan's death while sitting and talking with his three sons, some relatives and a few friends.

"The Rawdh Palace has seen them come and go before him, and if God spares us and we live and last, there will be still more to tell."

Some of the people had long known what a Moroccan astrologer was supposed to have told Prince Khazael during his travels when he was still crown prince. He had warned Khazael against one thing: moving into his father's palace, since that palace would be ill-omened for the present Sultan's successors. The prince was afraid and asked for more interpretation, but the astrologer only told him, "I've said what you need to know. Be warned!"

The people knew this story, which one of the prince's servants had circulated secretly years before, but rarely recalled or repeated it. The only person who never forgot it for a single day was the prince himself, but when he remained in his palace, so that Mooran looked to the Ghadir Palace instead of the Rawdh Palace, some of the people remembered the Moroccan story. Their hearts were filled with fear, but their fear gave way to brooding.

This was Mooran as it had been since the beginning of earthly time, but when the doctor arrived there for the first time he saw only a cluster of contiguous mud houses. Except for the Rawdh Palace and the emirate building, no building could be distinguished from any other. Even the crown prince's palace, the Ghadir, so much longer than the neighboring houses, seemed like one of them because it was so plain and low. It was flanked by a broad courtyard, edged by a wide border planted with vegetation and

flowers. Beyond the garden, under the palm trees, was a gate leading to the inner palace. High walls divided the inner palace itself
into several wings, out of consideration for the prince's wives and
for security reasons, to facilitate its defense should it come under
attack.

Mooran's neighborhoods were tortuous and overlapping, their
narrow streets crowded with dust, children and flies. Markets at
the fringes of the neighborhoods stretched to the east and north,
almost bordering the Rawdh Palace on one side and extending to
the Souq al-Halal, the major market, in the other direction. Homes
mingled with shops and occupied much of the market district.

Mooran was inhabited by bedouin, and though some had
settled, they kept their bedouin way of life. Camels roamed the
small squares and were tied by the doorways, tents were set up by
the mud rooms, and firewood was stacked in the larger squares,
where earthen ovens were dug. Not far away, on the other side of
the squares, were cookshops. Sheep were slaughtered in the
ditches outside the houses, whose walls bore old bloodstains, dried
a scabby brown.

The doctor's heart sank when he first saw the town; even Harran
was far prettier and better laid out. His opinion of the place was no
better after he moved and settled there. He tried to console himself
and convince others, being assured of two things: this was the capital, and thus certain to change and surpass the other cities, and
it was large, with three or four times the population of the other
cities.

Except for the Saffan district to the extreme west of the city,
where the houses were newer and better cared for, Mooran made
a visitor catch his breath and filled his heart with an obscure sorrow—sunk, as it was, in the gloom of centuries, and nearly
forgotten.

Even after the oil had begun to flow, and ships started arriving
daily at Harran to offload tons of cargo every hour, Mooran was
barely affected; she still waited for rain that never came, for caravans that had lost their way. She sent her sons away with every caravan and camel herder, in the hope that they would return
someday with some wheat or cloth, or send wheat, cloth or a few
coins from wherever they had settled. Mooran had the patience of

a camel in the face of thirst and hunger, except when hunger had nearly wasted her, and the tyranny of thirst had exceeded any bearable limit; at such times Mooran lashed out, killing herself and others in uprisings of fever, madness and death, until balance had been restored between it and its surroundings.

When the doctor took possession of the lands west of the Ghadir Palace and near al-Hawooz, Shamran made a remark that long resounded in the hearts and minds of the people.

"Mooran has never been the Garden of Eden, and I suppose it never will be; those parasites and pickpockets aren't satisfied with anything less than taking over the land itself. We have nothing to do with them and nothing in common with them. They prefer their infidel friends anyway; you'll see."

The doctor had kept busy in Harran and had no time to listen to what people said, or to respond to them, but had much to do here as well. Mooran was not Harran, and the people differed from Harran's, but despite his determination to stay and to adapt, he stayed far outside the thick shell enclosing the people and life here; rather, he kept to the things that he knew or had tested before. This meant concentrating all his efforts on that great boulder, as he called him: the Sultan himself.

All his time was the Sultan's, all his experience and ingenuity were at the service of His Royal Majesty, for he was confident that whoever won over the Sultan had won everything. And he was stronger than anyone else.

In the very earliest days the doctor chose a moment carefully for a word with His Majesty.

"Permit me, Your Majesty the Sultan, to say what must be said: you are the king of all kings and God's gift to the world! Your coming has brought blessings after anxious and miserable times.

"Mooran was forgotten, remote, a non-place: none but the lost or fugitive came here, and none but the toughest survived here, but you came, bringing blessings; when you touched the sand, it turned all to gold. You will do much here; you will make the land and the people into new land and new people. And we, Your Majesty the Sultan, are servants in your charge: order and we obey, command and we respond."

The Sultan was amazed by this eloquence and deeply moved by

the doctor's emotion. He laughed, as a horse neighs, showing his large teeth, and stared hard through his eyeglasses to see if the doctor meant what he was saying, or if he was making fun of him. He saw that he was serious and worked up, almost desperate.

"Trust in God, Doctor—God willing, only the best will happen."

"Your Majesty, my lord, you know better than any other man there has been oil under this land for thousands of years, untouched in its place, until your late father, after seeking counsel far and near, asking questions and making inquiries, told them, 'Now carry out the will of God!'" He paused and drew a difficult breath, then added, "The oil might have stayed in the bowels of the earth, Your Majesty, for hundreds or thousands of years, but divine care, approval and the good fortune that comes only from Almighty God, said, 'Be!' and it was. Now, more than at any other time, and here, above any other place, Your Majesty, you can transform Mooran into a paradise on earth and rule over the far and the near!"

6

THE ARRIVAL OF DR. SUBHI'S FAMILY IN
Mooran caused a great stir. Muhammad
Eid had announced several prospective
dates for the family's arrival, then always said that some unfore-
seen event had delayed the trip. He held forth at great length
about every member of the family, listing their names and describing each in detail. Two of the three, he said, had the doctor's looks
and intelligence. The middle son and younger girl were the
nephew and niece of Mrs. Mahmilji. Eid praised the almost legendary beauty of the Hayek family, male and female alike, so it was
understood that the doctor's wife was of that family.

The news spread quickly and was hotly discussed in the Saffan
district, in al-Munazah and the surrounding neighborhoods, while
Muhammad Eid busied himself trying to furnish and prepare the
doctor's house as beautifully as possible. He enlisted two servants
from the palace and had Radwan, the doctor's chauffeur, bring his

wife to help. He and the chauffeur pitched in as well, but their frantic effort to be helpful, which seemed more like clumsy sabotage, much to the hilarity of the women trying to work beside the men, slowed the pace of the work and forced them all to work as slowly as blind persons. Their mistakes were small, but Muhammad Eid grew angry and exasperated. Finally he felt compelled to send the women away, before the work was done, to finish everything himself—it was "easier on his nerves," he told Radwan.

On the last day before the family's arrival the doctor had a look at the balcony, which Muhammad Eid had decorated with pots of flowers and plants. When he asked in astonished tones where he had come by the potted plants, Muhammad smiled triumphantly.

"I borrowed them, sir!"

The doctor looked confused.

"I told Rushdy Laham we'd return them to him in a few days, probably even taller than they are now. We only want them for Umm Ghazwan's arrival, because angels don't visit a house that has no greenery."

A telegraphic signal to the emirate building gave a final date for the family's arrival. It read:

GATE OF HOPE HERE.

KINDLY INFORM DR SUBHI AL-MAHMILJI ON YR PART THAT

HIS FAMILY DEPARTED EN ROUTE FOR MOORAN IN GD HEALTH STOP

MOORAN ARRIVAL TOMORROW MONDAY BETWEEN

LATE AFTERNOON AND EVENING GOD WILLING STOP

TAKE NECESSARY STEPS AND KINDLY INFORM STOP

SALAAM ALEIKUM.

After shy refusal and short-lived hesitations the doctor permitted Muhammad Eid to use the white convertible to pick up the family. The doctor had brought this car from Harran the previous year, or, more precisely, had accepted it from al-Salaami in payment for treatment and a stay in the hospital. Although the doctor had used the car several times in Harran, he was hesitant to do so here. He consented now because Muhammad Eid's argument was cogent and persuasive: "First of all, the car is big, so the children can ride in it; secondly, Radwan can't keep right and left straight, so I'll have to lead the way for them." He added sadly: "The fact is,

Doctor, that we'll have to use this car sooner or later before it rusts away to nothing in the garage!"

The doctor had already given several subtle indications that he would not be on hand to greet the family at Wadi Riha, on the eastern outskirts of Mooran. He had decided that doing so would look idle, and not befit his new social position. Muhammad Eid instinctively understood this point, but wanted to test the doctor.

"What time shall we set out, sir?" he asked the doctor slyly.

"They are supposed to arrive in the late afternoon, so you should be there at least by midafternoon."

"And you, sir?"

"I'll be waiting for you here," chuckled the doctor.

"The children will be wild, sir!"

"Never mind, I'll take care of them, don't worry."

Muhammad, who usually prepared luncheon by himself, and took to supervising its preparation after the doctor hired an Indian cook he had brought along to Mooran, had no thoughts of lunch today, or even of going near food. After helping Radwan wash the car, he requested, albeit in the tone of a command, that they drive it out immediately to test it. They did this once in midmorning, just after the doctor had left for the palace, and then again shortly before noon, reaching Wadi Riha; they wanted to test the power of the car and see what speeds the road allowed. It occurred to Muhammad to stay there and wait, but the look Radwan gave him made him change his mind. He had a light lunch and was finished as Radwan was thinking of having seconds; Radwan's eyes took in the several platters of food; this was the largest amount of food he had ever seen here. When Muhammad's voice broke in urging him to hurry, he nodded silently but in a cold fury.

Muhammad's suggestion that they use the white convertible was a sound idea, and his road test attracted twice the attention the car usually got. The children of Saffan and al-Munazah, and the men who watched in astonishment, and the women who could not stay indoors—several went outside on the pretext of finding or retrieving their children—caused a commotion that caught the attention of the doctor as he was leaving the palace. He was amazed to see men stopping when he passed by and the children running behind the car; for the first time since he had come to Mooran he saw women standing outside the doors of their houses. He said to himself, not hiding his pleasure, *That scamp, he makes such a production of everything—what will people think?*

At home he asked Abu Abdallah what time Muhammad Eid had left.

"The instant of noon prayers—the muezzin had barely finished saying *Allahu akbar,* and they were off!"

The family arrived in Wadi Riha with the first fresh breezes of the evening, shortly after sundown. Their reception was rushed and a little chaotic, and Umm Ghazwan preferred to keep her children with her in the same car, though at the last moment Ghazwan decided to ride in the white convertible. When his mother did not protest, his brothers tried to join him, but a sharp and imperious shout from their mother put an end to that, and Muhammad Eid was greatly relieved; now they might arrive in Mooran before supper—before the streets emptied. He scolded the chauffeur for driving too slowly, and felt that the minutes between sundown and their arrival in Mooran were the longest of his life; their reception in al-Munazah would, he hoped, be noisy and emotional, to compensate for what he'd not been able to do here.

The two cars roared across Mooran to reach its westernmost point, Saffan, through darkness penetrated only by a few faint, scattered lights and silence broken only by the barking of dogs. The pedestrians caught by the cars' headlights were the last stragglers heading home, or heading to relatives or friends to pass the evening.

Mooran looked bleak, ugly and provincial to Muhammad's eyes as he sped through it from east to west; he could barely conceal his irritation as he answered Ghazwan's questions—the young man asked about the make of the car, when his father had bought it, how much horsepower it had. Muhammad's answers were brief and casual; he was concentrating on driving as slowly as possible down Mooran's main streets, in order to be seen. He had innocently asked Radwan, as they were en route to Wadi Riha, whether Qibly Street or Rawdh Street was longer, and whether people collected in Qibly Street after sundown. Radwan gave Muhammad a long and detailed answer, but ignored the actual question. He knew only certain roads, and had no idea whether they were longer or shorter than others. Even when the doctor asked Radwan to turn left or right, with the idea of exploring the city a little, he obeyed immediately but soon strayed back to the streets he knew well.

Muhammad Eid was filled with frustration and disappointment but had one last hope: that there would be a welcoming party in front of the house, and large crowds of neighbors.

No one was there but three boys, and the blind man who never left the corner of Saffan Street. Even Abu Abdallah had gone to great lengths to look excited, rushing back and forth and greeting the children several times each, and moved like a ghost. The doctor stayed out on the balcony at first, with a broad smile on his face, repeating the words over and over again loudly, but could not stay up there any longer—as he had made himself try to do, to test his feelings. When he heard Ghazwan calling, "Papa . . . Papa!" he rushed down the stairs. Ghazwan's heart sank when he saw his father's strange appearance; the beard, vanishing and reappearing as he passed from the shade to the light, and the bizarre, gaudy robes made the boy hesitate.

There was a babble of voices intermingling, and a great fuss over unloading their boxes and suitcases, and over showing the new-comers around the houses, and how to get in and out. It was a frantic blur of blind movement. The doctor found his way to the center of the crowd of people, hugging, kissing and weeping like a small confused child. Muhammad watched from a distance of about two or three steps, moved by the doctor's tears and the way he behaved and asked simple questions. Radwan and Abu Abdallah stood far off, pretending not to watch. Muhammad's heart filled with sympathetic sorrow, and he said to himself, *A man without his family, in a foreign country, is like a fish out of water.*

The neighbors in Saffan Street heard cries and laughter until very late that night. Abu Abdallah and Radwan remembered what Muhammad had told them, that the doctor had only three children, but when they'd counted them, there were five. They exchanged baffled looks, and the next morning they glanced at Muhammad and smiled.

7

MOORAN SEEMED A REPULSIVE CITY TO WIdad as she gazed out her window early the next morning. The semidetached houses, low and monotonous like an endless succession of hard mud bricks; the few scattered palm trees, naked and dead; even the morning breeze, fresh though it was, felt dry and stank of dust. She gazed out on the scene and sighed deeply. While drinking coffee with her husband on the balcony, before the children were up, she felt a peculiar mixture of relaxation, pleasure, unease and real fear. Her emotions were confused and unsettled: blurred. Between sips of coffee she watched him, wanting to see him in daylight.

The night before, as she slept by his side, his beard—which he had trimmed and perfumed several times that day—scraped and bothered her, more than she'd ever imagined when she first saw him bearded for the first time after long absence. At night she called him by a pet name she had almost forgotten, it had been so long: "Suboohi, what *have* you done to yourself? I'm really cross with you." He pressed her close to him to let his body answer, but she drew away slightly and continued, in the same whisper, "The beard isn't nice, it ages you and changes your face." She wanted to say that it made him look ugly, but did not want to hurt him. When his whole body shook with laughter, loud and resonant, in reply, she went on: "Even the children didn't recognize you, and Salma asked me, 'Mama, is that man going on *hajj* or what?'"

Now, in the first light of morning, after a sleepless night for both of them, except for intermittent dozes, everything had a new feel to her. After the long journey and this longer night, she was trying to find the man she had lived with for so long. She knew him well and yet hardly knew him; he was strange and familiar at the same time. It wasn't only the beard: his hairline had receded, his complexion was darker, but his eyes still sparkled with the same mixture of worry and self-assurance, lust and fear. She avoided his eyes and pretended to be busy. He asked her how the children had slept and whether they were still asleep, and noticed immediately that she had not changed: she had not aged, the journey had not tired her, and in the few mad, blazing moments she knew how to give him, he had rediscovered her. Even as she half-jokingly played with his beard, tugging it, he was happy; he wanted her to do it.

He spoke, answering a question she had not asked: he'd read it in her eyes, which circled around to take in the horizon of the city, as if seeing it for the first time.

"God willing, our house will be finished before the end of the year, Widad darling."

"God willing."

"That house is something else—it's not a house, it's a palace."

"It looks like this country has been good to you," said Widad, laughing out of pleasure but with a little fear in her voice. "Like you don't want to go home again!"

"This country is better than a lot of places, my dear," he replied a little tersely. Then he said in a different tone of voice, "It won't take you long to get used to it."

"All I want, Abu Ghazwan, is to be with you, to help you, but I'm worried about the children," she said, with hidden aggression.

"Leave the children to me, Widad," he laughed. "Leave them to me." He stood up and walked over to the balcony railing. She stayed where she was but watched him. He spoke without looking back at her. "Come here, Widad."

She came to stand at his side, and he pointed.

"That tall building, opposite us, is the Rawdh Palace, the palace of the late Sultan. See the palm trees to the right of it? About four or five hundred meters beyond the trees is our house." He smiled and went on softly, as if talking to himself. "If you went up to the roof, you could see the exact site better." He did not give her a chance to speak. "God willing, in a few days we'll go and have a look."

"God is good. I'm hoping for the best," she said a little re-signedly.

Widad would not have given in so easily had she not heard move-ment behind them. She turned around to see lisping Salma, with the golden braids, the girl who knew every corner of her heart. Salma had no memory of the question she'd asked her mother the night before, about the bearded stranger; now she ran to him and hugged his neck and rocked herself against his chest. Reflexively she stretched out her little hand to give his beard a short hard tug. On the road to Mooran that early summer day, she had asked, "When will we get there?" hundreds of times; she wanted to get there with the speed of lightning. After napping and waking sev-eral times on the long desert road, after looking around longingly, she had become bored and talked to her doll. Now Salma herself asked her father: "Daddy, when we will go back home?" He cuddled her and said, "This is our home," and asked her to be pa-tient. It was a revelation to him, how much meaning he gave her life, and a certain full rich melody, even in his silence!

The rest of the children followed, led by Nadia. She was between girlhood and adolescence, slender, neither tall nor short, friendly and well-behaved, with large, laughing, honey-colored eyes. Widad had told him the night before, after the children had gone to bed, that her niece Nadia had been a great help to her. "And after the girl finishes school," Widad had said, "she will be the perfect match for Ghazwan, so we should raise her ourselves." This had seemed a little premature to the doctor, who thought Ghazwan too young to think of marrying, but he had made no comment.

Now she came, laughing like a small bird as she balanced the empty coffee cups and asked Uncle if he wanted more coffee or if he preferred a glass of water. He thanked her and said neither. She giggled shyly and asked him if he remembered her, because she remembered him so well. The doctor's smooth, confident reply— that he remembered her perfectly, and that she had not changed a bit in two years—moved him and his wife to give Nadia a brief looking-over, mostly over her body, for two years ago she had not had this poise, nor had she looked at men this way, or felt the hidden, unruly sensuality that her age gave her now. Two years ago he had not noticed the full breasts and shapely buttocks so prominent now. Even the shy giggle of two years ago had become something very different.

Kamal and Hamed came in together. They were grown and young at the same time. They had their private secrets, their own way of talking, of obeying and rebelling. When he asked them if they found Mooran beautiful, and if they would like to live here, they spoke at the same time, but he saw that neither of them wanted to stay. He said, in an effort to teach them a lesson they would long remember, especially when he saw Ghazwan coming:

"A homeland is not just land or people; a homeland, I have come to see, is wealth. A man settles wherever he prospers, because riches bring him power. Wherever he is, is his homeland. Someday you'll learn this for yourselves!"

Ghazwan stood and listened politely, waiting for his father to finish speaking. He looked at their faces, and at his father with a look of love mixed with awe. When the doctor finished, he spoke up loudly.

"Good morning, Father!"

The doctor, who loved all his children equally, had long been at a loss to explain the special love he felt for this "imp" who "enchanted" him. At first he assumed that it was because he was the eldest son; later he came to agree with his sister Kheiria, who said that "Ghazwan is the absolute image of his father, in thought, word and deed—the only difference is that one of them is big and one small." During the doctor's last visit home, Ghazwan had seemed a man before his time: he loved to sit in with the men and listen to their discussions, and he acted like his father: he ordered his brothers around, and they looked at him in a way siblings rarely regard one another; even the neighbors, the doctor was told, regarded Ghazwan as a little man! He never hesitated to do anything adults did. Now that the doctor saw him in the light of day, he was taken aback by his son's downy mustache and deep voice. Now he was a man: even his gaze was bolder and more appraising than ever before. The doctor thought to himself that the boy had truly pleased his father; he felt the glow of his special love.

"Come, come here, Son!" said the doctor theatrically.

One glance was enough for Kamal to give up his chair beside their father; Ghazwan occupied it, silent, his head bowed.

"Tell me, Ghazwan, how was the trip? Were they sad to see you go?"

"Everything was fine, Daddy. Everyone back home, every one of them told me, 'Be sure to give your father our love.'"

The doctor laughed delightedly.

"What else, Ghazwan?"

"There's so much else, but I don't know where to begin!"

The doctor felt renewed confidence as he gazed at his son. He looked around to take in the rest of his family. He paused.

"And your studies, how are your studies?"

"I'm anxious about all their studies," said Widad worriedly. "Back there they were getting an excellent education. Now I just hope for the best."

"Look, Umm Ghazwan," the doctor reassured her, "I didn't send for all of you until I had really studied every detail of the situation myself." To cut off further discussion, he went on grandiloquently: "Mooran has a private academy, and its standards and its program of studies are just like in Beirut, even better than in Beirut. Nothing will change for the children."

"And it's a mixed school, boys and girls together?" said Kamal sarcastically.

Ghazwan frowned at his brother.

"Mooran is not Beirut. Be careful," said their mother a little ambiguously.

"Kamal told me he'll never get married to one of them," joked Hamed, stuttering a little.

Umm Ghazwan spoke up sharply to catch her husband's attention.

"Just keep quiet, all of you, you're barely more than babies and talking like grownups! You may have done just as you pleased back there with your father away, but now watch it or you'll get what you're asking for!"

"Be patient, Umm Ghazwan," said the doctor soothingly. "The children are bigger now. They know their responsibilities, and how to take care of themselves, and they know I know it!"

8

THE FAMILY HAD BEEN IN MOORAN FOR JUST A week when the doctor approached His Majesty very humbly and a little shyly, to seek permission for Widad to be received by Majda, the Sultan's wife, to pay her respects. The Sultan's response was brief and a little confused: no permission was needed—the women of the palace, including his wife, were unused to such protocol. The doctor went on to ask His Majesty if he might graciously spare one minute of time for Ghazwan to kiss his hands. Since his second day in Mooran, Ghazwan had begged to accompany his father to the palace "just once" to see where his father sat and what he did. Now His Majesty the Sultan nodded.

"Your son is like one of our own sons, Doctor. He is most welcome—we want to know him."

The doctor signaled Mleihan, the royal chamberlain, to summon Ghazwan, and addressed the Sultan.

"The prompt giver gives twice, Your Majesty. Ghazwan has come
with me today to carry out his duty."

As in stories of bright youngsters who had the chance to meet
kings or presidents, who knew how to speak and what rules to ob-
serve, Ghazwan remembered everything. He entered in his im-
maculately white Arab clothes, his face pink with health and
timidity, and spoke in a shout unsuited to the little room and small
number of people in attendance.

"Greetings—peace be upon you!"

He bowed his head in the direction of the Sultan several times to
express his devout respect, then bowed briefly to the right and to
the left. When he had completed these dramatic gestures, he advanced and kissed the Sultan's hand. The Sultan was delighted
with the boy's manners and spoke to him kindly.

"Come here, my boy, come closer."

Like a shy girl, Ghazwan looked to his father to see whether the
space the Sultan was indicating was too big for him or not.

"Sit where the Sultan orders," said the doctor firmly.

Ghazwan sat, gazing at the floor, his fingers enlaced on his chest.
When the Sultan asked him how he was and how his studies were
going, he appeared embarrassed as he replied in the words and
expressions that his father had taught him in the preceding few
days. The Sultan asked whether he intended to be a doctor like his
father, or whether he preferred some other career. Ghazwan
raised his head slightly, glanced at his father and then at the Sultan,
and spoke with a confident smile.

"I prefer whatever career you choose for me, Your Majesty!"

The Sultan laughed loudly and nodded, pleased.

"The fruit never falls far from the tree!"

The doctor kept his head bowed, not looking at the faces around
him; he even looked embarrassed, as if taken by surprise. After a
few moments he raised his eyes to Ghazwan and spoke firmly, but
not angrily.

"The visit is over. We should leave."

The boy started to rise several times, but did not know how to
withdraw; he stood and then sat down again, looking at his father
a little resentfully, for not having taught him how to take his
leave.

"Your Majesty," said the doctor, "would it please Your Majesty to give your servants leave to go?"

The Sultan was not yet used to being addressed in this fashion; he thought the doctor was overdoing it. He said only, "God willing, we will see a great deal more of the boy!"

Several days later the doctor's wife visited the women's wing of the palace with Salma. Although his wife made a major effort to recall the words the doctor had repeatedly taught her, and asked her to practice and memorize, she could not pronounce them as he did. In the first moments she decided to be herself: if she became a figure of fun, from the beginning, she would never live it down later. She reasoned, *Better they should smile at my accent than laugh at me.*

She was surprised by the palace women: she could not tell which of them was the Sultan's wife. She did not catch some of what they said, or did not quite understand it. At least she could tell which were the princesses and which the servants, by their clothes and the way they looked at one another, and she understood the questions they asked her. These were mainly about her husband: whether he had married her before or after he'd become a doctor, and whether he could handle every kind of medical problem. They asked, with knowing smiles, if he treated women and, if so, how he "examined" them—with someone else present or alone? She answered the questions with no trace of embarrassment or fear, though she wondered if their smiles and the looks they exchanged among themselves were provoked by her answers or her Levantine dialect. In spite of this, she felt quite pleased and proud as she spoke—these were women she could get along with; they would come to love her.

They all noticed Salma, who looked like a doll with her blond braids and elegant dress, and they seemed to approve of her manners and questions. At first she was like a timid kitten, clinging to her mother's side, but as the time passed she looked more boldly at the women and everything around her; she responded shyly to their questions at first, then with more confidence. One of the women rose and left the room briefly, only to reenter with a gold necklace. She asked Salma to come near; the girl held back, but her mother pushed and encouraged her, so that she stepped frightenedly forward. When the woman placed the necklace around her neck and kissed her, Salma felt a surge of happiness and security, and gladly sat beside the princess for a little while, looking up at her every so often.

When Widad tried to describe the visit to her husband, she was unable to give a clear picture of what they had talked about or what the women had looked like—her descriptions were vague. The old lady, the younger one, the one sitting on the right, and the one to her left. It all confused the doctor, who wanted her to talk about the Sultan's wife herself: her looks, how old she was, her likes and dislikes, and generally what kind of woman she was; but Widad was not sure of anything. Her general and abstract descriptions constantly changed and shifted; she answered his questions only in passing, with minor details. When she showed him the gold necklace given their daughter (which she had taken from the girl in the car, "because you'll lose it—you can wear it when you're older," as she told her; she put it in her own jewel box for safekeeping when they got home) he seemed ecstatic. He examined the jewelry closely and looked thoughtful.

"I'm positive that the one who gave this to Salma was the Sultan's wife!"

Widad looked very surprised, but he went on as if he had not noticed.

"It's usual in this country for the highest person socially to offer a gift—it's unthinkable that someone younger or of lesser standing would step in and do it."

"But she wasn't seated in the center!"

"They like to sit nearest the guest."

"And this other, older woman, whom they called Ummi Zahwa, she kept her eye on everybody, and no one spoke without looking at her for permission."

The doctor thought some more and asked more questions about the older woman. What did she say? How did she act? How had she looked at her and Salma?

The next morning Salma skipped around him, playing, reciting poems and singing songs that she had learned. He looked at her and thought to himself: *You and Ghazwan were born under the same sign, Aquarius, and your father was not far off.* The doctor immersed himself in thoughts and plans, but nothing came into clear focus. When Abu Abdallah brought his bitter coffee, the doctor smiled at him. "If things go my way, Abu Abdallah, I'll give you a bonus bigger than your salary!"

The doctor acted out a part as he drank his coffee, and looked supremely confident as he shook the cup gently after his third and last serving. He gave Abu Abdallah only a fleeting glance, exactly as the Sultan did when he glanced at Farhan.

As the doctor got into his car, he said to himself, *Capricorn and Aquarius turn sand into gold; God willing, I won't be disappointed.*

9

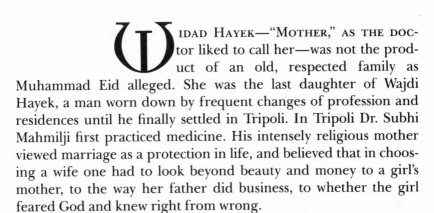

IDAD HAYEK—"MOTHER," AS THE DOC-
tor liked to call her—was not the product of an old, respected family as
Muhammad Eid alleged. She was the last daughter of Wajdi
Hayek, a man worn down by frequent changes of profession and
residences until he finally settled in Tripoli. In Tripoli Dr. Subhi
Mahmilji first practiced medicine. His intensely religious mother
viewed marriage as a protection in life, and believed that in choosing a wife one had to look beyond beauty and money to a girl's
mother, to the way her father did business, to whether the girl
feared God and knew right from wrong.

It was through his mother that the doctor met and married the
daughter of Wajdi Hayek, who had recently taken up a new livelihood, as an arbitrator of wills. This work, which suited him perfectly, led him to talk of nothing but Death and the dead: how
Death stole men but left their wealth behind so that the living

would quarrel over it; were it not for Death, people would be left to kill each other. He said that the dead went to their Creator in their shrouds, so that it was impossible to know any one of them from another, or to distinguish among them.

Widad heard these stories day and night, and as a result formed an antipathy toward this house, where there was nothing but talk of Death and the dead. When the doctor's mother came to look her over and arrange something, Widad gave the performance of her life and at last passed the test; scarcely had the woman come near her to smell her than Widad gave her, without being asked, a cup of the coffee she had convinced her own mother that she should have ready. While neither Widad nor her mother was in the room, Umm Subhi looked under the bed. "It couldn't be cleaner," she murmured delightedly to herself. "It's as clean as a mosque!" When the old woman was satisfied on every count, they discussed the betrothal and the wedding.

The doctor had already seen Widad and been enchanted with her long braid and fair complexion; she behaved better than other girls he'd known and always agreed with her mother. Her father's line of work did not much impress the doctor, but Wajdi Hayek, who stayed out of the preliminary negotiations, soon made his presence known, and his gentlemanly speech and behavior were a great reassurance to the doctor, who now hardly felt as though he were in the presence of a man who made his living dividing dead men's estates. Hayek referred obliquely to his profession and said, cleverly but a little defensively, that it was like any other line of work, that he pursued it because it was more congenial than many other professions. It was, he said, exactly like carpentry or haircutting, and he almost added medicine, but his little smile and general air expressed his meaning without words.

The doctor relocated in Aleppo to make a better living, where no one would misunderstand his profession. He did not make their marriage public. In Aleppo he made a name for himself and earned a good social standing, then moved on to Damascus and later to Beirut, where he became the physician for the *hajj* mission before settling, later on, in Harran.

Widad, who lived with the specter of Death she so feared and constantly fled from, because "my father's clothes stink of corpses, and my mother smells of the hereafter," never hesitated to move with the doctor from place to place. When he accompanied the pilgrimage to Mecca the first time, he returned complaining that he had been unable to accomplish anything decisive as far as "his family's rights" were concerned; time had been short, and "those elderly pilgrims never rest, and never let anyone around them rest." He would go back again, to settle the title deeds and because "that country has a future—with a little shrewdness, a man can get rich overnight there."

This kind of thinking struck Widad as premature, but she did not argue with her husband, since she had no clue that he was serious about emigrating there.

The following year, a few weeks before the date set for the departure of the pilgrimage mission, in order not to allow himself or anyone else to oppose his new idea, or even to discuss it, the doctor sold his clinic and referred away all his patients. In the final days, as Widad prepared his clothes and instruments, he told her that this time he would be away for a long time; he might send for her to join him. He gave her an unusually large amount of money and told her not to worry about the house—"Kheiria will take care of everything." Widad was used to being agreeable, and even more used to this man who always made his decisions without giving explanations, so she asked no questions, especially since she realized that the doctor might well change his mind about the whole business. After he settled in Harran, he made several short visits home to tell her about this city that throbbed with money and life and possibilities. He said that his clinic in Aleppo was smaller than the lobby of the new hospital he was building in Harran, and that he was beginning to realize dreams and plans he'd always had. She tried to believe him, but was happy to stay where she was, with the doctor visiting occasionally and sending enough money to take care of the house and the children.

During the years the doctor spent away from his wife and children, he visited Beirut only once or twice a year, and then only for a couple of weeks during which he was busy buying drugs and equipment and hiring nurses and doctors. He met with dozens of people to discuss projects that had nothing to do with his profession, then suddenly signed contracts for projects—their exact scope and nature, and who would run them, no one seemed to know. When Widad asked him about them, his brief replies made the projects seem even more mysterious. As to the family lands in Arabia that had been his original motive for going, he no longer mentioned them. When Widad once asked him about them, he looked at her as if trying to remember what she could be talking about, and when it came to him he smiled at her.

"I'm optimistic about them—it just needs a little more time!" He gave no details, and she never asked about it again.

In these years not only the doctor changed—Widad changed with him. Her complacent view of life, her unquestioning obedience, the philosophy the doctor tried to teach her in the early years of their marriage—all this changed. The change was not sudden, nor was it conscious or brought about by any one cause.

She wanted to escape from Death. She accepted her life with the doctor because he filled the house and every place around her, because she could find no other way out, because she did not know anyone. Now that the doctor drew further and further away from her, making only short visits that occupied him with new deals, Widad found that the life she was living was only another facet of the death she had been fleeing.

Widad enjoyed the days and weeks he spent with her, but felt that she needed more. The money he referred to, briefly and indirectly, was not real money because she did not have it in her hands, because it had not been turned into something she could enjoy; his great prestige in Harran, that unknown city that meant nothing to her, had little relevance for her as long as she was far away and forgotten, remembered by him in the way he remembered drugs, diseases and death. The children were growing up fast; he wanted them to be just like him, but they hardly saw him anymore. When he was home, they were not; when they came home from school, he was busy discussing new business deals with people—Widad had no idea where he conjured them up from; they came to visit once or twice and she never saw them again.

Her body bothered her. Before they were married, the doctor smoldered and burned—she felt it in the way he looked at her, in the way his lower lip trembled slightly. Her body was the focal point of their early marriage, but in the years that followed she felt that the doctor was drawn away from her by ideas and concerns that she did not even understand; she ascribed it to tiredness and over-work. She felt sure that he would be back, like a rooster on a spring morning after a light drizzle, to make up for the days of neglect, but he only became more and more preoccupied with his work, then began to travel a great deal. Her body, which she hoped would humble him, tame him, with both pleasure and anger, mutinied against her, made demands, especially late at night and at dawn. It was still roused and ready, as if awaiting her signal to rise, fight and offer itself.

1o

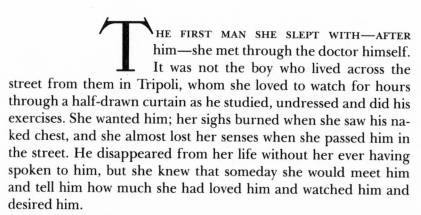

THE FIRST MAN SHE SLEPT WITH—AFTER him—she met through the doctor himself. It was not the boy who lived across the street from them in Tripoli, whom she loved to watch for hours through a half-drawn curtain as he studied, undressed and did his exercises. She wanted him; her sighs burned when she saw his naked chest, and she almost lost her senses when she passed him in the street. He disappeared from her life without her ever having spoken to him, but she knew that someday she would meet him and tell him how much she had loved him and watched him and desired him.

The man her husband brought home, three days before his departure for Harran, was also a doctor—the one who would take Subhi's place in the clinic. He came to the house to have "a last quick word" with the doctor and to settle the details of their agreement. Widad served coffee and sat with them briefly to get a fleeting look at the young doctor; he seemed much shyer than most young men his age, especially young doctors. He bore a striking resemblance to an Egyptian actor she had once loved and she almost told him so, but was prevented by modesty, or by the fear she felt when meeting a man for the first time.

Subsequently she went to the clinic to be treated for the pains she had felt all over her body in the months since the doctor's departure for Harran. Young Dr. Emad Qabbani gave her a complete examination and said that she was suffering from an unusual condition. He gave her tranquilizers, but the pains kept recurring. She felt relief—healed, almost—only when he touched her hands or body; she was sometimes untruthful with him, claiming that she had taken the medicine. She needed him much more than she needed the pills.

The fourth time, she told him, before he examined her, that she did not know how the pains came and went, that her problem had nothing to do with illness. She said this while staring into his eyes, and Emad understood immediately. When he asked her to undress for the examination, she did so and, within seconds, was trembling like a sparrow as she approached the examining table. She was frightened and intoxicated and feverish. She felt within herself a force greater than herself, untamed and defiant as the wind, and suddenly she realized that her arms were around Emad's neck, pressing him close to her. He showed no surprise, but controlled himself, responding cautiously, caressing her and gazing deep into her eyes, as if reading in them her ultimate consent, and when he was sure of it, he agreed to meet her that night.

On the first night, and all the nights that followed, Widad felt as if a stranger inside her were doing these things. The first time, she sobbed on his shoulder like a small girl, unable to look him in the eye, unresponsive to his caresses. After that night she was a different woman, helpless and confused. She decided, with a determination that bordered on anger, that she would never repeat her mistake. She punished herself. A few days passed, however, and her body began to burn again, and its hidden force romped again, charting its own course and making her forget everything she had said and the promises she had made, pushing her back to him more insistently than ever.

It went on like this for months. She used all her wiles and passion to find ways of visiting him with no one knowing or even suspecting, and never failed, although others, especially her women friends, had hidden eyes that knew without seeing, taking in the smell of things. Widad felt in the eyes of the women around her an accusing, malevolent curiosity; she strove harder than ever to disappear, to flee. If she stayed away for longer than Emad could bear, he always found an excuse to visit her: to pay the clinic rent, commissions, old water and electricity bills. He also had to pass by the house to see the children and check on their health as Subhi had asked him to do. These pretexts usually sufficed, and when they did not, he found others; when she tried to resist, he persuaded her, making her again aware of her body, so that in spite of her hesitations she always gave in. Afterward she was always haunted by the same feelings of depression, insignificance and resentment toward her body. Yet she was always quick to respond, with no limits or end in sight.

It plagued her from the beginning that she had planned none of this, but she was plagued much more deeply by the fact that Emad was a victim, that she had invaded his privacy and aroused him; she tried to forget or to bury this feeling in the wilderness of her memory, especially when she saw the longing and pleading of her victim, and his own sense of insignificance that reached the point of ruin in the face of her omnipotence, which grew time after time and month after month until she had to do something about it. When he told her that he had decided to get married, and that they would have to stop seeing each other temporarily, then devise a new way of meeting, she made an irrevocable decision. She listened to him with her eyes open, and when he had finished speaking, she smiled triumphantly and made a remark he would remember for years.

"I wanted it, in the beginning, and now you want it. Men always have the last word."

She did not say good-bye, indeed never spoke to him again, even when he came months afterward, carrying his medical bag, to examine the children. She asked Kheiria, Dr. Subhi's sister, to greet him and serve him coffee. The next time he came was during one of the doctor's visits, and she did not see him. She pretended to be ill, and told the doctor that she had a splitting headache and could hardly stand up.

Dr. Emad Qabbani was no longer part of her life, even though they lived in the same city for years afterward.

After Widad learned her lesson, judging that what had happened had been a slip, a whim stronger than she was that had overpowered her will, she devoted herself entirely to the children. The doctor, who considered the children his own appendages in the world, destined to carry on his family name, traits and traditions for generations to come, did not realize that the fleeting moments spent siring his children were nothing to the endless accumulation of changes since those moments, which was still going on and always would. His concept of these permanent and mystical appendages, his ineradicable insignia, was only a wish, a whim that no one else shared, which would disappear as soon as he was absent; and so it went. Kheiria's remark about the family resemblance, specifically between Ghazwan and his father, and what the doctor imagined in his great optimism, only strengthened the whim.

And her body? It weakened, angered, threatened and made demands on her—how could she deal with it? She would tame it and subdue it. And that was what happened in the period between Emad Qabbani's marriage and the appearance of Rateb Fattal.

The doctor saw Rateb Fattal as a lost youth, spoiled by an early inheritance. He had spent a number of years in Alexandria and Marseilles, first on the pretense of study, later claiming to be in business. By the time he returned to Beirut he had squandered a large part of his inheritance and earned no degree, though he had acquired vast practical experience and several foreign languages.

No one knew exactly what relationship existed between Rateb and the doctor, because the doctor was not proud of it. He tried to deny it, or at best did not expressly acknowledge it.

So it was for some time. Rateb felt no need to prove or deny the relationship, and went on changing his residence as each new deal demanded, then, bored, moved on, until one day the doctor—who had by then settled in Harran—came and offered him the deal of a lifetime, as he put it. The doctor needed an import–export office; he needed someone who spoke several languages, who had traveled around the world and understood people—above all, he needed "one of us," as he put it. He repeatedly stressed, in his indirect way, the strong bond between him and Rateb.

The idea would never have occurred to the doctor if Muti hadn't suggested it. Rateb saw in the offer a broad and dazzling horizon: he was, at the time, seeking a buyer for some of his land, but having no luck; so he was in financial difficulty and lost no time in accepting the doctor's offer. Rateb's only condition was that he not have to live in Mooran or Harran, that he be a "bird of passage." The doctor consented.

So two men founded the Oriental Import-Export and Transport Company, based in Beirut with branches in Harran, New York and Marseilles. In the course of dealing with all the details and technicalities, the men visited each other several times, and because family relationship was the cornerstone of the company, Widad was always present. On the first visit, she remembered distinctly the few times she had met Rateb before: once, at the wedding reception of the doctor's niece Zaina, and again at a party for Haj Wahib Shakhashirou when he returned from the *hajj* to Mecca; and a third time at Kheiria's.

Each time, Widad had felt that this wanton, cocksure young man was undressing her with his eyes as soon as he saw her. His eyes rested on her neck, then lowered slowly to take in her whole body from her neck to her calves. She slowly realized that this calm, slow stare could at any moment turn into an all-consuming conflagration. She feared and loved looks like that. She fled from them but felt totally encircled by them; no sooner had she gladly given in to them than she felt innumerable strange hands fondling every pore of her body. Once, she almost said this to the doctor, but lacked the courage, and besides what was the point? When Rateb left and their de facto estrangement took effect, he took his stares and searing lust with him.

Now that he was back and Widad listened to the two men as she carried the plates and cups, set the table, bustling about the room, she felt as if her clothes were flying off her body. They fell, one after another, some gently and others violently, until she was naked, completely naked. As soon as she had placed the dishes on the table, she ran her hands down her hips to check that her clothes were still there, and pressed them to her body. When her gaze met his, a wave of blood rushed to her head, like a cataract flooding back to its headwaters, and her mind clouded. She did not know how to act, where to go or what to do; his stare crowded her path, making her nervous and impulsive. When Rateb spoke to her as they sat around the table, she noticed how different he was from the doctor. He knew how to choose his words, how to speak and smile—more than anything else, he knew how to look at her. His glances across the dining table were like bolts of lightning, which ceased only to begin again, with a warm blaze that lit up her whole body, which had become hot, damp and white as milk.

Late that night, when the two men had agreed on all the details and gone off to bed, the doctor's body seemed to her soft and flaccid, almost like a pregnant woman's. When the hot embers inside her shifted, she expected it and could do nothing about it; when the doctor's panting breaths heated her body, she did not know whether he was just beginning or about to finish.

Before the third week was up, the doctor left. When Rateb called frequently at the house to check on the arrival of documents or to look up certain figures, no one's suspicions were aroused. He was one of the family, and people often saw Rateb and Widad together when the doctor was in town; now they heard that a new company had been formed, not run by the two men but by the family, their friends and anyone who wanted to work. Rateb, who was constantly on the move, in and out of the country to deal with details and seeking potential partners, acted independently, without fear or hesitation. Even when he went to the doctor's house and found a crowd of female relatives, or Widad busy with the children, he did not hesitate to plunge into a discussion of business matters and possible actions. During these visits, which took place both in daytime and at night, the threads intertwined, the ring tightened. Once he came very late, after the children had eaten and gone to bed. He gazed at her in a way that penetrated her utterly and told her everything.

This time Widad did not sin, nor did she lay blame. She suddenly found herself in the wolf's jaws. She made a mental effort to say no, to refuse, but her body was stronger than she was—forceful and tyrannical. The doctor, who could not understand this body or satisfy it, had fled it. On the same bed, on the same pillows, though her position had changed, Widad discovered for a certainty that Death, which she had fought for so long, encircled her on every side and would ravish her if she gave in to it. Now Rateb was making her body shiver, rerouting the circulation of her blood, breathing new life into her.

"Now I've been born again," she told him that night. She had never looked so tired.

Her new birth continued and grew as long as the Oriental Import, Export and Transport Company grew. The doctor moved to Mooran permanently and founded a contracting company to supply wood and building materials; meanwhile, most nights from March until the early summer became crackling infernos, their flames raging in every cell of Widad's body that was dead or could die. When the time approached to depart for Mooran, she found Rateb useful not only in taking care of business, but as the only man who could help her do things that required a man's muscles. His almost constant presence in the house was taken for granted by everyone, even considered essential. It was impossible for the two of them to be in one bed—each teased the other with words and glances and with their hands, often collapsing with laughter, laughing at themselves: two big, naughty children who did not know how to behave or what it was they wanted.

Widad wept like a child the last night; she wept from joy at having been so happy, at having really lived, from regret and from longing, and she wept because once again Death had begun to steal toward her. She explained her tears to the children and neighbors by saying that she was leaving home, and leaving them not knowing when she would return to see them again.

Rateb saw her happiness and enjoyed it, saw her tears and her pain, but could find no reason for so many tears. Nonetheless he pretended to be sad too, to mark the end of this phase of his life with dignity that he could always look back upon.

11

From the time the doctor's family settled in Mooran, al-Saffan and the surrounding neighborhoods talked of nothing but "the Syrians." And there was much to tell, about the children and the adults, the men and the women: how they talked, how they dressed, what they were doing today or had done recently. Muhammad Eid contributed, in his own way, to this public fascination with the Mahmiljis—he told stories and was constantly on the move in the city, which was in itself a source of popular comment.

The doctor accepted two or three invitations to visit his neighbors, but declined every invitation after that, pleading overwork at the palace and the poor health that Muhammad Eid had already spread rumors about. When his family arrived and the volume of invitations mounted, Abu Abdallah or Radwan always had the same unvarying excuse: "Madame is ill, and the children are fed at school." When the doctor's wife was seen, her first week in Mooran, accompanied by the doctor and their children as they went on an outing to the plot of land where their mansion would be built, she was not only unveiled but talking and laughing. Some youths saw her; she spoke openly to two of them, and this caused a great deal of talk, but what caused even more of a stir was the beautiful girl whose long hair flew behind her as she ran and played with the children. Nadia attracted attention right away, and everyone began talking about her. The boys who crowded against the fence were the first to spread the news, then the older boys, then the men were talking about her, and they all guessed that she was the doctor's eldest daughter.

The family was to become a favorite subject of the public gaze; their movements and family news were closely followed. When it was discovered that the girl was not the doctor's daughter, but only a relative, the thoughts of many mixed with dreams and desires, though they remained dubious and longing and never stopped wondering and waiting. Some of them who knew Muhammad Eid asked him where the doctor came from and what he would do here; others, more daring, asked directly about the family, how many there were and what their names were. No one dared to ask about that girl, though the question was constantly on their lips and in their hearts; it was never posed, almost as if asking it were a sin none of them could bring himself to commit. Even Abdallah and Radwan, who'd exchanged smiles and silent questions as they counted the doctor's children the night they arrived, realizing that there was one more than Muhammad Eid had said, dared not ask until much later, though the girl filled the house with her energy and vitality.

When Shamran al-Oteibi heard that the doctor's family had arrived, and that there was a girl who might be a daughter or only a cousin, he sneered.

"Don't worry, friends, his daughter or his wife, just say 'the daughter of the nobody' and you won't be far from the truth."

Even the doctor's sons, especially the young ones, who should have become part of the Saffan district, assimilating immediately into the society of children at play, failed to do so. When they did venture past the door, they stood, afraid, or at least very shy, watching the other children play. When they were invited to join in, they only looked at one another and smiled, then drew back. At first the children of Saffan made every effort to include them and to be friendly, but before long they forgot all about the "Syrians"— though not about Nadia, who was sighted every so often as she stepped through the doorway to order the small boys indoors. No sooner was her head glimpsed, no sooner had anyone seen her, than silence fell. The children fell silent before the adults and spread the news the quickest: when she appeared, how long she stayed out and what she did. She had no idea that her ventures outside the door or calls to the children were ever taken amiss by anyone, and her modesty and innocence were plain to see, but one day the doctor took her aside.

"Let the children be, Nadia. If they go into the street, don't go out after them." When she showed her surprise, for she did not understand what he meant, he went on. "Abu Abdallah has instructions to look after them."

The doctor chuckled and his voice changed.

"Mooran, my girl, is not like our country, and these people's values and customs are not like ours."

She looked at him, listened and nodded, but had no idea what she had done wrong or why he had scolded her. Only when her aunt explained to her that people here in Mooran had big mouths, that they spared no one, and that Muhammad Eid had heard gossip that he didn't like and then alerted the doctor—only then did Nadia smile and understand.

The doctor's relations with people in Mooran were correct and very limited. He had been careful from the beginning to allow his family to socialize as little as possible—he just found it "more soothing" that way—so that their acquaintances were confined to a few foreign families, among them the family of a German geologist. The families visited each other, though infrequently, but the families' children visited each other often.

The people of Mooran, who were used to a completely different kind of people and social life, could not conceal their bewilderment. They wondered how people could live like that—for how long the Mahmiljis would be able to keep their distance and isolation. Time and again they heard that the doctor's wife was ill and therefore unable to accept a dinner invitation or to pay a call, then saw her alighting from her car or going to the palace. They saw her give banquets for foreigners and grew more perplexed, and looked at one another and smiled.

The doctor, moreover, purposely left no opportunity for casual relationships to develop. When he arrived home he never paused or looked around him for fear of allowing one of the neighbors or passersby to catch his eye. He took care to attend Friday prayer services at a mosque as far away as possible from the Saffan district. The neighbors interpreted this as pure snobbery, but Muhammad Eid made a point of setting them straight, unasked. He pointed to the southern room of the doctor's house.

"He works until dawn—he doesn't sleep until he hears the morning prayer call." He smiled. "The light in that office is never even turned off!"

He let this sink in.

"The man doesn't know the meaning of the word *rest*. If he needs to take a break, he naps on the books on his desk—those books all have a thousand or two thousand pages apiece, and if it weren't for Umm Ghazwan telling him to go easy on himself, he'd be there days and nights on end."

Their eyes drifted toward the doctor's house, or at least in the direction it lay in, as Muhammad murmured, almost to himself: "Brain power! Brain power that can break rocks!"

Muhammad never discussed the doctor's relationship with the Sultan, on the doctor's own very strict instructions, reiterated almost daily in their first days in Mooran. Muhammad had to be content with gestures and allusions, always more meaningful than words.

"If it weren't for the Sultan's own wish, and the close friendship between those two, because they're more than brothers, you would never see the doctor in Mooran."

If anyone tried to explore the relationship, how and when it had begun, Muhammad chuckled inscrutably and told them, "How? When? Do you want me to talk all night?"

When they asked when the doctor would open a clinic or hospital, or when he would start taking people in and curing them, Muhammad paused with a hint of real fear, which confused them, and sighed, "If he lives!"

The doctor was immersed in his mounting worries and business concerns. He spent more and more time at the palace or traveling with the Sultan, and his meetings with Muhammad Eid were not what they used to be—the things on his mind were different and were constantly changing. Muhammad, who had always known what to do and how to do it, now felt "like the mother of the bride—neither busy nor able to rest."

It was not long, after moving to Mooran, before the doctor forgot all the ambitious plans he had cherished in Harran, or other concerns pushed them aside.

When the al-Hir Palace was nearly complete, largely thanks to Muhammad Eid's administrative efforts, Muhammad asked the doctor if he had any plans to open a clinic or hospital in Mooran. The doctor was silent for such a long time that it seemed he had not heard the question, or had no answer to it.

"By God, Doctor, we were a thousand times better off in Harran!" Muhammad finally said in exasperation.

The doctor's eyes settled curiously on him.

"Your problems here haven't left you with time to eat one meal or get a single good night's sleep!" Muhammad paused. "And for what?"

The doctor explained that their work in Mooran, however difficult, would be rewarded with triumphant results and that the hardship they suffered now was temporary and would soon ease or end.

"May God hear you, Doctor, but your humble servant is of a different mind," murmured Muhammad, almost to himself.

"Different mind?"

"I mean—"

It suddenly appeared to him that he could not say everything, perhaps out of shame or confusion.

The doctor spoke to him, slyly. "Mooran's changed you, my friend . . . hmm?"

"No, but—it's only that I feel I'm good for nothing. I don't know what to do with myself. All day long I do nothing but castrate calves!"

The doctor saw what Muhammad was complaining about. He was silent a moment, then smiled.

"Listen, Muhammad, it's true that the situation has changed on us. In Harran we hardly had time to scratch our heads: operations, examinations, needles, and so on and so on, but those days are over and done with. There are now more than fifty doctors in Mooran, and we have a new standard to meet!"

Their discussion ended with no agreement, but they seemed to have reached some kind of understanding, if only an understanding that the discussion would be postponed.

The doctor had long been aware of his need for Muhammad Eid: his need for him had been obvious and clearly defined in all the periods of their collaboration, and neither of them imagined himself capable of leaving the other; but things were different now and would never be the same again. Muhammad Eid would never consent not to be "Dr. Mahmilji's assistant." He delighted in this title and insisted on it, though by now no one knew what it meant or could assign it a clear meaning.

The doctor told him, a few months after this discussion, that he had decided to go in with Fahmy al-Hajjar to distribute pharmaceuticals, to keep himself busy. Muhammad Eid's surprise showed plainly, as if he had been slapped. He spoke with an almost mocking slowness.

"Have you had second thoughts about practicing medicine, Doctor?"

"Medicine as we used to practice it no longer exists, my boy. Every month or two I'll examine His Majesty, and if he needs anything, an aspirin or some . . . restorative, that's all."

This might have led Muhammad Eid to make a hard decision, and he might have left everything behind and departed for good, but what prevented him, what made him decide to forget and to behave as if nothing were amiss, was something he could not breathe to anyone.

12

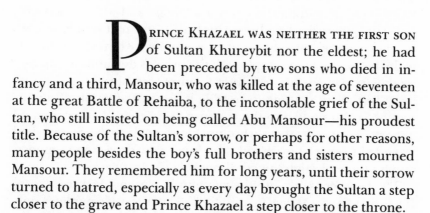

PRINCE KHAZAEL WAS NEITHER THE FIRST SON of Sultan Khureybit nor the eldest; he had been preceded by two sons who died in infancy and a third, Mansour, who was killed at the age of seventeen at the great Battle of Rehaiba, to the inconsolable grief of the Sultan, who still insisted on being called Abu Mansour—his proudest title. Because of the Sultan's sorrow, or perhaps for other reasons, many people besides the boy's full brothers and sisters mourned Mansour. They remembered him for long years, until their sorrow turned to hatred, especially as every day brought the Sultan a step closer to the grave and Prince Khazael a step closer to the throne.

It was true that in the beginning Prince Khazael gave it little thought, and never prepared himself to take his father's place or his brother Mansour's; perhaps he felt deep down that his brothers were better qualified or better prepared. Suddenly, however, he was the crown prince, and within a few days he forgot that he was younger than Mansour, and that he did not want to be Sultan, the more so since his maternal uncles made no secret of their grudge against Sultan Khureybit—he had deprived them of the immense wealth they coveted. The uncles abruptly forgot their grudges, ended their isolation and came once again to Mooran.

In Mooran, calmly and quietly, they surrounded the crown prince and waited for the death of the Sultan. The end came, with lamentation and fear on the part of the women of the Rawdh Palace, especially Umm Mansour and her sisters, who felt assured of imminent disasters. The new Sultan and his supporters pretended, however, to know nothing of what the women were saying or of the servants' gossip. The Sultan warily decided to keep his home in the Ghadir Palace, remembering the prediction of that astrologer years before.

Shrewdly, in great secrecy, a new circle of royal advisers was assembled, along with a formula for ruling very unlike Khureybit's. Sultan Khazael was on his guard and even fearful at first, because his brothers, who had pledged their loyalty to him and spoke movingly of their joy and wholehearted support, just as quickly fell silent and began to keep their distance. Some of them behaved differently toward him. When the Sultan saw this he resorted to lavishing money upon them, unhesitatingly and without accounting. His generosity had been checked in the past by his father's stern glances or outright rebukes; sometimes Khureybit even forbade the treasurer to comply with the prince's demands for money, on the pretext that the account was empty; but now this generosity burst forth with nothing to restrain it, for vast amounts of money had begun to pour into the treasury as a result of the rise in oil exports. So the brothers who, unable to replace the Sultan, had intended to share power with him, were now drowning in money, and finding in it undreamed-of power and pleasure.

The brothers sank into their wealth in varying degrees, except for three: Fanar, Misha'an and Torki. Fanar was his mother's only child, brought up in an isolation that had distanced him from his brothers; he was given to silence and contemplation. He pledged his formal loyalty to Khazael and quietly went his own way. For a time he stayed with his mother's brothers in Ein Fadda. A few months later he asked his brother the Sultan for permission to travel to Switzerland and America for medical treatment: he suffered from jaundice and more often than not looked tired and ill. Misha'an and Torki were sons of the same mother, a member of the large and powerful Huthail tribe. Like Prince Khazael, the two were preparing themselves for great things, even while their father was still alive.

Their mother enjoyed an exalted position; she had great influence over the Sultan, and he treated her differently from the rest of his wives. She and her brothers strove to arrange for the wealth and political power, "after His Majesty's long life," to be shared equally by Khazael, Misha'an and Torki, "because Khazael can't handle it, and all this money that's cost us so much blood and brainwork and sleeplessness can't just be left for him to squander."

Sultan Khureybit listened and said nothing, sometimes seeming to agree and sometimes not, never commenting or rendering an opinion as long as he was vigorous and in firm control. It seemed premature to him to plunge into this kind of bargaining at this point. On his deathbed, in the presence of his brothers and sisters, children and advisers, he named Khazael his successor, in order to prevent any family bickering. Misha'an, Torki and their mother felt abandoned by the Sultan—all the hopes they had cherished were now demolished, so that when they had pledged their loyalty to the new Sultan they lost no time in withdrawing from the court. Misha'an took up residence at his palace near Mooran; Torki said that he was leaving on a long hunting trip, for several months perhaps.

Sultan Khazael was perfectly content with their decisions and their planned absences. Any fears that he had in the long nights during which he was planning to succeed his father came to him in the form of those three brothers' faces, which inspired in him wariness bordering on outright dread—but none more so than Fanar.

Prince Fanar was the second oldest, after Khazael. His father had a special love for him, perhaps because of the close physical resemblance between them, or Fanar's constant presence at his father's councils. The prince had an abstemious nature and always strove for even greater austerity, both in the way he ate and the way he dressed, even in the way he talked. Now Fanar let it be known that he intended to travel abroad for medical treatment. He might return, he said, or he might not, but if he did come back it would not be soon. This satisfied the Sultan, who sent him a large amount of money to show his love and goodwill; he had never given such a sum to any other brother or to anyone else at any one time, but Fanar sent the money back to the treasury the next day, asking that the Sultan not be informed of this action. The courtiers who stood with the Sultan as he saw Fanar off remembered his sad words.

"Blessed Brother, your health is more precious to us than our eyes, and our only wish is that you set off and return in God's protection." Fanar nodded and tried to smile as the Sultan continued. "We've given instructions to our friends every place you'll be. Don't be stingy with yourself, Brother."

Thus Fanar began his long exile from Mooran.

In the absence of these three brothers, the Sultan was finally able to relax. His moodiness faded, and he appeared strong and confident—almost happy. His feelings of strength and confidence mounted daily as the oil revenues poured into his treasury; he distributed money generously in every direction, and the allocation to each member of the royal family—even newborn infants—rose steadily. The women of the Rawdh Palace and their servants and governesses had once all talked openly about the events surrounding the Sultan's death, but now they seemed to have suddenly forgotten it; or when it came up, they spoke in covert whispers.

At first the Sultan was very careful, spending uncounted hours receiving visitors and talking and listening to all his visitors; furthermore, he had to visit all the provinces, even the most distant, to inspect development projects, discussing their progress with engineers and the provincial emirs, asking if they needed more credit or any other sort of assistance. Now he was far less inclined to travel or to bother himself with those concerns; besides, there were now various departments in his palace to deal with government business, which relieved him of the duty of dealing with it himself.

One day the doctor and the Sultan were sitting on a balcony overlooking the new buildings of the Ghadir Palace.

"I remember, Your Majesty," said the doctor, "that Emir Khaled al-Mishari, when his palace was being built in Harran, used to inspect the construction every day, and go around slapping the walls and asking for more cement. And his own deputy would fill up the barrel!"

He laughed loudly at his recollection of the scene.

"Great things are for great men, Your Majesty, or, as one of the truly great German philosophers put it: 'Great deeds are only for the great; little deeds are for mere men.'"

13

U MMI ZAHWA"—THE SHEIKHA—WAS A FOR-
midable figure in Mooran and everyone
knew it; she was the most powerful person
in the Rawdh Palace. The young men talked about her, and so did
the children, imitating their mothers or whichever other adults
gossiped about her, but all they really could talk about was the
Sheikha the way they imagined her to be.

A woman, but unlike other women: she moved like a specter,
coming and going unnoticed by anyone, rather quiet, though in
her speech direct and sometimes wounding. Her complexion was
the color of moist earth or early twilight, her eyes like a cow's, large
and slightly protruberant, and at night as bright as candles. Her
nose was long, as hooked as a falcon's beak. Her high cheekbones
were like little hills in a determinedly watchful and stern face. She
was not considered short, despite her bowed old age and her twice-
shortened walking stick. Her hands were as long as a monkey's,
and her feet as broad as a camel's hooves.

Little was said of her past, so no one knew for certain whether she had ever married, or stayed single all her life. No one talked about it, and no one knew whether she had any children, but still everyone considered her their own mother, and that is why all of them, young and old, called her *Ummi*. Only the servants, foreigners and old men called her the Sheikha.

Truth was mixed with myth in their accounts of her past life, and imagination overruled facts, but fear also played a role in their conversations about her now. She was talked about only in whispers, cut off abruptly when she approached, since no one escaped her wrath at being the subject of a whispered remark.

Nothing was known of her past, and the exact relationship that bound her to the Sultan was obscure and could only be guessed at. Some said that she was the maternal aunt of Sultan Khazael; others maintained that she was a distant cousin or even an old family governess. In any case, her position at the palace, especially during Sultan Khureybit's reign, surpassed that of any other woman—or man, for that matter. She was said to have incomparable influence over him; at one point this was thought to be because she possessed fabulous wealth—treasures of gold she had given the Sultan when he was poor and needy, seeking loans so that he could pay his soldiers, who were on the point of mutiny or desertion. The Sultan, the story ran, repaid the favor when his fortunes changed.

Nashed al-Dublan, Khureybit's old coffee pourer, dismissed from the Sultan's service in his old age because of his shaky hands, was allowed to stay on in the palace, where he wandered from room to room. When people asked him about the Sheikha he shook his finger and rolled his eyes, signaling them to be quiet, but if they pressed him, and if he trusted them, he turned cautiously around several times, then muttered his reply as if talking to himself.

"By God . . . by God, if she had a finger's length more of flesh, *she* would be the Sultan!" He showed, with his finger, the measurement he considered, then looked warily around and went on. "And even without it she's a good rider and has a fine mind!"

Nothing could induce him to say more; he only replied fearfully, "Let's not talk about it anymore, my friends, there's no point, and the Sheikha hears everything that's said around here; and you know the cunning Suroor!"

For these and other reasons, the rooms and halls of the Rawdh Palace were filled with her presence and might. Although it was the custom of the bedouin never to mention women except in passing, the Sheikha eliminated this custom by becoming one of their favorite topics for discussion: how she had fought at Khureybit's side, and shown more endurance throughout the war than most of the men; and how she had disguised herself as a male horseman at the great Battle of Rehaiba, never letting the truth be known until the battle was over. Tales of her wisdom and the brilliant counsel she offered in times of crisis were beyond folklore—they were closer to the stuff of myth.

That was her position among men; but among women she was regarded with awe, even outright, ill-concealed fear. They fell silent when she came near, and seized any excuse to leave as quickly as they could. They agreed to any demand she made, viewing all she said and did with caution mixed with fear. When she left them or fell asleep, they sighed with relief, as if a heavy burden had been lifted from their shoulders. Their relief never lasted long, for Ummi Zahwa did not sleep as other people did, at appointed times; she needed only short naps during the day, especially in the afternoon or early evening. As far as anyone knew, she had never gone to bed and had a long, unbroken night's sleep. The servants insisted that at times her bed went unslept in and untouched for days on end.

There was so much to tell about her. She did not eat what other people ate. She always wore the same clothes, which she never seemed to take off. She moved with steps that seemed light and heavy at the same time, tapping her white cane, and all they ever heard from her were the same abrupt commands.

She had a special suite in the east wing of the palace but rarely used it because all the palace belonged to her. She did not even hesitate to pass through the men's *diwan,* which no other woman dared to do. In passing she gave the men an unseen appraising glance and sometimes spoke to them, in greeting or to ask a question. The men did not look at her long, out of fear or reverence, but kept talking among themselves, a little uncertainly, looking over their shoulders to make sure that she had gone away before resuming their discussion.

Those who loved the Sheikha saw a great deal of the compassionate spirit that filled her heart; she gave money to the poor and urged others to do so, and her short absences from the Rawdh Palace were to make charitable visits. There was no poor house that she had not visited, always bringing money and supplies of cloth and flour, and this she did at least twice a year. She cared for orphans, arranged marriages for women and had any number of prisoners set free. These stories were told with utter certainty, but no one could say that they had ever actually seen her go into a house or knock on a door. They made the excuse that "the Sheikha hates charity that's performed publicly." So her missions of mercy were carried out at unknown times, late at night or early in the morning, and no one knew about them until long afterward.

Those who disliked her, however, thought her lethally evil, and swore that she was a witch and practiced sorcery as naturally as breathing; they went to any length to ward off the spite she felt for everyone around her. To prove it they told stories about things she had done: she had killed people, among them Sultan Khureybit's Uncle Salman, a feared rival of hers. She had put poison in his food. She had ordered her slave, Suroor, to kill Salman's son, Jassam, for refusing, or delaying, his oath of loyalty to Khureybit. She still practiced various forms of magic: she used incense and enchanted water and special potions made of herbal ingredients she mixed secretly in order to marry off Khureybit to one woman after another. There were those who were convinced that in one period Khureybit married a different woman every night "so that he could have as many descendants as Noah and as many tribes as Jacob," as she was supposed to have said.

These same people, and others, said that a large number of the palace women, especially the Sultan's wives, died in very mysterious circumstances—and the Sheikha was behind it. On certain days a black slave-woman walked around and behind the women, carrying a pot of enchanted water, and the Sheikha had a small amount of salt; when she looked at any one of the women three times and then at the pot, the Sheikha sprinkled a little salt, and some evil thing befell the woman, and some women died.

They looked in her face now and saw an obstinacy that bordered on hostility, especially when she stared long and silently at them;

and this convinced many people that she could read their minds and knew what any man was going to do or wanted to do. Late in her life, in her old age, when her hearing failed, she began to hear with her eyes, and people discovered that only by chance.

In the last months of Sultan Khureybit's life, before his last illness, the Sheikha became totally unbearable. Her instincts told her that the end was near, she was sure of it, though no one had told her that, and she told no one about it. The bustle and the turmoil that reached the point of chaos created in the Rawdh Palace an air of tension unknown since the early days of the Sultanate. Everyone was filled with a vague but powerful feeling that something was about to happen—she had, in far less black moods, with no notice or lucidity, as if she were searching for something, or trying to raise a spirit from the dead, caused convulsions that had shaken the palace to its foundations and nearly killed everyone within. Now she did not limit herself to frantic movement or the curses she showered on whoever stood in her way, or the anxious, austere worry found not only in people's faces but in the very corners of the palace itself, and everyone was filled with anticipation more like dread. Even Sultan Khureybit noticed it and was filled with an eerie sense that the end was near. He frequently met alone with the Sheikha for long hours, in secret; it was rumored that she had tried to force the Sultan to make drastic, unreasonable changes. Others said that the meetings were only an effort on the part of the Sultan to exorcise the demon that had possessed her and caused her frenzy, rage and tension: that their long meetings were no more than an attempt to soothe her by listening to her meaningless jabbering; that any other explanation was nonsense.

After weeks of turmoil the Sultan suddenly took very ill, and everyone knew he was dying. Now it was assumed that his long meetings with the Sheikha arose from her desire to have an heir other than Khazael; she was trying to sway him. His condition worsened—he was delirious and then went blind, without the Sheikha having achieved what she wanted. They held more meetings, at her insistence, during his illness; she would ask all present to leave, in a rather commanding tone, and at other times made use of the time they spent asleep or busy; and she lay on the floor beside his bed, alone. In these meetings she was never able to achieve what she wanted, which gave rise to rumors, shortly after the Sultan's death, that his had been an unnatural death, or even that he might not be dead after all!

No one in the Rawdh Palace dared to say so out loud, but in the Ghadir Palace, which was a good distance away, and which the Sheikha had scarcely ever visited, it was said that the old woman was senile, and that she raved senselessly—so everyone in the palace held their silence on the rumors as if they had not heard them; surely they would die away as they had begun. If anyone responded to them, even to deny them, there was no telling where it would end, or how. That was not all, in the Ghadir Palace; for barely had the mourning rites ended and the last of the mourners left before Khazael went to pay a call upon the Sheikha in her private wing of the palace, and kissed her hand and forehead in front of a large gathering of people. A few days later there was yet another meeting, and then the Sheikha and some of her ladies left the Rawdh Palace and moved into the Ghadir Palace.

The Sheikha's old friends who saw her now found a resemblance, but no more than that, between her and this woman. She had changed, changed profoundly, and was no longer the woman who had been. The women were still afraid, and the men were still wary of the questioning, accusing looks and cutting words she sent their way; even so, the turmoil that had maddened the Sheikha for the past few months had finally crushed and consumed her. She could not even drive the flies away from her face. The grief that had overcome her since the last illness and death of the Sultan had changed her, as always happens with those obsessed by the pursuits of this world: they forget Death, they immerse themselves in lust and greed or in harming others, until they discover suddenly that it is all a meaningless distraction compared with the other reality: Death. Death was closer and more real than the fragile "realities" that had captivated them. So they withdraw completely, having been changed in the space of one day by this discovery.

Others said that the "old bitch," who had killed Salman and his son Jassam and still others out of loyalty to Sultan Khureybit, was now preparing herself, preparing her magic spells and poisons, and preparing Suroor, too, to start all over again—only this had made her agree so readily to move to the Ghadir Palace. Just as, when the warm season arrives, serpents reemerge after the long winter's slumber, so she would instinctively resume her mischief, they said, concluding with the warning that she would fill Mooran with catastrophes.

To soothe her, or at least to win her silence, in the same way the Sultan had helped her to outmaneuver her rivals, and to win their support, and to pamper her, the commodious south wing of the palace was put entirely at her disposal, along with three serving women. She was warmly welcomed and shown great deference, but it was clear to anyone that this was nothing more than a show— much as a child is put off with a new plaything.

14

SULTAN KHAZAEL INHERITED TWO TRAITS FROM his father—impressive height and a passion for women—along with the Sultanate. His tall, broad build attracted attention more than it communicated dignity, especially when it was accompanied by his ringing laughter and his deep, coarse voice that seemed to rise from deep within his chest, as if in thick layers or like pounding waves. When he was calm, he stroked his beard with gnarled but long and tapered fingers as thick as a small boy's forearm. His teeth, dominating the middle of his face, were like a broken wall after years of ripping tough meat and being cleaned with a small stick.

The Sultan inherited his height and broad shoulders from his father and both his maternal uncles; his half brothers' looks differed from his and from each other's according to the traits of their mothers' families. Prince Khazael was the tallest and most powerfully built of all his brothers. As a teenager he was addicted to a strenuous athletic regimen so that his size would not be a hindrance to him, but instead of enhancing his body's smoothness and symmetry it gave him even fiercer strength. He ate like a camel. He could eat, by himself, a whole one-year-old lamb and drink three vessels of curds. When he put a full waterskin to his lips, he lowered it limp, with a single swallow of water jolting around inside. He excelled at eating and drinking contests on his desert jaunts, much to his father's anger. Contests of strength, on the other hand, delighted Khureybit, for Khazael could wrestle a horse to the ground and force a camel to kneel—though the old man never showed his pleasure.

That was all in his youth; once he discovered the pleasure to be had from women, however, he would not exchange it for any other pleasure, and thought of nothing else. Sultan Khureybit wanted children and clans of descendants from women, as well as blood ties with all the tribes, to strengthen his dynasty and fight the injuries of time, but his son was different. He thought of none of these things, or rather did not think of them in quite the same way. He wanted women only for themselves, and pleasure only for itself; he did not use his body, and the power of that body, for any other ambitions or explorations.

He was nineteen when his father first spoke to him of marriage, and he was frightened and repelled by the idea, expressing a wish that it might be postponed for a few years, but the Sultan's words were stern and resolute and left no room for disagreement.

"We want children from our loins, to rule until Judgment Day. You must have a son!" His father added, laughing, "I was married and had children when I was still younger than you!"

When he was offered his cousin Hazla bint Torki in marriage, for she was the same age as he, he said nothing, voicing neither rejection nor approval—that was how he gave his consent. Things might have gone on in this way had not Ummi Zahwa stood against this marriage with the ferocity of a wounded wolf. She simply said, succinctly, "It will not happen." Sultan Khureybit was very cross at her opposition to the match, since he was trying to make friends with his brother Torki and he judged this marriage an excellent means of "purifying their hearts," as they said. He made his displeasure with the Sheikha's stance clear. Khazael hoped that the argument would prolong itself and grow more complex, which would keep him free for at least a short time. The palace women heard the news of the proposed match, then of Ummi Zahwa's opposition to it, and had great expectations of, at the very least, a feud between her and the Sultan which would lead to one of them giving in—perhaps even the Sheikha, which would end the whole nightmare, and mean that they could regard her somewhat more as an equal. The exact opposite happened.

For the Sheikha had a special love for Torki, preferring him to the others, but he did not understand her opposition, or rather misunderstood it: how she misrepresented or was able to hide her true feelings so perfectly. If she felt this way about Torki and his daughter Hazla, then what were her real views, her real feelings toward the others?

To the Sultan, marriage, like death, was an opportunity to bury old differences, to make new beginnings, build bridges, and forge new relationships. He saw secret motives in the Sheikha's opposition; for the first time, he distrusted her, thinking her more cunning and malevolent than he had guessed, and assuming that she had begun to play with others the game she had been playing with him.

A few days after she had made known her rejection of the marriage, and his anger had cooled, he spoke to her.

"There is a time for everything, Zahwa—"

She looked at him curiously, and he went on. "Torki was not there at the Battle of Rehaiba, but at al-Jamara he carried the day almost by himself. You've forgotten Rehaiba and remember only al-Jamara. Right?" She nodded. "And al-Jamara was fought about three years after Rehaiba, right?" She nodded again. "You've said that without Rehaiba there would never have been a Battle of al-Jamara, right?" She nodded. "And you've said that our men at al-Jamara all used to say, 'If you missed this day, you'll never see another like it; find some other place and some other nation.' Right?"

"Abu Mansour, that was the past," she replied angrily.

"So what happened then? And what's happening now?" he raged at her.

"Abu Mansour—" She laughed. "Do you want the truth, or something else?"

"Zahwa . . . Sheikha!"

"My dear man, you're his father!" she said angrily. He gazed at her in silence. "Khazael, Your Majesty, can't deal with women at all. Hazla? Today she's a wife and tomorrow a corpse—he'll kill her! Don't you see that?"

Khureybit flinched, as if he had just then awakened from a deep sleep. He gave her a searching, almost panicky look.

"My dear man! The girl's a weak reed—she's not suitable for him. Torki is my brother, and his daughters are like my own daughters. I raised Hazla myself! If you want her death, then I'll consent to this marriage."

The Sultan understood at last, and laughed, nodding, at the thought that he had missed such an obvious thing. He agreed that Khazael's first wife would have to be someone other than Hazla.

A few days later they found the right wife: Adla, a cousin on his mother's side. She was strong and solid, rather short, plump as a waterskin, and more amenable to marriage than Hazla. Khazael showed no great excitement, but laughed, and perhaps guessed somehow that Adla was more his type.

After their wedding night and all the nights that followed, Prince Khazael never ceased searching or exploring; he sought to discover the secrets of life and the world embodied in the tempestuous longing and perpetual regeneration of women, which knew no letup.

Once, food had been his most cherished delight, unrivaled by any other, but once he ate his fill he could not stand the sight of food and ordered it all removed. Later, sports captivated him to the point where he forgot everything else, but as soon as he was tired out he longed for sleep, from which not even a cannon could awaken him, as his friends, especially Zaid al-Heraidi, used to say. At still other times various hobbies obsessed him—breeding horses, hunting, poetry—but never for long.

Though the Sheikha pretended, along with the rest of the palace women, to be delighted with Prince Khazael's wedding party, she was deeply worried that the wedding night would turn out badly. Her friends remembered her pacing in circles like a tethered cat that night, not due to any of the usual worries of an old woman on such a night, especially for a young girl like Adla, whose strength and lust were being unleashed for the first time; no, she was pacing and praying that Adla was still alive, that she had been able to survive the experience. Very late that night, when the bride's mother appeared, smiling and laughing, all the women heard the Sheikha remark, "If she made it through tonight, there's nothing more to worry about."

This was a part of history known by very few, for after Adla came a huge number of women. The prince, who was once bashful or even afraid when it came to relationships with women, that other world that had so frightened and fascinated him since his childhood, was now immersed in this world and could not leave it, even for a single night. His close friends noticed this, and that he never left the Sheikha either. The fear that had filled her at his first marriage stayed with her through his second, and she played a direct role in choosing his wives, and she later discovered that things had changed, though she still gave the same instructions to the women who assisted her in finding him women: "She should be like a waterskin, supple and yielding yet strong, as big as a she-camel but as nimble as a cat—otherwise she'll never get out of his bed in one piece."

One by one they came and went, women fitting these specifications, with some minor traits to distinguish among them, since new qualities were required with the passage of time. The Sheikha required a strong and slightly plump body and large buttocks so that the pelvis would be large enough to bear both the prince and his offspring.

Soon, however, the prince became enamored of a young black girl. She was like a cat, like the stars in the night sky when she laughed, making herself shine, as if her teeth cast an incandescent white light that illuminated her from her head to the soles of her feet; it was, perhaps, this laugh of hers that caught the prince's eye and made him fall in love with her. He forgot that she was small-bodied and scarcely fourteen years old. He asked his first wife, Adla, to prepare the girl for her wedding night, saying that he would spend "tonight, and at the very most tomorrow night too" with the girl. For by this time the task of choosing new wives for the prince had fallen to Adla herself; she bit her lip hard and did not hide her perplexity, at the girl's youth or perhaps at the humiliation of her own position, though Khazael's deep chuckle left her no choice.

It was one of the Ghadir Palace's most famous nights. Even Adla did not think that the girl would live through the night: she was too small and weak to survive it. Other women guessed what the outcome would be, but Adla was absolutely certain that it was useless to offer the girl any advice. Likewise she made several last-minute attempts to convince Khazael to change his mind, or to postpone the wedding for at least a few months, but he would not listen to her.

Later, when Adla denied knowing the causes of the black girl's death, she said, "I told her, Wash yourself carefully there, and open and close your legs as far as you can, a hundred or two hundred times. And I told her, Put some oil there, and oil yourself again after you wash, and when he comes for you let him do as he pleases and then get out of there; give him what he wants and leave him, and if he gets on top of you, squirm around and keep moving, and God help you."

She went on in a different tone.

"So I stayed in the room next door, with just the wall between us. The poor thing was terrified. I was thinking, either he'll kill her or she'll die of fright. More than once I said to myself, Adla, don't worry, trust in God, go in there and see. Some time went by and I was still afraid, and then I heard her voice—she sounded like a cat that got stepped on. I said, "She's dead, he killed her; God had mercy on her and relieved her.' When I went in she was in convulsions, drowning in her blood and tears, crying and laughing. I asked her, 'What's wrong with you, girl?' and she said, 'I don't know, Auntie.'"

The prince's tastes changed again after that. "Our mother Eve turned Adam out of paradise," said the Sheikha, "and women today are enough to drag men and jinn all to Hell—you have no way of knowing what they'll do."

By the time Prince Khazael had become Sultan, sixteen women had passed under him, and he was still looking for the divine secret in man-woman relations. He spent long hours not only pondering the question but contemplating a woman's body; this body somehow drove him to distraction, but the arousal took several forms.

Everything about women aroused him. A woman's shoulder was not only the joint of a limb and torso, not only a fleshy oval; it was more than that. When she lifted her arm, or both of them, a whole world of delight suddenly sprang into view and he could not resist it. He wanted to follow the movement of every part of her body, to pause, to feel it with his fingers and his whole hand, to smell its odor; he even delighted in nipping at it with his teeth, though as soon as he began this physical exploration a scary electric shiver ran through his body, interrupting his meditations. He panicked, and his limbs and organs were in confusion: his fingers and lips became someone else's, and the palms of his hands strayed over these hills and plains, but he did not know how.

He wanted to pause at her arms, to grasp the undersides of her slender arms so that he might contemplate the armpits and come to understand what so tickled him about them. When she draped her arms around him he scarcely dared to touch her with his fingers at first, then he caressed her armpits until he felt his blood begin to blaze and thrust his whole head underneath the arm to gaze at it from below, always discovering something new, some beauty he had never noticed before.

Khazael trembled as he moved on to her chest from the armpits, about to lose control of himself, with the feeling that he was once again a tiny child lusting to fling himself on this breast and cling to it forever. He loved breasts so much that he could not leave them alone. He loved the slope, the firmness and continual give, and other features he did not even know. How often he dreamed of being a small, slumbering child cradled against a breast. When he nibbled the nipple with his huge teeth, the woman under him mewed from fear that he would tear her skin, and he often said to her, or to himself, "A little beast won't hurt his mother," and slid down, slid quickly, to stay there. And there he melted, revived, languished, panted, jumped like a rabbit, slept like a stone, in delighted disbelief, and like a rushing stream he never paused or stopped.

Adla remained his favorite wife. No matter how far he strayed from her he always came back, and when she had once again to find him another wife she did it with pleasure, in the knowledge that he would come back to her. It had happened so many times.

He might stay away slightly longer than she'd anticipated, but he was always back, with longing and exuberance and the same un-complicated joy of the early days of their marriage. He called her, though no one knew it, the Sheikha, and when she bit her lip a little apprehensively, he laughed.

"By God, there is no sheikha but you."

Eventually Sultan Khureybit noticed his son's long absences, and informants told him that Khazael had turned all his marital mat-ters over to Adla: she made the decisions about his marriages and told him to divorce this or that woman.

"Discipline your child even if his mother hates you for it," was Khureybit's response, often quoted by his children. He paused and sighed. "We have made some mistakes, and taken from these ex-patriates, but we won't give in to them, and we will never let them plot or plan to rule over us."

It was at about this time that Fanar began to spend much more time at his father's court; in fact he scarcely ever left it. There were clandestine whispers that the Sultan depended more and more upon Fanar and had come to love him more than any of his other children; that he might even appoint him as his successor. Fanar pretended to notice and hear nothing, and exaggerated his silence and indifference. When it was suggested that he should take an-other wife, he replied with calculated innocence, "These days it's hard enough to handle one!"

No one knew what the Sheikha was doing these days, or what she was telling the Sultan, though much was said, or rather whis-pered, about it. Mooran watched and waited, though many said, "We will not have long to wait."

15

O NCE THE DOCTOR SETTLED IN MOORAN AND
was appointed adviser to the new Sultan,
he became a permanent fixture at court,
and an even closer confidant of Zaid al-Heraidi, and a new plan
filled his heart and mind: he would rebuild the Sultanate of
Mooran from the ground up.

It occurred to him that one of the things the Sultan needed was
a private barber. He sensed this from the Sultan's nervous habit of
rubbing his head and adjusting his headropes; he noticed, too, that
His Majesty's mustache was asymmetrical, in its length and width.
Without any forethought at all—in a moment of "inspiration," as
the doctor called his luck—he suggested to the Sultan the importance, the necessity, really, of having a private barber.

"Yes, Your Majesty, it's absolutely essential," said the doctor excitedly, "because the Sultan's appearance doesn't concern only him, it
concerns all his people, because he is their symbol and an example

for them. The barber must be trustworthy, faithful, discreet, and of course an expert at his trade!"

The Sultan, a little doubtful, rubbed his head and straightened his headropes several times and glanced at the doctor out of the corner of his eye to be certain of what was being said to him. When he saw that the doctor's features were serious, he nodded as if remembering or thinking deeply, and spoke, as if to some other person.

"Little man, Doctor, it's more than enough to have my hair cut every month or two."

"But that's what must change, Your Majesty, because Your Majesty receives presidents and emirs every day. And the Sultan's barber should be no ordinary man, and the instruments he uses should be under direct medical supervision, otherwise—" The doctor looked several times to all sides to make sure no one was listening. "As long as you have chosen me as your physician, Your Majesty, and trust my advice, I must tell you that you should have your own personal barber."

The doctor interpreted the Sultan's silence as assent, so as soon as he left the palace, excited by his new plans, he found Muhammad Eid.

"Listen, Muhammad," he said paternally, "I have a plan I can't entrust to anyone but you. I want you, starting right now, to find me a barber, the best barber in all Mooran—because he is going to be the Sultan's barber."

Muhammad Eid, startled by the request, rolled his eyes and showed his surprise. This was the last thing he expected the doctor to ask, but he clenched his fist and punched the air, something he did only when he found the perfect answer to a problem, and because this habit of his derived from a certain incident during his first days in Harran when he had been trying to hang a door in the doctor's residence, after smearing the doorframe with oil; the doctor was helping him, to no avail, until Muhammad said, "One on top of the other, Doctor, male and female!" The doctor loved this expression and began to use it all the time.

Now he beat the air with his fist and repeated it triumphantly.

"I did it, by God, Doctor, male and female!"

The delighted doctor laughed like a child, but, longing to know, asked, "Do I know him? Have I met him?"

"Never mind—as I told you, Doctor, male and female!"

With uncharacteristic calm, Muhammad Eid then proceeded to explain to the doctor that his brother Badri was a barber whose like the Near and Middle East had never seen before—he had been a barber in the Foreign Legion, and become personal barber to Commandant Chevalier. Later, in Alexandria and Cyprus, he went on to practice shaving, not only as a trade but as an art and avocation.

The doctor's disappointment grew as he listened—he had not imagined Muhammad Eid to be imbecilic enough to propose bringing a barber all the way from Tripoli. Muhammad's face and gestures showed such excitement, though; and since the only barber the doctor knew in Mooran chattered and scarred his customers more than he shaved them, and the Yemeni in Harran was out of the question—"he's so boring it's a wonder people don't sleep through his haircuts"—he decided that he would think about it, albeit very cautiously. He had a sudden thought: *Suppose we choose a barber we know nothing about and he turns out to be some kind of lunatic?*

He looked directly into Muhammad's eyes.

"Someone you know is better than someone you know of. Your brother is our relative, and if he comes here and knows how to please the Sultan, we can't ask for any better than that."

With exaggerated calm he asked Muhammad to sit down and give him a detailed précis about his brother Badri: his age, his personality, and the chance that he would get along with the Sultan.

The doctor listened to some of what Muhammad Eid said and ignored the rest when he rambled on about irrelevant and contradictory notions. When he said that Badri could be in Mooran within a week, the doctor's delight was evident.

"Send for him immediately. Every day counts!"

Three weeks later, Muhammad's full brother, Badri al-Mudalal—"Abu Misbah"—arrived in Mooran.

No one would ever have taken him, at first glance, for a barber. A schoolmaster, perhaps, or a retired army officer. A careful look at his face, his long sideburns and pencil-line mustache gave the impression he might be a stage actor; when he spoke, he could have been anything in the world but a barber. The doctor met him the day after he arrived and was immediately delighted. The fact that he was called Abu Misbah, as Muhammad had told the doctor even before his arrival, counted hugely in his favor: the closeness between this name and the Sultan's filled the doctor with pride.

Badri's conversation brought him still higher in the doctor's eyes, to the point where he suspected that there was some secret he was missing. The doctor was filled with confidence and pride as he gazed now at the barber, now at the young man, trying to discover any kind of resemblance, but found none. He understood the secret of his affection for Muhammad Eid, and whence he inherited his perfect, captivating conversational gifts.

"Why not rest for a few days, Abu Misbah," said the doctor shrewdly. "Get to know Mooran and its people, and make yourself at home."

He did not mention the great, the momentous work for which he had been summoned, nor did he make any reference to the Sultan. Muhammad Eid had spent the whole previous night talking, explaining to his brother why the doctor needed him so quickly, what kind of future awaited him here, and how he would become rich in no time. He had alluded briefly to the likelihood that their entire family would move to Mooran and settle there for good. So, now, he was very surprised at the doctor's cautious stance, and wished, for the sake of his own standing in his brother's eyes, that he had acted differently. As the doctor stood to mark the end of their visit, Muhammad said to himself: *If this had been anyone but my brother he would have taken me aside and said, 'You take care of him; empty his pockets and then get back to me.'"*

"You got in too late, Abu Misbah," he laughed to his brother. "You haven't seen Mooran yet—take some time to have a good look around!"

Badri al-Mudalal waited thirty-four days, during which time he nearly decided to pack his bags and go home. Only the encouraging messages Muhammad brought from time to time, all of which assured him that "the end was in sight," made him reconsider and postpone his departure. One night, after yet another promising message, he spoke to Muhammad.

"Just as they say: A billy goat plays with a goat's mind, and for a month you've been playing with mine, and I believed you, only listen." He laughed loudly. "I swear—I'll divorce my wife!—that if the fortieth day of this passes and still nothing has happened, then neither you nor your big boss nor anyone on earth will keep me in this dump of a town!

"Look, Muhammad, it takes a woman forty days to conceive, and a corpse forty days to rot, and that's my limit, too!"

"Be patient, Abu Misbah. Just today the doctor told me that everything's all set, that everything's fine!"

"Oh, sure, that's him all right. Let your Sultan find another barber!"

"Don't be so hasty, Abu Misbah. Opportunities like this don't come along every day."

"By God, even the chaotic kind of living I was making before was better than all this Mooran and Harran of yours."

"Just be patient a few more days."

"Well, all right, but my patience has limits."

Then the doctor met with Muhammad Eid and Badri al-Mudalal two nights in a row. He came to see that the Sultan had been hesitant in spite of the doctor's attempts to bring him around; now he had agreed in principle and on condition that there be a probationary period. Any subsequent decision would be based on that— "and as to supervising the situation and their relationship," the doctor said, "both are friends of mine, so that's my responsibility."

Badri did not like the sound of it and would have told them then and there that he was going back home, but the doctor's swift and adroit change of subject, and the spasm of good feeling with this solution to the problem, helped everything to end on a positive note.

Three nights later Badri al-Mudalal was summoned to the palace to meet with the doctor in his office. When he entered, he found a third man there. It was obvious that this man was there to deliver a final decision, and although he did not ask him any questions or speak to Badri at all, his eyes never left him; his eyes stole all his secrets; they were almost hostile. When the doctor stood up to mark the end of the visit, he glanced at the man and spoke his parting words to Badri.

"Tomorrow morning be ready at twelve noon. A car from the palace will pick you up. You start tomorrow."

When Abu Misbah remembered the thirty-four confused, demoralized days he had spent in Mooran, always ready to go back home, he felt that that would have been an irreversible mistake, and that Muhammad Eid was absolutely right, for had he not been so insistent events might have taken a very different course. Muhammad often jokingly repeated what his brother himself had said before—"A billy goat plays with a goat's mind"—but it did not anger Badri; the events following that day, for years to come, were the fruit of Muhammad's stubbornness.

The Sultan seemed to have reservations, at first, about entrusting his head to someone he did not know and had never seen before; he made sure that the doctor, Muti, and two of his men were present, but did his best to appear relaxed. He appeared, in fact, merry, and when the doctor suggested, in a lighthearted moment, that the Sultan try a new look for his hair and beard, he agreed readily. Abu Misbah was the epitome of care and professionalism in making sure that he understood the new instructions perfectly, and before long his reserve melted and Badri al-Mudalal became one of the Sultan's boon companions.

16

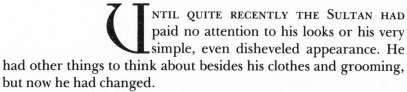

Until quite recently the Sultan had paid no attention to his looks or his very simple, even disheveled appearance. He had other things to think about besides his clothes and grooming, but now he had changed.

The doctor recalled that his first summons to Mooran had not been entirely guileless; the friendly welcome he had received, the hospitality lavished upon him, and Prince Khazael's speed in dispensing with the formalities of his station made him reluctant at first to guess what this all meant. The prince made no allusion to the doctor's prospects, but Zaid al-Heraidi did so on his behalf, for the doctor had been in the country only a few days when Zaid managed to spend an evening alone with him, and in an awkward but excited moment asked the doctor to secure a supply of "restorative" drugs. When the doctor slyly tried to find out what precisely were the discomforts or illnesses that required these "restoratives," Zaid looked away and gestured with his hand.

"Our friends in Harran told us everything—you know what we need, Doctor!"

The doctor was careful to laugh heartily, and after a pause told him, "Nothing could be simpler!"

This beginning was only a distant memory; what followed was much clearer and more striking. For Zaid, who came to Harran less than two months after this visit, seeming even bolder and more impatient than he'd been in Mooran, again made indirect but unmistakable references to the "restoratives" he wanted, in greater quantities than before; they were not only for him but for other persons as well. He laughed meaningfully and the doctor understood perfectly.

After that, events moved quickly and came into focus. The doctor's second visit to Mooran lasted two full weeks at the insistence of the prince, who seemed embarrassed, even ashamed, in the first days of this visit. The doctor hazarded at an opportune moment to ask Zaid, with fine ambiguity, about his health. When he answered that it had never been better and laughed delightedly, the doctor was emboldened to joke, "You're one in a thousand!"

Though the prince showed no interest, indeed kept gazing off in other directions, his nerves were taut. He secretly wished that the doctor would relax and discuss everything at length. The prince spoke to provoke the doctor into saying something.

"Life has rules, Zaid—a man gets old and his bones get hollow."

"We're still young men, Your Excellency, and besides, a man can be repaired just like an automobile!"

"Cars are iron, my friend."

"And everything in a man is like iron, even stronger than iron, Your Excellency!" Zaid could not allow the opportunity to pass. He turned to the doctor and asked, "What do you say, Abu Ghazwan?"

The doctor had, as he recalled, tried everything, even a variety of proverbs, to impress upon the prince the progress of medical science, especially when it came to enhancing a man's physical powers and prolonging his life. Doctors in Germany, Austria and America had discovered drugs that could give a man perpetual youth; he assured them quickly that he could travel to the great medical centers of Europe and America any time soon to check on the most recent discoveries and assess their effectiveness.

The prince listened closely and nodded wonderingly; he wanted a quick solution. He spoke to Zaid, but wanted the doctor to hear.

"Hear, hear, Zaid—live on with hope until the doctor returns from Europe and America!"

The doctor promptly turned to Zaid and asked him to have his small black valise and medical bag brought. Within minutes he had produced a vast selection of medicines and laid them out neatly in groups. Calmly, patiently, he explained the use and dosage of each, more to Khazael than to Zaid. The prince was obviously delighted but spoke to Zaid brusquely.

"Write it all down, Zaid, or you'll forget!"

At this meeting the doctor's rank was defined and established; the prince could not stop asking questions about the medicines, comparing one with another. He even asked the doctor for a thorough physical examination and detailed advice so that his condition would be perfect. The doctor did just as he was told, showing immense care all through the examination, and told His Highness that he was in superb condition—that "he had the heart of a twenty-year-old." He added that if His Highness lost a little weight, his health would be even better, and laughed.

What the doctor now recalled was a part of the ever-fading past, for the prince, who seemed at the outset embarrassed or ashamed, soon changed, with the help of the doctor, who spurred him on with stories from Holy Scripture and history, especially the history of kings and great leaders. He assured him that a man's own powers were the decisive factor in everything, and suggested that while ancient kings relied on popular medicine and folk remedies such as honey, almonds, pigeon meat and pigeon broth, the progress achieved by modern medicine had produced endless new services and remedies that had to be tried. After this visit there were regular deliveries of ever newer and more numerous medicines to the Ghadir Palace, accompanied by Dr. Mahmilji's detailed instructions and wishes for the Sultan to "enjoy himself."

Since settling in Mooran, the doctor had felt his duties and responsibilities mounting; he was responsible not only for the Sultan's health, but for helping to ease the burdens of ruling. All people, far and near, great and small, must know that this was a Sultan unlike any other, past or present.

This mission was behind the doctor's driving energy, his long spells of unbroken thought, and his ever more haunting uncertainty; he had not yet entirely adjusted to Mooran, and was unsure of the people around him. With the arrival of his wife and children, and Muti's evolution into a friend as well as a relative and a reliable aide, the doctor's state of mind vastly improved. One evening in the Central Province, where they had accompanied the Sultan on one of his tours, he told Muti, "Uncle"—this was how he addressed his nephew—"things have changed. I used to be alone, and the Sultan was just a prince, but now things are different."

He sighed worriedly and tried to gather his thoughts and focus them.

"Listen, Muti, you're an adult, your brain is mature and you don't need anyone to school you, but you know the saying: two heads are better than one and two men are stronger than one. Here we are, you and I together, and nothing will divide us but Death." He relaxed for a moment and added, in a different tone, "We have a difficult task ahead of us, very difficult, Uncle Muti, and at the moment no one may be envious of us, but they'll appear, don't worry, and perhaps enemies, too. We have to be prepared for them."

He smiled as his mind strayed among his memories.

"I've always loved reading history. Now we have to apply what we've learned." His tone changed. "I'm not a fool, and I'm not alone. You and I and a few others like us, if we come to terms and see things the same way, can change the face of this part of the globe!" He cleared his throat and nodded. "Perhaps you remember the story of the Englishwoman who created a kingdom from nothing, by taking a defeated king and raising him above all of the waiting, competing kings. She was a foreigner and she was all alone!" He took a deep breath. "Our position is much more favorable. The Sultan has given us all his keys, even the most secret, and we have to use them. If we let them slip away, if we let them get stolen, if we don't know how to put them to use, we'll have no one to blame but ourselves!"

Muti listened carefully to his uncle, and understood every word, but found that, put together, the words had scant precise meaning and followed no consistent line of thought. What did his uncle want? What exactly was being asked of him? It was true enough that he had found favor with the prince and made himself indispensable, having made several journeys to buy things the palace required and delivered several messages abroad, but now he did not know what was expected of him. He was required to confer constantly with his uncle, to answer his questions, to listen to him. Now that his uncle had moved to Mooran and they met daily and talked about everything, he found that the words he heard were full of hidden and divergent meanings.

During this tour, in his meetings with the populace, in his uncle's solemn and baffling remarks, he found new self-confidence and felt that he was not alone.

"You should have come to Mooran long ago, Uncle!" he said in a moment of deep satisfaction.

"Everything in its time, Uncle."

"Even so, I don't think we came too late."

"On the contrary, this is just the right time." The doctor laughed sadly. "As long as we know what we're doing."

17

IT HAD LONG BEEN FOREMOST IN THE DOCTOR'S mind that the Sultan should have by his side a trusted and efficient person to tend matters of "intelligence and security," as he thought of the secret agency he had in mind. He considered several people, and new names always came to mind, but he still had not found the right individual, since *the Mooranis are like nuts—you have to break them to see what's inside.* This person's mission would go far beyond knowing what the people were saying and thinking, it involved knowing everything about the princes: what they said, where they went, what they did, who their friends were, what these friends told them; in short, investigating and keeping records on even the smallest things, most of them secret.

The doctor, who knew many of the princes and noticed how they viewed him at first, and how they had behaved around him, could appreciate the immense sensitivity of his project: the princes were, even unprovoked, hostile and reckless; they went looking for trouble, as the doctor said to himself. Any one of them could kill a man without batting an eye, as easily as drinking water. If they knew they were being watched, their movements followed, if it were to be known where they went or what they did, they would have all the excuse they needed for the cruelest and most vindictive acts. So the doctor threw out one name after another, discarding especially anyone who was not a native of Mooran.

In Harran Muhammad Eid had been his eyes and ears; he told the doctor everything that went on, everything the people were saying. Here in Mooran it was completely different and much more complicated. When he asked Muhammad to fill him in on the local news and events or told him to stay close to what was on people's minds, he laughed.

"They're like deaf-mutes," said Muhammad jokingly. "They have nothing to say, truth or lies, and when they do say something you can't understand them. Once you get talking to them, they ask you about encampments and rain and the markets—'Ibn Saad's animals have arrived,' and 'Ibn Othman's beasts got lost and scattered,' and it takes forever to figure out that they're talking about camels and sheep!"

The doctor tried to explain to Muhammad that he was not interested in sheep or camels, and that the locals' dialect was not really that hard to understand, but he failed to arouse Muhammad's enthusiasm.

"If I do hear anything, Doctor, whom am I going to tell if I don't tell you?" said Muhammad to end the discussion.

Despite each man's efforts to explain his position to the other, each was convinced that he could not make the other understand what he wanted, so the doctor's thinking took a different direction: he had to find the man who could carry out the mission he had in mind.

One night the doctor brought it up with the Sultan.

"Your Majesty, as the proverb says, 'Close the drafty door before you rest.' The world we live in, sire, is heaving with unrest and anarchy. We can thank Almighty God that law and order reign in the Sultanate, that the people are contented, but the winds that are blowing from the four corners of the earth"—he used this expression very deliberately—"will find their way here sooner or later, and will be exploited by some dupe, some troublemaker, especially now that the Sultanate has become the envy of all her poverty-stricken neighbors. If it weren't for Your Majesty's wisdom and the love the people bear you, things might be very different."

He paused to watch the effect his words were having upon the Sultan, and changed his tone of voice when it seemed to him the Sultan was daydreaming.

"I am convinced, Your Majesty, that the presence of a trusted person, in charge of an agency directly answerable to Your Majesty, would be of the utmost value, at least in the future. Before any two men can plot, before a single bullet can be fired, you would know everything."

The doctor chuckled and shifted in his chair before going on, but the Sultan spoke up uneasily.

"So you've heard something, or know something, Doctor?"

"No, no, never, Your Majesty!" After a moment he went on. "I'm sure that there isn't anyone in the whole Sultanate liable to try anything, but you have to be in a position to know, Your Majesty, what any two people are talking about—you must be able to hear the ants crawl! Destructive ideas and extremist movements are spreading around us like fire through straw. It may be true that poverty, discontent and bad government are the main causes in the spread of these movements, but that isn't all—there are *countries* plotting, and atheistic ideas threatening our holy country to gain control over us and our religion. We have to contain them, and if necessary fight them in their cradle—that would be the task of the agency I am proposing to you now."

The Sultan loved the idea, which seemed to him valuable and essential. He gazed far off.

"What you say is true, Doctor, and we must do it. Whom do you recommend to us?"

"Give me time to think, Your Majesty, and, God willing, we will find the right person." And, in an effort to get a decision: "We have two types of medical science, Your Majesty: preventive medicine and therapeutic medicine. Preventive medicine is used to inhibit a disease from setting in or spreading. It has a beginning and no end; it begins with heredity and proceeds through every factor affecting the health—diet, avoiding infection, inoculations and so forth. With therapeutic medicine, a doctor fights an existing illness and uses every means to heal the patient: drugs, surgery, quarantine. As you can plainly see, Your Majesty, there is a great difference between preventing illness and fighting it once it has set in." He took a deep breath and raised his hands. "Our Department of Police and Investigations is excellent and efficient, God knows, but it's the equivalent of therapeutic medicine. It never is deployed until a crime is committed, to discover who the criminal is and how the crime took place. What we need now is to introduce preventive as well as therapeutic medicine."

The Sultan laughed and seemed absolutely delighted.

"As you say, Abu Ghazwan, before trouble starts, choke it—tie the fox with a rope strong enough for a lion!"

The plan was with the doctor in his waking and sleeping hours. He reviewed the names one after another; he did not even leave out Badri al-Mudalal, *because the bastard uses the Sultan's head to find out what's in every other head, and with all the chatter and shaving he gets the secrets of their minds and their balls.* But then he decided against him, since *his only asset is the fact that he's a barber, and besides he talks too much, he repeats everything he hears—he could be more harm than help to us, and ruin everything.*

He considered Prince Rakan. True, he was lazy, but if he straightened himself out he could be formidable. He was moody— sometimes he just disappeared and went to his farm. He was religious, always citing Ibn Hureira and Ibn Abbas and Ibn Malek and Thaalibi. The doctor pondered and then recalled that *the problem is, Rakan and the Sultan are from different mothers, and there might be factors I'm unaware of . . . then there is Prince Mayzar, but all his friends are traders and merchants, who talk of nothing but 'Such-and-such a piece of land is now worth so much, and So-and-So bought it.' Who has the time to listen to that sort of thing?*

The doctor had not forgotten Muti, Jaafar or al-Hajjar, but thought, as he ruled out each in turn, that *God has already given each of them something to keep him busy.*

A few weeks later he was close to abandoning the plan, since if he did not mention it to the Sultan, the Sultan would not remember it, especially since he himself was having so much trouble

choosing the right person. He did not know how it had ever occurred to him to be, himself, the chief of this kind of organization.
He imagined himself in a half-lit room directly off the Sultan's reception room, with dozens of intermittently ringing telephones, information pouring in from every direction. He would pass on to
the Sultan what he deemed necessary. He would have dozens of
aides, each with a special task. Everything would be done at night,
in secret; he even thought of giving his aides code names, or even
numbers. He tried to remember some of the books he had read
long ago about the great and dangerous deeds in the two world
wars, how intelligence services had played a decisive role in guiding
the leaders' conduct of the war, but no specific names or faces came
to mind. *Abu Ghazwan,* he said to himself ruefully, *if you had only
thought of this ten or fifteen years ago and done something about it, it might
have worked, but now* . . . In an attempt to check his momentary feeling of unworthiness, he laughed and thought, *All these possibilities
are now yours, Abu Ghazwan, all the energy and the information will be
your very own, but you have to be strong and equal to the task, and you
have to know what to do!*

After a great deal of waiting, thinking and evaluation, the doctor
reached a decision. *"Long ago I told Muti that a woman, yes, a woman,
and a foreign one at that; who did not speak Arabic, who did not know a
soul, founded a kingdom from nothing—and now, Subhi, Abu Ghazwan,
you are unable even to choose a man to head up the security service?*

"Your Majesty," he proposed to the Sultan, "I have a recommendation that will please you. I have found the right man."

"Who is it?"

"Hammad al-Mutawa."

"Hammad al-Mutawa? The son of Ibrahim, or of Saleh al-
Mutawa?"

"The son of Saleh al-Mutawa, Your Majesty."

"Do I know him? Have I seen him?"

"He was at court last Thursday, Your Majesty. He's the one who
sent the blind man away and told him to go to the emirate."

"Oh, yes, oh, yes, I remember him. Who put you on to him?"

The doctor chuckled before replying, "By God, Your Majesty,
my heart guided me to him."

The Sultan laughed loudly and nodded. "Excellent, Doctor—
the heart never misleads a man!"

The doctor sighed.

"His mission, Your Majesty, has easy and difficult aspects, and it requires, above all, loyalty and integrity. Hammad is equal to the job, and young, and you know, Your Majesty, that the Mutawas are a prosperous family. He can grow in Your Majesty's shadow to become your most faithful subject."

"How old is Ibn Mutawa?"

"About thirty, Your Majesty."

"Isn't that a little young for this kind of work?"

"A young man growing in Your Majesty's shadow is better than an older man who's grown up elsewhere."

"Is he educated?"

"As far as high school, then he came into his family's money, and now he is the head of his family."

The Sultan wanted to leave the matter undecided.

"God is great. Let us think about it and learn more, Abu Ghazwan, God willing, and hope for the best!"

18

SOME MONTHS BEFORE THE DOCTOR LEFT HAR-
ran, two men arrived there: Hosny Karkar
and Said al-Usta, half brothers from the same
mother. Hosny was tall and fair and slender; Said was stocky and
rather short, or at least seemed so because he was plump and
swarthy compared to his brother. No one would ever have guessed
they were brothers; no one, told that they were, would have believed it at first glance; if one or both of them were present and the
fact was mentioned, and either of them nodded, consternation
would be clear on the faces of whoever was there to hear it for the
first time.

Their unlikeness was not limited to the lack of physical resemblance or their different surnames: their temperaments were very
different, too. Hosny came across as tolerant, kind and religious,
whereas Said was a practical man, as he described himself, so it was
easy to get along with him in spite of his sarcasm and his reckless-

ness in moments of anger—there was nothing he would not do. Perhaps it was these qualities that caused the two to meet with failure after failure, and to leave Syria long ago to open a business in Amman. Hosny made a brief visit to that city to study its markets, since he had many acquaintances who had lived there longer than he, and he concluded that he could do business there. Their business in Damascus was failing anyway, and beset with problems they could not solve, so they moved to Amman.

No one was exactly sure of the date of the move, lost as it was in darkness and disagreement and the past, with no two people having the same account of the event—even the two men offered versions different from each other's and from even their own on other occasions. The reason the brothers left Amman was bankruptcy. They had opened a store different from any other in the goods and services it offered, and after an initial period of success, which came as a marked surprise to most people, Said overextended himself in real estate speculation and contracts for smuggled sugar— and, some said, narcotics—and this, or perhaps some other deal, bankrupted them. Hosny, however, had provided for the eventuality before it occurred, having transferred the title of most of the land and assets held jointly or in either of their names to relatives, women especially, so that when their business was seized for liquidation, some of their creditors waived their rights, finding nothing worth the trouble of confiscating.

Bankruptcy, or rather the prosecution of their bankruptcy, was what forced them to leave Amman, at least until things blew over. Since Said had business connections in Harran, mainly from his traffic in the smuggled sugar, that city seemed to him a good next stop, or even a final destination. He told Hosny, in an effort to persuade him to go along, that "our relative Dr. Subhi Mahmilji is rich, and in that country they can refuse him nothing, and he thinks the world of us," and since Hosny could not refuse and had not the capacity to be stubborn, he assented.

"The doctor is in the operating room, and it will be a long operation," and "The doctor has been urgently summoned to the emirate," were Muhammad Eid's answers when they came to the clinic and hospital on their first three-day visit to Harran. With this kind of reception, Said had to think of something, and once he started, or became angry, there was no way he could be silent or stand for anything. Within a day or two it fell to Muhammad to investigate the two men and look after them, as the doctor had told, or rather ordered him, to do, for "that madman Said can't deal with people and there is no telling what he might do." This in spite of the fact that the family tie, distant though it was, was between the doctor and Hosny, though to listen to Said's talk one would have thought, or even have been certain, that it was between the doctor and Said himself.

At the luncheon the doctor gave for them on their fifth day in Harran, to make up for Muhammad Eid's mistakes, he lavished all his attention and hospitality upon Said and was careful to show nothing but delight at their visit. He did not want to get embroiled with Said over the projects he proposed (demanding that they be implemented immediately) or reject them outright, for that would lead to another mad outburst. He praised Said's ideas and projects and asked for time to study them carefully until "we can find local partners." Until that was accomplished he assigned them duties relating to the hospital and lands he owned in Harran, "and after we've churned them we'll know the cheese from the whey."

Muhammad Eid did not hide his surprise or resentment at the doctor's fear of this "pipsqueak"—Said al-Usta—*because if he let me deal with him, neither he nor anyone else would dare presume upon the greatest genius in Harran*—the doctor.

The doctor smiled and spoke, as if to himself.

" 'Watch what you say,' as the Prophet said." He looked closely at Muhammad Eid. "The short and the long of it is, they are family."

Muhammad was still upset, and felt blamed for the mistake, and answered sharply.

"Some relatives are scorpions, sir, make no mistake!"

"There has been no mistake, and we have nothing to lose. The men and their deeds are all that concerns me."

Four months and a few days later the doctor returned to Mooran as part of Harran's mourning delegation for the late Sultan. He brought Said al-Usta and Hosny Karkar as a sign of his deep sorrow and the personal loss felt by his family, and to give them a chance to get to know Mooran for themselves and to decide whether or not to move there. He took excellent care of them and introduced them as relatives and as important businessmen not only in Jordan but in Syria, Egypt and Lebanon as well. Said was delighted and seduced by the friendliness and hospitality and began to act like a big businessman. After nagging one of the palace men to introduce him to some of Mooran's big merchants, he began to frequent the markets by himself, spending hours there every day, asking questions, haggling and getting to know people until he felt absolutely sure that if he went into business in Mooran he could not fail; this time he would not suffer the fate he had in Damascus and Amman. He was so swept away that he wanted to stay in Mooran while Hosny returned to Harran with the doctor to liquidate their business there; he would await them in Mooran. But the doctor's looks and smiles and gestures told him that he could not do without Said's services in Harran, "since you know everything and can do anything," so he agreed to go along with them, planning to come back to Mooran as soon as possible.

19

THE PERIOD OF THE DOCTOR'S ARRIVAL IN
Mooran with his whole entourage—Muhammad Eid, Said al-Usta, Hosny Karkar,
a cook, a servant and two security guards—was considered Mooran's golden age, or at least that was what the doctor called it. He
said it gaily, but added, with a completely different look on his face:

"God, may He be praised, has opened the gates of Heaven to this
poor, noble people; after long waiting, longer than Jacob waited
for his son Joseph, after years of subsisting on locusts, dates and
barley bread, after dying of malnutrition, the Almighty said to
them, 'My patient servants, You have known enough hunger and
suffering and plagues. I have taken pity upon you, and when I take
pity and show my bounty, I do so without measure. If I have tried
your faith in the past with starvation and tyrannical rulers, I now
relieve you of the troubles and cares of the world, which I will
reckon in your judgment on the Last Day, and now give you a Sultan unlike any other, and all the treasures of the world!'"

The doctor was lost in his most distant thoughts, and then spoke again, in a different tone.

"If you'd come to Mooran two years ago, you wouldn't have been able to live; you would have found nothing but misery and hardship: no work, no money, no people!" He smiled sadly. "But if you come here two years from now, there won't be room for you—there'll be more people than grains of sand, all more ravenous than flies!" He ended this speech to himself, or to his close friends, by saying firmly, "This is the day, and this is the golden age of Mooran!"

Within six months two firms opened for business in Mooran's Aoun Street: the International Import-Export Company, which dealt in foodstuffs, owned by Abdelaziz al-Ghamdi, Said al-Usta & Co.; and the Hissan Construction Company, owned by Muhammad al-Hissan, Hosny Karkar & Co. The first was at the beginning of the street, on the square, taking up three or four storefronts. Part of the space was used to display the company's stock—sugar, flour, lentils, boxes of tea, and large quantities of canned goods—and the rest was office space. The front part of the building had been converted into a large foyer for receiving distributors, wholesalers and the most important merchants.

Said's partner, Abdelaziz al-Ghamdi, had spent his boyhood and part of his youth as a shepherd; when he grew older and stronger he became a camel herder and worked in this line for a few years, during which he traveled to eastern Jordan, to Palestine, once to Egypt and to Houran in Syria, and became an owner as well as a herder. At first he owned two head of the flock, but within a few years became a fifty-fifty partner in a herd of thirty-two sheep.

At the time he came to know Said and helped found the International Import-Export Company, he had just returned from Kuwait, where he owned three trucks and a trade in wool and skins. Only pure chance had brought him together with Said and, later, with the doctor. It seemed to them that he had tired of travel and wanted to settle down, and when they offered to make him a partner in the food supply company he did not hesitate long; he sold two of his three trucks. The company obtained a loan and credit facilities from the government and went to work. Abdelaziz al-Ghamdi had one-third of the capital and the trade, Said had a third in credit assets plus trade and experience. Rateb al-Fattal, the "purchaser" and guarantor for the foreign firms abroad, held the last third.

The first third was Abdelaziz's alone, but the other two thirds were divided into fourths: the doctor had a fourth, since he was the sponsor for the firm's funding and had assured its success and reputation; Rateb had a fourth since he was the purchaser and link with foreign suppliers, and the brothers, Hosny and Said, each had one-fourth, in trade and experience.

Said was very happy with the partnership and with his share, and when Hosny grumbled about the doctor's role in the business, and Rateb's, Said clapped him on the shoulder and told him, "Don't be a fool! The only ones who've put up money are Abdelaziz and al-Hissan, and we're all partners—if the business makes a profit we split it evenly, and if it loses, those assholes are the losers!"

Hosny accepted this explanation, but still felt vaguely defrauded, since "the doctor is getting easy money—he put up nothing, he's not going to carry any lumber or steel, but it will come rolling in to him. And Rateb al-Fattal does nothing but sit on his ass, writing to companies—'Please send us one hundred tons of cement and twenty meters of lumber'—they send it and he pockets the cash!"

Once the company opened, however, all the partners were astonished at the volume of business and all forgot about the shares—they were too busy running the firm.

The doctor hosted a dinner party to mark the launching of the company and the end to his formal involvement with it; he spoke grandly, impressing upon them the importance of self-reliance, and addressing his words to each of them.

"Today there are no more excuses. Some people in some other places complain that they have no work, that there's no work to be had, and here, too, they complain—about the work they do, or about the amount and diversity of the work!" His voice became very humble. "As the holy proverb says, 'I fear not poverty for my nation; rather I fear insufficient guidance.'" He reverted to his earlier tone. "The doctor, my friends—God bless him—is a cipher in this business, don't ask him for advice or try to get him involved— he has a thousand other cares, so deal with your problems by yourselves!"

Hosny tried everything to make the doctor maintain some link with the company, to consult with the partners, but gave up, gamely accepting the doctor's refusal on the grounds that he had no time—besides, his brother bellowed at him, "Every minute of the doctor's time is worth the whole earth—the man has been hired by the top man in the country to be responsible for everything in the country! Do you think we're going to go running to him every minute and every hour—'Doctor, lentils, Doctor, onions and macaroni—sardines, Doctor, today's price is such-and-such, against yesterday's so much, should we buy or sell?" Said chuckled. "Have some sense, Abu Tayseer, let the man do his job."

So it was decided that the day-to-day management would be left to Hosny and Said. Rateb would make a long visit every now and then, and if necessary the doctor could attend discussions to render his opinion on some of the more important matters.

A huge neon sign giving the name of the company was placed on top of the building. "People care about appearances, Abu Homeidi," Said explained to his partner, "so looks are important, especially if it's foodstuffs you're selling—it's the eyes that eat, as they say. If we spend a little extra dressing up the company, we'll profit in the end. Business is the art of taking and giving. If someone comes along and sees buying and selling going on in Mooran, he can't go anywhere else." Said paused and looked directly into Abdelaziz al-Ghamdi's eyes. "Sheikh Abdelaziz, Abu Homeidi," he said excitedly, "business in Mooran will never be the same again. We are not vermin like these other traders. If we have a strong start, the market is ours—we control it. If we start out weakly, we'll stumble and then starve."

His partner did not look convinced. Said changed his tone of voice.

"Ask me, Abu Homeidi. I've been all around the world and I've seen a lot and learned a lot about the way people work and how they behave. It all comes down to three things: shrewdness, looks and advertising. Shrewdness is what keeps your eyes open—you know when to buy or sell. It is a divine gift, from Almighty God. And looks are what really grabs people, it's what's most important to people about themselves. And advertising, Abu Homeidi, especially these days, is the most powerful and important weapon. The name of the International Company has to be everywhere at all times—I want people saying it in their sleep!"

The two partners agreed that the company would be as Said al-Usta envisioned it: imposing, and in the city center. It was decided that the foyer, intended for buying and selling, while Abu Homeidi would handle wholesale deals in the inner offices—this was Said's concept—would be dominated by Abu Homeidi's desk, directly in front of the entrance, because he wanted to see everyone and everything. Besides, he said, the inner office assigned to him was "suffocating—like a tomb. Anyone who spent a month or two in there would end up mute or mad."

In spite of all the remarks, at first, about the prodigious and unnecessary costs involved in setting up, "because Mooran is not Beirut or Marseilles," as Rateb said, the company's profits in the first few months convinced everyone that Said was right, and made them curse themselves for not knowing more about business. Said appreciated the impact of the success. "As I told you, Mooran is a different place now, and business is no game for children. In the past they may have done business here, made money and lost it, but that was yesterday. Today no one is going to do business and make money, and lose nothing, who wasn't suckled by a lioness!"

Rateb and the doctor were delighted. Hosny, who had to content himself with a shop, though a wide and high-ceilinged one, more like a storeroom or caravansary, was depressed by his brother's success. *I know him like the back of my hand: he's scatterbrained and can't deal with this at all. If he makes money at anything, he keeps at it in the same way until there's nothing left, and then he has to start from zero again.* These thoughts, which obsessed Hosny, were expressed with great calm and subtlety, but Said turned his back and pretended not to hear; he would get what he wanted, and that was all he cared about.

Muhammad Eid watched, listened and took it all in, but did not understand what the people were thinking or how they viewed all of this, for "Yes-Man," or "Air-Pump"—his nicknames for Said al-Usta—was a pretentious loudmouth, incapable of any good: he "swindled everyone." Still, people in Mooran talked of nothing but the two brothers, al-Usta and Little Karkar, as he called them: how they had "gutted" the markets, leaving nothing for anyone else;

how they alone truly understood business, markets and real estate. Surely they would become the richest men in Mooran; everyone else would be eaten alive. Muhammad Eid castigated himself for not understanding people—they were *so complicated—virtual laboratories.* He told himself, a little consolingly, that *the important thing is honesty. Money isn't everything in this world.*

Said himself seemed unsure, unconvinced. First, "since money is everything in this world," and he possessed nothing but his shrewdness, and had to make his own way, whatever hardship it cost him, he soon became a different person. "Money, my friends, comes and goes, but the important thing that endures is here," and he tapped his temple to show that he was talking about brains. Once he started making money and basked in everyone's praise, his self-confidence returned and he could not have been happier. "With most business people, a fellow may deal in sheep or camels. He might sell a sack or two of flour. He produces nothing and has no motivation—all the ingenuity he has is in haggling. He'll haggle over a price until he nearly kills the other fellow, and since we're nothing but nerve endings and can't stand it, eventually we give in, and at the end of the day he's made a few cents' profit and the other has made a loss of a few cents. This is what they call business." He shook his head sadly and went on. "But to take a risk, to go for his competitor's throat, to win everything or lose everything—they know nothing about this, they've never heard of it."

Even Abu Homeidi, who was skeptical and worried at first by the bustle of activity around him, and moved his desk from the inner office to the center of the foyer from the first day so that he could see and hear everything that went on, though with no wish to interfere, leaving all the negotiating to Said—even Abu Homeidi was soon swept up in the excitement and as pleased as he could be with the profits that had begun to pour in. His worry evaporated.

He began to get involved, to take an active part, even to take on Said's own personality. "Our merchandise is not like the other stuff you find in the market—we ordered ours from abroad, and it came here from the ends of the earth with our name on it, at our expense. You all have eyes—judge for yourselves!" He would take a fistful of coffee beans, sniff them and heft them, then let them run through his fingers back into the sack. "Look all over the market—

you won't find coffee like this anywhere else: It's like gold. Better than gold—God bless the hands that planted it, that picked it, that sell and buy it." Once he had impressed all this upon the haggling buyers, he would add, very much in Said's manner, "My friends, all this is top-quality merchandise, absolutely first-class. Our agents abroad have sent us samples, and within a few months there may not be a single bag of it left anywhere."

Said watched, from a distance, the transformation of Abdelaziz al-Ghamdi: his behavior, his speech, even his looks, and felt a certain delight, which however did not overpower his natural restraint. He felt that he had needed just this opportunity to reawaken his skills and potential. "Mooran isn't Damascus or Amman—people here are simple; they want to learn, and a man here can really help the whole country to flourish. Back home, people are bastards, worse than the Devil, and you never know whether they're laughing with you or at you." Seeing the change in Abu Homeidi awoke in him desires, new plans and ideas faster than the stars ignite in the night sky. "There's no end of work to be done in this country, but you need people, worldly people who know what to do and how to work."

Hosny was at the opposite end of the market, sitting at a desk he himself had constructed from wooden planks, between the sacks of cement and stacks of tiles, not far from the steel girders piled almost to the ceiling. He heard everything that Said said and did, and all the gossip of the market, and was confused—he did not know whether to be happy for him, to be reassured, or to go back to his old fears. Now that things had started this way, would they continue to move in the same direction? He could not reach any clear conclusion, especially when he remembered their experiences in Damascus and Amman, and abruptly raised his voice in prayer "Lord, make things easy, spare us tribulation; Lord, make things easy, spare us tribulation, watch over us with Your grace!" But when they met, both of them, and Said began to describe the new projects he had in mind, how it would not be long before he began to make them reality, Hosny spoke up, almost rebukingly.

"Concentrate a moment, Said; just wait a minute. Get to know the people and the country first . . . if you think you can just plunder the place, run around getting your hands in a thousand and one projects, you'll just get screwed, and we'll all be ruined."

"Look, I'm your brother, Abu Tayseer," said Said confidently. "You just see if I don't make this place prosper—I'll even look after the ants! Take heart. Don't worry."

"Everything in its own good time, Said."

"The time is now, Abu Tayseer. If we don't get started, if we don't get to work, it will pass us by. Someone else will come along and snatch it away."

20

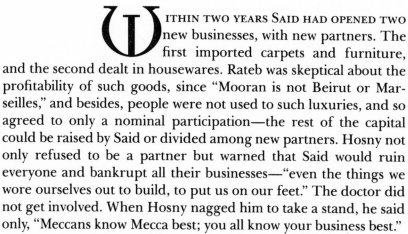

ITHIN TWO YEARS SAID HAD OPENED TWO new businesses, with new partners. The first imported carpets and furniture, and the second dealt in housewares. Rateb was skeptical about the profitability of such goods, since "Mooran is not Beirut or Marseilles," and besides, people were not used to such luxuries, and so agreed to only a nominal participation—the rest of the capital could be raised by Said or divided among new partners. Hosny not only refused to be a partner but warned that Said would ruin everyone and bankrupt all their businesses—"even the things we wore ourselves out to build, to put us on our feet." The doctor did not get involved. When Hosny nagged him to take a stand, he said only, "Meccans know Mecca best; you all know your business best."

Said ignored all this opposition and rejection; he had long since rented and furnished the new premises, and agreed, after distinct hesitation, that Abdelaziz al-Ghamdi would be his partner in the

Oriental Carpet Company. The Nile Houseware Company had not room for too many partners, he explained, and already had two, one of whom was Lebanese, who alone were capable of running the business.

Said himself would have been unable to tell how he got his ideas—the early stages blurred into the final phases, and he did not know whether he had dreamed up his plans or they had suddenly come to him; whether someone had suggested them or he had heard them in the babble of the market.

"As long as we sell coffee and tea, rice and sugar and all the other necessities—why, they're all for eating, not for fun." This is what he said to justify his plans. "Of course people consume them, so we have to sell them the means for doing so!" He chuckled delightedly at his logic, which had convinced him at the very start. "It's only natural that people need silverware just as much as they need food."

"Would you just use your head!" Hosny shouted. "A man eats three times a day, but in his whole life he buys only one saucepan and one carpet." His tone changed, to one of pity. "That's *if* he buys them."

"And there are people who never built a house," Said replied mockingly. "So by those standards it would be totally insane to open a business selling construction materials."

"But people do build, and we don't have to chase after business."

"But they all eat and drink!"

"But they don't buy pots and pans!"

"As long as they have money, they'll buy."

They could reach no agreement over the Nile Company, and disagreed even more strongly about the Oriental Carpet Company. When the idea came to Said, he was determined to start up the company, and told them, to decide the matter, "My friends, think big. Think of the future." He added smilingly, as if to himself, "You think like birds—you only think of today. If we only thought of furnishing the new Sultan's palace, that alone would be enough, we'd be buried in money up to our ears." But still they were not convinced.

The founding of those two companies was the beginning of dissension between the brothers; in addition to Hosny's refusal to participate, there were Said's daily moods and maddening adventurism. He took an exquisite pleasure in his risks, moving erratically from place to place and from task to task. Perhaps he had found in Mooran, and in his new wealth, new opportunities to do what he had been kept from doing in other places, in other times. They had rented a small house soon after arriving in Mooran, and now he not only found it too small and wanted to move; he wanted to rent a palace in the Saffan district. When Hosny stared at his brother, thinking that this was surely one of Said's practical jokes, his brother came back at him sarcastically.

"We're in Mooran now, Abu Tayseer—we're on top of the world!"

"And if it doesn't last?"

"Don't worry, it will last."

"You'll waste everything we've earned!"

"Abu Tayseer, the real danger isn't poverty, it's the fear of poverty."

"I don't want to hear any more about this!"

Finally they agreed on a solution, when Muhammad al-Hissan rented them the house he had built on the outskirts of al-Saffan, but the sumptuous life Said had taken up in this period provided new grounds for quarrels. Hosny wore shabby clothes and had to do dirty work in the shop, and in the course of the day, with its dust and exhaustion making his already glum temperament even more brittle and tense, he would meet the neat and elegantly dressed Said. On top of that, their partners had very different and even antagonistic qualities, for Abdelaziz al-Ghamdi did not consider a true partnership complete unless he shared in everything directly—in fact he went to great lengths to try to do everything himself. Hissan, however, never lifted a finger and spent much of his time in the coffeehouse next door. Whenever Hosny tried to make him work, or even to make him stay in the office, Hissan replied gently, with a smile that showed his enormous teeth, "God bless you, Abu Tayseer, with you at work, no one else is needed."

If he caught a reprimand in Hosny's eye, he went on. "The trouble is that the damned work is so backbreaking, especially figuring prices, and all those decimal places." He was referring to a miscalculation he'd made when the business had newly opened, which would have cost the company a fortune if Hosny had not found the mistake at the last minute, and asked Hissan to leave the cost accounting to him, since he excelled at figures: he could do any mathematical problem, no matter how large or complex the figures, in his head in no time.

These conflicts might have resolved themselves and disappeared, or at least not grown so formidable, had it not been for the almost idiotic recklessness that had taken hold of Said around this time. He had a fixed idea that hospitality alone could establish his commercial position, and while he may have hesitated to show his generosity in times past, constrained by the smallness of the house and the lack of servants to prepare meals, now he had solved these problems by moving into al-Hissan's house and hiring a cook.

Hosny grudgingly endured the first series of parties, since he saw them as repaying hospitality to others who had entertained Said, or as business necessities, but when the parties came more often, growing louder and more boisterous with card games, he began to lose his temper. He asked Said to have fewer parties, less often, and preferably in the afternoons, "so that we can get some sleep after the long days we put in." Said listened but paid no attention, made no changes or ever did as he was asked unless it suited his own wishes.

21

THE DOCTOR HAD ALWAYS DISTRUSTED SAID. It was a mutual distrust, though they both tried to conceal it, and indeed, pretended that the opposite was the case, especially in front of other people. As a result, those who knew them were convinced that the two men enjoyed a deep and special friendship. Even Muti, who had no secrets from his uncle, and consulted with him on all his plans and problems, and always took his advice, did not dare share with him his private opinion of Said. On the rare occasions when he did allude to it obliquely, in the form of a doubt or misgiving, he found the doctor's point of view immoral. In the beginning Muhammad Eid tried to hint at his opinion of Said but eventually gave up, or rather forgot about it in Mooran's never-ending stream of worries and concerns.

The doctor saw in Said a shining example of intellect and energy—"If we understand him and help him, he'll benefit and so will we," he would say, nodding. Privately, he saw him differently: *He's a cunning bastard—he could steal the perfume right off your face. And he's a swindler—he leads you to water and you go away thirsty. But as long as he's with you and you keep your eyes wide open, it's better than letting him go with someone else.*

That is how the doctor saw him. Even Hosny admitted that his brother was irresponsible, reckless and troublesome, but the doctor was more careful and always alert, and because he wanted to profit from certain of Said's qualities, he had Rateb watch him carefully and keep him accountable, and he had any number of other individuals following his movements.

Said held much the same opinion of the doctor.

"The doctor knows his medicine and doesn't need a certificate from anyone. In religion he's devout, he has many virtues. In politics he's an expert, he could ransom a corpse from the noose." Here he paused. "But that's about it."

Clearly his grand and general words were exaggerated, or more precisely, had no specific meaning; Said may have intended sarcasm, but his manner of speaking, so sincere and dignified, seemed to leave no room for doubt or misinterpretation.

Then there was his true opinion, as he summed it up to himself, and it was simplicity itself. *No power on earth could make me believe that man is honest. On the contrary, he's a fraud and swindler, with the nose of a bloodhound. He sniffs where a patient's put his money as he's examining him, as he's writing the prescription he's looking at the poor bastard's pocket, imagining the money, and if he can feel it, he'll know the higher denominations without even looking at them! After all his scandals, after all his shameless greed, he comes to Mooran and starts to eat the place alive, and this isn't hearsay, I've seen it with my own eyes!*

Said laughed, so enraged that his voice came out as a whistle, and went on, to himself: *And he wants me here for my dark eyes? My brother likes him more than I do, yet he can't stand Hosny, he screams at him! But me: "Oh, Abu Shakib, you're my brother and my best friend; before you came to Harran I was praying night and day for God to send me someone like you." What a liar. He never prays, and he has no need of someone like me—all he needs is money—he wants wealth. They think I'm a wooden cat, that I'll scare mice and eat nothing, or like the goose laying golden eggs. He made up his mind I'd be easy to fool. Hah! I can handle him, and his ancestors' ancestors—I've seen people a thousand times smarter than he is—only I'm broke, and I need someone like him, but once I'm back on my feet, no one is going to exploit me or make a fool of me. It's only a matter of time.*

If Said wanted to go on, to express his full opinion of the doctor, he recalled the expressions he repeated to himself, until he was grinning and almost laughing. *He's as fat as a pig, shiny as a cobra. He's in superb health—no hernia, no hemophilia—on the contrary, the blood just bursts out of his cheeks. But money takes care of that—it makes him totally bloodless! I can joke with him about everything except money. It would kill him to buy you a cup of coffee. If he shakes your hand, count your fingers! Anyone who says anything different just doesn't know him, or is a hypocrite. Money is his religion, his idol. Prayer, fasting and all the other rites are just the traps, the snares he sets out to help him hunt money!* He shook his head. *But by God, by God, he'll get what's coming to him, just as he's given it to others!*

This was how they saw each other, and how they acted, especially in front of others. When they met face to face, however, the doctor said, "Hello, hello, Abu Shakib!" They shook hands warmly, and the doctor spoke kindly. "Tell me—how are you?" And without waiting for a reply: "Your face is so pink, so healthy, you look wonderful!" He laughed. "Better knock on wood!"

All this was before Said had even sat down. If he tried to choose a seat at a distance or opposite the doctor, he heard, "Come here, man, come near—I've missed you! I haven't seen you in ages!"

Said responded warmly, playing the same game with the same skill. Before they could begin any serious conversation, the doctor resumed: "Are you, God willing, content? I hope you and your family are all well?"

This was the way their conversations began, most of the time, and how they went on. Said noticed the special treatment, and, affecting humility, knew how to reply.

"If you are pleased with me, if you look my way, Doctor, I enjoy a thousand graces from God!"

The doctor smiled and looked at him searchingly to see whether he really meant this; Said seemed genuinely to have meant it. To change the subject, he added, "If it weren't for all the important things that keep you so busy, Doctor, I'd like nothing better than to drop by, when I'm feeling down, so that we all could have a cup of coffee."

This was very Moorani, to say *all* for *we two,* and Said used the word on purpose to show the doctor that he had begun to learn the dialect.

"For Heaven's sake—you're welcome any time!" said the doctor quickly.

"Once things are in order and running smoothly, God willing, we'll have more time to get together."

"God willing, Abu Shakib." The doctor shook his head and sighed. "I don't know where the time goes."

"Really!"

"Even so, we should see more of each other. The work never stops, but life is so short."

"By God, that's true, Doctor, we barely got to Mooran yesterday, but it seems like a lifetime, an aeon ago!"

Having concluded these or similar formalities, they moved on to the business they had met to discuss.

This happened dozens of times. Each man made sure of the other's feelings toward him, and understood them perfectly, but they still needed each other. The doctor was amazed at Said's abilities, and the results that he produced, in terms of volume, profits and scrupulous accounts, greatly enhanced his optimism, if not his personal trust in Said. Said presented convincingly his plans for expansion—to add to their product line and open branches in other cities—which were studied carefully by Rateb and the doctor independently, and then accepted.

Their meetings usually ended in the doctor's house. The doctor always took care that no one else was present, particularly anyone from the palace. There were two reasons for this: so that the palace would not know anything about his other activities, and so that no one but he would have any connection with the palace. Said suspected as much. He had often asked to come to the doctor's office in the palace to discuss some urgent business, and the doctor always refused. At first Said hardly noticed, but later on, when he asked to be introduced to someone in the palace "to find out what their needs are, so we can take care of them," the doctor made a cryptic and somewhat mocking answer.

"Please forgive me this once, Abu Shakib!"

When Said sought an explanation, the doctor said, rather grandly, "The palace people know that I work on very important matters. If we go trying to sell them nuts, a kilo of sugar and a kilo of rice, we'll diminish in their eyes—we'll lose their respect."

Said insisted that the palace's business was immense, in the volume of their needs and the potential profits; that the whole market talked of nothing else. The doctor tapped the palm of Said's hand. He wanted to drop the subject.

"As I said, Abu Shakib, forgive me this once."

Said dropped the subject, with the doctor in any case, but he did not understand the reason behind his stand until one day when he went to the doctor's house for a meeting they had set up. He was intercepted by Muhammad Eid a few steps from the house, and told that the doctor had been called out. There were, however, three palace cars parked by the gate with bodyguards and officials around them. Everything indicated that the doctor was in, receiving a number of palace visitors in his home!

Even Muti—"the twanger," as Said called him, because he talked through his nose—who had seemed so generous when they first met in Harran, with whom he and Hosny had stayed for a whole week during one visit, had become a different person here in Mooran. Except for a few courtesy calls, always to the doctor's house, his absence was total. Obviously, he was avoiding them—he wanted to have nothing to do with them. Once, Said made a sly attempt to discuss with him the palace's needs and his chances of helping them, or getting to know someone in the palace, but Muti only gave him a perplexed look.

"God bless us, Said—please keep me out of your business problems!" He spoke these words firmly. Said could not hide his surprise at this answer, and Muti continued. "I have nothing at all to do with your plans, and I don't know what they are, so if you want anything from the palace, call the doctor!"

This kind of remark eventually persuaded Said that the doctor wanted him to stay away from the palace, and to have nothing— nothing whatever—to do with it. He also knew that the doctor wanted to share in their business ventures, but did not want them near his own business—let alone sharing it. This made him determined to attack the doctor in his own castle, but through the back doors, through doors the doctor did not know of and could not defend. It led him to look for others—it led him to seek help from al-Ghamdi and others.

When the doctor began, very secretly, to buy land, which Said found out about from friends of his in the market, he guessed at the doctor's interests at this point, though he never made any reference to this at all. So as not to tip off the doctor, Said undertook one night to reply to his brother, when Hosny had asked the doctor whether it made sense to buy a plot or two of land, as al-Hissan had suggested, with a view to reselling or building on it, especially since he had become knowledgeable about such things.

"Forget it," jeered Said. "Everyone in the market says, 'It's crazy to put your money in the sand!'"

He said this in a stately Moorani accent, and looking at the doctor, who blushed and trembled, a nervous habit—Said had noticed it at their first meeting—that afflicted him in any dilemma, or when things were not going his way. When their eyes met in that fleeting instant, he went on to try to create an affected warmth between them.

"Of course, they say lots of things in the market, and you never know what to believe."

Every time the doctor formed an impression, or reached a conviction, Said would do something to mar the impression or destroy that conviction—the doctor could not understand or anticipate him, for as intelligent and courteous and even guileless as he sometimes seemed, at other times he thought and behaved like an animal, a fox. Even when the doctor came up with new ideas after talking to people or reading reports or studies prepared for the palace, he found that Said already had similar ideas. True, he had them only in crude form, and sometimes they lacked clarity and precision, but he had "put his hand on the pulse," as the doctor liked to say, adding to himself, *He's incredible—the epitome of peasant cunning.*

Things grew more complicated as their business ventures expanded. Said, who had lived in a small house and was very modest in his habits and expenditures, now moved to a larger house and bought an expensive car. His whole way of life was now far more affluent, and he spent his company profits fairly quickly. He had an answer ready when the doctor, surprised, chided him.

"Doctor, money is like running water—you can't catch it, because its nature is to move. Better it should move in a way that pleases me than to please someone else—I might as well enjoy it, instead of someone else."

The doctor tried to explain the importance of saving, of spending in moderation, of being frugal, but Said only smiled and laughed.

"God bless you, Doctor—a man only lives once. If you don't enjoy money now, in this world, you'll never enjoy it afterward! Once you die, you've missed it."

Hosny gave him a look of reproof.

"Oh, Abu Tayseer," he laughed, "everyone thinks he has enough brains, no one thinks he has enough money, but I'm happy with the money I've got, and anyway money just pollutes the world. No one dies and takes anything with him."

The doctor had discovered a new quality in this man: *Money means nothing to him.* So there was no need to fear him—there was nothing to worry about. Moreover, it seemed to him that Said needed confidence and insight more than he needed money, since as far as he was concerned money was only a mark of power and prestige.

22

HAD HAMMAD BEEN BORN ANYWHERE BUT IN Mooran, in any times but these, he might have been a military commander, an artist, ringleader of a hundred-man gang, or have died—or been killed—at twenty.

The Mutawa family business, whose caravans of flour, rice and cloth moved across the desert throughout the year, held no appeal for him. The family's widely scattered land holdings, encompassing vast areas even the owners could not exactly define, similarly were worthless in his eyes, nothing but corrals for camels and sheep, or wasteland, since nothing was cultivated there, and they were so far from the cities. The family had bought them long ago, planning to use them for pastures or grassland, and since nothing had been done with them none of the Mutawa clan were interested in them, least of all Hammad. He was not tempted for long by the livelihood of his Uncle Shaddad, who bred horses and owned an inn, since the advent of the automobile which, in all its different varieties, became the horse of the new era. So the horses brought over from Egypt, bred so painstakingly over years, now went to his Uncle Shaddad. Hammad sold them to his uncle at no profit, with no regrets. Even the school so loved by his relatives and friends he left after battles, blows and insults that were the talk of Mooran.

As to why he could have been a military commander or an artist: he had that unruly tendency that marked him out for leadership, or to recreate and reorganize the world. This tendency caused quite as much unease among his family elders as it won him attention from his childhood onward, and led to disagreements among them as to how they should deal with him. His father thought commerce and "playing with money" would surely change him, but Hammad could not stand business and was not tempted by money. He returned from his own caravan travels having proved the qualities that slept in his blood more than showing the new qualities he had gained on his journeys. Within a few days he had spent the money it had taken him months to earn.

His Uncle Shaddad had other ideas. "If he's not tempted by money or horses, those brides that entrap even angels, that have the blessing of this world and the next—if they do nothing for him, there's only one thing left to try," and he laughed loudly. "A nice girl is what will catch him and hold him down—how many before him have been enthralled with women and ensnared?"

So Hammad married at age twenty, keeping just one wife until he was thirty. He changed only as a tree changes: he grew bigger, taller, sired children, and stayed essentially the same. The Mutawa clan, who were as possessive of their children as they were of their riches, stayed patient and bided their time. Muflih, their nearly deaf patriarch, understood Hammad's story only with difficulty and a great deal of time, only after his grandson Mutlaq shouted it all in his ear—Mutlaq was the only one who could make him understand. When Muflih heard it he smiled.

"Let him be, my dears. A seed turns and turns, but it ends up in the quern!" Then he began to rave. "Before him, all the Mutawa clan were just like him, until they got weary of it, and when they tried all they wanted to do, and some things they shouldn't have, they came back to their senses; if you try to change them you'll just wear yourself out and break your hand—they have to change for themselves. His grandfather before him, and his great-grandfather before that, all played the same tune until they flew into a rage, ran wild until they wore themselves out, and they turned out fine; then others came along." He looked at the faces around him and nodded. "Nowadays they're all like Hammad—unmanageable. God help us!"

So Hammad was left alone. His father did not pester him anymore, and did not expect of him what he expected of others. Hammad was himself just as confused and uneasy as he made others. If his mother told his father optimistically that now Hammad was interested in working in business, that he would surely take after his father now, it was never long before he proved her wrong. If his uncles brightened and smiled on him because he had begun talking about business and Mooran and jobs, he was never slow in informing them that he had saved no money and was not seriously thinking of getting a job. Sometimes he would add scornfully, "There's more to life than jobs and business."

During one of Rateb's visits to Mooran there was chance conversation about what was on the doctor's mind. Said did not know how he'd got this brilliant idea. Abdelaziz had told Said about the Mutawa family, their businesses and land holdings, their kinship, on the distaff side, with the Sultan, and about his lost friend Hammad. It seemed to Said that the game was worth a try.

After the agreement had been struck over the land at the southern entrance to Mooran, and Hammad and the doctor became friends with almost magical speed, events took another course.

The doctor knew, from his private inquiries, that the Mutawa clan owned immense expanses of land in Mooran, and that they were too immersed in their commercial ventures to have any idea of what the land was worth: too busy chasing camels and sheep. He was shrewd enough to realize that the time was ripe to buy some of this land, particularly in the more distant areas, in Hasiba, for example, where no one would even notice—this would be an experiment and an opportunity to get to know one member of the family.

Princes Mayzar, Rakan and Milhem knew, however, before anyone else how very important and expensive the land east of Riha would be within just a few years; the Foreign Ministry had bought a portion of the land for the construction of its headquarters, and the Sultan had read a proposal to zone the foreign embassies and ambassadors' residences in the same area. The princes knew that buying the land now would make them rich for generations, as Prince Mayzar told the doctor, who agreed fully—who had, in fact, been waiting for such an opportunity.

Hammad, who was close to his Uncle Salman, persuaded him that the land was worthless and would probably remain so for centuries. Should anyone wish to buy it, that money could be put to work in business, for productive purposes, and would double within a year or two at the most. Land, he pointed out, "stays where it is, does nothing and yields no profit." And the sum the doctor offered was very tempting and was available in cash immediately.

So the land deal was struck, and with it Hammad arrived in Dr. Subhi Mahmilji's office to take up his duties as chief of the Intelligence and Security Agency.

The land did not interest Hammad in the least except as it touched on his dream, though his dream was extremely clouded and confused. He was seeking a new, adventurous challenge, and did not know why he imagined or assumed that if he got close to the palace he would be able to realize this adventure.

23

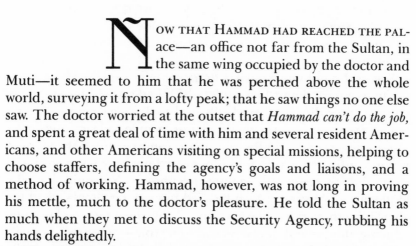

NOW THAT HAMMAD HAD REACHED THE PALace—an office not far from the Sultan, in the same wing occupied by the doctor and Muti—it seemed to him that he was perched above the whole world, surveying it from a lofty peak; that he saw things no one else saw. The doctor worried at the outset that *Hammad can't do the job,* and spent a great deal of time with him and several resident Americans, and other Americans visiting on special missions, helping to choose staffers, defining the agency's goals and liaisons, and a method of working. Hammad, however, was not long in proving his mettle, much to the doctor's pleasure. He told the Sultan as much when they met to discuss the Security Agency, rubbing his hands delightedly.

"The Mutawa family, Your Majesty, are more than great traders and horsebreeders—Hammad has surpassed all of them, and today, sir, you have an agency that can hear ants crawling in the dark!"

The Sultan seemed delighted and remarked with a laugh, "And the Mutawas have beautiful daughters, Doctor!"

The doctor shook his head as if surprised at this discovery, and replied, "Just as you say, sir, though for myself, I swear to God, I have never seen any of them, but anyone who looks carefully at Hammad and examines his features has to conclude that the women of the family are beautiful."

The doctor was quick to understand the Sultan's words, and agreed with Hammad on the necessity of marrying one of the Mutawa girls to the Sultan, to strengthen and renew the ties that existed between the two families. And this did happen three months after Hammad took up his new position, and not only strengthened and renewed their ties, but opened up new and grander horizons.

Hammad viewed the idea of allying himself with the palace as an adventure promising as much pleasure as possibilities to explore a new world, to go beyond business and the morose haggling his father was immersed in. He was moving in the right direction; true, he did not know exactly where he was headed or when he would get there, but the power he'd begun to feel and the information that flooded into his hands every day, the knowledge of Mooran's great and small secrets, even the palace's, what was happening all over the Sultanate—these discoveries made him question, think and dream more deeply, and transformed him, bit by bit, into a different person.

Events did not move quickly or according to any fixed plan, but the uneasiness, almost like panic, which had seized him in the beginning, now dissolved gradually and took a new course. He no longer went out into the world among people to learn and make discoveries; people and the world now came to him in the form of reports, informants who told him everything they had heard and seen, and his ceaselessly ringing telephones. Not only that; the loud voice of his past, which he used to mask his shyness, had become something more like a whisper. When he intervened in some ongoing affair—and he always had some role—only a word or gesture was needed for him to get his way, and this word was usually spoken over the telephone or through one of his subordinates.

At first Hammad took no action without consulting with the doctor; this formality created a warm friendship between the two men and enhanced the doctor's self-importance. Once he had wanted to run the agency by himself, changing his mind only because he decided that it did not suit his age or his position; now he was reassured that this new formula was far better. It was enough for Hammad to drop by for a half hour every morning, as soon as he arrived at the palace, to show him the reports he had prepared and take new instructions. This way the doctor was able to guide and supervise, and to control this agency whose importance grew with every passing day.

There were also routine Saturday morning meetings with the Sultan, and in the first weeks Hammad hardly spoke so that the doctor could present all the information and submit the "situation assessment" on the general state of the Sultanate. Hammad was gripped by shyness, even fear, in these meetings, wishing in his heart that the doctor would take charge, hoping that the Sultan would not ask him about anything. Later he lost this fear and helped to present the weekly report, though the "situation report" remained the doctor's specialty.

The doctor was always thinking up new ideas and implications that never occurred to Hammad. It was not enough for him to talk about events, or the information contained in the reports; he talked about the situation in the entire region: the dangers that surrounded the Sultanate, the subversive factors that could steal in from here and there. Hammad was proud that the doctor possessed such vision and could speak of such difficult and momentous issues; proud that he worked with a person of such worth. Perceiving this admiration, the doctor overflowed, bringing up more issues and citing historical events. The Sultan, for the most part, listened silently, nodded, and many times Hammad noticed an absent look in his eyes. Moreover, he saw that the Sultan's thoughts seemed to stray to faraway places and notions while the doctor was speaking. When the meeting was almost over, the Sultan changed, becoming cheerier and readier to talk on a variety of subjects, and in the final minutes, before they took their leave, the atmosphere became positively merry, as it always did with the doctor in the Sultan's presence—the doctor created that mood.

Hammad's relations with other people began to change. Before, one of his favorite pastimes had been to drive through Mooran in his open car, stopping often in the market to get out and greet people; he had a group of friends who did the same. Now he was a different person: he had a bigger and statelier car and was seen in the market only rarely—so rarely that people thought he had left the country. Even the friends he still socialized with did not know what sort of job he had in the palace, and he did not tell them. When asked, he gave brief and vague answers—he said that he worked in the Sultan's advisory office and left it at that. Even his Uncle Shaddad, proud of having recently acquired a black horse, said to be the most beautiful in Mooran, got only an exaggeratedly humble answer from Hammad when he asked him where he worked in the palace.

"With the Sultan's adviser, Uncle!"

"Do you advise him or does he advise you?" asked Shaddad al-Mutawa jokingly. "Because if you have any advice about my new Hamadani horse, or if he does, tell me. And if you don't, come and see—you can have His Majesty compare our horse and his!"

All his listeners understood that Shaddad was ready to sell his horse to the palace, to the Sultan himself, if the price was right, since this was a finer horse than any the palace possessed.

Hammad's father, on the other hand, did not know whether to be happy or sad that his son had abandoned business to go and work in the palace. He told some of his close friends that "the problem with a government is that you never really can tell—in business, nine men make a profit and one loses, but in the government, nine lose and only one fellow profits." He sighed sadly. "God willing, our Hammad will not be one of the losers."

The grandfather, Muflih al-Mutawa, was even deafer than before. His grandson Mutlaq had to use an ear trumpet to shout the important news at him, and he misunderstood the news, or wanted to; he nodded briskly and smiled. "I told you so! Hammad ibn Saleh, and Saleh ibn Rashed, and Rashed ibn Jeiham, every one of them got funny ideas. When Saleh's father died, he was one of ten children and poorer than a wolf in the desert, but today you can see how well he turned out. Rashed gave his family hell, and wore them out, and almost broke them, but all of a sudden he fell in love with the Persian girl, and when they let him marry her he stopped

fighting and became a lover, and that was that. And the grandfather of all of them—Jeiham—you all know his story!"

He said all of this with his eyes closed, trying to remember, and
when he opened them he said, "From the day I first opened my
eyes in this world and was able to think, I've always said, 'Someday
there will be one of the al-Mutawa, one of their sons who'll avenge
Jeiham," and this Hammad you've been talking about so much has
become a sultan, and now watch what he does!"

They all looked at him and then at each other, and instead of
laughing, as they usually did when they asked him about something and he gave a wholly unrelated answer, they looked a little
frightened—rebuking and expectant for Mutlaq to tell him the
news again, more precisely this time. When Mutlaq had done that,
loudly and enunciating clearly, Muflih gave him a surprised look
and said, "I know! I know, boy! Hammad is in the palace!"

Hammad's other relatives, friends and acquaintances interpreted the news as they chose, each imagining his own Hammad,
especially since things had changed with the accession of Sultan
Khazael and taken a very different course. The change was evident
not only in the reappointment of a few officials or the banishment
of some of the princes, Khureybit's sons; it affected everything in
the Sultanate, from the sort of names children were given to the
Sultan's new titles and new forms of address he demanded.

Even so, Hammad continued to improve his understanding of
his mission and grew comfortable with it. He sensed that the
Mooran he had known, the life he had been living, even the people
he knew, had all become something else, and that he had to think
and act within the boundaries of this new knowledge.

24

THE SECOND ANNIVERSARY OF HIS ACCESSION to the throne brought the memorable image of the Sultan receiving the princes, sheikhs and wealthy merchants who had come to pay their respects. He looked in perfect health, having lost a little weight, and seemed to most even younger than he had a year or two before, in part because he had changed his old, wide eyeglasses for a new pair that showed his big, laughing eyes. His clothes were gorgeous and suited him perfectly, better than the drab colors he had preferred in past years. Only slight changes had been made in his small beard—his barber let it grow a little up above, to conceal some of the gaps in the lower file of teeth, and trimmed the lower edge, "so that His Majesty's face will not look too long," as the doctor directed after seeing a particularly horse-faced caricature of His Majesty in an Egyptian magazine.

The Sultan stood, plainly overjoyed, to receive his well-wishers, looking even ecstatic at moments—as he embraced his brothers one by one, and the representatives of the different cities and provinces. When the large Harrani delegation arrived, the schoolmaster insisted upon reciting an ode in His Majesty's presence, which was well received, and then they presented their big surprise, the deed to a Hamadani horse, written in gold ink. The horse himself was shown that afternoon, first to the Sultan and later on to a number of guests and citizens of Mooran who had heard about it and wanted to see it.

The Sultan never doubted for a moment that anyone but the doctor could be behind a surprise such as this, and as a token of his trust and affection, he granted him that very night the title of Sheikh, and appointed him his chief adviser.

The doctor was happy and self-assured, the more so because his land purchases had gone virtually unnoticed. To explain the purchases, the story went that princes would build sports facilities, racing tracks for camels and horses; the rest would be used for schools, hospitals, and housing for tribes traveling to Mooran.

Rateb now visited Mooran much more frequently, which lifted the doctor's spirits, and he even spoke of moving there for good within a year or two—business was brisk, as planned, despite the turmoil Muhammad Eid reported from Said and the things the market people said. What gave real weight to the credibility of this good news that Rateb passed on to the doctor was the founding of a new contracting firm for the building of roads and the import of prefabricated structures. He indicated that the future of this company was extremely important, not only in the Sultanate but in neighboring countries; local branch offices would have to be opened quickly, before any competitors came on the scene—everyone in Beirut and other places talked of nothing but the huge projects in Mooran and the Sultanate's other cities; people had their eyes out for "their big break."

The doctor insisted on knowing what might happen in the future, how the business would be affected, both here and abroad, so he insisted that Rateb be his houseguest, since Mooran lacked a fitting hotel, and "so that we have enough time together to do business." He did what he could to persuade Rateb to move here to be with him. Rateb seemed hesitant, almost set against the idea—"I don't want to disrupt the household or bother anyone"—but was finally compelled by the doctor's urging to accept.

The doctor ascribed the changes in Rateb's life and behavior to his own personal effort, their discussions in the early stages of the company's founding, and his visits to Mooran, so full of stories intended to provide morals and examples, or a summary of all his wisdom. All this, in addition to their business successes, contributed to the great change. This boy, so aimless just a few years before, was now a new man; as the doctor said in explanation, "Most people go through an aimless stage, but it's a question of age," and he added, smiling, "age and upbringing."

What made the doctor even happier was the difference Rateb made in the house during his visits: the many gifts he brought, the tales he told, his ambitious travel plans—all these added a note of vitality and bustle, and it showed most of all in Widad.

Whenever Widad began to laugh and dance around like a little girl, holding the new clothes up against her chest to see if they were the right size and color, or to see the reaction of the others, Rateb had to tell the same story.

"I wasn't sure about the size, but as I was buying them I saw a woman who looked like Umm Ghazwan, and I told the shopkeeper, 'It's the same size as that lady!'"

"The last time we were in Beirut and we went to Hamra, you were with us and you saw very well what I bought!" Widad scolded him.

"But I didn't remember the size number, Umm Ghazwan!"

"I hope you forget the next time!"

They all laughed, and when they were quiet again the doctor said, "These will open a treasury.better than all the treasuries in Mooran!" In a different tone, he added, "Don't forget *them,* Umm Ghazwan!" He pointed in the direction of the palace.

"Of course, of course—what shall I wear—and when?" she asked, unable to hide her joy.

They were all pleased; the doctor, more optimistic, resumed his liaisons with many old friends after a long period of silence, because he had not been in the right frame of mind for socializing; they had been surprised by his behavior, wondering why he was so cold and distant. He had found not only that the demands of his work but the sensitive position he held in the palace imposed this distance; he blamed himself and decided to be a new man from now on.

Others noticed this change in the doctor and most of them ascribed it to the difficulties he faced.

"One hand can't clap," Muhammad Eid told people without any prompting. "That poor man is carrying the world on his shoulders!" And in a different tone, "When we were in Harran, I could lighten his load, but here . . ."

His words were meant to disdain and detract from the people who surrounded the doctor, and to provoke them as well, but the doctor pretended not to hear, and often even tried to change the subject. The doctor asked him about Badri and smiled, reassuring him that he never forgot anyone, especially after Badri had become important enough to move into the very palace where the Sultan lived—now he was indispensable for the little services he could perform, on which great and small alike depended. He had unlimited ability to tell anecdotes and stories and jokes, and the Sultan's children would not leave him alone. His salary was raised twice in one year, not to mention his bonuses, and he began to think of bringing his wife and children to Mooran.

Muhammad Eid could not understand the state he was in, happy enough some days to sing; constricted by grief other days to the point of tears. He lost himself in business having priority over the rest, but followed none of it closely, and yet found no time to listen to what people were saying. The doctor made constant demands on him. Eventually he became a different person. The change did not become evident immediately, but to a searching or practiced eye, or to anyone who had known Muhammad two or three years ago and saw him now, the change in him was obvious and alarming.

Widad could not stand Mooran or adapt to it at all. She fell ill several times, and the doctor made every effort to cure her, though he could not imagine what was causing her illness or how to treat it. She recovered her health, in most cases, only with the advent of mild weather, especially with the onset of autumn or winter, or during a family visit; the doctor reached the certain conclusion that *her homesickness has never left her for a single day—she has been trying to suppress or forget it.*

It was at this time that Widad's friendship flourished with the women of the palace, and she diverted herself from her illness, trying to cure it, as the doctor tried to explain to her the human capacity to adapt. When, however, she suggested to him that she visit Damascus and Beirut—this was just a few days after the Sultan's accession to the throne, and she said that the Queen had given her some gold to buy some special items, and that she had to get new clothes for the children, especially Ghazwan and Salma—the doctor found the idea useful in all sorts of ways. Too, the period of one month, which Widad had proposed for her visit, was enough for him to furnish and move into the al-Hir Palace, and the doctor wanted this move to be a surprise for her. She would improve vastly as soon as she found herself in a finer place. Her only reservation about the journey was the discomfort that might affect her condition, but she assured him that the first trip over had not tired her, and, laughing heartily, that a change of air would renew her youth and vigor, so he did not hesitate to agree that she should go.

Mooran, too, had changed in the space of these two years. While the change was minor, or, more precisely, was not entirely visible yet, it amounted to a telling indicator of what the city would become in the future. The wide boulevards that crossed the city center and outskirts, the lands enclosed by the Ghadir Palace, the immense quantities of building materials in piles around the southern neighborhoods, the armies of engineers and technicians, in addition to the large group of maps and surveys that moved from place to place, from office to office—all this spoke of the change that had taken place, and the one still in store for Mooran.

25

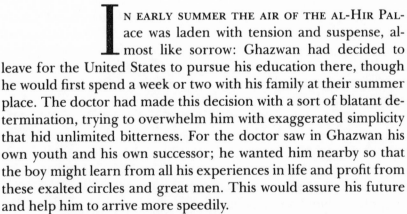

I N EARLY SUMMER THE AIR OF THE AL-HIR PAL-
ace was laden with tension and suspense, almost like sorrow: Ghazwan had decided to
leave for the United States to pursue his education there, though
he would first spend a week or two with his family at their summer
place. The doctor had made this decision with a sort of blatant determination, trying to overwhelm him with exaggerated simplicity
that hid unlimited bitterness. For the doctor saw in Ghazwan his
own youth and his own successor; he wanted him nearby so that
the boy might learn from all his experiences in life and profit from
these exalted circles and great men. This would assure his future
and help him to arrive more speedily.

In a hard but unavoidable moment—like an operation, for a patient—the doctor finally allowed the trip, though it was a difficult
and bitter decision. Ghazwan had dreamed night and day of going
to America but felt a twinge of fright, or something like it, when

his father gave his consent. It was the first time he had ever left his family, and he was going to a place so far away that none of his family or relatives had ever gone there before.

There were several days of expectancy and tension, and as the day of departure drew near the level of anxiety rose. When the doctor set up an appointment for his son to bid the Sultan a formal farewell, and the visit took place, the doctor felt the bitterness and difficulty of loss more than ever before. When His Majesty decided that Ghazwan's studies and travel expenses would all be paid as a royal gift, the doctor could not hold back the tear that rolled down his cheek.

The doctor's feelings of loss and bitterness were aggravated by the fact that he could not join his family at their summer place this year. Multiplying obstacles and great responsibilities pressed him here, and al-Ajrami, who had been gone for so long on a pilgrimage to Mecca that the doctor had almost forgotten him, had now returned even crazier than before; his provocations and attacks never stopped for a day, which worried and then actually frightened the doctor. Before long he gave up entirely the idea of traveling, consoling himself with the thought that *it would be stupid for a man to leave a building he's built with his sweat and insomnia to be ruined by others. When everything is secure I'll be able to go wherever I want in the world with no fear, and then I'll have the time to rest and relax and write, too.*

The day before Ghazwan left, the doctor wished that he could have stayed in the house to write a list of exhortations as a guide for Ghazwan during his stay away from them, to tell him so many things—how to behave, and think, and live, what sort of friends to cultivate—but at this point he had neither the ability nor the inclination, so he pretended to be busy, as if absorbed in his daily routine. He went even further by coming home later than usual in the afternoon, and when dusk came, with the sinking of the sun and the hour of departure, the doctor turned to his son and spoke to him in a sad but dignified tone of voice.

"You don't need my advice, Ghazwan; you've become a man and you know how to act. Any hope this family has, has been placed in you. His Majesty, who has undertaken to pay all your study fees and expenditures, will not forget you, but even so, this sum"—he handed him a sealed envelope—"may be of use to you and may help you through the ups and downs of fate."

The doctor kissed him three times, as he kissed his brothers, and stood for a long time by the door, until the car was out of sight.

Ghazwan showed great strength and self-control. He spoke like a man, bid farewell to Abu Abdallah and joked with him and Muhammad Eid, but could not wait to find out how much money was in the envelope, so as soon as Mooran was behind him he emptied the envelope and quickly counted the thousand dollars it contained. There was a letter with the money, and he read it.

My own boy, Ghazwan,

This is the first letter I've ever written to you, and you will remember it for a long time; perhaps you will tell your children about it. I don't know why even now I imagine you to be so far away, so distant, even before you have left. I feel the bitterness of our separation, and, even more, our haste in making this decision, but I have done many things in my life and not regretted them, and I think this will be one of them. I trust you as I trust myself, and depend upon you as I depend upon any grown and mature man; I beg you not to let me down, but to be my support now and in the future.

There are so many things I want to say to you in this letter, but I feel that my heart will not allow me to now. I will certainly be writing to you in the future, and my thoughts will be much clearer then; we will write to each other frequently and at length, each of us telling all about his thoughts and hopes, but for now, with you about to depart, I would like just to say a few words to you.

Take care of your health, Son, for good health is a crown worn by the wealthy, seen only by the sick. I have devoted my life to healing the sick and easing their pain, and I know, more than anyone else, the meaning of sickness. Never neglect your health. Once again I will remind you: warm surroundings, good food, early nights and moderate exercise are basic ingredients to good health; keep to them wisely and in moderation.

Be serious in your studies, my son, because the times we live in demand education, and an education will enable you to confront the problems of the future and to make money. Without an education, without money, a man is worth nothing, no matter what his origins are or who his family may be.

I caution you, my son, to choose your friends very carefully, and to test each one a hundred times before giving him your trust; even then don't give all your trust all at once. There is no need to tell you that good friends are few in this life. You will have many acquaintances, but friends are hard to find. Heed my advice and learn by the example of others so that you will not have to pay the price of your own.

I urge you, my son, to be frugal in life, for a little silver coin might save you some black day. Life is, by and large, powerful and treacherous. Never feel so secure today that you forget tomorrow, never put all your money in one basket, and never borrow money. If you must lend, give little and put it all in writing between you and your debtor, and never be ashamed to get angry. Try, my son, to keep away from what is illicit in what you eat and drink, and keep away especially from women. Remember God morning and night, and remember your father, and ask God to bless us both, as I raised you.

My dear Ghazwan, my eyes,

As I write this letter, my heart is full of pain, torn by love and sorrow, as if I were writing my own will and testament. You must try to understand a father's heart, and remember how much your mother and I have borne so that you could become the man that you are now. And until we meet again—and I pray God to will it soon—don't forget to write often—as they say, writing is half being there.

With much love, longing, and all my blessings and good wishes,

Your father

So Ghazwan left, and his father's wait began.

A few weeks before the doctor's family left for the summer, Muti left as well, though he returned, before the summer was out, with his bride, to a warm welcome and many parties. As a gesture of friendship, the Sultan gave him a new car and his wife a diamond necklace that everyone appraised differently, though they all agreed that it was very valuable. Muti was now far friendlier and more courteous than he had ever been before, and overflowed with energy and good spirits.

In this same period Abu Misbah left for a short trip, or as he called it "a mere errand—His Majesty didn't allow me to take any more than that," and brought back his wife, three daughters, his son Misbah, and a collection of birds: a parrot, a number of goldfinches and some canaries. He also brought some toys, though no one knew whether they were intended for his son Misbah or as gifts for other people. What was for sure was that Badri al-Hallaq—"Badri the barber," as he was now known—was in a state of rapture, to the point where people who had never seen him before or had no idea of his good qualities now discovered that he was an extraordinary person.

Muhammad Eid had refused a vacation. He would not even discuss it, even though his brother, Badri, insisted upon it and the doctor's wife thought he should go, because he could not "leave the doctor by himself." He tried to keep busy, and though he had thought about it before and even packed, he soon became ill, and despite the doctor's best efforts in examining him and referring him to two doctors he could rely on in Mooran, and despite all the complex analyses, they could not identify the malaise. The doctor could prescribe nothing but tranquilizers, and Muhammad gave a pained and sarcastic laugh as soon as he saw them.

"That's not enough, Doctor, I need the needle, too!"

The doctor laughed with him and then looked away. "Don't worry, my man, try these and trust me!"

26

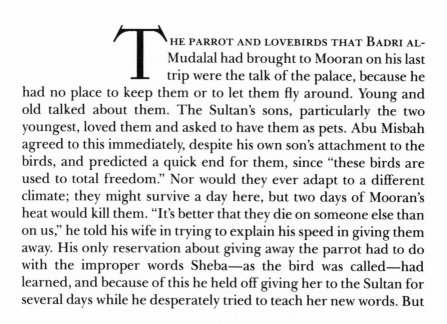

THE PARROT AND LOVEBIRDS THAT BADRI AL-
Mudalal had brought to Mooran on his last
trip were the talk of the palace, because he
had no place to keep them or to let them fly around. Young and
old talked about them. The Sultan's sons, particularly the two
youngest, loved them and asked to have them as pets. Abu Misbah
agreed to this immediately, despite his own son's attachment to the
birds, and predicted a quick end for them, since "these birds are
used to total freedom." Nor would they ever adapt to a different
climate; they might survive a day here, but two days of Mooran's
heat would kill them. "It's better that they die on someone else than
on us," he told his wife in trying to explain his speed in giving them
away. His only reservation about giving away the parrot had to do
with the improper words Sheba—as the bird was called—had
learned, and because of this he held off giving her to the Sultan for
several days while he desperately tried to teach her new words. But

no matter how many times he repeated, "Long live the Sultan! Long live the Sultan!" the bird replied, "Hi, ugly!" When he persisted, she cried, "Shut up!" Finally he had no choice but to keep the bird himself or give her away just as she was, and since the Sultan's children were not accustomed to being patient, he tried to explain his situation to Zaid al-Heraidi.

"His Majesty's boys have asked for the parrot. . . . I can't wait to give it to them, but I'm afraid this bird might cause a problem."

"Trust in God, man."

"Abu Omran, it's a rather impolite bird!"

"Impolite?"

"It has a dirty mouth."

Zaid roared with laughter, and Abu Misbah went on.

"And if it happens, what I'm afraid of, you'll all be after me."

"What does it say?"

"It just blathers."

"No, really, what does it say?"

"I have nothing to do with it—ask it and it will tell you!"

"Let me see it! And don't worry."

"On one condition."

"What is it?"

"That His Majesty knows nothing of it."

"Trust in God, man—do you think I have no more brains than the parrot?"

"If you assume all responsibility, I agree."

"Fine. Don't worry about a thing!"

So the birds were moved to the palace, to the Sultan's own wing. Although he did not notice them at first, they eventually provided him with a delightful pastime. Very few others were aware of this pastime. The Sultan became totally infatuated with the lovebirds: he watched them raptly and spent hours watching them embrace and feed each other, as they interlaced their beaks and wriggled. He urged them on. He gave them new names, and made a boisterous show of his delight when they hopped and twittered. The parrot was a special novelty to him, and though at first he never spoke to it for fear it might reply to him as it replied to all the others, eventually he began to joke with it, alone, at first, or with only a very small number of family members present, always with deep, reverberant peals of laughter from his great hoarse throat. His jokes were almost like curses.

"God protect us from you, you owl of death!"

Abu Misbah, who avoided any reference to the birds, especially the parrot, could not stop talking about them when the Sultan finally asked him about them, and when he promised to supply the palace with a magnificent selection of rare and beautiful birds, the Sultan was immediately enthusiastic. Within a few months the palace had a new annex full of large bird cages with many varieties of small, brightly colored birds. There were three African parrots, but no one could explain their silence or their aversion to speaking a single word. At first it was thought that they were too young but that they would soon learn. Later on it was decided that they would never learn if too many people tried to teach them too many words in too many different ways. Finally, when one of them dropped dead, it was said that they were old birds, ready to die at any moment, and that there was no point in trying to teach them. The Sultan, who in his more ambitious moments had thought of setting aside some time to teach one of them to talk, soon forgot all about it, though he kept his passionate interest in the lovebirds and still watched them for hours every day, making no secret from others of his fascination.

The doctor was downcast, to the point of utter pessimism, at the immense fuss these stupid creatures caused in the palace. The qualities they attributed to the birds, and the names and qualities they applied to men and vice versa, and the laughter, heated discussions and questions the birds caused made the doctor cranky.

"Your friend is responsible for all these birdbrains," the doctor joked to Muhammad Eid. "He'll be answerable to God for this. They just needed a bird to set them off, and the effendi brought them a thousand, and now there's no dealing with them."

He added bitterly: "All we think about now is, 'The dove flew,' and 'Now the dove is napping.' God help us."

With the flight and twittering of the birds, an idea, or rather ideas, began to glimmer in the doctor's mind. Why had he forgotten them? Why had the chattering of the birds revived them?

27

T HE GIRL IS USED TO BEING WITH US," WIDAD
told her husband, to explain why she
stayed by Nadia after Ghazwan had left.
She looked away. "Her future might be here, in this country."

The doctor sighed before answering, "Since the first day we
came here, Widad, I've been telling you: life isn't so easy to arrange. Ghazwan is too young to get married."

"He's gone, God bless him, and who knows what will become of
him now." She paused. "And girls mature before boys."

The doctor looked at Nadia the next day with new scrutiny and
discovered that she had grown up in the blink of an eye. She appeared to him a ripe, desirable woman. There was no sign of the
childhood that had brought her so near him when they had first
arrived in Mooran: it was gone, and in its place was a steady, almost
bold gaze and a supple body, about as slender as it always had been,
only firmer. Strange visions passed through his imagination, and

he said to himself, *The climate in Mooran stimulates and ripens things before their time, especially girls!*

He tried to remember Nadia again, tried to find some kind of link between the maturity he had suddenly discovered and the air of Mooran. He noted, a little regretfully, that *in childhood and early adolescence, there is a tendency to plumpness, except for the factor that differentiates the sexes; in subsequent phases, one notes that all the vital centers are suddenly active and ready to function, and manifest themselves strongly. This is one of life's secrets.*

But another eye had discovered life's secret and the genius of nature long before the doctor's, secretly and with no fanfare, without even theories, and that was the eye of Muhammad Eid.

From the moment he first saw her in Wadi Riha he'd felt that Nadia was meant for him alone, that she had come here because of him. As for the talk he'd overheard from Widad, of how someday Nadia would be Ghazwan's wife, he refused to believe it: Nadia was "better than that," too good to be married to "that bag of meat," as he secretly thought of Ghazwan. Ghazwan was too "small" to be a husband or a man, or so Muhammad told himself during the long Moorani nights, as he tossed and turned, trying to quiet his fears and sleep.

Now Ghazwan had left and Nadia was back from her summer vacation, riper and more beautiful than ever, her skin shining a luminous bronze; Muhammad felt that the illness that had so weakened him over the summer had been caused by Nadia's absence. He told no one, and barely admitted it even to himself. He felt that Mooran, whose heat and cold he tolerated along with its people and its ways, in spite of all its difficulties, was an unendurable city: cruel, arrogant, impossible to live in.

Now Nadia was back, and in these propitious circumstances Muhammad Eid felt healthier and more alive than ever before, as if he were capable of anything he put his mind to—and he would try fearlessly. Even the way he looked at the doctor now was more searching than trusting or companionable. He felt that he had wronged Badri and been too harsh when he'd told him those things about women and marriage; he did not know whether to have his brother talk to the doctor, or to take care of it himself. He did not know whether to speak to Nadia, to give her some sign, before approaching the doctor, or to knock at the door right away.

He was burning, but it was a sweet, passionate fire that enticed him more than it tormented him and made him work day and night only to think more and more of Nadia, to see her, to feel her close to him. The difficulties dissolved and the barriers between them fell. It was enough to see her every day, to hear her laugh, to feel the blood race through his body, jolting him and giving him indescribable happiness; he would do anything to make Nadia keep on laughing. He would say to himself in moments of intense weakness, *I'll do whatever she wants, I'll always make her laugh,* and lose himself in dreamlike thoughts. *If she doesn't like Mooran, we won't stay, we'll go somewhere else. If she wants to sleep late, as she sometimes does now, I'll go around on tiptoe, like a cat, I won't bother her at all. I'll even make her pregnancies as easy for her as I can.* He laughed loudly. *I can't carry the baby for her, but I can make it as light as a feather. I'll do the cooking and the laundry and everything, so she can rest.*

Such were his thoughts and dreams. To Nadia, who filled the doctor's house with such infectious exuberance, he was just one of those people she did not quite know how to handle. She called him *Ammu,* uncle, but so sweetly that she seemed to mock the title. He told her and all the doctor's children, "If you want to be friends, please don't call me *Ammu,* I don't like it." Ghazwan, who had always thought the word too formal and had trouble pronouncing it, was the first to call Muhammad by his name, and never called him anything else. Salma knew nothing but *Ammu* so called him that for years, and he never got angry.

He heard a fresh, sweet note to his name on Nadia's lips. He would look her straight in the eye and more than once she asked him, with a certain sly innocence, "Why are you looking at me that way?" When his embarrassment showed, she would giggle and not wait for an answer.

Widad was the first to sense the way Muhammad Eid looked at Nadia and behaved around her, but she felt strongly that Nadia was just a child, a little girl who did not yet understand the world of women; if she behaved in such a way as to inspire any particular feeling in Muhammad, that feeling would be merely a man's pleasure in a child's charm, or her way of acting or speaking. Otherwise it could not be. That is what Widad told herself. To make sure, every so often she asked Salma to stand next to Nadia to compare the girls' height; when she discovered that the difference was diminishing quickly, and calculated Salma's age, she became even surer that it was just a children's game.

Nadia had much unoccupied time in Mooran, and this, with the fiery, dry, quietly bodily-ripened heat that let up only in winter, apprised her early that her body was responding to her, obeying her. The breasts that used to embarrass her, that she even tried to conceal by wearing loose-fitting shirts as she continued to play the games boys did, began to change. Her body was firmer and seemed to her more symmetrical; she examined it carefully every day. Her breasts grew in size and roundness, as if raising their heads in a challenge or provocation; as much as she had to tried to conceal them before, she now considered them her body's greatest adornment and wanted them to be noticed first. She now chose clothes that emphasized the strong points of her body. She spent hours adjusting the length of her skirt, so that it was at or just beneath her thighs, to emphasize, as much as possible, the alluring curves of her body. She kept her hair long and flowing, carefully leaving it expertly tousled at all times. She knew how to strike poses with her head, and sometimes wore her hair in a ponytail tied with colored ribbons so that she looked like a big child. Widad kept a vigilant eye on how Nadia played with her hair, tied up one day and flowing loose the next, and told her in a tone of sisterly advice, "It really looks nicer when you wear it up like Salma does."

Nadia nodded in agreement but continued to experiment with styles she found flattering.

Was Nadia preparing herself to be Ghazwan's wife? Was she seriously convinced that she must?

Even Widad was not sure. She had mentioned it before, when Nadia became part of the doctor's household, or when she moved with the family to Mooran, but did not bring it up now. Furthermore, Ghazwan had begun to seem almost hostile. Nadia, who had been very taken by the idea at first, though she considered it in a rather unfocused and belated way, now decided that he was not the man she had in mind, not the one she would want for a husband, in spite of the show of masculinity he strove for, to the point of reverence; he did everything he possibly could to make himself appear to others as a man. He tried several times to use his father's shaver, but far from demonstrating that he had a beard, he only wounded his face badly. When his father had him order three suits from Hassan Sanjar before his trip, the lad insisted that each suit come with a vest. Both Sanjar and the doctor smiled; the tailor pointed out that young men his age did not wear vests, and that it was, moreover, "a rather old-fashioned look." Ghazwan, unconvinced, tried to explain to his father.

"But, Papa, where I'm going it's very cold—near the North Pole!"

The doctor told the tailor to make the vests, and to soothe Ghazwan's early manhood, said, "Yes, indeed, Ghazwan, over there a man needs more than one vest!"

Ghazwan had been in San Francisco a month when they received a letter from him.

> Dear Father,
>
> I kiss your hands, and pray to Almighty God that you and all the members of the family are well and happy. The only news I have now is of my safe arrival in the United States of America. I was lucky to be on the same flight as Uncle Rateb's friend Hassan Jukhdar, which was fun. He had wanted to spend a few days in Houston, but he decided to do that on the way back instead, so he spent three days with me in San Francisco, and after making sure that my living conditions and everything else were fine, he left, and I'm really grateful to him.
>
> Dear Father, dear Mama, the first few days far away from you were hard, and that's why I kept putting off writing to you, so that you wouldn't have a low opinion of your son Ghazwan. Now, however, I'm used to the city and the way of life here, and I've met some of the Arabs who live here. The life is pretty easy, and my studies are easier too, in spite of the language and the different course system. Once I've finished the preparatory section, I'll be able to choose which department I'll study in.
>
> In San Francisco there's only one other student besides me from the Sultanate, and it seems that his father has lived in Egypt for a long time. He hasn't visited Mooran in seven years. He gave me the new address of

the embassy, and I immediately wrote to the ambassador and gave him your regards, dear Father, and I brought up the subject of my allowance only in the most indirect way—I told them that I had opened an account with Citibank, and gave them the account number. (By the way, Father, I deposited the thousand dollars in a one-year certificate of deposit, and that way I'll earn interest. Everyone does that here.) Anyway, just yesterday I heard from the vice-consul and he said that the embassy had received instructions that His Majesty the Sultan was paying my fees, and they'll forward the monthly stipend to my bank account.

The weather is excellent, though rainy, and next semester the college will give me an on-campus room. That will be cheaper, and so close that I won't have to take the bus.

Dear Mother, I miss you and my brothers and sisters so much. Every time I eat the half-cooked meat here I think of your delicious meals, but don't worry about me. Write to me, and ask everyone at home to write to me— this letter is to all of you.

Dear Father and Mother, I send my kisses and best love to you; give my regards to Kamal, Hamed, Salma and Nadia, to Radwan, Muhammad Eid, Abu Abdallah and all our relatives and friends. Please write often and wish me luck!

Your loving son,

Ghazwan

P.S. I miss you all so much, but even so I might not be able to come home next summer; some of the Arabs here tell me that students work in the summer, more to get to know the area and for general experience than for money. I'm thinking about it and I'll let you know.

Love, G.

Widad wept silently as the doctor read the letter slowly and with paternal pride. When the rest of the children saw them, she was embarrassed and tried to laugh, and with her tears and laughter she looked so funny that the doctor intoned, "God love you, Umm Ghazwan, the boy has gone to college, he hasn't gone off to war."

"My little Ghazwan—how is he eating? How is he getting his clothes washed? Is he sleeping?"

"The Prophet, peace be upon him, said 'Seek knowledge, even unto China,' and America isn't so far away anymore. If he doesn't come home this summer, we'll visit him."

"That's a promise, don't forget and get so busy this summer that we can't go!"

"No, don't worry, it's a promise." He laughed. The children exchanged glances and smiled questioningly but said nothing. Nadia, who suddenly felt that Ghazwan was now very far away indeed, the more so since he would not be back this summer, had a sudden feeling of freedom and fear. True, she had little sympathy for him, she thought him rough, and perhaps he did not love her, but now he did not know her true feelings!

The only one whose reaction was nothing like the worry and apprehension of others was the delighted Muhammad Eid. When the doctor told him that Ghazwan had asked for him and sent his warm regards, Muhammad was consumed with curiosity about Ghazwan's news, but the doctor answered his questions with only, "He's fine—praise God." So Muhammad Eid asked the children instead, and thought to himself, unable to restrain his smile: *From the mouths of innocents* . . . The children told him everything Ghazwan had written in his letter and a great deal besides from their imaginations. Muhammad felt more secure and happier, and began to think a little differently than before.

28

THE DOCTOR WOULD NEVER HAVE GIVEN A thought to Rezaie, or even remembered him at all, had he not seen him again with his own eyes. His memory of the man had faded away with those days in Harran; he did not even remember what Rezaie looked like. In any case, the doctor's feelings, of both friendship and rivalry, had not been especially vivid, but now that he saw him again, and here in Mooran of all places, he felt a little uneasy.

After the guests flooded out of the dinner party he gave in Rezaie's honor, he thought, *Thank God I didn't go traveling with the Sultan—If Rezaie had come here in my absence, he would have ruined everything.*

In their first visit together, and later at the party, they exchanged lighthearted, nostalgic stories of Harran: how it had been then and how different it was now; about Emir Khaled and the emirate. Rezaie spoke at length of his adventures since his first arrival in Harran, describing how he had hesitated to come and with what trepidation he settled there, because the place was nothing like any city he had ever seen in his many travels. "Even the west and south winds, so sweet and refreshing everywhere else I've been, even the sea breezes—none of them are the same in Harran." The two men recalled how the Americans and others had launched tree-planting campaigns to give Harran at least a little pleasant greenery, and how quickly all the trees died: the ones that survived the drought died from the asphyxiating air or the gases that seeped out of the refineries. Yes, they agreed, Harran was an impossible city—no one would ever live there by choice.

When the doctor tried to find out whether Rezaie planned to settle in Mooran, he got only cryptic answers. Rezaie said that he had come to look into the possibility of opening a branch of his company, and to get some idea of what kind of people were here and what kind of place it was. He would make his decision later. The doctor smiled and nodded thoughtfully.

"It may be hot here, but it is certainly better than Harran!" Rezaie added.

The doctor politely assented, but he was still worried. They had been friends for as long as they'd been in Harran, where each man had his own separate affairs to tend to, but Mooran was not Harran and now they were both very wary, as if neither liked seeing the other here, or wanted anything to do with him.

After a few courtesy visits Rezaie vanished, much to the doctor's relief. *One less thing to worry about,* he said to himself, but Rezaie, who knew when to vanish and what to do, had vanished only from the doctor's sight; he had not left Mooran all summer long. The doctor never was able to find out how Rezaie had come to know Prince Mayzar, or how they had become such close friends—it took him completely by surprise.

An almond-brown Rolls-Royce arrived at the Rawdh Palace one day early that autumn. It was beautiful and immense, equipped with a telephone and a little desk. The backseat could open into a small bed. It had air-conditioning, and a compass that pointed toward Mecca.

They had never seen anything so elegant and stately. Zaid al-Heraidi, who accepted the car on behalf of the Sultan, could not hide his utter astonishment as he twirled the control knobs on the armrest in the backseat. The glass partition between the front and back seats lowered, the desk surface folded out. When he sank into the backseat cushions and turned on the air-conditioning full blast, two palace men in the front seat heard him murmur, "It's colder than Germany! It's colder than the peak of Jabal Simaan!"

With the car came a carefully worded letter containing a cordial invitation for the palace to send a representative to the grand opening of the Orient Automobile Showroom on Monday, the tenth of the month of Jumada al-Thani, at nine o'clock in the morning. The letter was accompanied by several beautiful full-color catalogues with pictures of cars, and two pictures of Rezaie, one in front of the showroom and the other behind his desk.

Rezaie remembered to invite several palace advisers, most importantly his friend the doctor, whose invitation had a short message scrawled at the end:

> My dear friend Dr. Subhi al-Mahmilji,
>   With my warmest brotherly regards,
>   With reliance upon God, with the encouragement of our brothers and friends, and as a result of your brotherly support, we have decided to establish ourselves in Mooran; aware, as we are, of your many and awesome responsibilities, we have tried not to burden you with our company in this recent period. We have seen fit to venture to open a car dealership, and it is my great honor and pleasure to ask you to honor us with your presence at the opening on 10 Jumada al-Thani, at nine o'clock. With you in attendance my delight will be assured.
>   With my greatest esteem and friendship,
>   Your brother,
>   Muhammad Ali Rezaie

When the doctor read the letter and heard the clamor all through the palace caused by the arrival of the new car, he did not contain his fury.

"That son of a bitch! That close-mouthed . . . *Mason!*"

Was Rezaie's business as much of a secret as the doctor supposed? Had he hidden from people so that no one saw him or knew what he was doing?

Work on preparing the showroom had not ceased all summer, but there were many doubts and different interpretations of what was going on; even after Rezaie and Ibn Dukheil became partners, and the news of their partnership spread through the market, no one knew precisely what sort of business they would go into. Ibn Dukheil traded in sugar and flour and sometimes in dates, and no one would have guessed that he would go into the car business; Rezaie was thought to be a dealer in jewels, silks and carpets, and when trucks full of rolls of thick cloth rumbled into his warehouse, everyone thought he was going into the home-furnishing business.

What made the people differ so widely in their perceptions of the business Rezaie and Ibn Dukheil would go into was Prince Mayzar's advice—not to say his firm request—to Rezaie one day, in Ibn Dukheil's hearing.

"Our people are like monkeys—whatever the biggest one does, they all just copy him, and no one knows them better than I do," said the prince. "So don't say a word—just open the showroom for business and let them see those cars for themselves, and they'll all be saying, 'Why didn't I think of this? Why didn't I do this first?'"

Ibn Dukheil nodded.

"That's the truth, Your Highness, as our people have always said: 'If you want to do something, do it secretly.'"

Then three English engineers arrived and threw themselves into the work in the final days before the grand opening, and the cars rolled out one after another in a tour through the city, before being driven to their places in the showroom, behind huge sheet-glass windows. The townspeople were flabbergasted—they looked at one another and recalled their guesses as to what the business was likely to be, or of what they had heard, and smiled.

At the grand opening, Zaid al-Heraidi was dispatched to represent the Sultan. He and the doctor came in one car, which had people guessing which of them was the Sultan's representative. After the ribbon was cut to signal the official opening, there was a great spectacle, not only in Rawdh Street or the commercial district but throughout Mooran—Ibn Dukheil suggested that every single car be driven through the city in a grand parade, and Rezaie agreed, albeit hesitantly since there were not enough drivers. Ibn Dukheil solved this by calling on his sons and some relatives, and Mooran saw a sight it would not soon forget: twenty-five British-made cars, packed with men and boys, cruising the streets and blasting their horns.

Shamran al-Oteibi heard the racket from the other side of town, and someone told him what it was all about.

"Remember this day well, all you merchants," he said, "because this is only the beginning—don't forget this day, because soon you won't have to worry about feeding horses and camels!"

That is what happened, and much sooner than even Shamran expected: for years thoroughbred Saqlawis and Hamdanis were the epitome of wealth and rank and were bought and sold, like fine camels, for immense sums, but the people changed overnight. Cars became the great status symbols, and a person's importance and social position were defined by the type of car he rode in and the number of cars he owned.

Until then only the palace and a very small number of rich men had ordered cars, generally from Beirut, and when one of those cars arrived after crossing the desert, dusty and filled with sand, and running roughly, it seemed like an old car. Now the people saw cars arriving in wooden crates, or enveloped in thick cloths, like precious cargo, and when the crates and wrappings were taken away, the clean cars emerged like shining fish right out of the water, with their distinctive new smell, and every person in Mooran vowed that they would buy one of those cars as soon as possible.

Rezaie agreed to sell only nine of the cars, "because the rest are for display, so that any buyer can order the model he wants, however many he wants, and register that with me along with half of the price, and he can take delivery two to three months after that." This kind of business was totally unknown in Harran and created a good deal of surprise and grumbling, even on the part of Ibn Dukheil. Several buyers came prepared to pay many times the price Rezaie was asking for a car, asking only immediate delivery. When Rezaie refused, or declined to negotiate higher prices, the company seemed to be facing real trouble and even perhaps closure, since "this place can't stay empty," as Rezaie said, "and people don't buy a fish still in the sea." "My good man," shouted Ibn Du-kheil, "everyone has seen the cars, either in the showroom or driving around the city, and they're ready to pay two or three times what we're asking, and we're telling them, 'Hold on, these cars aren't for sale'?" The problem had to be solved by Prince Mayzar himself, who ruled that one car of each different model should be on display in the showroom, notwithstanding their size or options, and that the rest should be sold. Rezaie made an urgent trip to order large quantities of different models.

The doctor did not comment on the car that so delighted the Sultan, except to say that "the color is all wrong for this country. If His Majesty decided to go out hunting, or went for an outing in the desert, no one could distinguish the car itself from the sand all around." Privately, however, he was filled with jealousy and rage; he had never seen such a powerful, well-built, luxurious car in all his life. *If it were just a question of doing business,* he thought, *Mooran's a big place, there's no problem in that, but if he's trying to worm his way into the palace, and using this car as bait, I'll make him sorry he was ever born.* The doctor blamed himself for not thinking of opening a car dealership first, and his friends for not suggesting it to him.

When he heard that Rezaie had gone on a trip, the doctor spoke rather crossly to Muhammad Eid.

"I've told you a thousand times, Muhammad, to keep your eyes open and tell me everything that goes on."

Muhammad looked confused.

"What do you mean?"

"Everyone in Mooran is talking of nothing but Rezaie's cars, and I didn't know a thing about it. You never told me one thing!"

Muhammad raised his hands in a gesture of helplessness.

"Abu Ghazwan, there are a thousand headaches in Mooran every day, and I can't bother you with every one of them!" He added, more sternly, "Besides, you have enough problems of your own to keep you busy—more than enough, in fact!"

"A few days ago Rezaie went away on a trip," said the doctor in a friendlier tone. "I want you to let me know the instant he gets back."

"Whatever you say, Doctor."

The doctor longed to know every move that Rezaie made or was planning to make, and feared his long absences more than his presence in Mooran, *because he is a sly devil—no one knows what he's up to.*

Other matters diverted the doctor's attention from Rezaie, but he did not forget about him completely. Every day or two he thought about Rezaie or was somehow reminded of him, as he prepared to choose a way of fighting or at least stopping him.

29

AT CERTAIN TIMES, ESPECIALLY WHEN HE WAS tossing on his bed, Muhammad Eid considered declaring his love for Nadia, or at least dropping hints about it, but once he reached that crucial decision he usually ran into Nadia the next day as she fluttered around the house like a butterfly. At that point he lost his nerve and changed; his face looked resolute, almost scowling, but he gave up his decision as the words vanished from his head or seemed suddenly stupid, or else he just could not utter them. He would, instead, address her with some perfectly ordinary and meaningless words.

Days, weeks and months passed without him knowing what he was doing or what kind of action he should take; now summer was closing in, and the warm and sometimes scorching breezes aroused explosive vigor in every living thing, driving them to act with fertility akin to violence, and stirring deep within Muhammad his dreams, desires and fears, and he decided to resolve the matter once and for all.

He had waited three whole years, day and night, tossing and turning on unceasing flames, had endured torment and insomnia, and endless waiting. Now he had to put an end to it, to act. He could wait no longer than he had already. Nadia was no longer a dream he could overcome with fear or hesitancy. She was a flood that rushed around him, drowning him; he had to struggle or sink.

He had not traveled in years, and now, for the first time, he felt that the earth itself was moving and that he had to move with it, to keep up with it. Harran had consumed him, turned him to stone. Since it had been so fraught with motion, and its people changing, multiplying and moving like the wind, he felt his strength increasing, sinking roots in the perilous, turbulent earth like a palm tree. Mooran, so tranquil, sunk in the desert and in silence the first year, soon succumbed to Harran's contagion and began to race earnestly in a clumsy competition, like a race of cripples or drunks.

Now he needed to act, to move, to travel to the end of the world. His luck had betrayed him before by abandoning him in this desert, which he had never left, though in his dreams he had visited infinite cities, but now the time had come to see them in the real world. He would not travel as a lone, lost tourist; he would put Nadia behind him on a horse and fly away; or they would cruise the seven seas on a ship. They would visit cities and landscapes, unbelieving that they were really there, perhaps never to return to this hideous desert—perhaps he would blame her, or she him, as they sat in the shade of a tree in a faraway land, for their not having gone there before!

What other thoughts and dreams filled his head in those days between spring and summer? What songs did he sing to himself, what daydreams came to him in the afternoons as Mooran's pitiless sun beat down? What beginnings and endings did he rehearse hundreds of times, with the briefest, most moving words, to open his discussion with the doctor?

The right moment would never come; life was rushing by with all its bounteous possibilities, and the love that spun its threads as the heat grew more oppressive. The mad haste to prepare his house for the summer made him postpone, time and again, his approach to the doctor. He was waiting for the most auspicious moment, which seemed to come often, only to be cut off by a cloud or falling star. The doctor only got busier and busier, Ghazwan's letters arrived less frequently; the house was in an uproar after Widad had a spell of illness; the Indian cook quit; the search was on for a new cook. Any one of these was reason enough to wait until the doctor was in a more receptive frame of mind.

Even Nadia, whom summer seemed to make more beautiful, now appeared to be more gentle and loving toward him as well; if he did not make his feelings known today, he reasoned, tomorrow would be even better. Now, with her condition, Widad was more insular and irascible than ever; had she been herself, she could have been useful and saved him a great deal of time, but as it was she was the person he was least likely to approach.

Days passed and turned into weeks. Time yawned before him like another desert. Muhammad's sensation of time passing was riven in two: it was so long that it was eternal and endless, and as short as a flash of lightning when Nadia was near him. Every day, every hour that he spent waiting for Nadia was worth the whole part of his life that was past, not only his time in Harran and Mooran but all of it, since he first opened his eyes on the world.

Once, Mooran had been bearable, and he had been able to tolerate what went on there, but now, with the onset of summer, and this tempest that encircled and choked him, he felt that his breath inched up from his toes on a mad, agonizing mission to his throat; surely he would suffocate any minute now unless someone, preferably Nadia, hurried up and saved him.

The heavy, unmoving air was like a weight on his chest. The searing heat pervaded every speck of dust, making everything rough and hostile; the hidden, unhurried readiness to travel was tantamount to a direct threat to him. He swore not to put it off any longer. *Tomorrow, no matter what, I have to tell the doctor and get an answer from him.* If tomorrow came and he delayed any further, he told himself scornfully as he lay his head on his pillow, *that's it—all this calculation will be lost.* His calculations filled his breathing, tormented him, flogged him, though he forgot everything as soon as he heard her voice, when she strolled in front of him. When she smiled or giggled, like a bird cheeping, his soul filled with light, it crackled like a fire, and he forgot; that was all he needed. She talked and laughed only for him, so that he could hear. She went from one place to another only so that he might see her.

He was readier than ever to leave; his soul thirsted, and he was in the grip of a depression that was more like fear. He had felt ill the previous summer when they left for their vacation, but surely the illness would kill him this year if they left before he said anything. If the doctor told him that Nadia was too young, that he might get engaged to her now but wait until she was eighteen to marry her, he would agree to that, though he would assure the doctor that Nadia truly was an adult, and tell him that girls in Mooran married far younger than that. "What do you think, Doctor? People here are like fruit—do you remember how the figs and grapes at home ripen at the end of the summer? In Mooran at the end of the summer you won't find a single fig left on the branch. The girls are the same—they marry at fifteen and sixteen and have two or three children by the time they're eighteen." If the doctor would not budge, he would ask, "But, Doctor, how old was Umm Ghazwan when you married her?" The doctor would not be able to deny it. *I saw it for myself when I had the passport—I saw all their ages, and it just took a little math: Widad got married at sixteen.* If the doctor said that he had to talk to Nadia's mother and father, his answer was ready: "You are her father and Umm Ghazwan is her mother—she has no one else. If you have to ask anyone else, ask her."

He lost himself in his dreams. *She might fall silent or nod, but if she smiles and looks at me, that doesn't just mean "Yes," it means, "Take me, take me now, and let's get out of here."*

His nightly dreams enthralled him still by day, like spells; even the brief, concise speech he was planning to give the doctor as soon as he could slipped out of his memory when the doctor looked at him, certain evenings, and asked, "Well, Muhammad, what's new in the world?"

Muhammad glanced around before replying, "Everything's under control, Doctor—it couldn't be better!"

"And the news, what's the news?"

"No one talks about rain and herds anymore—all you hear about are the prices of land, property, gold and cars."

"Everyone knows that—of course."

"Believe me, I have things on my mind, Doctor."

"No—what's on your mind?"

"Nothing to trouble you with, Doctor."

"No, really, what's the problem?"

He wanted to speak, to let it all out, but he was too afraid. After their silence had lasted several moments more, the doctor spoke again.

"What's the worst it can be? Trust in God, my dear boy, it can't be that bad."

Three days before Widad and the children left for Lebanon, it was settled that "within a week, or two at the most," the doctor would join them so that he and Widad could set off for America together.

Muhammad chose his timing carefully, and took one of the tranquilizers the doctor had prescribed for his depression and insomnia. They were alone in the garden, the children were in bed, and Widad had excused herself, taking Nadia with her to help her pack—"We'll have too much else to do the day we leave."

That night, under the trellis loaded with grapevines, beside the little pool where the doctor loved to spend his quiet evenings, after chatting briefly on an assortment of topics, Muhammad addressed the doctor in a voice he hoped was strong and even.

"There's something I have to discuss with you, Doctor."

The doctor glanced at him solemnly, with a touch of surprise.

"Go ahead, Muhammad."

"Something personal and, uh, private."

"Go ahead, my boy."

"I want you . . . to help me."

His voice failed. He felt afraid and began to sweat and could not go on. The doctor guessed the seriousness of the problem, and to help him along he chuckled and said, "God bless you, Muhammad, if there's a problem, something personal, you should have told me a long time ago!"

"Only you can help me, Doctor."

"So tell me—let's have it."

"Nadia, Doctor."

"Nadia? What about Nadia?"

"I want to ask you for her hand, Doctor."

The doctor started. He had not expected this and could not respond; perhaps this had occurred to him long ago but he had put it out of his head. He could not believe Muhammad had the audacity to make such a request. After a long, cruel silence the doctor found his voice and asked in a soft, neutral tone, "Have you mentioned this to anyone else?"

"No, Doctor, I swear."

"Nadia—have you spoken with her?"

"Not a word, sir."

The silence was heavier and more eloquent than before. Muhammad's breath hung upon the next words the doctor would utter; they would give him life or death. If he said yes, he would feel like the happiest and strongest man in the world, he would love the doctor more than himself, he would immediately kiss his hand. If he said no . . . Muhammad was dizzy. He did not imagine he could hear that word from a man he had spent his life with. He had always told him he was just like Ghazwan; now, again, he would surely reiterate how much love and companionship they had shared through the years. He heard a voice from inside the house. It was Widad calling Nadia. He flinched. He looked around several times. His eyes refocused on the doctor. He was waiting for a verdict of life or death, two things that were so close that they were really just two aspects of one thing.

There was the doctor's voice again, but it was the voice of a different man.

"Muhammad—Nadia is engaged!"

"Engaged? To whom?"

"To a nice boy."

"Ghazwan?"

"No, Ghazwan is too young, he can't get married before he finishes his studies."

"So . . . who is it?"

"As I told you—a nice boy."

"Why didn't I know?"

"It's your own fault!" The doctor chuckled mockingly. "She gave her hand some time ago, and God willing she'll be married before the end of the summer." The doctor sighed deeply, and he spoke in a different tone, so that he seemed to be a different person.

"A girl like Nadia isn't right for you, Muhammad." His tone was now paternal. "If you like, my boy, Umm Ghazwan is leaving in a few days, and she can find you a lovely girl, and you can marry her."

"Thank you, Doctor, I can manage."

"Just as you like, my boy—you know I only wish you the very best."

Muhammad Eid did not sleep that night. He cried into his pillow like a small boy, convinced that he was going to die.

Before the sun was up the next day, a huge assortment of plans had already passed through Muhammad's head, though he did not dare to act on any of them. When he heard the call to dawn prayers he got out of bed. He sat in the corner, thinking and dreaming, and he did not notice that the sun was rising and that the city was stirring around him. When the doctor called him, and asked him to go to Azmi Hajjar's warehouse to pick up some drugs, mainly some drugs for nausea, he could not look into the doctor's eyes. Had he looked at him, he thought, he would surely commit some crime or folly.

"And come by my office—there's something else I want to see you about," the doctor added in a neutral but stern voice.

"I'm busy. Find somebody else, Doctor!" He did not raise his eyes.

"You have something else to do?"

"Yes, I do."

"What is it?"

"I'm leaving, Doctor."

"Leaving?"

"Yes."

"Don't be silly, my boy."

"I've made my decision and it's final . . . Doctor."

"Fine. Forget everything else for now, and when I come back from the palace we'll see."

"Don't bother, Doctor. Give the money to Abu Misbah."

"Don't be silly—don't make a big mistake, Muhammad."

"Never mind, we'll see what happens."

"No—wait for me until this afternoon."

"I don't think so, Doctor. I can't wait. It's late as it is."

30

ONCE, HARRAN HAD BEEN A CITY OF FISHER-
men and travelers coming home, but now
it belonged to no one; its people were fea-
tureless, of all varieties and yet strangely unvaried. They were all
of humanity and yet no one at all, an assemblage of languages,
accents, colors and religions. The riches in the city, and underneath it, were unique in the world, yet no one in Harran was rich
or had any hope of becoming so. All of them were in a race, but
none knew where to or for how long. It was like a beehive, like a
graveyard. They even greeted one another differently from people
in any other place—a man greeted others and then looked searchingly in their faces, as if afraid that something might happen between his greeting and their reply.

At least this was how Muhammad Eid saw them on his return.
He had lived here for several years, and experienced the birth of
the city. He had seen the stones put together and stacked up to

become tall buildings, he had seen the streets paved to make passages for men, animals and cars, he had seen shops and restaurants spring up like mushrooms, and the emirate building, military command and Shifa Hospital. Now, as he arrived here again to stay for good, checking into the Desert Flower Hotel before strolling through the commercial district, he could not believe that he had ever been here before. He recognized nothing, he knew no one, nothing was as it had been. Even the emirate building, on the northern hill, had become the Harran Central Prison. The Central Command Center, Johar's old headquarters, was now a police station.

The Shifa Hospital, where he had spent most of his time in Harran, was now a hospital for foreigners. Dr. Mahmilji's clinic was now the Orient Dry Cleaners. The Friends Coffeehouse had been demolished and replaced by the Bahlawan Building. Rashedi Street had been torn up and rebuilt, and though it officially retained its name, most people now called it Old Market Street.

The emirate building stood in the rolling hills by the Ujra Road, and the emir's residence was on the opposite side of town; for when nothing remained in the city but refineries, the cargo port and smoke, the Americans built a new city twelve miles to the east, named for the old site where it was built: Ras al-Tawashi. Within this new city were districts for merchants, wealthy citizens and high-level employees, not far from where the Americans themselves lived, and this was where the emir lived.

The residential areas on the western hills, originally known as Arab Harran, had slowly become a commercial area, after having been pulled down and rebuilt several times. The people of Harran were separated from the residents of these areas in several directions, behind the hills, toward the quarries. The workers' camp, located midway between Arab Harran and American Harran, was now a storehouse for old equipment. One section of it was buried under junked cars, old tires and barrels. This had come about after the death of several workers by asphyxiation from the fumes of the nearby refineries; the workers were moved far away, to a site between Harran and Ras al-Tawashi.

What was true of any other place was also true of this one. The Friday Mosque, to whose construction the doctor had been so proud to contribute, still stood but was an eyesore, decrepit and black, smeared with layers of grime and smoke, and surrounded by tall buildings. When Muhammad asked about Abdu Muhammad's bakery and Abu Kamel the butcher, the people he asked labored to recall when the bakery and butcher shop had been demolished, but they could not be sure, and some had no idea at all.

Even the cemetery was gone. The new emir, Abdallah Shibli, gave the Harranis who had their dead buried in the cemetery fifteen days to dig up the bones from the graves; after that, bulldozers rolled in and destroyed whatever and whoever was left. Ibn Naffeh shouted at them and cursed them and spat in the faces of the bulldozer operators and ran to fetch a number of poor people to rescue some of the skeletons before they were crushed and torn by the bulldozers. Ibn Naffeh himself died a few days after the "opening" of the new cemetery on the Ujra Road, and the completion of the high wall around it.

This smell is horrid—it smells like corpses, muttered Muhammad to himself as he walked through the marketplace; now he remembered. *It is like no place else—it isn't even like itself. The people here know each other only by chance, and spend almost no time together, exactly like the passengers on Abboud al-Salek's trucks.*

Harran was deafening by day, but at night, under the blaze of the refinery, it was a city of shadows and silence; when the ships' sirens and roaring engines, audible from the cargo port two miles away, died down, you might have thought that Harran was part of the desert that stretched beyond it. Even the streetlights gave off a gloomy light you could barely see under the fiery black-orange sky that was the city's dreadful ceiling.

Muhammad had been able to endure several summers in Harran, but this time he began to suffocate almost on arrival, not only from the heat or the humidity, but from the heavy, malodorous air: a mixture of petroleum, cooking spices, sulfur, dust, the desert, leftover food, dead fish, burning tires—not to mention the smell of people. It was unbearable. Once, Harran had been easier; a person could get used to it or tolerate it. Now, at least in Muhammad's state of mind, it was an overpowering, malevolent city, more like a tomb.

Saleh Dabbasi had some trouble remembering him; he looked him up and down and slit his eyes and asked about the doctor and some of his important friends—were they still active in business, or had they moved on to something else? He listened to Muhammad's answer, then asked whether the doctor might want to sell the land west of the foreigners' hospital; he wanted to buy it and was ready to pay any price.

When Muhammad asked for help in finding work at the hospital, since Saleh was in charge of procurement there and was one of the rich and important people in Harran, or so people had told him, Saleh answered slowly.

"You work with civilized people—the doctor, and society people. Why would you want to do the little things we do?" He laughed, as if to repeat his question, and when Muhammad did not reply, waiting for an answer himself, Saleh went on. "Come back in two or three weeks, and we'll see what we can do, God willing."

Muhammad left Saleh Dabbasi's office vowing never to go back.

In the streets he saw throngs of poor people, foreigners and others; he could not imagine what they were doing here. He was surprised at how the police stopped people and examined their papers, asking them why they had come or where they had come from. Many of them had to go along to the police station, near the emirate; from there several were deported daily. Others were jailed, beaten or harassed, and even other things. Muhammad heard that Salah Dabbasi had built the prison—he had imported the building materials, and his trucks and al-Seif's were used to deport the detainees who had no job or no proper papers, or who had lost their papers.

Now everything was new and strange to him. It seemed incredible that these things had come into being during the short period of his absence from Harran. He felt estranged, as if the city had turned on him, but saw no alternative to staying here and settling down. He would find work, meet new friends, and renew his ties with old ones just as soon as he established himself. Saleh Dabbasi had been supercilious, almost insulting, but others would be different—*There are still nice people in the world. Saleh was always arrogant, and no one ever liked him, and he never liked anybody.*

Muhammad thought of starting his own business. He thought of

Harran's doctors—after all, he was not just any person looking for a job, he wasn't without gifts. He had worked in the medical field for longer than those doctors, and had he not been born poor and unable to complete his studies, he would have been a doctor before many of them—even as it was, he understood more about medicine than they did. He could recognize symptoms and indications, the stages of infections and treatments, and he could give injections better than anyone else in the world. Yet to everyone who saw him he was just an unemployed man looking for work. Others, not he, would weigh his abilities and usefulness. He would have to do a brilliant job of describing his skills; he would have to knock on doors, to be servile. There was no hurry, and nothing to regret.

If he had been in a better state of mind, if he had been in better circumstances, he would not have hesitated to go to the emirate and visit the emir himself. He still remembered that awful time he had had to go and examine Emir Khaled al-Mishari—he still remembered the emir's rage, delirium and seeming madness, and his murderous looks. He'd had to be restrained by the deputy emir and Rezaie. If he were to visit the emirate now, he would know many people and they would recognize him. Three years did not obliterate people's memories or change them; they could not deny him. Still he was not ready to go; he was not persuaded. He was different from other people, but he would find his way.

They told him that Emir Khaled al-Mishari had left for good and had never been heard from since leaving; the same was true of Johar. He had been replaced by his deputy, Emir Mishaal. Muhammad could not think why this name meant nothing to him; he seemed to remember that the deputy emir had been Abu Rashwan, whom some people called The Barrel. After Emir Mishaal came Emir Dari al-Suheil, who ruled for a year and a few months before being succeeded by Abdallah al-Mashhour, but al-Mashhour did not last long.

After the strikes in the refinery and cargo port, and many acts of sabotage against the pipeline and pumping stations, al-Mashhour came to be regarded as too lax and negligent, so he was replaced by Abdallah al-Shibli.

Harran had changed so many times in its few years that it seemed the new emir had come to give it new, unchanging features. He imposed taxes on merchants and peddlers, paved the sidewalks and moved the cemetery, but there was a great deal more to these moves, and to his having been chosen as emir. Many of the townspeople were apprehensive or afraid, but Muhammad Eid did not share these feelings. He would have gone to visit the emir if he had been in a better mood.

31

After three weeks of wandering, think-ing and asking questions, perhaps he would be able to put down roots again in this desert soil and start out anew.

He visited the foreigners' hospital, pretending to be ill, in the hope of finding someone he knew, or some opportunity to go back to work there. After a few minutes of waiting in the outer lobby, however, he actually began to feel sick, so, unnoticed by anyone, he slipped away.

Dr. Agha was very surprised at Muhammad's reappearance in Harran, and told him, after a long talk that touched many topics, "People in Harran are crazy about medicine. Bellies and genitals are big business now, you can guess why. Gold teeth and false teeth, no—they went out of fashion—the demand just died." He was smiling at his memories. "Right when you left, or two or three months afterward, I left the clinic and went into real estate. God

Almighty, may He be praised, has given me great success. The kind of profits I make on one deal are equal to a year's work in the clinic, without the bother of dealing with those filthy bedouin."

He chuckled.

"No . . . I got out of that line long ago!" Suddenly serious and a little sad, he added, "The doctor, with his foresight, picked up some pieces of land that were like pure gold, even better than gold. My guess is that he'll just hold on to them."

He reverted to his earlier tone.

"Listen to me go on, Muhammad—tell me, how is the doctor doing in Mooran? Is he rich yet? Is he making it?" He went on without waiting for an answer, as if talking to himself. "I've heard he's a millionaire, that he's sitting on millions!"

Muhammad Eid tried to answer, to be part of the conversation, but Agha was not listening and gave him no chance to speak. He concluded, a little sadly, "I wish you luck, God help you, but you've come at a bad time, because I myself am planning to move my business to Mooran in a few months. It's still the capital, and the economy there is a thousand times better than in Harran—especially in real estate!"

Muhammad visited many others; he asked them questions and listened to them; they all asked him about the doctor, and the land and buildings he owned in Harran, and whether he was interested in selling, since they assumed that Muhammad's visit to Harran had to be related to that. He tried to dodge their questions, and avoided giving any precise answer. When he asked them what the job market was like and what their advice was, they looked positively amazed that anyone would quit a job in Mooran to go to any place as small or insignificant as Harran.

They all avoided talking about the work they did. "Anything would be better than what I'm doing. It's just backbreaking and I'm not making a bit of profit." He listened carefully and waited.

He considered opening a coffeehouse; surely that would make a lot of money, since Harran, which was bursting with shops, restaurants and banks, had no place for people to take a break from the hustle and bustle, all the buying and selling and haggling. He asked about Abu As'ad and the Friends Coffeehouse, but while some remembered the place none remembered the man. When he gave the matter further thought and set out to learn more about opening a coffeehouse in Harran, he ran up against the incredible rents demanded by owners of seafront land and the landlords of the spacious buildings in the market district, so he lost no time in abandoning the project. *Harran is a stable,* he said to himself, *and that's all it will ever be until the last drop of oil is gone. Then all the men and beasts will walk away and leave nothing behind but wind and tombs.*

He looked at the site of the doctor's old clinic and considered opening a dye shop, but the idea really did not appeal to him very much. He thought of buying and selling real estate, or opening a small place for practicing his old profession, but smiled and thought, *Every hospital and clinic has plenty of doctors and Muhammad Eids, and a patient may get away from one of them but not the other!*

While thinking, waiting and looking for work, he noticed the police. The first time they saw him they glanced at him, then passed on; his clothes and general appearance were different from those of the types they usually followed and arrested. The second time they watched him closely and talked among themselves. The third time they stopped him. He showed no fear, but at the same time was not eager to get into a long discussion with them. The patrol leader asked him politely but firmly to accompany them to the police station.

Their faces were strangely repulsive. They asked him accusingly: Where have you come from? Why have you come? Where are you staying? Where is your work permit? Who is your sponsor? The questions were offensive and hostile, and he could scarcely answer them, but he was like anyone else: a suspect who had to answer all questions, hand over his papers and tell everything he knew. He wanted to tell them that he knew Harran better than they did, had known it for years longer than they had, that he had worked harder for this city than any one of them, that he was more Harrani than anyone else; but he did none of these things. He was not surprised that they did not know him, because he did not know any of them, and it seemed very unlikely they would listen to his story or take the trouble to verify what he said.

As he left the police station he thought of Johar and Mufaddi, and shook his head sadly. *God help this world—it always sides with the strong, the bully.* He thought a minute and then spat.

Muhammad almost decided to become a seller of fruits and vegetables. *People don't go a single day without eating—they'll snap up fresh
vegetables as fast as I can get them.*

In order to implement his scheme quickly, he visited a number
of buildings under construction to select a suitable place. *It's a roomy
place with frontage on two streets, and there's a huge cellar that's just right
for storage.* After long thought he made a security deposit, even
though it seemed a great deal of money—*It's true that it's a big deposit, but it's fixed capital, and in a few years, if I want to walk away from
this, I can get it all back with a little extra.*

He did not stop there; he was determined to lease two or three
large refrigerator trucks and to work out a precise schedule so that
the produce would always arrive fresh, and in quantities just right
for the market demand. This kind of business required yearly options in the contracts, *so that I won't be at the mercy of the truck lines or
drivers; fruits and vegetables are so perishable that you can become a millionaire or go broke overnight.* He considered going to Damascus, Si-
don and Amman to make some import deals. *Getting the produce is
the first thing. Then containers. The quantities will be ordered on a long-
term basis, with goods for individual shipments to be fixed on an order given
to the driver to submit to the exporter; then he accepts shipment.* He decided to let the business grow one step at a time; at some point in
the future he could bring in a partner for the refrigerator trucks,
and he would have to buy refrigerated storage facilities in Harran,
since *Harran would eat itself if there was nothing else to eat, and all you
have to do is blink and the fruits and vegetables will spoil.*

Without delay he went to vegetable sellers to have a good look at
what they had on sale, and he asked their retail and bulk prices.
He asked where the produce came from, how often it was delivered and by what means, and all the vendors were as helpful as
they could be in answering. They told him that the vegetables that
came from Australia, New Zealand and California were cheaper
than the produce from Ujra, and that as a rule produce arriving
by sea was superior to that which had been trucked across the desert to Harran. When he asked about the demand in Harran, as
against what was actually available, the seller gave him confused
figures and then said he did not know. When Muhammad asked
what he thought about a new, large produce-import and distribu-

tion firm opened in Harran, the man looked him straight in the eye and said: "In this place, brother, any business can succeed . . . and any business can fail. It depends upon—" and without finishing his sentence, he added, smiling, "Just be sure you deal with the right people."

Muhammad's last tour around the city was on a Thursday, and although he was a little hesitant he decided to start up on Saturday. He would make a deposit and pay rent and get right to work. *I must work harder than ever before. I must succeed!*

32

I T WAS A MIDSUMMER FRIDAY.
Muhammad woke up late that morning, because he had gone to bed late and had had
nightmares all night.

He remembered, as he tossed on his bed, trying to sleep, that he
felt alone and full of sorrow—even more, deceived. He tried to
banish the doctor's face from his imagination, as he had resentfully
made up his mind he must; the image of the doctor besieged him
on all sides. He remembered the first time he'd seen the doctor,
and his last words: Umm Ghazwan "can find you a lovely girl, and
you can marry her." He remembered moving with him from one
town to the next. Every time he caught himself in the act of thinking about the doctor he tried to stop, to forget him, to force him
out of his thoughts; at times he even tried to forget by counting up
to one hundred, but no sooner had he started than he forgot the
numbers and he went back to the doctor, or the doctor came back
to him.

Nadia—"Oh, what a beauty—I raised her myself!"—his feelings toward her were thoroughly contradictory. He loved her and hated her, wanted her and did not want her, but realized that she was not responsible, and had no idea what had happened, perhaps even now. His only enemy was the doctor. He made all the decisions, his own and everyone else's. Even his claim that Nadia was already engaged was a lie. Muhammad was well aware of every far more trivial event that befell. He had his ways of knowing everything. It was only a lie, like the many dozens that had come before it. Not only that, he knew exactly when the doctor was lying and how; he had been his accomplice in most of those lies. For the hundredth time he turned over in his bed, trying to sleep, and thought, *The bastard made up his lies with me, and he forgets that we were in it together!*

When he finally fell fast asleep he was assailed by nightmares again and again. He saw himself encircled by masses of snakes, and when he tried to escape from them he fell into a black abyss. He tried to grasp the stone sides as he fell, but he hurtled down through one chasm to another, screaming, trying to grab anything but closing his hands over nothing. He crashed on stony ground and heard the cackling of old women. He looked at them through his tears and blood, but none of them moved to help him, and he screamed one last time before he died—then awoke.

He woke up soaked with sweat and parched with thirst, exhausted and helpless. He could not reach his glass of water. In an effort to stay within the kingdom of sleep, he kept his eyes closed as he went groping for the spot where he had left the water the night before. When he collided with the side of the bed and pain shot through his left leg, he roared, like a wounded animal, "God curse Mahmilji's father!"

He sat on the floor, rubbing his shin to ease the pain, straining his eyes in the dark to see the writhing specters. He rubbed his leg with one hand and his eyes with the other, hoping to save his soul, which he felt failing. The apparitions came and went, loomed over him, surrounded him. He shouted abruptly, "In the name of God, the Compassionate, the Merciful!"

He got up, terrified, and switched on the lamp, which bathed the room in a beautiful yellow light. He looked all around him and saw on the nearby table the carafe of water and a half-filled glass. He looked several times just to be sure. The specters were gone; the room was full of silence. He nodded, and nodded again. He stood up. His leg still hurt. He walked to the table and drank a glass of water that was warm, almost like urine, and slightly bitter. He wiped his face and neck. He thrust his head through the open window and filled his lungs with the fragrant smell of Harran, and thought of the doctor. *The son of a whore. He grew a beard, like a goat, but his lie is as bald, as blatant as a baboon's ass. He thinks he has everyone in Mooran fooled, but someday they'll be hunting him. Then—that's the end of you, you hypocrite!* He banged the windowsill with his fist. *If I don't forget him, may I turn into a bigger bastard than he is!*

He lunged at the light switch, flipped it irritably and threw himself on the bed to try to sleep. The room was filled with shadows, but he could not sleep. He turned over and over, and the image of the doctor faded out and returned. He smiled sadly as he tried to remember Nadia. *The little bitch! She's like a flower, she smells better than jasmine—she has the perfect smell. Pretty, graceful . . . her color is just like coffee with milk, no, a thousand times prettier, and when she laughs the whole world laughs, she's like a bird! But that bastard, that rabbi, took her away. He doesn't love anyone but himself.* He did not know what he was thinking of.

He did not know when he fell asleep. His last thought before he drifted off was, *I'll turn out worse than he is if I keep thinking of him. What's past is over with. This is today.*

The next day he spent a longer time than usual with the bean seller. He drank two glasses of tea instead of one, and gave a large coin to the little boy who brought the tea. He strolled along the beach and spent a long time gazing at the sea and at the faces of the passersby. Suddenly he found himself having a last look at his store near Sultan Khazael Square.

The muezzin was calling a prayer when he got there. He left the square and walked toward the shop, where he found the builder and three men. He greeted them and smiled. A few moments later the builder resumed his conversation with the men; they seemed to be discussing the price of building materials and the men's wages. He left them and went down to the shop and examined it again, then paced it off in large steps he guessed to be about a meter apart. He stood in each corner and contemplated what he saw.

He left through the other door and looked all around from the sidewalk across the street. For a moment he saw the shop full of fruits and vegetables, crates stacked crookedly on top of one another with the fruit shining through: golden apples, McIntosh apples, pippins, sweet Zabadani apples, bananas, and all kinds of grapes: Damascene, Helwani, Zaini, white grapes and black grapes; and fresh figs as beautiful as children's eyes. Then he thought of the vegetables. He would not be able to handle the business all by himself; he would need an assistant. A boy would not be enough; he might carry the stock around and pile it up, but Muhammad would have to supervise the weighing and pricing himself. He would have to find a man who could get along with him, and with the customers, *and he'll have to be honest!*

He was happy; for the first time since leaving Mooran he felt that sadness waning. He crossed the street and saw the builder coming toward him.

"I hope you like the place. Will you open soon?"

"God willing. Tomorrow we'll sign the agreement."

"God willing. If you're free now, why not have some coffee with us? My house isn't far."

Muhammad accepted immediately. He wanted the prayer time to pass, and the builder seemed to have the same idea. To see if his impression was correct, he said, "I can only stay for an hour, because I'm busy for lunch."

"Fine!"

Muhammad considered himself similar to the doctor, and knew he had been influenced by him, but the one difference that had always separated them was prayer. Muhammad believed that "religion is conduct," and he could never pretend at piety to deceive others. Since God was not deceived, what was the use? The doctor, on the other hand, was very fastidious about appearances, more so than about anything else, and made Muhammad feel slightly mutinous for not being likewise. For as long as he had been in Harran, and later in Mooran, he had tried to avoid deferring to others or pretending to be like them.

Now he had accepted the invitation to have coffee. The prayer time would pass within the hour that he would spend there, and perhaps he could discuss the future of the work with the builder and see what kind of progress they were making now.

Before the hour was up, Muhammad wanted to leave, whether because of the smell of the house or some other mysterious reason he did not understand; he had to go, it was unimportant where. When he looked at his watch the builder knew that he had to leave, and said in a friendly voice, "So what are you planning on calling the shop?"

Muhammad stared at him as if he had not expected this question.

"The other grocers have taken all the names already!"

"Don't worry," Muhammad laughed, "I'm going to call it the 'Take Your Stuff and Get Out Grocery.'"

They laughed together, and Muhammad took his leave.

In the early afternoon Harran was tyrannically hot and oppressive. The air was still and heavy; the streets and buildings were immersed in a shocking silence. Harran had never been so steeped in unease and self-deception; never had it been so desolate and forbidding. Muhammad dragged himself along, trying not to die, and muttered, "God, give me the strength to bear mockery."

On his way to the square he wanted to walk by his shop. He remembered the name he'd given it—"Take Your Stuff and Get Out." He tried to smile but could not. He was profoundly uneasy, and there was a bitter taste in his mouth.

He looked again, but was still confused. He looked at the ground and the sky; both looked harsh. He hurried irritably toward the Friday Mosque in Sultan Khazael Square.

A sudden sense of peril came over him when he saw the crowds pouring out of the mosque, especially the boys and young men, then the women; a sense of gravity, then fear. What could it be? Why had he not known before or heard before?

He struggled through the crowds and the silence, and struggled to see. He saw two men getting down from a jeep—one was an old man and the other a teenager. The old man wore a torn and dusty cloak. His features were harsh, like dry wood, and, bareheaded, he looked like a weak desert animal. His helpless eyes peered about, bewildered. His hands were tied behind his back. The boy's clothes might have once been white, but were now so shabby and torn in the sleeves and chest that his bare arms and tanned, skinny chest showed like a bird cage. The two were roughly pushed along by the emir's men and some police officers.

The crowd gathered in a spacious circle. The emir's men seemed enraged to the point of savagery. A subdued buzzing was the only sound the crowd made. No one knew what would happen next. The tension and heat grew. The two with their hands tied behind their backs were forced to sit on the ground. "They're thieves," said one man in the crowd, "and a thief must have his hand cut off." "They have to announce what it was they stole," replied another man. "An eye for an eye and a tooth for a tooth," said a third. Yet another man said, "I've never seen anyone have his eyes pulled out before." "Those poor souls have committed no crime," a man said. "There is no power or strength save in God—He willed their actions, not them," another man said. A short man replied, "But man has a mind; he has feelings," and the first man repeated, "There is no power or strength save in God!" Another man said, "In death man needs only a shroud—he has no use for all the gold in the world." "Be quiet! Let's see how this calamity is going to end," said yet another. A child jostled in the crowd bellowed at his father, "*Baba! Baba!* Al-Alqami!" pointing to one of the emir's men. Al-Alqami turned around and whipped his stick through the air; it whistled. "They're innocent," said a man whose face no one could see, "just as innocent as the wolves were of Joseph's blood." "No talking allowed!" shouted one of the emir's men. Muhammad tremulously asked the man beside him what the men's crime was, and what would their punishment be, but the man only shrugged to show he did not know, and looked at Muhammad quizzically.

The sun rose vertically in the sky like wires of fire. The emir's men and the police bustled about blindly. The two prisoners looked around dazedly, yet quickly, as if looking for someone. They exchanged a glance between themselves, a look expressing patience and comfort; perhaps something would happen at the last minute. Their lips were pale. Their throats were full of bitterness and dust. The throng's movements were heavy and mechanical, and silence filled the air.

A short, stout man stepped forward, looking strong and confident, even aggressive. He was about twenty, and dark-skinned, almost black. He took heavy but firm strides. His clothes were white, and he wore a heavy bandolier draped from his shoulder to his waist. He looked like a fat chicken. He looked at nothing and no one, and would have seemed almost afraid had the short swipes he made with his sword not belied that impression.

The men were made to sit in a different position, almost as if kneeling, about to prostrate themselves. At first they struggled to get into the position, and when their hands were unbound and retied in front, then tied to their feet, they were nearly prone, as if begging for mercy.

"What you were told were all lies. The bastards!" said the old man. No one answered him. "Let me see the emir, you people!" Again there was no reaction, and he shouted angrily. "My offense and my blood are on your hands today, and every day until the Judgment Day!"

The boy began to babble.

"If there's any good in your emir, if there's any good in your Sultan, let them know what's happening!"

"We're innocent, those bastards have wronged us," said the old man. "Our blood is on all of you, far and near!"

"God's curse on the Americans, and on whoever laid the first stone to build Harran," said the boy.

"Don't worry, Hammad," said the old man with sorrowful anger, "our blood isn't lost. For our blood money we want his head. Our blood is on everyone who sees and hears this; you'll see."

Subtly, almost mockingly, the commander of the detachment signaled the executioner, and motioned for the emir's men to withdraw slightly but remain at attention. The executioner, who had been waiting for the signal, now stirred.

These gestures and movements were made in silence, and as the sky vented its full wrathful heat on the earth, a total, oppressive silence fell; even the subdued breathing picked up by the ear or discerned only by the eye seemed to stop, and in a moment of madness and fear the executioner advanced. He glanced briefly to either side, but saw nothing and no one, and at that moment, not before or after it, he appeared suddenly behind the two men. He shook the sword like a cane, and took one step forward with his left foot. He was above the old man. He pricked him with the sword at the bottom of his spine, just above the buttocks. It was a strong, painful jab, and the man's torso rose, seeming arched and strong as his neck stretched upward, and at that very moment of madness and fear, as his neck stretched out, the blade fell in a clumsy blow. The neck was strong, poor and sinewy, and the sword cut but did not sever it. It seemed tough and strong, even haughty, and the executioner's anger showed. He immediately struck a second blow, and the head flew and then rolled. It was ten feet away when it stopped, face upward. The eyes and beard faced the sky and the spectators, and still moved, still trembled. The body shuddered, stretched, contracted, rose and slumped, moved, and shuddered again. The blood spewed like a stream, a fountain, soaking the executioner's clothes and cloak, spraying even the boy, who, oblivious to any consequences, began to scream.

"Down with Khazael and al-Shibli—you sons of dogs!"

His voice was frenzied, almost like an animal's, and without waiting another instant the executioner snatched a rag from his belt, quickly wiped the sword, looked to one side and then the other, looking in the faces this time, still appearing, himself, wrathful and frightened. When no one approached, he jabbed the boy in the small of the back just as he had the man, and when the boy's body responded, like that of a dancer in a moment of ecstasy, or a horseman about to gallop off, the slender neck extended like a bird's, he brought down his sword and chopped the head from the body in one blow. The head rolled and rolled until it was near the spectators, actually brushing the feet of two or three of them. Its eyes were bloodshot and wet with tears; the long tongue hung out of the mouth, and several men drew back in fright. The body, which seemed determined to get up, rose to the height of a child, then fell down and began to shake.

Silence; silence; silence; then anger.

The emir's men pushed the people back. They gathered the pieces of the two men, and within a few minutes the spectacle was over. For the first time in his life, Muhammad Eid felt rage, shame and fear.

The commander of the detachment, trembling slightly as he hurried into his car, shouted at the crowd.

"Ibn Hathal's turn will come!"

The two men, who had been arrested the day before after a

shepherd had informed on them, were said to be responsible, with others, for blowing up an oil pipeline. Ibn Shibli decided within hours that the men had to be killed, whether they confessed or not, in order to strike fear into Miteb al-Hathal and his men; and for the sake of the nation and the people, as he said, and repeated; and because Sultan Khazael demanded it. There was no difference between an evildoer and someone who wanted to be one!

That afternoon a green Hudson sped through the desert from Harran to Ujra; Muhammad Eid had hired it by himself. Although Ibn Seif had been surprised by Muhammad's wish to go to Ujra, he was even more taken aback by his refusal to wait another day to make the journey, and deduced that Muhammad had a very important deal to close.

"The doctor is our brother," he told Muhammad as he saw him off. "Give him our regards and tell him everyone in Harran has happy memories of him."

Muhammad nodded but said nothing. His eyes answered the remark. His heart was filled with endless bitterness, and he felt horribly ill, dying even. When the car passed through al-Mattale' and the desert road stretched out before them, he saw the cemetery and some men sitting in the shade of its dusty gray wall. He tried to turn around to have one last look at Harran, but could not. He shot a quick sidelong glance at the grave, almost glum driver. He wanted to talk, to hear some sound other than the wind, but he did not have the strength or the desire. He said to himself: *The last of Harran is behind that wall; a sensible man can do nothing but leave.*

The car raced the sand and the wind on the endless level plain, and the hot air burned their faces to reach their fingers and toes, then swirled around to scatter the dust particles that formed billowing walls between all things, confusing vision, desires, and thinking until one could not be distinguished from the other.

"Hot!" said Muhammad suddenly.

"Yes, hot," said the driver awkwardly.

"Are you from Harran?"

"No."

"Where from then?"

"From God's wide world."

"No, really, where are you from?"

"Guess."

"You look like you're from the Sultanate, but your accent—"

"If I were from the Sultanate, someone else would be driving you right now." He added a little sadly, "If I'd been from the Sultanate, I'd have changed the world!"

After a silence the driver asked, "Were you in Harran this afternoon?"

"Yes, I was."

"Did you see it?"

"Yes, I did."

"Not one son of a bitch said a word or raised a finger for them, and those poor men were butchered. God help the poor." He sighed. "If there were any real men in Harran, if what happened there had happened anywhere else, no one would have stood for it. But people are like sheep, they make noises and are led around, and in the end a few bastards come and put them to sleep and do what they want."

Silence fell again. Sun, dust, and the rays of the sun. The driver spoke to break the silence.

"Are you going to Ujra or farther on from there?"

"Farther."

"Where, God willing?"

"I don't know."

The driver turned to give him a surprised look, then shook his head and curled his lip. "How come you don't know?"

"Because the whole world is nothing but shit. Every place is the same."

"You're like me!"

"We're all alike, cousin, and Harran might be rotten, but pretty soon everywhere else will be just like it."

Silence fell again, and the driver pressed the gas pedal even harder.

33

M UCH CAME OF HAMMAD'S FIRST THREE
years in the palace: he was promoted
from deputy head of the Intelligence
and Security Agency to its actual chief; from a wing in the palace
to his own building; and from living in Mooran to traveling
through the world visiting other such agencies in friendly countries.

Two years and three months after the Sultan married Anoud
bint Rashed al-Mutawa, she gave birth to a son, and as a direct result of that Hammad was appointed Director of the Agency; the
doctor informed him of that before the royal edict was issued.

"Hammad, the Sultan loves you, he loves you like a son," the doctor told him in a moment he had chosen carefully. He laughed.
"Either your luck is straight from Heaven or you're a magician!"

Hammad did not know how to reply to this, so the doctor
went on.

"Congratulations—really. You've been appointed Director of the Security Agency, on the direct orders of the Sultan; there is no room for mistakes now. You have to vindicate his decision completely."

Less than a month after his promotion Hammad moved into the newly refurbished emirate building; the emirate offices had actually been moved to a new building. This was necessitated by the expansion of the Security Agency and the hiring of several special "experts" from the United States and Germany, who, it was said, were to stay only a short time—all except five of them whose services were contracted for three years. The move was an urgently needed one, since special equipment for the Security Agency had arrived, and it was large and required a great deal of space. The engineers had suggested that they be installed far from the palace, so that they would not jam the radio systems there.

Despite the move, Hammad kept his office in the palace at the doctor's wish, which he had made known jokingly.

"For one thing, we can't stand to see you go—we couldn't let a day go by without seeing you. And we assume you feel the same way about us." He laughed. "Secondly, this room has luck—this is where you got your start. I'm happy just knowing it's here. And lastly, for security reasons, it's better for you and your work to be here in the palace."

Hammad thought the idea, which he assumed the doctor had come up with well in advance, was a good one. He made up his mind privately, however, not to give up any of the secrecy he had become used to; secrecy had a great allure for him. If he moved out of the palace completely and publicly, he would surely be confronting new difficulties and even embarrassments of one sort or another.

"You're right, Abu Ghazwan," he told the doctor. "I wouldn't move at all if it weren't for all these machines and God knows what I have to find room for. There's no place like the palace."

Muti had become one of Hammad's most trusted friends, and the two were hardly ever apart. He was listening to this conversation and now joined it.

"The office in the palace is indispensable! For receptions, storing important documents, and emergency meetings."

They were all in agreement on Hammad's continuing links to the palace, and the need for routine meetings, and the doctor said pleasantly, "Hammad's room is a refinery—all the data pours into it to be refined and assessed. We should call it the Situation Assessment Room." His eyes twinkled. "No, even better, we should call it the Operations Room, just as armies do. It's like the operating room of a hospital."

The three laughed, and decided that Hammad's office would be called the Operations Room.

By the end of that third year, too, the doctor bought large amounts of land in nearby Hasiba. Once again, Hammad was an excellent middleman and convinced his Uncle Shaddad to sell. Shaddad could not understand why any sane person would want to buy that land.

"My lad, Hammad, Hasiba is just an empty field," he said ironically. "No one would ever dream of buying it unless there was gold there, and if there's gold there, leave it for the Mutawa family, leave it for your Uncle Shaddad. That would be better than some stranger coming and taking the land and the gold."

"Uncle, if there was gold there, they wouldn't have named it Hasiba!" The name meant gravel.

"So that man, the Sultan's adviser—why does he want it?"

"He wants to build a hospital there."

"So he can heal Ibn Duheish's camels? Or maybe the jackals out there in the desert?" He shouted with laughter because no one would dream of building a hospital in that remote place, and then spoke with the same irony in his voice. "My lad, Hammad, I'll sell, I'll sell, to that adviser or anyone else who wants to buy, just give me the facts, tell me the truth—is this friend of yours sane or crazy?"

He did not wait for Hammad to reply, only laughed and spoke again, as if to himself.

"If he makes a habit of making decisions like this, if he advises the Sultan with the same wisdom he buys land with, then this country is in good hands, and curses on anyone who doesn't believe it!"

When their discussion was ended, Shaddad had agreed to sell part of the land, but he would not sell it all, "because I'm going to watch this crazy fool, and whatever he does I'll do; if he loses, I'll lose too, and if he profits, they'll say, even if it's a thousand years from now, that Shaddad had a good head, that he knew when to buy and sell land!"

Before the sale was made final, Shaddad insisted that "the land was sold with a horse on it," and that was the way the doctor bought it. He presented the horse to the Sultan on the third anniversary of his installation as Sultan.

A few months after Hammad had assumed leadership of the Agency, it was decided that he and three of his aides should travel to the United States for a three-month training course.

The thought of a journey, especially to such a far-off place, deeply worried Hammad. He could easily travel to Egypt, even to Syria or Iraq, but to ride an airplane over the ocean, to meet people he had never seen before, whose language he did not know; to become a student again, to do lessons, he who had not been able to finish his schooling here—the very idea gave him bad dreams. He considered asking the doctor to excuse him from the trip. He could select some aides to attend the course, and attend one himself at a later date. Now that he was Chief of the Agency he preferred to put the trip aside, but in the routine meeting that followed his learning of the course, the doctor told the Sultan that the embassy had urged them to send the Director of the Security Agency quickly, due to "urgency"—the doctor did not explain what this urgency was likely to mean—so Hammad was unable to oppose the plan or make any excuse not to go.

To combat the uneasiness and outright fear he felt, and to leave himself no way out, Hammad exaggerated his eagerness and readiness for the trip. He selected three of his men to accompany him, with the doctor's help, plus a fourth to translate, though this one could not be allowed to go along until he had joined the Agency.

A few days before leaving, Hammad kept one of his promises to Abdelaziz al-Ghamdi (and his partner Said al-Usta, though without mentioning his name); the palace's supply contracts with Othman al-Asqi, Sultan Khureybit's old servant, and the senior palace cook, Abdelmajid, which had been more or less informal contracts, were abruptly turned over to Abdelaziz al-Ghamdi, "because he is really the only local party who can supply goods to the palace that are first-class and meet all official standards."

This was a long-delayed gift that Said had awaited with enormous eagerness and impatience; he had begun to think "that Hammad is just like anyone else—he'll get one foot in the palace and forget all his friends." When Abdelaziz showed up with the signed contract, Said laughed and said, "At last!"

He read the contract and commented, "We underestimated him. I thought he'd forgotten us, but I swear to God he kept his promise."

"The best is yet to come, Abu Shakib." Al-Ghamdi laughed.

"God is good, Abu Homeidi."

Shaddad al-Mutawa learned of Hammad's trip three days before he was to leave, and made a long-remembered remark.

"There is absolutely no good in foreigners or strangers. As long as my nephew is tied up with those people, I don't think he'll come to any good either!"

Hammad's father was profoundly saddened at seeing him go. He could only repeat, "We belong to God and to Him we must return. We belong to God and to Him we must return."

34

HAMMAD'S DEPARTURE FROM THE PALACE
left a void for the doctor, much like the
one a daughter leaves when she marries
and moves in with her in-laws. Hammad's office remained and was
given all kinds of new names, some serious and others uproarious.
In the first weeks after the Agency officially moved out, Hammad
stayed in the palace; thereafter, he dropped in every day to have a
cup of coffee with the doctor and Muti. Nevertheless, his feeling of
isolation, or at least of distance, was very real and oppressive. The
doctor had been used to summoning Hammad or Muti several
times a day, often on a mere pretext, because there was fresh coffee, to check the accuracy of a verse of poetry, a date in history, or
the name of a person or place. At other times he would drop in on
them, saying that he was tired and needed to relax. These little
meetings were often prolonged by wide-ranging discussions that
the doctor considered a form of mental exercise, and that taught
him more about Mooran than any book.

All this began to change when Hammad moved. The doctor considered him on vacation, or something like a vacation, since Hammad would never be able to leave completely, or so he thought; he laughed and said to himself, *Hammad is like a policeman—he takes a vacation, and spends it sitting in front of the station.* What made him so sure of this was that Hammad did not leave the palace, and it appeared that he could not leave. If he did not join them for morning coffee, as he generally did to start the day, for a discussion interspersed with a general chat and jokes, descriptions of their dreams of the night before, real estate prices, news of friends who were out of town, and the latest happenings in Mooran—if he did not join them for morning coffee, he dropped by later on. Sometimes the doctor made bets with himself—*He'll definitely come in the morning, before noon prayers*—but Hammad would not come until somewhat later.

This was how they got along, and because their relationship was founded upon routine, the doctor assumed that it was unchangeable, though after Hammad moved he was worried about the turn things seemed to be taking. Hammad spent most of his time in his own new office and had no fixed times to come by for coffee or idle talk. It was true that he did visit and spent some long evenings there, but his coming, or awaiting it, had become a real anxiety for the doctor.

In spite of that, as with all things in this life, the doctor began to get used to the new arrangement and before long was accustomed to it. Telephone conversations with Hammad now took the place of their visits. They talked for a long time, usually several times a day, and always according to the same pattern: they began quietly, then briskly dealt with all the business at hand before gradually straying into other subjects, exactly as they used to do over their cups of coffee. The doctor found himself immersed in land deals and the price of construction materials. He did not hesitate to ask Hammad if so-and-so's daughter was really going to marry such a one, and whether it meant the union of two fortunes or the alliance of two clans, and what the repercussions were financially and, he added, laughing, ". . . politically!"

These telephone conversations relaxed Hammad; they were a diversion from the burdens imposed on him every day, and he never delayed in reaching for the phone to put aside his duties for the moment. What made it even easier were the Sultan's recent requests, on several occasions, to cancel their weekly intelligence and "situation assessment" meetings. The doctor insisted that the meetings be held anyway, just as if the Sultan were present, so that he, Hammad and Muti could exchange information, then engage in "situation assessment," claiming that "these habits create traditions, and in the final analysis nations are built on and rooted in traditions." He was another person altogether during the meetings, carrying sheaves of paper, taking notes whenever the other two men spoke, and assuming a serious, even harsh look on his face—the only time they ever saw him look that way. Sometimes, especially when the Sultan was not present, he summoned some of the high-ranking employees or officials to question them on certain affairs, or to ask their opinions on certain issues, "each according to his specialty or responsibilities," as he put it rather grandly.

At first this mode of work and of dealing with people occasioned no comment, but Hammad and Muti became much closer friends, and left almost no matter untouched by their close attention, until they had intruded into everything. As they concluded one of their weekly "situation assessment" meetings, Muti said half-jokingly to the doctor, "To look at you, Abu Ghazwan, one would think His Majesty were here at the table!"

The doctor gave him a surprised look, and Muti laughed.

"God love you, Doctor—why are you so serious? After all, in another minute you're going to be asking who married so-and-so and what about what's-his-name's divorce!"

The doctor smiled pleasantly and his voice came from deep within his chest: "My boy, Muti, work for this world as if you were living forever; work for your eternal afterlife as if you were dying tomorrow. Since I was a boy, when I began my studies, and after, I gave every task its full importance. I learned that lesson a long time ago—I learned it from the Germans. They were my model. They worked like donkeys, they ate like beasts, and played like children—other people confuse work and play."

He paused, shaking his head, inhaled loudly, and went on.

"Our job here is to build a new nation, to create traditions and to be examples for everyone else!"

Here Muti deferred to Hammad, who spoke up quickly and disingenuously.

"Brother, sometimes the doctor goes a little too far—he gets too strict. You can't tell whether or not he's really serious."

Hammad listened, watched and learned, trying to sort out and connect the events to one another in order, in the end, to formulate his own assessment of the situation.

After he went to the United States and was gone for so long, and wrote letters to the doctor and Muti—the doctor read all of them—he decided that he had been right all along: a trip like this was absolutely invaluable.

Hammad sent three letters to the doctor and three to Muti; the letters were all different, each written to suit its recipient.

His first letter, ten days after he left, was sent to the doctor.

> April 24 / Safar 7
> Atlanta, Ga.
> To His Excellency Dr. Subhi al-Mahmilji
> Peace and Blessings of God.
> Dear Uncle,
>
> I hope this finds you in good health. For myself, praise God, I have never been better, and lack nothing except the sight of you, my dear friends, and I pray God to correct that as soon as possible. The men with me send their best wishes and are all asking for you; they are, like me, praise God, in excellent health and doing very well indeed.
>
> Our friends here have taken good care of us since the very hour we arrived. They have assigned us guides and escorts and provided everything needed for our comfort: food, accommodations and translators. They have arranged a series of visits to various regions of the United States, and when we come home, God willing, we'll tell you all about it.
>
> Dear Uncle, I decided to write a thank-you note to His Majesty the Sultan, and did write it, in fact, but was ashamed to mail it; I am relying on you to convey to him, in person, my warm thanks, until I can thank him myself as soon as I return to our beloved land.

In closing, I send all my love and thanks to you, our
friends and colleagues, and especially Muti.
Sincerely,
Your servant,
Hammad al-Mutawa

Muti got his letter from Hammad three days after the doctor
received his:

Dear Muti,
I hope this finds you in good health, and that God
wills that we meet again soon.
I'm writing this from the hospital—I checked in here
four days after I arrived. The doctors say it's nothing serious—I just need rest and a little medication. The
American weather has affected me, and they've detected
what they call a hereditary disease after giving me a
thorough examination and some excellent nursing care.
If everything goes well I should be out of here within two
or three days.
I'm telling you this—which I haven't told the doctor
or my family—just to reassure you, since if you heard it
from anyone else you might worry. And if you're wondering how these people are looking after us, you might
be surprised by their concern and hospitality. But as they
say, I'm a friend in need—imagine. The doctors and
nurses visit me several times a day and make jokes and
ask about how I'm doing as if they'd known me all their
lives.
So I'm fine, praise God, and so are the rest of the men;
they all send their best regards, and so do I.
Your friend and brother,
Hammad al-Mutawa

The second letter to the doctor was much like the first. Hammad
wrote that they had visited Houston, Texas, and San Francisco.
These were very important visits, Hammad said, adding that "in
San Francisco they asked about you with the greatest interest and

respect. They said they had heard of you and hope that you will visit them."

The third and last letter to the doctor was written fifteen days before Hammad left the United States; it was written from Washington. He sent his warm regards to the Sultan and the doctor, and said, in part:

> Most of our meetings here were with people who spoke Arabic, who know the history of the Sultanate of Mooran and have the greatest respect for His Majesty the Sultan. They asked a great many detailed questions about His Majesty—how old he was, how many children and brothers he had and so on. We answered all their questions as frankly as possible, and they were very pleased. They also asked about their highnesses the princes—they know most of them by name—and said that they plan to invite them to visit the United States. We've seen equipment much like what was sent to the Sultanate, only more advanced, and the men with me have had a training course on how to use it. I'll give you more details when I get home.

The second letter to Muti was sent from Atlanta on May 14.

> I didn't tell you how afraid I was when I was in the hospital—not just of illness or death, but of death in a strange, foreign place, and as a precaution I asked—ordered, actually—that the men who had come along with me should, in the event of my death, ship my body back home. They laughed and said that things were not quite that serious, and so I sat up one night and wrote my will, and put that stipulation in it!
>
> Now that I'm better and the illness is just a memory, I go strolling with the men and the Americans around Atlanta and the surrounding areas, and look at these colossal buildings, streets, parks and automobiles. They fill me with a different kind of fear—I feel that we are as

small as ants before all this American greatness and American power.

Everything here is so organized, everything is by the clock: trains, planes, sleep, waking, work, even leisure. Several times they've made appointments for us all the way across town, but we always get there exactly on time.

The Americans really love us—I feel it every time we are all together. Their concern for us and their hospitality is beyond description. If it weren't for the cold weather, you would want to live here, or at least spend a long time here. There are other things I can't mention in a letter, but I'll give you all the details when I get back."

The third letter, from San Francisco, was dated June 18. Part of it ran:

If it weren't for my missing you and my family and home, I would stay here. It would take time to get used to, but it's a giant city, with every race and nationality, and if you spoke English well enough, you could live here for a good long time, in the city or the suburbs. It is like the paradise that God promised his faithful servants. There are buildings you can't even see the top of and streets so wide that it would frighten you to cross them, suspension bridges and the raging ocean, but nothing is more beautiful than San Francisco at night. The city doesn't sleep or let anyone sleep. Even in the wee morning hours you see men and women in the cafés, restaurants, the streets—everywhere. I asked our guides, "When do these people sleep?" and they laughed but didn't answer.

I think California is one of the richest and most beautiful places on earth, and the Arab students here agree with me. (By the way, I met up with Ghazwan, and we had a good time together. He seems to be doing well in his studies; we agreed to stay in touch. I'll give you the details when I get back. I told him that everyone at home sent their love.)

Everything is green in this country: forests, fields, streets. You would never believe it unless you saw it.

In this particular region there are lots of resorts and lakes. I asked our senior guide if it would be possible to come here with a family or group of friends to stay for a month or two. He said absolutely yes; all I'd have to do is to give them enough notice so that they could prepare everything for me. I think I'll come back here more than once, to get around without anyone hanging around me all the time, you can guess why.

When we have a chance, I'll tell you everything about this city, by day and by night, and we can plan to come back together in the future.

The last letter Hammad sent to Muti was from Washington, and dated July 9.

You have to visit America—I say so, and so do all the men with me, especially after the celebrations we've seen in the past few days in the American capital. You could simply never imagine festivities like these—it's impossible to imagine that there could be anything like them in any other place or any other time: horses, drums, torches, men and women, little children and old men, in the streets, the squares, everywhere. You should have seen us—we must have looked dazed. We just stared. Even our guides were like different people—they danced along with the dancers and laughed and sang, and if we had not been an important, high-level delegation we would have joined in.

America, Muti, is a country of unequaled greatness. As I've said in my other letters, the buildings, the streets, the airports, even the restaurants and hotels, even the people. We have only a few days left here. To me, this visit was crucial and essential. I have truly benefited from it and must come back here again and again; please God, we'll visit here together. I look forward to seeing you soon; we need to have a long talk.

35

H AMMAD'S RETURN HOME BROUGHT ON A
riot of celebration and excitement and a
babble of gossip and questions: everyone
had to hear from his own lips all about "this America." Hammad
himself was so excited that he repeated the same answers over and
over again; in any case, almost all the questions were basically the
same. The doctor chided Hammad for not telling him about his
illness, and was anxious to be the first to know what had come of
the visit and how it had affected Hammad. They met several times,
and the doctor asked many abrupt questions on totally unrelated
topics. As a student in Austria, the doctor had read studies that
proved that the ideal method of testing and measuring intelligence
was to question the subject rapidly on a variety of totally unrelated
topics. Intelligence and the capacity for logic were indicated by the
reaction, speed and clarity of his response. The doctor carried out
this little test, using questions he had prepared beforehand, and

his conclusion was that *Hammad is too talkative for this position or any other.* He arranged for an urgent meeting with the Sultan.

During the audience with the Sultan, Hammad did his best to convey his impressions of his visit, to describe all that he had seen. He realized that he was confused, that his thoughts slipped away from him and got mixed up. He did not say the things he had intended to, or said them wrong. The doctor intervened to help him out, by pointing to the letter Hammad had written to the Sultan from Atlanta and to the will he had written in his illness, with the result that the Sultan grew more interested in them than in anything else, and asked to see the letter and the will. Hammad was deeply embarrassed and felt that he had fallen victim to a minor but obvious plot, of either Muti's or the doctor's fashioning, but he went on and talked about many different things, though he doubted how important or interesting they were. When he got to the part about his visit to Washington and the questions they asked him there, especially about the Sultan, the mood in the room changed. It was now tense and even dangerous; the Sultan, who had been delighted with the stories, which he could not get his fill of, now opened his eyes wide in surprise and massaged his beard.

"You say they were asking questions about the Sultan and his brothers?" His tone of voice turned mocking. "Surely they didn't forget to ask about his womenfolk too?"

Hammad hastened to deny strongly that he had been asked anything like that, and said sharply, "If he had asked me that, sir, I would have cut my tongue out before I'd let him say a word!"

"Did they ask you about the princes?"

"They said they'd like to have them visit, and they'll send invitations."

"And Fanar—did they ask you about Fanar?"

"No, sir." After a moment he added awkwardly, "Sir, they asked me about the princes' ages, about the order of succession."

It was clear that the Sultan was displeased by the Americans' questions about him and their intention to give the princes invitations to the United States. He was silent for a moment before speaking.

"No one ever mentioned us, no one ever visited us or told us, 'Come,' before this oil started to flow." He sighed deeply. "God rest your soul, Khureybit—you told them 'This is gold,' and they all came running."

The doctor did not know how to get the conversation moving again or to lighten the mood. It seemed to him that the Sultan's words could be taken several ways, and that perhaps they were meant to be. So he tried to change the subject; when he felt the moment was right, he bowed and said grandly, "In my judgment, Your Majesty, it is absolutely essential that you be invited to the United States, invited by the American President himself—there are so many matters to be discussed with Your Majesty!"

"Would you accept that, Doctor?" replied the Sultan with a note of sarcasm. "Shall we say to them, 'Invite us, friends, we want to visit you'?" A rough laugh rattled in his throat. "If they were like us, with bread and salt between us, we tell them, 'Prepare a feast, good friends, tomorrow we'll be your guests!'"

"That's the truth, Your Majesty." This was the doctor's humble reply, and he added very earnestly, "They should run after us, and we'd tell them, 'No, we can't come today, or tomorrow either,' and once they're exhausted from running we'd say, 'Never mind, all right,' and we'll set the date when we'll visit and how long we'll stay and what suits us and what doesn't!"

The Sultan's features relaxed and he replied, "That's just what to say, Doctor!"

The doctor nodded, and it was settled. They talked of other things: the Sultan asked about the climate and the food, about the American President's health and whether or not he was loved by his people. He shied away from asking about certain subjects that interested him, but turned to the doctor and said, "They tell me, Doctor, that over there they make no distinction between what is allowed and what is prohibited in marriage—just whatever comes into their heads."

The doctor laughed to help lighten the mood so that Hammad would speak up, so when Hammad looked at the floor and said nothing, he asked him, "We forgot to ask you, Hammad, are the women over there beautiful?"

Hammad gave the doctor a look of embarrassed reprimand, realizing that the doctor had read the hidden references in his letters to Muti, and perhaps even discussed them with the Sultan.

"It's like any other place, Doctor," said Hammad to close the sub-ject. "You find some beautiful ones, and others who aren't worth the trouble."

Their meeting concluded with a few pleasantries and an item of advice the Sultan offered as he rose to bid Hammad good-bye.

"Keep your heart and your eyes open, my boy. The heart is even more important than the eye. God give you success."

No one was more delighted to have Hammad back than his fa-ther. He was as unable as a child to hide his excitement. He had vowed to slaughter a camel on Hammad's safe return, and wanted to bring it to the airport to slaughter it there. His sons and brothers talked him out of it, saying that it did not suit the dignity of their family and might anger Hammad. So he slaughtered the camel in the marketplace, with a large audience, and brought not even the smallest piece of meat home, having distributed most of it among the poor of Mooran. Saleh al-Mutawa received guests in a constant stream for two or three days. For the first time, he listened care-fully to what his son said about his travels; Hammad was unlike most travelers who stayed abroad for long periods of time. Saleh was convinced that his son had returned from a distant, very dis-tant and dangerous land from which only few visitors ever re-turned alive. He was not exactly sure how the idea had come to him or how he had become so sure of it, but he was absolutely positive, and his doubts were confirmed when he heard that Ham-mad had been ill there and had to be kept in a hospital to be cured. On the evening of Hammad's third day back, he told his son, "Our town is much safer, Son, with family and friends here; if a man dies, he dies on home soil, among family and friends."

Unlike his father, his Uncle Shaddad hid his feelings. When things had calmed down a little and almost everyone had paid their respects to Hammad, Shaddad told him, "Listen, Hammad, now it's our turn to give advice and have our say, not that fool who can't tell a bull camel from a mare. Let him be an adviser to whoever deserves what he has to say!"

Shaddad's words were taken to mean more than one thing, and to refer to more than one person. When he was alone with Ham-mad, he asked him, "My boy, what has come over you? We like to stay in our own place, here, among our own tribe, but you go rushing from place to place, from tribe to tribe, as if the Mutawa clan needed no more children—as if all our vendettas were history!"

Hammad laughed.

"Nephew, this place is better than a lot of others, and your people are better than a lot of others!"

The grandfather, Muflih, did not know about Hammad's trip until the day he arrived home. When he noticed all the commotion, he asked Mutlaq, "Hah, sonny, did someone die? Who's dead?"

Mutlaq shook his head vigorously, with a broad smile.

"Ha—who's getting married?"

Mutlaq fetched the newly enlarged funnel and used it to tell him that Hammad had arrived that day. His grandfather gave him a perplexed look.

"Where is he coming from? When had he left?"

"He went to America, months ago!"

"America!"

"Yes—America."

"Is that east or west?"

"West."

"People travel east, my boy—from the east you get wheat and cloth and every other good thing. What ever made our Hammad go west? Didn't anyone offer him directions? Didn't he ask anyone?"

The old man was deeply confused. He had never heard of this place, knowing only that most people traveled to the east; the fact that, unlike them, his grandson had traveled in any other direction, and to an unknown place, and made it back again, convinced him that Hammad had become important.

"If he comes here, tell him to come to me and tell me about it," he demanded.

Hammad seemed to be a new person—everyone, including his subordinates and friends and the women, thought so. His wife gazed at him silently, as if trying to identify the marks of the trip on his face and in his eyes; as if she were trying to discover whether this was the same man who had left. His mother, like his father, ran around not knowing whether to laugh or cry. Tears streamed down her face and she did nothing to stop them, or to veil herself in front of all the children and young men!

When Hammad visited his grandfather, at old Muflih's insistence, he sat beside him and the old man looked at him as if he were getting to know him for the first time. He smiled and slapped Hammad on the thigh.

"Ha, my boy, do you like this place or do you like the west better?"

Hammad smiled but did not reply. His grandfather waited and watched him for a long time.

"From the time God created the world, my boy, we've been traveling to the east, but you went west. I hope you found something good there?"

Hammad laughed loudly, but the grandfather did not understand. Mutlaq did not explain it to him, even though he was holding the funnel for that purpose.

"If we'll live, we'll see, let's hope it's for the best," said the old man.

36

How could three months change a man so profoundly? How was it possible for a man to change, to become someone else, within such a short period?

After the fuss died down, Hammad decided to rest for two or three days before reporting to work. When he tried to force himself to relax, he found that all his senses grew more tense, more aroused with every passing hour, that his mind flitted from one thought to another as quick as lightning, to the point where he could not remain in one place for long or concentrate on any single task. Suddenly, late the first night he was back, as the last shops in Mooran were closing, he found himself heading to his office.

For the first time since he had held that job he was going to the office at this hour. His appearance caused a stir and some anxiety among the office staff—anxiety only heightened by his request that a number of section chiefs and two cryptologists be summoned.

What could he possibly want at this hour of the night? What could not be left until the next day?

Within less than an hour most of the officials of the Security Agency were assembled for a meeting that lasted nearly three hours, in which they discussed the events of the past few months, the major crises of those months and how they were handled. The meeting concluded with some general instructions to the staff. Hammad remained at work for hours after that, and since he was there, several of his employees had to stay as well, although they had no work to do. Hammad studied various documents and files, and took from its box the beautiful clock presented to him in Washington. It was a yellow desk clock the size of his fist, in a dark-green velvet frame, and not only gave the time and date; its graceful but clear bell rang to mark that a certain amount of time had passed. If Hammad wished to limit a meeting, to a half hour, for example, the clock informed him and his visitor when the half hour was up, and reminded them five minutes later, and so on until he reset it.

This clock had another distinction, known only to Hammad, and he did not tell anyone in Mooran about it. The clock was really a recording device, and could record any conversation that took place in his office, no matter how far from the clock itself.

The clock was given to Hammad in his final meeting alone with the chief of Central Intelligence in Washington. No one else was present but the translator—not the one who had come with Hammad, but the one employed by this department.

In this and many of the other meetings between the Americans and Hammad, usually unaccompanied, much was said that he largely forgot but he remembered the general outlines at least vaguely; he told no one about it, not the doctor or anyone else, since the Americans' strong advice, given in more than one form, persuaded him that it would be best to keep it to himself.

Now he placed the clock on his desk and set it to three o'clock in the morning, and began to lose himself in his distant memories and dreams. Faces, places and smells mingled as he gazed out the window at Mooran, as sleeping and tranquil as a dead city, and at the thought that the only lit building was this, his headquarters, he was filled with feelings of pride, power and fear.

This was new to him. Although the feeling of power overwhelmed all his other feelings, it had nothing to do with the number of men he worked with or with the complex equipment that occupied the rear of the Agency building and never ceased working night or day; it was more. It was power, for now he knew more and knew better than anyone else, and, knowing that, knew that those who knew more and better than others were the most powerful.

They told him, in Washington, that they knew him well, that they knew all about him: who he was, his age, his order of birth among his brothers and sisters, his father's business and his uncles'. They told him the color, make and model of the convertible he drove, and yet all this was a digression on the part of the American he was meeting with, who read these facts out loud, then closed the file folder and laughed, having made his point that they had so much information, so very much, about him and everyone else in Mooran. It frightened Hammad at first, but before long he regarded them with a kind of respect.

At this late night hour in Mooran, after the meeting he'd held with his section chiefs, he felt that the mission entrusted to him was too momentous to be left to anyone else. True, he did not know exactly what he wanted or how to accomplish it, but he knew he would have to become a different person, even to himself. He had chosen to come to the office at this particular time, with no advance warning, and to stay until this hour, and he now felt that this was the beginning of a new and special path to follow.

He was a long time straying in these distracted dreams, but as soon as his clock struck three he roused himself first from his torpor and then from the remnants of his dreams. As he drove home he stared at the guards a little harshly, as if to reprimand them for lacking the right bearing and alertness. As he crossed the streets of Mooran he saw men lugging carts of vegetables and going to the mosque; he saw shepherds and travelers. For the first time he saw them differently: he counted them, scrutinized their clothing and general appearance, and wagered that he knew at least some of them. When his car careened past the Rawdh Palace, he gazed at the building carefully, as if seeing it for the first time, and fleetingly inspected the guards and counted them, too.

Hammad slept until the late morning. His father, who went to the marketplace early and came back to the house for his morning coffee, asked for him, and when he saw him still in bed, with sleep still showing in his face and eyes, he laughed.

"Remember, my boy: the mark of a free bird is that it soars the highest, sleeps little, and rests at dawn."

Hammad nodded and smiled, then explained to his father that he would need a few days to get used to the local time, since the time difference between Mooran and Washington was seven hours.

His father nodded to show that he had heard, but he did not know what was meant by the "time difference," or how such a thing could be. He asked around, but only got more confused, because they talked about things he never thought about and had never heard of before.

Later, when Hammad reached home at dawn or shortly after and saw his grandfather trying, with difficulty, to begin preparing his morning coffee, he took his place beside him to help, handing him what he needed. Muflih was delighted to have this help. When they were done, he asked Hammad to come near so that he could tell him a secret.

"I told them, 'Leave Hammad alone, he's making his own way and he'll get there, if not today then tomorrow!'" He laughed loudly and went on with a question in his voice. "For a few days now I've noticed you up at dawn, my boy, or even before, as if you were the imam of a mosque, or were going to prayers!"

He stared at Hammad with eyes barely visible in the last shadows of dawn and saw nothing but phantoms. He did not know what was happening in this world.

Had the Americans told Hammad to change his nights into days and his days into nights, or had this been his grandson's own crazed, headstrong idea?

If that had been all, he would not have found some explanation or not bothered to worry, but Hammad never stopped changing. Every day his mind produced another monstrous new idea, and since these ideas didn't apply only to himself but affected others as well, the doctor took notice. Two or three weeks later, Hammad had still not paid him a morning visit, nor even by noon prayers, and when the doctor tried to phone him in the office he was not there; the doctor was surprised. Eventually someone told him that

Hammad was spending his days at home and his nights, until nearly dawn, in the office.

"Abu Rashed, it looks like you've decided to stick with American time!" the doctor said to Hammad in their next weekly meeting.

Hammad looked at him with surprise; he did not know what the doctor meant by this. The doctor laughed.

"We try to call you in the office and they say you're not there, and in the house at night and they say you're not there!"

They had a long talk in which Hammad tried to explain why he worked at night; how his first experiment with the idea, in spite of the initial strangeness and difficulty, yielded such excellent results. The whole staff rushed to their work stations and worked diligently; additionally, he could receive friends privately, to get all their latest news and information. When the doctor heard this, he said jokingly, "I'm with you—the Agency is private, and in a situation different from other departments. Even if you have office hours at night sometimes—you shouldn't have work habits that become too fixed, or known to everybody."

The doctor chuckled as though his head were filled with conflicting thoughts, and added, "It's a great idea, to visit the office at night. It's vital to have someone there at night, following things, but don't force yourself or others to work at night."

Hammad, who nodded in agreement, decided to make the most of every person and every minute.

37

MUTI AND HAMMAD HAD BEEN CLOSE FROM
the earliest days of their acquaintance;
anyone who saw them even a month
after would have thought they were old friends. The doctor was
delighted by the intimacy that had sprung up between the two
men, and to explain this phenomenon, like so many other phenomena in man and nature, even among animals, the doctor
thought, casting his mind back on so many things, that *it is difficult
to ascribe certain phenomena, such as friendship, to direct, specific causes,
or even to volition. It's more complex than that; it's rooted in the subconscious, in the gray area, as scholars call it. Unknown, subconscious forces
are at work in that gray area, much as the heart pumps involuntarily, and
it is these forces that mold a person's affections and strivings, even his mind.*
The doctor was fascinated by these phenomena of life, of the
world, and other such puzzles, and often pondered them; he considered thinking an important and life-prolonging exercise. Why

did a man love and hate? Were love and hate simple, separate phenomena or complex and interrelated? Was it true what people said
about "the first moment" and "first sight"? To figure it out, he used
palpable examples: his relationship with Sultan Khazael, for example, had formed the hour they met, and all that followed were
confirmation of that and the details. Muti and Hammad: how had
they met and become close as if born to be friends? By contrast,
Muti and Said: although they were related, they seemed born to
hate each other—*they even hate the ground the other one walks on,* the
doctor said to himself.

Hammad and Muti's friendship grew stronger, and they were
able to exchange ideas and reach similar or identical convictions
with little effort and very few words, and one day the doctor said,
while speaking of this subject. "The heart is a brook, my friends;
man's task—the task of reason—is to open the brooks so that they
flow into a great river."

This central idea of the doctor's had several practical applica-
tions; that these two basic elements should work harmoniously,
with no coercion or intervention on his part, meant that half the
mission he dreamed of was already accomplished. This explained
his indecision and delay, early on, in selecting a chief for the Security Agency, but after chance turned up Hammad, and they got
along, and he befriended Muti, the doctor decided that the "gray
area," the hidden force, was still very much with him; and this is
what encouraged him to recommend to the Sultan that Hammad's
trial period be cut short so that he might be formally appointed
Director of the Security Agency.

Hammad's trip gave the doctor a chance to think everything
through again. He spent whole nights preoccupied, thinking—not
because he did not know what he wanted, but because he was
trying to gather in the net, as he told himself, to follow the seas
west of Gibraltar, because Mooran and its people, as far as he could
see, were simple, kind, and peaceful. Appearances were often mis-
leading, like the face of deep water, which was usually tranquil but
quick to change; on the whole he dreaded people more than he
understood them. Even the city, as gay and primitive as it appeared
to him, was hard, cruel, layered; no sooner had he uncovered one
layer, discovering what was underneath, than he was surprised by

yet more under that. He saw Mooran as a place with a violent temper that could flare up with no warning; just the opposite of Harran.

This was how he saw things. Hammad's letters helped him to overcome the Tempter (as he called his moments of doubt) and his fears, as did his talks with Hammad after he came home. True, Hammad did not speak directly to him, perhaps out of respect or shame, but he told Muti everything in great detail: the San Francisco nights, which were not restricted to touring the streets or standing on that great bridge at the opening of the bay, to see the glowing blaze that defined the features of the city—he spoke of the young women they met: unforgettable blondes of such beauty as to deprive you of reason. In bed, in those warm, perfumed beds, their embraces could turn the biggest man into a small child. They were so skilled, so lively and strong, never tiring, never sleeping, never allowing anyone else to tire or sleep. And this not only in San Francisco, but in most of the cities they visited.

Muti mentioned all this to the doctor very indirectly and jokingly ("the pampering those men got over there") and said that Hammad had come back totally seduced, "with the image of America engraved in his memory forever." After the doctor heard these details and made his choice, he was confident that he held winning cards in his hand—trumps, he said to himself: the press and security. The winning player was the one whose face showed nothing, whose face had nothing of victory or loss in it.

It was at about this time that the doctor decided to publish a new sort of newspaper in Mooran. Muti had spent months getting ready; he had traveled twice to Cairo and three times to Beirut to make deals with several journalists and technical people. He came back with results that, at first, did not impress the doctor, considering all the time and effort that had gone into it, but when the daily newspaper *al-Badiya*—The Desert—was a reality, followed five months later by the weekly magazine, *al-Waha*—The Oasis— all the pomp they entailed and the influence that grew with each new issue, the doctor was convinced that the power of the press was no less than that of the actual weapons that could kill, demolish and achieve final victory.

The doctor had great expectations of the press. True, he did not know precisely how much he expected or how he would attain it, but he felt it. Sometimes it appeared to him very clearly, only to fade again. Nevertheless, he believed that the role of journalism went far beyond the mere reporting of news events here and there, or providing entertainment; its role was total, comprehensive, self-regenerating, always remaking readers' ideas, feelings and out-looks, so that no man would think or act except on these bases—exactly like religion. He shook his head in wonderment and added to himself, religions—any religions, divinely inspired or not—were all so powerful that they stamped one mark on each of their followers, almost as if they were all one in morals, ideology, behavior, way of seeing—in a word, everything.

The doctor recalled something he had read about the gypsies: a people of inherited traditions, ideas and traits that were not actively taught. This was because of the mental climate they lived in—they were steeped in all the traits and ideas that had come before them and that were now a part of them, and thus, generation after generation, almost unconsciously, they absorbed and shared, so that, from grandfather to grandchild, it was almost as if they *took the same path and learned from the same teacher,* as the doctor put it to himself: *what journalism should do is to remake the mind, even the Sultan's mind.*

Thus he dreamed of the role journalism could play; when it came to making this happen, to deciding what should be said and who should say it, he was at a loss, though this did not keep him from plunging in to try. The effort would crystallize his thoughts and help him to know what to say and how to say it.

Since he was not free to do this, he did not consider the hours he spent with Muti or their conversations to be luxuries, nor yet a way of killing time, as others did—it was "gypsy culture," as he often told himself, and laughed.

Mooran was not an isolated or fortified island, and storms whipped around it: every day brought news of deposed or executed kings, of "brilliant and powerful" kingdoms that collapsed and vanished like salt in water. These reports frightened the doctor, because he feared nothing more than time. He used to say to himself wrathfully: *Our competition is not with others, as to which will succeed; our competition is with time.* He was afraid that his dreams would scatter and be lost before he could fulfill them. The challenge enthralled him as much as it frightened him. *We are not alone; we cannot run away from what is around us; all we need is enough time to perfect our weapons, and when we've done that—we'll welcome any battle!*

And until our weapons are ready, we must protect ourselves, immunize the country—immunization before the onset of disease will give us resistance against the plague that's coming over the region and the whole world. Especially since he knew what kind of madmen were being hatched in the region, and what they could accomplish, given the hunger and oppression that afflicted them every day. He told himself sadly: *When poverty unites with a dream, a revolution is born,* and when he recalled Muti and his shouting, he thought, *If we get them to read what we write and prevent them from reading what the others write, if we monitor everything and are careful to plug all the holes, we'll have won half the battle. As to the other half . . .*

He, Muti and later Hammad found themselves in complete agreement; they had to "start the game with the rules, to create a press and get some journalists." He consented to many of Muti's suggestions, and ordered him to get going without delay.

Muti selected a group of professional journalists, several of them famous, and paid them handsomely. On top of the large salaries, he gave them housing and travel privileges, "since we'll benefit in the end," as he told himself and the doctor, in defiance of the criticism and proverbs people kept repeating to him.

38

F ROM EARLY ON—FROM THE DOCTOR'S FIRST
meeting with Prince Khazael in Harran, to
be exact, and his subsequent visits to
Mooran—the friendship between Khazael and Mahmilji was
strong and close, though accompanied, on the doctor's part, by certain misgivings. Moreover, he was now thoroughly dissatisfied with
his way of life; he became more and more positive, with every passing day, that he was no mere adviser to the Sultan, but cut out for a
much greater task: building a nation.

To build a nation was no small thing; one had to possess extraordinary courage and unlimited acumen, not to mention superb ex-
ecutives, capable and loyal; most important of all, circumstances
had to be favorable. This was the practical side. When the doctor
weighed what he had accomplished and reviewed the faces of his
aides, he was filled with delight. Hiring Hammad had been a real
stroke of luck; the man had benefited from every ancient and

modern advantage, from city and bedouin life, through money and friendships . . . and through intimidation.

When the doctor thought back on the way he'd dealt with Hammad, he felt that his effort had not been wasted; even the gypsy culture, as he called their informal, wide-ranging discussions, had broadened Hammad's mind and strengthened his character. The visits abroad and new friendships he formed, especially within similar agencies, had also developed his mental powers. The doctor said to himself contentedly, *The bedouin are, as a rule, intelligent; you have to give them that. Perhaps that vast desert, the hard life, the long nights, plus other factors that sharpen their natural disposition toward contemplation, made them so unmistakably so.*

So the doctor no longer was anxious about the domestic situation; the flow of oil had made the people less inclined to waste their energy talking politics around the coffeepots. Even the princes, some of whom showed signs of unrest that unnerved the Sultan when he had just ascended the throne, now settled down to doing business and piling up money. They flew, like arrows from a bow, to trade, real estate, contracting, and speculation, becoming richer than everyone else in the country, then competing among themselves to see who could accumulate the most, and build palaces to inflame the others with jealousy. When a particularly beautiful girl came of age in Mooran, one raced the others to marry her, to fill Mooran with talk of nothing but him and her from the day the wedding date was announced. The wedding itself would turn the city upside down, turning the night into day with lights and rivers of gold, tables of food that seemed never to end, and gifts that beggared the imagination.

The doctor had told himself from the beginning that nation building required, in addition to the right tools, a philosophy. While time and other purely practical considerations compelled him to give the tools priority, he had not missed a single night of thinking about the philosophy the state would rest upon, since *philosophy is the basis of thought and science,* as he said to himself, and he was the only person qualified to deal with that task. *A state without a philosophy is like a ship without a captain.*

Now that his tools were ready, that he had placed the right man in the right job and satisfied himself that their position was secure, he could no longer put off freeing himself to deal with the basic mission. This did not mean starting from zero as he had done in Harran, or when he first arrived in Mooran. The philosophy whose tenets he wished to anchor was already clear in his head, at times even too clear, too vivid. He needed no more than a few months, at most a year, to implement it. After spending a great deal of time thinking deeply about it, he concluded that he was indeed capable of achieving this task; that he inevitably must.

It was only natural that he could not discuss his thoughts now— perhaps not until much later on. Recording his ideas and subsequently preparing them for public study would require time and effort.

As to how this rare congruence had come about, and the doctor had reached such a point of contentment, he attributed it to a hidden force, or the "gray area" as he liked to call it—perhaps he would use that same term while writing up his philosophy. The hidden force defined, initiated and led, making everything possible for man. If they were worthy of it, and were able to look beyond today and tomorrow, to do whatever needed to be done, and to do it right, they could change their lives and make a new life of stability and permanence.

To combine these qualities properly, to be at the peak of the pyramid, especially after the Sultan had delegated some of his powers to him, while the princes kept busy with money, women and palaces, something bigger and better than shrewdness or luck, more important than competence, was at work, giving the picture dimensions and horizons he had not dreamed of.

After constant effort and unceasing, untiring perseverance, he arrived at the philosophy of the Four Centers, or the Square Theory. This was no whim, nor did it resemble anything the doctor had seen in the history books he had been poring over for two years. It was his own theory. Even if he did not care to make it public just now, because it would need followers and adherents first, it had been tried and tested until it was like a perfectly aimed bullet: it could not fail.

The Square Theory he dreamed of day and night, which had begun to fascinate him utterly, was summed up in the reliance of the basic controlling forces upon man. These forces were not good and evil, as commonly understood; they surpassed the mind alone, and the mere physical senses; they were something special. They were a combination of all forces, in extremely complicated forms and proportions. When the doctor wanted to relax, to feel happy and superior, he contemplated man, the predestined force: the forces that controlled him, whether he knew it or not, were the "centers." There were four centers, which started at the top and descended to about the middle. The mind was the seat of the intellect, the means of reasoning, and could be called, metaphorically, the first, or highest center. It defined and guided, working with the other centers. The second center was the heart. The heart was man's emotional life, the pole, filling the other centers and being replenished by them. Faith and conviction were born here, and a man was capable of no success without the vigor and power of this center. The third center was the stomach, because if a man was hungry, unable to regain his strength, his other centers would weaken. He might become dangerous. So this center was linked to the heart, so as not to leave it any more freedom of movement than the second center, and the others, allowed. The fourth center, much neglected by thinkers, was sexual energy; the doctor felt fortunate to appreciate its importance and power. It had been easy for him to supplement, he thought to himself, his study of the influence of this factor, when he was a student in Austria, and it was one of the reasons that made him take particular notice of the sexual drive, and to study and then specialize in venereal diseases.

He smiled when he thought about how he had conceived the Square Theory. "Newton discovered the law of gravity from a falling apple," he said, "and before him Archimedes made his discovery while bathing—that's how I discovered the Square Theory." Then contracting his forehead, and closing his eyes: "All things express their essence, in this theory: it rests entirely on four bases; a chair, for example, in order that everything be strong and balanced, stands on four legs; so does a table; so does a bed, and everything else. Not only that—if you think, you find that nature itself is based on the Square Theory. There are four directions, and four elements: earth, air, fire and water. Creatures are designed by the Square Theory: animals walk on four legs, and so does man." He laughed, because it did not seem clear at first; but a man's leg was made up of two joints: the thigh and the shin. The thigh was useless without the shin, so two were needed to make one. The result was four, leaving the arms aside—they were for balance. Man could not walk without them.

The doctor spoke at even greater length of the Square Theory. "A man's face and body depend upon the principle of Four: if you consider him lengthwise, you find that same principle applies: the right eye, the right ear, half the nose and half the mouth, truly divided, one buttock, and half the penis—that's four."

The doctor could have gone on forever talking about the Square Theory; he had arrived in Mooran on the fourth day of the fourth month, in the fourth season—spring. He saw this as yet another sign of his precious good luck which had helped him to discover the theory with such speed and depth.

The Square Theory did not come from history, though all of history pointed to it. It could not be considered the application of practical hypotheses and experiments, even though practical theories, especially in medicine, offered new support for this theory every day. Even man's achievements in the sciences of clairvoyance, astrology, astronomy and theology were such that the doctor could not disregard them. Even so, the Square Theory had nothing to do with any other science or theory. It was the result of inspiration, on one hand, and of sciences, ideas and profound contemplation on the other. Although as it was concerned with purely theoretical matters, the practical side was no less important or effective; perhaps the practical side was the chief reason for its having crystallized so quickly and brilliantly.

In the context of his coalescing ideas and the arrival of his theory, the doctor posed a simple question: What was humankind? He did not see the necessity of bringing all his intellect to bear on this particular question, so asked himself another: How must we deal with humankind? To arrive at an answer, step by step, he was able to form his ideas.

While it was true that he faced a great many exceptions in his research, he remained convinced, he told himself, that the exception proved the rule, as the saying went, and that a number of issues still required further study. He would get around to that soon.

39

"NOTHING IS HARDER THAN STARTING FROM zero—or more impressive, or more firmly rooted." This is the basis on which the doctor reviewed his achievements so far. He was happy as a child and exhilarated as a drunk, because once again another "worry" had been added to the burden of worries he already had. The Sultan, who had always insisted on attending the Agency meetings, now grumbled that "it's always the same old talk, time and time again," and promptly made the meetings monthly instead of weekly. Still later he contented himself with written reports of the proceedings, which he never read. He scrawled the word *Perused* on the cover in green ink and returned them. In the third year of his reign, when he seemed the picture of good health, he nevertheless asked the doctor to stand in for him as the overseer of the Agency, in addition to his other duties.

This decision was only a financial formality, since some of the proceedings that required the Sultan's consent or signature were frequently delayed due to his absence or his wish to "look it over," or the interference of Malik al-Fraih, the treasurer. Malik was more watchful over signatures and official seals than over the actual treasury, which had led, from very early on, to strained relations between him and the doctor. Now, after this decision, the doctor had a free hand in taking whatever action he deemed necessary with regard to any government agency, and "that Jewish usurer, that milkmaid's son, can pay and be hanged," as the doctor said proudly to himself, feeling that he had struck a powerful if not lethal blow against Malik al-Fraih.

Their relations had been marked, from the beginning, by silent rivalry, though there remained a surface cordiality, which they sometimes exaggerated, particularly since the two enjoyed extremely refined and gracious manners and shared the Sultan's friendship and secrets. Malik had preceded the doctor in Mooran by several years and considered himself a native Moorani, since his father or grandfather—he was a little vague, using general words that could be taken in different ways—had been compelled to travel, like so many other thousands of Mooranis, in order to do business—camel trading, in most cases. He did plan to return, but put it off; he married and settled down, had children, and time passed. When he died, his sons were in no position to travel or return home, so stayed where they were, "until the time came when our homeland needed us, and we wasted no time," as Sheikh Malik explained his return to Mooran. Once in Mooran, he profited from a distant and vague connection with the maternal side of the Sultan's family, and since he could read and do sums, even in his head, Sultan Khureybit took notice of him from the very start. Later on he formed a firm friendship with the crown prince and became one of his close confidants. When the prince ascended the throne, Malik was made assistant treasurer, and within a few months he became the actual treasurer.

Having returned to Mooran and attached himself to the palace, to the prince's entourage, Malik al-Fraih, or Sheikh Malik as he became known, put right an error he blamed on others; it did not take long to come to his notice and he set about amending it immediately: he returned to his family and his country and did his utmost to renew his connections with them: the accent, the clothes, the cool stare, familiarity with his relatives and family history. He recorded his family tree back to the seventh generation in an elegant album, and began to give his ancestors' names to his children, one by one. Every time his wife gave birth to a son, she spent a month or two arguing with him over the newborn's name, which she had never heard before, nor had any idea where he had unearthed it.

Sheikh Malik took these ideas as far as he could, to the point where many people who did not know his life story assumed that he had never left Mooran for a single day in his life. At other times, especially when he spoke to the doctor or Muti, it was impossible to distinguish him from any long-established native. He purposely spoke in the native dialect, with its restricted vocabulary and soft articulation, to show how well he knew it, and so that any listener would know that he was talking to foreigners, who could not have understood him otherwise.

The doctor had made a dogged effort to speak the Moorani dialect, but could not master it, and sounded ridiculous, even mocking, to those who heard him try. Before long he was forced to give it up, and he never lost his bitterness over this. In an indirect way of getting back at Sheikh Malik, he abandoned his own accent and spoke only classical Arabic, exaggerating its already stately pronunciation to the point where people hearing him for the first time took him for a preacher, or thought he was trying to be funny. As time passed, however, his speaking improved, and everyone except foreigners and those meeting him for the first time were used to it.

It was easy for the two men to coexist in Mooran, they and so many thousands of others before them, since the city offered so many opportunities to divert and occupy them; it would have been possible to smooth over the feud between the two if some sign of it actually manifested itself, but this did not happen. It was exactly the opposite. Even so, the silent battle in the shadows never paused for a day, taking on subtle forms that appeared entirely innocent. Sheikh Malik never referred to the doctor, but tried to ignore him, to diminish his importance. On the other hand, if it was a financial matter, he was strict and painfully precise before releasing any funds, and always waited until the last minute, to prove to the doctor the extent of the power and authority he enjoyed.

The doctor still showed total disdain for money; he did not want his feud with the "milkmaid's son," as he privately called him, to be in this area: *that usurer will pay, sooner or later; he just wants me to cringe in front of him, to kiss his beard. Forget it!* The doctor was positive that if he played Sheikh Malik's game he would be the loser, because *he just wants me to yield, to give in, and after that there's no going back. It would just go downhill from there, giving in time and time again. That's what he wants, that's how he's planned it, but I know him, and time is long—we'll see what happens.* So the doctor was filled with resolve, bordering on contentiousness, to stand firm and ignore Malik, and to give in to no pressures at all. When the specter of the "milkmaid's son" floated through his mind, he would say, "Is there any madman on the face of the earth who would go to a starving, anemic, syphilitic dog and try to wrest a bone out of his mouth?" He would chuckle menacingly. Since Mooran's wealth was all the Sultan's, the doctor did not try to please or flatter Sheikh Malik. *You turn a horse's head in the right direction and he goes,* and therefore he went directly to the Sultan for everything he wanted. Not only that, the doctor felt above these matters—his responsibilities were far too grave for him to be concerned with, or curry the favor of that warden. *No matter how big he gets, a warden is there for you to tell him, "Bring me this," and he brings it. You tell him, "Come take this." But if you cringe and say, "Sir, could you give us this and this, you see, we're building a nation," he'll answer you, "I can't help you."*

In this way, and through the Sultan's orders, the doctor obtained all the money he needed all at once—for the newspaper, the Security Agency, and "gifts, honoraria and special expenses." Thus he was spared any arguments or embarrassments that would have befallen had he been obliged to submit to Sheikh Malik's wishes or policies.

Now that the Sultan had invested him with new authority, he was happier and more powerful than he had ever been, and began to make new plans.

40

OORAN, ONCE SUNK IN INDOLENCE, INTRO-
spection and apathy, began to stir itself
and change: endless new styles of build-
ings sprang up and multiplied all over, streets sliced through the
city center and its outskirts, and not far from the Palace District, as
al-Ghadir was known, the remnants of the houses, walls and trees
now resembled ancient ruins left behind by a sudden earthquake.
There were throngs of new foreigners every day, who lost no time
in settling in for good. Jobs proliferated and overlapped, so that
one hardly knew whether to go on the next day with today's work
or to move to some other job. Life, in brief, had become rootless,
hard, and unstable, with no one knowing what would happen next.

Of course, it was very different from what had happened in Harran or Ras al-Tawashi, in Badra, Umm al-Awali or Ujra, because
every building put up here and every street laid out added to the
existing pile new piles, new ulcers, until Mooran resembled scat-

tered intestines, or heaps of refuse on this endless desert plain. The very sight sickened any native citizen, made him tense and sad, wondering whether, after all that had happened in this city he had known so intimately since first opening his eyes on the world, the city would ever go back to its former state, or at least ever be orderly and familiar again. Foreigners arriving in Mooran for the first time wondered—had its citizens lost their minds, to take their pickaxes and wreak vengeance against their own city, pitilessly demolishing everything in it with such haste? Even the engineers—they must have been engineers—who led these groups of people, and their equipment, here and there, so maliciously tearing up the districts of the city and smashing the houses, did one job and then withdrew, only to be back again, their faces full of confusion and frivolity; even when they had disappeared in the rubble, lost in the twisting lanes and crossings, still others arrived to carry on their work and begin anew nearby.

A city that had no pity on itself or its citizens: a mound of debris that rose higher every day. People looked around them, bewildered or gratified, but with a single wish: to get this all over with. Because the doctor saw Mooran through the planners' drawings, he saw transparently into the future, a pleasant city with trees; he did not see the inconvenience and suffering of the people around him. Two things interested him: real estate and philosophy. By day he never paused in studying the developers' plans with rapt enthusiasm. He did not hesitate to summon engineers from the municipality and the emirate to discuss the smallest details of Mooran's future. He had spent days and months virtually memorizing the plans, and sent his men "to help the needy on the city's outskirts," offering to buy the fallow land they owned there; he was prepared to pay enough money, on the spot, to enable them to start a new life!

After a day's long, hard work, the doctor went back to the Hir Palace to give a large part of his night to pondering his Square Theory.

Those who knew what the doctor was doing, or who heard about it—how he was looking day and night for poor people, to save them from their poverty, finding work for them in the municipality or the emirate—curled their lips skeptically.

Malik al-Fraih knew that the doctor would try to buy every piece of land in Mooran, alone or with other investors. "By God, by God, he won't leave a single inch of Mooran for anyone to be buried in!" he said through his nose, shaking his head. When his assistant came, after being summoned, and stood wordlessly, without moving, he looked at him a long time, still shaking his head, finally asking him, "And what do you think of what he's doing with other people's money?"

The assistant curled his lip but did not know how to answer.

> " 'The hungry eat of my provision, and cling to me,
> That it may be said I am generous, as I intend . . .'

"Then flee!" The sheikh exclaimed. When the assistant flinched and seemed ill at ease, the sheikh concluded, "Be frugal, my boy— don't pay out a single coin until his sweat is dry, whomever you're paying!"

Shamran al-Oteibi heard what the people were saying in the marketplace and in Zaidan's Coffeehouse. "Don't believe it, my friends," he said acidly, "I know all about him, he's just a shark, he snaps and sucks other people's money!" He spat on the ground and added after a moment, "If all generous people were like that, who would want any part of generosity!"

He changed his tone of voice, now sarcastic again. "And that Qasr al-Bir, that Camel Palace of his—if those walls could talk, what they couldn't say!"

Zaidan had been listening, and now said, "A coin spent on land like Qur'a or Hasiba will just die, Abu Nimr, but if it works it will breed more coins."

"Trust in God, my man—ill-gotten money is fire that burns whoever touches it, as we may live to see!"

Al-Ajrami and other Mooranis who had been surprised, then angered at seeing their city knocked down on their heads did not wait long before going to the palace to meet with the Sultan.

"What is more spacious than the desert, sir? And it's nearby— why can't they leave Mooran as our fathers and grandfathers did? If these foreigners and freeloaders who just got here yesterday don't like it, let them leave us alone, and leave Mooran as it is—we like it here and don't want any other place." Al-Ajrami paused before going on. "It's not just a question of Mooran, sir—those wicked people are trying to turn people away from the Islamic religion, and want to sow corruption. You must have heard about the papers they printed up and left in our houses!" Again he paused. "You, sir, are the protector of religion here and of us—you're the protector of the Muslims. We want you to cut them off with your sword and root them out!"

The Sultan smiled and spoke a few words, which most of them did not catch, which were: "Trust in God, my friends, and God willing, everything will turn out for the best."

The doctor was more than ever absorbed by his theory; it so happened that Muti's trips grew longer and more frequent, and Badri's absences were longer too. The doctor knew some of what went on but still missed a great deal; he did note that al-Ajrami attacked an enemy with the ferocity of a bull, unable to give in or retreat, ready to exploit any opportunity and make his case before anyone he might meet.

The Sultan was in the habit of making an excursion to the desert in the middle of the spring; it was very private, composed only of guards, the royal entourage, and members of the Sultan's family. Officials and advisers were excluded, and this year, as a result of his brother's pressure and their fears of threats to the whole Sultanate, not merely the Sultan himself, the Sultan agreed to be careful, to take no one outside the royal family into his confidence, and reduce the powers of his advisers, who "never have anything but bad news," as Prince Mahjam said.

Abu Misbah told the doctor, very clandestinely, some of what was happening, adding that "life is false—a harlot," and the doctor agreed, nodding, but said nothing. He felt the earth shake beneath his feet; he blamed himself for neglecting and forgetting so many things.

When Muti showed up looking uneasy and frightened, and told him that the Sultan had appointed another secretary besides himself, and that it was a man he would not get along with, the doctor shook his head and looked worried. He was silent for a long time. When Muti tried to get him to speak, he was sharp and gruff, and looked into the distance.

"The Sultan is a sultan, Muti, he isn't answerable for what he does; he gives life and death. Secondly, we are, like it or not, guests here, and while they may have been hospitable to us up until now, jealousy allows no one to live in peace."

"And he wants everything done his way. I told him we have to decide which duties are whose, and to share the work, but he said, 'I have to know about everything, even if someone brings a glass of water in to the Sultan.' We can't agree on anything."

"Leave him alone."

"But he'll leave me nothing!"

"It's enough if he leaves you alive!"

"Is this why we came to Mooran, Uncle? So that we could stay alive, to eat and drink?"

"No, we are here for much more important reasons."

"So why are we doing nothing now? Why are we just accepting this?"

The doctor laughed coarsely as several ideas and notions flitted through his mind; he had an impulse to tell Muti everything about the Square Theory, but the time did not seem right, and he was not in the right mood to explain it fully. His gaze fixed on a distant point, beyond the walls, and he said, "Listen, Muti . . ."

He faltered and almost forgot what he wanted to say. The silence extended over them like the lid of a tomb. He went on.

"A lot of things you learn when you're young you think of as absolutely certain, unquestionable, but life teaches you that that kind of certainty is just an illusion."

Muti thrust out his lip to show that he was not very much interested in this; he did not understand a word of what had been said, but the doctor continued.

"A straight line, for example—no one disputes that it's the shortest distance between two points. If I asked you now, you'd give me the same answer everyone else repeats."

For a few moments Muti thought his uncle was raving, that what he was saying had nothing to do with the attack that beleaguered them now. The doctor paid him no heed.

"I'm the only person, or one of the few, who says that a straight line is not the shortest distance between two points—in fact, it's the longest way to go."

"What has that to do with our problems, with what we're talking about, Uncle?"

"Everything."

"I don't understand."

"Take your time, and you'll understand everything."

Muti raised his hand a little nervously, a gesture that said he thought his uncle was mocking him. The doctor kept talking.

"This is the first thing I want you to remember and never, ever forget, and the second thing too: learn never to get angry."

"By God, Uncle, I've made up my mind to pack up and go."

"That's what they want you to do, it's what they're pushing us to do, but we'd be making a big mistake to do what they want or what they expect. We have to do what we want, what they do not expect."

"To tell you the truth, Uncle, I'm not convinced. This is something I've done for you, and if it weren't for the respect I have for you, I wouldn't have stayed a single day."

"Give me another chance, Muti, and you won't regret it."

"What do you want me to do?"

"To be convinced that a straight line is not the shortest one, and that anger, or a show of anger, means losing half the battle in advance." The doctor was silent, then spoke in a different tone of voice, as if he had been preparing for this for a long time.

"Until now we've been in an exploratory phase, preparing for the days to come. If there is any stupidity in our enemies, their basic stupidity is not that they hate us—that's understandable, to be expected, and has never been out of my mind for a single moment—no, their real stupidity is that they're moving against us openly, in small battles. In other words, they've plunged into a war before the war actually exists. We, from this moment, don't acknowledge that a war's been declared, though it will be fought against us constantly. If we want to fight, we have to fight at a time and in a way they don't expect.

"This is half the proof of the straight line theory—the other half of the proof is that indirect wars, the wars among them, privately, with us not letting on whom we support, can spare us from getting into wars we'd have been in. Let there be a thousand wars, but our war is the last one—the last one for the victor!"

The doctor sank into a blissful silence, apparently delighted by his words. Muti understood and yet did not understand—he was more confused than before, not knowing whether to continue this frivolous conversation with his uncle or merely to let him go on talking.

"There's a big difference between what you're saying and the way things really happen," said Muti pointedly.

"Anger, irritability—they make a man seem naked, all his weak points exposed; the weapons he wants to use are exposed. His enemies can make him stand before their guns in the open air. So from this point on we must learn how not to be angry, or at least how to contain our anger, so that they won't know how we will act."

The doctor laughed as he remembered.

"More than twenty years ago, in Germany, I learned this lesson well. I was boarding with two other fellows in an old lady's house. She had a gray cat, which she adored, and she used to treat us according to how well we treated the cat. If you loved the cat and petted it, she liked you and looked after you; if you ignored the cat, she ignored you; if you bothered the cat or gave it a dirty look, you might last a month boarding there, but not a second month. Unfortunately I've never really liked cats, though I don't actually hate them either—I just leave them alone. I didn't know how strongly this woman felt, and she never spoke to me, and the cat stayed away from me. But Hans, who lived there and seemed enchanted by this cat, was treated royally and enjoyed privileges no one else did.

"Several times I argued with Hans over the cat—he'd throw her at me, or put her in my bed.

"One day the cat disappeared. Hans and I were in the house when the old woman went out for a while, and when she came back and didn't find the cat, she pounced on me and asked me angrily where I'd put her or what I'd done to her. I told her I knew nothing about it, that I hadn't seen her. Hans came in just then and smiled at me, and his smile and the way he looked at me, as if announcing that I was the criminal—that's how he was able to achieve his goal.

"Three days later, because of police reports and the testimony of eyewitnesses—the old woman and Hans—I found myself on the border with Austria, and that's where I completed my studies. That was how I learned not to get angry, or rather how not to show my anger until the time was right."

The doctor told this whole story to himself, to give himself courage and the proper frame of mind in which to face this new phase. Muti seemed convinced, or pretended to be, and decided privately to wait a short while; if things improved, and began to go his way, he would stay. Otherwise, he would feel no obligation to fight battles that meant nothing to him; furthermore, he felt sure that his uncle was taking unnecessary risks and certainly going too far with these losing battles.

41

THE DOCTOR LOST NO TIME PUTTING HIS
theory aside. While he had seemed for a
time satisfied, convinced that he had
closed in on some basic laws, he was disappointed not to have applied these laws. His theory, any theory, was meaningless until its
dimensions could be explored through application and practice.

When the Sultan appointed a new secretary without consulting
him, without even telling him, the doctor realized that things were
worse than he had imagined. There was a rumor going around
that a hospital might be established solely for royal use, and that
Dr. Muayad al-Daqqaq had been summoned two days in a row to
discuss it with the Sultan. The Sultan had mentioned none of this
to the doctor, who now was inclined to worry.

When Muayad al-Daqqaq was actually named to the post of
Royal Physician, the doctor decided not to consider him an enemy
or rival, "because he's just a doctor, and I'm something more—I'm

the Sultan's friend, his best friend. I have his balls in my pocket. Plus, I'm the adviser who does his thinking for him, his companion, and his private secretary. Most important of all, I understand how he thinks and what he wants . . . and that's the main thing."

The first thing the doctor did, with the obstinacy of a child, was to make friends with the new doctor. "If they want to provide me with an enemy, to stab me in the back, as Abu Misbah told me, I'll show them that they've miscalculated—that I can just pull the knife out of my back, as dervishes do."

His other idea, which he acted upon with great care and craft, was to make friends with anyone he considered a friend of al-Ajrami, since his own friendship with the Sultan did not mean that he had to hate or forget everyone else. He was a little rueful that he had not attached any importance to forming friendships with them—except with Prince Mayzar and Prince Rakan—in years past, but now he consoled himself by thinking, "Time waits for no man." He remembered what Badri al-Mudalal had said, not to put all his eggs in one basket, and laughed—"that illiterate chatterbox knows more than wise men. His life and travels taught him much." As to the enemies who had launched their war against him, he must not give any sign that he heeded their warning, indeed that he knew anything at all or was preparing for anything.

Al-Ajrami needed another Ajrami, as Muti had told him a long while ago; and this is what he would be. And there was Ibn Shaheen, who had visited the doctor twice and hinted broadly that he needed certain "restoratives" to regain his strength. The doctor had pretended not to understand, and said, to appease him, that he would refer him to another doctor, a friend of his, who was a specialist in gerontology and would "put him right." Now Ibn Shaheen was essential to him. The restoratives he needed were not merely to help him in marrying for the sixth time, but, most importantly, to help oppose al-Ajrami.

He did not summon Ibn Shaheen; he did not ask about him directly. He waited until he came to the palace one day. In front of the Sultan, with consummate craft, he asked him about certain religious matters. That was all Ibn Shaheen needed to talk, to speechify, for an hour, as if he were giving a Friday sermon, citing Koranic verses and ascribing sayings of the Prophet. The doctor nodded humbly, showing his support, and carefully chose his moment to speak.

"The Sultanate needs a Sharia College and learned people like you, Abu Muhammad."

This was the beginning, and the lure he used, so that instead of having to pursue Ibn Shaheen, the opposite happened. Within a few days Ibn Shaheen came to visit the doctor in the palace, and after some small talk, he asked him about the "sublime idea" he had suggested—what exactly he had meant and how it could be. The doctor went on at great length detailing his suggestion and said that if it were acted upon it would create generations of believers, building lofty edifices for religion on firm ground—unlike the present time, "with ignorance of religion spreading, its banner carried by people ignorant of the fundamentals." On his second visit two weeks later, the doctor spoke not only of a Sharia College; he asked solicitously about Ibn Shaheen's health and smiled, and at one point went over and opened a drawer and withdrew a bottle of medicine, which he handed to Ibn Shaheen.

"The restorative you asked for some time ago. I didn't forget it, Abu Muhammad, but then I didn't have it. Here it is—try it and let me know. I hope it has the desired effect."

Ibn Shaheen went home feeling young in his war and his pleasures, and in his nights as well. He needed no encouragement, no one to tell him what to do. The doctor was afar, watching, listening. Mooran, which so loved rain and war, had this year exchanged late rains for a cockfight. This fight took place everywhere and at all times: "Al-Ajrami doesn't know the letter *alif* from a stick. He barely qualifies as being among the living." "Ibn Shaheen's balls have befuddled him—he's missed out on this life, and he'll miss the afterlife, too, the poor bastard." "You tell a blind man, 'Look, the road's uphill—save your shoes and ride a donkey that knows the way!'" "Any idiot knows not to put a snake in the trash—when the weather turns warm he'll see why—we all will." "Al-Ajrami calls me a snake? Tell him a snake that grazes and lies is better than a snake of straw!"

Their battle dragged on and grew more complicated. The doctor pretended to take no notice; when he heard anything about it he evidenced surprise, and if it died down for a single day he said something to rekindle it. The stories that spread from al-Qil'a to Sabi and from Souq al-Halal to al-Awali soon reached the coffee-houses and homes of the city, growing like desert sandstorms with each retelling, aided by the fact that each man had qualities that could scarcely be exaggerated by caricature. Even so, the towns-people did embroider the stories as they told them, making each man smoke and smolder and finally burst into flames.

The ribald jokes that Ibn Shaheen was constantly telling were now amended to apply only to al-Ajrami, and his listeners laughed as hard as when they heard them the first time. Al-Ajrami re-sponded to the jokes and stories with angry curses. He went too far, lumping all together those who told the jokes and those who listened to them or laughed at them, and thus demonstrated his loss of the battle day after day.

The Sultan had heard some of what was going on, and it made him laugh. One night he asked the doctor whose side he was on.

"The two gentlemen, Your Majesty, are like the fingers of a hand," was the doctor's calm and calculating reply. "What's the dif-ference between one and the other?" He paused. "Of course, Mooran does need a Sharia College. If Ibn Shaheen runs it today, someday he'll die and leave it to al-Ajrami and that's the end of the problem."

Sharia College was founded in Mooran, and its first president was Ibn Shaheen, but he lived to a ripe old age, so al-Ajrami did not give in.

"Just as you said!" said the doctor to Muti not long afterward, delightedly, as he followed the cockfight. "Nothing blunts steel but steel!" Muti only stared at him. "One day you told me: nothing will solve the al-Ajrami problem but another Ajrami, and now you see what's happening between al-Ajrami and Ibn Shaheen!"

Muti was shocked—he had never guessed that his uncle was be-hind what was transpiring between the two men.

"Pride smashes pride. Each of them is rottener than the other."

"This is what you have to understand!"

The doctor began to explain his point of view again, somewhat differently.

"If al-Issawi asks you not to give the Sultan so much as a glass of water without reporting to him, let him bring all the water to the

Sultan. If he wants to discuss the genealogy of the bedouin with the Sultan, don't interfere. If he wants to spend more time visiting with the Sultan, don't compete. The important thing is for you to do things that no one, not Issawi or anyone else, can do. Don't compete with him in the place and time that he wants, where his strengths lie. Let him try to catch up with you in matters he knows nothing about and can't learn. Let him run until he's dead tired, and when you're sure he's weaker than you he'll submit to you. But don't push him to the breaking point."

Muti was tempted by the idea, but he did not see how to put it into practice. In an effort to have the doctor make the phosphorous in his mind glow, as the doctor liked to say of his inspired moments, he said provocatively, "Uncle, Abu Ghazwan, Issawi is no al-Ajrami!"

"Don't talk nonsense—Issawi is smaller than a louse's leg, and you're drowning in an inch of water!"

"I am?"

"Yes, you."

"No, you're wrong, Uncle."

"No, sir."

"So you don't know me!"

"I know you by heart." The doctor laughed and added, "Listen, Nephew, the proverb says that no one thinks he has enough money but everyone thinks he has enough brains. Issawi is like al-Ajrami—even smaller. He's in a hurry. After he and his family heard that the world was changing, and which direction the money was coming from, they broke into a run. Leave them alone, don't get in their way; wait in a corner, wait for the right time. Even if they make a mistake, if they fall, don't strike. It's better—wiser—for someone other than you to deal the blow, and it must be lethal."

"By God, Ibn al-Issawi, I'll show people what you are!" said Muti between his teeth. He looked happy as a child, as if he had finally achieved what he wanted.

"No, my boy, no—if you start out with that attitude you won't get there." The doctor smiled. "Plant a mine in every corner, in every word, and sooner or later the lamb will step on one, and it will explode. You didn't see it happen or know anything about it—this is what I tried to teach you about the straight line!"

The uncle and nephew had no deep discussion or argument. Each went his own way to plan patiently, to weave a thread as complex as a spider web. Issawi might escape one thread, but he would get caught in another, and surely fall.

42

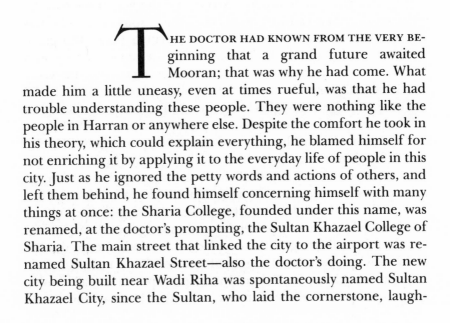

THE DOCTOR HAD KNOWN FROM THE VERY BE-
ginning that a grand future awaited
Mooran; that was why he had come. What
made him a little uneasy, even at times rueful, was that he had
trouble understanding these people. They were nothing like the
people in Harran or anywhere else. Despite the comfort he took in
his theory, which could explain everything, he blamed himself for
not enriching it by applying it to the everyday life of people in this
city. Just as he ignored the petty words and actions of others, and
left them behind, he found himself concerning himself with many
things at once: the Sharia College, founded under this name, was
renamed, at the doctor's prompting, the Sultan Khazael College of
Sharia. The main street that linked the city to the airport was renamed Sultan Khazael Street—also the doctor's doing. The new
city being built near Wadi Riha was spontaneously named Sultan
Khazael City, since the Sultan, who laid the cornerstone, laugh-

ingly told the project foreman that he would leave it to him to think of a fitting name for the city. Thus within three years of the Sultan's reign innumerable places bore his name in Mooran and through-out the country. No city or village lacked a school named for him, or a street or square.

The doctor's crowning ambition, however, in cooperation with Muti, was in the press: "the field, Nephew, where no one can begin to compete with us." He chose new sites for the newspaper and the magazine, in Rawdh Square, and replaced the old presses with the newest and most modern ones imported by Rateb from Germany. These were not confined to printing newspapers, but were put to use for many important commercial projects.

At first the princes, the Sultan's brothers and other relations were afraid of the doctor and other advisers, but presently they forgot them as they involved themselves in more important mat-ters. The land around Wadi Riha, some of which served as Moor-an's refuse dump, with others given to grazing and camel markets, was their main concern: who would acquire most of this land, and who would get the rest? There were also companies in the running.

Muti, meanwhile, polished the Sultan's image every day in his newspaper, with single-minded greed, and publicized some of the altruistic deeds and athletic events the princes sponsored. This was coordinated with the doctor, who was fascinated with this game and gave it a great deal of thought. He dreamed of writing a weekly column or article every few weeks, setting out and analyzing the Square Theory. He thought of serializing his memoirs. He did not entertain these thoughts long, since "our mission now is to con-solidate our position, to form some permanent alliances." His eyes had a dreamy look as he repeated the word "permanent." He did not define it or really know how much he meant by it, but in his heart he knew the strength of this word. He felt that the way to achieve this permanence now lay not in thinking about himself but about others: the Sultan and his power. As long as the Sultan's brothers held a share of power, he could not ignore them; he had to think about them, give them a place in his design, even though he knew what the Sultan thought of some of them, and what some of them thought of the Sultan. In any case, power was a complex game that had to be played by its own rules. He may have made mistakes in the past by letting people spread rumors about him or belittle him, like al-Ajrami and Ibn Fraih, or antagonize him, but this was his own fault. Man, any man, was only flesh and blood, a proof of the Square Theory (the Sultan was not, after all, the only one the theory applied to); the doctor had absentmindedly let some things get past him, and now it was time to put them right.

He would not squander his theory in newspaper articles, or let it appear distorted or fragmented. He would take great care to see it was presented to the public as clearly as possible, so that it would have the impact of a bomb. The common people would talk about it, those learning to read and write would learn it. It would be the topic of questions and commentaries, like any other major issue, but this would not exhaust it. He said to himself solemnly, almost sadly, *No, it would be more fitting for it to appear between the covers of a book, or a series of books, so that it doesn't get distorted, or become the talk of every mob of penniless morons and illiterates.*

So the doctor forged new ties with the princes, and so did Muti. True, it was done casually, or that is how it was supposed to look, but the ambition with which the ties were made, on all sides, could not be hidden. The third annual horse race in Mooran, which had previously been held in the desert, far from the townspeople and cut off from their participation, was now moved to Mooran, and sponsored by Prince Milhem. The doctor and Muti were guests of honor. The prince appeared welcoming and companionable and made every effort to make all his guests known to one another and to the horses, loudly made predictions about the race. He briefly pointed out the horses he owned, which had "run in Cairo and Alexandria and Beirut and won every time."

Muti jotted down some observations and asked the prince how many horses he had and which races they had won. He watched the race very enthusiastically. The next day he expressed his delight and appreciation in an article in the daily newspaper under the byline "An Observer," which was accompanied by several photos, with Prince Milhem appearing in each.

So it went with Prince Milhem, Prince Fawaz, Prince Rakan, Prince Munawar, and the younger and less important princes. Prince Milhem loved horses, but Prince Fawaz loved sports; he was the godfather of all sports in the whole Sultanate. He had spent a year and a few months in Cairo and Alexandria, and marveled at the sporting events and their popularity; he played soccer in Cairo but was not really very good at it, perhaps because of his age or because he was poor at offense, as the trainer told him, but in any case he was impressed enough to found several sports clubs and to become the godfather and overseer of sports and sportsmen in Mooran.

The other princes, too, had their pastimes, which the doctor, with a great deal of patience and diligence, was able to discover. Prince Rakan, for example, loved just two things: prayer beads and fine robes. Because the prince loved the doctor, he often invited him to his farm outside Mooran, where they had long talks about language and Islamic law and became close friends. Prince Rakan suggested that the newspaper reprint "Alfiya Ibn Malik" so that everyone could benefit, but did not insist.

When Widad was planning her visit to Damascus and Beirut that winter, the doctor ordered her to buy several sets of prayer beads, wrote her a note giving the types, color and number of beads so that she wouldn't forget, and told her to give the note to Rateb, "and tell him to do whatever he has to do to get them—these are for the highest-level authority." He also told her to buy two cloaks, "of genuine goat-hair, one light, the color of fresh new dates, and the other one dark, the color of figs. Spend whatever you have to, Umm Ghazwan, because all these will pay for themselves." They laughed together, and she asked him to whom he would give the prayer beads and cloaks.

"To the lucky winner," he laughed. When she gave him a quizzical look, he said, "Right now I'm planning to give them to Prince Rakan, but when you get back with the things, we'll talk about it and see who deserves them!

"Do you remember a certain saying of the Prophet—I don't recall his exact words, but I remember the meaning," said the doctor in a deep, sincere voice, trying to convince both his wife and himself of this important point. "He said, 'Give gifts, for gifts bind hearts together,' or perhaps he said, 'bring hearts together' instead of 'bind' them. It's true—gifts don't just create love and affection, they open hearts and prepare them to understand and accept even the hardest things." He nodded decisively, sternly. "When you go on your trip, Widad, don't forget to bring whatever you can, and two of everything, like Noah, peace be upon him. That way if we need to give a gift, it will be there and we won't be caught short."

Widad had always bought things for the women of the palace on her trips abroad—things they asked her to bring, and others that she thought would make a fitting gift for this or that princess. She usually forgot, once having arrived back in Mooran, that she had bought these as gifts, and when anything reminded her or if she noticed a particular such piece, she thought, *They have enough things to last a lifetime,* and smilingly put it back.

Now the doctor was asking her to bring back mostly gifts and talking about prophets and religion—this was strange.

"You say, Abu Ghazwan, they'll appreciate these things?" she asked dubiously.

"Gifts are the shortest distance between two hearts, Widad." He smiled. "If you want to get, you have to give."

This was a lesson the doctor had learned well from Badri al-Mudalal and practiced with great shrewdness and grace. He did not overdo it by giving too many gifts, nor did he always over-charge them, nor did he talk about the gifts once he had given them. He had a very clever plan. He watched the princes with an eagle's eyes, listened with an ass's ears and detected scents like a cat. If a prince rested his eyes on other people's prayer beads, and asked what kind they were, he would receive from the doctor that very day a set of beads better than any he owned or had ever seen. If a prince loved perfumes and incense and was fastidious about his personal appearance, he would receive a small, elegant case containing bottles of cologne, with the doctor's own translations of the foreign labels. He wrote in a fine hand, quite unlike that of the prescriptions he wrote out, "aftershave," "light perfume for day-time," "evening perfume—for bed," "skin bracer," and so on.

For the princes' children, who had no special hobbies yet, the doctor sometimes brought sneakers, Faber pens, Kodak cameras, even, once or twice, small pearl-handled revolvers. He showed these to the Sultan first, since he thought the Sultan might want one. The Sultan showed his huge front teeth in delight, hefted a pistol two or three times in his right hand, aimed it, then hefted it in his left hand. The doctor saw that it was a good gift for His Majesty, and bowed his head slightly.

"I hesitated, Your Majesty, to offer it to Your Majesty," he said in a voice fraught with humility, "because your station is so far above such things, but if you accept it, I will never forget it as long as I live."

But no matter how subtle his choices of gifts, whether in the kind of gifts he chose or his timing in presenting them, he always encountered the threat of Badri al-Mudalal. Princes were the doctor's specialty, more precisely the senior princes; Badri al-Mudalal would not offer a gift to a prince at this time, perhaps did not even think to, and yet the gifts he produced from his box, with the cunning and skill of a magician, were the talk of old and young alike.

The toy pistols, the pop guns he brought on his last brief visit to Beirut to buy colognes and scissors for His Majesty, and gave out to the Sultan's children, created twice the stir that the doctor's real pearl-handled revolvers had. Badri always bought toys from a friend of his in Bhamdoun, whom he told to reserve for him the best and newest toys. He chose from his selection and brought them every summer, then chose carefully what he would give to whom. These toys were the talk of the whole palace, and from there word got out to the princes' palaces, until all Mooran was talking about them: snakes made of rubber, scorpions that clacked along, driven by a spring mechanism, matches that sputtered and gave off beautiful odors and different colors. Adults were even more thrilled than the children. They beguiled the long, wakeful nights at the Ghadir Palace and other palaces, and gave rise to stories that were retold for days afterward: how, for example, Ibn Shaheen sat down on a snake and then leaped up, terrified, and ran out of the room, or how Ibn Khamis lit his cigar with a match that gave off a horrible smell, or how Ibn Mashat's beard caught fire when he lit his clay pipe.

Badri brought the sparklers and the fireworks and gave them out three days before Coronation Day, which led to a night Mooran would never forget. The blasts grew ever louder, and the sky was so filled with color that everyone in the city saw it—then the air was filled with gunshots. This was unplanned and unexpected, but it turned the night into a festival that lasted until the early morning hours, while everyone had their hopes and expectations for this anniversary of the king's enthronement.

The fireworks brought on the firing of all the firearms in

Mooran, which led to some soldiers deciding to fire off some bigger guns as a token of their joy and participation, which gave the doctor the sudden idea of recommending that the army and police be kept on a state of alert, so that they would not use their weapons.

To the doctor, the threat was that strong and that real, though Badri al-Mudalal was unaware of it—had no thought whatever, in fact, of provoking or challenging the doctor—but this was the fact of the matter, and the doctor, who was inclined to Badri, and considered him a vital friend, was enraged by "this diabolical force that makes him act like a devil!"

When Badri proceeded to marry off one of his three daughters to the head of the Sultan's bodyguards and another to the second in command of the Mooran Police, the doctor sensed a direct threat.

"The son of a bitch!" he muttered. "We taught him how to beg and now he beats us to the doorways."

The doctor attended the wedding party at the special request of the chief of police, who told him that he couldn't consent to his deputy marrying any less well than the head of the royal bodyguards. The next day the doctor exclaimed bitterly to himself, *Badri's done it all now, the son of a bitch! He's the darling of the bedouin and the city people at the same time, the chief of police on his right and the head bodyguard on his left!* He laughed angrily. *God help us from his third daughter!*

That very night the doctor decided that he would let no one outdo him.

43

S AMIR CAESAR—HEIR OF ALL THE CAESARS, THE
doctor jokingly called him—was one of many
journalists who came to Mooran after being
hired by Muti on a visit to Cairo. Samir had been strongly recommended by Rateb, with whom he had struck up a casual friendship
a few years earlier, when Rateb had been spending some time in
Alexandria.

Samir's arrival in Mooran would never have caused any great stir
had it not been for a memorandum from the American embassy a
few months after *al-Badiya* began publication. The memo referred
to three articles in various issues of the newspaper, the first two of
which were signed "Samir al-Sarih," or "Candid Samir," and the
second with the initials S.C., with the offending paragraphs
marked in red ink. Furthermore, the embassy supplied information from unimpeachable sources—according to the chargé d'af-
faires, Paul Andrews—claiming that "this Samir Caesar spent
several years in prison in Egypt for political offenses."

This information, which caused the greatest consternation, would have been sufficient to deport any other person from the Sultanate, but not Samir. He had come on Rateb's recommendation, and he became extremely close to Muti and the doctor; *al-Badiya* would never have become as powerful as it was, or even been published in the first place, without his help. So as soon as the embassy's complaint was submitted, the doctor informed Muti of the new development, and they considered what step should now be taken—possibly even Samir's expulsion from the country.

"If he goes, I go," shouted Muti. "Keep that in mind, Uncle." The doctor stared at him. "Look, we've spent more than three months getting ready to bring out *al-Waha,* and everything depends upon Samir. As it is, *al-Badiya* can't survive without him."

The doctor nodded ruefully in agreement, which emboldened Muti to continue. "Those things they told you are old and blown out of proportion." His voice softened. "I've talked about those things with Samir. He told me that's part of the past, it's over and done with, and that he's sorry he wasted years of his life in childish political activities."

Subtly, placing a great emphasis on the perils of publishing the sort of articles the Americans were alluding to, and with constantly rising incentives, Samir began to take on new qualities, to become a person with no relation to what he had been. True, this was the result of a profound inner contentment and total readiness—and perhaps he had misrepresented himself in the past—more than it was the outcome of any discussion he had with the doctor, for both of them loved to talk philosophy, unlike "practical Muti," as the doctor called him, saying that he and Samir "spring from the same source, which is the source of all springs: philosophy."

When Rateb visited Mooran and the doctor asked him almost rebukingly why he had said nothing of Samir's political past or imprisonment, Rateb laughed.

"God bless you, Doctor, he's made a break from his past—it's a pity to remind him of it, to dig up that corpse from the grave and shove it in his face!"

The doctor showed him the newspaper clippings and pointed to the red markings, and said that the American embassy was upset.

"Forget it, chief," said Rateb testily. "The Americans are afraid of their shadows, they're afraid of anything red, and they don't like anyone with a past." He sighed and his tone of voice softened. "Doctor, you don't need anyone to tell you that someone with a past, who is willing to put that past behind him, is a thousand times better than someone else who wants to build his greatness on our backs!" He winked and smiled. "I'm not a child anymore, Doctor, and I'm not about to get you into any trouble or to get myself into any trouble. Trust me."

A few days later, at lunch, the doctor was instructing his youngest son to hold the knife in his right hand, "because the right hand is the stronger, and it's the one God prefers."

"Now I understand," laughed Rateb, who was lunching with them. When the doctor gave him a questioning look, he smiled broadly. "Because Samir uses his left hand you think he'll always be totally leftist."

"An ounce of prevention is worth a pound of cure." The doctor smiled back.

"Doctor, don't worry—you can rely on me. Samir can write with both hands!" They both laughed.

Rateb's prophecies and Muti's ultimatum were vindicated when the same embassy, during a meeting on journalism and its current role, praised the "clear direction of the Moorani press, which sets a firm, strong and influential pace in molding public opinion with regard to the king, in supporting moderate ideas and traditional religious and moral values." Paul Andrews was careful to cite articles by Abdelhadi al-Bakri and Sheikh Othman Ismail, as well as "Samir Caesar's recent articles," and he smiled exultingly as he said this.

Muti found himself reveling in this atmosphere; he read his success in the faces of these people, especially the palace people. He wanted an incisive and eye-catching press, so every day had to bring some provocative event: that was what attracted readers. The doctor's proverbs and all his philosophizing meant nothing to him except insofar as they could be made into light, entertaining formulas to catch the eye and arouse some curiosity; this was what made him put so much effort into the technical department, especially photography, "since Mooran today is so illiterate, and even the educated ones, who can read and write, have no time to read long analyses or pointless theorizing. Modern journalism must rely on pictures, on unusual things, and that will be the only measure of success."

What Muti had in mind to impose, and longed to achieve, was not the result of logic, since he had no interest in journalism. Everything he had heard while organizing the papers for publication, the discussions that had taken place in front of him, in many places, about the kind of press that was needed, that had to become reality, plus some of his own ideas, helped to formulate his general principles, though he was not able to put them into practice himself. All he had to do was to supervise.

This was how the special, close relationship sprang up between Muti and Samir—each of them felt that he complemented the other.

They met by pure chance. One summer, years before, in Alexandria, Rateb had stayed in the Pension Rogina, where he came to know Samir, who was related to the woman who owned the pension.

They met in Cairo, again by chance, when Rateb and Muti were looking for journalists to hire to work in Mooran.

"Building a national press is completely different from working with an existing press system," Samir told them when they asked if he could be of any help introducing them to journalists. "It requires exceptional abilities, and there aren't very many people who can create a really great press. I'm not saying it's impossible, but you have to start big, to have some big names, to make it powerful and influential."

He shook his head dubiously until they had a chance to digest this, then added a little sadly, "I have experience in setting up newspapers—I've done it before, with many papers, and I'd love to help you, but . . ." Their eyes were on him. "I have many great, pressing commitments at this time."

"For how much longer?" asked Muti uneasily but hopefully. "I mean—"

"And life in Mooran and other oil countries is so harsh—I don't know how anyone stands it." Again Samir shook his head dubiously. "There aren't very many journalists who'd want to work there—not very many at all." He adopted his former tone. "Though I suppose I could convince some of them, especially if the incentives are there."

After much give-and-take, subtle haggling and argumentation, and after Samir learned what all the benefits would be, he asked for two months in which to think it over.

"In two months I can fulfill most of my commitments here and get out of the rest of them, and I can get in touch with some of my colleagues and persuade them, one way or another, to work with us. It won't be easy, of course, especially since we want only the best people, senior journalists, but with the incentives you're offering, some of them might agree to go in with us."

Afterward he cursed himself. Asking for the two months was the stupidest thing he had ever done in his life. What if they went looking elsewhere and found others they liked better, and didn't even bother to call him back? Anything could happen within these two months, leaving him lost, confused, and even starving. Could they play a trick on him, could this really happen?

He could not sleep that night. He was lost in a state of confusion and failure—in his heart he wished he were less intelligent, so that when he was upset or lost something like this new opportunity, he would not have to pay the price of this useless intelligence. In his brief, broken slumbers he was back in prison, being tortured, as he had been in the early days of his detention. When he awoke suddenly, remembering what had happened, he decided to correct his error, to shorten that waiting period by at least a month or even more.

And that is what happened the next day. Samir kept his emotions under control and did not let his joy show, but Muti could not. He thought that cutting the wait from two months to one was an unforgettable sacrifice on Samir's part. He asked for time before coming to final terms. "I just need a chance to think, to think and study the project," and promised to do his utmost to contact other journalists. When he finally signed a contract, Muti felt that half has mission had been accomplished, and so as to leave no room for second thoughts, he paid him a generous sum immediately, unasked. At first Samir disdained taking this money, saying, "This is premature—we have an agreement based on trust, which is enough for me." Eventually he took the money on Muti's insistence.

These "final touches," as Samir called them, were essential. He laughed and rubbed his hands. "Rateb knows I have a prison re-cord—he has to stand by me." He suggested that they go to Alex-andria, "since we've finished our business." Rateb, who still remembered Alexandria, agreed eagerly, but when Muti hesitated, Samir suggested that they cut the month still shorter.

In Alexandria, Rogina kept Muti distracted while Samir ex-plained everything to Rateb, who shook with laughter.

"Look, everyone has something in his past, and with most people imprisoned for political reasons, the charges against them were trumped up or very weak." He added paternally, "Leave the past to God."

Once Samir arrived in Mooran, he worked well with the others, among them his close new friends, Muti and the doctor; he under-stood what each of them wanted, and did his best to help get it. He was friendly and articulate, and so began the game that was to have such a lasting effect in and around Mooran.

44

BEFORE THE SUMMER WAS OUT, UMM HOSNY suddenly arrived in Mooran with her daughter-in-law and grandchildren. It came as a surprise to almost everyone that either Hosny or Said were even married, that each of them had a family and children. People had never thought about it, or talked about such things with either of the men, as if they had given in to the life here, even though each of them went away at least once a year to spend a month or two with family.

When the welcome parties were over, Umm Hosny began to investigate, to listen to her two daughters-in-law in order to learn things her sons had not told her directly. She learned that something had happened between the two brothers, that Hosny wanted to move out into a house of his own, because he could not stand it. He said to himself sadly: *My heart told me long ago.*

She remembered how everything had been in Amman: the

sisters-in-law, children and men had clustered around her like a brood around a hen, and nothing ever happened without her say-so or approval. Now she felt that she had made a mistake, letting her sons travel off all alone, and a bigger one in letting them stay away all this time. So, with untiring patience, she tried to repair the damage done by time by using innocent wiles and little ruses, especially with the children. She paid each child to cling to his uncle, and bribed each of the women to look after her sister-in-law more than her husband. She could not tolerate the idea of the brothers parting ways to live in separate homes. One night as she was going to bed she muttered eerily, "You'll see me under the ground before I let you break up."

She was a little reassured to see her sons being kind toward each other, albeit quietly, and was convinced that things were back to normal. She had a persevering spirit borne of her troubles and refined by tribulation since her earliest orphan girlhood—shuttled from one house to another, then married off, while still a girl, to a man three or four times her age, whom she lived with for just two years, during which time she gave birth to Hosny, whom she named herself, since her husband died several months before the birth—which guided her steps and her life. Hosny was a new burden but a good omen as well, and she clung to him with deep love. She remarried and had Said one sweet year later, but felt still that her first boy was special and different; in later years this specialness remained obscure and hidden, because the burden of the three, in terms of food and other cares, was one.

So when as she arrived with her little tribe, after getting Hosny's letter begging her to come—their living conditions, he reassured her repeatedly, were excellent—she brought along some of the "trade" she plied in Amman. She brought frankincense, henna, sheets of dried pressed apricot from Damascus, dried okra tied with string, dried *moloukhiya,* and fine and coarse brushes. These and other small items were the stuff of the trade that brought in enough, "profit-wise," as she said, to pay the household expenses.

Her business varied with the places and seasons, with the whims of her customers and what they could afford. In summer, when vegetables were plentiful and no one needed dried vegetables, she peddled combs, scouring pads, and even samples of silk and woolen fabrics, not to mention prayer beads and all kinds of Damascene sweets. Other times she brought men's headropes, incense, and, with enough advance notice, cloaks and furs.

Umm Hosny traveled between Damascus and Amman, in those days, every three or four weeks. Inevitably she also brought several surprises. She was wily with her customers, whom she sorted into order according to her priorities. She never announced her arrival in town until she had organized her merchandise, then sent word to families before anyone else and received them first, always knowing when to bring out certain goods and for whom.

That was Umm Hosny for all the years she spent in Amman. Now, as she arrived in Mooran, despite the long distance and hard journey and Hosny's reassuring letter, which she had read to everybody, she still carried bundles of goods that she felt sure would be in demand. She chose them carefully and packed them to withstand the longest journey. Once she was settled in and reassured as to Hosny's circumstances, persuaded that everything was going well, she began to think of once again opening her house to receive lady buyers from among the neighbors. When she hinted about it, very indirectly, Said bellowed, "Please—anything but that!" When she looked frightened, he explained, "If word of that got around Mooran, it would mean we'd be out, Mother—we'd pack our bags and leave!"

She stared at him in surprise.

"People in Mooran deal with us as big businessmen," he whispered. "We import from all over the earth. We never make small deals. If we start selling candy and chewing gum to every scullery maid, and wooden clogs and house slippers, you'll see, people will look down on us—we'll be ruined!"

His mother did not understand what he was trying to say. Very patiently and calmly, with unswerving assurance, he explained that they enjoyed wealth and prestige, that she was a woman of rank, higher than all the women of Mooran; and that the sort of trade she wanted to ply would be highly detrimental. He impressed upon her that the Mooranis were different from people in Amman and Damascus and that she would have to behave differently with them.

"What about all the henna and frankincense and powder that I lugged over here?" she asked.

"Take ten necklaces for it—just get rid of it!" This was what Said said to try to kill the scandal before it started.

"Don't you think the women in this town use henna on their hair? Don't they use powder? Or chew gum?"

"They do all that."

"Fine, so what are we afraid of?"

"We're not afraid of anything, but that isn't our business."

"So whose business is it?"

"Mother, Haja, when you've spent a few months here you'll see why, you'll see what these people are like."

"I have to wait all these months? What about the merchandise I brought?"

"Forget it all—bury it and forget you ever brought it!"

"And my happiness, my son, can that be buried?"

"In this country you can bury anything—people, happiness, even honor. What's important are appearances. We can't afford a mistake, Haja!"

Umm Hosny understood what her son was saying, but she was not persuaded. Hosny, at least, had not changed; success had not spoiled him; the clothes he wore, except for his Friday best, were just what he used to wear years before in Amman. He was more devout than before, not less, and his eating and sleeping habits were more modest. Said, on the other hand, had become a different person, one she did not recognize, but she comforted herself by saying that this was a phase, just a youthful phase, and that he would come back to his senses, or his senses would come back to him, as always happened with him after every crisis or misfortune.

The old woman agreed reluctantly but did not give in; all the primitive genius within her was fired up, as with animals. She knew how to cut her path, how to break the siege around her, and thus within a few weeks she set out, as an earthworm does, and amid the shadows of Mooran that enshrouded every woman there, she was able to find her way.

U MM HOSNY TOLD SAID SHE WAS ABOUT TO
burst with boredom; she was sure she was
dying. "My heart, my boy, is like a little
bird flapping in my chest," she said, pointing to her chest, then put
on her wide cloak and went out.

She walked. She did not know which direction she was heading
in, or toward what. She looked at the buildings and at the people,
from behind her thick wrap. Everything she saw was alien, like
nothing anyplace she had ever been before. She saw people buying, selling, shouting, screaming and laughing, and suddenly, after
hours of walking, she did not know where she was. She was thirsty
and craved a drop of water; to rest in the shade of a tree or a wall.
And all at once she found herself someplace else: in the palace.

That is how she first told the story of the time she went to the
palace alone. Later on she claimed that she had watched carefully,
so that she would not forget, the route their car took her and the

doctor's wife on their first visit to the palace. She said that she remembered the landmarks the second time. She left out the thirst
and the drop of water, her weariness and her wish to rest in the
shade of a wall or under a tree.

No sooner had she reached the palace than a black slave stood in
her way and told her to go away. Then he asked her whom she
wanted, and she remembered that she wanted to meet the Sheikha.
He asked her if the Sheikha or anyone else in the palace had invited her, and she replied that the Sheikha herself was expecting her.

The doctor's wife told a different story.

"That creature was almost the death of me! Every day, every
other day, she'd be trying my patience: 'Please, Umm Ghazwan,
you and your husband are the best, there's no one like you two. I
must go to the palace and get to know the women, and no one but
you can take me there.' So I don't say anything, but can she keep
quiet? I should be so lucky! She hangs on me like a leech. 'We're
family, dear, we're friends—we have no one but you. Without you
we'd never have come to Mooran, never have seen it, and if you do
someone a good turn you should finish the job.' So I ask her, 'Why
the palace, Auntie? Whom do you need in the palace—what would
you do there?' And she answers, 'Nothing but a little friendly chat,
just to see the palaces and the palace people for myself.'"

The doctor's wife sighed and went on. "A day might go by without her coming, but she'd come the next. 'Umm Ghazwan, I'll kiss
your hand, your foot, just take me to the palace.' I said to myself,
the same way she kept after her son until she got her way, this old
lady is not going to leave me alone, she'll cling to me.

"Anyway, we made a deal. I told her, 'Tomorrow,' and the next
day here she comes, all decked out, made up, henna on her hair,
snapping gum in her mouth—she has no teeth, mind you—'Oh,
God, Umm Ghazwan, I'm late, Umm Ghazwan, do you think
they'll be mad at us if we're late, Umm Ghazwan?' So we left. When
we are in the car she takes and clutches my hand and gives me a
piece of frankincense and says, 'Chew it, Umm Ghazwan!' and
laughs. After a little bit she turns and whispers, 'So that your
breath will be sweet in case they come up close or kiss you.' When
we get to the inner gate of the palace, a woman comes out to greet

us and Umm Hosny *attacks* her in front of the servants—hugs and kisses, hugs and kisses. They didn't know what to make of it—their eyes were wide open—'What's going on? Who is this?' They began to laugh and stare at her, looking at one another. I didn't know where to look, I was so embarrassed, I was covered with sweat, I didn't know where to look or what to say. I told them, 'Umm Hosny is our relative—she was so anxious to come and pay her respects.' They said, 'Welcome!' and nothing else. She was like a cretin; she stared them in the face and laughed. When the Sheikha, Ummi Zahwa, came out, she lost her senses—she left the rest and attacked *her*. She got into her like a cat, and you know the Sheikha's old and frail and dizzy, and this was just the beginning."

Umm Hosny did not hear Widad's version of the story, and no one dared repeat it to her. She had her own completely different account.

"After my first week in Mooran, the doctor's wife—I forget her name, the girl from Tripoli—visited. No, if I'm not mistaken, her name is Widad. She came to pay her respects and invite us to the banquet the doctor was having in our honor. After a little chat I told her, 'My dear, I'm not used to parties—couldn't the boys go in my place?' She said, 'Absolutely not, I don't want to hear that kind of talk—if you don't come, I'll be upset and so will the doctor. After all, the banquet's in your honor, it's for dear Umm Hosny!' So in the end all my begging off did no good; I went. Everyone ate—the food was all catered, she had nothing to do with it, she never cooked one dish. I didn't eat a thing, but I didn't let anyone notice. Anyway, after the meal she said, 'Umm Hosny, you've been here more than a week now, and apparently the palace people are offended, they're upset. I suggest we visit them today—the doctor agrees.' So I told her, 'My dear, I'm an old woman, I have nothing to say—what would I talk about with them?' She tells me, 'A one-hour visit, that's all, I'll come by with the car to pick you up, we'll go together, and once we've all said hello, you don't have to say anything unless they ask you—just leave it all to me.'

"Well, I was confused and worried to death, and I couldn't sleep. I tossed on my bed, and the whole world asleep around me, and said to myself, Be sensible, Umm Hosny, stay home—don't go out anywhere; if anyone cares that much about you they can come here to visit. If you go flitting around from house to house, people will think you're a meddlesome old fool, running around like you have no house of your own. If only they were normal people, like everyone else—but they're princes and kings, and even if they like you or want something from you they look down on you, as if you were a beggar, trying to beg from them.

"Anyway, I never did get any sleep. I was worried to death. Finally I said, let it be God's will. I got up and said my prayers and went back to bed and slept. And the nightmares I had! I was in the middle of a crowd of people, and they were all pulling at me and hitting me and saying, 'That's her!' I woke up terrified, and washed and prayed again, and vowed to God that if I got through this day I'd fast for three days. I sat out on the balcony shelling beans after I had a little food and a cup of coffee. I don't know how I decided to turn the cup over and read my fortune. Before the grounds were dry, and before I finished shelling the beans, the doctor's wife arrives. 'Let's go, let's go, Auntie, I sent word to the palace and they're expecting us.' I told her, 'Sit down, my dear, relax and have some coffee, we never got a chance to talk yesterday with all those people around.' 'We can talk in the car—I've had my coffee,' she says. 'We have to get going now because they're expecting us.' 'My dear,' I said to her, 'I really don't want to go.' 'Oh, no!' she says, 'I'll be angry with you and so will they!' She went on insisting until I gave in to her. I put on my cloak and ran along behind her. We rode in the car—it flew. I don't know where it went or how it went, it got us there in the wink of an eye. I was dizzy and my heart was pounding and my tongue was like a piece of wood until we got to the palace.

"And this they call a palace, I thought—this is what all the fuss is about? I said to myself, the Muftis' house in Damascus is a thousand times better. The Hayeks' house or the Tabbases' in Amman is a thousand times better, too. This place was nothing but high walls, mud walls, and not a spot of green anywhere, not one plant. The rooms were depressing—so dark—and the whole place smelled. I thought, alas for these palaces and those that have to live in them. I looked here and there: everything was filthy dirty and black—God knows, the place may never have been cleaned. My heart sank—I began to wish I had never listened to her, never set foot in the place, but ... A coal-black woman told me, 'Have a seat'—it was like an order, you'd have thought I killed her father, and she pointed to a pile of mattresses. I sat down. I was afraid and nauseated, as if I were sitting on fiery spikes. The black woman went away, leaving me and Umm Ghazwan. I looked at Umm Ghazwan, and all around me, and just felt sick. I figured, if you want to be friends with princes, you have to put up with their crudeness and dullness, and I was thinking like this when the door opened and out came four or five women. I stood up and greeted them, but, I swear to God, you couldn't tell the princesses from the servants. They all looked alike: sallow and emaciated, positively bloodless. I was shaking with fear and surprise—one of them asked me something, but I didn't understand her. Umm Ghazwan told her, 'Umm Hosny is our relative—the doctor loves her like his own mother, and our joy at her arrival in Mooran is rivaled only by our joy in knowing you—so I thought you should get acquainted— it's always nice for nice people to get to know one another.' "

Umm Hosny rested a moment, bringing back the confused mass of memories and events, then went on in a voice made smoother by a swallow from a glass of water. "That might have been my first and last visit if the Sheikha hadn't come in. They all became quiet, and if a pin had dropped you would have heard it. I said to myself, all mothers, all princesses, should be like this: her eye had a spark that could melt stone, and her forehead glowed like the dawn. She looked so strong and dignified—almost superhuman. She greeted me and sat down, but never took her eyes from me, and my heart bounded. She asked me a question, I asked her a question, and we found things in common, as if we had known each other forever."

46

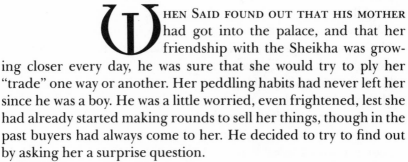

W HEN SAID FOUND OUT THAT HIS MOTHER
had got into the palace, and that her
friendship with the Sheikha was grow-
ing closer every day, he was sure that she would try to ply her
"trade" one way or another. Her peddling habits had never left her
since he was a boy. He was a little worried, even frightened, lest she
had already started making rounds to sell her things, though in the
past buyers had always come to her. He decided to try to find out
by asking her a surprise question.

"I was wrong, Haja, about what we discussed last week."

"What was that, my boy?"

"I told you to forget and bury the things you brought from Damascus." He added ruefully, "Did you get rid of all of it?"

She looked at him a little distrustfully. "Why do you ask?"

"In the marketplace today they talked of nothing but henna and
incense!" He let that sink in. "They were ready to pay its weight in
gold—apparently the palace was trying to get some."

Her eyes could not have opened wider, flashing with interest, not regret; he knew he had taken the right approach.

"I told the ones who asked," he went on, "to give me tonight, and I'd give them an answer tomorrow."

"So these things are very expensive now?" she asked yearningly.

"Nothing's expensive unless there's a demand."

"So they're in demand?"

"Well, the palace needs them—whoever can sell will get rich!"

She bit her lip remorsefully. He saw something happening but said nothing more; he wanted to give her the chance to say something now. She glanced around her in a way she did only when she had suffered a business reverse. He remembered the few times she had lost money: once, when an aristocratic lady bought some merchandise but never paid her; another time from a bad debt; she lost money once when a husband returned what his wife had bought, even though their children had eaten most of the apricot paste and almonds. Each loss taught her a lesson, and now Said saw that look in her eyes.

"That sly bitch," she said resentfully after a moment of silence. "She tells me, 'Sit down, sit down,' and a couple of days later she tells me, 'Auntie, I need henna,' and I give her some. She says, 'That's not enough, Auntie, my hair is so frizzy,' so I give her more, enough henna for her ancestors' ancestors."

"Who was this, Mother?"

She sighed deeply and said in a confessional tone, "The black slave who works in the palace."

"Is there anyone else, Haja?"

"I wanted to sell henna and incense, but I was afraid after what you said. I thought, they're strange, I don't know their ways."

"Did you give her all the henna?"

"No, my boy. A sensible person gives away a little at a time. Only a fool gives away everything at once."

"So you have some henna?"

"I'm your mother—I hold on to a stock of everything."

"A big stock, I hope?"

"Don't worry, my boy!" She laughed, showing her large and prominent front teeth. Reassured, he laughed too; now he would start again to get her where he wanted her. He waited for a pause

after they stopped laughing, then resumed his battle. "Mother—"
She looked at him questioningly, though she seemed to know what
was coming.

"Since the palace needs henna and incense, and as long as you're
here, we're on our way to great things, if," he added softly, "you
help me!"

"Me? How, my boy?"

"Yes, you!" He went on as she looked at him, curious and anxious. "The whole story is: you set the trap, throw out the net, and
then it's all up to your shrewdness!"

"Shrewdness?"

"Yes, of course!" He paused. "And shrewdness, you know,
doesn't always mean buying and selling."

She looked at him wordlessly; she was hearing something new.
She knew shrewdness as part of buying and selling; only in these
activities did one's power and intellect show themselves; she could
not imagine any others. Said went on as though he had noticed
nothing.

"The important thing is to get money—to know how to get it!"
She thrust out her wide, soft lower lip. He glanced at her and continued. "Just as a shrewd hunter puts bait in his trap, we have to
put bait in the gifts we offer the palace!"

"What are you getting at, my boy?" she asked warily.

"Since that's where the money is," he explained rapidly, "as long
as the palace needs henna and incense and a thousand other
things, instead of selling henna and incense to them, we'll say, 'Take
this,' and once they take it that's it—they're in. Instead of paying
once they'll pay a thousand times. That's shrewdness."

"Without buying or selling?"

"This is real buying and selling, Haja."

"We give these things to rich people, to princes, and don't charge
them anything?"

He tried again to regain control over this discussion.

"Listen, Haja—give me all the things you brought from Damascus."

After a great deal of unwillingness and misgiving, by which she
tried to keep her independence from him, so that she could sell
according to her own custom, while he tried to take her over com-

pletely, she brought out her bundles and small bags. He helped her. When it was heaped in a ludicrous pile in the middle of the room, he rubbed his hands together happily.

"Yes, yes, Haja!" He called her by this same title that the women in Amman used, though she had never made the *hajj* to Mecca—unlike Hosny, who called her nothing but "Mother."

She half-smiled at him, proud of her merchandise. "Is that all of it?" She nodded, saying nothing.

"Good. How much did all this cost you?"

She looked surprised and a little afraid, thinking he would ruin her, and said, to retain her position, now convinced that she was right, "My boy, it didn't cost much—we'll soon be giving it to deserving people, like alms or charity. Don't worry your head about these things."

"You're right . . . but I want to know what you paid!" He quickly corrected himself, laughing: "Never mind, it's not important what it cost—what counts is how much do you want for it today, in Mooran?"

"My boy—"

When he saw the entreaty and even sorrow in her face, he took a deep breath and spoke more kindly. "Listen, Haja, I am going to pay you whatever you paid for it, plus a little profit. Now are you happy?"

"It's not for sale!" she said coldly.

"Yes, Haja, that's right, first of all, but second, I'm not going to take it from you. I'm going to leave it with you, on one condition."

"A condition?"

"Yes, on one condition."

"What is it?"

"That you give it to the Sheikha and the princesses—in other words, to the palace!"

She raised her hands to show that she could not. "My heart won't let me." Her voice softened as if she were talking to herself. "People who have nothing to give will tell you to take—and now people with the riches of Korah take and don't give?"

"It's like cheese in a mousetrap, Haja!"

"It's poison."

"Wait a minute, Haja, dear lady. As I told you, I'll pay you whatever you paid for it, plus a profit. I'll leave it with you, just don't go selling it."

"That's it," she said a little angrily, "the hell with anyone who wants to buy or sell." Now she was sad. "'They asked, "What has made you so bitter?" and he said, "Something yet more bitter.'" And me—if it hadn't been for need, for poverty, so that you boys wouldn't have to beg—I took this burden away from you. I wore myself out so that you wouldn't go hungry, so that you wouldn't have to be servants in other people's houses. And I'm not the only one to trade, to profit or lose."

Silence fell, a sad and recollective silence that opened the doors of the past, that rushed back, rich, harsh and bitter. Said remembered long-lost days when his mother trudged from place to place, day and night, to make enough sales to buy bread, when she worked night after night, especially in Ramadan, or before the Greater Bairam, so that she would be able to afford new shoes and shirts for them. Her exhaustion melted away in the laughter of her homecoming, and on the morning of the feast day she looked rested, not at all as if she had stayed up for so many nights only so that she might see their happy smiles now.

Later on, in Amman, they experienced hardship at first and she took charge of opening the house, she who had saved up from her small trade, and still did, even now. Her sales were always small, since she sold each commodity separately, so that she would make no mistakes and not be cheated. She often displayed her goods spread out on the ground, with the price of each item shown in coins above it—she always made sure to have plenty of small coins to make change for women who never seemed to have any. When sales picked up and complicated arithmetic was needed, she got help from one or both of her daughters-in-law. She never ceased repeating, "No returns—only credit for mistakes," adding, with a chuckle, "mine or yours!" She often had to check her sums once or twice, re-adding the column of figures while examining the coins. When her stock of one thing was depleted, she replaced it with something else, but kept repeating to herself the name of the sold-out commodity so that she would not forget.

That kind of life left its mark, its law on the old woman, but she would not have exchanged one day or night of it for the life she had now. What Said was saying to her now was only one of the whims that filled his head, much like the whims of his father, who had left them to their hardship and poverty. He had trusted so many people without benefit of contracts or receipts that when he died his wealth died with him.

"By God, Haja," said Said, who wanted to dispel this sadness and please his mother, even at the cost of giving up what he had been trying to accomplish, "I was just trying to repay all your work and hardship with some effort of my own. I know how hard you worked for me and my brother." He nodded sadly. "Today and from now on, I want you to have every comfort. I don't want you to do one thing—you won't even have to fetch a glass of water for yourself." Then he changed the subject and began thinking and talking as if he were by himself.

47

U MM HOSNY HAD SOME PROBLEMS AT FIRST in her relationship with the Sheikha. She did not speak the dialect, and so found the queen hard to understand. And she did not know what to call her, either to her face or when talking about her. The doctor's wife, who acted as her translator on their first visit, thought nothing of calling the Sheikha what she heard all the other women call her— "Ummi Zahwa."

Now that Umm Hosny visited the palace on her own, she found herself compelled to invent a special new language in order to be understood, and to do that she made an effort to learn a few words, and an even greater effort to remember some of the unusual expressions, proverbs and verses she had memorized as a child.

She spent hours among the palace women, as if she were deaf. Tense and silent as an eavesdropper, almost in a trance, she followed their conversation with all her senses, trying to take in some of the words. On her way home she practiced the words—in the street and as she took off her cloak and talked to the children. Her daughters-in-law pretended not to hear anything, but looked at each other and smiled. Hosny heard his mother muttering feverishly to herself, repeating indistinct words in a subdued voice, as if praying, and sometimes she asked him the meaning of certain words. He was now positive that *the air in Mooran doesn't suit her— she may be getting a little senile.*

Said was the only one who saw that *the Haja is on the right track.* To encourage her he played the game with her, and so before too long the house was a circus; no one wanted to be left out. Every day he had a new list of words; he recited them and had the children, then his mother, recite them after him, in an uproarious atmosphere of laughter, until the words themselves became, from so much rapid repetition, comic but meaningless sounds, like puzzles.

With a great deal of persistence and patient skill, and agitation of her whole body in its secondary role, Umm Hosny resorted to gestures, her face and eyes to help her express herself, until she had perfected a special language, a comic one, but sufficient for communication. The Sheikha was delighted with this woman from the moment they met, though she did not know why; she found in her language a candor that helped her to defeat her sorrow. Umm Hosny understood this feeling, and kept the game going to strengthen her position.

A cup of coffee had opened doors for her in other places, and her instincts told her that it would not let her down here. She longed to invite the palace women to her house; there, telling fortunes with coffee grounds, she might at last spread out her goods. She would do it slowly, as if showing off things that were not for sale, one at a time; surely they would buy. She was certain of that. She knew how very rich they were. They would not tire her out with bargaining or return goods after buying them. Such an invitation would be a first for her; she did not know the people here, how they thought or behaved, but she knew that a mistake early on could cost her dearly. Not only that: *These are princes and sultans,* she said to herself—a sort of person she had never dealt with before. It was true that the rich, too, were a special class of people, but she knew them—how to talk to them, how to awaken their interest.

They were miserly, deep down, selfish and rapacious, and didn't want to pay for anything, but she never let one of them get by her. She even knew how to overcome their indecision. But these royals—were they like other wealthy people? Was money everything to them?

She was hesitant about inviting them over for coffee. She would not display anything for them the first or second time—but might they turn down her invitation? These were princesses; they had different blood and might not know proper behavior, any more than she knew how to behave around them. Even so, she felt that a cup of coffee would never fail her, and she would try it.

They served her their own coffee now: she studied the taste and found the savor of all the spices, but not coffee. She knew how much care and skill coffee needed: it needed to boil and brew in order to open all the pores of the body when drunk, to impart a delicious feeling of rapture. When it was drunk and the cup turned over, the sediment ran limply down, leaving tracks and blobs and signs marking and revealing the road to the future. This bitter, turbid liquid, so loaded with flavors she had never tasted before, could be anything but not coffee. She was impatient to make her own coffee, to invite them to her house and teach them a lesson!

In spite of that, she was indecisive throughout this early period. She still urged herself to seize her courage, and at one point the spirit of a she-wolf stirred inside her, with the wish to face the whole world fearlessly, to act, to live. She would not listen to Hosny. *And Said is dissolute—he doesn't care about anything except his own pleasure. He does nothing but sit around. I'm the one who's worked, and I'm the one who knows something about people.* She almost brought some of her merchandise along to the palace to display, to tempt them to buy, but abruptly thought better of it. *Don't cheapen yourself, Umm Hosny. All your life people have come to your house, and aristocrats have crowded in, asking and buying. And when was all this? Years ago, when you were needy. Today it's different; this place is not my home.* She rejected the idea, postponed it, but it came back to her. *What difference does it make, here or there—it all comes down to buying and selling. If they want to buy, fine; if not, fine. There are a thousand others who'll buy if they don't.* Her sense of magnanimity was reawakened. *Work at it, woman; it's only right to go to some trouble for once, so that later on they'll be chasing after you.* She relented gradually. *Coffee. The little pan and cups are light and easy to carry. I'll tell them, "I wanted you to drink my coffee, to try it, now that I've tried your coffee. Drink it, then judge!" After they drink it I'll tell them, "Now turn your cups over and I'll tell your fortunes!"*

She carried her utensils in a bag that she concealed in her cloak until the time was right. When the moment came, she asked the Sheikha almost pleadingly, for she was a little nervous, "Ummi Zahwa . . ." and when the woman looked at her curiously, a little surprised, "I have a request, if you would grant it."

"Why, certainly!"

"I'm going to make coffee, and I'd like you to drink some."

The Sheikha was not sure that she had understood, and looked at her questioningly. Umm Hosny opened her bag and took out her utensils, including sugar and coffee, and showed them to her to indicate how clean they all were and that her intentions were good. She then rose agilely like a cat and went into the little court-yard where the hearth and coffee pots were, and began expertly, as if she had been practicing for a long time.

Her eyes never left the ladies as they sipped the coffee. She watched their reactions carefully, judging how much they were enjoying it; would this coffee be a bridge, as it had been in other places and at other times?

The letdown she sensed in their faces and the looks they exchanged among themselves might have frustrated another woman, but she gathered her strength to continue her attack; her "trade" had given her many gifts in all these years, but a knowledge of people was the chief of these: the skill of understanding people, of seeing behind their masks, the strong and weak points of each. Her ability to see and act without giving away her own feelings had made it possible for her to survive and prevail. More than one cup of coffee had proved this. This small cup was sufficient to ensnare any woman, no matter how distant or powerful she appeared, and could open purses as well as hearts!

Now she was using this weapon. The time that had elapsed had enabled her to see and hear much; since these women did not reckon that she had learned their dialect, each of them exaggerated every word when speaking in front of her.

The first cup was the Sheikha's.

"Tell those who sorrow
That affliction does not last,"

was the verse of poetry she quoted; she had memorized it as a girl.
How often she had recited it! It had been part of her friendship
with many women. Now she uttered it and looked at the Sheikha
out of the corner of her eye, and when she saw her listening closely
she went on:

"None but the trustworthy hold a secret.
A secret with the best of them is preserved.
I keep secrets in a locked chamber
Whose keys are lost, and the door sealed."

The Sheikha's eyes were rapt—she seemed to want more, but
Umm Hosny's principle was to give a little at a time. "Trade" had
taught her that, and life as well, for whoever gave out much and
quickly had nothing left to give, and people always wanted more.
When she finished reciting the verses, she did not want to go on.

"And . . . ?" said the Sheikha.

Umm Hosny shook her head, in obscure refusal and a desire to
leave some matters undiscussed, at least for now, or in front of
other people. The Sheikha kept looking at her attentively, so she
added, in a different voice:

"Nothing surpasses sweet patience and piety.
What better things has our Master given his creatures?"

That was just the beginning, but the Sheikha understood Umm
Hosny's point and did not insist. She even seemed a little uneasy—
what if she did go on? And what if her coffee cup told everything?

"People are like soft wood, Umm Hosny," she said a little ambiguously. "It is hard to know one another; each heart is like a strong-
box."

Umm Hosny turned to the other women's cups. For a few moments it seemed to her that she had gone back twenty years in time.
She was beaming, full of cheer and excitement, just as she had
been in Damascus and Amman with the young women who came

to her to learn their luck in love and marriage from her reading of their cups. It was the same: she spoke in general, ambiguous terms, with smiles and winks. They could not make her tell everything, and though they were so delighted that they wanted her to go on with this dangerous game, she did not want to go too far. Each of them decided to arrange a private meeting with her, to discuss the past first, and, should that ring true, the future. Perhaps she could only detect the shadows of the past, but the future was more important!

They surprised her, for she had not expected them to be so stirred by what she said, nor had she expected their view of her to change so much; she felt changed herself. She felt more confident, more daring. At last she was able to ask them the meaning of certain words and to speak slowly so that she might learn. She even went ahead and used some Damascene expressions, though she felt sure that they did not understand them.

Just as one defeat leads to another, one victory leads to a greater one. On her next visit to the palace the women's gazes hung on her, embraced her, followed her everywhere to express friendship and discovery. They asked her, with mixed curiosity and playfulness, whether she preferred their coffee or her own, and she answered, with a broad smile, that she preferred hers, "because it cures and speaks and soothes." Then they clamored for her to brew some. Just as before, she began with the Sheikha.

> "Tell those who sorrow
> That affliction does not last."

She smiled and added,
"O excellency, O protected by God, had what has befallen you—what you have seen—befallen someone else, had they seen it, it would have annihilated them. It would have been the end. But tragedies can build and create, or as it was said,

> " 'God has a mishap to use on youth,
> In thrall to it, from which only God can give release.
> When you defeated it, it fled,
> Though I had thought it could not flee—'

"In the cup, Sheikha, I read signs and symbols, idle chatter, what has been and what will be and what cannot be known. Sight is long but our hand is short; what cannot be said today may be said tomorrow; peace and blessings upon our Prophet Muhammad and all his household!"

That was all for the Sheikha. She was secure in her silence, lost in the past, in her memories, in events that shook and disquieted and exhilarated her, and others that saddened her. She did not want to listen, at least not in front of these others.

Umm Hosny did with the women as she had done before, adding some new proverbs and verses that could be taken any number of different ways. The women laughed modestly; they understood some but not all of what she said, but they understood enough and were pleased.

Said noticed his mother's new status at the palace, particularly with the Sheikha herself, and showed his pleasure at this as plainly as a child would, but once again he had nagging doubts that his mother was taking the direction he worried about.

"I don't object to your business," he told her, "but let's be partners—I have to agree to the sales you make, before they're made!"

His mother laughed and nodded in agreement, but he was certain that she did not mean it, that it meant nothing to her.

"You taught us that giving money to charity at the end of Ramadan is a duty," he told her, "and the poor pass it on from one to another, down to the last, who has given too, even if it's just a cup of salt. Right?"

"Right, my boy."

"Now, God has been good to us and made us prosperous, and those alms aren't enough now, we have to pay the *zakat.*"

"Yes, of course we do."

"Well, my idea is that your merchandise is what we could give out for charity or *zakat!*"

"My boy . . ." she laughed sadly. "Are those things all you could think of?"

He laughed heartily to hide his discomfort, and to go on encircling her: "All I want, Haja, is to be able to sleep with a clear conscience and work hard because if I hear tomorrow one word in the marketplace, I'll lose my temper—that's it."

"What do you mean, my boy?"

"As I told you the last time: leave the business in this family to me and Hosny."

"You're harping on this as if you had nothing in the world to think about but my things!"

"It's my opinion, Haja," he said quietly, "that you should give the things you have to the Sheikha, as a gift to the palace."

"Yes, my boy . . ." She smiled broadly but ironically, and added after a moment, "They really deserve charity!"

"No, that's not what I mean! I want you to help me with the palace—that's what I mean, in plain Arabic, and that's all!"

Said had a terrible time making her see, persuading her, because she could not find in herself the power to change, to abandon values and manners it had taken her her whole life to learn. Nonetheless, because of her special love and the subtle powers this "little devil" possessed, she yielded, finding at the same time a certain pleasure in discovering this world, and in locating its weak points: how these rich people never had enough, how they took but never gave, and how well they understood giving and taking.

48

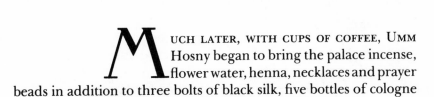

MUCH LATER, WITH CUPS OF COFFEE, UMM Hosny began to bring the palace incense, flower water, henna, necklaces and prayer beads in addition to three bolts of black silk, five bottles of cologne and thirty imported scarves.

The foods and luscious Damascene pastries she brought with her were devoured by her grandchildren in the first weeks. She could not hold out on the children or deny them, "because my heart wouldn't let me," as she said. Said ate the last piece of honeyed pastry, and when she opened the box where it had been kept he had a chance to exult and make jokes. He gathered the last fragments of pistachio nuts and gobbled them up, recalling that "the children of the aristocrats were always better than we were. You used to scream at us if we reached for the sweets you made for them! Now the paupers' children have eaten everything and left us nothing but a few crumbs. At least there's nothing left for the aristocrats!" He laughed. "Thank God we got something!"

"My boy, I was making those sweets for the children of the aristocrats so that you boys would have bread," his mother said quietly. "You were deprived, but it couldn't be helped. I wasn't being grasping—we had to earn bread. Do you think anyone was more precious to me than you two?"

"It's over and done with, Haja, just coming back to haunt us," he said jokingly, then added, addressing the children, "Did you eat, children? Did you get enough?" Without giving them a chance to reply, he went on, "From now on, for as long as you live, you keep this lady in your prayers. She raised you; if you become men, it's because that's what she made you; she's done, and is still doing, a lot for you, and you must never forget all she's done for you."

She was moved by this, and looked as if she were now receiving generous recompense: a confession. She had not worked so hard to save money or to get rich, but to protect her young ones, to spare them beggary and humiliation. Now she felt that she had succeeded. There was nothing more for her to do, and nothing left to tempt or frighten her. She still was frugal and had thoughts of business and such things, and wanted never to fail again. She had endured much. She knew the meaning of hunger and need, the looks people gave a woman alone and orphans, and she never wanted to endure them again.

The first gift Umm Hosny brought to the palace, to the Sheikha herself, was a prayer carpet with a compass that pointed in the direction of Mecca. Several of these had been sent to Said as samples after he opened the Oriental Carpet Company. He gave his mother one and asked her to give another one to the Sheikha. It caused a great stir at the palace and was given that same day to the men's *diwan*, where the men discussed it at length.

Umm Hosny had presented it to them in her capacity, as she saw it, as a messenger, but when the time came to give gifts from her own store of items, at Said's persistent nagging, she felt miserable and coerced, that she had been forced to do something wrong, something against her nature. For a day and a night, when she had unwillingly agreed to bring a few sticks of incense to the Sheikha, the woman seemed repugnant to her, to the point where she wondered how she had ever become friends with her.

What would remain of their friendship if they no longer did this buying and selling? Were they equals? Was that possible? Could she imagine her to be a friend as Umm Wajdi was, or Safiya or Naamat? Could that sort of people be trusted? She thought it over all day, feeling sad and useless, and was unable to sleep that night. The Sheikha seemed to her hateful and hard and full of spite; indeed, she was sure that the power that marked everything she did, and the effect it had upon the palace people when she came and went, was unjust. She was afraid, and even thought of cutting off her relations with the palace entirely. She did not know why two verses of poetry came to mind, which she had heard so many times about the gray-haired old lady in the old stories:

> Satan saw the ill-omened old lady.
> She taught him silent treachery.
> With politics she drives a thousand mules
> Harnessed with spider webs.

The next day as she was selecting some sticks of incense she took the weakest and shortest ones, wishing in her heart that this would be the last incense the "old witch," as she now thought of her, would ever smell. She recalled the words she might speak to her, "You're so sweet, so devout; you fast and pray, the light just shines from your brow, I've come to you, you noble women, daughter of your ancestors, mother of orphans and the poor, I've come to you with a wish—please grant it, you saint, you blessed creature!" She smiled bitterly, for the Sheikha now seemed to her the opposite of all these qualities.

Just as the cups of coffee had opened the palace to her, the smoke of incense, as it twisted in the air near the window, made a cage that enclosed the Sheikha on every side until she looked drugged and happy—like a completely different woman. She sucked the air in and looked smilingly at the faces of the women around her. Adla said to herself: *Someone has cast a spell on her, or foiled her own spell!*

Since Umm Hosny knew nothing but buying and selling, and to make her gift acceptable, she asked the Sheikha to give her in exchange a grain of salt. She made this request with a smile; she did not want to explain or to get into any discussion about it. The

Sheikha was surprised by this request and could think of no satisfying explanation for it.

"May He be praised who entrusted every heart with a secret," she said, nodding, and thinking to herself, to explain Umm Hosny's request, *Your Judge is your Lord—let us obey him.*

After Umm Hosny began to realize that there was more to life than business, and that business could take many forms besides the little transactions she had been obsessed with all her life, she started to receive heaps of gifts from the palace. This made her think: *The rich aren't like the poor. The rich never give away anything without expecting something in return. Even when they give to the poor, to beggars, they want to be thanked in a loud voice in front of other people. The poor give and expect nothing in return. They give little, but they have so little.*

She did not restrict her gift giving to the Sheikha. She saw that some of her merchandise was right for the young women—the cosmetics, powders from Aleppo, and special herbs could be useful to newly married women. The young palace women waiting endlessly to get married, especially those waiting to marry their cousins, found their salvation in Umm Hosny: she read the future in their cups of coffee and gave them cosmetics and powder from Aleppo to beautify their faces and make their hair shine. The women tormented by impatience to bear children or the fear that their husbands would take a second wife, especially once they got rich, clung to Umm Hosny; only she could help them.

That is how she became the center of attention at the Ghadir Palace. If she delayed her morning visit, the women searched for her but never lost hope that she would come, and if the day passed with a visit they were full of anxiety; even Ummi Zahwa was clearly surprised and subtly changed, whether because she could not adapt to the new situation, or from old age, no one could tell; it could have been the depression that affected so many of them around this time. The women were uneasy but expected the Sheikha to get stronger, to revive her spirits; surely everything would change, as it had in the Rawdh Palace. They were confident that her magic alone could change and destroy; now, in addition to it there was the magic of "the Damascene," as they called Umm Hosny; and so there was no doubt that everything in the palace would turn to salt. They were sure of it when Umm Hosny began to ask for grains of salt in return for what she gave, "for salt ruins and dissolves everything, the prophet Adam was too weak to resist salt."

Umm Hosny began to picture a new future, one which was an alloy of sympathies and resentments and fear, and the desire to avoid *the devils that drift through the Ghadir Palace like rushing winds.*

49

THE SHEIKHA'S VISIT TO UMM HOSNY'S HOME was a truly momentous event; in the three days and nights before the visit, preparations for it never ceased, and everyone in the neighborhood knew about it. Umm Hosny's nervousness never left her for a moment, and it grew into despair as the time for the visit neared. Umm Hosny began to wish that she had never thought so much of the Sheikha, or that she had postponed this visit, but she did not give in to her doubts. In order that she not lose time or fall prey to illness, she threw herself into the work of preparing the pillows and seat cushions and cleaning the house again and again. She even carefully supervised the rearranging of the clothes in the wardrobe—*God only knows if she might take it into her head to open it up and look inside, and if everything isn't in its place, clean and neat, she'll say, "How filthy they are—marble on the outside and a dump inside!" The creature might even decide to look in the kitchen or the pantry—we'll be trying to entertain her and she'll be peering around to see our trash.*

The chairs and other furniture in the guest room and the inner chambers were rearranged. Umm Hosny wiped down the ceiling and walls, shook out the carpets, and washed everything. She did it all herself, since she did not trust *these youngsters, who may rush through the job or forget things.* She sprayed every corner in the house with rosewater and burned incense for two straight days, and though she accomplished all this with the utmost care, her sense of unease never left her. *Suppose she lifts the edge of a carpet and finds dust? Or if she smells garlic or burnt onion? If the creature wants to freshen up or wash, and the children mess the bathroom up when we're not paying attention, whatever will she say about us?*

Umm Hosny treated her two daughters-in-law like servants, hurling hard, detailed orders at them, never taking her eyes off them. It seemed to her that they did not want this visit, even that they were scornful, and that worried her all the more. The two women wondered why she was making all this fuss. Their mother-in-law had never been like this before. Each woman asked herself: Why did the Sheikha matter? What would come out of this visit? Each asked her husband the same question. Hosny seemed pessimistic about the visit—he said it was a bad omen. He did not interfere or even say a word about it for the first two days, but on the third day, the day of the visit, when he came to lunch, and his mother asked him to eat in the kitchen for this once, he looked at her in surprise and anger.

"There's a good boy, it's only that I washed the floor just now and it's still wet."

"It's my own fault," he sighed like a bull, "for being stupid enough to come here in the first place. Weren't we happy enough just with ordinary friends—was it so terrible not having princesses and sheikhas around?"

"You have to keep up with the times, my boy. Every country has its own ways and every person has his place." She nodded and smiled entreatingly. "It's just once in a lifetime, my boy, and that will be it."

"Oh, Mother, I wish! But this is a long road—an endless road."

"No, my boy, once and that's all."

"Fine, whatever you say. We'll see!"

He ate only a small piece of bread and drank a glass of sour milk, standing up, before leaving the house without a word.

Said, on the other hand, put more effort into this visit than anyone else, perhaps even more than his mother. He produced, no
one knew from where, a number of plants and a sheep for the
occasion; he selected a big one with crooked horns. He brought a
quantity of almonds and walnuts, and wished he had been someplace where he could have bought a huge variety of things, "but
Mooran is like a village," he muttered to himself. He also had his
say about the way the house was cleaned and set up. On the third
day, the day of the visit, he took the three boys, his two sons and his
nephew, to get haircuts, and bought new dresses for the two girls.
He heard his wife's remarks about the visit on the first night, and
told her stiffly, almost rudely, "Nothing is too good for my mother
or my mother's guests, and I don't want to hear another word
about it." His wife said nothing and he might have left it at that, but
he exasperatedly asked her, "Do you understand?" and when she
answered, "I didn't say anything," he went on, "A man spends his
whole life and resources to get a visit like this, and all some people
can do is criticize!"

Said continued to offer his advice and assistance at every turn,
and spent a great deal of time alone with his mother. He told his
wife to wear her most beautiful clothes, and to smile and act right,
"because Hosny's wife, the silly bitch, will sit there like a owl and
not say a word, and the Sheikha might take her for a deaf-mute or
a halfwit. Try to be lively so that we don't come off too badly."

When Said was satisfied with all the arrangements, including the
bathing of the children, finding a butcher to slaughter the sheep at
the entrance to the house when the Sheikha arrived, and ordering
a cake of ice big enough to last a coffeehouse for an entire night,
he left the house with a final instruction loud enough for everyone
to hear.

"If you need me I'll be at the coffeehouse, Abdelrazzaq's Coffeehouse, do you hear?"

He chose Abdelrazzaq's Coffeehouse because it was near the
house. He wanted to watch the Sheikha's motorcade, to see the stir
it caused, and to be handy for any last-minute need.

That afternoon, with the approach of the time of the Sheikha's
visit, the commotion and noise reached a crescendo as the neighborhood children saw the Usta and Karkar boys in their new white

clothes, with their new haircuts, perfumed, standing at attention by the gate to give news of the Sheikha's arrival the instant they spotted her car. The noise and disorder of both groups of children grew louder and more confused as time wore on, and Umm Hosny grew afraid that they would mess up the spotless steps and sidewalk that she had scrubbed herself at dawn. She scolded them several times. She kept an eye on them and on her grandchildren and tried to keep them apart. All this cast an unexpected pall of tension and confusion over the visit.

Shortly after midafternoon the Sheikha arrived in two cars with her slave, Tahany, and two women Umm Hosny had never seen before. As they pulled up, the noise level soared and the children began pushing and shoving; the Sheikha almost slipped and fell down near the steps, but sharp-eyed Tahany noticed and grabbed her under the armpit. Umm Hosny, wearing a loose-fitting white outfit with what looked like wings, was momentarily embarrassed, the more so since she had raised one hand to her throat to trill the shrill traditional sound of welcome, and extended in the other a long-necked flask of rosewater to spray on the guests.

These were festive but tense moments, and Umm Hosny forgot to present her daughters-in-law in the manner she had rehearsed so much in the preceding days. The children came in and swarmed around to kiss the Sheikha's hand and those of the other women, as their grandmother looked on with bitterness she could not hide or do anything about. She saw that the sweets were passed around quickly, and it was done so quickly and consecutively with the other goings-on that it gave the visit a hasty feel that she had not foreseen and did not like. The butcher was gesticulating his questions as to whether he should cut the beast into small or large pieces; he wanted to have someone beside him to give directions. All the feverish activity and upset was compounded by the boys running in and out, asking their grandmother questions and making demands she did not know how to deal with.

The Sheikha had expected a calmer atmosphere. When she saw all this she looked a little alarmed; what heightened this impression of Umm Hosny's were the Sheikha's repeated glances around. At one point she asked Tahany to come near her, and whispered something in her ear. This really worried Umm Hosny and shamed her deeply, because she was in her own house and yet could not do as she pleased or behave as she wished. Even her flights of conversation with the Sheikha were brief, rapid and frequently interrupted.

The Sheikha had not come to eat. She had come in order to be alone with Umm Hosny, to have a private talk with no control, even from afar, and to hear exactly and fully what her cup had to tell her. This was what she had in mind and what she expected. Now, in all this clamor, with women rushing to and fro, she did not know which dishes she should try from those to be removed, nor could she talk, to say a single thing. She was no better off here than in the Ghadir Palace.

Umm Hosny's efforts to create a natural, calm ambience, to act simply and spontaneously clashed with the rising commotion, activity and excitement of the day, to say nothing of the noise from outside, which added to the general confusion and contributed to the visit's being abbreviated.

Umm Hosny had planned on the Sheikha's staying to supper. She at least wanted her to taste some pâté and other appetizers and appropriate light snacks. This situation led to complete chaos, and when the Sheikha stood up to leave, Umm Hosny felt that any attempt to make her stay would be in vain.

"Sheikha, this visit didn't count," she announced to the Sheikha. "It was too short. My sons and my daughters-in-law wanted to see you and pay their respects, so this visit was for them." The Sheikha smiled in agreement. "But you must visit again for Umm Hosny and it has to be something else!"

"The main thing is, we want to see you, Umm Hosny, here or there, it makes no difference, and here's hoping your house is never less lovely than this. Do forgive me for such a short visit!"

The visit ended amid the same noise and commotion and elegant ceremony, when the Sheikha left after sundown, but the talk about her did not cease and the noise that had accompanied her remained. Those who had not known of the Sheikha's visit before it took place learned of it now. The children who had for days been so excited and watchful, waiting for the visit, waiting for the Sheikha, were bitterly disappointed. Even as they came near the old woman and kissed her hand they were expecting another woman, any other woman but this one.

The daughters-in-law felt the same way, and their feelings were more obvious. To show that they did not care, they asked about the women who had accompanied the Sheikha: whether or not they were related to the Sheikha, whether they had had anything to eat. When they asked about the Sheikha herself it was almost with contempt. "Was she walleyed, or is it me?" "No, I noticed it too." "Her voice is weak, like she was paralyzed or had something in her mouth." "She looks around like a thief—she looked in this direction, then that, as if she were afraid." "Not only that, she kept passing her hand over her mouth and wiping it, and making a face, like she was swallowing thorns or was thirsty." "Did you see how teary her eyes were?" "I think she's walleyed in her right eye—she kept turning her whole head to see, like a puppet." "She's lame." "And her cane! It's half again as tall as she is!" "She's dark, too—as black as coal." "Everything about her made me sick." "I wanted to have some fun and ask her, speaking of women your age, did you know Eve?" "And the face on her!"

This was the first time Umm Hosny had heard them talk this way, but she pretended not to hear. She was distracted with trying to recall every detail of the visit, down to the smallest, from the moment she heard the noisy children knocking at the door and shouting that the Sheikha had arrived until the moment she left, and so completely absorbed was she that she let the two women go on like that, only catching the ends of their sentences and seeing their mocking smiles and laughter, without really hearing their words.

When Said came in, before the coffee cups and other remnants of the party had been collected, he was eager to hear his mother describe every detail of the visit, from the Sheikha's arrival to her good-byes. He seemed disapproving that the Sheikha had not stayed to supper, but his mother responded almost accusingly, as if the others were somehow responsible.

"I curse the day she ever visited us," said Umm Hosny rashly. She took an angry, resentful breath. "Alas for the day I met her and ever listened to her. Woe to me if I ever meet or listen to anyone else like her!"

She gazed at her daughters-in-law clearing up the mess. She held them responsible and wanted to complain, but thought better of it at the last moment. It would turn the two women against her, and as long as Said was with her, he would be able to deal with his wife; she would give in. If she started complaining now, and took a hard, emotional stance, the visit would seem like a total failure, exactly what she did not want.

So she was vague with her son. She said that the women had visited, and that it was like any other visit, and so there was not really very much to say about it.

50

THE DAYS FOLLOWING THE VISIT WERE NO-
table for their immense concealed tension
and vexation and the reverberant silence
that always warns of an imminent explosion, as if the weariness,
resentment and secret desires that usually filled her had found her
weak points and become congested, waiting until they could reach
her brain and explode.

For Umm Hosny, who had hoped for so much from this visit,
had been let down. She blamed herself, but bore it patiently, har-
boring it within herself instead of taking it out on her daughters-
in-law or grandchildren. She kept her distance from them at first,
then fell ill. This befell exactly five days after the visit, and lasted
for two weeks. She praised God for "striking me with the illness,
rather than the little ones or their fathers," but she did not mention
their wives. As a result of her high fever, and the medicines she
now took regularly, her health began to recover, though some effects of the illness and weakness did not leave her for a long time.

Hosny tried to act normally, or to pretend to, for the first few days, and was determined to say nothing, as his way of expressing his disapproval. The infection spread to his wife, Zakiya, who although she behaved nicely for actual visit, confounding Said's expectations—serving, laughing, wearing her best clothes, going on like that until evening—spent the following day gossiping and laughing with Adiba about the visit and the Sheikha herself. The next day she suddenly changed into a different woman: after Hosny left the house for his store, she secluded herself and the children in her room and did not go out or let the children out. When the children complained and began to scream, she reprimanded them harshly and kept them in there except to use the bathroom. She asked her oldest daughter to bring some food and water. So it continued until evening. When Hosny came home the children were let out again but only briefly, then she hauled them in again angrily. This went on in the same way the next day and the days after that, a little less harshly. When Umm Hosny fell ill and secluded herself in her bedroom, Hosny visited her several times, but his wife only peeped in the door twice to ask if her mother-in-law needed her, or anything else. When Umm Hosny was silent and turned her face away, Zakiya felt that she had done her duty, and visited her no more.

Said did not understand the cause of what was going on around him. He had expected things to take a different course; he wondered about it and asked his wife and his mother but got no convincing answer, so he assumed that something had somehow gone wrong during or after the visit, and that his mother and wife were not talking about it and did not want him to know. This assumption seemed true or at least possible to him, the more so judging from his brother's and sister-in-law's behavior, for although they tried to pretend that nothing was amiss, a certain coldness was obvious in their looks and in their silence. When he persisted in asking for an explanation, Hosny laughed mockingly, as if saying wordlessly, "Kill a man and walk in his funeral!"

Said had wanted a stunning beginning from this visit; it was all he thought about and hoped for. Even as he sat at a sidewalk table at Abdelrazzaq's Coffeehouse, he turned in obvious turmoil when the two cars passed, and said loudly, so that everyone around him could hear, "The palace cars, the palace cars, look!" In the next few days he confided in everyone he knew that the Sheikha had visited the day before, that she had "spent the whole day and nearly slept at our house, but the palace sent for her." "The Sheikha ate and drank and brought dozens of princesses, servants and slaves, all of whom extolled Umm Hosny," and "She almost sent the servants home and stayed with us for several days."

He circulated news of the visit and all that had led up to it, and followed it in many different versions, and he began to dream up new details that he rearranged again and again, almost without realizing it, and without considering himself inaccurate or boastful. When his mother became ill and that mood filled the house, he blamed himself for not getting more information about the small details of the visit from the very minute of the Sheikha's arrival until she left. When he tried to talk about it with his wife about a week later, she answered him in a voice of mocking rebuke.

"Good Lord, man, what did we get out of that visit but exhaustion and headaches!"

In the third week, the palace, or the Sheikha, sent a car to ask about Umm Hosny. The driver said that "the palace summoned her."

"Give my greetings to the Sheikha," Umm Hosny replied from behind the half-closed door, "and tell her that within a few days, God willing, Umm Hosny will show her face!"

The doctor also heard of the visit; from Radwan, who heard it from Said, and from Hosny ten days later. At first the news gave him pause, and he considered it significant, but then he persuaded himself that such visits happened all the time *between these old ladies, until the end of time.* He almost scolded his wife for not inviting over any of the palace women, especially the Sultan's wife or the important princesses. He consoled himself by saying that *any man who depends upon a woman, though, is like a man trying to harvest the wind!*

The doctor's wife heard the news of the visit late. She wanted to surprise her husband with the story, but found that it had already reached him, and instead of losing her temper over "that old crone" as she had begun to call Umm Hosny, she said merely, "If she's smart, and wants to play this game behind my back, she'd better know I'm no beginner!"

At the end of the third week, as Umm Hosny began to recover, signs of an approaching storm gathered at home. The "urgent message" from the palace—at least that is how Said thought of it, and what he called it—inviting his mother over, could not be put aside or ignored, because a very damaging construction could be put on that. He wanted her to visit the palace soon. Umm Hosny herself, who was bored with the sickness and with being confined to bed, felt her spirit fluttering in her chest; there was no overcoming this depression without getting out of the house. Where did not matter; the important thing was to get out, to get away a little, especially since her daughters-in-law were a pain to her, Hosny's wife in particular. They both made fun of her and her guests and were clearly indifferent to her illness. She wished everything would go back to the way it was before, when she was strong, independent enough to manage her own house, or to help out at least, and free to travel and do business as she used to.

Hosny himself considered his silence punishment enough; everyone would have to rethink his position, as he had done, to put aside his rashness and dispense with pretensions. He reckoned that Zakiya had got the message across for him even if his own message had not been clear. He was ready at this point to start anew, as he had done so many times before in the face of Said's follies.

Things might have gone on peacefully and normally, even this visit that had caused such bad feelings might have passed into the shadows and faded from everyone's memories as if it had not been, but Said could never let things take their normal course. No sooner had a new message arrived from the palace, with a gift, than he told his mother, a little chidingly and loudly enough for everyone to hear, "Haja, princes' and sultans' anger isn't like the anger of ordinary people!"

"Everyone who gets angry gets over it, my boy."

"Everyone except them, because they're not used to anger."

Hosny was listening. He was listening in silence, not meaning to interfere, but he detected in his brother's and mother's words an allusion to himself. He sighed and shook his head.

"And today is better than tomorrow, Haja," Said was saying.

"Listen, Mother," Hosny said, and his words came out angrily, even threateningly, "if you set foot in that palace I'll pick up my children and leave here."

"But whatever for?" asked Said, as if this attitude took him by surprise.

"God keep you all . . ." Hosny tried to keep his self-control, to keep his speech clear and slow, but he had begun to tremble. He added, "From the day God gave me life I've had nothing to do with the government. I don't like it and don't want to have anything to do with it."

"Who ever asked you to have anything to do with it?"

"Listen, Said, the first lesson we learned from the Haja, the first thing she ever told us, was to play by ourselves and come home happy. And she always quoted to us, 'Stay far from Evil, and sing to him'—don't tempt fate. But from the day we got to Mooran you've done nothing but look for trouble."

"Me? Look for trouble?"

"Yes, sir, if you want the plain, frank truth, you've been doing nothing but wooing the government and pushing the Haja toward the palace."

"Well, sir, I don't know what you're talking about, and I don't know what you're getting at."

"This is what I'm getting at: let's keep away from the government, not get mixed up in it."

"You mean, if the Haja visits the palace, if the Sheikha visits our house, then we've got mixed up in the government?"

"Yes, sir."

"You're wrong."

"Wrong, not wrong, that's my opinion."

"Your opinion is wrong."

"Listen, Said." Hosny sighed, then laughed bitterly. "The palace is the government, it's the state, you know that better than I do." He sighed deeply and shook his head. "And you know, sir, that the government, like a whore, has different friends every day, there's no right and no wrong, there's no heart and no Lord, nothing but self-interest. If you put yourself between the hammer and the anvil you'll be crushed, you'll lose everything!"

"Fine. So what does this talk have to do with us?"

"Said, my dear, play by yourself and come home happy. We came to Mooran to work, to make a living, and nothing else!"

"Who said we had to do anything else?"

"Every day: 'Let's go, Haja. We'll be late for the palace, Haja. You have to go to the palace, Haja.' If it were one visit, we pay our respects and shut up, fine; but look, one visit brings on another, and once we started visiting them they started visiting us, and as that man said: 'Talk leads to more talk, and more talk ends in the noose!'"

"Oh, my, my, my, now we're talking about nooses!"

"Yes, sir, and you knew how I felt when the doctor approached us about working in Mooran. I told him, 'By God, Doctor, a crust of bread, a morsel of onion and peace of mind are worth more to me than this job, more than being a government bigshot. Governments turn on you—there's no security, you have no real friends; that's if we're talking about normal governments. If you're talking about these phony setups like the one in Mooran!—a man is a Sultan one day, and the next day poof! he's gone, like salt in water, as if he had never been, deader than dead. And I'm not ready to die yet.'"

"Nor me either . . . sir," laughed Said.

"Fine then, since we agree, let's get away from the tombs—you sleep among tombs and get nothing but bad dreams." Hosny turned to his mother. "Say something, Mother. Why are you ill?"

"The illness is from God," she chuckled, "and so is the cure."

"And the Sheikha? The Sheikha's visit? Didn't she cause this illness?"

Said again tried to go on the offensive.

"Hosny, be sensible. Think. Our relationship with the palace will open a thousand and one doors. You know very well we're not the kind of people who get desk jobs, who make good employees. Look, I think the government is even rottener than you think it is, but we should develop a relationship with the palace so we'll get ahead—not so we can become cabinet ministers!"

"Oh, look, yourself—the government will be generous with you and take it all back plus ten percent. The government is the son of sixty dogs, there's no security, you don't have a friend you can trust there—things change every day. Every day it's a different government!"

"That's true for people who want to become ministers—for politicians. For people like you and me, in business, just making money, a relationship with the government opens closed doors. It helps us get where we're going. If we make friends there, if we pay a little here and there, we'll be in control—yes, in control. As they used to say, you feed someone's mouth and it opens their eyes."

Their disagreement stalled and there it remained, with Hosny absolutely rejecting a relationship, any relationship, with the government, and Said holding the opposite opinion: that excluding that opportunity, especially at this time and in this place, was intolerable, unforgivable folly. The old lady, baffled at their arguments, said, not to settle but to postpone the matter, "From the day God made us, we work and make ourselves miserable, and when we finally get a chance to enjoy a morsel, all we do is swear and fight!" She sighed sadly. "Be patient!"

51

After long thought, and with no reluctance at all, Umm Hosny decided to leave Mooran. It had to be; it did not matter where she went or for how long, but she had to get away. She would stay away until she was cured, and knew that when she came back things would be different. She would not be a ball to be tossed back and forth between them, that was for sure. Death might spare her this time, but the next time it might not. As to the Sheikha, Ummi Zahwa, she did not mean very much to Umm Hosny anymore. That woman did not understand love, and had never known it all her life. All she knew was hate, and how to increase her hatred for everyone around her with every passing day. And the other palace women—what kind of women were they? What thoughts, what dreams filled their heads! She knew all of them, and they seemed motivated by nothing but spite and trivial whims. While it was true that she did not understand some of the words they whispered to her, she could guess. They did nothing but talk about one another.

Each of them wanted her for herself, to talk to her, to tell no one else's fortune. She had had enough; she could not take any more.

Even Hosny and Said had changed. She would have to punish them as she had done before. It used to be enough for her to threaten them, to ignore them, or merely to put on her cloak and pretend she was leaving them. They would be terrified and immediately start to behave. Now she would have to do the same thing; surely it would work. They were still children, and only this sort of punishment, not a mere threat, would bring them to their senses.

She could not tolerate her daughters-in-law any longer. The two women had changed more in these few months than they had in all the years she'd known them. How had she allowed that? How had she kept her control, her mastery this whole time, then suddenly, through a little negligence or inattentiveness, noticed by the husbands, watched everything fall to ruin? Surely one day she would again be the woman she had been. She would know what to do. All she needed now was a little rest.

But where to go? And for how long? Would she be able to go back to living alone?

Going back to Damascus was not the answer. She had told every single one of her neighbors that her sons could not bear having her so far from them; they had demanded her presence in Mooran the day before tomorrow! What could she say now if she went back? Could she tell them that she was only visiting, as she had done before, or that she had come to stay? Would she be able to go back and be away from her sons and grandchildren and not see them? She would die of grief if she thought she would never see them again.

She had to do her thinking somewhere else, someplace that would save her, that would not expose her to the embarrassments of Damascus, the questions of neighbors and relatives.

It would have been possible to consider Mecca, where her soul might rest and regain its equilibrium, but it was not *hajj* season. Suddenly it occurred to her that the only place right for her was Medina, close to the Prophet's tomb. There she could catch her breath, restore her balance, withdraw from the world and rest, and, having soaked up the ambience and had her fill of its pure fragrant air and deep rest, she might even return a new woman.

Said tried to dissuade her from this idea: "Medina is so far, the timing is wrong—if you wait until *hajj* season I'll carry you there on my back." She was not persuaded and would not reconsider. Hosny, who like his mother was weary and careworn, did not have to think about it for very long before he agreed.

"I'll take you there and make sure everything's fine, then come back, Mother," he told her.

Just as Said had been shaken to see her arriving in Mooran with her bags, he was shaken to see her with the huge bag she would let no one else carry. He seized it and smiled.

"Haja, you're only making a visit there. Leave the business to someone else."

"A visit to the Prophet's grave, boy," she answered in a voice both angry and sorrowful. "The most important business in this world or the next. Don't worry."

"What about these bundles, Haja?"

"They're good things, my boy, they're useful!"

And so she left for Medina.

In Medina the people seemed to her different: light, almost like ghosts. They walked on tiptoe, spoke in whispers as if weary, as if too tired or unwilling to talk. They watched and did not watch. Their clothes were as light as shrouds: simple, graceful, flowing on their bodies like the wind. Umm Hosny felt that her past life now meant nothing. She was once again a mere grain of sand, a moment of light. Even food was a different thing for her here. She ate only to live, to be able to visit the Prophet's tomb, to get there. Again she was seized with regret for having troubled herself and others only to receive the Sheikha, for having done all she had done in the way of preparation. Even more, her life now passed before her eyes and seemed different to her, meaningless and void of accomplishments.

Before arriving here she had felt in need of months of treatment in order to get well. She had desired a long, unbroken sleep, but unexpectedly felt strong and unwilling to sleep. She had but a little time left on this earth; soon she would be lying underneath it. She had wearied herself so much—with travel, buying, seeing infinitely different kinds of people. Now she wanted to rest, to meditate on her life, to reckon her final accounts.

She was utterly mystified. How could she be herself and another person at the same time? Furthermore, how could she be drawing nearer to people and the Prophet at the same time? She chided herself for having spent more profits than necessary on the things she had sold; she chided herself even more for having charged the rich and the poor the same prices; she should have made distinctions, made allowances for people. True, the poor had paid, but in small coins. She had always welcomed these coins, which helped her, but she never once was lenient in taking what the price of the goods she was selling required.

Here, she did not know what to do with the money Hosny had left her. She always bought things and discovered too late that it was too much for her, more than she could handle. She said to herself, smiling as she remembered, *Children ruin you—we should have had more of everything, more than they could have wanted, so they never would have had their hands out again.* Now she did not know what to do with the second loaf of bread; one was enough for her, but she still found herself buying two. She had brought the two loaves to her room, near the mosque, in the first days, and continued to buy two loaves, but before reaching home she gave one loaf to one of the people standing at the gate of the mosque, and took the other one home.

There was more to it than one loaf of bread or the simple fare she was accustomed to here. Time lay heavy on her hands, for she needed only an hour or two of sleep, and since the night was too long to spend in prayer, she began thinking things over. She remembered her girlhood, her first marriage, then her second marriage; how her children were born, and how she raised them. She was surprised at the things she remembered for the first time, things she had never before recalled or thought about, which she now saw before her as if they were happening anew. She remembered the distant past best of all; even the first days of her stay in Mooran did not appear to her with the clarity of those far-off days. Everything from that far-off period had a special scent, yes, a scent she could smell now as it came back to her. Why had she forgotten these things for so long; why did they come back now?

She began to live again in lost days, the days of her girlhood; it delighted her to go back to those times. She suddenly remembered Hosny, Said, Zakiya; then she remembered her grandchildren; she saw the same faces come back repeatedly. They were the same faces, with the features slightly changed. She could not stay here, so far, so isolated. She forgave them all and felt no revenge against anyone. She loved even her daughters-in-law, in spite of what she had heard them say; in spite of the way Zakiya acted. She could stand it; she would say two prayers for them at the Prophet's tomb. *A girl can make a mistake—everybody makes mistakes—*it was not right to judge someone by these small mistakes.

She pondered all this and the night did not end: Ummi Zahwa, the Sheikha, baffled her. What did that old woman want? What was in her mind? Why was she stern, even harsh, with others when she appeared so serene, so resigned, like a little girl, with her? Why was she transformed into an intensely sensitive ear, to glean every word she said to her? Umm Hosny said to herself: *She must be waiting for something, otherwise she wouldn't be like this.* She recalled the whispers of the palace women when the Sheikha was absent, and how they looked and acted. Was it possible to kill or to create so evilly, for any reason?

She immersed herself in prayer in order to forget. She watched the people and things around her in order to avoid thinking. Even so, she had much time on her hands, and without noticing, without willing it, she found herself deep in thought.

Again, she overcame her cares and confusion with prayer. She spent her whole day in the courtyard of the mosque. But the night, that restless, unending ocean, besieged her, terrified her in her solitude. She would have felt stronger if someone had been with her. Even the cat, Yasmine, that she had kept long ago in Damascus, had kept her company after the children were in bed. It was enough for her to look around and see everyone asleep for her to feel strong and secure. The cat's purring consoled her and helped her to pass several extra hours of peace.

Now she felt alone and afraid. She might die here and no one would know, without saying any last words of advice to her children, and she did not want to die like this, to die alone, far away and forgotten. No one would know her grave or visit it. True, the poor visited the graves of the forgotten and lay green boughs over them, but there were countless graves here, uncared for and unvisited. She was sure that her sons would be sad when she died, that they would repent their sins when she was gone. They might build her a beautiful, sturdy tomb so that she would remain with them even after her body was consumed. If she died here, she would die utterly anonymous. No one would even remember her name; she would mean nothing to anyone. Months, or even years, later one or both of her sons might come and ask about her, and get no reply of any kind. Anyone they asked would push out his lower lip and shrug to show that he did not know.

No, she did not want that, even though this was sublime, sacred ground, and many people would have loved to die here; what she yearned for even more was to die among her children, among people she knew and loved. Then she would die happy, with no feeling of regret or exile.

The days passed and the months followed. Her days were filled with people, her nights with solitude; by day she was occupied with the cares and conversations of people, by night with her own thoughts. Everything she decided upon at night was forgotten the next day. When some of the people she had known in past weeks or months were no longer around, she knew that they had died; she mourned their deaths and promptly forgot until she recalled them again, when she was saddened less than the first time. Their features grew indistinct in her memory until they disappeared, and so did their names.

Eight months later Said came, made that pilgrimage with her and then brought her back to Mooran; she did not resist. She felt cured, ready and willing to go home. Most of all, she longed to see the children.

She was not reassured by his replies when she asked about his brother: how he had left him, and how they were getting along together. No matter how it stood, though, she was going back with him; for now, this lesson was enough for them. And the children, for what sin had she left them, despite her intense attachment to them? Even if their parents had sinned, why should they be punished or abandoned?

"Abu Tayseer thinks he's still in Amman or Damascus," Said told her when she asked about his brother. He sighed afflictedly. "Mooran is different!"

He laughed when she asked him whether the Sheikha or anyone from the royal court had been asking for her.

"The royalty only remember the people right in front of them, Haja." He shook his head. "A week, two weeks after you left, they asked, but after that they forgot everything."

52

SHE PERCEIVED, ONCE SHE WAS BACK, THAT HER sons were still living together in the house, because they could not decide, individually or as a pair, to make the decision to part. For all practical purposes, however, they were apart: instead of the one dining table, which had hosted so much boisterous festivity, there were now two tables, and usually one family started and finished at one of them without the others in the house even knowing. The daughters-in-law, who had enjoyed an intimate friendship in the past, now spoke to each other only when compelled to. Each of them took care not to enter the kitchen until the other had left it. The children, once the harbingers of love and harmony, were now sternly prohibited from mixing or playing together, and if one of them ate at his uncle's part of the house or brought something home from there it caused a dispute that lasted for days or weeks, not to mention the punishments and crying.

Hosny and Said had changed as well, in their relationship, at work, even the time each got home from work. The words they exchanged when they met were more like empty civility, or an attempt to avoid silence.

Umm Hosny was heartbroken and blamed herself for taking so long to get to Mooran the first time, but now she was discovering that everything was belated—too late. On top of all this, it seemed that her very presence here had become a new source of friction. Each of her sons wanted her to dine at his own table, to stay in his section of the house, to take sides with him and his wife. In the past she'd had some strength left and could prevent the wives from feuding, but now she was too weak to keep them apart, and her sternest words of rebuke were met with scorn rather than fear or respect.

It was with bitter despair that she answered Hosny when he insisted that she eat with them all the time.

"Don't bother yourself with my eating. I'll manage." When he insisted more strongly than before, she replied, "Eating is the least of my worries, my boy." She gazed at him with some surprise, then smiled sadly. "Since the pilgrimage and my visit to Medina, I've eaten like a bird. I could live on air if only I were happy and at ease!"

She was angered by his efforts to get her to eat with him and with Said on alternate days. "I don't want to hear any more about food!" she said sharply, her voice rising like a cat's yowl. "Just leave me alone, my boy, and don't worry about me!"

Said pretended not to see and not to notice. He asked for nothing and did not get involved; he was sure that all this would pass. At the same time, he did not want to be part of any plan of Hosny's. He had even put aside the issue of the palace, and whether or not his mother should cultivate ties that might help his business there, for he had found other means to achieve most of what he wanted.

What sorrow possesses a person who discovers that all her efforts, her whole life, have been futile, of no result other than this dark, forbidding atmosphere, and the pains everyone suffers in his own way? What good was wealth when all it brought was what she saw now? What was the meaning of leaving one place to travel to another if the new place caused so much pain and unhappiness?

And she . . . wasn't she responsible for all this? All she saw now, wasn't it the result of her own nurturing, of her way of doing things?

Mooran seemed to her oppressive and hostile, and the house like a prison. Her days and nights were full of loneliness, much more so than in Medina. Had she made yet another mistake in agreeing to come back? Was there anything she could do for these children who brought her from place to place?

She did her best to bring them together, or some of them at least. She cut a loaf of bread into small slices and placed sugar cubes on each piece, and fed the children like birds as she told them stories, but the shouts of Adiba and Zakiya, especially Zakiya, calling the children, cut short this sole pleasure left to her. The trembling child hastily getting up, wiping the corners of his mouth with the back of his hand to erase any sign of eating, filled her with endless misery, and made her incapable of any resistance. What could she do? How could she respond? The shout for the children to leave her and go to their mothers made her feel as if she had nothing left in the world.

She thought again of getting a cat or bird—*such animals never leave you, never abandon you, even if your children do*—but where would she find another cat like Yasmine? Was enough of her life left for her to begin afresh? If she died, to whom would she leave the poor animal? Reasoning thus, she gave up the idea.

Even prayer was no longer enough. She could pray and praise God for hours, but more often than not she found her mind wandering during these prayers. She begged forgiveness and started over again, but then the same thing would happen.

Her only remaining option was to travel yet again, to return to Damascus, back to Tiba, to be exact, where she could live out the rest of her days. She would give the excuse that the climate here had not suited her, and the water had affected her, and since she could not stand it she had come back. Her friends were there, and surely they would understand and help her.

So she began to think this way, to be filled with this desire, though she did not dare to discuss it with her sons or make a decision. While waiting to make that decision, she began to go out every other day or so, to visit a neighbor, or wander aimlessly through the streets. An hour or two out of the house was enough to keep her alive, to keep away sickness and death.

Zakiya was waiting for this, waiting thirstily, since she was positive that her mother-in-law knew only the palace and was surely visiting the Sheikha. As soon as she left the house Zakiya snooped through her room to see if she had taken any frankincense or depilatories; she was able to find out, most of the time, without even having to open any of the bags, since the scent in the room, and the extreme neatness that Umm Hosny maintained there, always gave her some sign of what her mother-in-law had been doing. When she came in from her walk, Zakiya thrust the children at her to make sure, since they pestered her with questions and begged her to give them whatever the Sheikha had given her. They acted this way and made these demands because their mother made them, and because of the constantly repeated lessons.

Hosny was not long in getting involved.

"From tonight, Mother, I've sworn a solemn oath: if you set foot in the palace once more you'll never see me again!"

"Damn the palace and everyone in it!" she replied angrily.

"It's none of my business, but you have to be careful!"

"Don't worry, my boy!"

This did not satisfy Zakiya; she wanted, in addition, proof, so that Hosny would have no excuses left. After the commands that he repeated dozens of times, which resembled threats, for her to swallow her tongue and keep her eyes shut, no matter what she saw or heard of his mother, she did not want to enter a losing battle, nor did she want a small or conventional victory. She had to have a total, decisive victory, and any misstep, however small, could be totally counterproductive. She had endured much from her mother-in-law in the past, and from Said and his sarcasm, but now the time had come to have a house of her own so that she could have a husband, not merely a mate, a partner, as she said.

So she did not let up in her search for some evidence, or cease pushing the children to bring some from their grandmother, so that when she had this proof, she could put it to her husband at an opportune moment and say, "You keep swearing oaths that you won't stay in this house another day if your mother goes back to the palace, but your mother hasn't gone there once, she's gone

there dozens of times—she was there today, and here's the proof!"
She would offer him some irrefutable proof, something no one
could find any doubt about.

This was how Zakiya was preparing herself, despite her certainty
that her mother-in-law had gone to the palace many times, though
perhaps in short visits, unlike before, when she spent long hours
there every day. Now she went on short visits when her sons were
not around, so as not to be found out. Zakiya was in no hurry; she
had waited a long time and could wait yet longer to catch her
mother-in-law in the act so that there could be no denying or cov-
ering up.

Now she did not want to put herself in a weak position, since
weakness always led to greater weakness; the quarrel was not between her and her mother-in-law, but between Hosny and his
mother. She must push him to keep fighting the war, and keep
herself out of it.

53

UMM HOSNY WOULD NOT HAVE VISITED THE
palace had it not been for the siege encircling her: she saw it in the eyes of the children and adults alike. And she would not have done it had the
palace not sent a car to her unexpectedly. What further induced
her to go was the fact that the Sheikha had opened the door: she
had extended the first invitation, and no one knew about it. True,
deep inside she resented the palace for totally forgetting about
her; as Said told her when she asked him, the palace asked for
people only when it wanted something from them, or when their
eyes met. Still, curiosity mixed with a certain craving, and her desire to violate this siege, to feel free to do as she wished—all this
together made her consider going to visit the Sheikha. Naturally,
she would not reply to the invitation immediately, but she would
not wait too long.

The Sheikha badly needed to see Umm Hosny, to have her read

her coffee cup, for these had been hard days at the Ghadir Palace: Tahany had fallen ill and died three days later, before the cause of her illness and death was learned. Just a few weeks later Suroor died. The Sheikha mourned Tahany's death, persuading herself that she had died of old age or something mysterious, but Suroor's death left her in no doubt: this was some secret she did not comprehend.

After Suroor fell ill, or more precisely when he was struck with fever and began to hallucinate, frightening people with his raving, the Sultan heard about it. Within hours, unasked and with no advance notice, Dr. Mahmilji visited.

He examined Suroor and gave him a shot and made him drink some medicine. Around noon the Sultan visited with the doctor, and at midafternoon, or just after, Suroor died and was buried before sundown.

Suroor's death terrified the Sheikha. She needed support, some knowledge of what the future held, and suddenly remembered Umm Hosny, who alone could save her and tell her what fate had in store for her, especially since the women around her had begun to look at her differently from before. Curious stares were no great injury, to be sure, but they had begun to unnerve her.

Three days later Umm Hosny came to visit.

The palace looked very different from before. Except for the gate, which had remained the same, everything was changed. Large sections of the inner walls had been demolished, there were spacious new wings and whole new buildings—she did not know how they could have been built so fast. Nothing remained of the Sheikha's old quarters except one room, which served as an entranceway to that wing.

The Sheikha, too, seemed a different woman: far more hunchbacked. Her cane seemed much taller than ever before, her hair was longer and whiter, and her skin was dark, almost bluish. The only thing that had not changed was her eyes. They still had their stern, obstinate and wary glitter.

The Sheikha received her as she never had before. In spite of her sorrow she hugged her tightly and kissed her, which she had never done on previous visits. Umm Hosny, who had planned on chiding her and keeping her visit short, promptly weakened in the face of this warm welcome and forgot the words she had prepared to say. She overlooked the Sheikha's forgetfulness and her failure to ask about her, especially after hearing, first thing, about Tahany and then about Suroor's mysterious death.

Despite her mourning the Sheikha wanted to know what the future held in store for her. Umm Hosny demurred, saying that she could not, at least today, and hinted indirectly that she preferred to put it off. The Sheikha took the hint and understood perfectly, even though she was burning inside to find everything out as soon as possible.

Umm Hosny did not prolong her visit. She left in spite of urgings for her to stay, left quickly with the excuse that one of her grandsons was ill and needed her by his side, since only she could nurse and comfort him.

She had barely arrived home in midafternoon when two cloaks were delivered. She hid them easily, but within an hour of receiving that gift, more gifts arrived: a pet fawn and some dates. Zakiya opened the gate and accepted the gifts while Umm Hosny was hiding the new cloaks, but she made no trouble; that is what she told herself. That was not all, however. The driver who brought the fawn and the dates told her that he would be back the next morning to pick up the children and take them, as the Sheikha and Umm Hosny had decided, to the palace. Then he would take them, with the other children, out for a picnic.

That night Zakiya was certain; she had proof. The time that had elapsed between the car's arrival and Umm Hosny's had been so short that Umm Hosny had not even been able to take in the situation or come up with a plausible excuse.

Hosny came home and found the children chasing the fawn, and the dates set out in the hall, and saw his mother shouting at the children to be quiet and leave the fawn alone so that she could tether it; and saw his wife sitting on the top step, looking gleeful and gloating.

He shouted angrily, "That's enough! You two—that's enough yelling!"

When the children stopped and the fawn calmed down a little—though he still seemed tired and afraid—Hosny turned to his mother and wife and, pointing to the fawn, asked accusingly, "Where on earth did this disaster come from?"

"Ask my aunt!" answered his wife defensively.

He turned to his mother, who was nervously holding a piece of rope, looking almost afraid.

"So, Haja,"—it was the first time he used this title—"what's going on?"

"Just what you see," she said sarcastically, irritated at the way he had spoken to her. There was a pause. "A fawn?"

"Yes, a fawn! I swear to God, a fawn, but where has it come from? How did it find its way here? Did it fall from the sky? Or sprout from the ground? Why did it ignore everyone else and honor us with its presence?" He was speaking slowly, mockingly, just as his mother had, but now his wife spoke up to get to the heart of the matter.

"They sent the fawn and they sent the dates—it's all from the palace, from the Sheikha!"

"The dates, too?" This, too, Hosny said in a sarcastic tone, and he looked straight at the dates.

"They told us to get the children ready," his wife continued, "so that they can pass by and take them to the palace."

"Well, well! This is just great, this is really something—what else?" He turned to his mother. "What else, Haja? What else do they want us to do?"

What sorrows can gather in the heart and lodge there, as if dead or dying away, when actually neither dead nor dying? What memories can vanish into the breast, that tenebrous cave, never stirring or expected to reappear, until they suddenly do reappear? What human capacity for tolerance, charity and forgiveness makes us forget and be contented, and to go on again, until suddenly the lid is lifted and blown off by pain, discontent and the inability to take any more, revealing everything that could not be kept stifled another moment?

In the few minutes it took for Hosny to ask his questions in that mocking voice, as if Umm Hosny were not his mother, as if she were a naughty little girl, a myriad of emotions, thoughts and desires crowded her heart. She recalled her life since girlhood, the doll with the blue dress that she had made herself. Then she and her doll were snatched away and thrown into the embrace of that old man, Abu Hosny, who played with her as she had played with her doll. He woke her late at night to keep him company because he could not sleep, to massage his feet and back, to chat with him before he began to recite the Koran. On other nights, when she was very drowsy and wanted only to sleep, he wanted other things: she did not know how to respond to him, how to help him, ignore him, or go back to sleep, she was so full of fear and revulsion. When he died, which he did suddenly, she was unable to tell whether he was asleep in the grip of some distant ecstasy or dead, never to come back to her.

She married again, and, having known enough pain in her orphaned state and first marriage, was ready at last to live her life as other people did. She gladly got pregnant and bore one child, then another, giving Shakib al-Usta a boy and a girl, as all women did, and though she was ready to do anything to give him more sons, he left her and went away: divorced her and disappeared.

She was busy with dozens of little tasks, from embroidery to knitting to selling firewood, started her little "trade," and moved to Amman. In the space of several years, as she moved back and forth, trading and making money, dividing her earnings into three equal portions (household expenses, children's clothes and working capital), leaving only a few coins for herself, she would stack her coins up to buy one thing special to her, never saying a word about it to anyone until she had saved enough money to buy it. Then she kept it far from her and still wrapped, now and then adding to it some few necessities. That was the one thing she possessed or considered truly her own; besides, all her life—of which so little was left, she thought to herself—she had worn herself out for them, gone hungry for them, wearied herself so that they would not have to weary or lower themselves. When they were grown she married them off. Now they had children, and once again she was wearing herself out, staying up at night and doing drudge work for them. She wanted nothing in return but a kind word, and if that did not come from the heart, from the depths of their hearts, she did not want it; it was enough that they leave her alone to live as she pleased. But to be called to account, bullied, watched, to be told "Do this" and "Don't do that"—no, that she could no longer tolerate.

Even the palace, the Sheikha, Mooran and everything in this world no longer gave her happiness or meant anything to her. All she wanted to do was something to give her the sense of being alive and free and strong—more than that, she wanted to stay "yes" or "no" according to her own convictions, her own wish, without anyone bossing her.

This is how she thought and felt and pondered; then she came back to herself and found him still watching her, and other eyes besides his were following her. She nearly forgot everything again. She had turned to the fawn and stretched out her hand to have it come near, when she heard Hosny's voice.

"You still haven't told us, Haja, the story behind that fawn!"

"The story behind this fawn?" She said this sharply, almost contemptuously. "There is no story, my boy. It's a fawn like any other fawn."

"Did it fall from the sky?"

"No, my boy, fawns don't fall from the sky. Angels come from the sky, and mothers' joy."

"Fine, so where did it come from?"

"From the Sheikha, my boy."

"So you went there—you broke our oath!"

"Only so that I wouldn't bother you or you me, I went, and I'm going tomorrow and I may go every day!"

"So my oath means nothing to you?"

"I have nothing but respect for your oath, my boy, but you must know: all my life, since I was a little girl until this very day, I've been held down and bound by oaths, restrained and useless, and told 'I don't pity you, I won't let God pity you, I won't let His mercy descend on you.' When you boys were small, I was held back; when you grew up, I was still held back; today and tomorrow you want me to stay that way. No, my boy, I'm the one who decides, and I don't want anyone deciding for me where I should go and when I must go and when I come back!"

"So I mean nothing to you!"

"Take it any way you want."

Said came in and saw how tense things were: his mother standing to one side with a rope, her face sallow and sick from anger and despair, Hosny circling like a hobbled animal, glancing from the fawn and the heaps of dates to his mother, and the children standing in the corners by the staircase. Only the fawn seemed happy.

Said knew that a storm had broken over the house, and he spoke pleasantly to put everyone at ease.

"A fawn is a good omen—and dates are our favorite fruit!"

"And the Sheikha is our favorite person," said Hosny dryly, and laughed.

"All people have good in them, dear brother!" replied Said, trying to assuage his anger. "Look, no matter how you cut it, half of a thousand is five hundred. There's no excuse good enough for a man to get his blood hot, to fray his nerves." He turned to his wife. "What's going on here, Adiba? Is everything falling apart? Is the world coming to an end? Well?"

"Nothing at all, dear . . . if they'd just be reasonable it would be simple. It's not worth all this."

He asked her to tell him, to explain what had happened, and she explained briefly that the palace had sent them the fawn and the dates, and that that was at the bottom of the argument.

"This is a simple matter," he announced to smooth things over. "We'll slaughter the fawn or return it to its owners, and there are a thousand people who'd kiss our hands if we gave them a few of these beautiful dates!"

But that was not the end of the problem. The next morning Hosny and his wife quickly packed their things and left with the children. Said did all he could to change their minds, to make them postpone this move, but Hosny was firm. To convince Said that this was the best solution, he said, as he pushed the children before him, "It's better for both of us, and better for the Haja"—as he now called her—"and this way we're parting as brothers who love each other. If we don't part today, we'll part tomorrow as enemies."

He tried to smile or laugh, and nodded to reemphasize that this was the best solution.

54

ITHIN A FEW DAYS OF HOSNY'S LEAVING the house, Umm Hosny fell ill again. The illness appeared to be a relapse of her old one, so this time Adiba, who was suffering pangs of conscience, as she felt responsible for that malady and some of its repercussions, and who was the sole lady of the house now, was moved to nurse and care for her. She had seen Umm Hosny prepare her medicines the last time, and knew which herbs were needed and which had to be crushed, and now wanted to do as she had done.

"Don't trouble yourself, my girl," croaked her mother-in-law. "You see, my illness now is something different from the last time."

Adiba stared at her, surprised and perplexed, and the old woman cleared her throat and went on. "Nothing can cure me but an herb from Wadi al-Tib!"

"What, Auntie? An herb from Wadi al-Tib?"

"Yes, my girl, an herb from Wadi al-Tib and the water of my own country!"

Adiba tried to persuade her, to insist, to cajole her into feeling a little better, but the old woman smiled sadly. Her voice was weary.

"Every person is her own physician, my girl. I know my condition!"

That afternoon and evening Said tried to soothe her, to persuade her that her condition was nothing, that in a few days she would be better, and then he would give in and let her travel—but in order for her to get better, they would have to call in a doctor. She refused, insisting more vehemently that her cure was *there* and that her health would revive as soon as she got there. If they turned her over to a doctor here, to Mahmilji or someone of his ilk to pierce her sides with needles, that would only hasten her death, and she did not want to die here.

To show him that she did not need any doctors or medicines, she had Adiba brew her a drink of certain herbs she described to her. After drinking it, she seemed livelier and her strength returned. She looked Said in the eye.

"I beg you, my son—send me back. Let me go back to my own country and my own people."

"Haja, we are your people. We are your country."

"You were my family, my boy, but today I don't have a family anymore." A tear dropped onto her cheek, but she was not ashamed and kept talking as if to herself. "And if you have no country, you have no country."

"Trust in God, Haja. Don't talk that way."

"There's no point in talking at all, my boy," she sighed sadly, shaking her head. "I've done plenty of talking in my day and no one listened to me!"

"If it's Hosny's getting mad and moving out, that's a simple matter. It's his own fault, but for your sake I'll kiss his head and make up, and if you stay here we'll be brothers again and love each other. But we have to put this sickness behind you."

The old woman shook her head, meaning that there was more to it than that. When silence filled the room, and Said was unable to create the kind of gaiety he always could, her voice sounded, weak and exhausted.

"Take me to the country and I'll ask you nothing more."

"Whatever you say, Haja, Mother."

"Can we leave tomorrow?"

"We'll travel as soon as you're able to travel."

The night passed, and Umm Hosny was filled with the odor of musk as she remembered how Wadi al-Tib smelled, and felt her thirst quenched by the very thought of the wadi's cold, fresh water. Said spent most of the night quarreling with Adiba because he was afraid that this would be the old woman's last night. He thought back on his past life and realized that it had been harsh and full of difficulties, yet pleasanter and more humane than the life he lived now. Here in Mooran he did nothing but run, run in every direction along with everyone else, convincing other people in an effort to convince himself, laughing, but ironically, as if laughing at himself; yet had had nothing better to do.

With the first rays of daylight Umm Hosny was completely ready. She put on her traveling clothes and sat on the steps opposite Said's room, her bundle set in front of her, waiting.

She did this after setting out food and a little water for the fawn, saying the required morning prayers and repeating some prayers of supplication; she wondered whether she should have something to eat, to strengthen her for the trip and the discomforts of the road, but found herself unable to touch anything, and not really wanting anything.

Just as he had done the night before, Said tried to postpone her trip, promising with ever-mounting fervor that as soon as she recovered from her illness and regained her strength he would travel with her. He would stay there with her if she so wished, and take care of her every need. He could move back to Damascus or Amman, leaving Mooran to its own people. She listened and did not listen. She was far away and filled with sorrow, secure in her silence, not commenting or replying to anything he said, but unmoving in her insistence on leaving this accursed city, this city of misfortune and beguilement and jobless men.

Days and nights passed, her health alternating with illness, Umm Hosny was like a candle, melting and disappearing, or like a nail refusing to bend or break. Said awaited the light of every new day, filled as he was with the conviction that death came only at night, in secret. He was utterly perplexed as to whether he should leave her—she might die away like smoke; to leave her to die without a doctor having been called, because only he understood her illness and how to treat it; or to watch her mental state, to consider that her illness was an expression of depression, for if the depression left her, her strength would return. Torn between these contradictory feelings, he tried to instill a little happiness and animation in the house, and did not hesitate to promise her whatever she wanted.

Hosny came on the fifth day to visit her, downcast and ashamed, and kept looking around every part of the house the whole time as if seeing it for the first time, or looking for changes in it since he had left. When he asked his mother whether or not she was better, and if her pains were the same she'd had before, she answered without moving her gaze from the ceiling, as she lay stretched out on the bed.

"Don't worry about me, my boy." Her eyes dropped. "God doesn't abandon anyone."

The visit ended after the time had passed in silence, except for the deep breaths and sighs Hosny heaved every now and then, which he wished were stronger and more expressive than words. Umm Hosny constantly stole glances at him, as if recalling past images of him and comparing them with the image before her now; she felt intense love and bitterness toward him at the same time. She wanted to rid herself of what was in her heart before remembering him as he had been, but she found that she could not.

He kissed her hand and said, "Forgive me, Mother, please don't begrudge me your blessing."

"Bless you, my boy."

"If I can't come tomorrow, I'll be with you the day after."

"This is your house, my boy. You are welcome here anytime."

He turned away and had nearly reached the door when she spoke wearily.

"Don't forget to give my love to the children, and Zakiya!"

Tears ran down her cheeks as he descended the stairs, as if she had bid him farewell for the last time. She felt the world contracting, collapsing in on her, and felt that she no longer needed anything or anybody. She had always been alone. No one had ever understood her or stood by her.

Adiba came in after saying good-bye to her brother-in-law, sat on the edge of the bed and looked awkward; she could not ask her about Hosny now for fear of stirring the sorrows anew, and since she could not think of anything else to say, she asked if she wanted anything or needed anything done for her.

"If my daughter Zakiya were here . . ." Umm Hosny answered, and added sadly, "She should have been here."

"I'm like your daughter, Auntie."

"That's true, my girl." Umm Hosny looked around her, seeming uncertain and confused. Adiba sensed that she had something to say, and asked her anxiously, "If you need anything, believe me, I'm here to serve you, Auntie. Tell me."

"I've said everything I have to say, my girl."

"Yes, Auntie, tell me everything you want. I'm here."

Umm Hosny turned on her side and pointed to what was under the bed. Adiba looked, questioningly, and Umm Hosny added wearily, "The bundle."

"The bundle?"

"What I prepared for the end is in there." Adiba's gaze did not leave her. "It's my shroud, my girl."

At dawn the next day, the darkness scattered and day began, one hour after the arrival of the doctor sent by Dr. Subhi Mahmilji from the National Hospital to treat Umm Hosny (Dr. Mahmilji had excused himself from coming himself, since he had retired from general practice, he told Said, who had brought him shortly after midnight); at that moment, between the last darkness and first light, as Said was traversing Mooran from one end to the other trying to find a pharmacy to buy the medicine, Umm Hosny died.

Three days later the Sheikha sent a palace chauffeur to inquire after Umm Hosny, and Adiba told him from behind the half-opened door that she was not there. When he asked when she would be back, and when he might return, since the Sheikha wanted her urgently, Adiba said, "Tell the Sheikha she is gone."

"When will she be back?"

"She's not coming back."

"Is she traveling?"

"It's over with!"

"What?"

"She is dead."

"Dead?"

"Yes, dead."

"God have mercy on her, and on us all!"

"I always had my eye on that bundle," Said told his wife two weeks after the decease. "I was worried by how big it was—I thought it was all of her things to sell—who ever imagined it was a shroud!"

55

MOORAN, LIKE ALL THE TOWNS AND VILlages of this obstinate, untamed desert, calm and peaceable for uncounted years, bothered itself with outside affairs only briefly before reverting to its natural and typical state: waiting. Mooran waited for rain, caravans, the Thursday market, and something yet more it could not see and did not know.

Rain, or the mere gathering of clouds in the sky, whether they burst here or somewhere else, filled the Mooranis with a sweet contentment resembling delight, for rain meant fewer days of hardship, a less wretched life for them, and could mean—though often it did not—that fathers and sons could remain at home instead of roaming.

Caravans meant the arrival of any number of long-awaited absent folk, in addition to the money, news and fragrance of far-off places the caravans brought. The people bought more at such times than at others, as they knew or guessed the new difficulties they might face as a result of the stability or changing of prices. When not welcoming the returning travelers and asking about those who had not returned, listening to the news of other communities, whether or not they'd had rain yet, Mooran lived these happy, unusual days with its people living and acting differently. They were livelier, less on their guard, and could not get their fill of talking among themselves and asking questions of the newcomers.

In any season but winter, or when the caravans arrived late or did not come at all, Mooran waited, in its orderly, serene way, for Thursday, which was the market day as well as the traditional day for weddings and banquets. People were livelier than on any other day. And it was on this day that the livestock that had been out in the desert for a long time were brought back in and that people from all around Mooran came to buy and sell, haggling and telling stories. There were arguments and double-dealing, and disagreements that ended in angry rifts or, occasionally, satisfaction, though each side hid his true feelings, so that the other side would not feel that he had been bested or successful.

Mooran's waiting, day after day, month after month, was mostly focused on the Souq al-Halal, a market which was virtually the lung by which Mooran breathed, the pole where things gathered and then dispersed. The most important men met here for the biggest and most important deals; money, livestock, foreigners, everyone came. The market was not in the center of the city, nor was it neat or beautiful, but it was the most important place.

The Souq al-Halal stood to the extreme east of the city and slightly to the south, not far from Wadi Riha, where most of the caravans entered Mooran: it was a broad expanse of land, flat and arid, with wells on one side and livestock pens on the other. These were simple pens, mere squares and oblongs of earth walled off by rows of small stones about three feet high, rented for trifling sums to foreigners to keep the livestock and beasts they bought from getting mixed with other people's animals.

On the borders of this land, or of the marketplace, as it was generally called, were several small and windowless shops, built primitively and with great speed, to sell everything the caravans needed and pursue several lines of business at once. Most of these shops were usually filled with people and goods and buyers mixing with sellers, especially from midafternoon Wednesday until noon on Friday; the climax of activity was on market day, Thursday. On all the other days the shops were empty of people, or nearly so, as the proprietors thought nothing of closing up for long hours at a time.

Not far from the marketplace, on its western flank, to be exact, stood the mosque, on a square plot of land enclosed by a wall of carefully selected stones set tightly one above the other—unlike the walls of the pens, on whose soil were spread simple mats of different sizes and colors, most of which were slowly rotting.

On the opposite side of the marketplace was Mooran's cemetery. Outsiders had a hard time picking it out, unless they squinted or saw it in daylight, but the people of Mooran knew every single one of its graves, though most were now level with the earth, the tombstones fallen down or removed. Each tomb and each stone marker was a powerful and living thing to every person in this city.

When the whole scene was assembled and viewed from a certain distance, it looked like a triangle: the mosque was the apex of the triangle, and the marketplace and cemetery were the sides.

Mooran was reconstituted time and again in this triangle. Its joys and sorrows and fears began here, as did its thoughts and all its news. Travelers and foreigners came here, and there was no citizen or resident of Mooran who did not have vivid memories of this place: a father returning from a long journey; the recollection of those who had gone and not returned; the confusion, advice and tears in the last moments before departure; and the wistful sorrow and anguish as the caravan rose up and embarked.

In this triangle of earth were stories of the poor of the market, so poor that they owned no more than a sack or two of straw, or a bucket with a few drops of camel medicine, but they hung on for the opportunity so long awaited that its coming meant all their happiness; they were rich. Others, whose wealth in cash and flocks had been proverbial, became penniless in the space of a day if their herds were wiped out in a drought year, or wandered into the desert in search of grazing, never to be heard from again.

Children who had opened their eyes upon the world around them passed over their houses and the neighborhood they were born in to discover, before anything else, the Souq al-Halal: from here they herded lambs for the holiday slaughter; here they bought a donkey or mule to carry water, before the houses got plumbing; uncounted marriage deals were concluded between fathers here; from here embarked the grand journeys to far-off places, which changed the lives of so many.

In the market, jokes and stories were told and carried to Mooran, after which short journey they were changed and embroidered, much to the laughter and delight of the Mooranis. In the market, titles and nicknames were given to people, which came to be used more than their own names; in the market, the people gossiped about one another and spied carefully on everything around them and learned all the news and even the most hidden secrets.

So the market had been for as long as Mooran existed. Every market has its landmarks, its characteristics and experts who know all the secrets and mysteries, though nothing in their dress or outward behavior gives that away, and nothing visible at first glance. There were two or three such men, whose features were sharply etched in the people's minds, not because they had achieved remarkable things or were richer or more powerful than the others, but because their existence was linked to the people's lives in some unaccustomed way, and because their actions were not governed by the logic that ruled others. If every state and city has its rulers and rich and powerful men, every city also has certain people who epitomize the life of the city, who set it apart from other cities and from other times.

Shamran al-Oteibi was one of those, not because he had money and livestock, or because he was the Sultan's representative, giving a receipt for every beast that came into the market or was sold there, but because he was the "wise man" whose opinion was sought on every important matter, especially when things became serious or there was a dispute.

If there was a dispute in the market, which happened often, the disputants would go to Shamran and he would settle it. He knew horses and the age and lineage of each, the going price for similar horses here and elsewhere, and who the buyers and sellers had been. He understood strong camels, their health and their illnesses, and how and when to treat them. In a dispute over livestock that had gone or come, and the share of those who had gone in on them, it was Shamran who mediated and delivered an opinion with long discussion or protest. When it came to the unwritten laws that governed the relations between people here and defined their rights and obligations without knowing how and why these had come into effect, Shamran, who could not read or write, was one of the few who heard them out.

Shamran also had a thorough and indisputable knowledge of the genealogies, intermarriages, and feuds that kept the tribes together or apart, whose details defeated the memory of most.

Shamran was neither rich nor poor; he was one of the thousands who passed through life without wondering, and without asking others, how a living was secured, because they actually got along by chance or luck, by their modest needs, ability to make do, or perhaps the secret planning and desires that never reached the point of greed. Had it not been for Shamran's children, each of them, since the beginning, with his own line of work he doggedly applied himself to without prodding, he would not have been able to spend these long hours in the market, in his unvarying spot: he sat in the shade of the mosque's wall, and all seekers after his counsel came here, along with the curious and those who wanted nothing more than to talk or listen to the stories.

Caravan news and the state of the market could be gleaned here by asking questions or simply listening in; someone might decide whether to buy or sell or wait, to decide what action to take today or tomorrow.

If it was not market day, and a caravan was not arriving, and it was not winter, then Shamran's getting up to say the sundown prayer in the mosque was the signal that his day was ended. He always set off briskly to perform this duty, cutting through the cemetery—his unvarying route—never ceasing to repeat under his breath his prayers of supplication. As he came near the western wall, his voice rose distinctly, because his father's grave was there. On the way home he bypassed the cemetery, crossing Mooran from east to west.

Shamran was only rarely absent from the market and still rarer were the days when his news or stories were not quoted. While his absence may not have attracted attention, it moved the curiosity of old and young alike and created a void in the wall of the mosque and the whole market. Many of the people claimed that silence reigned like a dark, mournful shadow over the market when he was not there.

The stability and conspicuous character that Shamran lent the Souq al-Halal were matched or even surpassed by those of Saleh al-Rushdan—Saleh the Warner, as they called him—because Saleh caused more commotion and outcry in the market than everyone else put together.

Saleh's main job was "shoeing horses," as he told anyone who asked about his line of work, his answer both insistent and ironic. No one had ever seen him shoe a horse, and no horse owners went anywhere near him, with or without their horses, out of fear that he would claim to have once shod their horses or given his opinion of them!

If there was a shortage of donkeys, or if their owners put off shoeing them for weeks on end, because they were poor or did not see the urgency of shoeing, Saleh would find someone to do it for them.

Every year, in the month of Ramadan and during the feast days, Saleh stayed out of the Souq al-Halal and went nowhere near it, giving no sign of life: he had important work to do, carrying a drum through the streets of Mooran with an ever-growing number of shouting and laughing boys. He beat the drum happily with special, constant rhythm, calling out words somewhere between prayer and curses directed at several people by name. Late at night he raised his voice higher than in the daytime, and, angry or exaggeratedly serious, especially when he got no response to his drumming or shouting, demanding that all sleepers get up, "because life is short, and people should spend it in prayer and worship, and because Death awaits everyone and judgment is at hand."

It was Saleh's habit to spend the last three days of Ramadan, and the feast days, carrying a green flag fastened expertly to his middle, and having been given quantities of wheat and barley as holiday alms, proceeded to distribute them secretly to the needy. This was a task that occupied him completely. He put the wheat and barley into bags whose size reflected the size of the needy family, sorted them, marked them with signs he alone understood, and after counting them dozens of times and rehearsing in his mind the names of the recipients, gave them out without anyone the wiser. It took days, after which he reappeared in the market, all set for long and burdensome work after having been gone for the whole period.

The people looked on Saleh as Mooran's village idiot, or one of them, because his behavior, and the notions that filled his head, and the speeches and opinions he came out with, especially against the rich and prominent, and his jokes about work and people, not to mention his very numerous fabrications, lies, and complaints, made them see him that way.

They said that he talked to animals and stones, and refused to talk to people unless he had to. When a donkey or she-ass was brought to him for shoeing, he spoke to the donkey and asked it more questions than he asked its owner. "Those tyrants," he would say, "they don't just exhaust you, they curse you and load you down with the whole earth. In this world everyone oppresses everyone else, but you're the only oppressed one who oppresses no one." He shook his head sadly and turned to his tools, starting his job and his monologue together. "Don't be a donkey all your life—keep your head high, kick and fight, kick a few blind men—don't be afraid!" When the donkey's owner laughed, Saleh would turn halfway toward him angrily and address him from between clenched teeth. "Have a little mercy! Remember, this is one of God's creatures and has to rest sometime!"

If the donkey's owner replied or kept smiling, Saleh would leave the donkey's leg and turn fully toward him. "You say, 'What can a donkey understand? A donkey has to bear burdens'?" Not getting a reply, he went on. "Without the beasts God created, without this market, you wouldn't be able to do one thing.!"

Saleh al-Rushdan could be angered by a mere word or an act; it happened every day. When angry, he interrupted his work, not to return to it for at least an hour, no matter how close to completion it was. Sometimes he would not resume it as long as the donkey's owner was there, so that the owner would have to take his animal some distance away and give it to someone else, pretending to have sold it, in order for Saleh to resume his work.

The price he asked varied according to the customer and the

day. He charged the wealthy more than the poor, and sometimes he dealt in bulk: if a poor man's donkey came in with a crowd of others, he demanded payment for it from those best able to pay.

He did this happily and subtly. When asked why he made distinctions between people that way, his answer was soft but sarcastic: "For whoever doesn't like it—Mooran is a big place, let him eat as much sand as he likes!"

People went back to him and got used to his ways, using arguments and haggling as a means of chatting with him and killing time, or to make Saleh lose his temper. When he began to curse, with froth appearing at the corners of his mouth, and insults directed at the ground, making threats and vowing to leave this line of work, and "these Mooran people can go to hell," then they would give in or pretend to give in, telling him grand and exaggerated things to please him, praising his skill, which was like no one else's, and describing the prestige and value his presence lent to Mooran. After a long session of apologies and pleading in God's name, Saleh would consent to go back to his work.

Because Saleh al-Rushdan was this sort of person, he became a powerful and vital part of Mooran. Everyone asked for him and joked with him and asked his opinion about important local issues: "Al-Dosari is buying up all of Mooran and trying to evict everybody—what do you think, Saleh?" "Mooran belongs to its own people, not to al-Dosari or anyone else, and they're not going anywhere!" "But he's bought it." "Bought it, didn't buy it, don't bother me with these stories of crazy people. Mooran is staying where it is, it's not changing—let al-Dosari go somewhere else."

When news spread that horses had been delivered for the Sultan, everyone sought out Saleh. "The palace is asking for you, Saleh. His Excellency said, 'Let Ibn Rushdan be brought to us and stay near us—no one but he can handle these horses." He looked unbelievingly at them, and when they swore that they were telling the truth, he replied, 'His Majesty knows where to find me—let him come or send me a messenger with paper and a seal—then we'll see." "That's no way to talk, Saleh—the Sultan will be angry!" "Anger is the height of silliness—I don't care who he is, let him come and ask for me." "But you know him, Saleh." "And he knows Ibn Rushdan!"

Beside Shamran and Saleh in the market was Obeid al-Tawil: a short, plump man whose beady eyes shone with insolence and irony. Anyone seeing him for the first time would have thought him to be the sheikh of the market or its richest merchant. His constant swift movement among the buyers and sellers, the orders her flung at this or that knot of people, demanding speedy acceptance of the offer he was making or consenting to one, bewildered the people. "We'll pay thirty per head—if you're selling, we'll buy," he might say, and if the seller was silent, he shouted, "Thirty and one-half," and if the seller looked away he again shouted, "Thirty-one," and if this met with a shake of the head and smile, Obeid shouted, "Why don't you sell, my good man—this is the market price!" and pretended to wash his hands of the deal, to turn away and address the other group of people: "My friends, the sheep are fine, well-fed, and each one is worth forty." "Are you buying or selling, Obeid? Those sheep are skin and bones and not worth anything! If he'll sell for thirty-three, we'll buy." "My friends, there are people all around him and they'll pay more." "Offer higher, and we'll see."

Rather than going directly into more haggling, Obeid circulated through the market to see which of his competitors were present and what prices were attainable, and when some time had gone by, he went back on the offensive. "If you sell at my price, my boy, you won't regret it." "God willing." "The market's dead—no one else will pay you what we're paying." "Get out of my face, man, I have to make a living!" "Look, here's my final offer: thirty-two." "Not even close! That's not the price of someone who really wants to buy."

Once again Obeid went back to his second group. "My friends, Shammari is cunning. He knows his sheep and he knows the market. My advice is for you to brace yourselves and pay forty." "You snake, are you with us or with Shammari?" "With you or with Shammari? God forgive you, people of Mooran—is nothing sacred?"

The haggling wore on, with Obeid shuttling to and fro, the price shifting, Shammari silent, shaking his head at every new price Obeid proposed; when Obeid pressed him harder, Shammari curled his lip to show a mocking smile, and uttered what he never tired of repeating: "Not even close." When the price reached thirty-five, which was the highest two of the Mooranis could possibly go, Obeid was told to close the deal for them. "You're still bedouin," Obeid told Shammari in bitter despair, "you don't know how to buy or sell. No one else would pay what I've paid, but it seems that you have no luck—you'll have to wait until next Thursday and sell at twenty." He sighed. "So—will you sell at thirty-four and a half?" "Not even close, not even close." "At thirty-five?" "You've got a deal."

Thus suddenly, as unexpected as a spring rain cloud, the sale was made. No one watching the long and arduous bargaining would have expected the bedouin to concede anything, but now he agreed and the deal was made. This was where Obeid showed his gift for control; he issued resolute orders to both sides to step aside with the sheep and urged the buyers to pay up, and when they did, he put it in his pocket and asked that the sheep be counted again, while the bedouin, who did not recall the number he had mentioned, and tried to recall it as his sheep were taken away from him, looked wary and worried that he had been the victim of a careful trap, the more so since Obeid, with the money in his pocket, was moving around here and there asking questions. The buyers of the sheep were busy examining the quality and fatness of the sheep. During this difficult period of waiting and worry Obeid shouted for the bedouin to follow him. He sat in the shade of the mosque's wall and asked him to sit, and after discussing the number of sheep, the price for reach and the total sum, the long and arduous task of counting began, since each man had his own way of counting. When that was over, with Obeid holding a portion of the total, they began to negotiate over how much Obeid was due from the bedouin. As a rule, given the air of worry and uncertainty, Obeid got more than he had expected, and the bedouin was too confused to know whether he had given him too much or too little.

Just as Obeid rushed around in circles to conclude a deal, and settled up with the bedouin, whom he described as being like a pigeon, since he did not know whether he was coming or going, he went back to his clients, the buyers, to show intimidation but insolence above all.

"If it hadn't been for Obeid wearing down that slob, he wouldn't have sold them for less than forty! He was ready to turn around and go home!" He repeated these words with different emphases to help them sink in while he probed the backs and tails of the newly sold sheep, and went on ironically. "Now, reach in your pockets and reward Obeid!"

If they delayed or seemed hesitant, he changed his tone of voice.

"Look, here's Shamran, Abu Nimr, he's right here and he knows these things."

"Be quiet now," one of them shouted at him, to leave him no more chance to display his shameless smoothness. "Let us see for ourselves!" When Obeid looked surprised, the other added, "Don't worry, man, you'll get yours."

"That talk is no good to me," sneered Obeid, "it doesn't give me bread. Come on now, reach in your pockets and pull out some money!"

"Be patient, man, trust in God!"

With unscrupulous cunning one of them led away the sheep while the other stayed behind to deal with Obeid, and after much strain, shouting and anger as people gathered, Obeid got his way.

Great sums of money made their way to Obeid, albeit sporadically, and might have been enough for him to go into some easier work, and thus avoid this racing around the market, but he loved his work; it made him, in his own view, a gentleman.

"He's a mess," Shamran said of Obeid. Others, who laughed at him and needed his services, called him the father of the market, while those who hated him were quick to call him a thief and swindler.

There were a great many more characters in Mooran's Souq al-Halal, whose faces came and went, either because they had no steady work or had left it, and many of them traveled frequently. Juma passed through the market—he was the black doctor who treated camels. There were two brothers who worked as slaughterers, because there was a demand for butchery in the market, but Mooran changed and so did the brothers: one got himself a restaurant and the other became a chauffeur. The same could be said of Abu Ghoreifa, who used to make coffee and hawk it in the market, or stand at the gate of the mosque, until one day he joined the court of Sultan Khazael and became another person entirely.

All this was a part of Mooran's history fast vanishing from its people's memory. And just a few years into Sultan Khazael's reign Abu Ghoreifa announced, through Juweiber al-Duweihi, Mooran's town crier, to the crowds of worshipers leaving the mosque, that beginning from the following Thursday the market would be held in Awali; and that they were to pass it on. Owners of shops in the market found this out from the police, who ordered them to move out.

56

BEFORE JUWEIBER AL-DUWEIHI, MOORAN'S
town crier, stood at the gate of the mosque
to tell the people leaving it after prayers
that the Souq al-Halal would move to Awali, and that they should
tell everyone else . . . before that, a number of things happened:
the nearly forgotten doctor, forgotten even by Shamran—who,
more properly, had not forgotten him, but remembered him as an
old illness is dimly remembered—came to visit the Souq al-Halal.
He came three weeks before the decision to relocate the market.

It was late afternoon. Shamran was in the shade of the mosque's
wall, listening more than speaking, and it was an ordinary day, not
a Thursday; nor was any caravan arriving. The doctor parked far
away and got out with three palace men, to give the visit an air of
simplicity, and headed first for the mosque. They said some brief
prayers in honor of the mosque, and spent a considerable time in a
state resembling submissive supplication; then they got up and

headed west, cutting through the full length of the market. Shamran was watching them perplexedly in silence, as if he could not believe what he was seeing.

"So what is prayer but prayer, my friends."

Those with him looked back and forth between him and the slowly receding doctor, but his eyes never left their faces. He smiled and added, "But those prayers have nothing to do with God!"

While the doctor's visit left little impression on the people, since he did not speak to any of them, and the visit had such a guileless and pious stamp, a certain unease affected Shamran and within a few days turned to fear.

Several days after this visit Prince Mayzar made a visit, though his was marked by a great deal of noise and spectacle. It lasted longer than the doctor's, and he talked to the people and asked questions and joked with them.

Prince Mayzar's visit delighted most of the people, since they remembered the old days when the Sultan himself used to visit the Souq al-Halal. They remembered how the talk went, how people were then, especially when they listened to Prince Mayzar tell them how rich the market would become; it would become a green meadow, so that anyone seeing it a year or two from now would not know the place. He said all this smiling and laughing loudly, which made many of them join in the talking and laughter. For Shamran, who stayed in his spot by the mosque listening to the distant laughter of the prince and the noise of the talk and questions of the men around him, this was the day his unease turned to fear. *We haven't seen them for years,* he said to himself, *or heard anything from them. And I don't think today is any better than yesterday.*

The very next day, a Wednesday, in the very late afternoon, as the market throbbed with animals and people, and sellers mixed with buyers, traversing the whole length of the market to check on the quality of all the sheep before making decisions the next day, Prince Mayzar arrived with Price Fawaz and Prince Milhem. Despite the fanfare of their arrival—for they drove their car to the center of the market—most people took little notice of their visit because of the shouting, the rush of people, and the fury of the camels at the general noise and crowds.

Shamran noticed, however, and while he learned of it only shortly before it ended, he immediately abandoned his conversation and insisted on going to look for Saleh. Saleh was completely absorbed in shoeing a donkey, unaware that anything unusual was happening in the market, unaware even that Shamran was standing over him and calling him.

When he raised his head, he looked at Shamran with questioning eyes.

"Don't worry, Saleh, you have nothing to worry about," Shamran told him in a voice mixed with sorrow and irony. Saleh said nothing, but continued to question with his eyes. "A few days ago the sheikhs paid us a visit, you know who, and today His Majesty's brothers are visiting. Tomorrow or the next day the big man will come and you'll deal with nothing but Thoroughbreds—you'll be minting money!"

"That's the last thing on my mind, Abu Nimr."

"Look and see! They're wearing white robes like bridegrooms, and they haven't spared anyone in the market—it's all 'How are you!' and 'How do you do!' God knows what's going on."

Saleh glanced around in all directions and saw nothing out of the ordinary, because the crowds at that hour obstructed his view and made it hard to distinguish one person from another. He looked at Shamran, who spoke.

"God help us from all three of them!"

When Saleh saw that Shamran meant what he said, he tossed aside his hammer and slapped his hands together.

"Do you remember, Abu Nimr, when Khureybit used to come to the market—do you remember how he'd boom, 'My friends, my good men, I swear by God you have borne much; there is yet a little to go. Be of good cheer—when we are done we won't forget what any one of you has done, but for right now we need your help, men.' A little time comes and goes, some die and so much for them; if they left orphans, so much for *them*, and Khureybit became a Sultan of salt, and—he forgot it all. When a catastrophe or two hit the market, it was 'God help you good men, how are you, God go with you.' When anyone asked him a question he raised his voice over everyone's: 'With the sword we conquered. We took pity and gave pardon. We. We.' And the ones who fought, who suffered and died, no one remembers them. He used to fool everyone with his fine talk of 'I swear to God you are true men, great heroes.' And that's all we ever got from him!" He added with a sigh, "God, how much has Mooran seen!"

"There's more for her to see," said Shamran meaningfully.

"Don't worry, Abu Nimr, you'll see. You can't build without tearing down . . ." He paused. " 'Who thinks that time will last, his pleasure/Will not endure.' "

Saleh was more at ease than usual. When the donkey's owner pressed him he resumed his work, still repeating, "Pleasure will not last; no, pleasure will not last," and working fast in order to go and see what was happening. He had a feeling that today was different from other days, and that Shamran needed him, because "Abu Nimr is the linchpin of the market; he's the light and the rain." That was how Saleh described him when they were on good terms; when they were not, he kept quiet and ignored him, very unlike his behavior with other people.

The two had a special and unusual friendship, unlike the relationship between any other two people. Shamran had a memory like the earth and the rain, and Saleh was the same: he knew people by their voice and could identify them without raising his head. He could smell the rain hours before it fell by twitching his nose, as a rabbit does, and then he would say, "My friends, the rain is on its way!" or, if he was expecting a sandstorm, "Beware, my friends! Sand, dust and hardship are coming!" He knew from the movement of the wind, and his unerring gut instinct.

This was how the Souq al-Halal knew Saleh, and because he was fearless and forthright, people tried to provoke him—they told him big news as soon as they heard it; that got him started, and he didn't stop.

At one time it had been no more than a joke—all he heard were allusions. When someone told him that the Sultan had begun to wear gold brocade and silk, Saleh said something that engraved itself on people's memories: "Beware, people of the market! These are the first steps of a dangerous dance!"

When news spread of the Sultan's marriage to a half-Arab, half-Circassian woman, Saleh refused to work that day. "Stop your buying and selling, people!" he told anyone who asked him why. "This is the wedding day!" When, nonplussed, they ignored him, he came back at them angrily. "It's my father who's getting married! He's marrying a bedouin girl, with a town girl in her womb!" Then they saw what and whom he was talking about.

"Ibn Rushdan," someone shouted, "careful what you say! The evil eye!"

"Anything can happen." Saleh laughed.

Everyone within earshot laughed, and after their laughter and smiles faded, they sank into thought or got into discussions with one another.

That was Saleh, and Mooran, which tolerated him and found in him a relief from its enveloping monotony; through him the city said what could not be said directly or officially. Some discerning souls urged him to tone it down or to stop it, or to "put a stone in his pocket to weigh him down." So far the palace had been patient and tolerant, or pretended not to hear, but one day its patience would wear out.

Saleh himself did not imagine that the palace could quarrel with him or become an enemy, because "the palace is our palace and the state is our state, my friends. If it weren't for us—Khureybit, Khureybit's son, who are they? We don't want a palace for any criminal or clown, we want a palace for God." Al-Ajrami heard what Saleh said and spoke up: "Just as I've told you all, this is a city of faith and will never be a city of blasphemy—until now we've put up with that fancy white man, but someday he'll break his neck and die. You go to Sheikh Saleh al-Rushdan and listen to what he has to say!"

Stories, jokes and rumors circulated between the Souq al-Halal and Mooran, but the people were more amused than upset by them; the talk made life easier to take. If the Sultan trimmed his beard or changed his appearance, if he married again or got a new favorite boy, or if his motorcade headed in this or that direction, Saleh was the mouthpiece of the market: "My friends, since he first came here, dressing up and perfuming himself and carrying on, we've got nothing but camel piss; we've been moving backward every day."

The people knew that the Sultan had cut his beard and begun to wear new clothes, unlike before, and when al-Ajrami heard it he raised his voice: "This dervish"—he meant Saleh—"has a link with the heavens—his prayers are heard!"

The people looked to Saleh and looked around them, and Saleh raged on day after day, his words of warning becoming ever more dire: "Be watchful, people of Mooran, the world is heading for desolation. If Judgment Day doesn't come tomorrow it will be the day after, if you don't die God's death you'll die a slave's death! Your money won't do you any good, this world is passing away and man is but a speck in all creation—you must not be deceived! Every soul will taste death, and then money and offspring won't do you any good!"

That evening, after the princes left and the clamor in the market died down, Shamran arrived uncharacteristically late. Saleh came and found out what had happened, and addressed Shamran and those around him.

"Since the first day the foreigners came, they've been like the lids of his eyes. . . ." And he pointed to the Ghadir Palace so that they would know whom he was talking about. "You see how low he's sunk, and if you live until tomorrow, you'll see with your own eyes."

When the decision was made to move the Souq al-Halal from its original site to Awali, it was more than Shamran could bear. Saleh refused to obey the order, and for weeks insisted on coming to the market every day; he spread out his tools and started his fire, but was eventually forced to move, as everyone before him had been forced to move, by the earth-moving equipment that came and began its work.

57

SHAMRAN LOVED HORSES MORE THAN ANYTHING else, and was more attached to them than to any other thing, "because their forelocks impart enough luck to last until Judgment Day," as he claimed the Prophet once said, adding, "When a man is depressed, or oppressed by a Sultan, he finds a new family, new loves, new lands on a horse's back." A moment later he whispered conspiringly, "It gives him one of the two 'red things': blood or gold," and smiled as he concluded, "God knows, he may get both."

The Sultan was, in Shamran's eyes, a tyrant, no matter how he might change. "He loves his power more than he loves his subjects, and loves himself more than he loves his Lord."

Shamran did not bequeath horses to his sons, because the ones he had were consumed by the flames of this new age; he bequeathed them out of malice to the Sultan, a malice that became irrevocable when he was forced to run his horses—he owned two of the finest horses in Mooran—in the al-Rahba Race. His Ham-dani and Saqlawi were sent away in Ibn Maheid's truck, but the truck caught fire and the two horses were killed. Shamran said that the Sultan had asked Ibn Maheid to do that, so that Shamran's horses could not win the race. Ibn Maheid said, in front of the sheikh, "Death and God's will, my good man—I've lost more than al-Oteibi: my truck burned!" but within a few months Ibn Maheid had three trucks and Shamran had no horses, for a few days after the fire he'd sold his other horses to Shaddad al-Mutawa, saying, "I've lost my finest—I don't want anything."

What camels he had left were lost after the huge trucks and ce-ment mixers filled Mooran and turned it upside down upon itself and its night into day—he was compelled to sell his camels because he could no longer afford to feed them, and "no one would haggle for them." He sold them cheap as dirt and slept that night without cursing the Sultan.

What he bequeathed to his four sons, or what they inherited from their ancestors, without knowing or wishing it, were marvel-ous things: in Nimr's case, knowledge. He was the only one of his brothers to learn how to read and write. Even while he learned how to write letters for travelers, and to do market accounts, he left the office, and just as his father had a corner in the Souq al-Halal he too acquired his own corner, and just as his father talked about the features and bloodlines of horses, Nimr talked about people's concerns and problems, and just as his father changed, he changed. He began to talk of nothing but politics. He read, lis-tened, probed and studied, so that he came to know everything that went on in Mooran. Now, day after day, Nimr not only wrote letters and petitions, but talked with the people of Mooran about everything, until he became known as Nimr the Newspaper!

Badr, on the other hand, had never held a pen in his life or traced a letter; his substitute for the pen was the screwdriver. No one knew how he learned to repair electrical appliances, or when. He was especially gifted with radios.

"Don't fool yourselves," his father said when asked about it. "Badr has learned only one thing: how to tear things apart—he even tears cars apart!" When he was asked about it again, as this reply was understood to be joking or sarcastic, he said, "If you don't believe me, go look at the cemetery behind our house and then you'll believe!"

Badr began this way, "killing" dozens of electrical appliances, especially radios, making his difficult way. He could fix any electrical gadget, no matter how new or complicated, and never asked what the problem was or how to repair it; just "leave the receiver with me and come back in three or four days," and in that time, with very patient tinkering, he would reach one of two results, either "This died before it got to me—it's no good," or "Take it and see—is it better than before or not?"

That was his beginning, but before long he became a specialist in unusual things: how to defeat the jamming of certain programs, and how to "steal" electrical current for the homes of the poor. He was happy to do these things without any pay or profit.

Just as Nimr was called Nimr the Newspaper, Badr had several nicknames: Badr Radio, Badr Shortwave, and Badr Mediumwave, but the name that stuck, especially when anything electrical was mentioned to him, was simply Ibn Shamran.

Shamran's third son was Najm.

Najm was raised by his uncles, the Bani Murra, and from the Bani Murra he learned tracking, caution and knowledge of others; he came to Mooran only at the age of twenty, already grown and matured. He was extremely wary, even of his brothers and the other members of his family, silent as a rock, and stubborn as a mountain. His father and brothers tried to find out what kind of man he was or could be, but in vain. No one knew when he had learned to read and write, or whether he had learned in Mooran or from his uncles. Unexpectedly they discovered that he could write and read, and while his brother Nimr sought out others, to write their letters and petitions, Najm wrote for himself, and read without knowing others and without sensing. Shamran explained his son's "skittishness" by saying that he was not used to their ways, having lived with his uncles. "Let him be—he'll come along." Najm had grown up and developed very much with his own temperament, with no one else involved.

Some time later, Najm asked his father for money to go into business, and when Shamran asked him what sort of business interested him—horses, sheep, or buying and selling in the market—he was surprised to hear him say, "I've been thinking, Father."

Shamran looked at his son and smiled a rather puzzled smile.

"In all Mooran, Father, no one sells books but Bukhari and Ibn Hazim. There should be another bookstore."

"Will you sell paper, my boy?"

"I'll sell books!"

"Do you think people will buy?" He went on without waiting for a reply. "Unless I'm deceived, my boy, the only customer you'll have will be your brother Nimr, so that he can tell it all to the people and confound Mooran!"

Shamran laughed loudly but sadly. He knew that people could trade in sheep and merchandise, and had learned that some traded in land and buildings, but he had never imagined that people would buy and sell paper. What books were there but the Koran and the tales of Antar and Zeer? The Koran was given freely, not sold, and that only once in a lifetime; even then it might never be opened, since people found it blessing enough to have the book there in the house. He absolutely could not imagine what else there might be.

Now there was this boy—no one knew how he thought or what he wanted—asking for his help. Should he help him or abandon him? Should he close his ears to him and lose him as he had lost him for the first ten years?

He talked it over with him. He told him that Mooran needed work and subsistence more than it needed paper, and that Bukhari and Ibn Hazim were enough for Mooran and did not want competition. He told him that the misfortune of Nimr and Badr was enough, and that he would lend him assistance in herding sheep or camels—if he didn't want that, why, then, cloth was rather like paper—everyone in Mooran needed clothes to wear, and nobody in Mooran read. Najm said nothing; he went silent. Shamran, who feared his son's silence more than his words, gave his consent in the end. He sold and bought to secure what his son needed, and Badr helped, so that Mooran got a third bookstore: the Abu Zarr Bookstore.

Saleh, the youngest son, was raised by his father, at first in the Souq al-Halal and with Shaddad al-Mutawa after that. When his father's horses burned to death and the rest were sold, he had only Shaddad to turn to. At first Saleh worked as a rider and groom, then bought a quarter share in a horse, then half, and because he had no world but this one, knowing how to ride horses, to breed and groom them, Shaddad came to think of him as a son, and for a long time many people thought that Saleh was of the Mutawa clan.

The bookstore had been open a year or slightly more before the Souq al-Halal was moved to Awali. Shamran, who gave Najm the money he needed to go into business, never asked about the business. It was his custom never to interfere in his son's affairs, because he trusted them and was completely immersed in the details of the relocation of the Souq al-Halal. After the market moved, leaving Shamran lost in Mooran, one of the places he visited to pass the time was the Abu Zarr Bookstore.

It never occurred to Shamran for a moment that his son had made a wise choice of careers, but he agreed to give him the money voluntarily, though he did not go along with the idea. Now, however, that he sat in the store, watching his son scurry around and the people going in and out, buying and making inquiries, he reproached himself for knowing about nothing but horses, and did not miss the Souq al-Halal. He said to himself rather sadly, *The Mooran we knew has gone, it's dead, and in its place we have this Mooran—God willing, it will be for the best!*

Even so, he did not really like the bookstore, or electrical gadgets; even Nimr, who lived with him in the Souq al-Halal, and knew more than his other children, was a different person: his mind and concerns had changed completely. He tried to remember how things had been for his father and grandfather and the people around him, and realized that everything had become something different. Cars had replaced horses and camels, tall houses with walls and locked gates had replaced the tents and mud houses that had been part of their surroundings, with their doors always open. And trade? The streets? People's manners? Their relations with one another? Everything had changed, everything he had known had collapsed and ended. He preferred to sit in the coffeehouse. There he could find people he knew and talk to them or listen. They knew him well, they knew how to talk and ask questions, and even those ruined by Mooran and corrupted by cars had something to say for themselves, or at least knew how to listen.

He tried to forget his horses, consumed by fire, and his stolen land, he tried to forget the Halal Market, not to feel upset about it, but with every day that passed he felt more isolated from everything around him; more than that, he felt hostile. This—or perhaps something else—kept him far from the bookstore, or at least no nearer than absolutely necessary, and it was the same where the Technical Workshop for Automotive and Household Electrical Appliances was concerned.

Before, in the Souq al-Halal, he had felt like a part of his surroundings. When the animals were ill or in pain, he even knew what made them sick or suffer—he knew it from looking into their eyes or from their breath. He spoke to them and asked them questions. Now he could only wonder how Badr could take in these dead, inanimate appliances and know how to deal with them. How could they tell him of their sickness and pain, and how could he restore life to them? The books that Najm sold—who read them and why? Were there actually people who needed more learning, with life boiling boisterously around them, changing every day, with people never ceasing to tell stories and ask questions? He said to himself despairingly, *The Souq al-Halal was a teacher, and people there learned. Ever since it closed, everything has been like flour scattered in the wind.*

Had he been in a better state of mind, as in the old market days, he would have hesitated to criticize his son Najm and the "business" he had chosen; he would have spoken of him as he did of Badr, or even better, but now he felt lost and saw that everything was in vain. Money was more important than before, but it was devoid of blessing and meaning, and very few people became rich, taking their share and others' as well. All the others now ran like dogs after money, and no sooner did they get it than it was spent and lost. Not only that, people's manners and morals had changed—as if they were not the same people he knew. Even his own children had changed. He said to himself with deep sadness: *Praised be Him who is eternal and never changes.*

Najm opened the Abu Zarr Bookstore after a three-month visit to Cairo and Beirut, during which he bought large quantities of books, some of which he brought back with him and others which came in batches. Many people expected and even bet that his "business" would end within its first year with an assured loss; for

Mooran, which understood food, real estate and gold, had not yet learned to read. For if Bukhari made a living selling large and small Korans, *The 1001 Nights,* the folktales of Antar and Zeer Salem, and Ibn Hazim stayed clear of Korans, stocking smaller books, greeting cards, stationery and school supplies, then only a madman like a son of Shamran would think of opening the Abu Zarr Bookstore.

Because Mooran did not stop to think, and since its people knew nothing but what they opined to one another, the bookstore did not entice or even interest them, and so was soon forgotten. The people even forgot that they had predicted it would fail.

Unbeknownst to them, however, a new Mooran was taking shape, and it was this Mooran that made the bookstore live and grow, forcing Najm to seek yet another partner and to travel once or even twice a year to buy huge quantities of new books.

Just as Mooran had taken in tens of thousands of people of all kinds, from all places, and was able to find a place for each and offer each a living, the city was able to take in and absorb thousands of books each year, which were made available by the Abu Zarr Bookstore.

Furthermore, two Mooranis opened up another new bookstore near the Sultan Khazael Mosque, bigger and more diverse than the others, called the Ansaf Bookstore. Bukhari and Ibn Hazim cursed and shouted in the marketplace, but Najm found an ally in the Ansaf Bookstore.

Najm read as many books as he sold or even more; he spent most of the night reading, and during the day he read between dealing with customers. It was this habit, which he'd had all his life, which had led him to choose this career before all others, and his books and business travels transformed him into a different person, one no one knew. The change took place slowly and quietly, attracting no one's notice; even Najm himself was unaware of the person he had become. He had been shy and afraid since boyhood, even of his brothers, but was changing, talking about the books he sold as if he were talking of friends: who had written them, when, what they said and what people said about them. This way of dealing with sales endeared him to most people and made him many friends. Even his brother Nimr, who fancied himself an expert on every subject and read the newspaper assiduously every day, never sleeping at night until he had listened to several radio news broadcasts, was surprised at how much his brother knew, and surprised at how much broader the world of books was than he has supposed. Nimr began to spend part of each day in the bookstore, and often helped out when he could.

Had it not been for Nimr's thirst for revenge against Muti, and his feeling that some hidden force drew him to that chair near the passport office, whence he could watch the palace and its people, writing petitions in his special way—had it not been for the revenge and the hidden force, he would not have hesitated to go over to the bookstore and spend his time reading, so that if he was to argue with the "parasites," as he called Muti and his kind, he could crush them. But he changed his mind and decided to stick to his own work, fully aware of how common this was in Mooran. His relationship grew stronger and deeper both with Najm and with the books Najm recommended to him.

When Shamran heard that Nimr was spending some of his time in the bookstore, and saw at home how inseparable the brothers had become, reading and debating, he shook his head and muttered, "Monkey see, monkey do—God help us!"

58

IF THEY HAD LET SHAMRAN KEEP HIS HORSES, HE
would have been gone in one day. If they had
let him keep his land, they would have seen
how reasonably he could bargain and would have avoided his
tongue. But when the Souq al-Halal was moved to Awali, where, as
Shamran said, no one but "a madman or some distracted wan-
derer" could find it, they has pushed him too far, and he cursed
and said things considered unsayable. Most of the time he never
held back from saying just what he wanted to, not only in words
but using his hands as well, saying with gestures as much as could
be summed up in words.

Hammad knew Shamran; they had once been friends. Now he
received reports, written and verbal, saying that Shamran did
nothing but curse the government—they quoted him exactly and
said he spared no one but the Sultan. Hammad shook his head
sadly and closed the reports, saying to those who had quoted the

curses, "Shamran can get away with things other people can't. They burned his horses, they took his land, they pushed him away from his father's grave. Let him say whatever he likes. In a day or two he'll get tired of it and be quiet."

Shamran did not tire, but sank into this new Mooran he had not known before. He changed noticeably and grew spryer. He was overwhelmed with curiosity, and silently awaited something, or perhaps his anger reached a pitch where silence was impossible. He was between passivity and rage, between watchfulness and dazzlement, not knowing how life worked or how it passed. Once he had been concerned with how to earn his living, but now his children had assumed that obligation, in particular Badr, who, as his father said, "was playing some money game."

Mooran had once needed Shamran. People had surrounded him just as a bracelet surrounds a wrist, and every problem demanded his role in a solution. Now that the Halal Market had been relocated in Awali and people cared less about horses and camels, now that shepherds no longer crossed the whole desert to get to Mooran, since butchered meat was imported from the four corners of the earth, and cars had replaced camels, he felt weary and senile before his time and contented himself with sitting in Zaidan's Coffeehouse in Qadi Street. He spent his whole day there, listening to people more than they listened to him. He saw faces he had never seen before and heard talk he had never heard before: cars, the different models, how much they cost, how much they could carry, how fast they could go. He heard about spare parts and tires. He did not know whether to join in asking questions or just listen. Even the bedouin here whom he had known in the Souq al-Halal were changed. Why had they gotten like this? Where were their camels and sheep? If they were like this today, what would they be like tomorrow?

After prolonged meditation, worry and anticipation, Shamran wanted to test himself: after all he had seen, heard and remembered of the names the people around him constantly repeated, would he be able to tell apart the cars that were parked near Subai's Garage?

That was what he wondered, not to test his knowledge, but in order to say to his son Badr, who had told him a few nights previous that he was ready to buy a car if there was someone to accompany him on his travels. "If we rely on a driver he'll cost us the earth and ruin the car." He was talking about himself. Shamran went to Subai's Garage and looked at the cars, scrutinized them carefully, especially the front end, as others always did. He looked at the tires and in the trunks to try to see what kind it was and how much it would hold, and went back to Zaidan's Coffeehouse, chiding himself. *Alas, Abu Nimr, you used to be able to distinguish at a glance a she-camel who'd had one pregnancy from one who'd had two, and immediately match a foal with his mother, and a mare with her mate; when she had weaned and when she might foal. But these metal things stump you— they might as well be stones!* He never again tried to play this game.

He did his best to forget the pain that gnawed at his heart when the doctor took over his land, which had almost killed him, especially after he heard so much about the lands "bought" by the princes or the doctor; there was no parcel of land in or around Mooran that had not been bought and sold several times over, the price multiplying with each resale, to the point where the mere mention of the numbers made Shamran's head spin. He heard people say, in Zaidan's Coffeehouse: "It's business—and in business you always have profit and loss." But why had it never been like this before? He had lived, he had even been brought up in the marketplace, and knew how buying and selling were done; he knew the stratagems they resorted to, buyers and sellers both, but what he was seeing now was more like a secret; from what he heard it had no resemblance to selling or commerce; it was something completely different, something he could not name or explain.

The Souq al-Halal had been a refuge and stronghold for Shamran, where he met with people he liked and did not like. It was not his habit to receive any visitor in his house, with the exception of Shaddad al-Mutawa, with whom he could spend long delightful hours, surrounded by horses. That was blissful: they talked and showed off those magnificent animals "whose back is a sanctuary, and whose belly is treasure," as Shamran liked to say as he stroked the croup of a mare or stallion. These visits were before al-Rehaiba; after that, when Shaddad wanted to see him or get his opinion on something, he came to him in the market as everyone else did, even though Shaddad was more worried about his horses, afraid they might shy or hurt themselves, but afraid, more than anything else, of people's eyes.

After the market was uprooted and Shamran emigrated to Awali, he was visited only as a tomb is visited, and settled down in Zaidan's Coffeehouse. Everyone who wanted to see him came there, as Shaddad did many times. Shaddad tried to persuade him to visit him at home again, because "the blue mare calved," or "because she's given me priceless horses—there is nothing like them in this world or the next," or "the white-footed Hamdani that the palace wants, Abu Nimr, needs to be appraised"—in spite of these efforts, Shamran was unbudging in his refusal, so that Shaddad had to give in.

Just as Zaidan's Coffeehouse was near the original site of the Souq al-Halal, it was far from the Rawdh Palace and the Ghadir Palace. Shamran considered that "the crookedness is from the old bull," and so did not want to see the Sultan or hear anything about him, using this disregard to express his scorn, or as a form of punishment, since the Sultan was at the bottom of the whole calamity that afflicted Mooran.

On the other side, not far from the Ghadir Palace, near the Passport Office, Nimr presided, writing petitions and letters, helping with travel formalities and watching the palace: who went in and who came out and what they did there, after reading the newspaper, "every letter of it," and listening to several news broadcasts the night before and that same morning.

Nimr learned more about Mooran from the radio than from reading the newspapers, "even though the radio is there and the newspapers are here, O servants of God!" He had no difficulty in deducing the reason why. When Muti's car sped by, headed for the palace, and he was inside, "cozy as a rabbit" in the backseat, only his eyeglasses visible, Nimr slapped his newspaper on the table in front of him and said out loud, "God—God help us in these times we live in, when a leprous goat minds the sheep!"

If any one of his hearers looked at him in surprise, he added in a conspiring tone, "That one passing just now is the sheikh of liars—he has nothing else to do but lie and be proud of it!" Then he motioned crossly at the newspaper and Muti's car as it turned right to enter the palace through a side gate, and the petition he

was writing, inevitably intended for the palace's Office of Griev-
ances, would become stern and vehement, reflecting his resentment.

When office hours ended and the sun's power ebbed, Nimr relaxed by strolling around Mooran; he traversed the city from one
end to the other, telling people what was going on: who and what
he had seen and what he had heard. He knew what to say and to
whom to say it. His tour always ended at Zaidan's Coffeehouse,
where he found his father, deep in thought or listening raptly to
the talk of those around him, of the new cars that had appeared in
Mooran that day, and who was driving them. Within minutes Nimr
would spread his news through the coffeehouse, leaving uneasiness in the hearts and on the faces of his listeners; when his errand
was complete he left, taking his father with him.

What puzzled and amazed the people more than anything else
was the sheer volume of Nimr's news—he knew more than anyone
else. Even the information that was incredible at first, that seemed
so fantastic and exaggerated, was later proved true by facts that
emerged. At any mention of the doctor or Muti, Shamran could
not keep himself from speaking up, usually voicing sarcasm or
curses. If the four—including Ibn Rushdan and Obeid al-Tawil—
were all present, his news would spread even more quickly than
usual that night, and, more likely than not, reach Hammad. Nimr
was quiet at first, as if averse to speaking, looking around cautiously to be sure of the place and the people, in order to decide
how to begin and what to say, then suddenly gave in under the
pressure of questions and encouragement, saying, "Mooran today
is like a graveyard, no one's buying or selling," "The Sultan's getting married," "The Sultan has a new baby," and "That Maltese
bought Harran's graveyard, and tomorrow he'll buy Mooran's
graveyard." And here Nimr and his father would have to brace
themselves for the scoffing around them, for there was a certain
sequence whenever Shamran spoke that always ended in mockery,
because Ibn Rushdan would join in with a criticism or curse, and
Nimr would give his customary impersonation of a radio.

"We first bring you, gentlemen, the news. In Mooran's news today His Excellency is considering a new marriage, possibly within
days. The Maltese has sold the lowland west of the mosque to

Prince Mayzar, and gone in with him to buy another piece of land west of Wadi Riha." Then, sighing dejectedly, "And now for today's editorial. Each of you has a mind and an intellect; ever since the wolf went in among the sheep, the world has gone astray and perished!"

He drew a newspaper from his inside pocket; it did not matter whether it was that day's or another day's, as long as those around him could see Muti's picture on it. Muti was his primary enemy, and his picture was run so often that it always seemed to be the same one: Muti, standing beside the Sultan at a party or reception, his hands humbly clasped over his chest, his eyes set admiringly on the Sultan.

"This is Musailima, the legendary liar," said Nimr, pointing at the photo. "He lies as naturally as drinking water, as breathing, but truth is like the sun, and you can't block out the sun with a sieve."

Shamran did not like this sort of news and commentary. Experience had taught him not to believe what the newspapers said, "because these sheets of paper, and everything written in them, aren't worth a hair, aren't worth a turd." He would steer the conversation in another direction—toward the doctor, perhaps.

"Gentlemen, you remember Mooran before that blot on humanity and his ilk; everything was wonderful. But since they set foot here, everything has gone downhill, and God protect us from what is to come."

Since Shamran's references were obscure, and the people did not know whom he was talking about, Saleh would interrupt.

"What blot? Please, Abu Nimr, tell us just whom you are talking about!"

"Do you think I'm afraid?"

"How should I know?"

Saleh al-Rushdan winked at those around him to provoke Shamran, who held back no longer.

"Listen, Ibu Rushdan, the one you're thinking of, you and I know who he is, the poor bastard, he's at God's gate. He could massacre his own family and be snoring five minutes later. And the other one, that parasite, forget him. He can't sleep at night for all his trying to think, to come up with ideas from God knows where. He's my enemy . . . today."

"The poor bastard you referred to, Abu Nimr—"

One of their listeners would say this, to raise the tension, but Saleh would break in, "By God, *we're* the only poor bastards around. That bunch we're talking about eat both the dates and the pits and leave us nothing!"

"If you're talking about money, friend, you're exactly right, but there's something much more important," said Shamran, taking a long, tired breath. "His father broke the backs of good people. He committed unspeakable crimes. We thought, well, it's revenge, but he told me, the day will come, Abu Nimr, when nothing will happen here except the people will it. That's what he said. I told him, 'Bless you!' But you all have seen what has happened, with your own eyes!" Again he signed. "Just as I told you. That blot on humanity is the head of the viper. As we used to say, if you put a horse among donkeys he'll learn to bray!"

"He's still a horse, Abu Nimr!" said Saleh al-Rushdan, and Shamran laughed heartily.

"That's true, Ibn Rushdan. All the horses have turned into jades!"

Nimr and others interrupted to change the subject, but Shamran was dogged in his conviction that the doctor was the head of the calamity and that the Sultan was his willing tool; it was the doctor who drove him, and if he was to hit out or run, the Sultan would have to retreat and things would get better than before.

This is how the stories and discussions went in Zaidan's Coffeehouse. Sometimes Saleh al-Rushdan was beaten up; informers were stationed openly in the coffeehouse, which was why Shamran might show up one day and stay away for several more. Nimr no longer cared whether or not he passed by the palace, and when asked would explain that "Mooran itself is a big coffeehouse, and you can spend your money here or there—Zaidan doesn't depend on me for his living!"

59

HOW IS IT POSSIBLE FOR A CITY TO FIGHT A man as Mooran did Saleh al-Rushdan? And was there any man, apart from Saleh al-Rushdan, capable of showering a whole city with the profusion of curses he did, in an attempt at vengeance?

When the Souq al-Halal was moved to Awali, Saleh al-Rushdan was lost. He did not make the move, because "no poor son of a bitch with a donkey could get there." Mooran was unable to find a place for him or offer him work, though every year the city took in tens of thousands of people coming to her from everywhere in the world.

Saleh walked all over Mooran looking for "any poor soul with a mule that needed shoeing," sometimes finding one and sometimes not—donkey owners were far rarer than before, and since they used their animals less, they did not shoe them as often as before and "the beasts could scarcely earn their own keep," what with the profusion of cars and trucks that had taken the place of animals for transport. The owners of horses who had never acknowledged Saleh's existence disowned him even more emphatically now; when they saw him hovering around their stables they sent for someone to get rid of him, as if he were a disease that threatened their horses. It happened many times, as if they had all agreed among themselves to do it.

So it went for long months, and with every passing month the siege around him came in closer and his life grew harder. For forty years he had plied his trade; he knew no other. He had shoed Mooran's donkeys from the cradle to the grave, and horses and mules too. In the past they had crowded around him, waiting for hours and hours, heaping praise on him and using big words to please him. Now no one even looked at him or asked him for anything; when they spoke it was usually to mock him: "My truck needs shoeing, Saleh—are you too busy? Shall we come back some other day?" "My stallion needs his nails cut and new shoes, Saleh, but on one condition—you do this other little horse for free. What do you say?" They would be pointing to a truck and a small car behind it.

Saleh spared not one of them: "You people of Mooran! Your donkeys are worth more than you are. Back when you had nothing but donkeys, you were human beings, but now you're shit." He would say, "I shoe donkeys hammering their feet, but the sort of donkeys I see now need it on the head." They would laugh loudly at what Saleh said, then start their cars and go away, leaving him alone.

When they used to tell him that he was needed at the palace to shoe the horses there, his reply was that "the palace is no better than anyone standing in line here—if they need something done, let them send someone over and I'll see." Now, he was determined to present a petition to the palace seeking that work, even at reduced pay, and people told him that that was a reasonable proposition. Nimr grudgingly agreed to write out the petition, feeling sure that no one would read it or reply to it. He wrote it in a spirit of irony, dripping with contempt:

"To His Majesty the Sultan, Father of his People, peace and greetings. I am Saleh al-Rushdan, native of Mooran.

After Your Majesty's edict removing the Souq al-Halal from its place, calamities have pelted down on the heads of your people and I am one of them. Work has dwindled away and doors have closed for good. As you know, I have been shoeing horses for forty years, but the arrival of cars has slashed my income, and I thereby beg you to appoint me master of horses in the palace.

" 'And say, work, for God and his Prophet see what you do.' "

For days and weeks he hardly left Zaidan's Coffeehouse, expecting the palace to send for him, but it never happened. In this period, when some malicious persons heard that he was awaiting a summons from the palace, and that it related to important business, they took mockery of Saleh further than it had gone before: whenever someone walked into the coffeehouse, especially some new customer, they would start whispering their comments: "Don't worry, Saleh—at last!" "That man who just came was asking for Saleh earlier. We said, 'Fine,' and he said, 'Fine,' but we were just whispering among ourselves. We told him, 'Saleh isn't here now, but he'll be coming. Do you want us to tell him you came or go get him?' He was afraid you'd be busy with some other work." Saleh would look on carefully and wait, but in vain.

"What's your advice, Abu Nimr?" he asked Shamran, not looking at him, but keeping his eyes fixed on the door. "The palace is silent as the cemetery. No news? Nothing?"

"Pile dirt on them and shit on it."

"You mean there's no news?"

"There's no use depending on others. You'd be better off looking for some other work."

"His Excellency has forgotten Saleh al-Rushdan?"

"He's forgotten us all, old man." Shamran chuckled sadly. "Who is Saleh al-Rushdan to His Excellency?"

"And who is His Excellency without us? What would he be worth if we left, if we weren't here?"

"Saleh, my good friend, I told you to forget all that palace nonsense. It will bring you no bread."

"But you can see with your own eyes, Abu Nimr, everyone connected with the palace is up to his ears in rice and meat, eating and cleaning his teeth!"

Saleh gave up on the Sultan, for the time being at least, and began touring around Mooran once again. He trudged to Awali and the villages around Mooran, but to little avail. "Even the loathsome bedouin have left their camels and horses—their religion now, their idol, is the pickup truck! But never mind, another day is coming. We shall see."

His resentment was not limited to people; it extended to the cars themselves. Whenever he walked past a parked car in a deserted street he would find a way of expressing his contempt; if he was unable to piss, he would ask his son to: "Come on, my boy, do what you can." If neither of them could manage, he would cough up a large amount of phlegm in his throat and spit it at the car, adding, "*Tfu* on you and these times." He did not hesitate to "sow" a large number of nails and pieces of broken glass in the street. He spread them in what struck him as the most strategic places, especially in the street leading to the Ghadir Palace, but that cost him dearly: motorists beat him and "played with him" from behind the wheel of their cars. They were quick to call the police, and the police punished him.

The siege around him closed in further. Shamran tried to help, not only lending him money occasionally but looking for a job for him. At first he asked Badr to "do what he could," but Badr, who agreed readily enough, did not know how to employ him or how to make use of him. He told him to "Sit down, Uncle Saleh, have some coffee and talk to us, and if we need anything from the market, you can go instead of me." Saleh was content, but before long was causing trouble, particularly with motorists who brought their cars in for the electrical system to be serviced, so after putting up with him for a few months Badr had to fire him.

Shamran found him work in his old friend Subai's garage, but only a few days after being hired as a security guard he was the cause of several disputes between car owners and the garage, so he was fired from that job after being beaten.

Work and idleness alternated. Saleh al-Rushdan was bewildered and lost, going from one job to the next, but each ended as badly as the one before, until there was nothing more Shamran could do

for him, and, tired of all his problems, he told him, "How right
your family was to name you 'Saleh'—'proper' and 'right.' They
weren't wrong. Now if you don't act properly and do the right
thing, you can find someone else besides me to get you out of
trouble."

"No one is as troubled as I am, Abu Nimr."

"You're troubled and you won't let anyone else rest."

"Do they give *me* any rest?"

"You've started looking for trouble, Saleh, but people can take
only so much. They may stand it today but maybe not tomorrow."

"Are you like them now, Abu Nimr?"

"May God guide you, Saleh, I've had enough, I've had all I can
take."

That was how relations between Shamran and Saleh ended after
thriving for years and years, though in spite of the break between
the two men they did not forget or neglect each other. Shamran
could do no more for Saleh than he had already done, but got his
son Nimr and Obeid al-Tawil to check on him every now and then
and help him out.

Every time the people thought that some kind of peace had finally taken hold, and that Saleh had given up his cursing or found
something else to keep himself busy, he came back at them like a
hurricane, at Zaidan's Coffeehouse, at the mosque, or standing in
the middle of the street. "Say whatever you want to say about me,
people of Mooran; say I'm sane, say I'm crazy—I wouldn't give a
date pit for your opinion, but I want you to tell me, by what religion, by what law do people build these high buildings and palaces
and play games with money? No one knows where this money
comes from. Other people haven't got a crust of bread! There's the
keeper of this nation and this faith, why has he closed his door—
he doesn't hear and doesn't reply, like one of the Sleepers of the
Cave in the Koran." He paused briefly to stare at the faces that
watched him, shook his head sadly and opened his hands in a gesture of despair. "Just a few years ago we were all so happy, but then
all these calamities came and you all started showing off your
trucks and pickups. You used to appreciate hard work and faith,
but now you say, 'Let's fool Saleh.' Saleh goes around looking for
work, and not a day passes but you slam your door on him like *he*

does." When he again heard them heaping praise on him or telling him to relax, that they would help him out, he screamed like a wounded man, "You and your money are worthless! I don't want it—I want to work, I want to sweat!" And whether he found work or they found work for him, it was only days or at the most a few weeks before there were more problems.

"Saleh," Obeid al-Tawil told him, at the end of his patience, "listen, man: get these ideas out of your head. The Mooran you knew is gone, it's dead. We are now in a different Mooran, so forget horses and horseshoes. Find some other line of work before you starve to death." He explained that Saleh had two choices: the first was to do as he himself had done, leaving his job as a sheep and camel auctioneer to become a real estate agent; he pointed out that the new work was not only profitable, it was easy, and most deals could be concluded within a few days. The alternative was to do as Shamran did, to sit in Zaidan's or some other coffeehouse, to be silent or learn silence, "because everyone has something against you—they may do nothing about it today, but who knows about tomorrow." In an effort to make him choose one of these courses, he restated his readiness to help him secure work, "for the last time, Saleh." If he chose to be like Shamran, then Badr was willing to hire his son, and what he would earn, "a coin here and a coin there will be plenty—the important thing is to stop creating problems, Saleh. I'm not the only one who feels this way—so does Abu Nimr, and everyone else. So choose, or we're through with you."

Every village, every place has a memory and a heart, but big cities, especially those which have grown and changed quickly, lose their memories and learn a proficient cruelty. Mooran, which had known Saleh in the past, and accepted his cursing and his way of behaving, soon neglected and then forgot him. Even when his two-year-old son died, there was no one to help him or walk with him. As Saleh carried the child's body wrapped in cloth to the cemetery, he provoked more mockery than pity: "Look! Saleh has stolen something! He's hurrying, like a thief—he's going to fall on his face and then we'll see what he's stolen." "Why the hurry, Saleh? Something's wrong! What have you done now?" He did not raise his face, he did not hear, only gripped the child's corpse with even greater bitterness, as if to draw strength and stolidity from it.

He tried to learn silence, but it did not come easily to him, and since no one listened or turned his way when he spoke, he began to talk to himself. He began by thinking of what he might say to the Sultan if they were to meet someday, how he would start talking and then turn the conversation in the direction he wanted. In order not to make mistakes or stammer, he assigned things around him the names of people he knew or would have liked to talk to. He would look at the door or the wall and begin: "Your Excellency, life is in God's hands; this is a transitory world and may be long for some and short for others. You know me, Your Excellency, or at least you know my story. I am Saleh al-Rushdan—all Mooran knows me—just ask anyone and they'll tell you. I've lived my whole life in the Souq al-Halal; no animal has come here in thirty, forty years without passing through my hands. I was as much a fixture there as Shamran. We don't know who advised you that the market should be torn up from its place—it must have been someone depraved, a son of a bitch—but since then everyone has been in a state! They all say God won't bless such a thing—this God, Your Excellency, is the Avenger, the Almighty, and no one escapes his punishment. If I were in your place, Your Excellency, I would start an investigation and find out whose idea it was, and give him the severest punishment. For now, you must give orders to replace the market where it was before." Saleh was delighted by this outcome, and imagined the market returned to its former site: the dizzying motion of men and beasts, everyone having something to do or something to say. He did not notice what was happening around him because he had so much work to do. He worked harder than others, and did not stop working until everyone else had already stopped. Sometimes it soothed him to take a day or two off from work, to sit and listen to Shamran and the others talking to one another, but "no one waits, no one gives me any rest, and my customers need me!"

He moved from the Sultan on to others. "Nothing gets past Saleh—he may tolerate some things for a while, and not say anything, but nothing stays hidden from him." He summoned them one by one to say what had to be said to each: "These are living witnesses—people don't forget you!" Because there were so many he wished to talk to, he had to give names and faces to everything around him, and he forgot no one and nothing.

All this went on as Saleh roamed the streets alone, looking for a donkey to shoe; his son had gone to work for Badr. Saleh wanted to work, not for money, but to prove to himself that he was still able to work, that he still could be useful to others; but no one responded, no one asked anything of him. Even the curses that used to amuse people before meant nothing to them now. He did not know how to rest or even to stand still, and found no one who would talk to him, so he talked to himself loudly, oblivious and unafraid.

When Shamran heard about the state Saleh was in, he said, "May Almighty God help this to end well!"

60

THE DOCTOR'S PROJECTS WERE EXPANDING and branching out. He was no longer able to attend to every little thing by himself, nor even could his staff, so he persuaded Rateb to move to Mooran. He also went to great lengths to summon Wasfi Agha so they could discuss a partnership, for new horizons had been revealed to him by the activities of none other than Hassan Rezaie. Before long he achieved both of these goals, and it was at about this time that the doctor showed his greatest strength and self-satisfaction. His family shared his lively and cheerful mood, especially because Ghazwan, who had visited them during his spring vacation, would soon graduate from college. He was plumper and more manly in his appearance, and in his speech and behavior, which filled the doctor with optimism. Deep down he wished that Ghazwan could stay near him; that way he might gain experience, share effort with him to make the most of their time, and embark on real life, for the doctor, despite his love of science, believed that only life could polish a man, define his potential and his place in society.

Nor did the doctor forget his "duties," for Rateb, who had been staying at the doctor's house, now found it necessary to take a house of his own; he had also found that a bachelor's life, in a place like Mooran, was impossible, and that people's opinion of a man such as himself, of his age and financial status, would suffer if he stayed single. And so Widad took it upon herself to find him a wife. It had begun as a joking proposition but became a serious one, until it was raised on various pretexts whenever they were all together. As a rule it was the doctor who brought it up and Widad, who found that her health was improving and felt changed and reinvigorated during Rateb's visits, decided that Rateb's move to Mooran was a joy unequaled by any other. At first she had been worried at the thought of his marrying, thinking she could not bear seeing him married, but soon she convinced herself that the only way for her to keep him, for him to stay put and not to travel, but remain virtually at her side, was for him to marry, with her knowledge, and her help. This would guarantee his presence near her, and her own choice of his bride.

After much searching and thinking, Widad traveled to Beirut on a trip lasting two months and ten days; but just ten days into her visit she sent a telegram to the doctor:

PLEASE TELL RATEB HIS BRIDE IS WAITING STOP HIS GUIDANCE NEEDED
NOW TO MAKE PROPER DECISION

The doctor went wild with joy at his wife's brilliance, which she did not always show, and which he had not appreciated before. He warmly congratulated Rateb and pressed him to travel as soon as possible—"the day before tomorrow—this matter allows no delay." The doctor laughed heartily. "This is a matter of your future, Rateb, your destiny!" He shook his head in delighted mirth. "We have already entered the gilded cage, and because you are so dear to us, we want you to join us!"

Rateb tried to make excuses, claiming that he had much business and could not travel until he had concluded it all. "A nice girl will wait, because she has no choice other than to wait, especially since Umm Ghazwan has prepared her and told her of the happiness that awaits her—the wonderful husband who'll share her nest!"

After several discussions full of laughter and seriousness, Rateb left and waited two months for the right girl to be located. Widad explained to her husband on her return to Mooran that "things got complicated several times. Rateb didn't like the first girl we got him, nor the second. He was thinking of giving up the whole idea of marriage, but at last my aunt Umm Ihsan changed his mind and found the right girl. He got married and left." She sighed and smiled at the heavy burden she had rid herself of, and the doctor, who could imagine the difficulties and frustrations of matchmaking, replied pleasantly, "That kind of thing comes up only once in a lifetime—thank God and rest easy now." He guffawed, then added, "There is no one like us!"

"Yes, by God," she replied with a sort of simulated anger, "this is one thing you all lack!"

"Why, my dear—are others better than we?"

"No, no, but everyone has his own way of doing things."

"Don't you like the way things are done in Mooran?"

"No—no, sir!"

"My dear, I have become a Moorani: their ways are my ways, their values are my values. I want to do as they do!"

"What do you mean?"

"I'm going to take a second wife, just as they do!"

"I'll tear your eyes out so you can't look at anyone else!" She flung herself on him and kissed him, hugged him, and looked straight into his eyes. The doctor felt bliss. Widad loved him more than he had guessed, more than she had ever shown, but she was proud and hid her feelings. Now, after this period of separation and longing, she was showing her true love, the sentiments and yearnings she had fought in her heart. He was full of tenderness.

"You mean everything in the world to me. You are more precious than my eyes!"

The doctor was also preoccupied with Ghazwan—he had visited him in the United States the previous summer, and found his son bigger and very changed; he had noted new poise and intelligence in him from the moment they met in the airport. Every act, every movement of Ghazwan's after that, during the whole visit, convinced the doctor that "this lad—if that's the right word—is a living ideal of intelligence and conduct ... and ambition." Ghazwan

talked effusively about San Francisco and took him on several out-
ings, each with a set itinerary, always to the surprise of his father
and mother. Their visit to Chinatown and stroll among the throngs
of Chinese brought back to the doctor memories he thought he'd
forgotten in the long years. The colossal forests near the city held
two surprises: until that point he had not imagined that his son had
learned how to drive a car. He had rented them a car the night
before, selecting one suitable for the family, then drove it over to
the house with no one knowing. In the morning his father asked
him what was on the agenda that day.

"Seeing it is better than hearing about it," Ghazwan answered.
Slowly, confidently, he drew out the keys to the parked car, opened
the right-hand door and asked his mother to get in. She looked at
him and then at her husband, not knowing whether or not to comply; the doctor's eyes darted all around, as if he had just woken
from his sleep. He was astounded. Ghazwan's clear, self-assured
voice was asking them to get in the front seat, his mother in the
middle, leaving them no choice. Ghazwan's expert driving, his familiarity with the roads, the songs he had taken care to bring along
and put in the tape player, all gave their trip a special joy, helping
the doctor to forget his fear for a large part of the drive.

The second surprise to startle the doctor utterly was the fact that
such gigantic and ancient trees could exist. The family glided
through the redwood forest among trees that aroused not only his
delight but amazement and almost stuporous wonder; the doctor's
mind strayed into strange, distant worlds. He recalled confusedly
the history he had read. Everything seemed possible in this life.
Eternity depended, more than anything else, on man's will and his
abilities.

He was too dazed to find the right words to say to himself or
anyone else. He knocked on the trees, looked up at the branches
and examined the roots, on this visit that had not come to an end,
with a look of wonder on his face, endlessly repeating the same
words, "God be praised! God be praised!" Ghazwan had prepared
for this outing with so many facts and anecdotes that his father and
mother were astonished at all he knew. The pictures he took, which
he made sure included all of them, and which he enlisted other
tourists to help take, were the source of fond and exhaustive talk

on the part of the doctor after his return to Mooran, and it so happened that in these pictures a great many of his friends caught their first glimpse of Widad!

The Sultan listened raptly to the doctor's descriptions of his trip, to how immense the United States was, how magnificent and varied its resources were, and carefully scrutinized the photographs brought by the doctor, who apologized that "Umm Ghazwan was obliged to unveil her face—the traditions they have there didn't allow otherwise." The Sultan expressed skepticism about the Americans' claims about the trees' ages; no man could believe them, because "How can they be more than seven or eight generations old? And how do they know that this tree is one thousand years old and that one two thousand years old, when they didn't plant them and they don't know who planted them?" The doctor tried to turn the subject in a direction that the Sultan could understand or grasp, and spoke of "scientific methods," but he could not continue long in this vein, in view of the Sultan's sarcastic smiles, which plainly showed his disbelief.

Whenever the doctor referred to "Noah's Forest," as he called it, the Sultan's interest was aroused, or seemed to be, and he took the pictures back to examine them afresh, as if restudying the age of the trees. In fact he was gazing at Widad, gazing at her hair, her neck, her height, studying the kind of woman she was compared to the women he had known. At an opportune moment the Sultan asked about Ghazwan's studies and "how far he has progressed in knowledge," and added, with a grin that showed all his teeth, "By All-knowing God, I see, Doctor, Ghazwan takes after both you and his mother!"

After a spell of conversation on various subjects, centering on the United States, the Sultan asked if any of the doctor's children had made the trip with them, then without waiting for a reply he asked how old the children were. This question delighted the doctor; it showed how much the Sultan valued and loved him, so he answered in great detail, giving the name and exact birthday of each of the children.

When Ghazwan came back to Mooran, his father thought it essential that he visit the palace, to pay his respects to the Sultan and offer thanks; this was also a chance for the Sultan to ascertain the age of Noah's Forest and look again at the photographs, to look, without reticence, and compare the pictures and Ghazwan's face and the doctor's face. He began to repeat the same words he had said months before: "I see, Doctor, Ghazwan takes after both you and his mother!"

Ghazwan was a different person on this visit. He persuaded his father that it was best to visit the Sultan in the same clothes that he wore at "State," and to act just as he pleased. That is how it went, and the visit left the doctor feeling very cheerful; the Sultan praised Ghazwan on his appearance and his studies, saying at the end of the visit, "We must visit Noah's Forest, Doctor, since Ghazwan is there to be our guide and tell us all we need to know."

Ghazwan's vacation, "shorter than lightning," as the doctor found it, came to an end, and as he bid him farewell, the doctor felt that he had barely had a chance to talk with him—that he had not seen nearly enough of him. "We haven't got enough of you," he told Ghazwan at the door of the plane, "but your education comes first. God willing, you'll be home again soon; God protect you and grant you success!"

61

THE DOCTOR WAITED IMPATIENTLY FOR Rateb to return from his honeymoon. His waiting grew longer and longer until the summer was gone and he was deeply anxious, for he wanted to begin the "great launch": the research phase, the "conclusive" phase to be followed by "internationalization." These were terms of his own choosing. He was like a wolf: one eye slept while the other was open wide as a saucer, knowing no rest or slumber, to watch the wily Said, or to discover what Rezaie was doing, especially during this blazing summer, which seemed to the doctor longer and more brutal than any other summer. He felt that he had made too many sacrifices, tolerated too many unbearable things, and put off too many urgent affairs.

After Rateb came home from his trip, supremely happy and self-confident, and after the parties organized for him, which were renowned events throughout Mooran, the doctor appeared in a fit of almost offensive haughtiness and said, with poorly concealed testiness, "I've had to take so much this summer, though God doesn't burden you with more than you can bear—but now it's your turn!"

Rateb knew the doctor's sense of humor and was always tolerant of it. He smiled and said nothing.

"Listen, Rateb," continued the doctor with a wink, "if you aren't prepared for the birth of a sheep, you'll get a goat."

"Some goats are better than others, Abu Ghazwan!" joked Rateb.

"But a goat always remains a goat," the doctor answered.

"The poor goat is so maligned, Doctor—he's brighter and braver than a great many other animals."

"My friend, the important thing is for a man to be on top of his work, because some of our esteemed competitors are a matter of grave concern!"

This was understood by all who heard him to mean several individuals, but most immediately thought of Rezaie.

With Rateb's return the doctor was able to act, to devote more time to what was on his mind, especially since the summer, despite its difficulties, had been one of his richest and most important times: Samir had stood by him, as a gesture of solidarity—this was how he interpreted the postponement of his annual vacation—and seemed more friendly than ever before. The conversations between the two men lasted, most nights, until nearly dawn. It so happened that Ramadan fell during the summer that year, and the doctor, who was by nature conservative, almost narrow-minded, found that Mooran forced him to be yet more conservative, and so Widad, when she came back, did not appear in front of their guests, and was in fact seen by a very small number of men.

With Samir it was a different matter, especially at the end of this summer. The meetings and conversations that took place in the al-Hir Palace, most nights, and on the western balcony, which were at first limited to the two of them, now generally included Widad. At first she was only being hospitable, but stayed longer in order to hear what was going on. She loved to know what interested her husband and what he was thinking about, and to see and hear this man her husband never stopped praising: his sterling qualities, his intellect, his suavity.

Their meetings began toward the end of the summer. When Rateb went away on his long trip, he was gone much longer than Widad had anticipated, and came back much happier than she had
expected, which threatened her in a way she did not quite understand. Stirrings of this kind had begun before he came back, and
the doctor noticed it; she had become very high-strung and sharp
with the servants. He thought it had something to do with the
weather in Mooran, or perhaps the month of Ramadan, although
Widad fasted only according to her whim. She was moderate in her
religious observances and fasted, sometimes, as children did, and
the doctor, who knew that, told her affectionately that "the merit is
for those who can bear the hardship—children and women have
many excuses. An hour in Mooran," he added with a smile, "is like
days. It's enough for a person here to fast in intention only, or according to what you can stand."

At the parties held in Rateb's honor, in which Widad functioned
more or less as both the mother of the bride and mother of the
groom, she overflowed with joy and anxiety. She helped to prepare
the bride for her presentation to the guests and the palace; she
offered advice to the newlyweds about what sort of friends they
should have and about decorating their house. This atmosphere
possessed her and changed her life profoundly, for with every
passing day she began to sense how much she had lost; she felt that
she had made a mistake for which she would never forgive herself
by insisting that Rateb get married, then doing everything to complete the whole charade. Her feelings were reinforced when Rateb
came back: he was like a different person to her. When she looked
at him in the certain way she knew so well, knowing, as well, how it
aroused him, and how he responded, he fled from her, pretended
he was listening to other people or that he was busy. If she persisted, and if he continued to distance himself from her, she would
know what to do—she knew how to humble him.

If only she were in Beirut. Had she been alone with him, she
would have been able to get him into her embrace as if he were a
small boy. In the past he had sometimes tried to rebel, to remain as
he was or behave as he pleased, but she crushed him with her omnipotence—no, it was not omnipotence, it was something else,
hard to describe or identify, something crippling that he could not
resist. She would raise her voice, or cry, or refuse him, or not let

him rest or sleep for a single moment; she came to him as beautiful as a spring cloud or stayed aloof, like a teenage virgin. She knelt by his feet like a slave girl and rubbed his thigh or tickled the sole of his foot; she attacked and ravished him, like a lioness, without his voicing any consent or even desire. He always fell, no matter how prepared or secure he thought he was; he found himself in her arms, like a child seeking warmth and love, seeking something he had lost.

Now she felt that she had lost him; that this young girl, only nineteen years old, had stolen him from her and was trying to escape with him. How was it possible to allow this, to surrender to this naive girl? How could she withdraw and content herself with the horrible role of mother-in-law? And Rateb, who was so proud of his experience and his past, could he be satisfied with that frightened chicken of a girl and forget her, Widad? None of this struck her as remotely possible. She would leave him now, leave him for a while, giving him time to get bored with that pallid body, like a meal with no savor, with a taste like water; of course he would get tired of her, perhaps even sooner than she expected, and he would come back to her.

When that happened, would she take him back at his mere request? No—that was part of the past, gone forever. She wanted to torment him to the point of misery, to begging. He would have to weep to compensate for her weeping in these past few days, he would have to knock at her door hundreds of times, and she would respond by showing that she was in there but not anxious to see him. Not ready to see him, even if he died, if he kissed her feet; after he had waited and tied himself into knots she would rescue him, she would restore him, but so that he would now be hers alone.

That is how she wanted things to go, but she was uneasy and not prepared to wait. She would not be like an abandoned woman with nothing to do but wait; she refused to be remembered by men only after they found no one else or had nothing else to do. No, she would not accept this. She would give him insomnia, she would make him crazy about her, and when? Just as he was sure of his victory, at the moment she felt he was leaving her, or no longer loved or needed her, and when that infatuated girl thought, in her heart and her buttocks, that she had won, she would find that she had won nothing but an illusion; then she, Widad, would submit to him, with greater humility and total obedience.

Jealousy, then, was the means she would resort to in order to rouse him: to have another man in her life, and not only a man she met with in the shadows, when others were asleep, as she did with him, with no one aware; no, this man would be a powerful presence. Rateb would see him with his own eyes and all his senses, to see how coveted and desirable she was, how impossibly beyond his reach. This role in the risky game was not to be played by the doctor; it would go to someone he would never expect: Samir!

She remembered . . . one night he had asked her a question and touched her, after the doctor had gone to bed; she'd stolen up to check on him and then murmured to Samir, whispering only, "Like all devils, he's worn out and powerless!"

Rateb knew the meaning of her sarcasm, and did not ask her again. On later occasions, when Samir was talking to their other guests but looking directly at the doctor as if he were his only listener, Rateb detected in his gaze a certain irony. At the end of the soiree, when the guests had left, the doctor spoke to Rateb without being asked.

"If Mooran had more like him, I'd have plowed the whole place and left them kneeling."

Rateb had other things on his mind and said nothing, but at dawn, when Widad at last slipped into his bed, he asked her somewhat accusingly, "You're late, why so late? What's wrong?"

She pinched his cheek and hugged him tightly. She was warm and desirable, and when the cool dawn breezes woke her, he asked her again if the doctor was asleep or not.

"Are you that afraid," she said sarcastically, "or just tired of me?" She did not know why she wanted to toy with him, to arouse his jealousy. Samir was like a ghost to her. She asked dryly, "Did you enjoy the party? Did you like Samir?"

She remembered Samir's jokes over dinner; she had pretended to be shy, but underneath the discreet veil of diffidence her dissembling was sly and insolent, and they had given her a good laugh; even Rateb kept looking at her with the same look whose meaning was unambiguous. Now that she asked him this, and remembered the suggestive jokes, she sensed his jealousy. When he said nothing, savoring their warm embrace, she said, to provoke him, "What would you think if I fell in love with Samir and slept with him?"

He answered this with his whole body: he threw himself on her as if to punish her, to beat her. He twisted her arm a little sharply but did not hurt her, and when she tried to get away from him, to escape a small distance to see his face, to read his answer in his eyes, the pale darkness prevented her from seeing.

"What's your answer to my question?" she asked, to go on with the game.

"Shut up!" he growled through clenched teeth, in a tone of anger, abuse, amusement and disbelief. That night they slept as they never had before, feeling bliss as never before, and closer to each other than ever before. When she heard Abu Abdallah coughing in the garden, she started suddenly and stole out of bed like a cat, leaving the door ajar so that the sound of it closing would not wake the doctor.

Her instincts told her that Samir was the only person who could help her to get Rateb back, and so with no further holding back she started her game. When the round of official parties for Rateb had ended that winter, she proposed a system for certain families to exchange visits, with Rateb as its basis, and Samir too. The system for paying visits would not have pleased the doctor at all were it not for what preceded them: Samir, who had shown such decency by staying in Mooran that summer to give the doctor all his time and the benefit of his ideas, had not only impressed the doctor, he made himself indispensable; that conclusion was reached by both the doctor and Widad. One of the doctor's greatest fears was that that mysterious, gloomy suffering would come upon her again, that she would isolate herself and reenter that cycle of illness and depression and nagging. This would thwart everything he had been trying to accomplish. When he saw how Samir's youth and good humor cheered Widad as no other guest did, and that she no longer was annoyed by the long discussions they had, he thought himself the luckiest person alive. *Some higher power, mysterious and powerful, guided his steps and fulfilled his mission.* He praised this "nobility" to Widad and said that her sacrifices and self-denial would not be forgotten, and it was this that moved him to consent to her proposal.

It was a winter full of thunder and lightning, and the young girl who was so delighted with the white dress she wore for the first time as a bride in Mooran, and looked like a doll amid all the parties and festivity, who had seemed nervous and ashamed, not knowing how to behave or how to answer questions put to her, fell ill within only a few months. "She hasn't adjusted," said the doctor. "The result is depression and loss of appetite." Her neighbor, Umm Jamil, was positive that the problem was "pregnancy fears, but without the pregnancy," and gave her two types of medicine to treat her abdominal swelling and dizziness. Only Widad knew what ailed her, but she said nothing. After several noisy evenings she assured the girl that she should not decide by herself, but that she, Widad, would decide on behalf of everyone, especially on her behalf, so the girl lost her power to act on her own and fell ill.

Rateb thought that Widad, who had been his plaything yesterday, would remain so today and tomorrow, and so acted with supreme confidence and self-assurance; he would go back to her as soon as he'd had enough of this child. Soon he would revert to his high-flying goose and get her back; he would go back to her whenever he needed her, but he began to discover that the goose was veering off, and that from this distance she was mocking him, saying plainly that she was ready to fly far off to join another flock, to discover a new world. Not content with that, she even knew how to toy with Samir right in front of him, to flirt with Samir, laugh at his jokes, and to make her words, once meaningful only to Rateb, mean something different and serious.

Rateb pretended that her game did not affect him, that it was a provocation that would end as it had begun, with a gesture or wink on his part, but with each passing day he found that this game was more in earnest than he had expected or could stand. He told himself that *man can please God and Satan at the same time, but to please two women is impossible,* and still waited, vowing never to forget this.

The only one to join the game in a calculated fashion was Samir, and he was sure of his calculations. Mooran, its Sultan, its doctor, everything standing on its soil and lit by its sky, meant nothing more to him than forced servitude in exile. True, he had chosen this exile, and would stay here for several years, but he would return home rich, to start a new life. This determination had blocked women out of his mind, or almost. He had forced himself to forget them during his prison years, to lessen his torment, but was incapable of turning his dreams into reality, especially here in Mooran, and so he kept to this game, not out of integrity or lack of desire, but because *all Mooran masturbates and never has sex, because the opposite sex is absent.* He said this to convince himself more than anyone else, to prove that women were absent or at least inaccessible, and to keep himself from pointless daydreams.

Money was his major goal, perhaps his only one, and he had dedicated all his desires toward that divine goal. After Widad had begun to sit in on his discussions with the doctor and become such a hospitable lady of the house, he judged her "an ornament in this beautiful desolation," meaning Mooran and its people. That ornament freshened the air a little, cooling the fire of the sun and taming the dust.

Widad was certainly not his idea of a desirable woman, he told himself. She excited no interest in him when first he saw her, nor did she arouse him the second time, protected as she was by her silence. Her eyes wandered in the middle distance without settling on anything or anyone.

Later on, especially during the parties for Rateb, or the soirees held at the Hir Palace or Rateb's house, or the houses of other friends, Widad seemed to him a different woman, younger and prettier than before, and he meant something to her. He was surprised that he had not noticed her youth and looks before, or her gaze so full of sensuality and appeal. When she picked a fight with him the first time, she put her hand over his and squeezed it, and he got nervous, and seemed even annoyed at her behavior. Rateb, who processed these signals immediately, understood them and smiled, making Samir even more nervous.

The next few days that passed were the longest Samir had ever lived through in Mooran; he was sure that the doctor would find out and teach him a lesson he would never forget. He would have him thrown into the deepest dungeon in Mooran, and after years with no glimpse of light or of any other person, wasted by disease, he would be plucked out like a rat and tossed across the border: poor, abandoned, sick, old and destitute.

After those few days the doctor summoned him, insisting they meet that very night; the chauffeur was emphatic and peremptory about that. Samir was sure that his moment had come and that the punishment in store for him would be harsh, as a deterrent to "those expatriates." When he arrived at the Hir Palace shortly after sundown, gaunt and frightened, wishing that he had never come to Mooran or even heard of the place, he found the doctor waiting for him on the balcony, hardly visible. He seemed wary and nervous, with a brooding expression on his face, which frightened Samir even more. He greeted the doctor in a nervous, even pleading tone of voice, but the doctor said nothing, only came toward him looking more brooding than before, now looking straight into Samir's eyes. Samir almost spoke, almost screamed that he had nothing to do with what had happened, that he would never dream of such a thing, let alone try it, but the doctor's timorous words prevented him at the last moment.

"I was telling myself that there was something wrong, not seeing you around . . ."

"I've been ill, sir, terribly ill!" His words were sad and pleading, as if seeking pardon or trying to delay his punishment. The doctor raised his hand and laid it on Samir's forehead to see if it was warm. Widad appeared in the doorway to the balcony with a laugh filling her face. She was wearing a rather tight blue dress that emphasized her haughty chest.

"You've been avoiding us, Mr. Samir!" she said as she came toward him. Then he knew that his assumptions over the past few days were just wild imaginings. When the doctor hurried inside for his medical bag, Widad said to him in a near-whisper, "You have no right to stay away for so long—or are you mad at us?"

Samir stretched out on the hammock on the balcony, and the doctor examined him carefully but to no avail. He was confused by the symptoms Samir described, so gave him a tranquilizer and said he would give him a follow-up exam if his condition did not improve within a few days. But before that night was through, with its uproarious conversations and the delicious supper Widad prepared, Samir recovered his strength and energy and seemed like a new man. When he rose to take his leave, the doctor suggested, as a measure of caution to reassure Samir, that he spend the night as their guest, but Samir declined. Widad said it would take her just a few seconds to prepare his bed, and to convince him she said that the doctor would be right nearby in case he was needed, and laughed, but he wanted to leave, and in light of his insistence they both decided to leave home in their car, "since the drive will be pleasant, at night, with Mooran so quiet."

In the car, her hands touched his more than once, and her hands said what her words and eyes had not. Samir felt as though he were moving down a one-way street he had to follow to its end.

62

"LOVE AND TALK, HATE AND TALK!" SAID THE doctor to Rateb, shaking his head a little sadly after listening at length to his change of mind regarding Samir; how miserly he was, and how "you don't really know him until you've worked with him."

Silence fell between the two, then Rateb added, "After I got to know him up close, I changed my opinion of him; I really came to doubt him and lose confidence in him."

When the doctor tried to remind him what he had thought of Samir when he first came to Mooran, Rateb replied crossly.

"God bless you, Doctor, you know better than anyone else that only Almighty God never changes!" He sighed vehemently and added, "Money, Doctor, can turn a man's head, and high position can change him. You can see that Samir has changed—as to *what* has changed him, your guess is as good as mine."

"My boy"—the doctor smiled broadly—"if the man has put

aside a little money, tell me who in Mooran isn't buried in money! If the issue is position, he's not even ambitious—he's nothing to worry about."

"I was just saying what I think, Doctor, and if it weren't for my high regard for you I wouldn't have opened my mouth." He paused and added sadly, "All the same, don't forget what I said—we'll see what develops!" He looked at the doctor apprehensively, because his confidence was unusually high this time.

"Look, Rateb," asked the doctor a little doubtfully, "have you maybe been hearing things I don't know about?" There was a pause. "Hmm? Heard anything?"

"No, not at all, not at all, the whole thing, the only thing is that he's just become a different person, not the one I knew."

"Fine," said the doctor a little menacingly. "Suppose we get Muti or Hammad in on this?"

"Sir, God keep you, it doesn't call for that."

Rateb wanted to sow doubt, to banish Samir more than to hint at his relationship with Widad, because he was still confident of his ability to get her back, and had not become so much of an outsider as to need help to eliminate this rival. This allusion was enough for now; if he tried to go further, Widad might be able to persuade her husband that it was he who was causing trouble with her, and that could cause him problems he did not need now, especially in the first days of his marriage.

And Widad, that lioness who had only belatedly discovered her body, who knew her husband to his fingertips, now wanted to make up for everything she had missed. Whoever talked about sex as much as the doctor, who filled his evenings with friends with the endless details of the importance and effects of sex on the attitudes of the individual, and of countries and societies, could not have the time or energy to discover it for himself, let alone practice it with Widad. Widad remembered Samir, that mole, as her husband called him jokingly, saying something she did not understand too well but whose meaning she sensed deep down. One night after one of the doctor's lectures on morality, Samir had told her—after the doctor left, as was his custom every evening, for a long bath—that "whoever talks that much about chastity has no time to be chaste!"

Now she wanted to discover the genius of the body, to test it, to explore everything it could express, defying every limit.

Rateb still made her lose sleep; he stirred her blood. The very sight of him provoked her and filled her with a challenge. She had become like a cat which sees a morsel of meat or cheese and cannot keep calm. She felt a need for him; she wanted him every night, and at the same time she hated and felt an aversion for him. When she saw him she felt weak and lost and found herself unable to forgive or forget, yet unable to yield to him. He would have to come to her, to kneel and beg, and then he could be with her. She could accept that they would part ways, but this: his confidence, contentment and presumption, his being aware of her only as one among many others—that she could never forgive.

She was not thinking or making decisions; her body was. It mutinied, it tyrannized and disregarded her. The doctor, who took his medications and seemed like a shining youth, flickered out and disappeared. She hated his snoring so much that she wanted to smash him. She often spent the whole night trying to doze off, but the monotonous, unvarying sound, so laden with security and contentment, left her weak and wrecked her nerves, and she could not fight it or retreat.

Furthermore, she did not know the truth of her feelings toward him: she loved and hated him at the same time. She wanted him and did not want him; while he represented an atmosphere of happiness and security, he was cold and distant, even hostile. Even his body was not loving or affectionate, and his moods were unlike the moods of old, ill or feeble men; he was a special case, unique; she did not know its real nature or its essence. What concerns, what ideas filled his head and ruled his body? What were his dreams and desires? She gave this a lot of thought but found no answers. Money? He had made enough money for at least two lifetimes—if he knew how to live. Power? He was already bigger and more powerful than anyone else: "the Sultan's shadow." He made decisions on the Sultan's behalf, did much of his thinking, and took executive action. He told her this very proudly, even boastfully, in moments of candor, but then would suddenly withdraw, exactly like a turtle, to be silent and inaccessible, as if he had retreated to some faraway place.

She wanted to know what he thought about and what he wanted, but in spite of the years they had spent together she did not. His air of mystery led her into labyrinths whose exits she did not know how to reach. In other places, at other times, she had known that he was not earning enough money, that Tripoli was too small for him, that he wanted to change the clinic or the household furniture. He told her so. After their move to the Sultanate, however, she no longer knew how much money he had, what he was thinking or what he wanted.

The doctor lived in another world. *How to begin my big launch?* he asked himself, putting off a decision or beginning day after day. He had collected a number of elegant leather notebooks, and none of his acquaintances traveled abroad without his giving them the same instructions: "Don't wear yourselves out bringing back gifts, all I want are some top-class notebooks, like ledgers, preferably big and leather-bound, preferably all different colors." With a high-pitched laugh he would add, "And if you happen across any—a Parker or Sheaffer pen!" Now full of enthusiasm, he would elucidate, "Whatever you spend, remember, we deserve it!"

He could not begin his "launch," as he imagined it, as he wished it to be, until he enjoyed perfect mental and emotional serenity, no aggravations from his daily work, and nothing to interrupt him. He was planning his launch to be powerful and stunning; he wanted to soar. Once he was aloft and had taken a direction, he would fear nothing and stop at nothing.

Every day he cast a fond look on the collection of notebooks he had arranged carefully on the big table near the west window in the upper room. In an effort to force himself to work he had named this room the *mihrab,* or prayer niche, and named the table he had revarnished the *sakhra,* or rock. He had also given titles to the first seven notebooks, after numbering them: the first was the introduction, and he had written in careful, decorative calligraphy, "In the Reader's Hands." The second was "The Wise Man's Ticket to the Secret of Immortality." He called the third "The Deepest Secret of Perceiving the Variations of Night and Day." He named the fourth "A Selection of Knowledge from Bygone Ages Relating to the Present and the Future." The three last notebooks were marked with brackets where he would enter the titles he would choose; he was still hesitating among several titles. He had not forgotten to write in rather modest script, "By Doctor Subhi al-Mahmilji." He was going to add, "Master Physician," but changed his mind. He thought of dropping the *Doctor,* since it was a foreign word, in favor of *al-Hakim,* which had a stately ring to it, and so many different meanings and implications. He wanted a resounding title for the book as a whole. He considered several titles but could settle on none of them, though the closest to his heart was "Constitutions through the Ages." He was still undecided, because he wanted his Square Theory mentioned or implied in the title.

The problem that really bothered him was how to bring peace to the al-Hir Palace: how to satisfy Widad, to make her happy, to include her and to achieve peace with others—i.e., the four principles of his theory—so he was extremely careful that she not fall ill or feel isolated; and should she turn disputatious again, or should others trouble him with their problems or reminders of his own duties, he would postpone his project until some other time.

Much to the doctor's surprise, Samir was not only a civilizing influence but a calming influence on Widad, who was pleased by his visits and his friendship with the doctor; he concluded that "every woman is suspicious of her husband's friendships with other women, but is reassured, and relieved of her doubts if she's sure that he has a good male friend." This was another of Samir's good points, and the doctor was sure of it because he listened very carefully to the conversations between the two.

At first Samir paid no attention to the looks Widad gave him, or could not explain them, then became deeply upset and afraid for several days when she flirted with him openly and he saw how it was with Rateb. She pinched his hand and laughed, and placed her hand on top of his more than once. He became absolutely sure of her invitation when she and the doctor drove him home in their car that night.

These hints were all he needed to begin. True, Widad was over thirty-five and was slightly overweight, but she took good care of herself and looked young. Since Mooran was a ghost town—a man scarcely ever saw a woman or could get near her—Samir resorted to taking longer vacations, on the pretext of having business in scattered places, and on these visits to Beirut and Cairo, and even a few times to Athens and Rome, he "made up for it" and "got his revenge," as he thought of it.

Now that Widad had invaded his world and he had seen her power and the doctor's devotion to her, he was filled with the desire to try this temptation. *Rich women don't age like poor women,* he said to himself, *and they must be wonderful and delectable, especially in rotten old Mooran.* He lost himself in rich and luscious daydreams. *For one person to control another he has to know what keys make him work, but a woman in love is no ordinary key—she's a master key that opens all his doors and shortens distances. The doctor fears Widad's silence and is terrified of her anger and isolation, and she could make me rich in no time; she can help me get out of this lethal city!* The ghost of Rateb flitted through his mind. *That son of a bitch can just leave well enough alone. Why can't he let her live a little, since he sleeps with the prettiest bosom in Mooran?*

63

DESPITE ALL THE PROBLEMS THAT KEPT HIM busy, the doctor did not forget his intellectual questions or his world philosophy; he was "committed to issues bigger than Mooran, beyond the few days man spends on the face of this earth." These were the issues that occupied him, that made him miserable because he did not have enough time to devote to them. That is why he decided, after setting his other business in order, to spend part of every night pondering these big questions. He could spend hours in deep meditation, almost in a stupor, trying to get to the heart of the matter—as he called the point upon which he concentrated his intellect when he closed his eyes and knitted his eyebrows, fixing on a certain question, and no sooner had he found a solution or formulated an idea than he wrote it down quickly, in his special way. He might write: "It is essential to monitor the wind through the four seasons of the year; it confirms the theory." Or: "The sand dunes in Mooran's desert are shaped like crescents, because the winds blow from the northeast to the southwest, which proves my theory." Or: "When two lights shining from two sources intersect, they become four." Or, finally, delightedly, laughingly: "Sexual intercourse follows the Square Theory!"

This sort of meditation and notetaking relaxed and delighted him, but made Widad tense and depressed; not only did she not understand the meaning of the notes he took, she considered them a waste of time unseemly for a man like him. She was so irritated by his long periods of silence every evening that she was often compelled to leave the room and take to her bed, leaving him to "the Devil's daydreams—talking to phantoms."

The doctor had always insisted on being "like a closed nut," as he described himself; he did not breathe his secrets even to his closest friends, because of his conviction that "if a secret is known by two, it is public," so he kept all his thoughts and dreams to himself. If he wanted to test a certain proposition or make a difficult deduction, he resorted to one of two methods or perhaps both: he invented a debate or raised a series of questions, and in most cases he was able to push the debate toward questions whose answers helped him to draw a conclusion or make a decision. The second method was in measuring his "desire," for he loved this word and insisted on using it, and if he found that he inclined to a certain thing he stuck with it. He had done this since his youth, he did not know how or why, and he had often recommended it to Muti and other friends as advice, especially when things were complicated. "If I propose two things to you, see which one is closer to you, and choose that one."

The doctor was like this in everything he did, but in his world philosophy things were more complex and critical. He helped his friends to understand and participate in practical, everyday issues, but they would never be able to grasp the simplest of his philosophical goals, so he did not expect them to take part; they were too fainthearted to know the extent of the inner fire that raged in his depths, and not sensitive enough to realize the importance, the momentousness of these questions. The upshot of it was that he preferred his ideas to crystallize apart from them. When an idea glimmered in his mind and he saw it come into line with his theory, he noted it with exultation; but at other times, when he spent long hours in profound meditation, with solutions eluding him, he attributed it to Mooran's "villainous atmosphere," which caused his thoughts to *evaporate and scorch with the heat and burning dust that blows around most of the year.* Or he pleaded overwork, overburdening responsibilities which "robbed" him of thinking over subjects he loved.

Now that he had organized himself, and felt settled and self-confident, he was more inclined to crystallize his thoughts, especially since he had discovered that Samir was not merely a competent journalist but a *devotee of mine, and of great questions.* After their conversations—for Samir had studied philosophy in college, and always considered it one of his interests—the doctor realized that his pending or postponed problems had solutions. Of course he would not tell Samir everything, or ask him—at least at this stage— to take part directly; for now, their discussions could stimulate his thinking and induce him to record his thoughts more clearly than before.

Samir perceived, from the first weeks, the doctor's philosophical bent and thought it all arrant nonsense, since it had no real basis and showed no intellect whatsoever—it was just showing off, more than anything else, in the same way that society women memorized a few clever expressions in order to entertain their guests, or as dullards memorized endless jokes to convince others that they were witty.

This is what Samir really thought, but he never said so. As long as Samir was dependent on the doctor, who was the "mind" of Mooran, and one of its most influential men, and he needed him— not only needed him but saw him as an avenue to power and wealth—he would put up with this nonsense, since it pleased him. He would listen and pretend to be convinced by what he heard, since this was the way to show his own brilliance and to draw closer to the doctor.

This game had an exciting, even festive aspect, and a boring, stupid one, but both men played it with enthusiasm and obvious gusto. Just as the doctor reserved every Saturday morning for the Security Committee meeting to set policy, he set aside two nights each week, Monday and Thursday, for questions of philosophy and the media. That is how he put it. He was joined by Muti and

Samir and some of his friends in the Information Ministry, and subsequently a representative of the Security Agency began to attend these meetings.

It delighted the doctor to talk in these meetings of his "information philosophy," rather than of information or the media as mere mundane work. What did Mooran require of the media, and how would it be accomplished? "How can we put the media in the service of higher questions? How can the media make people more moral?" Samir always agreed emphatically in these discussions, and offered ideas to "deepen and crystallize" the dialogue, but was opposed in this by Muti, who wanted to discuss work problems and possible solutions; he often tried to put an end to the "discussions of higher questions so that we can deal with some lower ones," he would joke, and start in on the work before them. This made the doctor resent him deeply, for Muti "interrupted his train of thought and brought him from the highest of the high to the lowest of all low planes, with his excursions into the mundane."

Because they took up so much time—what Samir had one day called "mental calisthenics"—before taking up their other business and devising solutions, the doctor came up with an ideal solution: "A day for God, a day for the heart, a day for practical questions and a day for intellectual questions." The Thursday night meeting would deal with "higher questions," in the doctor's phrase; this meeting bored most of the participants, who were not eager for debate or to volunteer their own opinions, and so before long it was attended by only two, the doctor and Samir, and instead of the palace or the head office of *al-Badiya* it was held in the al-Hir Palace.

This solution struck the doctor as clever, not to say ideal. He felt more secure in his own home, and found that when he was alone with Samir his mind ignited better, and he was more brilliant than before. When they began their fruitful discussions on mankind's "motives" and "hidden powers," and the doctor recalled some of the articles he had read in his youth, and how they were furthered by his medical studies, especially in Austria, and described his ideas and deductions, he felt proud and brilliant—even more, felt that he was very close to "closing his hand over the theory, and not over mere ideas."

In order to give these meetings a feeling of complete and intimate friendliness, he spoke about himself at great length, about his childhood and youth. He spoke long and leisurely about his medical studies in Germany and Austria, and repeated the same stories so often that Samir had them memorized perfectly, though he always pretended to be surprised and impressed by them, as if hearing them for the first time, and his attention gave the doctor real pleasure and made him cheerful.

Once, when the doctor was talking about the old days, his youth and first years of medical practice and describing, for the third or perhaps the fourth time, how he had left Tripoli for Aleppo, Samir told him half-jokingly, "If I may be so bold, sir, your life has been so rich that it must be written, so that you can be an exemplar for future generations."

The doctor was pleased by this remark but said nothing. He was really delighted because he had never given the idea serious thought. While it had occurred to him fleetingly before, when, to improve the standard of the Sultanate's newspapers, he considered contributing articles on his theory or on his life experiences, the notion had never lasted long or developed fully, since *the theory has to appear in its fullness, and completely refined, not mangled on the pages of newspapers and magazines in front of every good-for-nothing and vulgarian.* He found the idea of autobiography premature, but when Samir brought up his idea, his life resounded in his memory and he saw the days and nights of his past as clearly as if they were reoccurring before his eyes. "Everything in its own time," he said, to dissuade himself.

These meetings were the beginning of a new bond between Samir and the doctor, a close and mutual friendship, for the doctor, who had varying, even ambiguous or contradictory feelings toward others, felt that this friend was a compensation, "for just as bellies need nourishment, so do brains—even more so, but most people don't realize it, especially in Mooran." He was content with his friendship with Hammad, because Hammad was well educated and possessed remarkable insight, but "he's a little slow to understand things, and lacks imagination." He added, laughing, "The centers are the world, and most central is the most powerful." He could not really consider Said a friend, or even trustworthy; he was a likely enemy, "because his centers are off-line and undetermined, unequal in effect." Muti was "a relative, and blood ties determine character; and character must be molded." He nodded and went on confidently: "Even so, he never acts against my advice, and does nothing without consulting me."

The doctor reviewed, in his mind, other people he had known, or who had passed through his life, and paused when he came to Samir, saying to himself that *you never meet such a mind twice in a lifetime: a wooden cat that hunts but doesn't eat, who amuses, adorns, eats and goes home,* but even so he was careful not to make his affection or admiration for Samir too obvious, *because quiet affection is the most lasting and strongest affection of all.*

Samir, after his former misadventures and disappointments, knew why he had come to Mooran and what he wanted: *Mere chance created this wealth, chance drew me here; otherwise I'd have stayed far away and Mooran would have stayed, as far as I was concerned, lost and forgotten, an insignificant tribe in this endless desert; but as long as I've come, and since I have a role to play and I'm talented, I should gain the maximum benefits in every way. This whole era is going to be very limited, very short, even fleeting, and it will never happen again. I have no illusions, and I have no one to trust and no reason to wait.*

When he looked around he said to himself sadly, *How can a man ever reach any understanding with these bedouin, no matter what concessions he makes? They're desert animals—they have animal traits they'll never lose. I'd be crazy to think I could ever get along with them. I could laugh at them, joke with them, but we would still be from two different worlds.* When he thought of Hammad and Malik and others, he sighed. *They get so difficult after getting all this unexpected money that they didn't earn. Every one of them thinks he's a lord and master, a genius—there's no point in talking to them or trying to agree on anything with them. They're more stubborn than rocks.* He smiled at the thought of the doctor. *What a snob, what a simpleton—he thinks he's gifted, he's powerful, but really only his profession got him to Mooran and into the Sultan's confidence. Power is a delusion, especially political power—it breaks like a balloon, in an instant, but even so I have to get along with him or at least pretend to. And these delusions of philosophy and deep knowledge—what a pack of lies. He dallies with them the way other men dally with women, thinking, as they do, that they are loved and desired, able to assume some kind of control, when actually, when the night's over, when the struggle is over, they see how deceived they were, they have nothing—and they can't believe how gullible they were.*

He looked back on his life and shook his head resolutely. *No, I'm not ready to relive my mistakes. Now I know who I am and what I can do and how I can do it. Those questions I learned in college, that I thought were so simple at the time, are now the hardest and most fascinating things I know. How wise they are!*

64

I N ONE OF THE "DEEPER" DISCUSSIONS THE DOC-
tor now had with Samir, he alluded indirectly
to a theory of his that he wanted to apply him-
self to writing about, so that people could read it and improve
themselves, and indicated that on the strength of this he had
looked through a great many old books and intended to hold dia-
logues with people in specialized fields; he would record his new
ideas, quotes and commentaries in a special notebook which he
called his "daybook."

The doctor did not know how he had decided to wear a black
cloak while working, perhaps because he had begun his project at
the beginning of the year when Mooran was at its coldest. It struck
him that the black cloak was essential, because it looked like the
robe of a judge or monk; and he, in his work, would be a judge,
issuing his sweeping and conclusive judgments, and he would be a
monk, in the monastery of the mind, keeping his vow to make the
Square Theory available to all people.

The picture was clear to Samir, despite the doctor's discretion and secrecy regarding most of his papers, and Samir found it all amusing and different enough to make life in Mooran a little more bearable. He played the game: he brought books to the doctor, having marked several of the texts, and had any number of rambling discussions with him, and in a lighthearted moment began to call the doctor "master instructor," as Avicenna had been called. The doctor showed him the proposed title of the book, and after a contemplative pause Samir voiced his opinion that the book should have a subtitle, and suggested a provisional one, "The Fundamental Law of Political Thought by Abu Ghazwan—Master Physician Subhi Mahmilji al-Tarabulsi."

All this left the doctor at a loss, for Samir was speaking very much in earnest, and his offer of help was undoubtedly sincere; even his frequent suggestions that they go on with their discussions at the onset of night, and Samir's willingness to spend the night at the al-Hir Palace—all this inclined the doctor to consider him serious and to believe that he meant every word he said. Comparing him to Avicenna this early on, before his theory was published and circulated, was surely a bit much, but it came from love and not any bad intention. "Tell me what you think about," said the doctor to soothe himself, "and I'll tell you who you are—this man knows what I'm thinking about and what I intend to accomplish!"

That was the end of that, or almost. The al-Hir Palace enjoyed a certain peace, because the doctor was nearly finished with his preparations, awaiting only the beginning of the year so that he might begin; even so, he was a little perplexed, especially when he got the idea of dedicating the book to the Sultan. He sometimes thought that the importance of the book went far beyond its times, its author and the people among whom he lived, whatever their level. He did not know how *the world's ornament, the genius Mutanabbi* appeared to him, or more accurately had taken possession of him. He asked himself in a moment of irritation: *Who was that lame dwarf patron he had—who'd remember that black who was half nose if it weren't for Mutanabbi?* He seemed more inclined not to dedicate the book to the Sultan. *He's just an ordinary man—if it weren't for the advice he gets, he couldn't do anything.*

Still, he could not ignore him, could not bypass the Sultan with no mention at all. He thought of alluding to him at the end of the introduction, but retreated from the idea—*Some mischievous people might read the book, including the introduction, and then tell the Sultan that in a book hundreds of pages long he was mentioned only at the bottom of one page, just when the problems begin!* He considered writing a preface before the introduction, stating that he had written the book while he was an "inmate of Mooran," during the reign of Sultan Khazael, but gave up this idea as well, because he had never liked the word *inmate*—it reminded him of inmates of prisons or mental sanatoriums, and besides, he did not want to *show himself to the world, announcing that he was not Moorani, that he was merely a guest in Mooran.*

He finally dispelled his unease, in order to go to *the body of the text, not the footnotes,* by deciding to dedicate the book to the Sultan. *I know he doesn't deserve this gem, but he's like any king or president—he has to be the center of attention and interest, so that everyone will look his way and think he's the genius of the age when in fact he's not worth a kick. A man has to laugh at those kings and presidents, and could deflate their follies with a word, and that word would be his passport, a passport with which he could go to the stars.* He thought of having the dedication printed in gold ink on the first page. The Sultan would look at those golden words and see his name shining like the moon among the stars, and would have to give him more than he had ever given any man; he would order the book to be distributed everywhere, and overnight the book would be in the people's hands and they would be reading it and memorizing passages. Those who could not read would grab their children or other educated relatives and ask them to read aloud a few pages of the great tome so that they could memorize a few sentences, as they did with the Koran or their favorite verses of poetry. Best of all, he saw the book translated into a large number of foreign languages, published in several capital cities simultaneously, captivating all the newspapers, radio stations and universities, carefully studied by key statesmen, not merely because it was an important book but because it came from an eminent man who represented the present and future thinking and policies of the Sultanate of Mooran. For that reason its every word would have to be studied, every sentence pondered; otherwise there would be no way to understand Mooran's policies or the thinking that guided every step she took and every policy she adopted.

German, he thought, should be the first language into which his book would be translated, because first of all it was the language of philosophy, and second, because the Germans, more than any other people, were ready to comprehend profound and brilliant ideas. As soon as it was published, he would send a copy to his old landlady, who had been so gruff with him, never once thinking that the man she had evicted from her house would become so powerful and eminent. Perhaps the old woman was no longer alive, or might buy the book for herself, but he would have to send a copy to her anyway, with an inscription; it would teach her a lesson, and she might be sorry, *but alas! what good would her sorrow do her?* If she had died, her heirs would get the book and pass it around, read and admire it, it would be their nightly occupation. They would give the book to their friends and tell them that "the author lived in this room, in this very house," and no doubt they would point out just where he used to sleep and do his studying.

He considered going beyond the grueling schedule he had imposed upon himself, or the time he had set for the writing, and beginning immediately. *What's the difference between starting now or at any other time? Who'll call me to account, who'll even notice?* But he promptly gave up and decided that the project go according to plan, that it submit to the unvarying schedule, since in his view the schedule was part of the theory and would have to remain binding in every detail in order to produce the results he wanted.

These were his ideas and his concerns, the hesitations and unease that seized him, but in spite of them he was able to persevere toward the answers he sought, and he postponed certain questions so as to give them more thought.

Widad was queen of the whole autumn, days and nights alike, and then of the winter; no sooner did she perceive a challenge than it made her appear younger and more radiant. She smothered the doctor with solicitude and asked him dotingly how much longer he would need to finish his book, and whether his book was a novel or something else; she asked if she thought her capable of reading and understanding the book. The doctor was delighted with her attitude and considered it a good omen and explained to her very simply that his book was everything—"a comprehensive book, with stories from history and the ancients, wise sayings and poetry, which any person could read and profit by." Widad understood some of this. Her question was meant only to encourage him and reassure him that she was with him, that was all.

In the bustle of preparing for the "launch," their discussions intensified and took a practical turn; every autumn evening that year the doctor established a topic for discussion. Sometimes it was a verse of poetry or an aphorism, by way of introduction, and when they had exhausted a discussion of it, and reached a satisfactory conclusion, they made a note of it, and did not hesitate to read what they had written to Samir, and called their conclusion "the lock."

Widad sat in on some of these discussions. She listened quietly, looking now at one man, now at the other, but only rarely hearing what they said. When she grew bored with their talk she withdrew to direct the servants or to help them prepare supper, and when it was ready she called them to the table. At the table their talk took a new turn, light and gallant, including everyone, which pleased the doctor, delighted him even, and when at the end of supper she asked whether they intended to continue, Samir would reply politely, "Whatever the doctor says—whatever he orders!"

The doctor would laugh, pleased as a child, for he had scarcely imagined that people still had such fine manners. He would enthusiastically insist that they do another hour or two of work, "in order to make another lock or two." Widad prepared to leave them, filled with happiness, for this is what she had hoped for.

"Look, I don't need to tell you—a man needs rest, too!" She laughed flirtatiously. "Don't wear yourselves out!"

The doctor reassured her that "our ideas are all ready—I don't need to tire Samir or bore him," and he would whisper loudly to him "not to turn on the light because it would wake her," and Samir would nod willingly.

In the last humid hours of the night, with the gentle breezes, Widad made sure that the doctor had glided to his bed like a cat and sunk into his sleepy kingdom. Then she slipped out. She tiptoed downstairs like a ghost in the silence unbroken except by the doctor's snoring, and, like a lovely perfumed dream, or like a tame animal that knows how to tease its master, how to endear itself to his innermost heart, and without Samir knowing when or how she had come in, she slipped into bed beside him.

These were hours of bliss mingled with fear, the sort of fear that transforms every movement and every touch into stinging electricity. Neither of them remembered ever feeling this kind of pleasure before, or even being aware that such sensual delight was attainable. When the shadows dispersed, and the shapes of things began to appear almost distinct in the twilight before dawn, and the sounds of birds were heard, Widad stirred involuntarily at these signs that another night was about to end. Often, after her movements preparatory to leaving, she threw herself on him again and hugged him and kissed him as though she had no plans ever to leave his bed. He felt satisfaction and terror, and his response was less ardent and less longing; when she had stolen away, leaving his door half open, he got up to close and lock it, then fell fast asleep.

In the morning the doctor ate his breakfast out on the balcony if it was a sunny day and solicitously directed the servants not to raise their voices or make any noise, "because our guest is sleeping, and he must be tired from last night." Widad came in late, as a rule, after lying in bed or keeping busy with little tasks until noon, when Salma got home from school.

Such nights were frequent. Widad, who at first was motivated by the effects of jealousy and the need for a challenge, soon saw Rateb as stupid and inane. *He's a coward. He doesn't understand anything but money—he's just like the doctor—he even looks like him. He got fat after he got married, and he looks so smug you'd think he was king of everything.* Furthermore, she found that Samir *is really different from that bunch of tradesmen,* in his looks, his age and his behavior.

Without fear or hesitation, sometimes even with almost mocking menace, Samir became one of the people who hardly ever left the al-Hir Palace. The sort of friendship he had with the doctor demanded that he help him work on the Square Theory, and the doctor even considered that they might formulate it together, and though he considered this notion premature and possibly even frivolous, he decided that *that suggestion should come from him. If he suggests it, it will take a lot off my mind; I can dictate to him, or tell him my thoughts and he can formulate them.* Then he became uneasy. *Someday, when the theory is published, envious people will say, "Samir Caesar created this theory, he conceived it and wrote it down, and the doctor only embel-*

lished it, maybe putting his name on it only to help sell the book." So he very regretfully changed his mind.

Rateb had the sharp eyes of a wolf and missed nothing. "Doctor," he said to him one day, "nobody invites a bear into his vineyard!"

"Bear? Vineyard?" asked the doctor, taken aback. "What are you talking about, Rateb?"

"I'm talking about Samir, Abu Ghazwan."

"What about Samir? What's wrong with Samir that's not wrong with everyone else?"

"Doctor, everyone's saying it—'Samir is so cheap that he's left his house and he's living off the doctor.'"

"Rateb, people say all kinds of things and no one is crazy enough to believe half of it."

"But, Doctor, he's really gone too far."

"Look, let me tell you frankly, I'm the one who asked him to stay, and I need him." Very confusedly, the doctor explained to Rateb that he had some important literary plans. He reminded him of the books he had entrusted to him on his past visits to Mooran, and said that the effect of his plans, in their grandeur and influence, would not be limited to Mooran, nor to these times they lived in; they would affect the whole region, and for a long time to come. The doctor alluded very bitterly to the instability sweeping the world; it was caused by "a lack of capable philosophers to undertake the formulation of ideas to protect morals and religion and their countries"—and ambiguously, with a touch of humility, he hinted that *he* had undertaken this task and that only Samir could assist him.

As he had done the first time, Rateb postponed his battle until circumstances were more favorable.

65

HAMMAD HAD BECOME ONE OF MOORAN'S IM-
portant dignitaries and his name was on
everyone's lips, but his Uncle Shaddad
found this very strange. Shaddad had not seen him in months, but
when next he saw him he asked mockingly, "Hammad, boy, two
years ago, when I asked you where you worked, you told me 'The
palace'—that you were an adviser to the Sultan. Now I see you
dashing around, in a different place every day, as if the Sultan
didn't want to hear your advice!" He guffawed. "Tell your uncle
the truth, Hammad—are you advising the Sultan, or someone
else?"

Hammad smiled but did not reply. Shaddad turned to those who
were listening.

"Don't forget, people! Just as we've always said, Hammad may
not want people to know of his travels, and may think they don't
know, but time comes and goes and everything becomes known—
so what else is there?"

"What your own eyes can see, Uncle! The Sultan tells me to go somewhere, I go. The Sultan says, 'Do this,' I do it. The Sultan says, 'Sit,' I sit. You think there's something behind every trip I make, but that's not true." This was Hammad's playful answer, which was taken several ways; his uncle nodded and decided to understand it in his own way.

Hammad had changed not only toward his family and friends but even toward himself. The city of Mooran, rather than the Sultanate of Mooran, had become his world, and he never left it except for the nearby desert or a few excursions with caravans, which he never accompanied to their final stops. Now, day after day, he was possessed by the hobby of discovering the world, which he did with great interest and pleasure, and in his own special way. The Americans came to him in order to minimize his appearances in public places, and had him use a pseudonym on some of his travels, for added caution, and saw that he had plenty of ready cash so that in case of need he could use it directly, without asking anyone or going through anyone else, which pleased him beyond measure. His mind raced to invent new names and titles, and he prepared for himself several passports in several different names and disguises, and could not keep from laughing out loud when he looked at the pictures glued into the passports, especially when he remembered when the pictures were taken. He had put aside some of the money at his disposal in his iron safe, which also contained a number of revolvers and some passports ready for use as soon as he entered a new name and photograph.

The doctor was the only person, or at least one of the few, who noticed no change in Hammad. All he saw was continual improvement, which came from his almost frenzied absorption in his work, and which went along with his developing new expertise every day, and the acuteness that the doctor ascribed to his own efforts to train and polish him; and Hammad's travels had broadened his mental powers and alertness.

The doctor was delighted both with the choice of Hammad and the progress he had made, which facilitated and hastened the shifting of much business from him to Hammad, and which no longer required his intervention; and, ultimately, the independence of the Agency. This happened without any formal announcement or decision; it happened, for all practical purposes, before the doctor even decided to transfer some of his powers. Hammad used his instincts at first, and before long could foresee the consequences of every policy or measure taken; especially given his visits to the United States, and the recommendations of the Research and Reporting Center, which were submitted to him to let him know what needed to be done. Lastly there were his productive discussions with his aides, especially the Americans, sometimes even in the presence of the embassy adviser, Paul Andrews—all these had decisive and useful consequences.

Now the doctor was voicing his fears of the "red winds," as he called the ideas and movements sweeping through the region, and appeared reckless and upset as he demanded that Hammad "take firm measures to destroy this germ before it becomes an entrenched disease, like cholera or bilharzia or trachoma." He rejected the idea that Mooran should spend a fortune on a system of "gifts and grants," and Hammad agreed placidly and with gradual understanding. The doctor's views gave rise to thoughts and worries he had tried to push away or ignore in the past, which came back to him: why was the doctor so harsh and bigoted against the "expatriates" as he called them, and why did he put them all in one basket? Why was he so covetous about Mooran and the Sultanate— much more so than the native Mooranis or the Sultan were! And money—if Mooran had spent a little here and there, as it pleased, rather than as others pleased—what did he see wrong in that?

In spite of all the advice he heard, not to get excited, not ever to say a final "yes," or "no," never to show any emotion too openly, Hammad found himself unable to be silent or passive, and spoke to the doctor in a voice loaded with sarcasm.

"Please, Abu Ghazwan: spare us until we get rid of Malik Four-Eyes." This was what the doctor called Malek Abu Fraih, who always wore eyeglasses. "We used to tell him, 'Pay,' and he'd say, 'There's no money.' Today we're still not rid of him, but God has blessed this Sultanate with so much, and if we want to spend a little here and there, we're not the losers—as we used to say, whoever eats the Sultan's bread fights with the Sultan's sword!" He paused to take a deep breath. "I think, Abu Ghazwan, that if we spend a few coins here and there we can silence some of the insults we hear morning and night. We can put an end to the dissent and the arms they smuggle in over the border, waiting for the time to point them in our faces."

He lowered his voice until it was nearly inaudible.

"You know the saying, 'Fill a belly and close an eye.' "

The doctor was not convinced. He stood by his opinion, and Hammad did not wait for his consent to act or to speak his mind, nor did he tell the doctor anything. In the atmosphere of action and excitement, of hidden rivalry and rapidly changing events, this discussion between Hammad and the doctor was not resumed, nor did they have any conflict of opinion, partly because the doctor was occupied by new ideas and worries.

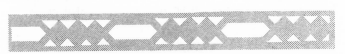

H E MARRIED ME TO HIS DAUGHTER, AND wants to be my only uncle—but he's wrong. He's dreaming," said Hammad to himself as he recalled the doctor's ironic smile after asking him about Rezaie and the others, and how he had told him nothing of any new projects under way.

It was not the first misunderstanding between the two. They had also disagreed on what sort of regional policy to adopt and on the relationship between the Security Agency and other government agencies. Hammad had learned many lessons in the years that were passing, but perhaps the most important was: be silent, and listen well. He did not speak unless asked to; when he did answer it was very briefly, and without his customary smile before answering—it covered his whole face, like a veil—he would have been badly misunderstood.

He learned silence and perfected it, and saw and heard much.

He was surrounded by people whose greatest delight was talking about other people. Hammad found their talk odd and fascinating at the same time, and reckoned that it would be useful someday, so he paid attention.

The doctor, on the other hand, considered that the service he had rendered Hammad by getting him appointed to the Agency would make Hammad pliant and obedient to him, and so he treated him, from the beginning, rather condescendingly. He showed off his knowledge in front of Hammad, not to teach him, but to make him conscious of his ignorance and poor education. At first Hammad listened mutely as the doctor's talk moved all around the world, delving into many complicated subjects, but before long he saw the uselessness of most of what the doctor said— *He does not know what's happening around him, or anything about the people nearest to him*—and Hammad knew the facts that proved this.

That was not all. For a long time the doctor loved to reminisce about the early days of the Security Agency, only to remind Hammad of the favors he owed him and his importance to him. Even the paternal tone the Sultan used when asking for something or informing him of something, to which Hammad listened very happily and eagerly, made an impression on the doctor, who loved this lofty tone and adopted it himself, much to Hammad's annoyance. It even made him furious, but he masked his fury with his now habitual patience and silence.

On the other hand, Hammad did not mention or make the slightest reference to the many favors he had done for the doctor, the first time or the second time, when he acted as a mediator between him and his Uncle Rashed, then his Uncle Shaddad—and the doctor himself had forgotten all this. Furthermore, when Rashed al-Mutawa asked to meet with the doctor to discuss his Hasiba land—more properly, what was left of the Mutawwa family's Hasiba land—the doctor was surprised at the request.

"The land your uncle is talking about is worthless, Hammad," said the doctor almost sarcastically. "I sold the land I bought from him at a loss, but for your sake I can help him out—I'll find him a buyer."

Hammad shrugged nonchalantly; none of this concerned him.

"If he wants to sell the land south of the riverbed, we can talk about it," said the doctor. "We can reach an understanding."

Hammad did not need anyone to tell him whether that or any other piece of land was sold or not, or at what price: he had, in the Land Records Office, a number of agents who kept him informed of all land that changed hands, of all purchases and sales in the city of Mooran and outside the city limits, even some of the real estate agents and merchants. His uncle had told him that land was like any other business, leading both to profit and loss; he wanted to pacify and please him as much as persuade him.

Hammad also remembered the story Said had told him long ago, about how the doctor had acted in certain land deals, notably with his Shifa Hospital in Harran. People had scoffed at him for building it on such a desolate site. They even thought it was part of the oil company. But construction began even farther out, and the site had become part of the city center. The doctor had ordered that the surrounding land be developed as a park, but within two years, after half of it had been planted, he cut it off from the hospital and enclosed it with a cement wall topped with an equal height of barbed wire; shops would be built there. His move to Mooran compelled him to slow and then give up his construction plans, so that only the foundations got built. The government bought the hospital and decided to build a road westward, passing through land owned by the doctor, and so had to buy all the land and pay its owners compensation. The doctor's response was less than half-serious: his words were the farthest his project ever got.

"Do you need the land west of the hospital?" he asked the head of the Appropriation Council.

"Most of it, for the Sultan Street project; we have to appropriate it."

"What about the Central Market buildings?"

"Central Market?"

"Everything's ready! The plans, the maps, the foundations—the market will be standing in a few days."

"The road has to pass through there, Doctor."

"And the compensation?"

"We'll pay compensation for the land."

"And the structures?"

"You can see for yourself that the structures hardly exist!"

The doctor laughed and look directly into the councilman's eyes. "Let's suppose the appropriation is delayed a month or two and construction begins—what would you do?"

"We'd buy the land, demolish the buildings and open the road."

"And you'd pay for the buildings, the construction and trucking away the materials?"

"Of course!"

"If I save you the trouble of the demolition and trucking, would you thank us and say 'God bless you good men'?"

"We'd say it."

"So why not pay us for it, and we'll say 'God bless you'!"

The council head seemed taken by the idea and asked the doctor to postpone making his decision. He consulted with his colleagues, sought the advice of the emir, who in turn contacted Mooran, and they struck a deal to compensate the doctor for the land, demolition, and trucking away the materials.

It was enough that Hammad knew Said in order for him to find out the deepest and most detailed secrets. Once he got to know everyone around the doctor, including Radwan and Abu Abdallah and Widad's maid, he knew more than he would ever need to know, and was familiar with his weak points, his hobbies, what he owned and where, though he pretended to know nothing about him; moreover, he even began to play a certain cynical game with the doctor, agreeing with everything he said, but never doing what he asked, unless it pleased him to.

When the relations between the two men took a critical turn, especially over their divergence of opinion over the Sultanate's policies toward its neighbors, Nadia's marriage became an issue. The doctor remembered her when he remembered Badri, and before long, he prepared her and got Muti to broach the subject with Hammad. The idea came as a surprise to Hammad but charmed him too; the oddness of the idea derived at least partly from Widad, whom he found enormously attractive, feminine and full of life. As soon as she got involved, in her customary way, he consented and the wedding took place. All this happened in a very short time. After the honeymoon, which the newlyweds spent in the United States, Hammad began to suspect that the marriage was a new trap the doctor had set for him, and so, after all the parties given in their honor, he took a deft stance: he showered Nadia with gifts and at the same time pleaded a terrible workload to excuse him from accepting most dinner and party invitations. This way he saw less and less of the doctor, gradually at first, but insistently, and then still less. Very patiently and persistently he was able to win Nadia over, and satisfy the doctor with a different kind of relationship.

Bit by bit, the doctor came to be a secondary thing to Hammad. His ideas and analyses seemed stupid to him, even idle and full of unreality; they had no basis in real information and were full of contradictions. He exploited with primitive cynicism the Sultan's whims—what he hated and what he loved, what he wanted to hear; he courted him in this way without going to the trouble of showing consistency in what he said today versus what he had said yesterday, with the result that Hammad no longer placed any value on his analyses or proposals—he left him to talk as he pleased. He nodded when the doctor spoke to show his agreement and consent though he resolutely disagreed with every word. Even the weekly and later monthly meetings that busied the palace with the first phase of forming the Security Agency soon lost their usefulness with the Sultan's persistent absences and the doctor's bossy vanity toward the aides and employees whom he summoned, not to listen to them, but to teach them failed lessons in politics which had never existed in any place or time.

Still later, though not much later, an attempt to assassinate the Sultan was discovered, and Hammad followed the whole conspiracy by himself; he found out every detail and presented it as a gift to the Sultan, without telling another soul, least of all the doctor. So as a result Hammad achieved a special friendship with the Sultan, and the Agency was given lavish funds to be spent at Hammad's discretion, without needing anyone else's approval.

Hammad needed this sort of self-confidence, as well as that kind of money in order to act. Within a few months of the Sultan's decision to stop attending the Security Agency meetings, Hammad did the same. At first he timed his trips to coincide with the meetings, then more boldly excused himself on the pretext of other urgent work, sending instead his deputy or some other official of the

Agency. The doctor considered travel a valid excuse—"force majeure," as he called it—and soon got used to Hammad's trips or his absences.

"The important thing, Abu Ghazwan," Hammad once told him, in response to the doctor's inquiries, "is that somebody from the Agency be there." He smiled broadly. "Unless you want to postpone the meetings time after time, or have me cancel my trips!"

"The important thing is that we all be in the picture—that we all stay informed."

"Have no fear, Abu Ghazwan, no one from the Agency attends unless he has all the information—I'll see to that myself."

So the direct working relationship between Hammad and the doctor was over, for all practical purposes, especially after the doctor's two visits to the United States. During one of Hammad's visits, the Americans told him, when they were discussing the doctor, that he was a "chatterbox" and laughed, adding that "he's harmless, in any case, and might be useful in the future."

The doctor now owned huge tracts of land in and around Mooran, in addition to what he owned in Harran, and had registered them in the names of his wife and children; only the al-Hir Palace was held in his name, with some of the first land he had bought in Mooran. Speculation had begun, and as a result prices had shot up; princes started buying and selling land as well as numerous houses in Beirut, Mount Lebanon, Tripoli and Damascus. Every now and then, between lulls, the doctor raved about ideas and plans for books he wanted the time to write; Hammad was sure that "this man knows as much about politics as I know about medicine." Everything he said and did was nothing but cover. He had quarreled with Said and was beginning to quarrel with Rateb. "As for that scarecrow"—he meant Samir—"he has no right or wrong. Whatever he wants to do, he does, and doesn't bat an eyelid."

It would have been possible for Hammad not to see all that went on, or to ignore what he did see, but "the doctor's friends and relatives don't ignore or forget anything." A day hardly passed without one of them saying in Hammad's face: "The man's crazy, absolutely crazy, sir! He wants to invent a new theory of the world, the Square Theory—have you heard anything about that, sir?" Sa-

mir would pause, then: "He wants me to write it—he's out of his
mind, sir—I mean, if a man has a theory he should write about it
himself, right, sir?" And Muti: "Listen, you and I are friends, Abu
Rashed—I wouldn't breathe a word if we weren't. The doctor has
gotten unbearable. He thinks of no one but himself; he doesn't get
along with anyone anymore, and pretty soon he won't even get
along with Rateb. Ibn Caesar is now ruling the al-Hir Palace—the
doctor does nothing without consulting him." And Rateb, who
talked but did not tell everything: "Believe me, Brother Hammad,
I was on top of the world in Marseilles, and when I was in Beirut
everything was fine. But the doctor's insistent letters and cables, all
nagging me to come at once—and when I got here he forgot me—
nothing—he pays attention to nobody but Samir. They chatter
back and forth all day long. The doctor tells him he's going to do a
book, a ten- or twenty-volume book." He paused before adding,
"It's a nuthouse, Abu Rashed—a mental hospital!"

Hammad listened, surprised, in silence, but he hankered for this
information, which would undoubtedly come in handy at some
point: it told him what kind of man the doctor was and who his
aides and relatives were—but where did he find the time to think
about writing books? And the theory Samir was talking about—
what kind of theory was it? What did it mean, for whom was it
intended, and what were the implications?

Hammad needed this game to continue. He slipped an envelope
full of money into Samir's pocket and smiled broadly. "Forgive me,
Samir—just a little gift!" Samir made a show of protest. "Mooran
has grown very expensive, my man—one is always in need of a
little extra." And then: "Come now—no formalities between
friends!"

Samir accepted the money with affected pain, but began to visit
Hammad weekly. Muti refused to accept money the first time and
the second time, but when Hammad seemed angry—"This money
is not from my pocket to your pocket, it's something for you to use,
to give to some of the deserving workers on the newspaper"—Muti
accepted his explanation and said, to rationalize his acceptance,
"I'll give you a receipt for every sum I pay out, no matter how
small."

"God keep you, Abu Rushdy, but never mind—it's too trivial."

He offered nothing to Rateb, but told him, after listening to him at length, "It's true that things are harder now than they used to be, but we have a thousand and one things to do."

Before Rateb went back to his office, Hammad phoned the director of the Armed Forces Supply office and asked him "to give some help to Mr. Rateb Fattal, our brother and friend, because he's earned it." Within three days the Oriental Foodstuffs Company was given the contract to feed the defenders of Mooran. "This is strictly between the two of us," Hammad told Rateb delightedly. "Not a word to Abu Ghazwan—he wouldn't like the Agency getting involved in business, and he doesn't like to see anyone do better than himself."

Rateb winked and shook Hammad's hand warmly.

"Don't worry, Abu Rashed, I'll never forget your help—you've saved my life!"

"Don't mention it. If we keep in touch, everything will be fine, everything will go smoothly."

Hammad owed nothing to anyone, and acted as though no one owed him anything either. He smiled as he always had, and kept his friendly demeanor; the only thing that had changed was his absence from the office whenever any of them wanted him. His secretary, Abdelmawla, was extremely polite and friendly: "Abu Rashed left town two days ago and hasn't informed us when to expect him again," "Abu Rashed was needed at the Palace," and "Abu Rashed is in an emergency meeting—we don't know how long it will last."

Sometimes Hammad returned calls, sometimes he forgot, and because some people could not bear to wait or to be put off, and since Hammad had a large number of aides, he directed some of them to receive his "friends" and talk to them. "But if it's a personal matter, something that can wait, I'll get to it as soon as I get away from what I'm doing." And so his aides were told much, and other things were postponed, but it was becoming ever clearer that Hammad had become a high official and trustworthy friend who could be relied on when needed. All the doctor's friends thought so, though none of them said as much to the doctor or anyone else.

67

EVEN HAMMAD DID NOT KNOW HOW HE HAD become so powerful, or at least he could give no clear explanation. Not long after he began working in the Agency he noticed a growing number of people all around him, all of whom wanted to talk to him, or to please him, and because he had learned how to smile and listen, and also to give orders, they loved and feared him at the same time. When he learned to give and simplify things for others, he was loved even more than before. Every day he grew in self-confidence and in the conviction that he meant much to his colleagues, and his visits to the United States, Germany and other countries proved this to him. He became a new man: he knew what he wanted and how to get it.

He had decided early on that the Agency was for all Mooran, not for any particular person or interest, and since he was the Agency chief, he made the decisions, he knew everything, and no one criticized or came near him, not even the Sultan, if only because *the Agency has saved his life several times, even saved him from his brothers.* And the Sultan had a great deal on his mind; he was always receiving delegations or visiting the provinces, and when these tasks were accomplished he was at leisure for the one thing he never wearied of: women. Hammad, who had planted spies everywhere, did not omit the palace; in fact, it was one of the most prominent and vital targets. He planted them expertly and with great care: "His Majesty's life is the most precious thing we have." He hand-picked the palace agents after first testing them on several missions, and sent special crack units to the United States for training, keeping both groups under direct Agency supervision. He had agents among the servants and guards and the palace women, so that he even knew which woman the Sultan slept with, and whether he had left her during the night to sleep with another woman. He knew when the Sultan went to bed and when he got up, who visited him and everything that went on in the palace.

At first some of the princes did not understand what the Security Agency was for and thought little of it, but slowly they began to discover that Hammad could be very helpful to them: in gathering information, and filling their needs from within and outside the Sultanate. Above all, Hammad knew how to serve others, how to make himself useful or indispensable at the right time. No sooner had any of the princes spoken of the telescopic hunting rifle His Majesty owned than he was given one, within a few days or weeks at the most. There was much more to it than that. If another prince wanted to know who owned the land south of the Khalidia palaces, Hammad needed just a few hours to deliver the needed information, or even more than was needed. If a prince or princess planned to travel, Hammad had to prepare them a staff of bodyguards and servants, and instructed the embassy to provide accommodations, cars and escorts.

He did all this and more with overflowing humility, as if it were part of his job. When he got richer, he discovered that people loved money more than any other thing, and that they would perform any service in order to get it.

The palace often gave gifts and grants, and before long turned this task over to the Agency; so many mistakes had been made and complaints received about Sheikh Malik. Three of the plotters who had tried to assassinate the Sultan were of a tribe whose chief had not received his allotted grants for that year. The Sultan smiled meaningfully at Hammad when he assigned him this task.

"They're our people and we know them better than anyone else. If you fill their mouths, you stop up all their trouble."

"That's the truth, Your Majesty."

"Two birds with one stone: placating them and binding them to us."

This was something Hammad did not need to be told. He had already given gifts to a number of sheikhs who had helped him uncover some of the arms smuggling that went on, and on another occasion because they provided him with men to build storehouses for the Frontier Guards. Now that all the sheikhs were paid fixed sums by the Security Agency and enjoyed confidential relationships with it, they flocked to Mooran and spent days there with Hammad as their doting host. When a separate building was constructed and named the Desert Bureau, the sheikhs crowded in not only to obtain their grant money but to have some of their many problems mediated, and to pick up the flour, sugar and other supplies they needed.

Even the tribal sheikhs from neighboring countries who had been accustomed to visiting the Sultanate every now and then since the days of Sultan Khureybit, always returning home empty-handed, now came more often and prolonged their visits. The Sultan was not stingy with them: in addition to a warm welcome, they were given money they had never received before—never dreamed of before. The Security Agency was responsible for liaison activities and disbursing the gifts.

One day Shaddad saw the horse his brother had been given by Milhem bin al-Meheid as a gift, and said, "Abu Fawzan, I don't like that horse. Something's not right!"

"There's no other like him, Abu Ghanem. You know horses!"

"I mean, he's descended from his owner, that's all—what about that day in Zarqa?"

"God keep you, man, you never forget anything."

"A man never forgets, Abu Fawzan, he can overlook some things but never forget them."

The two brothers fell silent, as if they did not want to remember the day in Zarqa, when Milhem had betrayed them to the Frontier Guards; all the goods packed on their camels were confiscated, and Milhem received a third of those goods, as he had admitted in front of several people, among them Shamran. Shaddad now resumed his attack.

"Khureybit had his bad times, once or twice, years ago—you remember, Abu Fawzan—but they used to be welcoming; now they've got a bauble instead of the welcome, and horses and a Mauser instead of a handful of dates, and they'll want your daughter, too!"

"Look, they're sorry, Abu Ghanem—remorse is natural."

"Remorse or money, Your Excellency?"

"I'll give you this horse," snapped Abu Fawzan in an effort to quarrel. "Take it—it's yours!"

"A wicked man's horse will only get worse, Saleh, and spoil the good horses. Listen . . ." Shaddad said bitterly to his brother. "Listen, Abu Fawzan, I'm not the first to tell you that Mooran is no place where favors are done for free. His Majesty told Hammad to open his moneybags and hand money out, and he has—to everyone they've dishonored, everyone with a revenge to exact. Now Milhem wants to make up the day in Zarqa to you. You may forget, but I remember, and you may be weak, but I can still do plenty."

Saleh laughed and ended the discussion, for the time being at least, but Shaddad spoke aloud, although almost to himself: "Someday we'll pay for our own horses and other people's nags, and the one who has nothing will pay!"

Hammad was no less masterful at wielding power than he was at winning people over, and he could threaten with it. One day Paul Andrews told him, "The policy that makes Mooran so stable is a simple one, but it needs to be applied cleverly," and added, with a friendly look, "the carrot and the stick!" When Hammad looked at him quizzically, he explained, "force and money," then laughed and clarified: "not money and force."

Very calmly and patiently—the opposite of the way the doctor spoke—he explained to him that the new circumstances in Mooran had helped to create a climate of stability and contentment, which required just two methods, or at least one: incentive and force. Incentives for those who saw the status quo alone as being their business, since it affected their interests; force toward the others, dissidents, those who were never satisfied with anything.

Hammad had made a vague conjecture that most people in Mooran needed money or fear, and that those who were not won over by money could be frightened by the stick, even if the stick was never used. Experience had taught him that no one ever had enough money, which deeply disturbed him; in spite of the wealth he had amassed, he felt that he needed something more, and saw that money was not everything in this world. Perhaps that was the reason, or one of the reasons, that made him view the doctor as he did.

Days passed and the people of Mooran were occupied with the constantly changing life around them, straining to earn their livelihoods. They forgot their fears or engrossed themselves in other things, but Mooran was part of the wide earth, full of hunger and oppression, boiling with frustration, burning for something other than what it was told and what it heard; and like the muezzin whose voice splits the dawn twilight to announce the start of another day, the voices of the frustrated and hungry echoing also in Mooran, heard from place to place throughout the sorrowful Arab lands, echoing also in Mooran, where people ceased their mad race and let their memories catch up with them. Once again their fears returned; they wondered and waited. The rich, and those whose riches increased with every passing day, grew more afraid as they grew richer, and the poor, who had known how to cling to life and earn a livelihood in past years, found that this life had now grown more powerful than they, and more mocking. It threw them from one place to another, and they did not know where it would shove them next or where their graves would lie. They strained their ears to hear sounds coming from far away in the future.

The Sultan did not like this anger. He feared it, and often wished deep down that electricity had never come to Mooran, and that airplanes had never found it; the people would be living in contentment, as their fathers and grandfathers had, but since all this had happened, and since Mooran was now rich, they could afford to give, so he issued orders to Hammad to act: to give. Hammad knew better than anyone else not to wait for a fire before going to Mooran to put it out; he went to it before it flared up, to prevent it with money. With the arrival of money and the contest over dividing it, the frustrated and hungry were occupied and the rulers heaved a deep sigh; the middlemen got rich, and the anger receded, losing its urgency.

The doctor opposed this policy, as he had been saying for some time, but Hammad paid no attention; he listened very politely and attentively to him, but that was all. The doctor spoke of prayers and Islamic proseletyzing and explained some of the Square Theory, but only awoke Hammad's sarcasm and pity, and sometimes his annoyance. Even when the doctor telephoned him to seek an explanation for the events that echoed through the radio news, he considered it an intrusion into affairs that were none of his business; sometimes he took these calls and other times asked his secretary to handle them. The doctor knew nothing of the amounts of money paid out, or to whom they were paid, and was told nothing.

Hammad moved around putting out fires, or sent money, but here he kept his hand closed over the Agency. He wanted Mooran to be as quiet as a grave; he wanted to hear nothing, nobody. He planted agents everywhere, to count the breaths that people took, to watch every movement and weigh every silence; even in the palace, on the pretext of fearing for the Sultan's safety, he demanded more scrutiny and more vigilance.

He sent a man to Nimr to tell him, "Bite your tongue; one more word and it will be as if you were never born. Put a stone in your mouth. Shut up." Nimr laughed mockingly, seeing the threat more as an expression of fear than a show of strength.

"Tell Abu Rashed I send my regards," he told the messenger, "and tell him blood is thicker than water—the people of Mooran are all one family and they know what's right and what isn't; they beware of parasites and people who wear glasses on their nose!" He was referring to Muti or Samir, or perhaps both of them. When Shamran heard about the threat to his son, he spoke to those around him in Zaidan's Coffeehouse.

"I don't think Hammad's behind it—he's a good boy and knows his horseflesh." Then he added suddenly: "But even so, he or whoever it is, near or far, should know that all wars start with words."

When Hammad learned what Shamran and his son had said, he laughed angrily and could not stop himself from saying, "Believe me, I know more than they do and better than they do—just let them try something and they'll see."

68

PRINCE FANAR HAD BEEN AWAY FROM MOORAN
for several years, roving through Switzerland, Austria and the United States in quest
of rest and relaxation or seeking medical treatment. He made only
short visits to Mooran in these years, never exceeding a few weeks,
always packing his bags suddenly and setting off again, pessimistic
and suffering a relapse of his ailment.

This time, he showed up with three weeks left in the year. "One
of his usual visits," most people said. "It's just the cold weather that
brought him here—as soon as spring comes to wherever he came
from he'll pack up and go back, the way birds do." Others said, with
sad faces, that "he has something incurable. They told him, 'It's
better for you and for all of us if you die in your own country'—so
he came home."

Sultan Khazael, who saw nothing unusual in his brother's visit
and was neither curious nor fearful, looked after him lavishly but

soon felt alarmed. Fanar had always been a quiet man and some-what mysterious, but now he was completely inscrutable: he had never perfected anything as much as he had this silence. The Sultan's alarm, then fear, mounted when the prince turned down the recently built Saad Palace, which was one of the most beautiful palaces in Mooran. His refusal was almost curt. He preferred to go back to his old house, which was so dilapidated that it looked abandoned, because no one had tended it in his absence.

"A disposition never changes," murmured the Sultan when he heard that his brother had declined to take the Saad Palace.

This was interpreted all sorts of ways. When the conversation moved to other subjects, the Sultan repeated the same remark twice for no obvious reason, smiling; then added, "A man has to do as the times demand."

Most saw a link between the two sentences and assumed he was talking about his brother Fanar, but they were not completely sure. The prince had assumed that Mooran was as he had left it, in his father's time, but he had erred: nothing was left of that Mooran. The city had not only grown three or four times bigger, it had changed. There was no link to the city it had been a few years before. The prince expected to eat dates and sour milk as he had always done, as his father had done, to please the citizens and win their loyalty when they saw him near them and doing as they did, but Mooran had not eaten dates or drunk sour milk in years, and the Sultan's importance and influence now, and the people's attachment to him, had more to do with how strong and generous he was, how distant and lofty he made himself.

Mooran no longer needed sultans like Khureybit, austere or pretending to be, and would never again be as it was. As for Fanar coming back with his illnesses and silence, thinking that living in his old house gave him some sort of distinction—he was wrong. Mooran had been seduced by the earliest cars years before, though there had been no more than twenty or thirty cars in the days of Sultan Khureybit, and most of those belonged to the palace; their mystique had faded now, like a toy with which a child gets quickly bored so that he ignores it in favor of another, then another, and now cars were piled up in Mooran like discarded toys, changed as often as socks. And then Mooran moved on from cars to the love of a new game: palaces. People suddenly discovered that the tents that had shaded them and the mud houses that had sheltered them were hateful and degrading.

The doctor had been one of the first to build palaces, and had named his German-style palace the al-Hir Palace. Most of the people who criticized or made fun of him soon joined the game: instead of one palace they had two or three, instead of one story they had several, instead of wide windows there were glass panels from wall to wall, which, they said, made them feel still a part of the nature around them. As they once named their horses, they now gave their palaces unusual or even ridiculous names and titles. They raised animals, especially sheep, inside the palaces, and the sheep roamed to the windows and sliding glass doors to rub their snouts against the glass and butt it, to the hilarity of passersby.

Within a few years Mooran was a wondrous city. Due to the journeys its people had made to a variety of countries, the magazines they brought back with them, the blueprints they planned for the houses they saw on these trips, and the existence of the al-Ghazal Villa and Palace Construction Company, palaces began to appear like creeping plants, like Japanese gardens: an assemblage of colors, shapes and forms the eye could not stand; houses so spacious that one could only wonder what they could be used for or who would live in them. Dozens of rooms beyond corridors and passageways as dark as tunnels, which broke the house into separate wings, accessible through double doors, revolving doors or hidden doors. Most walls were paneled in wood or lined with colorful velvet; the floors were covered with wall-to-wall carpeting, as were the corridors, and even some of the kitchens and bathrooms. At first English fireplaces were the rage, especially after Prince Mayzar built his palace on the Riha Road, but before long most people began to prefer French and English stoves.

The feverish competition among palace builders never let up or stopped, and everyone was taking part. The Sultan was ahead of everyone else, for he had a new hobby to add to his old one: he now lived with each wife in a different palace, and built a new palace for each new bride. Before long, however, the Sultan was advised (by al-Damiri, who arranged most of his marriages) that the citizens now knew how many wives he had, simply by counting palaces, so he bought large expanses of surrounding land and walled it in.

Shamran said that it took a man one full day to walk all the way around the Ghadir and Khalidia Palaces; a horse going at a trot could do it in three or four hours.

Cars had come to Mooran, air conditioners, jewels and ever-rising numbers of foreigners, and with all these came Amin al-Wardani, director of the al-Ghazal Contracting Company: a broad-shouldered, rather short and fat man, cheerful and practical in every sense of the word. He arrived in Mooran suddenly in his small private jet, with a party of aides. For three days in a row they toured Mooran from end to end in a long motorcade; people said they had gone as far as Rahba and al-Rehaiba, and that the Sultan had given a banquet for him in al-Mileiha. No sooner had the dust from their activities settled than the news spread that Mooran was to be demolished and rebuilt; it was even said that the capital would be moved to al-Mileiha, because the water there was more plentiful and the air sweeter.

When Shamran heard this he made his oft-quoted remark, "This town is beyond any help scarification and cautery could offer—it has to be destroyed!"

Within a week of Amin al-Wardani's arrival the Sultan agreed to have the al-Ghazal Company build him a new palace in the Khalidia district, in the style of the palaces of the Abbasid Caliphate, with a mosque beside it in the style of the Hagia Sofia Mosque—this was the doctor's suggestion. Amin al-Wardani asked insistently that the palace be the gift of the al-Ghazal Company, "so that the Sultanate can see the variety and quality of our work," but the Sultan refused, though in the event that the project did not go as al-Wardani expected, it was agreed that the company would present its accounts of expenses incurred when the work was completed, "and not ask for one extra coin."

The al-Ghazal Company's arrival marked the beginning of the madness in Mooran. At first the doctor appeared deeply worried by Amin al-Wardani, but it did not take long for him to see his mistake, for the prices of the land he had bought went up ten times, then a hundred times, which helped him to forget or at least ignore everything else. The friendship that sprang up between the

two men in the short time Amin al-Wardani was in Mooran convinced the doctor that *we complement each other—we could never be
rivals or enemies.* Amin al-Wardani needed huge amounts of materials, which *the doctor, with his experience and connections, can help secure.* Food and housing for the workers would be supplied to the
company "by subcontractors, which cannot be chosen, or any
agreement with them reached, without the say-so of the state, or at
least its consent."

That was how the wave of madness began, and it widened and
grew to carry along everything and everyone with it. Even Shaddad, who was immersed in his own madness, so distant that he
heard only faint echoes, and cared nothing for them like the rest
of his friends, was told that "the Hasiba land is like gold," and that
the doctor, who had bought it to build a hospital, had sold it to the
palace because "the Sultan wanted to build three guest palaces on
it." Shaddad heard this and could not sleep that night. He went to
his brother at dawn, and when he found Muflih, the elder of the
al-Mutawa family, he spoke to him, though he was sure that he
could not hear.

"Brother—Abu Daham! You told us, at the Battle of Rehaiba
and even before that, 'Let Khureybit alone.' We said, 'Abu Daham,
he's digging our graves.' You told us he was only digging his own
grave and that this was the time for it. Not a day passed without his
saddling up and riding out; you said that if he flew his banner we'd
ride out too. We held our peace and rode out later."

Muflih looked at him but heard nothing and did not know what
was being said. He nodded and stoked the fire to prepare coffee.

"Abu Daham, you said, 'Let him be,'" continued Shaddad.
"'There's no point, a hunchback knows how to sleep.' Now the
hunchback is on top of us!"

Saleh—Abu Fawzan—stood a few yards away. He was listening
but did not know what his brother was talking about. Shaddad
turned to him.

"I told you, Abu Fawzan, from the day Hammad started working
with that Maltese and became the Sultan's adviser, he hasn't been
our Hammad—we've had nothing to do with him—he's no good
to us. You said, 'Put your faith in God,' and we kept quiet and conceded that patience was in order; we gave him the benefit of the

doubt; we told him everything; we told him, this is Mooran and these are its people; this is what goes here and this is what doesn't. But he disappears and goes off God knows where, and no one knows when he'll come back."

Shaddad was worked up, almost angry. Saleh still did not quite understand what his brother was talking about or what needed to be done, but he smiled and replied, "Trust in God, Abu Ghanem, be patient and in time everything will be fine."

"Our time is past, Abu Fawzan." He added sarcastically, "And what the thieves haven't taken from us, the Maltese has!"

"Maltese? Who on earth are you talking about and what has he taken?"

"But my real enemy is Hammad."

"Our Hammad?"

"He's not our Hammad anymore, Abu Fawzan—he's sold us and forgotten us."

"Trust in God, man."

"Coffee is like water," said Muflih. "It washes away poison!" He had drunk the first cup, and offered the second to Abu Ghanem. He did not know what his brothers were discussing, but he knew they were arguing. Shaddad took the cup and drained it calmly, and spoke, as if planning something.

"By God, you bastard, you Maltese, I'll get you!" He paused, and then, as if having reached a decision, "Just as we used to say: to beat someone at his own game, you have to play."

Shaddad explained heatedly to his brothers that he would never have sold the Hasiba land without Hammad's intervention, and that he had sold it because "the Maltese wanted to build a pharmacy there," but instead the doctor sold it all to the palace and made a fortune; Shaddad said he would not get away with this, and he would not be quiet about it.

"Abu Ghanem, our advice is good only for women and children," said his brother bitterly. "Those who have grown up, who have gone and come back, don't know what they're talking about—only time will teach them!"

69

L IFE MIGHT HAVE GONE ON UNCHANGED AND uninterrupted into the spring and the migration of the birds, but it was not known whether Prince Fanar would stay or go, whether he would remain in his old house or move into another; someone told the Sultan that his brother had come to stay, and that he would not move from the house he was in. This report was confirmed by a number of palace women, who had been told by friends of theirs who knew the prince's womenfolk.

The Sultan had always appeared strong and confident, and knew how to deal with all his brothers and make them think his way—except for Mujham, who was always busy with his falcons, and had come to Mooran only once in three years, when he was said to have fallen ill and nearly died from sleeping indoors; he was carried back to the desert on a stretcher and was never heard from again. Except for Mujham and Rakan, all of them immersed themselves in Mooran and its new games, and began to compete among themselves for palaces, women, jewels and trips around the world—"the four corners of the earth," as the doctor said.

Prince Fanar's coming and all the attendant news and gossip made the Sultan profoundly uneasy and fearful, and with the Sultan uneasy and afraid the palace changed. The earliest and most noticeable changes were in the doctor. He had waited for months and completed his preparations for his "big launch," had even worn a black cloak most nights, replying to Samir's stares with a remark Samir long remembered: "As they say in Mooran, it fights the winter cold and tames the spring cold."

He laughed and explained to Samir that the desert cold was dreadful; it invaded the body as water invaded sand, it crept in unnoticed until it was too late, and so had to be avoided and protected against. But the spring air, despite its coolness, did a man no harm—in fact it did him good.

This commentary was necessary to explain his elegant, cozy black cloak, which gave him the appearance of a venerable, wise and educated sheikh.

The new year, which the doctor awaited with impatience and a little anxiety, was only a few weeks off when Prince Fanar came. When the doctor heard the news of the prince's arrival he struck his thigh and said, without thinking, "God help us now!" He nodded sadly, almost despairingly, and said resignedly, "God willing, it may be for the best."

He told Muti and a new man he had recently hired to keep his appointments straight that he'd had a terrifying dream the night before: he had seen himself surrounded by flames. Whenever he tried to escape, masked men—only their angry red eyes were visible—pushed him back among the flames. Their voices were like rolling thunder.

As the doctor described the vision, he made a connection between it and the arrival of Prince Fanar. A few days later he learned that things were even worse than he had thought or had ever imagined. The Sultan was worried and gave orders for the Security Committee to be summoned for an emergency policy-setting meeting, and even attended it himself for the first time in more than two years.

In the meeting the Sultan hid his real concern by talking about events in the region. "Evil forces are afoot in the world around us; people are like mad camels, running wild as if they were being chased or led on by demons—running around like madmen."

Then the Sultan asked innocently about the security of the Sultanate and its borders, but when Hammad reassured him that "things are held in place by an iron hand; people are busy with their work and care about nothing else," the doctor voiced his fears. "Not from within—this land is blessed, God be praised, thanks to His Majesty the Sultan, with peace and prosperity, and its people with contentment. What we really have to fear is what can come from beyond our borders, from our neighbors—we can only fight that threat with thought, with a cause, and so the most important thing for the Sultanate is to have a strong, coherent, philosophical viewpoint."

The doctor paused and looked at the Sultan, adding, "Just as all great historical causes have had a basis in thought and means of persuasion, the Sultanate of Mooran must have its thinkers and propagandists, its own cause, to combat unbelief, secularism and corruption—not within its borders, but outside them."

The Sultan, whose gaze met Hammad's several times, spoke to end this discussion.

"We have to watch over our borders and our country—nothing else concerns us. What I want from you, Hammad, is for you to keep your eyes and ears open and let nothing pass, however small or large, without telling me about it—even if it relates to one of my own sons or brothers."

It was understood that the Sultan was talking about his brother Fanar and no one else; he did not respond to the doctor's remarks in this meeting. At a second meeting the same week, the Sultan asked the doctor to come near, and told him, "Abu Ghazwan, we've taken care of our friends abroad, here and there, we've bought them or given them some of God's bounty—we've told them to accept it and be quiet. Don't let it bother you, what you hear on the radio or in the newspapers—it's just farting. It doesn't mean anything."

The Sultan looked around several times before adding, in a whisper, "If we have trouble, Abu Ghazwan, it will come from behind us, from our own, from the people closest to us!"

The doctor tried to set his mind at rest, and as the year moved toward its end, he forgot this urgent item of concern; he would have resumed the task he had vowed to complete had it not been for the quarrel that arose between Rateb and Said. For the company founded a few years before, which had been a success and made huge profits at first, was now beset by splits, misunderstandings and quarrels.

The quarrel began over the sale of raw materials; that problem was remedied and put behind them, but as Said's plans and connections flourished, he became less enthusiastic about his partnership with Rateb, though he did not want to be the one to end it.

The split first showed when the doctor and Rateb refused to go in on two companies for carpets and household goods; they figured that Mooran was not yet advanced enough to need such companies. Then, thanks to the new horizons Hammad had opened by giving the palace supply contract to al-Ghamdi, plus contracts for furnishing all the palaces—all of which he did without consulting the doctor—things changed. When the Oriental Carpet Company furnished the Sultan Khazael Mosque with the costliest types of carpets, the doctor thought it excessive to the point of folly, and could not forgive it, though it did not cost him anything. His point of view was clear.

"You can give a gift of a cloak or prayer beads, Abu Shakib," he scolded Said. "If you really want to, you can give a cloak *and* prayer beads, but to do this—to give away carpets worth hundreds of thousands, and every carpet finer than the one before, and so many that they all overlap—why, the people in Mooran won't stand for it—they'll all say, 'These people have come and robbed us—they've eaten the egg and the shell, leaving us nothing! They own everything, and not only that, they're not only filling a room or a house with expensive carpets, but a whole huge mosque!'"

Said listened and smiled and tried in every way possible to explain to the doctor that the gift was to God's house and that he had vowed years ago that he would give the first profits he ever realized as alms, for the souls of the living and dead; he was not sorry for what he had done, because he did not think his action wrong. After this explanation he pointed out that he had not given it all himself—al-Ghamdi had gone in with him out of the kindness of his heart. The doctor, however, was in no mood for a discussion.

"Look, Said," he said at the end of their talk, "you've put us in the public eye now. Let's hope the public forgets us."

Said tried to please the doctor by promising that the mistake would never be repeated, and the matter was closed. Later on, a rumor circulated that the furnishings of the Sultan Khazael Mosque had been donated by several persons, among them—the first among them—the doctor. It was also rumored that a number of donors refused to make their names public because the donations were for the house of God, "but that the names of some were given out on their behalf."

After this bitter lesson Said decided to have nothing more to do with the matter. *We want grapes; we don't want to fight the warden,* he said to himself, deciding to ignore the doctor until the right moment came *to shaft him from behind and pull the shaft out of his eyeballs.* So he paid little attention to the foodstuffs company and applied himself to other business.

After Rateb settled in Mooran and discovered its business possibilities, the feuds and threats began. He wanted to impose a new order: whom to work with, whom to refuse to work with, how to price goods and other procedures. Said, who thought himself a genius, capable of dealing with the devil himself, found that he could get nowhere with this person who had fallen from Mars. He left it to Abu Homeidi, but before long even he gave up.

Toward the end of that year, in a meeting of all the partners, Rateb made an attempt to settle with the doctor.

"Abu Ghazwan," he said, "you are the father of us all—without you none of this would have happened."

"Please—please!" said the doctor very humbly.

Said looked at Rateb from the corner of his eye.

"God forgive what's past—our concern is today!" He turned several times, and his eyes met the doctor's; they seemed to be in agreement. "Whatever the doctor says is fine with us. You make the decisions, Abu Ghazwan—we'll stick by them."

"Yes, whatever Abu Ghazwan says," interjected Said, "but this is really not his concern." He laughed ironically. "A few years back we had a problem and wanted him to help us out—we were kissing his hand, but never mind—and he said that this company was not his concern."

"Back then I was up to my neck in other things—over my head, Abu Shakib!" said the doctor irritably. "Anyway, we're all brothers here, and any disagreement between brothers is just a summer cloud."

They could get nowhere. At the end of the meeting Said observed that "We started out as friends and we're breaking up as friends—there's plenty of work for everyone in Mooran!"

And that was how it all ended, despite the doctor's efforts; this ending left him deeply depressed. "Just as everything was ready to succeed, and Rateb had lightened my burden, all the problems hit us at once." Sadly he recalled Prince Fanar's arrival, and how he would have to postpone his work yet again.

"'Thou shalt be afflicted by naught but God hath decreed for thee,'" he quoted to Rateb, sadly and resentfully.

70

THE DOCTOR'S SLEEP WAS ANXIOUS AND troubled that night. *Another year of this life is gone,* he said to himself while trying to doze off, *and I don't know whether I'm going forward or backward, or what I'm moving forward or backward toward!* He drifted off to sleep still pondering this difficult question that weighed on his chest like a great stone.

Sultan Khazael was calmed by Hammad's assurances, which were endorsed by still other friends and officials; he believed that *money chips away at boulders, and Fanar is like anyone else—he'll take a hard look around and go back where he came from.* His fear had faded to mere unease, unease that came and went.

It was the doctor who was truly prey to doubts and misgivings. *Rateb is an office type, a foreign executive type, not a man at home in the marketplace.* Seeking partners here, or attracting them from abroad, was a difficult operation, or at least more difficult than before. Not only that: Rateb himself was a different person now, *like a man possessed.* He was very quiet, ill at ease, at times cross. This caught the attention of the doctor, whom it confused—*maybe the man is embarrassed to say what it's about?* The doctor looked through his medical references, especially in the field of sex; he recalled a few cases like this, and the misery they caused; he also remembered the old stories about Rateb, how he had squandered much of his inheritance on women and travel. The doctor considered talking to him about it, at least to get him in a mood to reveal something, *so that I can help him and solve his problem for him,* but then he repeated to himself, "The important thing now is to solve the material difficulties, not cure his mental complexes." He added, remembering Said, "The bastard left us with the work at its peak," and the words Muhammad Eid had pronounced years before, when Said and Hosny first arrived in Harran, now rang in his ears: "God bless you wherever you go, Eidou"—a nickname he used in sentimental or affectionate moments—"a man doesn't know his good fortune until he tries something else." The doctor sighed deeply as he said this.

After enormous trouble the doctor found a new partner: he reached an agreement with Fleihan al-Zaubaii for the management of the Foodstuffs Supply Company, to replace Said al-Usta and Abdelaziz al-Ghamdi. The doctor and Rateb agreed to give al-Zaubaii fifty percent in return for his name and work, for among the new regulations laid out in Mooran was one stipulating that every business had to have a Moorani partner holding at least half of the equity.

"Tell me, Widad," the doctor asked his wife one night, "how are things with Rateb and his wife?"

"Rateb and his wife?" She asked this in a rather shaken voice, as if she had been challenged, or as if he meant something else.

"I mean, how are they getting along? Are they in love?"

"They're married, aren't they?"

"You mean they're getting along?"

"Yes, *sir!*" She said it mockingly, and the doctor understood it to mean the opposite of what she had intended. He looked at her carefully and nodded, because his guess now took root in these few words.

"It's still early for them—they didn't know each other."

"No, Abu Ghazwan, you misunderstood me. I meant that they were enthralled with each other, as if God had created none but the two of them!"

"So?"

"Not only that, I've seen them when he couldn't believe how she flirts and carries on—she dazzles him!" She laughed ironically. "We thought if he got married he'd settle down, he'd start to act human—but he's turned into a boy! She says the word and he runs and fetches. She understands him, and she plays with him—seriously! One day she has cravings. Then it's an aching back. Then it's, 'Sweetheart, I'm so bored, take me to visit my family.' And he'll do anything to please her and spoil her! Necklaces, earrings, chains, jewels, and 'My darling' and 'My eyes,' and she loves it!"

The doctor shook his head in surprise and disbelief that he had noticed none of this or foreseen it, though he was usually a keen observer who "caught things on the fly," as he constantly described himself. He added a little sadly that "being wrapped up in a theory made me forget people."

Widad saw his mind wandering and brought him back by demanding, "You didn't tell me why you ask."

"The truth is, Widad, that the man has changed toward me—he's hard to get along with."

"It's your own fault, Abu Ghazwan. You gave him ambition, you encouraged him—now he thinks he's important. He's forgotten." She added angrily, "He needs a chance to find out what he's worth—to remember who he is!"

"Take it easy, Widad, things aren't that bad."

"They are, and worse. You don't notice, but I see everything!"

"My dear girl!"

"From his first day here, or his first week or two weeks, he talked big, he wanted to be known. Abu Ghazwan, you have such a good heart, you don't hear anything. I heard everything and understood perfectly." He looked at her, even more surprised than before. "He was terrified of you, he didn't dare say a word, but now he makes jokes—he's insolent. If you don't check him, he'll go even further—he'll start talking about you—or about me!"

"Oh, let him try! I'd cut his tongue out!" The doctor replied angrily, as though already insulted or intimidated by future possibilities, but after a moment he added sadly, "Strange, Widad, everyone we've treated nicely, everyone we've helped, has turned against us. People have no morals these days, no religion, no values . . . but never mind. We'll see what happens."

"You have to look out for yourself, Abu Ghazwan!"

"Even so, Widad, life gives and takes away. A man can't isolate himself, he can't live alone. He has to put up with people."

The doctor needed Rateb desperately, especially now, and could not afford to think too badly of him or to let his feelings show. At some point he would deal with him, decisively and prudently, but wouldn't overdo it, as other people did.

The second jolt was not long in coming: it was the contract between the Ghazal Company and Rezaie, some princes, Said, and al-Ghamdi, to build three airports in the Sultanate of Mooran: one in the capital, Mooran; the second in Harran; and the third on the northern border near the city of al-Beqaa. The contract included a network of international highways linking the cities of the Sultanate with the surrounding countries.

The doctor could not imagine how such a deal could have been made without him, first of all; and, second, how it could have been made without his knowledge. The sums were huge, too huge for him to comprehend clearly, either in terms of expenditures or of the profits each of the partners would realize. The real injury he felt was that all this could happen without his knowing, without anyone consulting him at all. Where was he? What had he become? And his friends who knew about the deal—how was it possible that they had said nothing—and why?

He asked Rateb if he knew or had heard anything about it, and why he hadn't told him.

"God love you, Doctor," replied Rateb with a hint of exasperation, "I'm lucky if I know what's happening in the foodstuffs company!" The doctor did not like this answer and looked it. Rateb went on, with veiled sarcasm. "Al-Zaubaii is like mercury, Doctor, he's a sneak, a swindler. You can't tell when he's lying or telling the truth. How long have I been in Mooran? How am I supposed to know these things?"

The doctor asked Hammad how it was that he'd heard nothing about the subject.

"You know, Doctor, that the Agency has a thousand things to

keep track of," Hammad replied coolly. "Each of those is more cru- cial than the last. We haven't the time to find out who's buying and who's selling!" He smiled politely. "Your Excellency, you told us, 'Follow political issues, security issues, and don't get mixed up in anything else!'"

The doctor nodded in agreement, but it was obvious that he did not mean it.

"If you had only asked us, Doctor, we would have told you every- thing," said Hammad.

The doctor had no choice but to be satisfied with these explana- tions or excuses, and to consider the subject closed—with them.

He wanted to bring up the subject when he met with the Sultan, and told him somewhat bitterly, "I am afraid, Your Majesty, that the palace's Economic Consulting Committee does not realize the importance of wealth, though Almighty God has blessed us with wealth; they don't understand how it must be spent. People are talking about some of the projects that have been approved re- cently: Who will undertake them? For how much? Are they neces- sary or not?"

The Sultan smiled his broad horsey smile.

"Abu Ghazwan, if the people keep busy playing with money they'll forget everything else—that's what we want. Let them run around and get tired out—when night comes they'll drop like rocks and sprawl out and sleep."

"Your Majesty," said the enraged doctor, meaning what he said, "man does not sprawl out for money alone. For money and for breasts."

The Sultan guffawed delightedly and licked his lips. He looked at the doctor and nodded. "That's the truth, Abu Ghazwan!"

"Money should go to people who deserve it, who've earned it, but sometimes it goes astray and causes harm. As the poet said:

> "I keep my coin from every man
> Mean-tempered, lest I forget.

"You see, Your Majesty, money becomes spears and swords in the wrong hands. As the poet said,

"Don't let him ride too much on the breast,
Lest he not think horseback a better steed
Or wean him off too soon,
Lest he prefer to drink the blood of foes."

"By God, that's the truth, Abu Ghazwan."

The doctor had reached one conclusion, and the Sultan another, but the subject was closed, with the doctor determined that no project would slip past him again; he would overlook nothing. When he made this decision, he saw that it was not a mistake to postpone writing his theory; it could wait, especially since it applied not only to this particular time but to all time, not only to this generation, but to all generations to come. What strengthened his conviction was that he had neglected weighty affairs during his thinking and planning phases; if he kept that up, even more crucial and momentous matters might get past him; this is what he told himself in order to concede, with difficulty, that he had to put off his great "launch."

If these had been the doctor's only problems, he would have known how to face and solve them, but what worried him was Ghazwan's failure to come home that fall, and the boy's many letters, all of which alluded in some way to the possibility that he might delay his homecoming and even cancel his spring visit. The doctor needed *a man of steel, of flesh and blood, to be near at hand for support, after all others had quit the field.* He wrote several letters to Ghazwan asking him to come home.

The first weeks of spring passed with no visit or word from Ghazwan, and the doctor was upset. *He finished his studies last summer. He has no excuse. He must come home—the idea of graduate school is an indulgence—I can't agree to his staying there. If he wants to stay there because of a woman who has him in her clutches, that's the worst tragedy. That's the end of a man—he dissolves, he disappears like a candle, leaving nothing and no one behind.*

This is how the doctor's multiplying fears were embodied; they haunted him all the time, when he was with other people, when he was alone, even in his dreams, from which he often awoke with a fright. If he hadn't had plentiful information explaining dreams, he might have fallen prey to delusions or even illness.

Now, the spring was coming to an end; Ghazwan was home at last after the long wait, and seemed to his father—and to many others who had known him before—a man in every sense of the word. He had put on weight, and his hairline had receded a bit, and he looked and acted the part of a man. The doctor was reminded of his own youth, though his hair had not thinned like that. *In some things he favors his mother's menfolk,* he thought rather proudly, *especially this receding hairline business.* He was astonished at how many people Ghazwan knew: he knew a number of princes and appeared to know them well, in addition to senior officers. The doctor was amazed at first but then very proud, as he saw that *the boy has pleased his father; the lessons he learned in childhood are showing now.*

Ghazwan's arrival was an opportunity for the doctor to renew his vitality and regain his respect; his isolation in recent months had been followed by the insulting and demoralizing reverses suffered one after another, which everyone in town had discussed, first in whispers, then openly, at last with scorn, costing him his self-confidence and his confidence in others. But Ghazwan's arrival and the warm welcome his friends and acquaintances gave him cheered the doctor and made him optimistic. Even his winter back pains, which had compelled him to wear the warm black cloak, despite his delayed plans to write his theory, vanished.

The doctor reshuffled his deck, as they say. He consoled himself: *A man learns from his mistakes; he must try and try again until he gets results, until he achieves perfect balance. Some people call themselves relatives or friends, or pretend to be, but they're usually motivated only by greed. These days one can rely solely on blood ties, on true relatives, on flesh and blood, on one's children especially.* He thought of his two sons studying at a private school in Broummaneh, and how close to them he felt, how his love surged in his heart; sometimes it even made him sad. When would he have all his children around him again, as cubs stayed close around their father, the lion? He would talk to them as he now talked to himself; he would reveal to them even his most secret and complex ideas—the opposite of what he was doing now, for he could not share his feelings or beliefs with those closest to him. *It's not easy to trust people, or even to know them. A person can be explored and understood only in very few instances: when he's afraid, or*

when he's dealing with money or women! Images of people he had
known or helped now passed in front of his mind's eye, and the
clearest image, blotting out all others, was of Said. *When the son of a
bitch came to Harran he was like a beggar. I fed him and gave him to drink.
"Here, my boy, all you have to do is work." It went to his head and he turned
away from me. Not a word, no "Thank you, Abu Ghazwan." And whom did
he go to work for? The people who want my head, who are longing for my
funeral. He turned out to be vile, despicable, as if I never did anything for
him, but that's the way of the world: people out for what they can get, no
morals, no honor.* Then the image of Ghazwan, a confident and fully
grown man, appeared to him, and he comforted himself with,
Enough tribulations; let's look to the future.

The doctor talked to his wife a great deal. He told her that a
believer never gets stung twice; he would have to begin anew, with
Ghazwan. He discussed many of his ideas with her, but always got
confused and abruptly broke off the discussion. Sometimes he did
not know what he was saying, or how to express the ideas that filled
his head. At other times Widad seemed distracted, her mind wandering. Once, when he was talking to her and saw how distant she
was, he thought, *She must be thinking of a wife for Ghazwan. She's re-
viewing possible faces, eligible relatives, comparing them. If Ghazwan gets
married and settles down, that will really change things!* He imagined
Ghazwan married, with children, and thought that despite all his
duties he would have time to play with the little ones and entertain
them. He said to himself that *the first thing they should learn, the first
word they would remember, would be:* family . . . *and the name of the family.* Al-Mahmilji seemed to him a strong and beautiful name, even
if it was a bit difficult. He nearly told all this to Widad, but decided
it was premature.

He spent three weeks thinking and dreaming, but resolved not
to discuss anything specific with Ghazwan or to talk about the future in any serious or detailed way; the bedouin never ask a guest
about the purpose of his visit to them for the first three days of his
stay, and since Mooran was still sunk in its backward bedouin men-
tality, despite its money and pretensions, *I'll outdo them, yes, I'll outdo
them in everything. I'll let him bring up the subject, even though he's no
guest, but my own flesh and blood, the pillar of the Mahmilji clan, the pillar
of the future* . . . and he chuckled proudly.

By the end of the third week Ghazwan had not told him. Widad told him; she did not seem upset.

"Abu Ghazwan, Ghazwan has something he's ashamed to discuss with you himself."

"What is it?" asked the doctor, as excited as a child. "Tell me—speak!"

He thought the only word she could pronounce was *marriage*. He felt happy—delighted and relieved—and watched her impatiently. His eyes besought her to speak.

"You won't get angry?" she asked uneasily, almost fearfully.

"Angry? God forbid a man should get angry at his own son!"

"Ghazwan wants to leave." Her eyes were on the floor. "To go back to America."

"Leave? Go back to America?" he asked weakly, as if he could not believe his ears. When he grasped the meaning of his wife's words, he dropped into a nearby chair. The world turned black in his eyes; he felt banished, rejected and alone, abandoned by everyone. No one was left standing by him; now even Widad seemed distant from him—otherwise how could she deliver this news to him with such cold impartiality, as if it meant nothing to her—though it meant death to him? She could have told him some other way, or prepared him, or, before this, tried to prevent Ghazwan from leaving. That's what she would have done if she were a true mother, if she really knew how to get what she wanted. Now, he, a man of experience, of his age, was never deterred or prevented from trying to get something he really wanted. He always succeeded—so what about this young man?

So he remained for a time, absent from his surroundings, no longer sensing them; Widad stayed by him for some time, taken aback by his reaction, then got bored and went away. He did not notice when she left, or when she looked in on him once or twice.

He did not know how he went out or got into the car; when Radwan asked him where he wanted to go, he gestured with his left hand for him to get moving, but said nothing.

When Radwan had driven a good distance, he twisted around slightly, questioningly, but the doctor only repeated the same gesture to keep going. They drove the whole length of Mooran, which appeared to him a harsh, repulsive city. This had been his first impression upon his arrival, though the city had changed drastically over the years and become filled with villas, with Japanese-style and English-style buildings, and still others that were a mélange of styles; in hidden places, behind the wide streets and the tall new buildings, lay the low mud houses. Broad boulevards and sweeping traffic circles had blanketed the city in the last few years; people's circumstances had changed, and so had their looks: they were fatter. To the doctor they looked like barrels—as he used to call the deputy emir of Mooran—but even so he did not like this city and still was not used to it.

Now as he traversed the city the brilliance of the sun showed him only dark clods of hard, unruly earth that throbbed with hostility. He wished that he had never come to this city. He wished he had never heard of it.

He said to Radwan, he did not know why, "Take me to one of the friends of God, my boy!"

Radwan turned his head and part of his torso to him to make sure that he had heard correctly.

"A friend . . . a friend, my boy," repeated the doctor. When Radwan's face remained stolid and uncomprehending, he sighed and asked, "What kind of friends do you have in Mooran? Good men?"

"All people have good in them, Doctor."

"My boy, people die and leave nothing behind but their graves and their good deeds."

"Like so many in Mooran, Doctor." Radwan saw that the doctor was acting strange, that he was ranting, or that he did not understand what he was saying. He observed him in the rearview mirror; he watched him change and blink, then open his eyes wide and shake his head in anguish. These movements frightened him, but he said nothing.

"Take me to the cemetery," said the doctor suddenly.

The car glided as smoothly as a snake, as if driving itself; Radwan too was now in something of a stupor. He had been surprised from the first by the doctor's wish to ride in no specified direction, but attributed it to a desire for fresh air or to enjoy the sun on this spring day. Then the doctor asked to be taken to see friends of God and good men, and mentioned the dead, though he knew that Mooran quickly forgot its dead—not only forgot them but obliterated their remains with a few heaps of earth, so that they became part of the earth around them. Then the doctor asked to be taken to the cemetery, and Radwan knew there was something here that surpassed his ability to grasp or understand it, but realized that there was no choice but to comply; he resolved to be cautious and, should the situation call for it, firm.

At the cemetery the doctor looked all around the ample expanse, seeing nothing but a few stones scattered here and there, stones as big as skulls, some bigger and some smaller, but he did not see the graves. He looked behind him and saw Radwan standing two paces away, his face stern.

"These are the graves of Mooran?" the doctor asked softly.

Radwan nodded but said nothing. The doctor recited a prayer, the *fatiha,* wiped his face, walked back and got into the car.

"Home," he said.

As the car sped through Mooran from the east to the west, the doctor said to himself, *Nothing has any value, not to the living or the dead, in this city. If those are their graves, their death is even more miserable than their lives.*

Late that night Widad saw her husband cry for the first time. He cried in silence and then sobbed, trying unsuccessfully to hold in the sound. She asked him gently what was wrong, and he answered without looking at her.

"Our hope was in Ghazwan, and he knew it, but he can't stand Mooran . . ."

She tried to talk to him, to explain, but he did not listen or respond. It seemed to him clearer than before that she had not even tried to dissuade Ghazwan from leaving; perhaps she wanted him to leave. There was nothing he could do.

Subsequently Ghazwan explained to his father that he had accepted a job in San Francisco and would report to work on July fifteenth; he could not start even one day late because he had signed a contract. He said that the company had important business in the Middle East, including the Sultanate of Mooran, and that several of his princely and military friends had urged him to join the company, especially since he would be working in the sales department and would be the first Arab the company ever hired in sales. He was not interested in getting married just yet; when he was, he would take no step without his father's counsel.

Rateb and Samir were with Ghazwan, and helped, not to convince the doctor, but to ease his pain: they told him that their work and the future of their work would require someone who was, like Ghazwan, on good terms with foreign firms. Any rational person planning for the future had to think this way. Mooran, as Samir said, "had, in terms of commissions, reached sky-high. Any potential expansion will require direct contacts with suppliers abroad—with foreign companies." The doctor listened and did not listen, but could not protest, because it seemed to him that events were taking a course he was powerless to influence.

The one promise the doctor could wrest from his son was that he would write constantly and visit them in Mooran twice a year, staying with the family for no less than a month each time. So Ghazwan left and the doctor began to wait, again immersing himself in his work and the atmosphere of Mooran.

71

THE ONLY ONE TO CRY INCONSOLABLY WHEN
Ghazwan left was his sister Salma. She
cried as she never had before. She clung to
his neck, in front of everyone, and begged him not to go, and when
he smiled and did not answer, her tears flowed and she began to
sob and stamp her feet. Her mother cried too, or at least her tears
flowed, but Widad was not sad. His father was composed, almost
aloof, and even tried to laugh, but his throat did not oblige him.

This young girl whose age was impossible to judge, though
surely she was no more than fourteen, put everyone in a sad, almost depressed mood. The doctor thought to himself that *if Widad
had done some of what this child is doing, Ghazwan wouldn't be leaving*.
Widad said, "She's young and lonesome—she doesn't know what
makes her happy or what makes her cry. Tomorrow this will all
pass." Nadia hugged Salma and stroked her hair and guessed that
the departure of her brothers, one after another, was the reason,

and that after Ghazwan had gone she needed someone to hold on to. That is also what Rateb and Hammad thought, and Samir too, though Samir saw something besides the tears that he could not identify. True, he had seen the girl many times before, but he did not know why her breasts caught his eye now. She had always been too young for him to notice, and he had thought her nothing but a little girl, worth no more than a smile from him or a word at most. Now, as he saw her again, he was surprised first of all by her crying, and then more so by the pathetic, nervous, harsh breaths, like the beating of a drum.

No matter how difficult or cruel things seem in this life, they all pass away, and so these moments passed. When Ghazwan looked upset and ready to lose his composure and cry, his mother pulled Salma away by the hand. Widad told her that his trip was a short one and that he would return, and that in two months' time she would take her with her when she went to visit Ghazwan. The doctor remained calm and told a few jokes to make these moments more endurable for him, if not for anyone else, but failed, and so fell silent, watching the scene with a sense of almost suffocating sorrow. But in an instant it was all over. Ghazwan embraced the men and shook hands with the women. When it was Salma's turn, he spoke firmly.

"If you don't laugh, I'm not going to hug you!"

She did not laugh, but he kissed her several times, buried his face in her hair, then pinched her cheek. He waved as he headed for the plane, after the VIP lounge had been opened especially for him; within moments the scene was ended.

It took the doctor several weeks to regain his serenity. He considered resuming work on his theory; he reviewed his "drafts" again and again, and underlined passages in red or green ink, and delighted in reading it all aloud to himself, but the early onset of summer that year spoiled his mood and ruined his nerves, especially since Widad had suggested going on vacation in mid-June. She proposed that the family spend the whole summer, or most of it, in Alexandria, "because we're tired of Beirut and Mount Lebanon, and the children need a change." The doctor wanted to spend the summer in the villa he'd bought three years ago in Duhour al-Shweir, "because the cool air freshens the brain cells—and if two years go by with no one staying in the villa, the village people will think the owners have died or abandoned it—and there are plenty of rascals up there." Widad was not convinced, so the doctor considered spending part of the summer in Alexandria and the rest in Duhour al-Shweir, "since I'm no swimmer—the sea is my bitterest enemy."

Samir's intervention was decisive; he skillfully convinced the doctor that "Alexandria isn't just the sea—it's cafés along the coast, restaurants, the refreshing sea air—and there we can go on with our research and get things done."

Samir traveled on ahead. Widad was to leave a few days later to pick up the children in Lebanon, and the doctor and Salma would go directly to Egypt and they would all meet in Alexandria on July fifth—Widad agreed on this date "only for the doctor's sake," and planned to do a little shopping in Beirut.

Early that summer Prince Fanar suddenly and unexpectedly agreed to move into the Saad Palace. This delighted the Sultan, who saw it as a sign of his own farsightedness, for he had expected it from the first. "Blood is thicker than water, Abu Ghazwan," he told the doctor when he imparted the glad tidings. The Sultan was so relaxed, even to the point of bliss, that for the first time he dispensed with some of his usual formalities; for he usually declined invitations, and had never been to the house of any of the palace officials, but now he made it known that he wished to visit the doctor's palace.

The wish delighted and frightened the doctor; there were only a few days left before Widad's departure, and an affair like this demanded weeks of preparation. The state of excitement that filled the al-Hir Palace, that spread like electricity from the doctor to Widad herself, made the task easy and difficult at the same time. The doctor saw the Sultan's visit to his home not only as a mark of respect but as a confirmation of his influence. It might open new horizons for him; he began to ruminate on what Ghazwan had said—that he could engineer a special relationship between the Sultanate and the company he worked for, that would help the Sultanate to re-equip its army and set up a network of military installations. The doctor wished that Ghazwan had put off his trip a month or two; he would have been able to explain it to the Sultan and obtain his direct approval.

Even so, the doctor decided to prepare the ground for the project until Ghazwan could come back to follow it up, and it was for this reason that he began to rethink the timing and duration of his vacation. Widad, whose excitement had reached the point of utter confusion, did not know whether to be happy or angry, or whether to start preparing without delay. Her life had been full of the Sultan all these years because of the constant talking about him from the doctor and others; the ruler seemed grand, impressive, and even young, to judge from his generosity and the frequency of his marriages since moving to Mooran. And the doctor had told her how closely the Sultan had studied the photographs they had taken in America, and how he had noticed the resemblance between her and Ghazwan. She was dizzy with pleasure that the Sultan had looked at her picture and studied it carefully, and she yearned to see this man up close, to see what he was like.

There were three days and nights of continuous preparation, during which no one in the al-Hir Palace was able to sleep or even rest, except as cranes do, on one leg. The workmen took two days to repaint the stairs, the front and back balconies and the entrance. Two full days were needed to weed and trim the garden, grapevines and other foliage; three workers were still at it on the day of the Sultan's visit. The cooks, servants and decorators so oppressed and maddened Widad that she actually screamed several times and cried in front of them at least twice. The doctor hovered like a bee, not knowing what to do or how to make himself useful in the frantic bustle of activity around him, and was told that the less he did, the more smoothly things would go; the workmen did not want to be interrupted or to feel watched.

The noise and chaos was so bad in the very early morning of the Sultan's visit that Widad was certain that she could not receive the Sultan with things in this state. "You have to tell him not to come," she told the doctor after her sleepless night, "or else I'll lose my mind or kill myself." She had brought in three women to help her arrange the rooms in the palace. The doctor, who had not slept either, and gave up trying to help, went away to compose a speech of welcome for the Sultan, and spent hours writing and tearing up paper. He used up several pens, "because some of my pens broke or ran dry, and some of my notebooks were sterile—they produced nothing." So he decided to give an extemporaneous speech, and he made a short list of the points he wanted to cover to make sure that he omitted nothing important. He also prepared a few verses of poetry. He was in a state of confusion and panic when he heard Widad's screams and weeping, and her demand that he cancel the visit or do something to save the day, before she went mad or killed herself.

Very affably and patiently, he explained to her that the Sultan was a simple man who never noticed anything or asked questions, and that he would come alone or with only a few men. He told her to get an hour or two of sleep; he would start supervising things, and he gave her a glass of water and a tranquilizer. Abruptly she stared at him searchingly, which made him a little afraid, and his heart thumped. Then she smiled, took the pill and told him coquettishly, "On one condition."

"What is it?"

"If the Sultan comes alone, I want to greet him!"

"But, Widad—"

"I insist."

Widad slept until noon, a deep and unbroken sleep that she had not known for three days. She dreamed that the Sultan came and held her in his arms. She was frightened at first, but when he laughed like a horse she smiled. When he laughed even more she laughed with him, and when he touched her upper arm, near the shoulder, clasping her flesh, she shivered with pleasure and fear. He pinched her cheek and she screamed in pain and lust, then he asked all those present to leave, and they left. She was alone with him. He was strong as a bull, but simple as a child. He looked into her eyes and looked at every part of her body. She was as ashamed as she was happy, but still felt desire. When he climbed on top of her, she felt a blazing fire, a dry fire that crackled through every cell in her body, and so remained for a long time; she was laughing and trying to escape, but the fire surrounded her everywhere. When she awoke she saw that the doctor had closed the double curtains; she did not know whether it was day or night. She remembered and got up, frightened, looking fearfully at the bed as if trying to make sure that no one had been in it with her!

The doctor was disturbed by the state Widad was in, and was afraid that it would deteriorate or lead to undesirable consequences, but more than anything else, he was bothered by the condition she had imposed on him: she wanted to see the Sultan! What if she insisted? What if the Sultan brought other people? What would the Sultan himself say—how would he take it? The doctor's thoughts were more scattered than before, and he almost gave up the idea of the speech, especially since there were two verses of poetry he could not remember no matter how hard he tried. He spent the whole morning, until noon, moving from place to place without doing a thing. When Widad woke up, radiant after several hours of sleep, his optimism came back, and he even was ready to go along with her request . . . if the Sultan came alone, or with a few men.

The Sultan stole in like a spy, alone except for seven bodyguards. He even left at home, this time, the black Cadillac he called "The Hoof," which he preferred to all his other dozens of cars, as it was scarcely less luxurious than his bedroom. He did not take the gray Rolls-Royce—"The Ostrich," as he called it, because it was higher than the other cars. Nor did he take "The Steed," either. He came in his Chevrolet, like the one the palace women used. One of the bodyguards' cars was parked by the inside gate of the palace, in front of the Sultan's car, and the other in the left side of the garage.

At first the doctor was overcome with awe and nerves. The Sultan glanced all around the room several times, looking repeatedly toward the inner doors. When he said that the palace was pleasant and beautiful, the doctor told the famous story of Haroun al-Rashid, which he had told his sons many times; he half expected the Sultan to ask a question, as the Caliph of Baghdad had asked of the clever boy—how would he answer? He would say, like the boy in the story, that wherever the Sultan was, was the most pleasant place, thanks to His Majesty's mere presence.

The men were meeting for the first time outside the Sultan's palaces or camps. Now, in the doctor's palace, what an honor the Sultan was showing him, what feelings of gratitude flooded through him! He longed to say so, to express his feelings, and thought of standing up and making his speech, but decided it was too early for that; perhaps a speech like that, delivered in front of the Sultan alone, might seem inappropriate, or even groveling, so he gave up the idea. He considered telling some jokes, but he had learned long ago that unless jokes were told in context, with a relevant point, and, as he told himself, *truly memorable,* they seemed unsuitably frivolous. Should he ask the Sultan about Fanar, how he had been acting lately, and how the two were getting along? He held back, since *he might think me intrusive, and it's unseemly to ask the Sultan about things that annoy him.*

These thoughts passed through the doctor's mind as, nervous about the silence, he began to smile too much and rub his hands more than he usually did. *There is no cat weaker or edgier than I am now,* he admitted to himself. Time was passing very slowly. He recalled that he had written some penetrating remarks on the concept of time, under the heading "Mahmilji's Concept of Time." He also recalled how torn he had been between the terms *time* and *duration.* He had been determined to research the fine difference between the two terms, and could not understand how he had neglected to do so.

"Air conditioning is a mercy from God, Abu Ghazwan," said the Sultan in a friendly attempt to enliven the atmosphere, "especially in daytime! But at night God's air is nicer."

The doctor took this in hastily, and in evident confusion asked, "If you prefer God's air, Your Majesty, we shall sit on the balcony."

"That would be better for us, Doctor."

And like a camel he stood up. The doctor had assigned three servants to come in at fixed times, each through a different door, according to his precise instructions, and at a precise moment: to bring the water pipe to His Majesty, then some incense and flower water. He told them where to place the coals, when to bring the coffee and how to serve it. Now that the Sultan was going to sit on the balcony, the plans were upset and there might be awkward problems. His Majesty continued his badinage.

"The builders did some fine work here, Abu Ghazwan." The Sultan looked all around to examine and explore the palace.

"Good construction and good weapons pay for themselves, Your Majesty!" the doctor replied pleasantly.

"May it be a blessed and prosperous home, Abu Ghazwan."

"Thank you, Your Majesty."

"Not at all—you've earned it, and God willing, you'll enjoy it for a long time."

"Your presence is our greatest pleasure, Your Majesty, and may you reign over us for a long time!"

On the balcony the doctor sat in his usual chair, and the soft, sultry night breezes invested him with feelings of joy and self-confidence. He talked of Mooran as he had first seen it, what a simple city it had been: "No water, no electricity, and the streets! The buildings! The life!" He shook his head and smiled as he remembered. "And now . . ." He talked about the other cities in the Sultanate and how they had grown and the life of ease the people now enjoyed, and how all this was due to His Majesty's wise and rightly guided policies. He said that the future would be even better than the present. "All Mooran needs is a strong army and modern weapons, which is not the hardest thing to attend to."

The Sultan, invigorated, nodded in agreement and laughed happily every now and then, but he also needed some light and comic conversation, and another mood altogether, so when the doctor suggested that they stay out on the balcony and take their meal there, he noticed the huge table that had been set in the indoor dining room, and things fell into place.

"If you prefer to dine on the balcony, Your Majesty," said the doctor in a tone of apology, "Umm Ghazwan can serve us."

The Sultan could not find the right response to this. He laughed, a sound like the neighing of a horse, to express his pleasure and acceptance of this plan. The doctor did not wait, but sprang up like a cat, and within a minute or two the procession had begun: the doctor, rolling along in his white robe, minute beads of sweat gathering slowly on his forehead; Widad followed two steps behind, in the tight black dress that emphasized her radiantly light complexion, especially her neck and the upper part of her bosom, and, one step behind her, Salma, in a sky-blue dress embroidered with white roses, her auburn hair braided and tied with a black ribbon. She looked as young as a girl and as grown as a woman, the more so since her mother had touched up her cheeks very lightly with rouge, and, for the first time, applied kohl to bring out her wide, dark, wary eyes.

The doctor read the monarch's reaction in his eyes, and carefully watched his smallest movements. For the first time the Sultan seemed as bashful as a boy as he greeted the two women, and the muscles of his face twitched as he settled his gaze. He remained standing longer than was his habit with guests, and this extraordinary gesture on his part embarrassed the doctor.

"For Heaven's sake, for Heaven's sake, have a seat!" he told him. "Have a seat, Your Majesty!"

The Sultan looked around questioningly, to see whether it was going to be permissible for the women to sit down too, so the doctor intervened.

"Have a seat, Umm Ghazwan, join us for a while, and later on you can arrange how we sit." He laughed to gain extra courage, and added, "His Majesty desired that we dine under the stars rather than stay cooped up indoors under those air conditioners."

Widad took a seat opposite the Sultan. Salma remained standing, so that it seemed that the others had forgotten about her or turned away from her. The doctor, looking all around to test the mood to see how hearty it was, noticed his forgetfulness and said apologetically, "Come here, dear, come near me."

"The Sultan's visit lasted three hours and thirty-eight minutes," gloated the doctor as he reviewed the visit with Widad.

"He might have stayed even longer if we had insisted more," was Widad's reply as she reclined and conjured up the man's image in her mind's eye: how he had laughed and eaten and looked at her so sweetly.

When the doctor ticked off the events of the visit, one by one, minute by minute, he conceded that pure luck had played a part, though "cunning and inspiration played the decisive role." The idea of the visit had not, after all, been a passing whim or a coincidence. The doctor said that he had long been planning this honor, and made his wish for it known on several occasions. And the visit, had it been to anyone else—not to detract from the Sultan—could not possibly have been this lively, friendly and thrilling. He had lavished some civilized touches on the visit from the moment His Majesty stepped out of his car until the moment he left. Sitting out on the balcony, surveying the green gardens and canary cages; the sprigs of basil he offered to the Sultan at just the right moment; the easy flow of conversation and his own unprecedented heights of brilliance. The fact that Widad and Salma joined them had enhanced the gracious, perfumed atmosphere, and awakened in the Sultan an affability that the doctor had never seen before. The women had not stayed with them the whole time; they moved around quite a lot, which allowed the doctor to tell some jokes he would not have told had they been present.

The tape wound through the doctor's memory, how he had arrived at the brilliant idea, which glowed like a meteor, even he did not know how to explain, so he attributed it to inspiration; for before broaching the topic of arms, "by luck, by sheer luck, Ghazwan was able to make connections inside the world's biggest and most important company for weapons supply, and we can benefit from his knowledge and connections; he is willing to be of service to the Sultanate, to help it obtain the best armaments available, in any quantity we need."

This proposal might not have sounded practical or succeeded had it not been for the sudden glimmer of his brilliant idea.

"Great men, Your Majesty, must remain in the memory of generations and be mentioned by every tongue, and it is not the task of future history, but the responsibility of the present, to see that that happens. I beg you to allow me, Your Majesty, to gain your consent to a certain proposal: to write Your Majesty's biography, from childhood until the present moment."

The idea seemed to appeal to the Sultan, but he did not know how to respond to the request, so he smiled, showing his enormous teeth.

"We would call the book, Your Majesty, *The Eagle of Mooran.*"

The doctor went on at length, explaining the importance of his idea and the necessity of carrying it out. He would personally supervise every phase of the project. He said that he had the best person to undertake the job. The Sultan was trying to judge how serious these words were, and how much the doctor meant by them. During a lull he asked:

"Wouldn't it be better to write about my father and the history of the Sultanate?"

"We'll touch on both topics as background, Your Majesty. Some of the early chapters would be devoted to your late father and his founding of the Sultanate, and of course we would cover the history and geography of Mooran." The doctor had smiled at the Sultan, then at Widad, and added, "This book, Your Majesty, is not only a history, it is the biography of a great man, and would contain a whole collection of pictures, illustrating your boyhood, youth, and adulthood. It would have to be widely distributed, to people and institutions, and translated into several languages."

The Sultan was convinced, but the doctor had one more surprise in store for him.

"Samir Caesar, Your Majesty, is ready to begin work on the book. All we need from you, Your Majesty, is the setting aside of enough time to tell us about your childhood and youth. Samir and I will do the rest, and it will definitely meet with your approval and the approval of anyone who looks at it."

The doctor did not know how this idea had come to him; he suddenly found himself thinking of it, then took the leap and proposed it, and might not have pursued it had it not been for the Sultan's friendly and confiding mood. He was also heartened by the encouraging looks Widad gave him when their eyes met. She winked twice, as if urging him to persist. Late that night the doctor suggested to her that they go out and sit on the balcony, after their long talk and long silences; they both felt like draining these delicious moments to the dregs in their special way.

"You know, Widad," he told her affectionately, and then laughed and shook his head delightedly, "so many things come down to—providence." He did not want to say *brains,* since he thought she might misunderstand, and he did not like the word *luck*—he always called luck *a crutch for the lazy.* When she concurred, he went on.

"Even your decision for us to spend the summer in Alexandria, with Samir near us, will be a crucial factor in completing *The Eagle of Mooran.*"

She laughed coyly and said, "You should always believe me and take my advice!"

"There is no one else like you—you princess!"

72

I'M WILLING TO DO IT," SAMIR TOLD THE DOCTOR three days later, "but only on two conditions. The first is that we need several sources for facts on His Majesty. The second is that he set aside several working sessions for us, so that we can ask him questions we've prepared."

"Don't worry, leave it to me. I'll take care of everything."

"How much is he paying?" Samir smiled.

The doctor had not thought about this question; more precisely, it had not occurred to him. He had assumed that with a book of this importance, which could be written in just a few months, there could be no talk of hardship. Unconsciously, in the same tone of voice Samir had used, the doctor repeated his question.

"How much is he paying?"

"You know very well, sir, that a book about the Sultan is not like any other book; it requires uncommon effort, and there can be no question of any error of any kind; the whole thing has to be handled in a special way." He smiled broadly and looked directly into the doctor's eyes. "With any other book, of course, it would be different."

Their discussion was not a long one. "Don't worry," the doctor told him, "if the book comes out the way I imagine it, and the Sultan is pleased, you won't need to ask for recompense; you'll be swimming in money, from me and from His Majesty, not to mention special disbursements!"

The deal of a lifetime, Samir said to himself. *It's a lifetime insurance policy; it will open up opportunities for a future I can scarcely imagine now. I have to do this right.* He considered various sums: ten thousand, a hundred thousand, five hundred thousand . . . a million. He said, "A million," and laughed giddily: a million what? Pounds? Francs? Dollars? He imagined what he would do when he got the money. *I'll put it in the bank and live on the interest. I'll invest it in a business, but I'll have to study it very carefully; I may be able to double my money within two or three years.* He thought of founding a publishing firm to surpass *al-Ahram* and *Akhbar El-Yom. Enough of being an employee; let me work for myself now.* He thought of founding something in his own name, that would last his lifetime, even after he was dead. He thought on ahead, imagining his publishing firm and the names of the newspapers and magazines he would put out, and where the head office and presses would be. *We'd have to form a distribution company to get the newspapers all over the globe, so as not to be at the mercy of some local distributor.*

He thought of keeping a daybook, as the doctor did, in which he could duly record everything he saw and heard. From this raw material would rise *The Eagle of Mooran;* he approved of this title and thought it clever, but left the rest, including the rare photographs of His Majesty, until the proper time. They would come in handy in many ways and at different times: the Sultan might die suddenly, or be exiled or assassinated, *and if I have all the raw material, I can take out whatever I want.*

The doctor spent just two weeks in Alexandria. He was unable to stay longer, since, as he told Widad, "I'm not a king; I can't just stretch out and forget the king and the government. And I'm expecting Ghazwan—he'll be arriving soon, and I can't leave him on his own." He and Samir spent much of this period in deep discussion over details of the book: how many chapters it would have, the title of each chapter, and whether the photographs would come at the beginning or the end. He did not omit how many copies they would need to print, and other technical details. He was stumped by the issue of his introduction to the book: was it suitable to put his name on the cover, as the writer of the introduction? Would the introduction itself consist of ordinary remarks, as so many introductions did, or be a profound treatise on the social and political philosophy the Sultanate was founded upon?

He was undecided and hesitant until the day before he left, when he informed Samir of his departure.

"I have to get back quickly. I have to get some crucial sources for you, and make the appointments with His Majesty."

Samir made a show of trying to persuade the doctor to postpone his trip, since he could "get nothing done during the summer," though he finally conceded that the doctor could at least "seek out sources" while he got started on the work immediately; the doctor asked him, almost urgently, to lose no time.

Those two summer months were the most momentous ever in their lives. The doctor was gravely disappointed by the collapse of some of his dreams, but found in these new circumstances a chance to win back what he had lost; furthermore, he wanted to do something on his own, still stung by his dealings with others and the way they had collapsed, or at least run into difficulties. He said to himself, to settle this decision he regarded as crucial: *Play alone and go home happy.*

Widad had been in turmoil the night after the Sultan's visit and even now did not know what her true feelings were. She had become, in Alexandria, a woman tiresome to herself and others, as if she were unable to accustom herself to the clamor of having so many family members around her every moment. She did not know what to do or how; the doctor did not object to her wearing a bathing suit or spending much of her day on the beach, but in spite of her protestations he refused to undress or go into the water himself. That was part of the trouble, and since she did not know how to swim and could do no more than splash a little water on her body, though all the children tried to teach her how to swim, she spent the rest of her time sitting on the beach with a book whose pages she hardly turned.

She was not used to reading books and rarely read anything; it surprised her how people wasted their time with something as silly as reading. That amusement held no appeal for her, but a great deal had gone on between her and Samir. She was not the only woman he knew. Widad discovered that he had numerous liaisons and knew many women with whom he spent a great deal of time. Even when he was with her and the children, he thought nothing of ogling any woman who passed, following her with his eyes as she neared and again as she walked away, an obvious look of lustful appreciation on his face. He did not hide it; in fact, he took special pleasure in showing Widad.

Sometimes when they were in bed, to be away from the children, or when Widad wanted to go into town to shop, and other times they were together, he was a different person than he had been in Mooran: he was easily irritated and used crude words. He used them half jokingly but meant them. The charm that characterized him in Mooran was totally gone; instead, he was harsh and even uncouth.

Widad might have understood this behavior if it had stayed within bounds, and she might have sought excuses for it, had it not been for the thing that surprised her the most: his wily, quiet attempts to seduce Salma. She saw this not with a mother's eye but with a woman's. She watched how he taught Salma how to swim. She saw how he looked at her on the beach, or as they sat on their balcony. He was constantly talking to her and asking her questions, even sometimes patting her shoulder or thigh. Salma was like a newly blossomed flower, and here, with her brothers and thousands of people around her, in a permissive atmosphere after long months in the prison that Mooran seemed, she was ready to respond, to drink in this new life. Salma did not know what Samir wanted of her or why he looked at her that way, but she was fascinated by it all, especially the way he looked at her and behaved around her.

Widad saw this, and kept her eyes on them, seeing also how Samir tried to avoid her, and she grew upset and filled with rage. She had never imagined she could be treated this way or that anything like this could happen, but at the same time she did not want to acknowledge anything or to surrender. She gave up the one-piece bathing suit she'd worn during the doctor's stay for a bikini, and intended to buy three more of them in flashy colors she selected because they suited the tone of her body. The fear of the water that had possessed her in the first days of the vacation now left her, and she tried in earnest to learn how to swim, with the children and with Samir. In the course of doing this she swallowed enough salt-water to make her ill, and thereafter was content to "swim" in the shallow water. She sent invitations constantly, day in and day out, each in the name of one of the children, with Samir always the host and the guest; her aim was to hold him, to keep him in her sight. She had dozens of other tricks, all to get him back, to convince him or herself that he was still the one she knew and wanted. Samir was there one moment and gone the next, like the water: she could not hold him or know him, find out what he wanted or what he was thinking.

It was a solid month of effort and blind struggle. After the doctor left, whenever it seemed to Samir or Widad that he was approaching or arriving, they discovered that he was heading in the other direction, the wrong direction. Samir wanted to keep his relationship with Salma but really wanted Salma for the future. Widad wanted to get him back, and tried to draw closer to him while pushing Salma away, making of his relationship with her daughter a childish and innocent one that could never become anything else. Salma, fascinated with this new life, and the attention of her brothers, the young men around her and Samir, felt her body maturing and filling out, attracting the others as much as it attracted and embarrassed her, but she felt nothing more. Her two brothers were taken aback by their little sister's growth and were not sure of their feelings toward her: she was still young, still a girl, but now had a body they needed to protect from others, and so they had a hard time sorting out their ways of expressing their affection and jealousy of her.

Mooran reappeared in Widad's mind again now: there she might be a queen. Everyone desired and pursued her, even His Majesty. She had felt bliss when he looked at her that way, because she knew the meaning of that look and what it could lead to. Here, in this prodigious mass of naked bodies, in which men were scarcely able to avoid the women, she had no opportunity to make a show or attract anyone; she was only a number. *Men make so many mistakes with numbers; they always make mistakes—otherwise how can you explain how men know so many women before they marry, so many beautiful women, but when they marry, they marry a specific woman, perhaps less beautiful than the ones they've known before, but she's the only one they want.* She resolved to fight from a position of strength, at a time of her choosing. And that was not all: she had to protect Salma, to remove her from the wolves swarming around her. And she had to get to Beirut, to put the children back in school and do some shopping for them.

Thus in a sudden and turbulent moment, after Samir had promised her and failed, she decided to leave. Within hours they had packed. When Samir came that afternoon, there was only an hour left before their train to Cairo, and he tried desperately to persuade them to postpone the journey. He claimed that he had been ill and unable to go to the Café Araby, but Widad's mind was made up.

"Thank you, Samir." Widad smiled as she extended her long straight arm to shake his hand and keep him from coming closer. "God willing, we'll be seeing you soon in Mooran."

"Thank you for what? I'm very upset!"

"Upset?"

"Yes, ma'am! What do you mean, leaving so suddenly?"

"The children have one week left before school, Samir, and I have to get them there and buy them their things."

"So that's how it is." He chuckled and turned to Salma. "Are you leaving, Salma?" When she nodded and laughed, he said, as if to himself, "A pity . . . by the Prophet."

73

*A*FTER A FEW MONTHS, WITH PRINCE FANAR'S acceptance of the Saad Palace and his move into it, and the subsequent visits and receptions, it became clear that the Sultanate was again enjoying an unprecedented period of wealth and stability, especially since the princes, all brothers, were on selfless and friendly terms with one another. That reminded the Sultan of the days following the Battle of Rehaiba, when the sons and brothers of Sultan Khureybit hurried from one place to another, with selfless energy, helping the new state to put down roots, to strengthen its control, so that it might confront all enemies and dangers resulting from neglect or laxity.

It was the same now for the Sultanate. What compounded the strength of the feeling now, unlike before, were the power and riches that flooded the place; the Sultanate seemed dreadful and desirable at the same time. While Sultan Khureybit had sought the help of many men to establish his reign and destroy his enemies, he had had relatively little money and was often compelled to skimp them, delay their pay and urge them to tighten their belts. Now unlimited riches flooded the country in a way that no one had ever imagined. And whereas Khureybit had been tough and scrupulous, even stingy when it came to money (he had spent as little as possible and had given it away only after prolonged reflection, and even then in installments), Sultan Khazael never scrimped, and thought nothing of spending money or giving it away; there was no one in the palace, no one connected or friendly with the family, who had not been given something. His prosperity was evident in the way people acted, in their faces, in their clothes, and in what they ate; everyone was proud and content . . . everyone except Malik al-Fraih.

Sheikh Malik, who once had been willing to avert his eyes and let things pass, could no longer tolerate the extravagances that grew wilder every day. In the meetings scheduled to debate project funding, which he was expected to attend, there was always a profusion of talk about the importance of some projects and the urgency of securing adequate funding to implement them, and Malik often ended up shouting as if he had been stung.

"It's not our problem, whether a project is good or no good— that's your business and up to your consciences, but for God's sake, where is the money going to come from?" He would turn to his aide, who kept the account books. "Give them to me, my boy."

And without his aide coming forward to give him the books, and without speaking further to him, he went on: "My friends . . ." and laughed angrily, glancing surreptitiously at the Sultan to see how closely he was following this. "We have nothing but a few coins left, Your Majesty, and if you want to spend them on this project, that is your decision, but that has to be the end of this." But if he perceived the Sultan inattentive or preoccupied, he would shout, "I'm going to roll out my carpet and say everything!" He would again demand the account books from his aide and wait for him to come up and hand them over; then he sat down to listen to him.

"His Majesty is present, and the carpet is spread; let every man give his opinion." And before opening the books, and before anyone could say a word, he snapped at his aide, "Take some paper and write this down!" And he would steal a look this way and then that, as if wary and fearful, then go on in a hushed, even conspiratorial tone: "My friends, money comes by His Majesty's order, and he has the final say, but, as we used to say, 'Even a traitor doesn't betray his benefactor,' and it would be a sin to throw our money away."

There was always a great deal of discussion and pressure and sarcasm, for Malik was always on one side with everyone else against him, and the Sultan never said a word. He watched the dispute in progress before him until it was ended, and when he came to a decision, Sheikh Malik, pleased and happy, was the first to support it. "This is the way it will be; each of us has a conscience and wants what's best for the country—I assent!"

The doctor understood this veiled hint better than anyone else, since the basic contest here was who was a native and who was a foreigner: who was thinking of the interests of the state of Mooran and who was here to enrich himself!

This assent was only half the battle for Sheikh Malik; perhaps even the easier half. When anyone came to get money from him, Sheikh Malik, who had no paper or pen, would stare at him and ask, "My friend, don't you do anything but ask for money? Don't you know how to say anything but 'Give me'?" If the person laughed or got angry at being put off by Sheikh Malik, the sheikh's serious and angry response was, "What money do you want?"

"What His Majesty has decided for me."

"What His Majesty has decided?" He paused. "Leave His Majesty alone, my friends, give him a rest! You've made him dizzy with all your 'We want, we want.'" When he had given them this lesson and calmed down, he asked his petitioner with the utmost innocence, "By God Almighty, all you have on your mind is money?" And if the man nodded yes, Sheikh Malik would go on to say, "Dear cousin, the money is mine and the king's both. In this world we follow a course like water down a hillside, and the wise people, my friend, are the ones who know that after this world comes death, and then accounting and judgment."

Most of the time this speech met with no interruption, and the sheikh was not in the least troubled if it met with silence. He would pull out his yellow prayer beads and tell them deftly three at a time.

If his guest coughed quietly to remind him of his presence or the purpose of this visit, then the sheikh raised his gaze with deep annoyance and anger in his eyes, and snarled, "If no one listens to God's word, then let's hear from His slave." Then, with a mocking smile: "Speak, my boy!"

And since they would have nothing to say, nothing at all to add, he would only repeat the sum of money His Majesty the Sultan had promised him and say that he knew all the details, and that there was no reason to go through it all again. The sheikh would try to remember, but most of the time his memory did not fully oblige him; he needed more explanations, which he interrupted at several points to ask exactly when this had happened or who had been present, what His Majesty had said. He responded to the details with nods and careful looks directly into his interlocutor's eyes as he slowly muttered, "Good, good, now we understand the whole thing. . . ." Then he would pause, smiling, to add, "There's one more thing, my boy."

"One more thing?"

"A note from the Sultan." Malik would smile broadly enough to show his teeth, so that it was hard to tell whether it was a smile of doom or of delight, and add, "Don't forget, it should include the Sultan's signature and his seal, and then that's it—for God is munificent."

On the second try, when the visitor showed up with a signed and sealed letter from the Sultan, Sheikh Malik would negotiate over whether it was required to disburse the total sum now or only part of it, whether it would be possible to reduce the amount slightly; all this with much vehemence and sarcasm, many mentions of Heaven and Hell, and after all that, when the visitor was insistent and unprepared to renegotiate or haggle, the sheikh replied stonily, "I've taken to heart everything you've said, and there's no question of disobeying His Majesty's command, but what if I told you we don't have the money you want? It just isn't there."

Sheikh Malik summoned his clerk and told him to bring the account books. The clerk brought them, but the sheikh left them shut and the clerk standing, and said sadly, "I'd like one of you to be in my place—just for one day!"

Sheikh Malik often got what he wanted, or part of it: a reduction in the payment, an installment plan, or a postponement. When he got something like that, he was delighted, he changed, he became a different person, he got very talkative and ordered coffee or tea for him and his guest, most of the time, always talking about how Mooran was the target of a conspiracy, hatched by foreigners who were attacking like locusts; therefore it was necessary to "open our eyes, to watch every coin, because when our money is gone, our fire will go out and no one will remember us." One way or another he would steer the conversation in such a way that he could tell a story he had heard from many different people: "A camel rider came from Mecca nine days' distance, bringing the news that the Franks had taken Kamran and were besieging the city of Sawakin. The Sharif, the emir of Mecca, went out to Jeddah with his chief agent and a party of Mamelukes from there in Mecca, and they stayed in Jeddah from fear that the chief of the Franks would attack them. They sent word to inform the Sultan of that, and the Sultan was sore grieved by it, especially since he was cut off in al-Dehaisha because of his eye, and the people were sore grieved. When Friday came, the Sultan went out and said his Friday prayers, and a Shafei magistrate, Kamal el-Din al-Tawil, came out and mounted the pulpit and preached an eloquent sermon about the meaning of the incident that took place because of the Franks. He took them to a number of towns on the coast of Yemen, and when they had prayed, the muezzins said, 'Despair follows prayer.' And the Friday magistrate despaired as he made his final genuflection, and the Sultan and the princes and everyone in the mosque despaired, one and all."*

When he had told this story, he asked himself and his guest, "After the news reached the Sultan of Egypt—what happened?" And without waiting for a reply, he said, now ironically, "He grieved, yes, he grieved, and waited until Friday, then despaired, and after he despaired he remembered no one and no one remembered him!"

The sheikh talked on and raged on, with one aim, to convey a message: "Dr. Subhi al-Mahmilji is Mooran's enemy, and if there is mischief awaiting Mooran, or a foe lurking, it is he—or will come

---

*Ibn Iyas, *Marvels in the Injuries of Time,* Part IV, p. 308.

by way of him." But he never once mentioned his name and never alluded to him.

The doctor, who had borne much and no longer had any direct relationship with Sheikh Malik, could not ignore this, and could not forget revenge. Now that things were different, he felt that the time had come.

After the meeting in which it was decided to build the tower and the Khazael Sports City, and as a result of Sheikh Malik's laughter and scorn at these projects, and his saying that they were pointless and that those who proposed them were enemies of Mooran, the doctor's anger exceeded all limits. He spoke to the Sultan, who had attended part of that meeting.

"After you left the meeting, Your Majesty, that devil Ibn Fraih must have lost his senses: 'I won't stand it—you'll never see that money—that tower won't be built.' We all said, 'It's His Majesty's command, Sheikh Malik; that project has been finally approved.' But he would have none of it, Your Majesty. He laughed and stuck his tongue out. I think he has gone too far this time, Your Majesty, by being insolent toward your high station. He needs to be curbed, as a warning to others."

The Sultan was not long in firing Malik, but kept him at his disposal without appointing him to a new job.

74

THE DOCTOR FELT EXHILARATED AND POWER-
ful now that he was rid of his enemy; he
had long awaited the right time, and when
it came he showed no pity. *It will be an example for the others; they must
learn who Dr. Mahmilji is!* he said proudly to himself. He found that
the Sultan was in a very good, even exuberant mental state, and
felt that many of the ideas that had occupied him in the past, and
the dreams that he wished to accomplish, had moved closer to reality; surely he would realize them all soon.

His intuition was not wrong, for the palace and everyone who
had any connection with it had changed: the bustle, life and people
all suggested exuberance, as if the return of Prince Fanar and the
accord that had been reached—for him to stay, and to co-govern,
though no one talked about it explicitly, or too loudly—had been
everyone's long-awaited wish. Though he chided himself for not
having foreseen the importance of this and what its consequences

would be, the doctor was not long in deducing them. He wasted no time in calling on Prince Fanar, with the aim of talking over some issues with him, of gauging his acumen and the range of his knowledge. His conclusions from the visit were that *the man is ordinary, practically illiterate, speaks no foreign language, can't tell a good joke, and he's very conservative, in his clothes and the way he acts.* He found the prince to be a simple man, who asked him about several of the diseases common to hot climates, and some of the steps that could be taken to fight or treat them. He asked how such diseases were fought in similar regions of the world. The doctor held forth at length about the hot climates, and how infant mortality was at an all-time high in most of them; in Mooran, he pointed out, the rate was far lower and would certainly decline in coming years. The visit concluded to their mutual satisfaction, with the doctor convinced of the soundness of his prior judgment.

Prince Fanar had done more than merely move into the new palace and respond to the invitations he received, which he had, in the past, brusquely, almost rudely, turned down. When he did attend functions, his demeanor and everything he said expressed his simplicity and feelings of true brotherliness. It is true that he was not a graceful speaker, but he was friendly; he showed great courtesy even as he listened to his brothers talk, asked questions, and expressed his agreement and understanding. The other princes, who had been deeply worried by Prince Fanar's return and his subsequent actions, and those who wished he had never come, regretted their poor opinion of him and were doubly happy now.

The same happiness spread to the Sultan and all the palaces. The Sultan had thought, in an inspired moment, of having all his brothers, the sons of the late Sultan Khureybit, take new wives in one night; this would spread lasting joy throughout the Sultanate for days and nights on end. It might be a good omen and become a tradition for generations to come, imparting a certain pride to future generations, especially when they saw the marriages recorded along with the new births occurring all at once, or at around the same time, just as was the case with many creatures. This thought shimmered in the Sultan's imagination for several nights, but he abandoned it at a party Prince Mayzar gave for Prince Fanar; after all their long and merry conversations, Prince

Zaal told his brother Prince Fanar that he looked younger and stronger than he had in years, and received a somewhat rebuking reply.

"Some know, Zaal, and those who don't, say whatever comes to mind!"

This was understood to mean that Prince Fanar still suffered from poor health, though he bore it stoically, and that had it not been for his desire to be among them, to die in his own country and among his brothers, he would have preferred to stay abroad. For a few moments each of them who had been following the conversation entertained in his memory past joys and sorrows associated with this traveler who had come home at last. This is what made the Sultan think better of his plan.

It was time for those seemingly endless private meetings that the Sultan and Prince Fanar attended with only a very few of their brothers, and the two met three times a week for discussions of their own, twice at the Ghadir Palace and the third time at the Saad Palace. It was said that the prince attended because of his wish to help and foster harmony, and on the orders of his brother the Sultan. What gave this credence was the report that the prince had taken an office in the new royal palace in Khalidia.

This violent outburst of enthusiasm and change, which lasted for weeks and was the talk of almost everyone in Mooran, for it affected all of them in one way or another, soon faded and passed away, then reversed. Prince Fanar himself helped to demolish it, by way of a press interview he granted to Samir Caesar, with Muti in attendance. He asserted, indirectly, that his status had not changed when he came from abroad to resettle in his homeland, and that he had put himself in the service of the Sultanate and the Sultan, though he preferred merely to rest for the time being.

Statements he made before and after the interview were more explicit and meaningful. Prince Fanar was careful not to give anything he said any striking outward significance. He allowed the newspaper to print only one picture of him because he preferred not to be too prominent, so that people would not make much of him and affect his health adversely.

The doctor was obsessed with getting the most precise information and the very smallest details. He questioned Muti and Samir, he questioned them both together and listened to every word they said, then questioned each of them separately. He monitored the parties they gave from up close and very carefully. These were limited to princes and their families; foreigners never attended. When the doctor was asked how he assessed Prince Fanar's future, he replied, as if in deep sorrow or pain, "God help him and us both!"

He did not seem eager to offer a clear opinion, but a few weeks after the newspaper interview he did speak more plainly.

"A man must never despair of two things: God's mercy and the progress of science. Now I'm speaking as a physician—it's true that there are some irremediable cases where no known remedy does any good, but there's always the hope of new medical discoveries, which can bring about great changes, as long as doctors keep in touch with the world's research centers and leading universities."

His listeners took this to mean that the condition of Prince Fanar's health gave cause for concern, even for grave alarm. They all remembered the rumors of his initial arrival: his doctors were said to have told him, "We've done all we can for you; now the best thing is for you to die in your own land, among your own family and tribe." It seemed all the more plausible because the doctor had visited Prince Fanar in the early weeks, then again in the Saad Palace, and, for the last time, around the time of the newspaper interview, at the request of the Sultan himself, and made it clear that this was the extent of his relationship with Fanar and he had no desire for any stronger relationship.

Hammad was amused when the doctor asked him how he assessed this new situation.

"Mooran stands as she is, Abu Ghazwan, she's not changing or going anywhere!" When the doctor sought a clearer answer, he added, "What I think, Doctor, is that things are as they were, and that it's best for none of us to get involved with them. It's best not to see or to hear, or become food for eagles."

Once again the doctor recalled the book that he would, with Samir's help, unburden himself of—*The Eagle of Mooran*—and felt a surge of pride at having chosen that particular title; for in addition to its significance, it was both powerful and eloquent. What Hammad was saying now only pointed to his farsightedness, but even so he did not feel that he had taken a clear position or shown decisive sympathies with regard to what was happening.

All this had happened before the doctor's summer trip, but now, after his return, he felt his previous convictions confirmed. He heard nothing of Prince Fanar, who had, perhaps, vanished again. He explained that biliousness generated melancholy, which might ease or not manifest itself clearly. A sick man clung to his final days of life, so that what looked like vigor in early summer was really no more than a freak occurrence, a temporary thing, which might recur one or two more times, but be essentially meaningless.

The other thing that caught the doctor's attention on his return was the Sultan's obvious and bountiful affection. He told the doctor that he had stayed away too long. He told him that Mooran's weather had been far more bearable this summer than it had been in many years; more so, specifically, than last year or the one before. This affection spurred the doctor to make grand strides forward, though he deeply regretted that he was fighting alone, and that the others, even the children, in spite of the sacrifices he had made for them, were not responding actively enough. How else could he explain Ghazwan's delay, or Samir's?

He had cut his trip short, spending only three days in Dhuhour al-Shweir after leaving Alexandria. He had not even been able to sleep in the villa, which was in sore need of repairs and renovation. He spent his three days going back and forth between the little front balcony and the entrance, to let everyone know he was there. He hired a new gardener, since the old one had died several months before his arrival, though one of his relatives who came to collect the deceased's wages claimed that he had died just fifteen days before the doctor's arrival. The doctor pretended to believe this, but turned several times silently toward the garden, to show that the man had died at least a year before—the state of the garden made that clear.

He sent two cables and three letters to Ghazwan. The cables asked him to come as soon as possible, and the letters could not have been misinterpreted, but still he had not come. Ghazwan replied in a brief letter explaining that his company was sending him to Brazil with a delegation, but that as soon as he got back he would put his affairs in order and come. He did not say how long he would be in Brazil or when he would return, and gave no approximate date for his arrival in Mooran. The doctor consoled himself by finding justifications for Ghazwan: *The absent need not make excuses, but when he gets here I'll give him a scolding.*

By this time, Samir had prepared most of the material he would need for his work. He hinted briefly at his appointments with the Sultan without seeking exact times, since that seemed a little premature, and the timing would be affected by several different factors. He would take charge of them, *since there's no room for error, and they have to be subject to my own judgment and done by me personally.*

The Sultan alluded more than once to the evening he had spent at the doctor's, and smacked his lips as he praised Umm Ghazwan's cooking. He asked, a little mysteriously, about "the family," and declared that he hoped for more such evenings in the future. The doctor listened with amazement to this praise, smiling again and again, recalling the events of that evening with delight. He remembered everything about that night, how upset and frightened Widad had been, how she'd cried and asked him to offer their excuses to the Sultan. Smiling and reminiscing, he said to himself that *women are a little lacking in brains and faith,* for without his insistence and his own efforts to calm Widad and to act and speak normally during their soiree, events—and his subsequent relationship with the Sultan—might have taken a very different turn.

Even Rateb, with whom some of the "errors" originated—"stupidities," as the doctor called them—now seemed friendlier and more balanced. When he asked the doctor to recommend a doctor for Nabila, "who is pregnant, Abu Ghazwan, and has back pains," he was nervous and almost ashamed; the doctor reconsidered his past preconceptions about Rateb and was quick to suggest a suitable doctor for his wife. Nor was he long in finding a truer explanation for Rateb's situation: "At a certain age, a baby becomes the most important and cherished idea to a mature and experienced man. Our friend's wife did not get pregnant right away and he got scared, but now he feels more balanced and self-confident." What convinced him of this new view was the vast improvement in the performance of the Foodstuffs Company, its new contracts with the army for foodstuff supplies and the fact that Rateb and Zaubaii were getting along so much better.

Muti had come to love journalism, and it diverted his attention from almost everything else, much to the doctor's dismay; he took notice and felt it necessary to intervene. "The column in the newspaper, Nephew, is not worth the news printed in it. You are, at all times, the father of journalism, not its son, and if you want to shut your door for hours and hours and have your work lights burning, not seeing anyone and letting no one see you, not overseeing the newspaper or giving direction, only concentrating on writing a few words that no one may read, we're going to fail badly, as anyone else might do; we won't have been journalists or editors." This is what the doctor told Muti two or three months before his vacation, and it annoyed Muti, though he only said, with an angry chuckle, that he was doing a good job, and had given up his daily column, which Samir helped him to "edit," with a weekly article in the magazine *al-Waha*. This was not only an article in the magazine's first pages, but an article with a picture of him: Muti had chosen an old picture of himself in profile, in deep thought.

The doctor took in these developments, and praised them without referring to their conversation of a few months before. This came at the same time as the "happy event" Muti awaited any day now, which would have meant little to the doctor except for the fact that Muti wanted to name the newborn Subhi or Ghazwan, if it was a boy; he was still undecided between Salma and Naama if it was a girl. All these names had something to do with the doctor, so it was essential to ask his advice.

Muti was a little shy and did not know how to broach the subject. The first son, named Rushdy for his father without anyone's being asked, did not much appeal to the doctor, though he did not say so directly. Now he wanted to try new names, and the name closest to him, and his favorite above all others: Subhi. If the doctor was too embarrassed to choose this name the alternative would be Ghazwan, so he had to be consulted.

The subject would not have worried Muti at all had it not been for past discussions the doctor plunged so enthusiastically into with his guests, which seemed to him both important and entertaining, in which he mocked certain names, especially common ones in Mooran, chosen by people who knew nothing about naming children. He recalled what the doctor had once said while considering the popular names in Mooran: "These jackasses—they must be blind. There's nothing in the world cheaper or more plentiful than names, but they leave all the names that would make you proud, to choose Kalb—*dog*. Or Jahsh—*donkey*. Fleihan—*little peasant*—what will they think up next, *little shitter?* As if there were no names like Ghazwan or Hamid, Kamal or Salma"—the doctor virtually sang these names. He said that the only way to create a balanced, wholesome future generation was to give suitable names to their children, and to impose a punitive tax on any father who did not give his son a grand and dignified name.

These conversations now echoed in Muti's ears; he was eager to discuss this very subject with the doctor, and in order not to be deluged in scorn, he smiled brightly and said to the doctor in a moment of candor: "As the Mooranis say, Uncle, any day now God is going to bless me with a child, and I've been trying to decide between two names: Subhi and Ghazwan. You have to choose for me!"

The doctor laughed heartily, enchanted by this gesture of Muti's, which, among other things, demonstrated clearly that the man was not only deeply influenced by him but regarded him as an ideal and exemplar, *otherwise why would he corner me like this?* The gesture showed more than loyalty—it was even above that—and loyalty had to be rewarded with loyalty, and confidence with mutual confidence.

"There's no lack of fine names," said the doctor, still smiling, "but if you prefer one of those two names over the other, then trust in God and choose it."

"You're his uncle—you name him!"

"Don't embarrass me even more than you have, Nephew!"

In a warm and genial mood, the doctor let Muti name the new baby whatever he wished; though he had no objection to the name Subhi. For a girl, he proposed, with a hint of finality, Loubna, instead of Salma or Naama. Muti was very pleased and agreed instantly: "Subhi for a boy, Loubna for a girl."

The doctor was delighted, despite the mistakes of the past; furthermore, he considered those mistakes small. They could have happened to any man; other people had made far worse mistakes. What consoled him was that his aides and coworkers loved and trusted him; he was an example to them. That was why they rallied around him, asked him questions, sought his advice on small matters and large. *They don't even name their children without talking to me—that's respect!* He did not want to remember Hosny or Said, Muhammad Eid or Mufaddi. He slept comfortably that night, bothered only by the delay of the travelers: Ghazwan, Widad and Samir.

75

THE FIRST "ELECTIONS"—HELD IN EARLY AU-
tumn, to select members of the Mooran
Chamber of Commerce—came as another
blow to the doctor. He might have accepted the defeat of his list
and the success of someone else's, but what he could not accept and
had never imagined was the success of the enemy list: Said's and
Rezaie's. Al-Ghamdi had been elected chairman of the Chamber of
Commerce, and Rezaie the deputy chairman, *but the fact remains
that the list—in its members, its setup, even its slogan—was the work of that
vile Said,* so the doctor saw it as a threat, even as an insult.

The doctor had seen the difficulty of the contracts won by the
Ghazal Company several months before, and devoted his time and
energy, since that time, to respond through Ghazwan and his company. But Ghazwan had come for only three days in the late summer and offered "ideas," as he said when received by the Sultan,
and left Mooran with proposals, which he promised to study and
"respond to as soon as possible."

Two months passed, two very long months for the doctor, for he received no reply except for two letters. The first was a personal letter from Ghazwan in which he referred to the proposals only obliquely, asserting that "the results will be positive." The second was from the corporate administration of the firm, confirming that they had received the Sultanate's proposals, which were now being studied with great interest; as soon as the studies were complete, appropriate steps would be taken. The firm concluded the letter with profound thanks and gratitude "to Dr. Subhi al-Mahmilji and his son Ghazwan, who has shown, in the short time he has been at the company, his ample qualifications and abilities, earning the approbation of its directors."

Now, with the victory of the "enemy" list, the doctor's position was badly shaken. *Everything we've done at one end has been undone at the other.* He was also upset that a tradition observed since Sultan Khureybit's day—the Sultan's lengthy desert excursions, with the princes and their sons, never taking along any advisers or foreigners—was not observed very closely by Khazael. One year it happened, the next year it might not, and even then would last for only two or three days instead of for weeks. Sometimes some of the princes did not go at all. This year it was a totally different event, with Prince Fanar in attendance—perhaps because of that. What really enraged the doctor, or seemed to him an evil omen, was that Hammad received an invitation to join the excursion the day after it set out, as Muti told the doctor, and three days later Hammad's deputy was summoned, but no one asked for the doctor. Hammad and his deputy remained away for the full duration of the excursion, but when they came back he shrugged off the doctor's questions.

"Telling old stories and hunting—not another thing went on, Abu Ghazwan." Hammad added, when the doctor gave him a skeptical look, ". . . and there was a horse race!"

The doctor nodded a little despairingly; he saw that Hammad did not want to talk, and, even more clearly, that they were excluding him and did not want him to know.

If things had been better at home, between him and Widad, the doctor would have known how to deal with others, or at least to strike a certain balance to protect himself, but she had tarried in Beirut and Alexandria, tending to the children and refinishing the house in Beirut, and arrived back in Mooran a changed woman: flighty, silent, almost ill. The doctor did all he could to help her snap out of it, but felt, deep down, that the problem was the stress she'd been under. He blamed himself for giving her responsibilities she could not handle, especially since she had been in Beirut all by herself. So, with understanding and self-denial, he bore up under the awkward and gloomy mood of the al-Hir Palace but felt, more than ever, that he was alone, utterly alone, and that even those closest to him did not understand him.

That was not all. *Samir Effendi is being a bastard.* "My dear doctor, I can't possibly put ink on paper until we agree on two things: first, my payment for this job, and, second, ten working sessions with the Sultan. I have to know everything about His Majesty and debate some of the small details with him."

The doctor had done everything in his power to make Samir abandon these two conditions or not to insist on them. "It isn't in your interest to set your price now, Samir, because His Majesty might order it doubled; and you can't set the number of working sessions in advance—it might end up being less or more. They won't be useful unless you read the history of the Sultanate, and after that we'll agree on the questions and other details." He pushed toward Samir a number of history and geography books for him to read preparatory to writing an outline of his book. Three or four weeks later when he asked Samir if he had finished reading the books, he found out that he had not touched them "because our friend Muti recruited me on some urgent business, sir, which seems to be of importance to the palace."

So the doctor's fortunes were liable to rise and fall with whatever wind was blowing, and with however people happened to be treating him. Muti, who visited him every now and then to discuss names for his boy, if it was going to be a boy, took on no work without consulting him, but the doctor heard from others that Muti had taken certain actions and struck up new friendships that he never alluded to; and that Rateb was now—unlike in the early summer—very happy and self-confident. And so many others were doing better or worse without his knowing; all this was, to the doctor, clear and timely proof that he was prey to conspiracies and whispers, though he did not know whether it was his fault or the fault of the others.

He said to himself sadly that *the hardest thing in this life is for a man to be alone, or to feel alone, with people and activity all around him.* He sank into a depression, convinced that he had wasted his life; his whole life had been a stupid race, and even if he had got somewhere, or thought he had, he now saw that he had been running in the wrong direction, toward something he did not want. Even his own wife and children had changed in this new era. He did not know what they wanted or what they were thinking, so his feelings for them were shaken and uncertain. He had worn himself out for them and spent his life making them rich, and now that he had arrived and could offer them this security, he found them distant and unmindful, as if riches meant nothing to them. He wanted Ghazwan to be with him, by his side, but Ghazwan preferred to stay there, for God knew how long—was it possible that his life in America was preferable to his coming back here and having everything given to him? And Widad—she had loved him more in the past, or at least he thought so. Now she gave her time to trivial things: clothes, cosmetics, going visiting; any spare time she had, she put into the house and furnishings. She no longer felt his presence or his importance as she once had. When she asked him about his health, it seemed to be out of courtesy, a formality: his answer meant nothing to her, and when she had pretended to listen to it, she was again immersed in silence. He generously brought her clothes and gifts, perfumes and jewels from his trips, and when he had emptied his suitcase, mostly of presents for Widad, and she thought that was all, he would surprise her with what he had kept in another suitcase. But despite her happy, brief laughter, it all ended rather quickly, and she went back into her own world—but why was that world so sad, so full of tension and silence? What could she want above what he had given her? Was there any woman who lived better than she did?

These thoughts consumed the doctor; as convinced as he was that he could explain even the most difficult problems, he found that the problems facing him were too complex: they changed form and distorted themselves so that he could explain nothing.

And Samir—why was he acting this way after coming back from his vacation? Even his visits had become short and perfunctory; he did not conceal his wish to leave almost as soon as he had come, as if he were making a courtesy visit. *Perhaps there was some offense given during the summer vacation,* the doctor said to himself, *some offense of mine or the children's!* He tried to remember the days and events of his visits but could recall nothing, so he asked Widad if she had noticed any change in Samir, any difference in his behavior. Her answers were so brief and noncommittal that he understood nothing. When he asked if the children might have given any offense that she had not noticed, she denied it vehemently, but showed no desire to discuss it any further.

How could he reassemble and reorganize a life this fractured and lost? What madness had afflicted his friendships and relationships with people to make them incomprehensible, unstable and open to any threat?

So it remained for the whole autumn and the onset of winter. The Sultan came back from his desert excursion a different person: he seemed senile, or convalescent from a long illness. He was almost mute and preferred to be alone, and spent far more time than before in one of the palaces far away from the Ghadir Palace. All this worried the doctor even more than before; he was on the brink of fear, especially since it coincided with Prince Fanar's new visibility: the prince presided over Friday prayers three weeks in a row in the Sultan Khazael Mosque, and made a monthlong tour of the provinces accompanied by a number of his brothers, bodyguards, aides and journalists. What had been said before, about the possibility of Fanar's getting a headquarters and offices in the Khalidia palaces, had become a reality; the English furniture the prince so favored arrived even before the palaces were finished, and was kept temporarily in the Saad Palace. The doctor's efforts to cajole Hammad into telling him about the desert excursion, about what was new and what might be happening soon, all failed miserably and left him more muddled than before.

". . . And you know, Abu Ghazwan," said Hammad, in an effort to avoid telling him anything, "the Sultan loves his brothers the way he loves his children—it's a trait he inherited from his father, and all the people of Mooran know it. Prince Fanar was in ill health, but after God granted him a respite, and restored his health, he became like any other one of the princes."

Zaid al-Heraidi visited the doctor twice in one week, with one aim which he did not hide or disguise as he had done before.

"His Majesty sends greetings, Abu Ghazwan, and requires some of that blue medicine you gave him some years ago."

The doctor tried to learn more, pretending not to know which drug Zaid wanted, though he knew very well what it was—he was the one who had given it that name—but was unable to find out anything specific or reach any conclusion.

"If anything was wrong, Abu Ghazwan," Zaid told him on his second visit, to reassure him, "you'd be the first to know—no one is closer to His Majesty than you are!"

The doctor gave him the medicine he needed, with a clear admonition.

"Please convey my respects and warm regards to His Majesty, and tell him he mustn't exert himself too much!"

The doctor's anxiety eased for a time, but he was not wholly reassured, because he had seen the Sultan only twice in two months, and even then there were others present so that he had no chance to discuss anything really pertinent or personal. He decided sadly, almost despairingly, to let it pass, though he was in agony because he was fighting alone, with no one lending him the kind of support they should have.

"The worse I get, the happier he is," said the doctor as he read Ghazwan's letter that arrived in December. It was a long letter, which read in part:

> . . . joining me in the delegation will be the vice president in charge of sales and three of his aides, plus some of the company's technical and legal advisers. It is essential, Father, that this delegation receive the best possible welcome and attention; the program must include an audience with His Majesty, especially since the vice president in charge of sales speaks fluent Arabic (I'll tell you about him), but in the Moroccan dialect. The company wants him to say something in front of His Majesty the Sultan to describe the close ties between the United States and the Sultanate of Mooran, and the mutual benefits of their cooperation. And, please, see that the delegation is given appointments with the Minister of Defense, Minister of the Interior, Army Commander

and Chief of Intelligence, because there is much they can talk about and cooperate on (and the company president himself, Father, has requested a private meeting with you, in addition to the other meetings and parties). By the way, please do make an extra effort to arrange parties, so that we can show them that what they've read in history books about Arab hospitality is not a thing of the past, but part of the present too. You and I have a lot to discuss, Father, but for right now I need you to do as much as possible to help organize this matter. If you give this your serious attention, the results will be very encouraging; the guys are more than ready to cooperate at the highest level.

In closing the three-page letter, Ghazwan reminded him of the need to book the fifth and sixth floors of the Grand Mooran Hotel, since those floors were all suites rather than rooms, and to provide cars for the delegation. "Lastly, Father—gifts. You know that gifts have a very *nice* effect." He underlined the word *nice,* and went on to say that the delegation could stay no more than one week, so a Moorani negotiating team should be named, "to discuss things and sign contracts." He set the delegation's arrival for December ninth.

The doctor did a double-take when he read the date, then looked at the wall calendar and said worriedly, "We only have six days!" He did not rest during these six days. He requested an urgent meeting with the Sultan, and told Zaid al-Heraidi it was "top priority."

"Your Majesty—have no fear—" The Sultan, who was dressed in a garment as simple as his nightshirt, looked at him and neighed, as he always did when he was happy, and the doctor continued. "What we have been waiting for has finally come."

The Sultan neighed again, and stroked his beard, and said very calmly and affably, "Have a seat, Abu Ghazwan, and let us ask you, first of all, about your health and how you're doing—then we'll discuss other things."

The doctor was shamed by the Sultan's words, as if he were offended that he had not asked about his health, and tried to make amends.

"God curse Satan, who makes us forget, Your Majesty!"

"Don't think of it, Abu Ghazwan."

"And how is Your Majesty's health, sir?"

"God be praised—as you see." He neighed again. "As long as you're our doctor, Abu Ghazwan, and keep sending us the blue and red tablets, and as long as God wills it, everything is fine."

They both smiled; the doctor wished he could laugh like the Sultan. His Majesty looked in excellent health—unlike the last time the doctor had seen him, three weeks before.

"You needed rest, Your Majesty," joked the doctor, "but are you sure the desert air did you good? Maybe you're even more tired!"

"People go to the desert for a day or two. This time it was longer—twenty days! I got a little tired, but one week ago, two weeks—God be praised!" The Sultan did not neglect to ask about the doctor's family. Once again he recalled Umm Ghazwan's cooking, saying, in a longing effort to recall it, "God willing, before too long you'll see me in your house again, Abu Ghazwan!"

"You are most welcome, sir—a great honor, Your Majesty." The doctor laughed meaningfully and added, "And it might be appropriate to make it soon, sir."

"What? Tell me more!"

"Your loyal servant, Ghazwan, sir—you asked him to look into weapons for the army, and from the time he set off he's had no other idea in his head, and has done his research and made his inquiries and now he's produced an extraordinary success!" He paused to smile and look at the Sultan very humbly. "Yesterday, Your Majesty, I received a letter from him. The largest arms manufacturer in America is ready to supply the army of Mooran with the most modern and effective arms—and at low prices—as cheap as dirt!"

"We're not concerned about the prices, Abu Ghazwan—what concerns us is that Mooran should have the best and strongest army anywhere—after that everything will fall into place."

"Exactly, Your Majesty, that's the important thing. With Almighty God's help, Ghazwan has got the most important company—in a few days you'll see for yourself!"

The Sultan nodded his head happily several times.

"I have a favor to ask, Your Majesty," said the doctor cautiously.

"Granted!"

"The company directors have asked to have an audience with Your Majesty during their visit to Mooran, because there are several things they need to bring up with you personally." He added, with a dry and cracked laugh, "I have sent several letters to Ghazwan, Your Majesty, to remind him of some of the proposals from Mooran, and the need for him to follow them up scrupulously, and yesterday, only yesterday, I received his letter confirming everything. They will all be coming on the ninth, for a week." He assumed a different tone. "In my opinion, Your Majesty, you should receive them on the second to last day of their visit—a courtesy call, to show how strong and deep relations are between the Sultanate and the United States. Such a reception would strengthen the company and support it, should there be any parties within the American government that would oppose such a large and significant arms deal with the Sultanate."

"Shall I give a speech?"

"Not at all, Your Majesty. You can ask the directors about their health, about how they are enjoying their visit, and what they've seen in Mooran, that's all."

Very slyly, the doctor succeeded in winning the Sultan's consent to receive the delegation, though he wished circumstances had been more favorable; he might have persuaded the Sultan to invite the delegation to a luncheon or dinner party or to accompany some of the princes on a hunting trip, and spend a day and night in the desert. That was the sort of thing the Americans loved—he had seen that and put it to the test during his stay in Harran, but he did not dare to make any such request now.

He had one card left to play, if necessary, to get one more concession out of the Sultan: the "biography." He had to set a time to receive Samir so that the book could then get under way. He brought it up in an inspired moment, when the Sultan had returned to the subject of the blue medicine.

"Your Majesty, there are all kinds of things that can strengthen a man." He laughed. "Strength, Your Majesty, has nothing to do with age or medicines. Strength is in confidence."

The Sultan nodded, though the doctor did not know whether the nod indicated agreement or curiosity.

"Do you remember, Your Majesty, that I told Your Majesty some years ago that you were a symbol, an example for this nation, and people look upon this symbol with great respect and love; and yet many people do not know as much as they should about Your Majesty."

The Sultan smiled but said nothing.

"Now that the time is right, all I ask of you, Your Majesty, is that you fix an appointment or two for us to complete the information we'll need to organize in the book that will be published about Your Majesty, and for you to tell us of any ideas or statements you wish to appear in the book."

The Sultan was not sure whether the doctor was asking him a question or making a specific demand, or whether he was speaking about the project he had brought up months before. He tried to avoid giving an answer.

"Everything in its own good time, Abu Ghazwan."

"The prompt giver gives twice, Your Majesty."

"Yes, indeed, Abu Ghazwan."

"May I expect that you will fix an appointment, or two, so that we may complete our information?"

"Whatever you say, Abu Ghazwan."

"We'll begin one month from now, Your Majesty."

"God willing."

76

THE SULTAN'S RECEPTION FOR THE AMERI-
cans was a cordial but splendid affair: it
was the crowning of an important long-
term accord between the United States and the Sultanate of
Mooran. Ghazwan, to the admiration of most, had played a prominent role in getting it signed, and the Sultan was quick to allude to
Ghazwan's role during the reception. What also caught people's attention was the special treatment the Sultan gave to three of the
delegation: the group leader, his Arabic-speaking aide, and Ghazwan. Not only did he talk to them warmly and at length, with Ghazwan interpreting between His Majesty and the group leader; he
gave them as gifts swords that were even more elegant and expensive than those the others received. The Sultan was clearly dazzled
by Ghazwan, and made Zaid al-Hureidi repeat, so that everyone
present might hear, the words he had spoken to the doctor: "Now
you may be sure, Abu Ghazwan, that none is dearer to us than you
are—as you can see!"

The doctor, deeply affected, glowed as he replied, "God give you long life, God keep you, for without you we are nothing!"

The doctor had himself played a major role in preparing for the delegation's arrival and this happy conclusion to the visit, and Ghazwan's brilliance had been a decisive factor at every stage. His contacts and his use of his own and his father's friends had been crucial to the successful result, and he'd not forgotten to emphasize to the company, from early on, the necessity of bringing gifts. Upon his arrival, he spent two hours with his father deciding how the gifts would be distributed, to avoid any blunder. Even Prince Fanar received a gift: several parchment pages from a fourteenth-century Koran, bought in London for this purpose. The Sultan was given many gifts, among them several firearms with the emblem of the Sultanate and his name engraved on them, and some battlefield binoculars to use while hunting. Most of the other gifts were sidearms and hunting rifles, though the company had also brought four gray Scottish falcons.

The doctor was presented with some valuable golden pens; Ghazwan had kept this surprise from his father until the last minute, and when the doctor opened his gift he looked at his son tenderly, and when he embraced him he could not hold back the two tears that rolled down his cheeks. This gesture of Ghazwan's toward his father came about after their talks during the short visit at the summer's end, when the doctor mentioned his hope for the leisure, some years hence, to write his memoirs. He referred in passing to his needs for that undertaking: among other things, the right atmosphere, state of mind and the right tools—by which, he explained, he meant pens and paper.

The doctor longed for Ghazwan to remain for a few days after the delegation had left, but he did not dare to discuss it, since he would not be able to bear a refusal. He had his wife bring it up, and Widad, who was in a better state of mind, held nothing back in her effort to persuade him, but Ghazwan was unbending in his resistance to pressure.

"Mother, you have to accept it," he told her. "If I linger one day later than the delegation, they'll get ideas—they'll think I'm up to something behind their backs. And that will ruin everything." In order to show self-denial and to console his parents, he had agreed to spend most of his evenings at home and to sleep there, "even though I have a hotel room reserved."

On the nights Ghazwan stayed at home, which lasted until the early hours and were usually confined to him and his father once his mother withdrew, "since I'm sleepy, and you two never stop talking," the two discussed many things. The doctor discovered that the studies in America had benefited Ghazwan and changed him greatly. Ghazwan told him that in the modern age, and especially in recent years, huge changes had taken place in political thinking and international relations; Mooran was vitally important to the United States and the West in general because of its strategic location, oil wealth and regional role, so that its fate was more likely to be decided outside of Mooran than within. "All this business about the Chamber of Commerce, Father, or whether or not So-and-so and What's-his-name aren't getting along, is meaningless." He insisted that the interests of the region, since they affected the future of the world, could not be left in the hands of a few sheikhs, princes and bedouin, "because they're much too serious, too important for that—just as war, any war, is too important to be left to generals, as one philosopher has said."

The doctor shivered several times, as if chasing sleep from his eyelids, as he listened to his son; he was shocked by what he heard. He had wanted to discuss the Square Theory and his thoughts and conclusions about it, but found that Ghazwan thought differently than he did, *and perhaps doesn't realize man's hidden and profound motives*—that was why, when he tried to remember some of the theories that had failed to explain human behavior, he could not recall them. *But this America is a miracle—how else has it been able to gain control over the world?*

The doctor was muddled and disturbed, for what he heard did not fully convince him, but the proof he saw left him no room for doubt. What Ghazwan quoted from that philosopher, about war being too serious and important to be left to military people, filled him with uncertainty—what his son was saying was mere words learned in a schoolroom, repeated by some madman who fancied himself a philosopher—otherwise who decided to pursue a war, who prosecuted a war and decided its outcome?

Most of their discussions began from a specific point but

branched out and digressed, and they generally forgot their starting point or what they had wanted from it, and the doctor forgot
that unnamed philosopher, but he did not forget the daily problems and difficulties that beset him. He wanted to understand
Mooran's future so that he would know how to act, what actions to
take, but Ghazwan insisted ever more vehemently that taking the
decision had an inverse effect on the relationship between home
and abroad: the more important any country became, the less able
it was to determine its own policies, and so his father need not
bother himself with what he considered to be problems. The doctor pretended to concede these points to his son, and tried to recall
what he had been thinking at his age, what ideas had possessed
him, how he'd regarded life and people. He recalled how he had
changed from year to year, how experience and friends had matured him—and how those experiences and friends not only did
not conform to what he had been taught in college, but contradicted it outright. He said to himself, trying to reach a balance, *The
little scamp has a brilliant mind, a great mind—he'll make a masterful
politician, but only after life refines and trains him.*

"Anyway, Father," joked Ghazwan, seeing that his father was not
convinced by what he said, "the important thing is that this deal
should go through—it will be a good start. It will open endless
doors to us, because right now, in this part of the world, arms are
the most important thing."

The doctor smiled with his son, assured that all the effort he had
put into raising him was bearing fruit, and that yet far greater
things were in store.

The next night, when Samir joined them for some of their talk,
they were all radiantly content, but their conversation took a different turn: the doctor talked about his memoirs, saying he had kept
a diary since an early age—"of major events, of course, not daily
goings-on." He said these diaries would help him when he wrote
his memoirs, "which will be a record of fifty years of the region's
history." Samir lauded this habit of the doctor's and said that he
expected the memoirs to be of monumental importance. Ghazwan
thought differently but laughed.

"Do you remember the thousand dollars, Father?"

"The thousand dollars?"

"That you gave me the day I left."

"Of course, how could I not remember?"

"I turned it into twenty-five thousand in these few years!"

Widad whistled like a bird at her son's words; she was having a wonderful time. She said, like a little girl, "Oh, my baby, you're rich!" The doctor was flabbergasted. "You mean it multiplied twenty-five times?" he gasped.

Ghazwan explained in great detail how he had invested the sum, how the banks in the "States" helped investors and offered opportunities to reinvest their money; he had transferred the money from one investment to another until it reached that amount, and he concluded with a smile, "If a man knows how to invest his money and how to work, he can become a millionaire!"

"It's fantastic," said Samir, shaking his head.

"You're wasting your time and energy, writing memoirs, playing politics and these thousand other things," Ghazwan told Samir amicably, though he really intended these words for his father, almost chidingly. That was when the doctor knew that his son would surpass him in intelligence and great deeds; that Ghazwan would accomplish some of the things he had been unable to do. He said in self-defense, "Things are different with us here—and the world is changing!"

On the second to last day of the visit, the doctor gave the delegation a sumptuous banquet at the Rabia Hotel; it was Ghazwan's idea: "The guys aren't used to lamb and rice every day, for one thing, and for another they need to see you, Father, as someone different from the Mooranis. Lastly, a dinner in a public place, a hotel, isn't hidden from anyone." The doctor liked the idea, though it was a little uncommon in Mooran, and he considered wearing the clothes he'd worn before settling in Mooran. He also thought of giving a speech of welcome in English, but his English was not very good and they might laugh, which would make him think badly of them; if he gave them a speech in German, they might get the wrong idea. He thought long and hard over whom to invite; he wanted this occasion to be a devastating riposte to his enemies and detractors, and so he immediately and unhesitatingly excluded two names: al-Ghamdi, because he did not accept him as the head of the Chamber of Commerce, and Said, because he wanted everyone to know he would have nothing more to do with Said. He had invited Rezaie before and would invite him again now: perhaps this banquet would succeed in splitting the Chamber of Commerce or cultivating a new power within it. The doctor considered a great many names, discarding some and including others, then checked it again, until he had a suitable guest list, *because hospitality isn't a matter of numbers or grandeur or expense, but of good manners and good cheer and a certain civilized touch, especially with a bunch like this.*

The doctor and Ghazwan were like newlyweds as they received the guests at the main banquet hall, and at the cocktail party during the forty-five minutes before dinner, at which the guests chatted and got to know one another. Ghazwan and the deputy head of the delegation, who spoke such good Arabic, were instrumental in introducing the guests and interpreting . The doctor was like the father of the bride, spreading hospitality and cheer equally among all, though he chatted with the leader of the delegation and his aide longer than with the others and mentioned, without knowing how it occurred to him, that he was currently writing a book about the history of Mooran. This detail caught the attention of the aide, who showed great interest. All the guests, especially the Americans, were delighted with the doctor's extemporaneous speech, which included a joke. Ghazwan translated it, speaking in the same cadences as his father, which the guests noticed and which deeply impressed them.

The doctor's party was the talk of Mooran for some time, and the echoes reached the Ghadir Palace, especially since a number of princes and courtiers had attended. What gave it such great and long-lasting interest were the numerous incidents during and after it: during cocktails, though no one knew how, anti-American leaflets opposing the arms deal were put by all the plates in the main banquet hall. Each leaflet was folded carefully and placed neatly under the plate, so that most guests did not notice it at first, but one of the guests opened the leaflet and read the first few lines, grew frightened and turned to see more leaflets under the plates all around him. There was an effort to collect the leaflets after they were noticed, which was in vain because those who had not seen the leaflets now noticed them, and those who had not kept them now wanted them, which caused some temporary embarrassment for the doctor, but he told a joke to dispel their surprise and bewilderment, and the matter passed.

The second thing that caused some complication later, after the banquet, was Saleh al-Rushdan and his drum. The steady beat of his drumming reached the guests as they dined, and when one of the Americans asked what it was all about and why it was so loud, Ghazwan was confused and did not know how to answer. But he translated the question for his father, who looked all around quickly, as if for a reason, then smiled and said, "It's a Moorani wedding!" As soon as Ghazwan translated, the doctor's smile became a laugh and he added, "In our weddings the drum is the leader—the master!"

"But today isn't Thursday, Doctor!" al-Zaubaii contradicted him in a surprised tone.

"Every day is Thursday in Mooran now, Abu Omran—thanks to His Beloved Majesty!" replied the doctor, as pleased with himself as a rooster after a rain shower, and when this exchange was translated for the Americans they looked delighted, and so did everyone else. When the doctor said his good-byes to the guests at the hotel's outer gate, Saleh's voice and the beat of his drum were clearly audible.

"Spread the news!/Tell the killer he's going to be killed/Tell the thief he's going to be poor!"

He chanted these words and beat his drum, then paddled the drum harder, turned and sang: "Our black day was the day you came and we saw you/Our holiday is the day you show us your backs!"

He pointed to the doctor and laughed as he chanted, and after repeating the second verse mockingly he sang:

"You oppressed, you who may/Rue this place and rue this day."

He repeated this verse and then seemed mocking and sorrowful at the same time, and his tone of voice turned sharp.

"Those that flew may still fly,/But all will shortly fall and die."

The doctor was clearly disconcerted by the words and curses he heard, and tried to remove from his sight and hearing and from the sight of the others this man who had come to ruin everything. The Moorani guests, who knew Saleh al-Rushdan, or who had seen him during some Ramadan past or on one of the two big feast days, beating his drum to honor the holiday, had never dreamed that he knew curses like those he was using now, or felt the bitter sarcasm that dripped from his words. They were even more shocked by his drumming at this time of the year and this time of day. When he stopped, some of the guests went over to chat and joke with him, and he had a ready answer for their questions why he had chosen this place and this time.

"You have to tell the blind man that he's blind, so that he knows and everyone else knows," he said, pointing to the doctor. "And that tyrant doesn't see his own hump, only other people's humps, but we have to tell how things are."

The doctor wished none of this had happened, and that Hammad had been present; Hammad would have known what to do, how to curb this mischief, these little insults that were, perhaps, Said's doing, to ruin his banquet and remind him that he was still around and capable of revenge. And he wished he had given this banquet at his house. He sank in the backseat of his car after Ghazwan led the delegation back, and the doctor told himself that the envious bastard was catching up with him, and that he would take his revenge against that infidel Said—this was all his doing. He thought back over the evening's events: how it had begun, what he had said and how he'd said it, and the others, how they'd reacted. His thoughts revolved around one key matter: the reaction of the Americans.

77

"SALEH ISN'T RIGHT IN THE HEAD," IS WHAT Hammad said when he heard what had happened at the doctor's banquet. He shook his head as he considered the people who had been there and the likely explanations and added, as if to himself, "That was no Ramadan or feast day drumming—nothing godly about it."

When his assistant suggested that Saleh should be arrested and punished, Hammad said ironically, "No—leave him alone. It makes no difference. Let him drum, and the sound will always tell us where to find him, and that's what we want."

Hammad's response to what had happened was calm, almost cool and unconcerned. Everyone who had been expecting to see Saleh harshly punished was surprised to see him strolling haughtily through the streets, fearlessly repeating for anyone who asked him the words he had pronounced at the Rabia Hotel, right in the doctor's face.

"You should have been there, Abu Rashed," the doctor scolded Hammad. "For one thing, everyone was asking for you, and you could have prevented that scandal from happening!"

Hammad smiled and tried to get by with only this as his response, but the doctor's sharp and inquiring looks compelled him to speak.

"You know how busy we are, Abu Ghazwan, and anyway I don't go to most parties—and that's no recent thing. I never have."

"And this scandal—who do you think could be behind it?"

"God knows, Abu Ghazwan."

"What's your guess?"

"I don't know."

"Could it be the Chamber of Commerce?" He wanted to say Said, but instead used this generalization.

"The Chamber of Commerce?" repeated Hammad incredulously.

"That's what I thought, because I purposely didn't invite any of them after what went on in the last elections."

"Trust in God, man, they're all fine fellows. I don't think any one of them would ever dare think of something like this."

"And that beggar who was drumming and raving at the gate—who put him up to it? Who gave him a few coins and told him, 'Drum and curse and wake the dead'?"

"He's feebleminded, Abu Ghazwan—no one listens to him!"

"You must arrest him and make him talk—he's the end of the chain, but there are lots of other links."

"I don't want to turn this fool into a hero and martyr, I want to get the people who are behind him."

"But if you arrest him, you'll find out who they are."

"Never fear, Abu Ghazwan, we'll find out."

That was all they said on that subject, but it was not the end of the affair. The doctor, who was profoundly uneasy that evening and for several days that followed, and who was positive that Said was behind the incident, now felt less inclined to think Said had acted alone. The thoughts that began to fill his head, and the suspicions that tempted him, made him sure that the matter was far more serious than that. Said might oppose him personally and speak against him, but what had happened exceeded all boundaries—it went far beyond a mere feud or rivalry between two men. Hammad, who had always been ready to discuss anything with the doctor before, or at least to listen to him, was immersed in new problems, and they hardly saw each other anymore. Hammad had a new telephone number that was given only to a very few people, and the doctor was not one of them, so they spoke rarely. Polite Abdelmawla was even more polite when he found the doctor on the other end of the line, telling him that Abu Rashed was not in or had left town just a few hours before. The doctor's anger mounted; and so did his fear. He did not know what to do or how to respond to this neglect, this disregard.

Furthermore, he was living with the apprehension of hidden, evil powers pursuing him, aiming, perhaps, to kill him, without his ever finding out who the powers were and who was behind them. Still, he was not about to mention his fears to a soul; he lacked the courage and had no proof. He regretted not taking a gun when they were giving out the gifts—*Guns give a man entertainment and security both*—but decided, after all, that the question was too serious for him to face alone with a gun: it was a huge conspiracy, so cunning and clever that it constantly reshaped itself, taking on endless new faces and aspects. Perhaps even Said was only the instrument of someone else.

Hammad's worries were of another kind. From the time Saleh had stood at the gate of the Rabia Hotel, Mooran—which Hammad wanted to be as tranquil as a tomb—seemed to him a city he did not know, a place he had never lived in, a mocker, an impostor among cities. Worse, it seemed to him dangerous. He hid his anger, because Saleh was too paltry an enemy; not only that, he wanted to know who was behind those leaflets, who had distributed them and why. Saleh was a mere decoy; he would use him to hunt the others. He would let him go where he pleased; he would not hinder him or allow anyone else to hinder him, but would watch him from afar, and when he was able to put a hand on the enemy he would crush him unmercifully, to teach Mooran a lesson for years and years.

Since this was his plan, he was in no hurry. *When the prey feels secure and ignores the danger, the hunt is easier. A fool doesn't hunt or let others hunt,* he said to himself. Everyone told him that Saleh was still marching through the markets, cursing and speechifying, as if the night at the Rabia had killed the fear in his heart, which made Hammad laugh. "My friends," he said softly, "let Ibn Rushdan be. It's enough that God has deprived him of comfort." When they told him that he held nothing back, that he spared no one, he said, "Let him spit out whatever he has to say—if he doesn't, we'll have no trap and no bird."

A month passed, then another. Hammad did nothing, and his voice was not heard. The doctor's fears of the plots against him, of daily attempts on his life, had eased somewhat; he felt a little safer and had regained some of his confidence. Samir had finished reading the books on the history and geography of Mooran after postponing reading them time and again, always with the excuse that Muti had given him urgent business to attend to. And, too, the Sultan had decided to make a tour around the Sultanate, just as he had when first ascending the throne, and he wanted the doctor and Muti to be included in his entourage. The doctor thought about it and made Samir go along as well.

The tour was, in a way, a response to Prince Fanar's tour: the Sultan's expression of how much he cared for his people. The doctor thought the visit ideal for achieving a number of goals: Samir might have chance meetings with people who could help to shape the biography, *since artists need inspiring sights, and the book will be, basically, a work of art,* as the doctor said to himself. And he himself might at last see the new factors at work since Prince Fanar's arrival and the desert excursion. That excursion still troubled him as much as ever, especially since the Rabia conspiracy, as he now called that night, seemed to him bizarre, perhaps even unfathomable. While certain things may have escaped him for some reason or another, surely the Sultan must have heard about them. *Nothing, small or large, can be kept from him, and from one conversation to the next I will surely get something; as for me, perhaps they're just being cautious, or perhaps they don't want to alarm me unnecessarily.* The last major thing on his mind was to follow through on Ghazwan's admonition, repeated dozens of times, that the Sultan should send, every now and then, letters of inquiry about the arms deals, delivery dates, and, of course, cost overruns; this would enhance Ghazwan's standing in the company and help him to conclude future deals, with the Sultanate and other countries as well. The doctor expected, on this tour, numerous opportunities to press the demands that Ghazwan had outlined.

The doctor could not have arrived at these convictions without Widad; after the depression and solitude that had dogged her since her arrival, she seemed, by late winter, so energetic and happy that the doctor was reminded of his youth and the early days of their marriage. Before, she had stayed away from him and avoided her "duties," which he had ascribed to illness and over-work, but now she was a new woman: she welcomed him home impatiently and pampered him, showing all the love that had been hidden for months, even years. And then there was her usual joy and playful nagging; and though he had accepted these things with caution, thinking them perhaps a passing fad or fit on Widad's part, his confidence in himself and everything around him was en-hanced when they lasted and flourished. He began to think that the idea of a conspiracy may have been an illusion brought on by his isolation and loneliness, or his failure to understand others. When he observed his surroundings he saw that at this time of the year nature, according to the Square Theory, was changing and coming alive, firing the vitality of plants, animals and men alike.

Full of excitement and desire, the doctor reveled, bodily and spiritually, in Widad's new attitude. And Samir told him that he expected to complete the biography shortly. "Sir, if I'm feeling rested, and have the materials to work from, and the will, I can write it in record time."

Widad wanted the doctor to travel, to get out of her sight; the challenge to herself prevented her from sleeping most nights. She wanted to test her powers, to discover whether or not she was still strong and capable enough to make decisions, give orders and take revenge, as she always had been. She had to accept this challenge and triumph, without fear or hesitation.

And Samir? He was a different person now, for while he re-turned to Mooran the same person he had been before his trip, Widad's aversion, or more precisely her cruelty, rendered him un-able to know how to act. For a certain time he was cut off from the doctor, kept busy with all the business that had mounted over the summer, and given urgent tasks to complete, all related to the pub-lication of a new newspaper, but he also felt that he could not be more disregarded than this. Without a great deal of intelligence, and because he knew the doctor's weak points, he had been able to get back to the biography, *The Eagle of Mooran.*

And Salma? She returned from the summer sojourn dreamy and full of longing, but Mooran deserted her again, besieging her with the terrors of her mother's stories, which did nothing to relieve her caution or wariness of men, how they were wolves who spared nothing and no one—especially young girls! When Widad spoke to Salma she saw the phantom of Samir lurking, waiting to ravish and destroy her; it was always Samir she was referring to. When he'd had enough of her, he looked around him and saw only Salma. Would she let him ravish her? Would she offer her to him? She was ready to do anything only to get rid of him.

When the Sultan's tour was fixed, with the doctor and Samir to accompany him, Widad saw it as the most opportune time to win back "this traitor, this coward" who had tried to escape from her. She did not know why a vision of the Sultan shimmered in her imagination: his immense size, his neighing laugh, his glances at her that she could not explain. *There are two things about Mooran no one can understand,* she said to herself, *its politics and its men.* She recalled the state of mind that had possessed the doctor over these past months, and his vague talk of conspiracies and the Sultan's isolation, and about the book he was writing with Samir, but she understood none of it.

78

S HAMRAN, WHO HAD NOT SPOKEN TO SALEH AL-
Rushdan in years, did not lose a minute in
embracing him warmly, in front of the crowd
at the Zaidan Coffeehouse, when he heard what had happened
that night at the Rabia Hotel. He did it sincerely, as if apologizing
for the past and blaming himself for being so cold and indifferent
toward him. Saleh, too, was affected and could not look at the faces
of the men around him. He appeared ashamed and embarrassed,
even though ever since that night he had marched haughtily
through the streets of Mooran, as if avenging everyone.

The two men reminisced, and the others with them, about the
Mooran of long ago: how peaceable and contented it had been;
how people earned their livelihoods despite life's hardships. They
had always found the time to talk, to listen to odes, and, some
nights, to sing and dance. That was life then, and they had been
happy. Since the coming of the Americans and the discovery of oil,

the life and people had changed, had turned upside down. Even money meant less now than it had then. The foreigners, who now outnumbered Mooran's own citizens, were a mixed rabble; they came and went and no one cared, and others came to stay. Even those would have been tolerable if they'd been real people, but they weren't. They came to steal, to rule over others and to exploit them, and they were insatiable.

As they conversed in this way, the image of the doctor was not far from any of their minds; for what Saleh had done, word of which had traveled through Mooran with the speed of light, was thought to be appropriate, whether the palace liked it or not, and many of them thought that the message Saleh had conveyed, which Mooran had long felt, had to be understood, or they would do what he had done. Some said that what Ibn al-Rushdan had done would change nothing and would not prevent the doctor and his ilk from buying up land and putting up buildings, whether the people liked it or not; they went further and said that the life we were living now was no better than that to come, "for blessings lie in the future."

Shamran listened, reminisced, and reminded others. Every few moments he gazed at the man before him: how time had altered and wearied him, but not humbled him. Saleh had never lost his obstinate, almost mischievous look; no, it was even clearer and stronger now. In the Souq al-Halal he had pretended to more anger than he actually felt; he knew how to forgive or forget most of the injuries people had done him, and now he had become a total stranger to fear—he was readier than ever to do anything.

Hammad's face appeared to Shamran. He leaned over to Saleh and whispered in his ear.

"From today on, Saleh, your enemy isn't that scoundrel—you gave him what he deserved and then some. Now take a good look at Ibn Mutawa. You might ignore him, but he's not ignoring you."

"Who cares!"

"Tie up the fox with a lion's rope—you can't be too careful, Saleh."

"All we have is our happiness, Abu Nimr."

"Treachery is worse than the cold of winter."

"By God, Brother, all I have is my life and my cloak, Abu Nimr."

Mooran sank into its cares and forgot yesterday's cares. The night at the Rabia faded from memory. The doctor came home robust from his tour with the Sultan, stronger than before, his picture in all the newspapers and magazines: beside the Sultan, chatting with him, whispering in his ear. Nimr was one of the few who actually read the newspapers and magazines, so he was the one who told everyone else in the Zaidan Coffeehouse and the market what was going on. The rest listened and shook their heads, and it all ended in silence or a curse word from Saleh, if he was present, or a word and expressive gesture from Shamran.

"After it rains, you remember the lightning that came first—the thunder and rain come after," said Shamran to Nimr one day.

Nimr did not know what his father was getting at, and waited for him to go on.

"That night at the Rabia was the lightning. The thunder and rain are coming, or upon us. Today or soon we have to be on our guard!"

"Why are you telling me this, Father?"

"Wolves never sleep, my boy."

Shamran explained to his son that Hammad would never overlook or forgive what had happened at the Rabia; they would have to be very careful, very wary. Hammad would use anything as a pretext, any flimsy excuse, any false slander, to take his revenge. Nimr understood and said, "Father, they've killed and robbed us before—aren't you afraid?"

"Fear, my boy, died in my heart long ago, but now I smell rain—and the rain will come."

This is Shamran's doing, is what Hammad said to himself. *Shamran and Saleh are one, and the whole market knows it.*

His thoughts and suppositions churned on. Even his Uncle Shaddad came under suspicion, but Shaddad was too busy with his horses, and if he wanted to quarrel with the doctor he would have done it long ago and in person. And what Saleh had done was not important: *Saleh's brain is a shriveled thing—anyone can tell him, "Take these coins, go drumming and chanting," and that's that.* What bothered him were the leaflets. Who had printed them? Where? And was it just a matter of leaflets? That's all it might be today, but no one knew what tomorrow might bring. And him—where had he been

through all this? Why had he not known before? His lazy, chattering men had said that it was a wedding in Mooran, that the people
didn't know how they had spent the money they'd been given, that
they'd done nothing but call upon His Majesty. Those who had
cursed, who had left nothing evil unsaid in the leaflet—who and
where were they? Even the Americans knew about it while he, a
native of Mooran, who had spent millions here and everywhere . . .
how was it that he did not know?

An apparition of Nimr the Newspaper passed in front of his
mind's eye. *Ibn Shamran just has a big mouth—I don't think this looks
like his work,* he said to himself. Nevertheless, he planted a rival
scribe named Qahtani near the Passport Office. *Perhaps professional
jealousy will help Nimr to let us hear what's on his mind.* Weeks passed,
but instead of becoming enemies, Nimr and his rival became
friends, and not only that, when people came to Nimr asking him
to write their petitions or to follow up their transactions, he sent
them over to Qahtani, "so he can make a living and stay in business."

The reports that reached Hammad informed him that "Nimr
knows nothing that hasn't appeared in the newspapers."

When Hammad asked Said if he knew or had heard what had
happened in the Rabia Hotel, and who might be "behind that
old madman Saleh al-Rushdan," Said laughed heartily and answered, "I heard—and I know, Abu Rashed." He laughed again
and went on in a different tone: "If you want my opinion, the doctor himself is behind the whole thing. He's the one who gave
that drummer some coins and told him, 'Come on and entertain
the group!'"

"Fear God, my man—you aren't serious!"

"The doctor—and I know him as well as I know myself—loves
fame, even if it comes on a shaft."

"Forget that, man."

"Fine, Abu Rashed, time goes on, and we'll see."

"And the leaflets?"

"Those? Ah, that's another story."

Hammad neglected no one and no place, even what Said had
told him, which he considered only half serious, without thinking
it over again, but he got no closer to any conclusion or ray of light.
There was only Saleh, whom he nevertheless let alone. "It's better

to give him more rope; we'll soon pull him in." He planted spies in the Zaidan Coffeehouse and near the Passport Office, and assigned two men to follow Saleh like his shadow, without Saleh's ever noticing. Not content with that, he planted a beggar near Saleh's house, whom Saleh's small children often gave whole loaves of bread.

At one point Hammad thought that what had happened was only a trick of one of the Rabia Hotel guests, some ambitious, competitive foreign guest who wanted, perhaps, for Ghazwan somehow to lose face in front of the Americans, so he did what he had done. This explanation reassured him for a time, but it did not eliminate the fear from his heart. He saw himself as responsible not only for the security of Mooran; he was preparing himself to be one of the few men responsible for the security of the whole region, from coast to coast, especially since the Sultanate had bestowed its wealth on so many, made them a part of its institutions or formidable commercial and financial interests, and since ties of friendship bound Hammad himself to so many of the other intelligence chiefs in the region.

He felt threatened, even insulted. If even the most local troubles eluded him and he had no idea who was behind them, then someone was deceiving him, or at least was incompetent. He charged at his Agency like a bull, reorganizing and expanding it, reshuffling many of the positions and creating new departments. He reached an agreement with Mr. Andrews to have a number of Americans come to Mooran, and he worked closely with them, studying certain options and strategies. At the same time, he saw no one and took no calls. He changed his home and office telephone numbers. No one knew whether he was in Mooran or abroad. The doctor pursued him day and night and finally caught him. He asked Hammad whether he had "caught the perpetrators, because the problem is far more serious than you think, Abu Rashed. It isn't just Dr. Mahmilji's problem or someone else's or any individual's. It's a plot to bring down the government, to tear it up by the roots. As I told you: arrest that scoundrel and everything will come out."

Hammad listened on the telephone to what the doctor said and shook his head, not knowing how to respond. Their conversation ended with Hammad's promise to take all necessary measures with appropriate speed, and to contact him later on, but he never took any action or called the doctor back.

Hammad had been scheduled to accompany the Sultan's tour, on which the doctor hoped to solve all the problems deviling him, most particularly to discover "the dimensions of the conspiracy," but Hammad excused himself the day before the departure "for urgent reasons," and assigned his deputy to go along, saying that he'd catch up with it as soon as he could. His absence disappointed the doctor, who had much to accomplish during the tour, but who nevertheless overlooked this point and put it out of his mind until he arrived in Harran, when he suggested to the Sultan that they say their afternoon prayers in the Sultan Khazael Mosque. He was proud to accompany the monarch to the mosque he had helped to build, and he wanted to let everyone know it, especially Hammad, who had never sufficiently acknowledged his generosity.

When the Sultan returned to the capital to boisterous celebrations, Mooran truly looked like a city celebrating a wedding, much to the surprise of the doctor, the tour party and the Sultan himself. It had all been arranged by Hammad, for one of the stipulations of the recently arrived American team, one among many, was that all the people sense, very palpably, the presence of the state, especially the Sultan, to fill their hearts with contentment and fear at the same time.

Four miles from Wadi Riha, in a motorcade of hundreds of cars, most of them the same color, the Sultan entered Mooran after the lavish reception accorded him on the outskirts of the capital, in which many of the princes and high officials participated and during which dozens, even hundreds of sheep and camels were slaughtered. Only Hammad did not take part in this celebration; he remained holed up in his spacious office on the third floor of the new building the Intelligence and Security Agency had occupied several months earlier. He stayed there to keep an eye on everything and protect everyone, and when the motorcade passed by, he looked out the window without opening it and nodded several times, smiling inscrutably.

Shamran al-Oteibi glanced at the end of the motorcade as he came out of the Zaidan Coffeehouse, and stopped. He watched the cars pass by slowly, almost at a crawl. He tried to see if he could recognize anyone in any of the cars but could not. He said to himself: *The shrouds of the dead have been white since Noah's day, but these bastards, these worthless cheats, their shrouds are as black as their faces.* A man who had been standing on the street corner now approached him and indicated, with a silent movement of his head, for Shamran to move on. Shamran moved off slowly and said, though he did not know whether or not the man heard, "Others have lasted, but not these."

79

ITH THE SULTAN'S HOMECOMING, THE doctor seemed to have got what he wanted, and perhaps even more: everyone had noticed the Sultan's friendliness toward him, from the beginning of the tour, which filled the doctor with added importance and unlimited confidence; this confidence, in turn, helped him to realize other hopes. Samir told him that the biography was "in his pocket." After several sessions in which the doctor directed the discussion, Samir jotted down a great many thoughts and insights, like sketches—*croquis,* he said—or a backbone for the structure he would erect as soon as he got back to Mooran.

This achievement, together with the cheerful air of the whole tour, encouraged the doctor to think of new issues, such as the general political situation in the Sultanate, especially since the Sultan, who only recently had seemed careworn and deeply uneasy, now saw his brother's return as his salvation, for Fanar was highly capable, and what had bothered Khazael before was Fanar's aloofness, his refusal to help out. Now that he was responsive and willing and had shed his obduracy, their cooperation would make Mooran immensely powerful; the Sultan alluded in passing to Fanar's poor health, and, by extension, to the likelihood of his having to travel to resume treatment, and that would leave open the possibility of a new crown prince. The Sultan did not want to expand on this particular point; the succession was both a complex and constantly postponed issue.

The other point on which the doctor wanted to see some definitive action was arms. "The Sultanate cannot be at the mercy of others and their threats; it must rely on one dependable source, and obtain long-term contracts, for ten or twenty years, instead of having several different sources for arms, at the mercy of importers we can't rely on, and who, every day, say something different than the day before. That's not all—the Sultanate should review its past orders, and even demand delivery dates—conditions in the region demand it." The Sultan, who had no need of all these reasons and rhetoric to be convinced, was ready to agree, and ended the discussion on the subject.

"When we are safely back in Mooran, Abu Ghazwan," he said, "in our first meeting with the Minister of Defense, you only have to remind me, and, God willing, we will do just as you suggest."

The Sultan began to talk about his impressions of Ghazwan: how different he was from long ago, how promising were the signs of his intelligence and acumen—"and he speaks American like a native." He also pointed out that the Sultanate had a pressing need for such knowledgeable young men. "He must return to Mooran soon; we prefer to have him by our side, giving us advice and assistance, than to have him far away."

The doctor did not know how to thank the Sultan or how to express his gratitude. He felt full of pride and glory: his labors had not been in vain. The silent sacrifices for which he expected nothing in return now bore their fruit, before even he had expected.

Nor did the Sultan forget to ask about the family. He did not name anyone in particular, but he seemed seriously interested to know how they were. The doctor answered briefly and a little timidly, as was customary in Mooran, feeling more than ever before that the friendship the Sultan offered him was greater and more copious than what he offered any other subject.

In view of this milieu, the doctor did not see the necessity of asking the Sultan about the "Rabia plot." He did not want to disturb or disquiet him with details he might not have heard, "because it was, in retrospect, the work of jealous people and madmen." When he asked Hammad's deputy, after carefully but indirectly bringing the conversation around to it, he received a very clipped answer.

"I was in the United States then—I don't know anything about it."

The doctor changed the subject, *because great men don't occupy themselves with idle chatter.*

On the final day of the visit to Harran, the doctor spoke before the Sultan and others on one of his favorite subjects: Harran and how it had been the day he arrived there in a truck, when there had been only one small hotel and a few shops, and how it was now. He spoke not only of his role in founding and developing Harran, but of its history. He said he was considering writing a book about "this grand city with its tall, modern buildings, its well-planned and modern streets, and its hospitals that resemble the hospitals of Houston." What he needed most of all for that book, he said, were photographs. Photography had been a hobby of his since his student days in Germany and Austria, and some of the recent photographs he had taken could truly speak. It suddenly occurred to him that the best title for this would be: *A City Speaks.*

I will call this book A City Speaks, he concluded, *or* A City Speaks of Itself.

The Sultan seemed very pleased and proud as he himself thought back on his visit to Harran many years ago, the first time he'd met the doctor.

"I remember your gift, Abu Ghazwan," he said pleasantly.

"Don't mention it—don't mention it, Your Majesty!" The doctor bowed his head, humble and abashed, and said, without raising his head, "Your gifts and favors have been lavished upon all of us."

The Sultan neighed like a horse, laughing at these words, and then said, "Now that we are in Harran, Abu Ghazwan, I want to give you a gift—name it."

The doctor glanced at him and lowered his head again, waiting for silence to fall, and when he felt that the Sultan was still awaiting his reply, he smiled and said, "Your Majesty, I want only happiness and long life for you!" He paused and raised a beseeching face to the Sultan. "The greatest gift, Your Majesty, is that you be happy with us and bestow your gaze upon us all!"

The Sultan turned to Zaid al-Heraidi and winked to remind him of something. Zaid nodded in understanding, and the Sultan turned, smiling, to the doctor.

Within a week of the doctor's return to Mooran, a black Cadillac was delivered to the al-Hir Palace to join the palace's three other cars. It came with a letter signed by His Majesty, closing with the words ". . . and this gift is for Dr. Subhi al-Mahmilji and his family as an expression of our gratitude and deep affection." The doctor could not hide his elation. He and the family went out to inspect the car twice within an hour; the greater part of his delight was watching Widad, who was as excited as a small girl. She insisted on sitting in the driver's seat although she did not know how to drive, and hugged and kissed the doctor despite Salma's presence, and laughed from her heart. She said that she would use no car but this one for her visits and errands, even if she had to take it abroad. Her joy was infectious, and the doctor could not help noting that since her return she had been a new woman: happy, tender, very attached to him. He thought back on the time before she went away, certain that the Square Theory not only explained it, but was proved by it. For a moment he wondered what would have been if circumstances had allowed him the time to write his theory, but he realized that the many obstacles and delays still to come would permit the theory to ferment, to ripen, in a way his leisure would have prevented.

Within a month of the Sultan's tour, the Ministry of Defense sent several letters requesting delivery dates for their arms and the dispatch of a delegation to discuss a new long-term contract. This was on the Sultan's orders, though Hammad also played a role—he seemed a different person. While he had not participated in the reception for the Sultan, he visited the doctor a few days afterward and called him a few times to ask for Ghazwan's telephone number so that he might contact him. The doctor reflected that people's negligence was sometimes due to worry and overwork, or perhaps forgetfulness; it did not always have something to do with love or hate. It was for reasons outside their control. He could only explain Hammad's behavior by *all his daily projects—of course the man can drown in an inch of water, because he doesn't know anything about strategy. He never studied in any institute or university—well, even so he has a good mind.* So he reciprocated his friendliness, and in an effort to show him that *money means nothing to me,* he decided to invite him and a number of his friends to a splendid banquet in the desert. He wondered whether he should also invite His Majesty the Sultan, but could not make up his mind until the last minute.

The woman . . . yes, the woman, she is the source of life, fertility, and all permanence, said the doctor to himself. He was noting Widad's interest and enthusiasm in making up the guest list; when he hinted that he might invite the Sultan she positively lit up, and tried to demolish all his reasons to hesitate or hold back. "The man loved our house and my cooking—of course he'll accept." She kept after him day and night, as he drank his morning coffee on the western balcony, and in bed, too, trying to overcome his fear of inviting the Sultan. "Even if he sends regrets, we'll have done our duty." She kept after him until he gave in. When he pondered Widad's excitement and insistence, he said to himself, *A woman is like sleep—a man may resist and avoid her, but in the end he always has to give in.*

80

THAT SPRING DAY IN LATE MARCH, IN THE Mileiha Desert on the road to Harran, not far from the Safa springs, three tents were set up with the flag of Mooran flying in from the top of the largest, middle one. This tent was furnished with a red and blue Kashani carpet laid out all around with thick cushions with gaily colored flower patterns. Pillows were strewn about in luxurious disarray. In the corner of the right-hand tent lay a collection of hunting rifles and three military rifles engraved with the emblem of the Sultanate of Mooran.

The sun diffidently, almost lazily, caressed the sand and cleansed away the night's dew and dampness, but with the coming of day and the sun's ascent, the caresses became a hot embrace between two lovers clasping for eternity; the grains of sand stirred and changed color, from pale yellow to waxy white, took on a bluish tinge in the dark night air, then became, uniformly, the color of freshly mined salt or liquid gum. Every wafting breeze slightly re-configured the landscape with gentle agitation, beginning on the farthest horizon and ending at the eyeball.

Silence is the true king of the desert: intense, ubiquitous and absolute. Even the sounds that do erupt are quickly absorbed by the sands and transformed into new sand. When the silence co-heres with the sun and sand, they breed a secret sound like that of suffocation or drowning; even the gunshots that pass through space for a moment do not overcome the silence—they mar it for an instant, then slip into the deep current of the wind, like extin-guished shooting stars, or birds trying to take off.

Thus the desert has been for as long as it has existed, since the first eye beheld it, but on this spring day the desert seemed a strange and unfamiliar place to every eye beholding it: there were hundreds of cars and hundreds more sheep, a small number of guests, and a Sultan who arrived one hour and seven minutes after the other guests; the doctor knew that because he checked his watch.

For the first time in her life Widad saw the desert in all its phases, from the first ray of sunlight until the last: she had been so pos-sessed by the anxiety that something would go wrong and spoil this gathering or alter her careful plans for it that she had been unable to sleep, except as a sparrow does in a new nest. She woke several times during the night, looking time and again at the clock by her bed, reminding the doctor, several times as well, that she would be going, and that he would go, too, several hours early, "because we have so much to do." She had also wished to spend a night, just one night, in the desert, under the stars, but her fears quickly stifled this wish. When she heard the call to dawn prayers she arose and woke the doctor, and by the time the sun rose the new Cadillac was nearing the Safa springs. When she got out of the car, which was parked by the tents, the cold morning air brushed her face and neck, giving her gooseflesh. As the sun rose and warmed the air, she came out of the "observation tent" and the doctor went into the one beside it, reserved for women. She entered the middle tent, which she had seen the night before, to see it now in daylight, straightened a few cushions, especially the big one the Sultan would sit on, and added two pillows to it, then perfumed the place and the whole tent with a light, subtle perfume, and prepared some sticks of incense to light at the proper time.

She performed these and other little tasks with her anxiety still not having dissipated, because she still did not know how things would go. In the al-Hir Palace she could be in total control, to have her own way, no matter how complicated things were, but here, in this endless space, she felt lost and afraid: the blowing sand might ruin what she had arranged; the sand might get all over the carpet and cushions; the sun might get so hot that no one wanted to move. She now faced an unknown enemy, cunning, elusive and unpredictable, not knowing when or where he would strike.

She scarcely noticed the brisk bustle coming alive all around her, but when the vanguards of the king's men arrived she withdrew, with Salma and the five palace women who had come to help her, into the observation tent, in accordance with the doctor's wishes. He had seen nothing wrong with her moving around among the men who had been stationed there for the last three days, but "Now, you must withdraw, Umm Ghazwan, because our guests are due at any moment."

In the hour she spent changing her clothes and selecting jewelry, the guests began to flock in. She looked out the tent's opening and saw her husband standing amid a group of men, facing east, and recognized Samir and Rateb among the men, but she did not know the three others. She busied herself with Salma, adjusting the collar of her dress and combing her ponytail. When that was done she looked out the opening again and saw that a group of new guests had arrived; she recognized Muti. A few minutes later the space before the middle tent was crowded with men. She felt anxious and a little afraid; she wanted to see the Sultan the moment he arrived. She had seen him once, by himself; now she wanted to see him among this throng. She imagined him, so powerful that he was scary, and the men darting around him. She wished she might shake his hand in front of everybody; if she did, the men would all discover that the Sultan knew her and that she knew him, and they would mutter among themselves. She laughed at the idea and put it out of her mind.

From this distance of more than one hundred yards she saw the doctor appear and disappear as he moved among the guests, and her anxiety gripped her without seeing his features clearly. He had told her that the Sultan would arrive between ten and ten-thirty. She looked at her watch: a few minutes after eleven. She tried to see beyond the tent to the road, but the area was full of cars, which blocked her view. She left the tent for a brief instant and looked east. "His motorcade is huge—it will raise dust you can see for miles." But she saw nothing and heard no noise, so she went back in and sat by the opening and asked Salma to come and join her there.

At eleven-twenty-five two helicopters landed not far from the tents, and all the men broke and ran like camels to welcome the Sultan, who had surprised everyone by arriving by air. Most of them ran as fast as they could to get there in time, and the stampede, together with the wind from the choppers, raised huge clouds of dust that soon enveloped the tents. Widad was sad, wishing with all her heart that the dust would settle.

Abu Abdallah hesitated, very wrought up, between the tents, giving orders, passing on bits of news and comments. He had arrived this time after the Sultan, and went into the tent to order the water pipes prepared. He declared, unasked, that he had never seen so many cars in one place in his life, and that he had never seen a plane this close up before.

Radwan said that they had been slaughtering sheep since dawn, and it continued until late morning; he said that there was enough meat for an army of seventy camel-mounted platoons. Abu Abdallah disputed that and said that there was enough meat to feed all Mooran for two or three days, and added that there were too many cars for anyone to count. "In the hundreds of thousands," he said to settle the matter, gesturing to show that it was beyond him, or that he did not care. The guards formed an unbroken wall so long that an observer at one end could not see the other end.

The doctor had racked his brains to surpass all his previous speeches—he had spent a whole night until dawn trying to compose an ode for the occasion, but it ended in failure, so he contented himself with three verses he composed and inserted in his speech. When the verses came, he smiled a half-smile, "as the poet said," and if anyone asked him who the poet was he would give any name, because he did not want to admit that it was himself.

More bullets were fired than in the seven days of the Battle of Rehaiba, as Abu Abdallah said; Radwan claimed that by himself he collected one hundred and seven spent shells. When the Sultan danced the traditional *ardha* that afternoon, he waved a rifle instead of a sword, and rested it on his hip and fired it.

There were many things that could be said about the day of al-Mileiha, but they could never be counted or summarized. The contests that took place, the bedouin poetry that was recited and sung, and verses on the Arabs' choicest odes about valor, generosity and loyalty, as well as dalliance with women were so numerous that they all melted in the memory. Their jokes, many of which the doctor told—for he had come prepared—were retold for months. The young princes, two of the Sultan's youngest sons, and Mansour, one of the middle sons, were the darlings of the day, both because of the little speech the youngest, Milhem, gave, and the ode Miteb recited. He was six months older than his brother. Mansour was the center of attention when he danced along with his father and showed true mastery of the dance.

Widad, who had at certain points been afraid, forgot her fear when the Sultan showed up. When he stood in the entrance of the tent, enjoying the whole panorama, he asked the doctor, who stood at his side, about the next tent, and then the third one, and the doctor seemed to point toward Umm Ghazwan in the observation tent. The Sultan nodded and laughed, or so Widad surmised without being sure. From then until sundown her confidence grew, especially when Abu Abdallah came, looking afraid, to tell her, on the doctor's instructions, to prepare to return to Mooran in a helicopter.

In Widad's mind the whole day was like a dream that would never recur. She saw the Sultan strolling near the observation tent. She saw him laugh like a horse. She saw him dance. She saw his monumental size and the way people saluted him. She saw him fire a gun. She was terrified by the suddenness of the doctor's order that she prepare to fly back in the Sultan's helicopter, that she and Salma board it before anyone else. Why was this happening? How would she comport herself? What would she say if someone spoke to her or asked a question?

When Salma said that she would prefer to return in a car, her

mother shot her a look of rebuke to prevent the recurrence of any
such thought, and turned to ask Abu Abdallah when and how to
go, but he did not know. Widad did not know whether to take or
leave behind the valise she had brought from Mooran; she looked
at her things bewilderedly, as if seeing them for the first time. She
looked at the middle tent and wished Abu Ghazwan would come
for one minute so that she might ask him if he was coming with her
and Salma, or coming later, and learn other details that would help
her decide what to do. But the doctor was far off, deep in the tent
that seemed darkened and mysterious to her, but that did not for a
moment stop the thousands of images she saw in her mind.

As the sun sank toward the horizon and shadows began to
lengthen grotesquely, Abu Abdallah came running, summoning
her immediately to the aircraft. The Sultan was ready to depart.
She could scarcely drape herself in the black cape she had brought,
so she asked Salma to do it, and within a minute the Cadillac was
parked by the tent, waiting to take her away.

In the helicopter there was only a greeting: the Sultan nodded
grandiloquently. The doctor and Hammad were behind him. He
looked behind him once or twice, but their eyes did not meet, and
she could not catch his features, other than to see him incline his
head questioningly. Why he laughed, why he looked down, she
could only guess.

The doctor came to her once before the helicopter took off, to
whisper in her ear that the Sultan had thought of landing the aircraft at the al-Hir Palace, but due to the thickly planted trees and
lack of a wide enough clearing, it would land at the Ghadir Palace.
He told her this unable to disguise his exultation. When the helicopter landed and the Sultan disembarked, causing a great stir, she
and Salma remained seated inside for a considerable time, until
she began to think that they had been forgotten, but when the
noise faded away a little and the Sultan's motorcade sped off, a
number of palace men came in a car to the helicopter door, with a
brief order: "The doctor will join you shortly."

She felt a joy almost like bliss that filled every cell of her body,
and when she placed her hand over Salma's and pressed it, she felt
that the movement tickled her; a shiver ran through her body. She
had not had such a feeling as this in a long time. She wished she

were alone in her room so that she could look at her body, and look deep into her own eyes to see the pleasure, the delight that was mounting with every passing moment. Why was she like this— what was she thinking—what did she want? She could not say; she was confused, but her tender, delightful confusion was slowly being transformed into a numb daze. She wanted to be alone, but also wanted to see the doctor to ask him about every detail of the day, from the Sultan's arrival until the last moment. She wanted to dance, to shout like a child to express the joy that filled her chest, to look, through the light shadows, at Salma, who sat beside her in the car, looking the other way, but she had no desire to talk, and spoil and lose this rapture.

She tried to remember the scene once more, but it was all so blended together that she could not recall one fixed scene. All the faces and events came to her in one mass; even the Sultan's laugh as he passed by the observation tent rang in her ears again as if she really heard it again. She turned around more than once and stopped when he passed by, pretending not to hear what was being said; he was stopping only because of her; otherwise why would he want her to come back in his aircraft? In the helicopter, when he passed and greeted her, his nostrils flared as he inhaled her perfume. She knew it when she caught the slight twitch of his nose— like a rabbit's. This was one of her hidden secrets; even when the doctor buried his head in her neck, he was made a little dizzy by the perfume she used; she knew how to use it and where.

She was restive and confused, going from room to room the whole time the doctor was gone. She asked Salma dozens of questions, questions she knew the answer to, questions no one could possibly answer. She smiled involuntarily and stood in front of the mirror to try to remember all that had happened, but all the images were scattered and mixed. She threw herself on the bed and closed her eyes, feeling the fire flowing from her body—even her fingers burned. She lay her hand over her forehead and cried out aloud, but no one responded. She got up and walked to the balcony and looked out toward the Ghadir Palace, saying to herself, *He's late—he's very late.*

The doctor was back shortly, rushing like a ball of fire, a smile filling his face, full of excitement, not knowing what to say or where to begin. He wanted to say everything at once. He wanted to tell her the smallest details, and between her questions he told her everything: how the Sultan had laughed until he fell over backward at the doctor's first joke, and laughed even harder at the second one after recovering from the first one; how the little princes laughed at the grown-ups' laughter, then asked what the joke meant and why everyone was laughing so much. He told her that the Sultan asked attentively about the observation tent and smiled broadly when he was told that it had been Widad's idea to invite him. Why had he insisted that they go back in the helicopter? To see Mooran from the air at night. He told her how delighted the Sultan had been—he had never seen him this happy, in all these years—and how he regretted not having given parties like this before. He praised her for her insistence on inviting the Sultan.

"But pictures, Widad." This was the only error he'd made for which he could not forgive himself. "We should have taken dozens of pictures. All of this should have been on film—they would have come in handy for *The Eagle of Mooran!*"

Widad listened and her heart soared; every moment took her back to al-Mileiha, which she saw again in all its endless space, and she saw only one person: the Sultan. She wished she'd been smarter and kept the guest list to an absolute minimum. Just a few people, and a very limited number of wives. Had she done that she would have shone the brighter—she would have known how to talk, move, and engrave an unforgettable day on every memory.

Despite the late hour, the insomnia of the previous night and the day's exhaustion, the two wanted to do nothing but recall the delicious moments and every detail that had made up this day. When they went to bed, Widad felt her body exploding, nearly out of her skin, to be one with the sand, the wind, the whole day. When the doctor leaned toward her and inhaled her perfume, he was dizzy for a moment, then threw himself on her and hugged her tightly, and she responded with warmth and welcome, more than ever before, more powerfully than any other night, but she was imagining him to be someone else: she imagined him, this time, to be the Sultan. The doctor was alarmed when she moaned and clutched him, and he almost pulled away, but she clasped him even more tightly to her, and soon they were asleep.

81

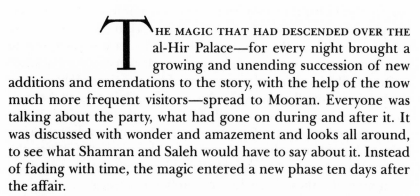

THE MAGIC THAT HAD DESCENDED OVER THE al-Hir Palace—for every night brought a growing and unending succession of new additions and emendations to the story, with the help of the now much more frequent visitors—spread to Mooran. Everyone was talking about the party, what had gone on during and after it. It was discussed with wonder and amazement and looks all around, to see what Shamran and Saleh would have to say about it. Instead of fading with time, the magic entered a new phase ten days after the affair.

Hammad, who had visited the doctor at the Ghadir Palace only once, and telephoned him twice, informed him on the tenth day that he would visit him in his palace that same night "on important business," without further explanation. This call and this message worried the doctor, who spent the whole morning wondering and guessing what the important business might be, and why Hammad was being so secretive, but he got nowhere. When he went home

he did not want to ask Widad, especially since no one had said anything about work visits in the evening or at home, and because he
knew how Hammad thought and acted. He assumed that Hammad wanted to talk about the Rabia plot; perhaps he had arrested
the persons behind the plot or found new dimensions to it that
required discretion. Since Widad was still in a state of rapture, as
the doctor himself put it, he had forgotten or at least not concerned himself with these darker matters.

From the first moment, Hammad appeared to be a completely
different person: a smile filled his face and there was no sign of his
former reserve. He radiated ease, exchanging pleasantries with the
doctor, Widad and Salma, who came in a little later. It all made the
doctor jovial far beyond his usual habit, especially around Hammad. He even forgot about the Rabia conspiracy. *It was a mistake for
Hammad to leave the Ghadir Palace so early,* the doctor thought. *We
never got a chance to talk and grow closer.* He blamed himself for not
giving Hammad a chance, now that he seemed so different from
before, and vowed to behave differently in the future.

An hour or more passed with no reference to the "important
business," and indeed the doctor forgot all about it, but when he
invited Hammad to stay and have some supper, he declined, saying
that he had to get back to the office; he was expecting an important
telephone call.

Widad joined in most of their conversation; she loved bringing
the discussion around to the party at al-Mileiha and how the guests
had enjoyed it, what they had said and how they felt about it. Salma
was very quiet, and eventually withdrew, without anyone noticing.

At one point when Widad was out of the room, Hammad smiled
at the doctor and said, "I have something to tell you, Abu Ghazwan—just between you and me."

All the doctor's senses were alerted, and his fear and feelings of
danger came back to him. *People in Hammad's line of work are heart-
less—they'll kill a man and then march in his funeral procession.* Their
faces were usually expressionless. Once again questions and apprehensions filled his mind. He looked at Hammad: the same expression, the same glee. When Widad reentered the room, the doctor
said to her a little brusquely, "My dear, Umm Ghazwan, please
leave us to ourselves for just a minute."

She looked, smiling curiously, into the doctor's eyes, a little surprised and chiding, then looked at Hammad, whose friendly smile was wider and brighter, as if he, too, wanted her to do as the doctor asked. She said pleasantly, to hide her embarrassment, "You men and your secrets!"

Later the doctor would not remember how Hammad led the discussion, how he said what he had come to say to the doctor, because the shock was too great at first for him to grasp what was going on. There was a sort of preamble, then a flood of affectionate and respectful words the Sultan had entrusted to Hammad to convey to the doctor, since he could not say them directly himself. Finally the surprise came, brief and clear: "His Majesty wants Salma."

Widad had been listening to some of the men's noise and thought that they were whispering when their voices fell. Hammad asked his question but did not expect an immediate answer. The doctor could not make a decision this quickly, so the two men sat in silence.

"I'll drop by tomorrow, Abu Ghazwan, and we'll have a talk," said Hammad after a lengthy pause.

The doctor looked at him and swallowed, then nodded in agreement and stood up to see his guest out. "A simple matter—God is magnanimous!"

Hammad paused for a moment and cleared his throat more than once; he wanted to see Widad, to say something to her, but when she stayed in her room, he said loudly, "Good night, my friends."

The doctor walked out with him in silence as far as the outer gate and stood there until he drove off, then turned slowly back up the stairs. He wanted some time to prepare himself for telling Widad the surprising news—should he tell her right away or put it off until tomorrow after he had thought it over? And Salma—should she know? What would she say—what would she do? He had erred in not asking her for her impressions after the Sultan's visit, or in these days past. She was too young for him to ask her about such important things. She really was young; her fifteenth birthday had been only a few weeks ago. He remembered the day she was born—it seemed only recently, but nevertheless she had become a woman in her looks, her silence, and the way she behaved. He had married Widad when she'd been Salma's age or only slightly older—so why was he so taken by surprise?

Could he refuse?

Widad pretended to be angry. He found her in the living room, and before he had prepared himself sufficiently to speak, she said, "After all we've done for him, to civilize him so he can go around just as he pleases, now he has secrets—he decides he can tell us about something, or maybe not!" When the doctor said nothing, she added sarcastically, "Really—for God's sake!"

Very earnestly, almost aggressively, he said, "Just wait a minute, Widad—this is a serious matter!"

She looked at him, wondering and afraid, and seeing him anxious and silent, said, "Is it bad?"

"Come here, darling, so we can talk about it." He answered her slowly, wearily and very sadly. She felt a pang of fear; her rebuke was becoming a nervous state almost like rage. She did not have a clear idea what Hammad's job was; she sensed that his work filled him with bitterness and cruelty, and sensed, furthermore, that she disliked him. He had spent a full half hour with the doctor and must surely have told him about Rateb—perhaps even about Samir. Not about Rateb exactly—for after the doctor left on the tour and prolonged his absence, Rateb had paid several visits to the al-Hir Palace. Someone must have told Hammad. *But Rateb is our friend, he used to live with us—this isn't anything new.* How would she handle this? She had to decide. If a man was going to complain, it was his own affair—so she was thinking, so she told herself; but for a stranger like Hammad to get involved, she could not understand or accept this.

When the doctor saw her sullen and silent, he said to her lightly, "We have to talk, darling, and make a decision!"

He sat on the western balcony, preparing himself. She went in and out a number of times for little things, trying to prepare, to bolster herself—just as he was doing. Finally they sat facing each other.

". . . on serious business, Widad," he was saying softly. She looked at him without speaking. "Something that cannot be put off."

With difficulty he explained to her that the Sultan had an exceptional love for their family; he had asked Hammad to pass that on, because the Sultan could not express his love and appreciation directly. After the two parties, His Majesty's affection was even greater. Widad relaxed and smiled, feeling included in this affection, and felt a light shiver of delight in her limbs. She wished she had heard these words from Hammad, so that she might have drunk in with her own ears how the Sultan had said them. Why had he deprived her of this pleasure? Why was he so primitive, such a coward, afraid of any sentimental kind of talk in front of women?

"Very nice," she said, her anger still with her. "If that's all the message he had, why was he so ashamed of it? Why didn't he say something? Why so secretive?" She saw that the doctor was silent and avoiding her eyes. She added, "Why was he shy about saying so in front of me?"

The doctor rose and closed the door to the balcony. Widad was surprised by this and his evident tension and silence, and she spoke up impatiently.

"He must have told you something else to upset you this much, Abu Ghazwan!"

He nodded in agreement, then gathered his courage and told her, "His Majesty, Widad, has asked for Salma's hand!"

Like a desert hurricane, Widad's world veered abruptly; she was hauled to a giddy height, near the stars, then dropped. She was speechless, so sad that she was almost in pain, yet rapture rang in every part of her body; she felt, all at once, totally abandoned and fiercely combative, deeply perturbed—though with anguish or rapture she could not tell.

Neither of them knew how long the silence lasted. When the doctor got up and laid his hand on her shoulder she trembled, then found herself clinging to his neck and crying. She wept silently, her tears rolling down her cheeks. He did not understand why she was crying or what it meant; he did not know whether she was happy or sad. He had never seen her like this before. She was like a different person, like someone he was seeing for the first time.

He stood up and put his hand under her arm to help her rise; she was heavy as a stone and as light as a breeze, near him and distant at the same time, both happy and sad.

"Widad," he whispered, "let's go in and think about it later."

Trapped and resigned, she walked along with him. They sat in facing chairs drawn close in the bedroom.

"Where's Salma?" he asked in a conspiring whisper.

"Asleep."

82

MOORAN HAD NEVER SEEN A PERIOD OF SUCH feverish activity as it did between mid-April and mid-May that year. The movement between the Ghadir Palace and the recently completed Khalidia palaces on one hand, and the al-Hir Palace on the other, never stopped, never even paused. Messengers never wearied of bringing news and gifts at all hours of the day and for much of the night. Everyone could see the things sent to the al-Hir Palace, because the trucks were too big to drive through the outer gate into the palace courtyard. Many more flights than usual were landing and taking off at Mooran Airport. The doctor even thought of cutting down the trees that grew in the back garden of his palace, to clear enough space for a helipad, but decided, at the last minute, to leave that until next autumn.

Summer, that year, came early and was far hotter than usual: in mid-April the air was redolent with the sticky, narcotic heat that bred as much languor as warmth, and the Sultan was inclined to move his travel date up a week or ten days from the original date. The doctor, however, told him that the climate in Europe, especially Germany, Baden-Baden to be exact, was far cooler than Mooran's, and that the move from a hot place to a cool one, a very cold one, to be honest, could lead to undesirable health complications. The Sultan listened to the doctor and agreed with him; the marriage would take place in Mooran, and they would leave after that. This decision meant that preparations had to be speeded up, so that Widad had to rely on the seamstresses who would come from Lebanon to prepare the wedding dresses. "Their work can go on, with a few adjustments—the dresses themselves we'll buy off the rack in Paris."

The Sultan agreed enthusiastically, and as a mark of his enthusiasm put his private plane at the disposal of Umm Ghazwan and the bride. This favor, which the doctor had foreseen, and which had never been accorded to anyone before, not even Prince Fanar, meant an extra burden for him, since he had to settle all the preparations in the first ten days of May.

This wedding kept the palace busier than any other in its past, and there had been many—people disagreed as to how many. Most said that there had been twenty-seven, but some of the Moorani women with connections to the palace said that this new wedding would be the thirty-fourth, because the Sultan had brief marriages with four or five girls who had been brought up and lived in the palace. Othman al-Dimeiri, who had arranged most of the Sultan's marriages, told two of his friends that he alone had contracted forty-two women to the Sultan—he told them that and asked them please to forget what he'd said, "because there's death in that statistic—there's head-cutting."

The palace hummed with activity. The Sultan himself was very pleased with this marriage, which he wanted to take place as soon as possible. He also wanted some special event to mark it in Mooran, because it would be the first wedding in the Khalidia palaces, and since the new harmony within the royal family, and Fanar's move into his new offices in these palaces.

Princess Adla, the Sultan's wife, was taken aback by all the commotion and tried to remember what Salma looked like. She knew that she had seen her, and that she'd been as small as a toy, with blue eyes and a long braid. When she'd been asked to come near,

the girl started and hid behind her mother. This was the only picture Adla remembered, because Widad, who had visited the palace
many times after that, never brought Salma again. When the girl
grew up, the Sultan was captivated by her but she could not see
why. She knew that the Sultan had visited the doctor at home, but
she knew no more than that. She had heard about the party at al-
Mileiha, and knew that the doctor's wife and daughter had been
there; the women who'd helped to prepare the water pipes told her
that the two women had never left their tent, and that none of the
men saw them. Even on the flight back with the Sultan there'd been
no conversation, and nothing happened—so when had the Sultan
become so attached to her? How had he arranged it?

Adla was sure that she would meet with the doctor's wife before
the wedding party, and then she would have a chance to give her
advice, especially about the first night, *because more than one woman
has been badly injured.* She would do this out of sympathy, not love.
She set no store by the wives coming after her, feeling sure that she
alone would last; he would never forget her or learn to live without
her. Even so, in this affair she sensed some secret she did not
understand. Her mind moved on to the doctor. *He bewitched him,
the bastard. From the day he met him, he's had him under a spell.*

Since the wedding was to be held in Mooran, there was work in
the Ghadir, Khalidia and al-Hir palaces, and for all sorts of men
and women as well: they were buying gifts, sewing dresses, and
buying jewelry from Paris, London, and America. These, or at
least most of them, were tempted to find some way to tell the doctor and his wife that they, too, were perfectly capable of buying
some things: the doctor and his wife were not special, and there
was no excuse for their air of superiority. Yes, the doctor's daughter was marrying the Sultan, but that meant little and would not
last long. The Sultan had married many, many women, and just as
he was marrying the doctor's daughter today, he would marry some
other girl tomorrow. But the wave of preparations moved on, with
every person doing what he could, in his own way.

Ummi Zahwa seemed to be in a stupor. She was desperately sad
after the death of Surour, and spent most of her time in her own
wing, where almost no one saw her or was aware of her presence
until she suddenly burst out like a cyclone. The Sultan had moved
to the Khalidia palaces, and his visits to the Ghadir Palace were

short and very infrequent; he had forgotten the Sheikha, or at least did not remember her as he once had. Those who had been close to her now saw her shiver like a cat, shriek and threaten, and pound her cane on the floor repeatedly, all the time cursing, sparing nothing and no one; though no one who saw her like this was too worried about it. Nashed al-Dublan watched it all in silence and said to himself, *It's the wakefulness before death—I don't think she can do a thing.*

Adla's relationship with the Sheikha had never changed; she was still very close to her and listened to her. She had noticed before any of the other women what Suroor's death had done to her. The grief had changed the Sheikha. Now Adla saw her raging, and said to her, in front of two of the younger princesses, "Ummi Zahwa, it's like a dust storm—it will pass, as everything passes."

The Sheikha shook her head in disagreement and to make clear her intention to keep fighting: this marriage would not take place, just as his planned marriage to Hazla, so many years before, had not. Adla understood, but went on to say, "That was before, Ummi Zahwa—these are different times!"

When the Sheikha found no understanding or support from those around her, she turned to others; it was said that there was not a single prince, young or old, but she had cursed the doctor in front of him as a murderer—that was what she now called him—and demanded that they intervene to block the Sultan's marriage to his daughter.

The princes who heard her out laughed and shook their heads and did nothing.

So the wedding preparations moved forward, and with them the bustle and noise until no one could hear anyone else anymore, but the Sheikha's voice was absent from the clamor. The Sultan heard about what the Sheikha had been saying, but ascribed it to spite and senility. When Zaid told him what she said, he told him, "As soon as we're back from our trip, safe and sound, we'll drop in on the Sheikha and win her over again."

The other Mooran was busy, too, in its own special way. Shamran al-Oteibi had heard about al-Mileiha: the sheep that had been slaughtered, the odes and songs, the Sultan's dance with a rifle instead of a sword. He looked around in disgust and asked mockingly, "Where are you, Ibn Rushdan—this is your day!" He lowered his voice, but most still heard him: "I don't think a drum is enough—I don't think words are any good anymore!"

When a rumor about the Sultan's approaching marriage to the doctor's daughter spread, Shamran said to a gathering of men in Zaidan's Coffeehouse, "When a man's morsel is too large, he chokes, my friends." They looked at him with questioning eyes, and when he added, with a laugh, "Who will have that nobody's daughter?" they understood that he was mocking the doctor, and one of them winked at Shamran to warn him against someone sitting behind him. With the laugh still on his face, Shamran replied, "And who cares, Abu Ibrahim? There's nothing left in life—we've seen it all!"

Shamran turned completely around to see the man Abu Ibrahim had warned him about, and asked, "What do you think, my good man?"

"You said it, not me, Abu Nimr."

"Our crowd in the Souq used to say, 'Beware the rich man when he's hungry, and the poor man when he's fed.'"

The man looked worried. He did not know how to reply, or how to deny the suggestion that he was one of the "nightingales," as Nimr called the agents of the Security Agency that always affected a shabby and poverty-stricken appearance, and were to be found everywhere. "But they always sing, and all stick out like black goats among sheep." When this man saw that all eyes were upon him, he got up, saying, "God save you, people of Mooran, you never rest, and never let anyone else have any rest!"

Nimr's news was garbled and confused these days. After the court moved to the Khalidia palaces, watching the Ghadir Palace was hardly worth the effort, since "even our one-armed friend"— he meant Muti—"has moved to Khalidia." So Nimr believed it when he was told at first that the marriage was going to be between the Sultan's son, Mezid, and the doctor's daughter. When people disputed this, he told them that his information "was from inside the palace," but three days later he admitted the information was wrong. "It's the big stick himself who's getting married."

Each new day brought heightened activity and more news. It was expected that schools and government offices would be closed on the wedding day, and that government employees would be paid a bonus. The wedding celebrations were expected to be on a scale of size and grandeur unprecedented in Mooran. Reports of new uniforms for the palace guards spread fast, and this story was given strength by the news of the formation of a new musical group under the direct supervision of the palace.

Saleh al-Rushdan was ill, but the news that reached him, in greater detail every day, was all garbled so he was forced to get up and go to Zaidan's Coffeehouse. When Shamran saw how weak and weary he was, he winced and rebuked himself for having forgotten him again, and to lift Saleh's morale, and to hide his shame over his own negligence, he joked, "You've come—rather, God has sent you, Saleh!"

Saleh peered at him, his large eyes prominent in his gaunt, ailing face.

"His Majesty has been asking for you," added Shamran.

"Why?" Saleh laughed mockingly. "What's his problem now?"

"He has big news this time, Saleh."

"Tell me, Abu Nimr."

"He's going to marry your enemy's daughter, and he wants you to go drumming and informing Mooran: 'O people of Mooran, here's the news, pass it on to your neighbor'—and whatever you care to add."

"Stop talking in riddles—tell me what's going on, Abu Nimr."

"That's what they say, Saleh, and if you don't believe me, ask your friends."

Saleh swallowed with difficulty and looked at the faces around him as they waited for him to speak.

"Well, my friends?"

"Abu Nimr is telling the truth."

"God help us—so fleas still stick to dogs! We used to say that His Majesty is fine, there's no one like him, our real enemy is the nobody. Now we don't know what to say anymore. Get ready to present your heads, bald men!"

His seated listeners burst into laughter. Saleh still did not want to believe it, he did not want to think that this was true, what they

had told him. The doctor may have taken no revenge on him before, but he would this time. He was not afraid of revenge, but
he did not feel, in his body, the energy he would need to fight this
war to the end. When the men stopped laughing, he turned to
Shamran.

"Listen, Abu Nimr, His Majesty found someone else to shoe his
horses, and neglected Saleh. Now, I don't care if he sends legions
of men and djinns loaded down with signed and sealed requests—
Saleh doesn't hear and won't comply!"

"Trust in God, Saleh, the world isn't ending yet."

"It's ended, whether we like it or not. A hunchback knows how
to sleep!"

Still Mooran strove and changed. Eventually every citizen heard
the news, and while some were not affected, seeing nothing out of
the ordinary in it, they soon found that they were indeed affected
by it, one way or another. Housewives were very curious, and asked
about it loudly, as did schoolchildren and government employees.
There were rumors among the downtown merchants that public
decorations would be mandatory, and delegations would have to be
nominated to go and congratulate His Majesty—the same thing
went for small businessmen and shopkeepers, many of whom were
worried and curious—had Mooran lost its senses? Would the place
be turned upside down, as it had been when the Sultan returned
from his tour, and all buying and selling was ordered to stop?

There was no end to the commotion in and around the al-Hir
Palace. Even Samir, who had completed four chapters of *The Eagle
of Mooran,* seemed a different person when told that the Sultan
would wed Salma. He took a break from the biography to write a
series of articles for *al-Waha* magazine, under the overall title "Man
and Power." He included in the articles several ancient Egyptian
and Greek legends, all of them dwelling on the power of money
and the influence of the powerful and the divine. These powers
pursued men and tested them, and only those who were intelligent
as well as powerful could survive these trials. The weak failed, and
that is what still happened. As soon as he completed the fifth article
he became a new man: he resumed work on the biography, con-
vinced that *a crisis that doesn't kill me strengthens me. I'll get through this.
Man is a social animal, a modern animal with unlimited intelligence.*

When the doctor asked Samir if he would like to accompany the Sultan on his honeymoon trip to Germany, he was willing to go, even enthusiastic.

Hammad, who had not been slow to inform the Sultan of the doctor's consent, which they had expected with no trace of doubt, was a different person from that night onward, in his concern and kindness. Now even Abdelmawla sometimes telephoned the doctor, and was more delicate and more easily confused, too. His conversation had been clearer in the past, despite his friendly flattery. Now he was different, and although the doctor did not notice, he was struck by how much he liked this person, or valued him. Abdelmawla very solicitously asked the doctor about his health, and whether or not he was calling at a convenient time, and when he was satisfied with the answers, he informed him that Hammad would like a word with him.

Even Badri al-Mudalal, whose relations with the doctor had cooled considerably after Muhammad Eid's sudden departure, especially after he discovered why Muhammad had left, rarely even saw the doctor except when he discharged the "duty" of visiting him on the religious feast days, and kept up with him mainly through listening to gossip, which he helped to spread. He did this when the doctor had his falling-out with Said and when the Rabia incident happened. He paid no attention to the doctor's other news, or merely muttered when he heard it. Now, with this fresh wave of news, he could no longer feign neglect or disinterest, and phoned the doctor on some trivial pretext—not to congratulate him, as he was quick to say, but to respond, indirectly, to something the doctor had said years before, when two of his daughters were married off, one to the assistant chief of police in Mooran, and the other to the commander of the Desert Forces, and with a certain cunning he made a particular reference, albeit a clear one, to his happiness at the news. He said that the Sultan had asked him about Salma, and in reply he had praised her beauty, conduct and diligence; he wanted the doctor to understand that he had played a central role in this marriage. The doctor accepted his good wishes and tried to steer him away from this subject as quickly as possible. He asked him about Muhammad Eid—"God willing, he's made a success of himself?"—and about his life and Mooran and his family. Badri answered these inquiries briefly and moved on the final message he had for the doctor.

"For myself, Abu Ghazwan, I've done the needful: I haven't left a single white hair in his beard—not only that, I dyed all his hair. The Devil himself would not know him or notice him!"

The doctor listened to this with mounting rage, and said softly, as if taking revenge, "God give you rest, Abu Misbah, and bless your hands!"

Said refused to believe the marriage news that everyone in the market was talking about. He said that the doctor was spreading stories like this to make people forget the hotel incident, and to regain his social standing. When he met up with Hammad, who confirmed the stories, he said, "The bastard is like a cat—no matter how you throw him he lands on his feet!"

He thought a moment and then winked at Hammad.

"The best thing is for a man to pet it, to stay out of sight for a few months, until God gives him release."

Things moved along smoothly enough, despite a few difficulties. Widad went to Paris for ten days and returned with a fabulous haul. That was her view, and the doctor agreed. Salma, who was all aflutter, not knowing what to do, felt as if she were in a dream, scarcely believing, despite the dozens of dresses she tried on every day, and the shoes and handbags thrust upon her, that all this was really happening: that she was to be married, and to the Sultan himself. She was, on the whole, resigned, as if spellbound, especially when she heard her mother tell her, almost order her, to show her father the dresses she had brought. She asked her to wear the tailored skirt with white shoes and white handbag, and Salma put them on and showed them both how she looked. When Widad asked her to wear the light aqua dress with the slit front and open back, Salma hesitated, because it was a scandalous dress and she did not want her father to see her in it, but her mother gave her a stern look, and she submitted obediently, like a tame cat.

After much preparation and postponement, Salma's wedding was set for the tenth of May.

THOSE WHO HAD WAITED IMPATIENTLY AND
made bets over the pay bonus, day off and
celebrations were not disappointed, and
credited themselves with profound intelligence and precise calculation. Those who had placed bets lost little or won a lot, because
all government employees, police and guards received bonuses
equal to more than two months' pay, plus a pay raise.

In order that it all not seem part of the wedding, there were
allusions to two other occasions, "the Battle of Rehaiba, whose anniversary falls this month, and the thirtieth anniversary of the
founding of the Sultanate." This came about at the doctor's urging,
"because our detractors are lying in wait, and they would be enraged by a wedding celebration on this scale." In fact, he was worried that what had happened at the Rabia Hotel banquet might
happen again here, *because everything that isn't complete is damage*, as
he said to himself; he did not know how to hide his confusion and
fear. He told Hammad that he wanted security provided for all the

palaces, meaning for his palace; he wanted all vagrants and troublemakers rounded up, because he was haunted by the image of two men, Mufaddi al-Jeddan and Saleh al-Rushdan, and found that the most fitting way to refer to them was as "vagrants." Hammad nodded and laughed, and told him that the al-Hir Palace had been closely monitored for a long time, and that he had taken steps to see that nothing would mar the celebrations.

Delegations poured in, just as they had when the Sultan ascended the throne, and pitched their tents all over Mooran. The celebrations began the day before the wedding: two musical troupes, one belonging to the palace and the other to the army, wound through the city streets, and some people thought that the Sultan had moved up the wedding day, but the more knowing and informed people corrected this error and told them, "This is nothing compared to the festivities tomorrow." Loudspeakers were mounted throughout the city, as were decorative triumphal arches and torches that turned Mooran's night into day. Some of the customers at Zaidan's Coffeehouse and other coffeehouses said that they saw three palace cars driving through the streets, and that the Sultan himself was probably in one of them. They could not be sure, because the cars drove by too fast, and the man in the backseat of the middle car drew a veil over his face to hide his features.

The horses and fine camels which were brought to Mooran made people think back on the days gone by, and they were reflective and sad until airplanes flew over and dropped gifts from the sky, which led to a certain amount of trouble arising from the running and shouting and arguing, among the youths and children, with the oldest winning out. On the wedding day colored cards were given out to be exchanged for gifts.

The Khalidia palaces looked like a flaming torch—they were easy to spot from a good distance, and people streamed toward them the night before the wedding in the hope of seeing grand games and celebrations. In fact, the show was limited to the palace's musical troupe and free coffee given out to anyone who rested in the huge tent set up by the palace's side gates. The visitors, especially the ones who got close up, noticed the frenetic activity and immense cargoes being taken inside the palace, but they could not make out what they were.

Hammad, true to his custom at such affairs, stayed at his post in the Security Agency, but followed everything by giving orders and asking questions over the telephone. Now, more than for any previous occasion, he did not leave his office, except once when summoned to the palace to meet with the Sultan; he spent an anxious half-hour there and returned to his office.

The doctor was edgy and afraid, not knowing, as he watched and listened to all this, whether he might be happy or express his happiness. Should he rejoice in front of the others or be quiet? He was at loose ends; he could not go back to the al-Hir Palace, which had become a beehive of activity, full of people whom he did not know, who did not know what they were doing, nor could he stay confined in his wing in Khalidia. Muti, the closest to him, was thoroughly immersed in the commemorative issues he was publishing for the special occasion, and he strode back and forth, watching, supervising, making sure everything was going according to plan, and yet he was filled, at the same time, with the fear that his article was not as good as he wanted it to be or as good as it might have been. He and the doctor had exchanged two brief and confusing telephone conversations, in which the doctor said that he wished he were in a better mood or surrounded by people with whom he felt more comfortable. The Sultan asked to see him, but they talked for only twenty minutes, during which the Sultan seemed tense and preoccupied, and his questions seemed to the doctor to be mere courtesies.

Widad had been mistress of her nerves for the past few days, but now was troubled again by insomnia and headaches. The doctor was afraid she would fall ill, so he did everything in his power to calm her and relieve her nerves, but for the most part she did not even listen to him, and often got up while he was talking to her, to check some item of business or look for something, all the time looking irascible and giving orders.

The day before the wedding she came in from the palace, where she had been visiting with Princess Adla, the Sultan's wife, who had telephoned her several times asking to see her on "important business." Widad postponed their meeting more than once, on the pretext of the overwhelming demands on her time, but visited her at last, and Princess Adla told her directly, without euphemism or ambiguity, what had to be said.

Widad escorted her husband to a room far from the commotion and told him. Her emotions were scattered and confused, between fear and delight. She asked him, in his capacity as a specialist, and on the basis of experience, if that woman could possibly have been in earnest and meant what she'd said, or whether it might have been only a spiteful attempt to ruin the wedding. The doctor listened carefully to what his wife had to say and assured her that he would prepare an appropriate medicine for Salma, and he furthermore considered "ruining" the Sultan for the wedding night, or at least rendering him weaker; but in the end he thought Widad's fears women's foolishness unrelated to science.

Dozens of events enlivened Mooran in the days before and after the wedding. There were wedding presents brought from all over and kept, as surprises, until the right time. Delegations made their way to the Khalidia palaces to pay their respects, banquets were given, and there were horse shows and races for three days running—the day before the wedding and the next two days. The torches carried aloft by schoolchildren for two nights, the sports festivals presided over by Prince Fanar, during which uncounted expensive gifts were given out, all changed Mooran—even turned it upside down.

Shamran had vowed not to set foot in the market for a full week, "until they cart away all this garbage littering Mooran and the last croaking raven has gone home," and told two visitors at his home, the night before the wedding, that "Marriage is a religious institution, my friends, but what you see now isn't marriage, it's just depravity and godlessness, and my feeling is that no good will come out of it."

Saleh al-Rushdan's ears were ringing from the noise, and he felt his blood boiling in his veins from what he heard all the people around him talking about. He was filled with the urge to take his drum and go out to the streets, to every single street in Mooran, until he reached the Sultan's palace to say what no one else would say, but he gave up the idea, since *if everyone went around drumming in this world, and singing psalms in the afterlife, what good is your drum, old man?*

Saleh toyed with the idea of a boycott. He decided to stay in his house, and when his wife and children went out to stand on the sidewalk or in the street, he remained alone. He looked back on all his days, on his life as a young man, how everyone in the market had feared him. They had feared him because of his strength and because he spared no one. He felt that he had exhausted his strength except for a mere trace, which even now was deserting him, slipping away one day at a time. He said to himself, as he watched the fireworks fill the sky, *We used to have real exploits and real men, but now that we've lost our strength and sold our horses, we throw saddles on dogs and tell them, "Swim!" "Fly!" Hah!*

When Shaddad was told that Mooran was full of horses and that he should bring his horses down for the races, he sneered, "Thoroughbreds have no place beside those pretty pets!" This was taken several different ways, but he did not hide his hatred for the doctor.

Muflih al-Mutawa's hearing had deteriorated even more than before, and his eyesight had weakened, but he noticed all the commotion and knew something unusual was happening.

"My friends! Who died?" he quavered.

Mutlaq was out that evening, and everyone took turns shouting in his ear that the Sultan was to marry the next day, but still he asked, "Hah? Who died?" When they said nothing, he yelled, "Who!"

Nimr was bothered by the newspapers advertising their "special issues": "The newspapers lie once on a normal day, but they lie one hundred times on a special occasion. What a gang of hypocrites and parasites, each competing to be a greater hypocrite than the other! Liars! And for what occasion? The wedding of the virtuous daughter of al-Mahmilji to His Beloved Majesty, Khazael bin Khureybit—as if it were the first wedding on earth, as if it were the wedding of Adam and Eve!" He was silent a moment, then continued. "And of course, at the head of the liars and hypocrites is their sheikh, the one-armed Muti. But by God, by God, the day is going to come when these articles are going to be found out. Like this, my friends—'Who wrote this?' 'Why did you say that?' You'll see their tears; they'll beg for the intercession of those sons of bitches—as if they don't carry their book with their unclean left hand. They think people will forget and be easy on them, they think no one knows how much they've stolen. Never mind, someday we'll see." And he listened, unmoved, to the clamor around him and the mad bustle that filled Mooran.

Badr was different; when he saw how depressed and pensive his father was as he watched the fiery rockets shoot through the sky, and the city of Mooran was immersed in brilliant light, he asked him, very seriously, even excitedly, "Father, if you want me to cover Mooran with darkness, just say the word!" He began to explain to his father how he could easily cut the electric current to all of Mooran, so that no one could find him out or repair it for days. Shamran nodded to show that he understood, and said, as if to himself, "The darkness of the grave would be better for them—there's nothing like that, my boy."

They did not quite understand this. Najm came home at his usual time and found them talking about the old days, sitting in darkness illuminated only, every now and then, by the fireworks. He greeted them and sat down to listen for a while, then said, "This isn't the first or last wedding in the world, and this Sultan is the son of a Sultan, and tomorrow his son or his brother will become Sultan . . . unless Mooran changes."

His father screeched as if he had been threatened.

"The Mooran that was, our Mooran, is gone. There's not a stone of it left, my boy, it's changed. This one has brought disaster to us, and you want more?"

"What I want, Father, is a different Mooran, a new Mooran, not like what you see today."

"Let us be, my boy! Wait until people have had a chance to say, 'God rest his soul, poor Shamran,' and walk in my funeral procession, before you give us this new Mooran you're talking about!"

"It's coming, Father!"

"By God, my boy, we've lost the best, the most precious that we had—it won't be the same thing."

The three still sat watching the fireworks, reminiscing and dreaming. Mooran would get no sleep this night or the following one, the night of the wedding, which brought the city celebrations that no one had expected or even imagined.

84

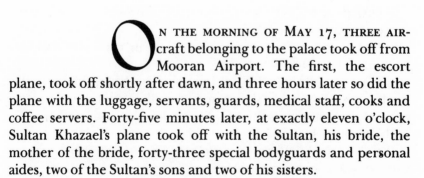

O N THE MORNING OF MAY 17, THREE AIR-
craft belonging to the palace took off from
Mooran Airport. The first, the escort
plane, took off shortly after dawn, and three hours later so did the
plane with the luggage, servants, guards, medical staff, cooks and
coffee servers. Forty-five minutes later, at exactly eleven o'clock,
Sultan Khazael's plane took off with the Sultan, his bride, the
mother of the bride, forty-three special bodyguards and personal
aides, two of the Sultan's sons and two of his sisters.

The doctor stayed behind in Mooran because of his enormous
workload, but he solemnly promised Widad that he would join her
in early June after visiting the children in Lebanon, to see that they
were fine, "and to give them the good news."

Samir had left on the Sultan's plane and encountered the Sultan
twice, first, when His Majesty was on his way to the bathroom, and
second, at the bottom of the stairs just after their arrival. The sec-

ond time, he tried to fix a time for more appointments so he could get on with the biography, but the Sultan looked at him and neighed and then added, jokingly and a little annoyedly, "Give us a chance to rest, my boy, and after that we'll see what God will provide."

Mooran, quiet after all the festivities and the "great days," as Muti called them in his article, was trying to return to normal, but it took several days to dismantle the decorations and sweep the streets and public squares, to take down the loudspeakers and tents. The people seemed, after all that had filled their eyes and ears, to be in a weary daze that they could overcome only by going back to their normal routine lives; within a day or two they had to start a new week like all the old weeks that had passed before.

As the sun sank toward the west on Thursday, losing its brilliance, Shamran began preparing his cot on the roof, as he did at the start of every summer. He sprinkled water over the flat roof until it was damp, made his coffee, took off most of his clothes, and did not forget to carry up his radio to listen to "The Desert," a program he listened to every Thursday to bring back memories and give him hope.

He was alone on the roof, because "the little old lady," as he called Umm Nimr, had chores to do downstairs. Shamran was more active than usual. He threw back the carpet, rearranged the cushions, kindled the fire, and rewashed the coffee cups, and he did all this unconsciously, without design, only to keep himself busy. When he finished these small tasks, he lay on the cot. He wanted to shout or sing. He considered standing on one foot. He smiled because he could not imagine how he thought of such an idea, and said to himself that *a man remains a child, in some ways, for his whole life.* He remembered Saleh al-Rushdan and thought, *He'll never change until he dies, he'll always be the same.* He recalled the doctor and what had been said in Zaidan's Coffeehouse: "The girl will be miserable, from the first night," and that the Sultan's trip today had more to do with his health than with anything else, and he said to himself, *If a man sells his own flesh, what will be left for him and his Lord?*

He relaxed as the first comfortable breezes began to blow, and reached out for the radio. He never listened to anything but "The

Desert," since *the other programs have their own audience,* and he hated and disbelieved the news on Radio Mooran. *They just look you in the face and lie—they're shameless, impudent.* Nor did he like the "dervishes": *All they're selling is "God said," and "The Prophet has said," and they don't know anything about God or his Prophet.*

Shamran turned on the radio. *If it's anything but "The Desert," I'll turn it off, I'll kill the sound.* Music. *That's fine.* He shifted on his cot, retrieved a pocket watch from under a cushion and examined it, holding it at a sharp angle so as to catch on its dial the faint light from the lower story of the house and the streetlight. *Three minutes to seven.* He put the watch to his ear to make sure it was running, closed the lid, wound it and replaced it under the cushion. He poured himself a cup of coffee and drank it slowly, savoring it. The radio still broadcast only music, and he remembered that he had heard music like that on other occasions. He made a gesture of futility—he felt that more than three minutes had gone by. He looked at the sky, then all around him, and pulled out the watch again: *Five minutes after seven.* He curled his lip at this surprise. *All these bastards have is this jingling, and they begrudge us the desert program!* He moved the radio dial to make sure that it was tuned in correctly, but the other stations were distorted and fainter. *The jingling is Mooran,* he said to himself, and adjusted the dial so that the music gushed out again; he shook his head resentfully. *Let's see what comes next.*

Suddenly the music stopped. *They're sleeping, the bastards,* thought Shamran. *They forgot to broadcast "The Desert"!*

"Noble people of Mooran, stand by for an important bulletin," said the announcer in a husky but tremulous voice.

Damn you and damn your parents, thought Shamran, and cast his gaze around in the falling darkness. *Important bulletin?* He shook his head. *They had their wedding, they're married—what next? More weddings?*

The music hummed in his ears again, and he said to himself, *God damn your parents, you bastards—am I to have nothing but jingling?*

His mind wandered to the events of past days, and abruptly he remembered Khureybit. *Ivory comes from big bulls. That cloud gave us this rain.* Images of Mooran passed through his head like a fiery film: the past, and how it was now. People struggled to earn a coin, moved frenziedly from one place to another, and never wearied of haggling. *Now everything has changed. Money comes to the laziest people—all you have to do is be a hypocrite, kiss the shoulders and beards of the royalty, and you don't have to work.* Money was no longer a pleasurable or important thing, nor had it anything to do with status or abilities—it was just the meaningless piling up of wealth, and no one knew what this would lead to.

Suddenly he was pulled from his reverie.

"Noble people of Mooran, stand by for an important bulletin!"

"Oh, you needless bastards, you're like gravediggers, with all this 'noble' and 'God' business—damn you and your bulletin!" He said this aloud, then added, "You take away the only good program you have, 'The Desert'—may your hand turn against you!"

Once more, as the music blared from the radio, Shamran repeated to himself, *Important bulletin, important bulletin,* and tried to imagine what the important news could possibly be, but could think of nothing. He smiled and said, "His news is usually that he's slaughtered more sheep, or has some new favorite."

The first to join him was his son Najm.

"Have you heard, my boy? On the radio they're saying to wait for an important bulletin."

"The market is full of tanks, Father!"

"Tanks?"

"Tanks and the army and all the calamities under the sun."

"More parades, my boy?"

"I don't think so, Father. I tried to get home before everything blows up."

Badr arrived, clearly frightened and rather confused, saying that he had been listening to his big RCA radio, which brought in many stations, such as the BBC and Voice of America, and that there were reports of serious incidents in Mooran. He had wanted to continue listening, but soldiers came and told him to close his shop at once and leave.

"Umm Nimr! Umm Nimr!" shouted Shamran as soon as he heard this. "Our sheikh is lost—his fire is out!" He looked at Najm and asked, "My boy, are they with us or against us?"

"No one knows, Father."

Badr turned to the radio and tuned it from station to station;

perhaps he would be the one to hear the news and tell the others. His father listened raptly and leaned toward the radio, hoping that "The Desert" would be broadcast, in spite of this delay. Najm had secluded himself in his room, gathering books and burning papers, running from one part of the house to another, paying no attention to the voice of Badr, who was busy hooking up an extension cord to move the big radio up to the roof and shouting for his father to help him.

Nimr was the last to arrive. He came after Zaidan's Coffeehouse had been closed by cars cruising through the market announcing a curfew and demanding that everyone go to their homes at once; violators would be shot. Nimr was angrier and more bewildered than he had ever been in his life; he did not want to hear the news, like everyone else, he wanted to see it, to witness it with his own eyes. He had gone around to several places to see the tanks, and counted them around the Ghadir Palace and the Khalidia palaces; no one was allowed anywhere near the Saad Palace. He was especially upset because Officer Ghanim al-Suhail, who was commanding three tanks in Sultan Khazael Square, had smiled at him and said, "It's all over, we've taken control of all the installations and strategic points." Nimr wanted to know more and asked him to explain, but was told only, "Wait for good news in the morning." Then al-Suhail got busy with his soldiers and refused to say anything more.

Nimr could not wait or calm down or let anyone else calm down. "Don't forget—every man is responsible for his own deeds, and this is the day of reckoning." Images and apparitions passed through his mind. "No mercy for anyone, no last cigarette. 'Come and hear the verdict. Aren't these pictures of you? Aren't these your words? You were puffed up with praise and glory, and you thought people were like sheep—and that this world would last forever.' " He laughed vengefully, but his apparitions and dreams scattered when his father asked him what he had seen and heard.

"Ghanim told me, 'It's all over,' and I saw it for myself—I went everywhere and saw it." He was silent for a moment before adding, in a different voice, "Tomorrow will be a bloody day."

"Whose blood, my boy?"

"The blood of traitors and spies, of parasites, hypocrites and sons of bitches, and every enemy of the people."

"Enough has happened in Mooran as it is, my boy."

"Nothing has happened yet, Father—you'll see, tomorrow."

"What's already happened is enough and more, my boy."

"Don't be afraid—it's just a time of reckoning."

"Don't talk like that. Only God decides the reckoning."

Shamran was sad to the point of despair. He wanted no blood or reckoning. He did not trust what he saw around him. His son was speaking of gallows and newspapers, which doubled his sorrow and made his despair feel like an incurable illness. Nimr was moving like a pendulum, looking all around and imagining faces and scenes that made him laugh and shake his fist and head menacingly. He was muttering what sounded like threats. All this worried Shamran more than it reassured him, and provoked him above all.

"My dear boy," he said angrily to Nimr, "just live your life and let us find our own path. The time will come when we see what is reckoned for and against us."

"It's all over, Father. I heard it from Ghanim with my own ears—it's not a rumor."

"And the Sultan, and Khureybit's sons?"

"Nothing will be left of them but a memory."

85

THAT SAME THURSDAY, IN THE AFTERNOON, Hammad telephoned the doctor. It was a brief and mystifying call, confined to one item of business: "I'm speaking to you from the palace, Abu Ghazwan. Crown Prince Fanar wants you to stay at home. We are going to call you back."

The doctor was tense, almost depressed. He wished his friends were near him, and at first felt relief when he heard Hammad's voice, but soon felt alarm instead. He wished the call had lasted longer, or that other, clearer things had been said. And it was unusual for Hammad to talk to him that way. *Prince Fanar must have been right beside him,* said the doctor to himself, *so he was embarrassed. He wasn't at ease enough to take his time and talk longer.* He did not like his wording, either—what was "Crown Prince Fanar wants" supposed to mean? *Does he mean that His Highness is going to pay a call on me? It would have been easy to say so in a nicer way, in a civilized way, but they're just bedouin. They have no idea what decorum is.*

A little while later the doctor thought of calling Hammad to get an explanation, *because, Abu Rashed, this is the first time Prince Fanar has ever visited me, and I want it to come off well.* But where was Hammad now? He had disappeared within moments of arriving anyplace—he had just vanished. The doctor remembered how Hammad would arrive at the Ghadir Palace or the Khalidia palaces—he would walk out of the room and vanish. He did not know which palace Hammad had been speaking from.

Abdelmawla was even more reticent and mysterious than Hammad. He told the doctor that his boss was not in; he did not know where he was or when he would be back. When the doctor told him that Hammad had called him an hour ago from the palace, Abdelmawla said he knew nothing about it, and went silent. The doctor asked him again how he could find Hammad or contact him, and was told that it was impossible, and there was more silence. Angrily, the doctor shouted that he had to find him.

"If he calls in, Abu Ghazwan," said Abdelmawla, "I will convey to him that he should contact you urgently."

The doctor was bewildered. From the rear balcony, in an effort to prove his importance and nonchalance, he moved from one chair to another, looked at the trees and at the sky; then a moment later he was on the front balcony, watching the entrance, the garage and the guardhouse. He listened quietly to the street, then retreated into the house to look hatefully at the telephone. He wanted it to ring, but the silence in the house compounded the stolidity of the instrument until it seemed like death.

He was more bewildered than before. What was he doing? Should he stay this passive? He would have been more clever, more courageous, if only Widad were here; she would have helped him do something besides move doltishly from balcony to balcony and from chair to chair.

He said wrathfully to himself, *His Highness is like this. Like a tortoise. He hides behind silence and chaos to hide his impotence and iniquity.* He saw Prince Fanar in his mind's eye, *a perfect, living example of a desert tortoise: static, vague, endlessly silent, unthinking, not knowing what he wants. Even the Sultan doesn't understand him.* He considered leaving the house, going anywhere at all: *They have their moods, and so do I—I'm not a child anymore.*

Less than an hour later he called Abdelmawla again.

"Well, my lad, has your boss come in? Has he called?"

"Not at all, Abu Ghazwan."

"Have you called him? Have you tried to find him?"

"I tried everywhere but couldn't find him."

"So—what's the solution?"

"Whatever you say, Doctor."

"Fine. Do what you can, my boy, and let me know what you come up with."

"Yes, sir, Doctor."

The doctor said to himself, *This Hammad should have been squashed like a louse. He should be under my foot. The instant I left him, I gave him more rope, he ran; he thinks he's something big. And who is he turning against? Me—but I can deal with him!*

The doctor considered forgetting the whole thing. *I have too much to do, anyway, and should stay in. And if someone wants to visit me, fine.* He tried to stretch out and relax, but suddenly remembered Muti. *Whom do you have if not your own family?* He telephoned Muti, but he was not home: "He went out after getting a phone call." Nor was he in the office: "He isn't here—he was called to the palace." The doctor tried everything he could to find out where Muti was or who had summoned him, but got only maddeningly vague information. Muti's secretary told him that "he had started writing the preface, but at about six o'clock they phoned from the palace and he went out. I don't know any more than that, Doctor."

He telephoned Nadia.

"I need Hammad, Nadia, I need to contact him—where could he be?"

"I don't know any more than you do, Uncle."

"He didn't say anything about where he was going?"

"Not a thing, Uncle—he never does."

"Fine, Nadia, but if he calls, tell him to call me at once."

"Yes, Uncle."

To himself he said, *Never again will I allow anyone to treat me this way, to talk to me like a telegram. Things have to be clear, perfectly clear.*

He paced time and time again between the rear balcony and the front balcony, passing the telephone on each trip and giving it a hateful look. When he walked away from it, all his senses were concentrated in his ears as he tried to hear it ring.

The sun's light abated as it sank toward the west. A fresh breeze blew, and the doctor felt more inclined to forget all about it as his apprehensions melted. *I used to scrawl a few words in a notebook—I'm out of the habit, thank God. The theory has been sleeping like the Sleepers of the Cave.* He considered writing something about those days gone by. *They were great days.* He had used this expression many times in front of Muti, who had not hesitated to use it as a heading for one of his chapters. He gave up the thought of doing any writing—he was too tense. *Writing and mental commotion are enemies. A man can write only with a cool head and cool nerves—otherwise he'll write like some kind of poet. Everything in its time.*

The house was empty and eerie. *Why did I allow them to go?* He wandered from room to room, looking at the furniture and the walls that reminded him of his absent family. He felt how very far away they were—very far. Why had he delayed? Why had he not gone with them? he asked himself with a certain bitterness. He considered writing a letter to Ghazwan; his feelings toward him were rich and inspired—he could write a stirring letter!

He looked out from the front balcony and saw Abu Abdallah carrying a pitcher of tea in the direction of the garden. *Always to the same altar.* Abu Abdallah spent hours each day resting by the palm trees, stretched out, listening to the radio. *They've been worshiping those transistors in place of God ever since they discovered them. They always have them against their ears. They'd have them under their skin if they could.* He almost called out to him that he needed him for something, but dropped the idea. *Their heads are emptier than the heart of Moses's grieving mother.* The doctor's education relied on books and other primary sources, or, as he told himself, *wherever it can be found,* and he considered the radio a vulgar means of education. He recalled the stories that had circulated in Harran about Khaled al-Mishari and the radio and smiled as he followed Abu Abdallah's careful footsteps.

Distant sounds reached his ears between seven and eight o'clock that night. *Mooran,* he said to himself. *Mooran—and Thursday.* He smiled broadly and thought, *And it's spring.*

He stood on the front balcony and listened quietly, then saw Abu Abdallah running, the radio to his ear, glancing around in bewilderment. He looked at the doctor strangely. The doctor said to

himself, *The halfwit—his brains are addled by the music.* He leaned
over the balcony and asked jokingly, "What is it, Abu Abdallah,
dances? Folk songs?"

Abu Abdallah looked up and shook his head.

"Something Oriental?" asked the doctor weakly.

"It's nothing like that, Abu Ghazwan!"

"Tell me what you've been hearing!"

"They're talking about an important bulletin."

Abu Abdallah turned up the volume as loud as it would go. The
music abruptly ended. He waited for an announcement of the kind
constantly being broadcast. When the doctor heard, all his senses
trembled and confusion gripped him. *An important bulletin? What
could it be? Is he listening to the news on the radio? Does anyone else know?*

Once more he began to telephone. Hammad had not called in,
and no one knew where he was, Abdelmawla told him. Muti was
still at the palace and no one knew when he would return. The
doctor called Prince Mayzar but no one answered the phone.
When he called the Ghadir Palace he waited a long time for an
answer, and it came before he could say anything: "Call back Saturday."

He made another call to Nadia, who told him that Hammad was
not home; she did not know where he was or when he would be
back.

"He didn't tell you anything, dear?" he asked uneasily.

"Not a thing!"

"And you haven't heard anything, Nadia?"

"Like what, Uncle?"

"You know, this or that."

"I don't understand, Uncle."

"Fine, fine, Nadia, I'm at home. When he gets in please have him
call me."

"Yes, of course, Uncle. Good night."

The world collapsed on the doctor. *Is it possible that the Sultan's
plane might have crashed and I still don't know of it? Have they kept the
news from me to break it to me gradually, so that I can prepare myself for
it? Would they do that on the radio? Is everyone else listening?* It occurred
to him that Widad, Salma, the Sultan and everyone else who had
been on the plane might now be nothing but ashes, their corpses

scattered over large areas of land or in the sea. He struck the edge of the table, and it trembled, as did the radio on top of it. He asked himself, almost as a dare, *What if I went to the palace?* He felt insulted—how could they forget him or put off visiting him? Hammad had called him from there and had promised to call him back, but something had come up. Even Muti had been called to the palace and had been there for hours. Was it logical of them, the doctor wondered, to forget him or purposely not return his calls? Prince Fanar—was there any connection between his imminent visit here and the important bulletin? And the Sultan—had he agreed to everything?

He tried to imagine every possible kind of important news: a pay raise for employees, increased loans for home builders, marriage loans? His thoughts leaped as he imagined the possibility that Prince Fanar's marriage might be announced. This was Thursday, after all. Or perhaps a surprise was being planned for him, and the Sultan was in on it. It would be announced after he left. Perhaps he was going to be appointed a minister or given special duties. He did not know why he had not thought they might be awarding medals to a number of important personalities: *Right now they're all in the palace discussing which medal to award to Dr. Subhi al-Mahmilji in recognition of his services to the Sultanate of Mooran—and of course they cannot discuss that in my presence.*

Each notion passed through his mind like a shooting star; they did not stop or recur. He had no way of confirming or ruling out any one of them. He was as mystified as he could be, mystified and unable to concentrate; he had no idea what to do. What compounded his confusion was the fact that he could not go out, *because they might all come at once, and at their head the Prince. They might have the medal decoration ceremony here, in the al-Hir Palace, as an added mark of respect for me, and Prince Fanar might ask me to award some of the medals on his behalf.* He chided himself for having allowed Radwan to leave Mooran that afternoon to attend the wedding of one of his relatives near Rahba. Had Radwan been here he would have given him some errands to do; he did not think highly of the palace drivers. It would have been easy for Radwan to ferret out Hammad and Muti and bring them back here, no matter where they were. He would know how to find them—everyone knew him. *But this halfwit*—meaning Abu Abdallah—*can't even be trusted to drink water, and if he weren't in such a state I wouldn't even have let him stay inside the house!*

Every time the radio made the announcement about the important bulletin, the doctor's bewilderment mounted, as did his hesitancy to call anyone to ask for an explanation.

Hammad did not call and neither did Muti. Nadia did not call. He considered calling Said or Rezaie, and a vision of Badri al-Mudalal appeared to him as he remembered their last moment at the airplane. *Don't give it a thought, Abu Ghazwan.* Abu Misbah had smiled. *I'll keep an eye out day and night.* The doctor had not liked this last word but had not been prepared to answer him back at that moment.

He thought of taking the black Cadillac himself on a drive through Mooran. He might drop in on the headquarters of the Security and Intelligence Agency to find Hammad or one of his aides. There he would find out everything. The idea did not tempt him very much, though. *I haven't driven for some time, and at night you never know who else is out there.*

After more hesitation and waiting he decided to call Hammad again. Abdelmawla was not there. Someone else answered, and when the doctor asked for his name and position, he replied roughly, "A friend," and said nothing more. When the doctor asked him to tell Abdelmawla or Hammad that he had called, he said only, "Fine."

When the doctor called Muti, the answer was that he was still at the palace. When the doctor asked what was new in the world, the office manager said, "You tell *us* the news, Abu Ghazwan!" And then he laughed.

The doctor did not know when his telephone line was cut. Between nine o'clock and nine-thirty, after deep thought and more waiting, he decided to call the Saad Palace and talk to the crown prince directly. Just then Abu Abdallah, his eyes wide as a cat's, came in, looking terrified, and informed the doctor that a tank was parked near the palace. Soldiers had chased him away when he tried to ask them questions, and had told him to get back in his house at once or they would shoot him.

· · ·

After all the commotion, waiting and disquiet, the bulletin was broadcast at ten o'clock:

"In the name of God, the Compassionate, the Merciful. Noble people of Mooran! With conditions in Mooran having deteriorated to their current sorry state, characterized by dissipation, neglect, failure and straying from the right path, their Royal Highnesses, the sons of the late Sultan Khureybit, have reviewed the state of the nation and taken action, deciding unanimously to remove Sultan Khazael from the throne and to name Prince Fanar Sultan of Mooran."

For a few moments Nimr seemed unable to understand the words he had heard. He was confused and dazed, and the smile on his father's face only added to his confusion. When the announcer had repeated the bulletin a number of times, Shamran spoke.

"Haste," he said, "is always from Satan!"

"There must be some mistake!" said Nimr, almost to himself.

Before midnight Shamran's three sons were arrested. The soldiers did not ask about Saleh, who usually slept out with his horses, or show any interest in him; perhaps they had already arrested him without anyone's knowledge. Shamran raged and cursed and tried violence to prevent his sons' arrest, but the three kept calm and even listened to the charges, which prevented them from coming to worse harm.

Shamran did not sleep for a moment that night. He paced back and forth between the roof and the interior of the house, and his mind cleared with the onset of night and then the coming of the dawn. His emotion subsided and he saw things differently. He told himself, *It will be for just a few days—they'll come back.* His wife, who was sleeping, or pretending to sleep, rose at dawn, as she always did, to bake bread and start the new day. When she asked him if the boys had come back, he tried to smile.

"Don't worry, Umm Nimr, they'll be back, either today or tomorrow."

The doctor spent that night and the next morning, until noon on Friday, wondering how he was getting through this alive. He was assailed, in turns, by fear, weeping and sickness; he heard voices and saw phantoms, or so it seemed to him, and was convinced that he would die before daybreak. Abu Abdallah did not know whether the meat cleaver the doctor kept by his side was a weapon for self-defense or a means of suicide; when he took the cleaver and tried to remove it, the doctor shouted at him in such a frightening way that he dropped the bag of mint he had brought in to cool him off and calm his nerves.

At noon on Friday Hammad's aide arrived and informed him very quietly that he should prepare for a trip, on orders from the palace; he had one hour to report to the airport.

The doctor was unable to recall all the details. He listened with great composure, but not very attentively, to what Hammad's aide said, understanding only one word: *departure*. Other things were said to him, but he forgot them all. Ivory Coast was mentioned, and the Comoro Islands, or perhaps it was Korea or Morea; he definitely heard Malta, too. In any case, the important thing was to be at the airport within an hour, before the curfew.

The doctor put all his pens in his small suitcase, and selected the seven ledgers. He considered taking his black cloak, but hesitated and then changed his mind.

Three security officers escorted the doctor to the airport. When they drove by the Sultan Khazael Mosque, one of them spoke.

"From now on there will be no thievery and no drums in Mooran. Whoever doesn't lose his head now will lose his tongue."

The doctor trembled and looked the other way to avoid seeing the throngs, or what was happening in their midst. After he boarded the plane, when the cabin attendant brought him the glass of water he had asked for, he drank it with his hand shaking and felt, for the first time, that water had a delicious taste, more delicious than he had ever realized.

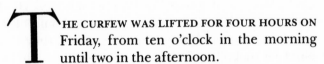

THE CURFEW WAS LIFTED FOR FOUR HOURS ON Friday, from ten o'clock in the morning until two in the afternoon.

Shamran dressed and tried to go to Zaidan's Coffeehouse, but one of Hammad's men posted at the door told him that he might go only as far as the mosque and warned him to go no farther. Shamran may have forgotten to curse the previous night, but he did not forget this Friday noon. He did not merely curse, he used both his hands and his right leg to express himself, and then asked the man to convey every word he had heard to Hammad, and to add some curses of his own if he liked. The man, who seemed a little fearful or perhaps embarrassed, said something that pleased Shamran and pacified him slightly. He said, when silence had fallen after the defiant tirade, "Abu Nimr, I understand everything you're saying, but I'm only a slave taking orders!"

Shamran nodded sadly and contained his rage; it appeared to

him that his battle would be tiny and trivial if it was limited to the man in front of him. He wanted someone important to fight, Hammad or even one of his superiors, if not today then some other day. He glanced all around, as if disposing of his anger or sending it away with these looks. Abruptly, in a paternal tone, though not completely devoid of sarcasm, he asked the man, "What if Shamran wanted to go to the Souq—or must he remain shut up at home like a woman?"

"Uncle Shamran, Abu Nimr," said the man confusedly, "the world is a different place today. It's best for a man not to expose himself to danger."

"Trust in God, my boy, don't worry."

Zaidan had opened his coffeehouse, though not officially, during the curfew. He left the door ajar. He wanted to see the people and hear what was going on; he was deeply afraid that some of his friends, particularly Saleh and Nimr, or perhaps Shamran, might have been harmed. When he saw Shamran walk into the coffeehouse, he virtually attacked him with a warm bear hug, as if he had not seen him in ages, and asked him about Saleh and Nimr. Shamran smiled.

"Shamran's three sons are the guests of al-Mutawa. He told them, 'You're our guests,' and there they are!" He shook his head and said, "A few days, and they'll come home." He paused again before adding resolutely, "They're young, they can take it. They could eat rocks!"

Then his voice changed completely. "What worries me, Abu Jasser, is Saleh. He's old and can't take it." His voice changed again; now it was conspiring. "If Ibn Mutawa didn't get him yesterday, we have to take care of him. We have to keep him out of their sight for a few days. You know what they say: Keep your head when fortunes are changing!"

"You're speaking the truth, Abu Nimr." And after a moment: "I have a storehouse, Abu Nimr, like Joseph's well—even devils could get lost in it. If Ibn Rushdan goes in there, all Mooran can search for him and never find him."

Thus, as more people were coming in to ask questions and glean information, someone said that Saleh al-Rushdan had been taken from his house even before anyone else had been arrested.

"They're going to finish him off, Abu Jasser," said Shamran in real pain. He sighed deeply. "But death is a mercy for us."

"Trust in God, Abu Nimr. Mooran hasn't changed, and people don't change. Revenge can still be taken, even if after forty years."

"Everything about Mooran has changed, my dear friend, and no one has changed more than Hammad."

"But Mooran itself hasn't changed."

"We shall see!"

Though Shamran heard the call to prayer, he did not move. Other things were on his mind: he was thinking of passing by Saleh's house to bring the family a few things and leave them some money, and almost got up, since Zaidan was busy, but decided to leave it until after prayer time; if Zaidan came with him, he reasoned, Saleh's children would think that they had many uncles.

Zaidan was asking one of the "nightingales" what was going on.

"Zaidan, we have an errand for the ones still alive!" When Zaidan looked at him in surprise, not having understood what he meant, Shamran added, "Saleh's children are our responsibility, friend. We have to visit them."

Zaidan reluctantly released the "nightingale" and asked him to drop in the next day since he had some important business to see to. "You know, the curfew begins in an hour."

Suddenly, like misfired bullets, a mob of children and youths burst on to the scene in front of the coffeehouse, as if they had known instinctively what was happening, and in clamorous, stammering voices they said that something important and terrible, which affected the coffeehouse people, was happening near the mosque.

Shamran sensed, from the disjointed words and terror-stricken faces, that what was happening affected him more than anyone else, and without waiting any further or hazarding a question, he was off. Zaidan set off after him, leaving the coffeehouse door open. He was full of confused thoughts: *Nimr ibn Shamran? His brothers? Someone else?*

Prayers at the Sultan Fanar Mosque—as the imam had renamed it—were over. The people surrounding the open plaza in front of the mosque on all sides were now stealing away after witnessing the punishment of "thieves," whose hands had been severed. Shamran hurried over and looked at their faces—he did not know whether he was looking for someone or merely curious, but he was filled with rage and resentment.

Everyone who was in Sultan Khazael Square and saw Shamran as wild as a camel said that the mosque's dove was no less agitated than Shamran: the dove flew right over their heads, which it had never done before. The flapping of wings and Shamran's voice were the only sounds, but they filled the square. When Shamran pulled off his headcloth and black headropes and waved them, as if declaiming or threatening, the dove hovered above his head and seemed to join him, dipping and soaring. Shamran penetrated the crowd like an arrow, and people immediately cleared a path for him. When he reached the middle of the plaza, he saw Saleh and screamed.

"The abodes of the oppressors shall be ruins! We are onto them—time is long!"

Saleh was wearing his winter cloak that covered, nearly buried him; all that was visible was his face, as emaciated as palm wood, and his eyes filled his face. Shamran embraced him and buried his face in his chest, in his cloak, and then looked at him: his large, sad, radiant eyes shone, as he shook his head again and again, saying everything. When Shamran asked him haltingly whether anything had happened, Saleh shook his head. Shamran looked at him again to be sure, and he seemed stronger and more vigorous than ever before in his cloak.

That night Zaidan tried to defeat the heavy silence that resounded over the men crowded around Saleh, who insisted upon remaining by his side that day, by talking of diverse things. He declared that he would be proud and happy if Saleh would agree to help him in the coffeehouse, and Saleh answered him, though he seemed to address Shamran.

"Like Jaafar al-Tayar, Abu Nimr, if you lose the right hand, the other becomes strong and firm!"

"If these calamities continue, it won't matter anymore, Saleh," said Shamran in despair. He paused and added, as if to himself, "Anger begins with madness and ends with regret. We live and see, and tell . . . or those who come after us will tell."

87

B Y THE END OF THE SUMMER THE CABINET HAD
been reshuffled. Hammad became Minister
of the Interior, Malik al-Fraih was named
Minister of Finance, and Muti was the palace press secretary. In
early autumn a Chamber of Industry was established with Rezaie
as president; al-Ghamdi still headed the Chamber of Commerce,
with Rateb Fattal as his vice president. Ghazwan visited Mooran
three times in this period and seemed to all who saw him a different
man. He visited the Sultan on each of his visits, though the newspapers did not mention that, and at the last minute he had to cancel several of his appointments and some of the visits he had
planned to make, because his time was so short.

Before the autumn was over, some of the detainees were freed,
among them Badr. It seemed that Nimr and Najm would have to
stay in longer, as even Badr told his father, so Shamran prepared
himself neither to wait nor to expect anything. He went back to

Zaidan's Coffeehouse and the same chair he'd had before. Saleh, who had agreed to work in the coffee shop, after weeks of pleading and hoping, was a different person: his curses were part of his work, and he held up his hand to whoever hindered him, as a powerful sign that he could do things others could not. No one who knew Saleh or was used to him from before ever hesitated to go along with whatever he said, but newcomers to Zaidan's Coffeehouse, and the "nightingales," could only marvel at "this uncombed creature who fears no one." Zaidan was embarrassed by Saleh, yet tried to protect him, and had a variety of answers when asked about what was said or heard in the coffeehouse, which were reported by others as well: "Since that day Saleh has been like a butcher's scale—he's lost his balance, but he's free, he's his own man—and no one has to listen to what he says." For those who refused to believe this claim, and there were many such connected with the Agency, he told them cautiously, "Be careful, my friends—Saleh is really off today, and he wants to see how far he can push you. He wants to get you into trouble. My best advice is to pretend you see nothing and hear nothing—I'm giving you this advice as a brother."

Saleh spared no one and was scarcely able to stay at the coffeehouse, to be tied down or confined, especially when Shamran did not come. He would leave the coffeehouse for the neighboring shops and sometimes wandered far away. Zaidan felt that his absence was more helpful than his presence, and did not ask for or want any explanation for his absences; he only wanted him to stay out of trouble so that no more would happen to him than had already happened. Saleh listened to what Zaidan told Shamran about his behavior, and commented acidly: "My friends, it's like the old days in the Souq—let Saleh say what the rest of you cannot."

Shamran agreed by nodding his head; he thought this remark of Saleh's perfectly correct. He turned to Zaidan and said loudly, "Abu Jasser, they asked Pharaoh, 'Who made you Pharaoh?'" and he said, 'No one prevented me.' If we act like sheep, they'll eat us. They won't spare us." He sighed. "And if we're afraid, let someone say what's in our hearts, let him speak."

Mooran moved on. When Shamran was asked about his sons, whether or not they had been released from prison, his answer varied according to the weather. If it was hot, he said, "They're in Jebel Semaan. The Sultan of that town said, 'You're my guests, and you must stay.' And you know that a guest is the prisoner of a royal host!" When autumn came, and then winter, he answered, "They're in the serene valley, they're warm and safe!" Then, with bitter sorrow, "But they'll be back!"

Shamran might have kept up his waiting and disdain, but, unlike everyone else, he ceased his Friday afternoon visits to his two sons, and so did his wife, since it did not befit either of them. He had Badr visit and make sure that they got everything they needed, until one Friday in winter, after a short visit to the prison, Badr was not allowed to bring in the food and clothes he had brought. He saw how swollen Najm's face was, and black-and-blue in several places, from beatings and torture; and told his father what he had seen. Shamran hid his rage and said nothing, but the next day, in the coffeehouse, when he saw Shaddad come in, he spoke with anger tinged with mockery.

"Dominion is God's, Abu Ghanem, and while it was shared with some it won't be shared with all!"

He wanted to send a message to Hammad by way of his uncle, and when Shaddad nodded and smiled and exchanged greetings with Shamran and the others, he spoke, as if replying to what he had heard.

"Only a visit, Abu Nimr. A short one. It will end."

"It hasn't been very short, Abu Ghanem."

"It will pass. Don't worry, Abu Nimr."

"Fear has died in our hearts, my friend, and so has patience." Shamran shook his head as if thinking or reminiscing, then his voice rumbled. "Do you remember our group in the Souq, Abu Ghanem, what they used to say, the stories they used to tell?"

He cleared his throat.

"They said that at the end of time there would be nothing but bastards, riffraff and robbers, and gravediggers, you'd see nothing but murderers, pimps and middlemen—and from the stench of the pit will come the depraved, scribes with black paper, eunuchs and rabble covered with medals, carrying seals, courtiers and Sultans' hack writers. Before them you'll see astrologers and fortune-tellers, people who dance with snakes and milk birds, and none of these have anything to do but flatter and pat you on the back and kiss your beard, and say, 'Even if it flies, it's a goat.' " He nodded to show his bitterness and continued, in a different voice, "Yes, at the end of time the earth will be full of orphans, widows, madmen, hashish addicts, dervishes and refugees from tyranny. The streets will be full of the starving and oppressed, and the whole land will be a huge prison; whoever enters it will be lost, and whoever leaves it will be born, but it won't last."

Saleh raised the stump of his arm proudly and brought it near Shaddad's face.

"Look with your own eyes, Abu Ghanem. For this I may thank the noble men Abu Nimr is telling you about."

Shamran cleared his throat and his voice was sharp, almost angry.

"You know, Abu Ghanem, that at the end of time there will be no difference between white and black, between good and evil, and there will be a gathering up of the false prophets and those who carried rags and flags, and the blind and the quacks will be exposed. And those who take charge, who pronounce judgment and lay down rules at the end of time, Abu Ghanem, will exalt themselves and suffer no pity or mercy in their hearts. They will think themselves builders like Noah, peace be upon him, and let their men kill and plunder, but when the calamity comes, the child will deny his father and the slave his master, and drop dung on them and weep from terror, and play with the present and absent, and say, 'If only I had been a forgotten thing, with no memory!' "

"Trust in God, Abu Nimr. God willing, everything will be fine," said Shaddad al-Mutawa, to soothe Shamran, who went on as if he had not heard.

"That's what you'll see with your own eyes at the end of time, and it may come sooner than any of us think."

"In the time it takes a blinking eye to see again, /God changes the world into another world," recited Zaidan from far off.

With strenuous effort Shaddad was able to convince Shamran to go along with him to visit Hammad, to look into getting Nimr and Najm freed. Shamran refused at first and then seemed reluctant but could not resist for long, especially when Zaidan and his other friends intervened. "We'll have coffee," said Shaddad to end the discussion, "then get our children and go."

Shamran was taken aback by the silence that filled the Ministry building, and at first he thought it was empty—for it was like a graveyard—but he saw some men in the corridors, going in and out, and he wondered if they were deaf-mutes or sleepwalkers. He looked at them and then at Shaddad. When they reached Abdelmawla's office, after passing through several other rooms, the man welcomed them as thieves welcome one another when they meet at night to do a job: he spoke almost inaudibly and answered telephones—they did not know when or how they rang. When that was over, he rearranged the papers on his desk. Shamran was very sorry he had come; he felt a shudder of aversion and something akin to terror, but Shaddad's shouting and behavior helped him to forget, and to give no importance to all he saw.

Hammad seemed friendly and restrained when they went into his office. He remained behind his desk and had to answer his telephone several times. When he was ready to hear them, his uncle addressed him with rough familiarity.

"Look, Hammad, boy, this is Mooran, and these are its people"— he indicated Shamran—"and blood doesn't turn into water."

Hammad smiled but did not reply.

"Get up and kiss Shamran's head, and ask him to forgive you!" urged Shaddad.

"If you really want to make fools of men, kiss their beards," said Shamran, alluding to a royal habit; then added softly to Shaddad, "I will never forget what you've done for me, Abu Ghanem." He turned to Hammad. "Since your Uncle Shaddad and I have come here, let us say what we came to say. If my boys are guilty, they've paid for their sins. They're young, they can take it. But if they are innocent, release them."

Hammad laughed loudly to cover his embarrassment, and when he stopped and silence fell, he cleared his throat and spoke without raising his eyes.

"With Nimr, there's no problem. If he promises to keep his

mouth shut, not to say a single word, to leave the government and its business alone, he'll be released."

He was quiet a moment to test Shamran's reaction or hear his answer, and when there was no reply he resumed speaking in a sterner voice.

"With Najm, it's a different story." He quickly pulled a thick file from a drawer of his desk and flipped through it, shaking his head. There was a long silence, then Shaddad spoke.

"Spare us those papers. Look at me, Hammad."

Hammad showed him a firm, expectant face.

"Whoever gives you your information is lying to you, Hammad. That's not Najm."

"Uncle," said Hammad testily, "Najm and his group wanted our blood, and that's not idle gossip. I heard it with my own ears. We can be gentle with Nimr, and say may God forgive the past, if he can be quiet and learn some manners, but Najm is something else!" He looked at Shamran and a questioning smile filled his face; then he turned to his uncle. "What do you say?"

"Let's go, Abu Ghanem," said Shamran as he stood up. He started to leave.

"Hammad, boy, the world will last longer than a day or two," said Shaddad, rising. "I'm afraid you'll regret this."

"Everyone will get his rights. Let Nimr keep his brother company, Hammad," said Shamran as he walked to the door. "We'll see!"

And still Mooran listened expectantly, and waited.

Translator's Note

The Trench is the second volume in the trilogy entitled *Cities of Salt*. The English title of the trilogy happens to preserve the alliteration of the Arabic title, *Mudun al-Milh*. I used that overall title for the first volume of the three, whose original title *al-Tih* was far too allusive to translate. *Tih* has three distinct meanings: "desert or wilderness"; "labyrinth"; and "lost." All the meanings apply to the people or setting of that book.

Munif entitled this second novel *al-Ukhdud*, which could be translated as *The Trench* or *The Ditch*. (The image is not of a wartime trench but of a hole one is likely to fall into.) I decided on the title *The Trench* after a conversation with the author, in which he described the reference as the undersea geological structure that we call a trench and the Arabs call *ukhdud*. As with the capital city in this novel, Mooran (from the word *mara/yemoor*, "to oscillate or shake"), the novel's title is meant to suggest seismic activity and, by extension, the precarious civilizations built by Arab oil.

P.C.T.

About the Author

Dr. Abdelrahman Munif was born in Jordan circa 1933 into a trading family of Saudi Arabian origin. He was stripped of his Saudi citizenship for political reasons. He earned a license in law from Baghdad and Cairo universities, and his Ph.D. in oil economics from the University of Belgrade. He served as director of planning in the Syrian Oil Company and later as director of crude oil marketing. In Baghdad he was editor-in-chief of *Al-Naft wal Tanmiya (Oil & Development)*, a monthly periodical. He now devotes his time to writing fiction. Munif resides in Damascus, Syria.

The Trench is the second novel of Munif's *Cities of Salt* trilogy; the first, *Cities of Salt*, is currently available in Vintage International. Among his other novels are *Sharq Al Mutawasit (East of the Mediterranean)*; *Heen Tarakna Al-Jisr (When We Left the Bridge)*; and *Alam Bila Kharait (A World Without Maps)*, written with Jabra Ibrahim Jabra.

About the Translator

Peter Theroux was born in Boston in 1956 and was educated at Harvard and the American University of Cairo. He has lived and traveled in Iraq, Syria, and Saudi Arabia. He is the translator of *Cities of Salt*, and the author of *The Strange Disappearance of Imam Moussa Sadr* and *Sandstorms: Days and Nights in Arabia*. He resides in Long Beach, California.